OUTSIDE THE GATES OF EDEN

LEWIS SHINER was born in 1950 and played in rock bands from high school on. Previous novels include *Black & White*, the award-winning *Glimpses*, and the cyberpunk classic *Frontera*. He's written about music for the *Village Voice*, *Pulse*, *Crawdaddy* and others. His short fiction has been reprinted in a number of best-of-the-year anthologies, and his latest collection is *Heroes and Villains: Three Short Novels and a Fable*. He lives in North Carolina.

OUTSIDE THE GATES OF EDEN

LEWIS SHINER

HEAD
ZEUS

First published in the UK in 2019 by Head of Zeus Ltd

Copyright © Lewis Shiner, 2019

9 7 5 3 1 2 4 6 8

A catalogue record for this book is available from
the British Library.

ISBN (HB): 9781789541137
ISBN (XTPB): 9781789541144
ISBN (E): 9781789541120

Printed and bound in Great Britain by
CPI Group (UK) Ltd, Croydon CRO 4YY

Head of Zeus Ltd
First Floor East
5–8 Hardwick Street
London EC1R 4RG

WWW.HEADOFZEUS.COM

For Jean-Paul
with love, always, from Raul

And, always, for Orlita

PART ONE

1965

THREE-THIRTY, Cole's first day at the new high school. He hit the courts in his tennis whites, carrying his Jack Kramer racket in its wooden press. The St. Mark's courts were like nothing he'd seen outside of TV. Bright green composite surface, clean white lines, cloth nets on steel hawsers instead of the chain link he was used to.

He was one of two dozen boys. After ten minutes of basic calisthenics, they milled around, waiting. The coach was named Fleming, young and skinny and earnest. Freshman English teacher, somebody said.

"Cole?" Fleming said, reading from a clipboard, and Cole raised his hand. Fleming glanced at him and said, "You and Montoya take Court Six. Let's see what you've got."

Montoya was small and wiry, light-skinned despite the Mexican name. Short black hair parted on the left. Good-looking and confident—hell on women, Cole figured.

"Alex," Montoya said, offering his hand.

"Jeff," Cole said. "But everybody calls me Cole."

"What year are you?"

"Junior."

"Me too. Transfer?"

"Yeah, I was in Midland. You know where Court Six is?" He slacked off the wing nuts and slipped the racket out of the brace, then swung it in large circles to loosen up his shoulder.

"The back forty." Alex pointed with the head of his racket to a second row of concrete slabs behind the elegant composite courts. He grabbed two balls from the bucket at Fleming's feet. "Your dad in oil?"

"Kind of," Cole said. "He's an accountant."

"Much money in that?"

"Not really. I'm here on scholarship. And against my will." Alex cocked his head and Cole said, "No girls."

"It's a drawback," Alex said.

The date was September 7, the day after Labor Day, and the colors of the distant courts rippled in the Dallas heat. Cole had already felt that first, cooling break of sweat under his arms and on his upper lip. Alex took the far side of the net, dropped a ball, and casually swatted it before it hit the ground.

In two minutes Cole had his number. He was exactly the kind of player that made Cole crazy, a scrambler who could get to anything and whose wild shots always nicked the line. Cole had made up for a lack of natural ability with hours of practice, focusing on technique, drilling against a backboard until the daylight was gone. He was a power player, with a hard topspin backhand that he liked to follow in to the net. Unfortunately, he wasn't powerful enough.

They took a few practice serves, then Cole said, "M or W?"

"M for Montoya."

Cole spun his racket and the Wilson logo on the handle landed upside-down. He hit both balls to Alex.

It went as badly as Cole expected. Alex's serves were nothing special, but every time Cole went to the net, Alex hit a deep lob that sent him scurrying to the baseline. Between that and the drop shots and bizarre spins, Alex easily won his serve.

Cole himself had a nasty American twist that Alex couldn't handle. If Cole got the first serve in. When he fell back on his second serve, Alex got up to the same tricks. Cole held his first two serves, trailing 3–2 when Fleming showed up.

"Montoya, get out of no-man's land. And quit hitting when you're out of position. Cole, if you're going to take the net, put it away. And you're hitting late on your ground strokes and killing your power."

Cole dug in and pounded two serves in a row, and Alex sent both of them into the fence. "Nice serve," Fleming said. "Let me see you mix it up a little." As soon as Cole complied, Alex was all over it and took the game.

Fleming moved on. Cole couldn't get the service break back and lost the set 6–4.

As they walked toward the net, Alex flipped his racket around and held it like a guitar, pointing the handle up and contorting his face as he pretended to tear off a hot lick.

Interesting, Cole thought.

They shook hands across the net and walked to the sidelines. "I guess you don't know much of anybody here, right?" Alex said.

Cole shrugged, still annoyed with himself for losing.

"Why don't you come to my house for dinner Friday night?" Alex said. "My father is always after me to bring people home, and the food is pretty decent. I can bring you over after school."

Over the years and many dislocations, Cole had developed the habit of making friends quickly. "Okay," he said. "Thanks."

COLE FOLLOWED ALEX out to the St. Mark's parking lot after tennis on Friday. Their books were stacked on their notebooks under their left arms, their rackets in their right hands. They were in their fall uniforms, khaki pants with Ban-Lon polo shirts in a particularly fungal shade of taupe. Cole was a little nervous about being branded queer, though Alex seemed straight enough. And popular, based on the number of people who sat with him at lunch, a club that Cole had joined.

Montoya's car turned out to be a red '65 Corvair Monza. Sleek, compact, sporty, engine in the rear. Cole stopped to admire it. "This got the one-ten horses?"

"One-forty," Alex said. "Not that I get much chance to open it up. You know cars?"

"I used to help out in the motor pool."

The red tuck and roll upholstery was hot enough to pop the sweat on Cole's freshly showered back. He followed Alex's lead and threw his books and racket in the back seat.

Alex had a cushion to put himself higher behind the wheel. He cranked the engine and the radio came on with it, blasting rock and roll. Big, skating-rink-type organ and tinny piano and a tired-sounding singer. "Check it out!" Alex said. "You heard this yet?"

Cole shook his head.

"It's the new Dylan single. Dig it."

Cole had heard of Dylan but not heard him. Midland was solidly country-western, and his father ordered him to get up and change the channel whenever music groups came on TV. Most of the rock bands that Cole had heard sounded crude. He liked movie themes and John Coltrane, the Kingston Trio and Bobby Darin. His parents had an ancient monaural phonograph and Cole didn't have any records of his own.

The song was over by the time Alex exited the parking lot and made a left onto Preston. He turned the volume down and said, "You like Dylan?"

"I don't know," Cole said. "How come you've got your license already? Are you even sixteen yet?"

"Sixteen next month. It's a hardship license." He looked at Cole and grinned. "My parents felt like it was a hardship to drive me around." Cole's parents felt the same way, but in his case it meant he didn't get out much.

"How long you been in Dallas?" Alex asked.

"Since June. Worked all summer in my father's office. Making coffee, running errands, shit like that."

"It's cool that you got to move around."

"Mostly from one armpit to another. Before Midland I was in Egypt for a year. That was where I learned to work on cars. We got out just before Nasser nationalized the oil. Midland for two years before that, Mexico for a year before that, New Jersey before that."

"Which armpit of Mexico?"

Cole flushed. "No offense, but we were in Villahermosa, which was in fact not very hermosa."

"Why should I be offended?"

He wants me to point out that he's Mexican, Cole thought. He shut up rather than give him the satisfaction. It was starting to look like a long evening.

"Relax, Cole, I'm just giving you shit. My father's from Guanajuato, which is in fact pretty hermosa, and I agree that Villahermosa is pretty much an armpit. I myself have lived my entire life in Dallas, and I'm not convinced that you haven't landed in an armpit yet again."

ALEX WAS NERVOUS despite himself as he parked behind the house. You could see there was something about "this Cole character," as his mother already called him. Alex felt like his own attempts at coolness were transparently lame, whereas Cole was the real deal, standing outside looking in, not with hunger but with indifference.

They got out of the car and he watched Cole take it all in, the pristine driveway, the perfectly rectangular hedges, his sister's red T-bird convertible, the privacy fence and the pool beyond it, the two-story brick house, less than ten years old. "Nice," Cole said. "What does your father do to get this kind of bread?"

"Import-export, real estate, he's got a piece of the Cuauhtémoc brewery in Monterrey, I don't even know anymore where it all comes from. Once you get past a certain point, being rich is a full-time job all by itself."

"You don't approve?"

"It's not that simple. I love my father. I just don't want to be him."

The garage door was up and they walked between his father's Eldorado and his mother's Impala, through the laundry room, and into the kitchen. Alex's mother was washing lettuce in the sink while Frederica sliced potatoes on the counter. His mother's hair was in a loose ponytail and she was wearing Capri pants and a tight sweater like somebody half her age. She'd barely turned 20 when she had Alex, and she was fanatical about watching Jack LaLanne and working out to fitness records. She dried her hands on her apron as she kissed Alex and said, «Hola, m'ijo.»

"Mom?"

"Sorry, sorry. Hi, *Alex*. And this is Cole?"

"Hi," Cole said. He took her hand European style, like he was going to kiss it. "You must be Alex's sister?"

"Points for charm," she said. "You can stay."

"Dad home?" Alex asked.

"Not yet." Alex wondered if her false cheer was obvious to Cole. "Susan's here for the weekend." She looked at Cole. "Susan really is his sister. She's a freshman at UT."

"Alex told me."

She nodded to Frederica. "And this is Frederica."

"I'm Cole. Anything I can do to help?"

Frederica shook her head like Cole was crazy, and Alex's mother said, "Is he always like this?"

7

"I barely know the guy," Alex said.

"Like what?" Cole said.

"You guys run along," his mother said. "I'll call you when dinner's ready."

Alex led the way upstairs. He'd remembered to make the bed that morning, at least. He sat on the bed and Cole pulled the wooden chair out from the desk and sat backwards on it. Cole eyed the guitars and amplifier, the stereo and the stack of records leaning against the wall.

"What kind of music do you like?" Alex asked. You could see from Cole's shrug that he was embarrassed. "C'mon, man, what's the big deal? You into opera or some shit like that?"

"No, it's... I don't know much about rock and roll."

"Yeah, I figured. Like, 'rock and roll' is oldies, okay, like the Platters and shit. Just plain 'rock' is what's happening now."

Cole nodded like he was taking mental notes. "You play guitar?"

"At it," Alex said. "I'd have to work a lot harder to be any good. Lately I've been playing bass because it's easier. If I was in a group, that's what I'd play. Did you like 'Positively Fourth Street'? That Dylan song in the car?"

"I think so. Maybe."

Alex thought it over and said, "Here's the deal. You help me clean up my tennis game, and I'll help you with your appalling ignorance about music. Okay?"

Cole nodded again.

Alex took out *Highway 61 Revisited*. "Lesson One," he said.

FIFTY-SOME MINUTES LATER and Cole's head was spinning.

The instruments on the record were clangy and some of them out of tune. Instead of ruining everything, it only made the music sound more urgent. Then there was Dylan's voice, like something he used to know and had forgotten. The voice of somebody too clever for his own good, hurt and lonely and rejecting before he was rejected. Like looking in a mirror and seeing somebody far more mysterious than he'd ever seen there before.

Alex surprised him by not asking what he thought, which Cole did not want to put into words at that moment. It must have been all over his face, because Alex said, "Okay. Now we're getting somewhere."

They went downstairs. Half of Cole was still out on Highway 61, or in the rain in Juarez, or maybe on Desolation Row. The other half dimly registered an oak-paneled dining room, a chandelier, an oval table 12 feet long laid out with linen tablecloth, candles, real silver. A two-foot-tall wooden crucifix next to a framed picture of the Virgin. At one end sat Alex's father, five-ten and massively built, with short, curly hair and a neatly trimmed mustache. The only other person at the table was a younger, blonder version of Alex, maybe a fifth grader, sitting in front of a glass of milk.

Alex's father stood up and held out his hand. "Al Montoya. Good to meet you." Only the slightest hint of an accent, more in the rhythm than the pronunciation.

"Jeff Cole." He was ready for a firm handshake and he got it.

Alex hugged his father and his father kissed him on the cheek. Cole, startled, looked away.

"And this is Jimmy," Montoya said.

The kid shook hands too and said, "Hi."

Alex's mother came in, holding a bowl of something in a red quilted mitt. From the look of it, Cole thought it might be potatoes au gratin, something he'd read about but never eaten. Then again, he'd never known anyone with a black maid before, or cars for everybody in the family old enough to drive.

"You're here, Cole," she said, pointing to a chair one away from Montoya. "Go ahead and sit down."

He didn't, of course. Being poor didn't mean you couldn't have manners, his mother had told him a million times. She read Emily Post and Amy Vanderbilt and never got to use them.

"You want a beer?" Alex asked.

"Um, sure." He didn't let himself look at Montoya to see if they were pulling his leg.

"Bohemia all right?" Alex said.

"Whatever you're having."

Montoya said, "If you're not familiar with it, it's got a richer flavor than the US beer you're probably used to."

Cole nodded as if he were used to anything other than an occasional pilfered sip of his father's Schlitz.

"Let me know what you think," Montoya said.

"I'll do that," Cole said.

Alex's mother set the potatoes next to the rest of the food on the table. Huge wooden bowl of salad. Fresh green beans instead of canned, cut diagonally and sautéed with mushrooms. Loaves of French bread torn to pieces and poking out of a checkered napkin in a basket. Glass butter dish and silver butter knife, steaming bowl of wild rice, pitchers of water and lemonade. She sat at her husband's right hand and said, «Susana! Ven, estamos listos.»

Alex, who'd come back with two brown bottles of beer, glared at her. Montoya cleared his throat. Cole shifted uncomfortably, and then Susan walked out of the kitchen.

She was darker than Alex, with lustrous black hair that flipped inward at her shoulders, like a fashion model's. Petite, graceful, completely out of Cole's league. Except for the wounded look in her eyes. It matched the pain in Dylan's voice, and Cole wanted to believe that no one saw it but him.

She carried a Pyrex serving dish full of rare steak, sliced into strips and garnished with parsley. She set it on the table and held out her hand. "You must be Cole."

"I suppose I must," he said, "but I can try to change."

She offered him the charity of her smile. The only unclaimed chair was next to his, so he pulled it out for her. She thanked him and then Cole, the last man standing, finally took his own seat.

No matter how hungry you are, his mother had taught him, be patient. Watch the hostess and follow her lead. What she did was hold her hands out, palm up, and the others around the table joined hands and bowed their heads.

"Jimmy?" Montoya said. "Will you do the honors?"

"Bless this food to our use and us to thy service," the kid said. "Make us ever mindful of the needs of others."

Cole, a devout atheist since age 12, didn't join the chorus of amens. He let his attention linger on the feel of Susan's hand in his. Small, soft, warming to his touch. He was careful to release it at the first sign of her letting go.

He took small portions as the serving dishes came around, said, "Everything smells wonderful," and braced himself to tell his life story over again. Instead Montoya asked him what he thought of the Gemini V flight. "I can't imagine," Montoya said, "what it must be like to be stuck inside a big tin can for a week. I would go crazy."

At Cole's house they ate on TV trays in front of the big black and white console set, and Cole's father complained if anyone tried to talk over the news. If Cole's father was home, the TV was on, so they never had any conversation at all. Which was okay with Cole, as his father found something to object to in most anything Cole said.

"It might be worth it for the sights," Cole said. "The thing that would drive me crazy is having so little control. It's all done by computers and the ground crew." Cole had all 55 Topps Astronaut Cards from two years before.

Montoya nodded. "That would get to me, too."

At the first lull, Cole looked at Susan, who hadn't spoken since her "amen." "How do you like UT? It's really big, right?"

"Thirty thousand," Susan said. "Some of my lecture classes have two or three hundred people in them. The hard part is getting the prerequisite classes for your major. Sometimes they don't have enough sections and you can get stuck in a holding pattern for years."

She was acting, Cole thought, as if he were a human in his own right and not just her little brother's friend. "Do you know what you're going to major in?"

Jimmy, barely audible, said, "Football players."

Susan blushed and her mother said, "Jimmy! Apologize to your sister."

"Sorry, Susan." He drew the words out in a singsong.

Cole's own face felt hot. Of course she was dating football players, and probably majoring in Home Ec. What had he expected, Russian Lit?

"No," Susan said. "I don't know yet."

The pain in her eyes was connected to this, and he couldn't possibly ask her about it at the dinner table. Or anywhere else, he reminded himself.

*

ALEX PLAYED IT COOL, keeping one eye on Cole as they ate. You could see he knew how to handle people. Say something to make them feel good about themselves, the oldest gimmick in the book, and that shit always worked, even on his father, who prided himself on not getting bluffed at the poker table. The trick was in the delivery, pretending he was kidding while at the same time coming off like he really meant it. It was a kind of non-sexual flirting, and he must have figured it out early on. You would need to make friends fast, moving around like that.

Cole finished his beer and smoothly got Alex's father talking about the brewery. "You want another?" Alex asked.

"Uh, sure," Cole said.

"I'll get it," Susan said, pushing back her chair and ignoring both Cole's token protest and their father's raised eyebrow. "Anybody else?"

Alex raised his own nearly empty bottle, pleased at the way he and Susan and Cole had taken advantage of the situation. Yes, Alex thought. I think he'll do.

Alex and his father and Cole stayed at the table until after nine. Cole didn't give up his attempts to help with the dishes until Alex's mother promised him, "Next time." Cole had eaten three helpings of everything and completely won her over.

"Cole lived in Villahermosa for a year, Pop," Alex said.

"Really? How old were you?"

"I turned ten there."

"Do you speak any Spanish?"

"I can get by. Between that and Spanish classes at school."

You could see that Cole wanted to ask why they didn't speak it at home, why the dirty looks when his mother used it. Even so, he'd read the mood well enough to answer in English.

Eventually Alex said, "It's late. I'd better take him home."

"You've had two beers," his father said. "You're not driving. Susan can take him."

Alex stood up abruptly. "Let's go, then."

Cole thanked everyone extravagantly, including Frederica,

and then he and Alex went outside to wait on Susan. "She's got to brush her teeth," Alex said, "and fix her hair and freshen her makeup. In case Prince Charming pulls up next to her at the light."

"She seems nice."

Alex shrugged. "Don't forget your books."

Cole got his stuff out of the Monza and after an awkward minute said, "Are you pissed off about something?"

"I hate it when my father treats me like a kid."

"We're fifteen years old," Cole said. "We *are* kids."

"When he was my age, he was working twelve hours a day and bringing home most of the family's money. And he didn't take shit from anyone, including his old man."

A floodlight snapped on above them and Susan made her entrance. "Shall we?" she said. She'd carefully tied a scarf over her hair and her lips shone. Cole moved quickly to open the driver door of her T-Bird, then glanced at Alex and said, "Shotgun."

Alex got in and stretched both arms across the back of the seats. Cole gave directions while Susan backed out. They cut over to Marsh and cruised north, three lanes each way, traffic sparse, the late summer wind pinning Alex's shirt to his chest. The nearness of fall made him lonely and impatient.

"The Dylan concert is the twenty-fifth," Susan said. "I'm getting tickets Monday morning before I go back. You want any?"

"Cole?" Alex said. "You interested?"

"I have to ask my parents... but yeah. Definitely." He looked at Susan. "Do you need money tonight?"

"Alex knows where to find you," she said.

"That's right," Cole said. "Whenever you need me."

THE GIRLS IN Mr. Casey's Civics class had pronounced him "a hunk." All but Madelyn. She found it alarming that he was so clearly aware of his good looks and that he took so much pleasure in the way the girls responded to him. His dark hair was unkempt and slightly too long; his tattersall shirts and knit ties were daringly casual; his smile radiated inappropriate warmth.

"Miss Brooks?" he said. "Will you tell the class the subject you chose for your essay?"

Madelyn had been dreading this moment. They'd spent the first few weeks of class discussing a major paper due mid-semester, and on Monday they'd had to turn in preliminary topic paragraphs. Now Mr. Casey was calling on the students he thought had provided good examples, with the idea that this would somehow inspire those who hadn't. Rather than, in fact, make them sullen, jealous, and resentful.

Madelyn's strategy for surviving high school centered on the avoidance of negative attention. On a tactical level this meant not doing anything to emphasize her quiet good looks, not binding herself to any of the social cliques that she easily moved among, and above all not making a display of her erudition.

"It's, um, about the crisis in Greece."

"I don't think," Mr. Casey said, "most of us know about this crisis. Can you explain it? And stand up, please, Miss Brooks, so we can all hear you."

She reluctantly got to her feet. Keep it simple, she reminded herself. "Well, it's a monarchy there, and the new king just took over, and he's very young and kind of pushy. He forced the prime minister to resign, but the prime minister is really popular, so none of the king's replacements have been able to win a vote of confidence."

"And this is important because…?"

Madelyn felt herself get caught up, against her will. "Because the power struggle is over who controls the army. Like in most countries, the Greek army is deeply conservative, and they don't like the wave of liberalism that's been happening over the last few years. If the civilian government can't hold power, the army could take over and impose a right-wing dictatorship."

She must have let some emotion into her voice because she heard, from the back of the room, Ed Wallingford say, "Big woo." Ed, the kicker and the smallest boy on the football team, was given to deflating what he saw as pretension.

Mr. Casey said, "Your title is 'The July Apostasy in Greece.' Can you explain that?"

His wrongheaded attempt to hold her up for admiration, she knew, would only end in ridicule. "That's what they call it over there." She looked at Mr. Casey and saw that he wanted more. "The prime ministers that the king appointed were members of the first guy, Papandreou's, party. So Papandreou's people called them apostates. Traitors, basically."

"Where did you get all this?"

"We listen to the BBC sometimes." In fact she and her father ritually tuned in the BBC Overseas Service—since March called the BBC World Service—nearly every weeknight.

"And Greece? Why Greece?"

That, Madelyn thought, was none of Mr. Casey's beeswax. "Greece is the cradle of democracy. If they became a military dictatorship, the symbolism would be pretty ominous."

"Excellent, Miss Brooks. I very much look forward to reading your paper."

"Me, too," muttered Ed Wallingford, prompting antiphonal sniggering on the back row.

When the bell finally released her from her agony, Madelyn got out of the classroom as fast as she could, unable to bear any more of Mr. Casey's veneration or Ed Wallingford's hostility.

It could have been worse, she supposed. Mr. Casey could have kept at her until he got to the truth of her fascination with Greece.

As much as her father doted on her, Madelyn's mother was the one who read her to sleep when she was little. They must have started with the usual Little Golden Books and then moved on to A. A. Milne; what Madelyn remembered was the night her mother set *The House at Pooh Corner* aside and said, "Would you like to try something different?" Madelyn was three, and this would be her earliest memory.

"Yes," she said, not having a real opinion of her own, responding purely to her mother's excitement. Her mother went away and came back with a thick book wrapped in an orange paper cover. She turned a few pages and began to read.

"'Tell me, O muse,'" she began, and then she said something about heroes and sacks and Ilion.

Her mother looked up. "Ilion, of course, that would be Troy."

Madelyn had laughed then, because she had no idea who Troy was either, or what a muse was, or what it was that was getting put in a sack.

Over the years, she returned repeatedly to that S. O. Andrew translation of *The Odyssey*, sometimes reading no more than a few lines. She'd absorbed enough about romantic love, long before the upheavals of puberty, to grasp the concept. The perfect lover was always available, always consoling, able to sweep you away from mundane reality, to obsess you, to steal your heart.

How could the Mr. Caseys of this world, let alone the Ed Wallingfords, ever compare to books?

DAVE HAD COME to Greenwich Village for the first time on a stifling Friday night in August of 1961, six-foot-minus-a-little, scrawny, 25 and already losing his hair. He'd never set foot there, despite growing up in Yonkers and two years at New York City Community College and four years working in midtown after graduation. From childhood, his parents had warned him about the Bolsheviks and gypsies and dope fiends of the Village, to the point where, even as an adult who knew better, he feared that if he went and got into trouble, God forbid, he would never hear the end of it.

On that particular night, he'd fled his airless Brooklyn apartment after another horrible scene with Rachel, her shouting, him retreating until he'd found himself in the hall, smelling overcooked cabbage and exhaust fumes from the air shaft, sick to death of his life so far.

For no conscious reason, he'd gotten on a train headed into Manhattan. A self-destructive impulse, planted by Rachel's venom and brought to fruition by the sight of the Bleecker Street station, had sent him off the train and up the stairs and out onto Lafayette.

As he walked up Bleecker past NYU and into the Village proper, he could see the history in every brick, some of which had no doubt been hurled at policemen. From the bohemian painters of the twenties and thirties to the radical theaters and playwrights of the forties, from the beats of the fifties to the current jazzmen and folkies, the Village had witnessed a continuous outpouring of dissent that was as alien to Dave as fakirs walking on hot coals.

Back when his name was Fischel Cohen, he had grown up with Zionist folk songs, and when the Weavers put "Tzena, Tzena, Tzena" on the flip of "Goodnight, Irene," he was permitted to buy a copy. The guitars and the unrestrained power of the voices touched something in him as frightening as it was compelling. Years later, still in college, he heard the same thing in the Kingston Trio's "Tom Dooley." So he knew the names—The Village Vanguard, Gerde's Folk City, The Cock and Bull—even though he'd always believed himself too old, too married, too square to ever act on that knowledge.

At the intersection of Bleecker and MacDougal, the excitement seized him in the pit of his stomach, a feeling indistinguishable from the terror he felt when he walked past a cluster of duck-tailed, Lucky-smoking, motorcycle-jacketed hoods on Flatbush Avenue. This crowd was more benign, dressed the same way as Dave, in white short-sleeved shirts and narrow ties and shiny black Florsheims, yet they had an air of knowledge and purpose that had always eluded him.

He followed a group of them up MacDougal and ended up in a line twenty people long that led down the stairs to the Gaslight Café. Fifteen minutes after that he crowded into a damp, unbearably hot basement where every table was filled and the overflow leaned against every inch of available space along the bare brick wall. The only light came from the occasional fake Tiffany lamp that hung from the ceiling and Dave had to walk with his hands in front of him until his eyes adjusted.

On stage, a guy in an elegant suit and a neatly trimmed brown beard manipulated the microphone to produce startlingly realistic sound effects, creating characters through weird voices and then tossing them aside, dispensing with punchlines in favor of building and abandoning entire surrealist worlds. When he finished, everybody snapped their fingers instead of applauding, and Dave began to suspect he was asleep and dreaming in Brooklyn.

"First time here?"

Dave turned to see a stunning black-haired woman in black-framed glasses, jeans, and a black sweater that was coming off one shoulder. He nodded.

"Apartments upstairs," the woman said, pointing. She spoke with exaggerated clarity to be heard without raising her voice. "Same airshaft. People complained about the noise." She ended on a smile.

"Who was that guy?"

"Hugh Romney. On staff here."

Overwhelmed by shyness, Dave nodded thanks and turned away.

A hugely tall man with a thick moustache and brown hair that fell in his eyes arrived on stage and sat on a stool with his guitar. He joked with the crowd and then began to pick intricate patterns and sing in a raw, powerful voice. Some of what the man played was what Dave had always thought of as folk music, and some was blues, jazz, Dixieland, gospel, and anything else that came into his head.

Between two of the songs he turned and gave the black-haired woman a questioning look.

"Dave Van Ronk." She seemed amused.

He'd heard of Van Ronk. Everybody in the music business expected him to be huge, and nobody would take a chance on him other than the Village's own beatnik label, Folkways.

Van Ronk played for half an hour and then announced Brownie McGee and Sonny Terry, a guitar player and a blind harmonica player, both Negro. Dave's parents had told him that in the Village the schvartzers mixed with the goyim on the streets, in the clubs, even in the bedrooms. It still struck Dave as very odd, not objectionable, merely strange. And speaking of mixing, Van Ronk had obviously paid close attention to McGee's guitar playing and singing style.

Eventually he wandered out onto the street and let himself be drawn up MacDougal to Washington Square. In April there had been a so-called Beatnik Riot there, after the city had tried to shut down the Sunday afternoon folk singing. Naturally the city won.

Dave arrived to find the police enforcing a six-PM curfew on musical instruments. He sat at the central fountain anyway and listened to the kids as they passed around cigarettes and argued, mostly about ideological purity of one kind or another: clawhammer versus Scruggs-style banjo picking, Negro blues versus Childe ballads, hammered dulcimer versus guitar. After that he'd walked the streets until daylight, fueled by espresso and an anxious, irresistible excitement.

That had been the start. After he separated from Rachel, he rented a cheap fourth-floor walkup on Sullivan Street and over the next six months began to make sense of the emotional onslaught. Seeing Fred Neil at the Café Wha?, Bob Dylan at Gerde's, and Tim Hardin at the Night Owl had shown him why Van Ronk was not going to be famous beyond the Village. The zealots in Washington Square had missed the same thing that Van Ronk had. The problem was not a failure of authenticity, but rather an excess of it. This was not shaping up to be a decade of reverence.

DAVE HAD BEEN an engineer at Columbia Records since 1957, since he'd shown up with his two years of college credits and convinced them to give him a try. That first week, an old Jew in accounting had looked at the name on his paperwork and shaken his head. "Fischel Cohen? I don't think so."

"What do you mean?"

"You get credit on an album cover, that's what people should read? We can fix this. Fischel, Fisher. Cohen, Ken. Turn it around, Ken Fisher."

"Ken? You want me to be a Ken?"

"What else you got for me?"

"Well... my middle name is Dov."

"Perfect. David Fisher."

The deed was done before he had time to think, and it seemed a minor thing, until his first paycheck arrived made out to David Fisher. Accounting said it could take months to correct, and it would be simpler to open an account in the new name. Within a month, the pressure of trying to maintain two identities was driving him meshuge and he gave up and went before a judge and made it legal.

It wasn't like he had any affection for Fischel. He'd been called "Fishbreath" in grade school and "Fishy" in the Army and it was only stubbornness that had kept him from changing it before.

Telling his parents was another thing. A month and a half went by before they let him in their house again, and even then they barely spoke to him.

Rachel had been even worse. Though she had watched the process unfold and nodded along with each step, she managed to hold it against him in the end. Then again, Rachel had held most everything against him.

IN FEBRUARY OF 1962, Dave told Mitch Miller, his boss at Columbia, that he wanted to record some of the new folk music. He had by that point worked his way up from second tier easy listening dates to full orchestra sessions with Tony Bennett and the latest *Sing Along with Mitch* album, even as the TV show was burning up the ratings. Miller had sneered. "You mean they actually use engineers on that garbage? Why?"

Dave had always had a grudging respect for Miller, though many considered him a schlockmeister for stunts like pairing Sinatra with a howling dog and letting a 13-year-old sing "I Saw Mommy Kissing Santa Claus." Miller had invented the idea of the record producer, along with the idea that a record could be an art form in itself and not just a souvenir of a live performance. He was the absolute monarch of "the Church," Columbia's 30th Street Studio, generally considered the best sounding room in the world, 100 feet long, wide, and high, with an echo chamber in the basement that was the envy of the industry.

Miller's shovel-blade beard, two-armed conducting style, and tight smile were national icons. The public never saw his self-confidence cross the line into arrogance, or heard his contemptuous dismissal of contrary opinions. Dave's penalty for his disloyalty was exile to Studio A, uptown on 7th Avenue. Miller never spoke to him again, even when they passed in the hall.

Once free of his influence, Dave began to see that Miller had helped turn the musical culture of the 1950s into a sterile wasteland of artifice and made-to-order sentiment, had created the very famine of authenticity that the kids in Washington Square were rebelling against. The contrast between Miller's world and the future that was barreling toward them became more obvious every day. In February of 1964 on the *Ed Sullivan Show*, The Beatles served notice of that future to every pop musician in the US.

The following May, Tim Hardin showed up at Columbia to record a set of demos. Dave had fought to get assigned to the session, only to have it explode into chaos before it started. The schedule listed it as a solo recording, and Hardin arrived with an entourage that included musicians, hangers-on, and his own producer, a six-foot-six baritone blond named Erik Jacobsen who was the banjo player in some folk group with a kooky name. John Sebastian was there, the harmonica player that Dave had seen playing with Fred Neil. So was Gary Burton, the jazz vibraphonist, and Sticks Evans, with his left-handed drum set and his dapper three-piece suit and pocket handkerchief. So was a huge, loud woman named Cass, a wild man named Zalman, a kleptomaniac named Pompa, and various other musicians and women of little or no virtue.

It quickly became apparent that Hardin was completely loaded on heroin. Cass, Zalman, Jacobsen, and Sebastian began smoking reefer in the hall. Every time Dave turned around, Pompa was gone and something else was missing: a typewriter, a chair, pictures off the walls. As soon as Hardin got a few bars into a song, he would nod out and the other musicians sat and waited until he drifted back in and picked up, in perfect time, exactly where he'd left off.

God watches over fools, Dave's mother had always claimed, and somehow they got through the 12-hour session without the intervention of police, firemen, doctors, or Columbia executives, and when he replayed the tapes afterward and heard, amid the endless variations on the "Hi-Heel Sneakers" riff, the beauty and pain in Hardin's voice on "How Time Flies," his heart swelled up and he phoned Jacobsen and babbled incoherently until Jacobsen invited him over to his apartment on MacDougal, where he and Sebastian were listening to country and blues and jug band music on reel-to-reel, and where they told him their stories, how they'd been living in adjacent rooms in a transient hotel in the Village unbeknownst to each other until one night Sebastian came knocking at two AM asking Jake to turn the music up, and how Jake had heard The Beatles on a jukebox in a White Castle while on the road with the Knob Lick Upper 10,000 and started to hear sounds in his head that he couldn't make as a musician, but thought he could create as a producer, and how Cass had introduced Sebastian to Zally at her apartment on the night The Beatles had debuted on *Sullivan*, having already decided that they should be in a band together, and they'd played together for the first time then, Sebastian the technician, Zal the free spirit, dripping influences from Floyd Cramer's slip-note piano to Louis Armstrong's air-raid trumpet to Clifton Chenier's blustering accordion, and now it looked like Zal was part of their conspiracy, the band they were going to form as a sort of American armed response to the British Invasion, and Dave, his judgment perhaps affected by the clouds of pot smoke floating in the room, had said, "Take me with you."

Columbia understandably passed on the Hardin demos. Dave assumed that was the end of it, but when The Lovin' Spoonful finally materialized, Jake remembered him. The band cut their first demos at Bell and Allegro, top-notch rooms with state of the art gear, and Dave moonlighted as engineer to be part of it. He found to his surprise that he belonged there, in the thick of the creative whirlwind, putting a pickup on an autoharp or under-dubbing to create new hybrid instruments that blended guitars and pianos or guitars and tubular bells. Jake taught him how to splice tape to resurrect brilliant fictional performances from the ashes of failed takes. They created every sound they could imagine and went beyond that to create sounds even they had never imagined before.

AND THEN, SUDDENLY, September of 1965 arrived and "Do You Believe in Magic" broke nationwide and here, on this Thursday night in the Village, Dave was walking down Third Street to listen to the Spoonful for possibly the last time ever at the Night Owl, because after extended dates in LA and San Francisco they had outgrown not just the club but the Village itself.

He saw then that he had blinked and missed another cultural warm front that had blown through and changed everything, had swapped out bulging, long-necked acoustic guitar cases for flat Fender rectangles, banished jackets and ties, grown hair over collars and ears, put women into jeans and sandals and jangling jewelry.

We did this, he thought, the Beatles and the Spoonful and the bands in garages everywhere. We electrified the world.

The street around the Night Owl's famous yellow awning seethed with kids, locals and tourists both, a testament to the success of the record. Dave knew from experience that the volume of the band made them a more pleasant auditory experience on the sidewalk than inside. Jake knew it too, and Dave found him fifty yards from the club, his blond head poking up past the crowd around him. Dave made his way over and Jake threw one arm around him and pulled him into a hug. Jake was dapper, as always, in a double-breasted suit and no tie, while Dave, who had no instinct for clothes, wore a short-sleeved sport shirt and gray slacks.

"This guy," Jake said to no one in particular, "this guy is going to be huge, once he flies the nest and starts producing on his own."

Dave felt the opposite of huge, dwarfed by Jake's physicality and outsize personality.

"You want to go inside?" Jake asked, and Dave shrugged. The crowd made way for them, and Jack the Rat, at the door of the club, gave them a gap-toothed smile and waved them in.

The interior was barely more than a hallway, 20 feet wide and long enough to disappear into darkness at the far end. The stage protruded from the middle of one wall, so small that Joe had to set up his drums on the floor at stage left, the PA speakers pointed outward from the sides of the stage so that the vocals rode high above the instruments. Zal was in full wild-man mode, dancing jerkily back and forth like he had to take a leak, tall and lean in vertically striped stovepipe pants and a top hat. He was to blame for the crippling volume, cranking his guitar until the rest of the band had no choice other than to go along or be swallowed up.

They were in the middle of Chuck Berry's "Almost Grown." Sebastian waved to Jake and smiled happily, and Zal nodded and raised his guitar neck in salute. Heads turned, and failed to recognize who the salutes were for. Dave saw Jake's gaze move over the room, checking out the girls, winnowing out the underage, a more difficult feat every day.

Suddenly Dave felt a hand on his shoulder, pulling him down toward the floor. He turned and saw Tim Hardin, feeling a surge of disappointment followed immediately by guilt. Hardin had turned Jake around at the same time and now he was smiling, arms open wide, his long brown forelock falling to his eyebrows across the wide plane of his forehead, one eye glittering with mischief and tragedy, the other squinting against the smoke from the cigarette parked in the corner of his mouth. He looked fairly straight, Dave thought hopefully.

The volume prohibited even the pretense of conversation. Jake gripped Hardin's shoulder in greeting and Dave nodded awkwardly. Hardin pointed to his ears and led them to the street.

"I thought you were still in LA," Jake said.

"What's the matter, aren't you glad to see me?" Hardin never expressed fewer than two highly volatile emotions at once. Here his petulance teetered on the edge of laughter.

"Sure, Timmy, always." Jake was less than convincing, on the verge of losing patience while Dave was willing to cut Hardin more slack on the basis of the incredible music they were in the midst of recording. Jake had come up with the idea of buying Hardin a portable tape recorder and paying him $50 for every demo that had at least two verses and a chorus, $75 if it had a bridge.

The scheme was working. These were brand-new songs that finally did justice to that amazing, heartbroken voice and the virtuoso guitar playing that sounded like Robert Johnson dueting with Django Reinhardt, the lyrics deceptively simple and full of surprising images and naked emotion. Once Verve released the album and Hardin became a household name, bigger than Dylan, bigger than Sinatra, Dave was sure that the recognition would chase away the demons that were riding him so very hard.

"Do you want me to set up some studio time?" Dave asked.

"Tomorrow, definitely."

"What time tomorrow?" Jake said.

"I don't know yet. I'll call you."

Inside the Night Owl, the band wrapped up "Good Time Music" and Sebastian said, "You folks stay groovy for just a few minutes and we'll be right back."

Somewhere in that elegant pearl-gray suit, Dave knew, Jake had a couple of joints, and his attention was already in the tiny dressing room downstairs where he and Sebastian would light them up.

Hardin saw it too. "I've got a new song," he said.

"You got it on tape?" Jake said.

"I can sing it for you right now. 'Got myself a red balloon, got a blue surprise…'"

"You know the deal, Timmy. No tape, no advance."

Dave wanted to hear the rest of the song. Such was the power of Hardin's charisma that Dave wondered if he had fifty dollars on him, which he didn't.

"Listen," Jake said, "I've got some business to attend to, but if you're around later, we could do some work tonight."

"Aw, man, not tonight. I just got back."

"All right, then. Later." Jake nodded to both of them and ducked back in the club.

Dave felt abandoned. If Hardin noticed his discomfort, he didn't show it. "Did I ever tell you," Hardin said, "about the first time I saw Susan, here in the Village?" This was the actress who worked under the name Susan Yardley. Hardin had met and fallen in love with her in LA, and she had inspired the sudden outpouring of songs. "She was living in this apartment over on Christopher, this must have been sixty-three, and there was a bar there on the ground floor. And I walked in there one day and she was dancing to the jukebox, all by herself. 'Fly Me to the Moon' was playing. God, she was beautiful. I just stood and watched her, never said a word to her. The minute I saw her in LA, I recognized her. I knew right then it was fate, man. Destiny."

"Sinatra, was it?" Dave asked.

"Sure, man, Sinatra, who else?"

"That record just came out last year. August of sixty-four."

Hardin shook his head in disgust. "Maybe it was Mathis. Maybe it was last year. You're not hearing what I'm telling you, man. You got no romance in your soul."

If that's true, Dave thought, why do I think of Rachel and cry every time I hear "It'll Never Happen Again"? And then he thought, what a tissue of lies we all make out of our pasts, pointed little narratives that prove something, the hand of God or the lack of God, how smart we were or how blind, how funny, how sad.

"I've got to meet somebody," Hardin said. "Can you loan me five bucks?"

Dave knew where the money would go and still, for no reason that would hold up in daylight, gave him ten.

Hardin responded with a heart-melting smile. "Tomorrow," he said, and Dave raised one hand in farewell as he disappeared into the crowd.

He briefly considered looking for Jake and Sebastian, then decided he'd had enough of the future for one night. The Gaslight was around the corner. Maybe Van Ronk was playing.

EARLY AFTERNOON, the Saturday after Cole's first dinner at the Montoya house. He sat in his parents' living room and waited for Alex to pick him up. Pee Wee Reese and Dizzy Dean were calling a Yankees game on TV, the monotony of their voices hypnotic, sleep-inducing. Cole's father slumped in his recliner with drugstore reading glasses halfway down his nose, sketching some new piece of furniture that he would eventually build in the wood shop in the garage, with Cole's grudging participation in the cleanup, sanding, staining, and all the other parts that his father didn't have the patience for. Cole's mother sat across the room, knitting yet another pair of slipper-socks.

Alex, being polite, rang the doorbell instead of honking from the driveway. Cole reluctantly brought him inside to run the gauntlet of his father's disapproval. "Mom, Dad, this is Alex."

Cole's father looked at Alex over the top of his glasses. "Jeff says you've been a big help showing him the ropes at school." It sounded like an accusation.

"It was nothing, really, sir."

"No?" He glanced at Cole as if this confirmed his suspicions. To Alex he said, "And you play tennis?"

"I try, sir. I'm not as good as C— as Jeff."

"I see." He stared at Alex as if he expected further confessions.

Cole cleared his throat. "Uh, we need to get going, Dad."

"You're going to be home for supper?"

"No, I'm eating at Alex's. I already cleared it with Mom. I'll be home by ten."

His father nodded brusquely and looked down at the sketchpad. Cole grabbed the paper bag full of stuff that he'd left by the door and hustled Alex outside.

"Holy shit," Alex said. "Is he like that all the time?"

"No, most of the time he's not in such a good mood."

They drove to St. Mark's, where Cole tried to normalize Alex's strokes and get him to follow through. As soon as they started to keep score, Alex reverted. "I don't like to lose," Alex said. "I can't help myself."

"If you put discipline on top of your natural ability, you'd be really good. You could make the team."

"Then I'd really have to get my ass in gear. Don't worry, Cole, you're not responsible."

Still, Alex's occasional efforts at good form threw him off enough for Cole to take both sets, 6–4 and 6–3.

Cole tried not to show his disappointment when the red T-Bird was not in the driveway, lest Alex give him one of his pained looks. They changed into swim trunks and Cole swam a few laps to work the kinks out. Then he did a flip turn and rolled over into an easy backstroke.

"Don't you ever goof off?" Alex called out to him. Alex was in the deep end, both arms up on the rough concrete edge of the pool.

At his next turn, Cole hesitated, hands gripping the edge, feet planted against the tile. "What do you mean?"

"You know. Hang on the edge of the pool and look at the sky."

"I never really thought about it."

When he'd tired himself out, Cole made a few simple dives off the board and stayed underwater as long as he could, gliding the length of the pool. In his dreams he was able to open his mouth and breathe underwater.

Later, he showered in the guest bathroom upstairs and changed into clean clothes from his grocery sack. He'd brought the pint-sized Japanese reel-to-reel that had been his last year's Christmas present, and he set it up to record *Highway 61* and *Bringing It All Back Home*, The Rolling Stones' *Out of Our Heads* and the Animals' *Animal Tracks*.

They sat in the den downstairs while the albums were taping and Cole tried to get a line on the female situation. He'd heard about an all-girl's school called Hockaday that was the distaff St. Mark's.

"No, man," Alex said. "Hockadaisies are a bunch of stuck-up prudes. There's going to be a party at Arch Walker's house in a couple of weeks. I'm talking about drama club girls, art girls, music girls, a live band. Action guaranteed."

Cole nodded.

Alex said, "You're still a virgin, right?"

After a silence, Cole said, "Yeah. I've been in Midland. Nothing's happening in Midland. You?"

"Close," Alex said. "Not all the way. Not yet." They'd snuck a couple of Bohemias out of the spare refrigerator in the garage and Alex took a long drink. "We go down to Guanajuato every Christmas for a week or ten days. It would be pretty easy to, you know, go with a professional. A lot of my friends down there have done it. But… that's not really what I want. You know?"

"Yeah," Cole said. "I would want her to want it too."

Cole went upstairs to turn the record over and when he came back he said, "That's why I wanted to go to public school. I've been in Dallas for four months and I haven't even *met* any girls my age."

"Your dad is like my dad," Alex said. "He wants you to go further than he did."

"And I don't even want to go in the same direction. Meaningless job and wife and mortgage and car payment."

"Yeah? You already know what you want to do?"

"I've known since I was little."

"Tell me."

Cole shook his head. "Nope. Unh-uh. If I told you, you'd mock me."

"Now you *have* to tell me. I swear I won't give you shit."

"I always wanted to work for like the FBI or the CIA," Cole said. The beer, he thought, was loosening his tongue. "Field agent, overseas, undercover, the whole deal."

"Like James Bond."

"I've read all of those. And John le Carré and Len Deighton and people you've never heard of. Philip McCutchan, Donald Hamilton, Philip Atlee. And that's just the fiction."

"You are seriously into this."

"Right now I can only work in Latin America because Spanish is my only other language, except for a few words of Arabic. That's why I'm going to take Russian in college."

"Do you really think you could kill somebody?"

"Oh, hell yeah. I think it would be very satisfying. Once you were in the middle of it, kill or be killed? No question at all."

"Cole, have you ever considered the idea that you might be completely fucked-up crazy?"

"No," Cole said. "If it's either me or the rest of the world, I know who I trust."

ALL THAT WEEK, Cole put on the Dylan tape as soon as he finished his homework. The walk-in closet in his bedroom was his secret headquarters, furnished with an old armchair and a lamp and TV tray. He listened to Dylan there to lessen the chance of his father hearing it and going on a tirade. When he sang along, his voice was no more than a whisper. By Saturday night, both albums played continuously in his head.

Alex arrived alone in the Monza to pick him up. "I thought Susan was coming," Cole said.

"She went with her own friends. Are you kidding? Why would she want to go with us?"

"No reason," Cole said. "Never mind."

Moody Coliseum was the smu basketball court, a red brick box like all the campus buildings. They parked two blocks away in a student lot and joined the crowds on the wide flight of concrete steps outside. For all of Cole's father's talk about "beatniks" and "long-haired weirdos," what they mostly saw was short-haired college boys in slacks and sport coats. A few balding guys in black turtlenecks, some women in their thirties with straight hair halfway down their backs and skirts above their knees who looked like they'd taxied in from New York.

Cole got his ticket out. He'd been carrying it in his billfold all week and it had started to show some wear. They passed through the big glass doors and followed the signs to the steeply raked seats of section M. The stage was below them and to their left, a set of risers with white cloth backdrop and a rough scaffolding for the lights. He could make out instruments in the dimness of the stage— piano, organ, drums, amplifiers. He had trouble getting his breath.

The sight of Susan climbing the steps toward them made him sit up straight and try to look casual at the same time. She was squired by a tall, massive guy in a yellow blazer and a narrow tie that looked like it might choke him. Behind her stood a girl with a blonde flip, cat-eye glasses, and an equally large date. Susan spotted Cole and Alex and waved. Cole smiled and waved back and watched her settle in, three rows down and a dozen seats past him, eclipsed by her date's bulk.

The wooden floor of the basketball court had been covered with a gray canvas tarp and folding chairs, nearly all of them full. The stream of people into the side sections had slowed to a trickle. Expectant silences passed over the crowd, followed by bursts of nervous talk. Cole saw that he was drumming his fingers on the wooden seat between his legs and forced himself to stop.

At last the lights faded. A spotlight picked out the front of the stage and a disembodied voice introduced "Columbia Recording Artist" Bob Dylan. The applause was nearly drowned out by shouts and yelps and whistles.

Then Dylan was there. Small, not more than five-eight in his boots. Some kind of ultra-modern tan suit with no collar or lapels, hair standing up like a rooster tail. Acoustic guitar, harmonica rack.

He waited for the applause to fade, and then he leaned toward the mike and said, "Hi." Laughter, more applause. He stroked the guitar strings, and the strokes turned into chords, and he started to sing. "Of war and peace, the truth just twists…"

Until that moment, Cole had been detached, watching the movie unfold. Now, suddenly, the reality of it hit him in the solar plexus. He smelled the hair oil of the guy in front of him. He felt the density of the concrete beneath his loafers, heard the PA echo off the rear wall of the coliseum, saw a kid in the front row of chairs lean forward to put his elbows on his knees. He felt the chill and dampness of the air that lay over the city, the curvature of the earth, the tidal pull of the moon.

The piercing notes of the harmonica, Dylan's voice itself, nasal and whiny, his curiously emphatic "the," his chilly distance, all meant more than the tangled symbolism of his lyrics. They were the secret handshake, the tap on the shoulder, the beckoning hand from the alleyway. They separated the curious from the initiated.

Toward the end of the acoustic set, a girl with long, ironed blonde hair walked slowly out of the center aisle and floated toward the stage as if she'd been hypnotized. She reached out a hand to touch Dylan's boot and before her fingers made contact, two cops materialized out of the shadows and gently led her away.

Dylan finished the set with "Desolation Row," a song that Cole was sure nobody else in the audience understood half as well as he did. None of the places he'd ever lived, not the mud-brick houses and palm-lined suburbs of Suez, not the pastel-colored plaster walls and oily air of Villahermosa, not the blasted, salty plains of West Texas, and certainly not the high-rises and miniature mansions and paved-over scrublands of Dallas, had ever felt like home. The only space that the word defined for him was inside himself, a space that Dylan had mapped to the finest detail.

The lights came up and Alex asked if he wanted anything. He was talking about getting a Coke, Cole realized. He shook his head. The four dollars he'd paid for his ticket had wiped out his allowance. As Alex ran lightly down the steps, Cole wondered what Susan's friends had made of Dylan. The two boys had stood up and turned to face their dates, brawny arms folded, talking and laughing. Cole willed Susan to turn around and see him, to see that he understood that this was no laughing matter. She resisted his psychic powers, as so many had before her.

His awareness kept returning to the stage. Tilted, overlapping circles of drum heads and cymbals, worn guitar necks propped against the silver fabric of the speaker cabinets, cables wrapped like vines around the trunks of microphone stands. Their hum ran up his spine. He was content to be in that fulcrum moment, knowing that once the electric set started, it would be on its way to being over.

When Alex finally made it back, he had two Cokes and handed one to Cole. "In case you changed your mind. The lines were really long."

"Thanks, man." He took a long drink.

"So what did you think?"

Cole opened his mouth, and nothing came out. He thought of the blonde girl, drawn toward Dylan by currents of magnetic force. It was more like that than words.

"Yeah," Alex said. "Me too."

The lights began to dim. The last voices in the audience fell silent at the same moment that the room went dark.

Somebody moved on the stage. Shadows passed in front of the tiny red lights on the amplifiers, the bass drum gave out a single, muffled thud. A voice counted to four and the stage lights came up behind a tidal wave of noise. So loud and so distorted, so garbled by echoes off the hard, flat walls, that Cole couldn't distinguish the individual instruments, let alone any semblance of melody or rhythm. Terrifying, exhilarating, uncontainable, triumphant. It blew harmlessly through Cole's body even as it leveled Western civilization around him.

Dylan had the same suit on, now under an electric guitar, and the electricity arced through his legs and made him jump stiffly across the stage. He charged the microphone and spat lyrics into it, his expression no longer distantly amused but aggressive and defiant. He'd been booed, Cole had heard, in New York and LA, and was clearly expecting it again.

Cole felt a chord change more than heard it, and that and the lead guitar riff told him that the song was "Tombstone Blues," the second cut on the first side of *Highway 61*. The chaos of sound clicked into focus and now he could make out the words and hear the surging Lowrey organ and the pummeling bass.

Cole had grown up in the era of cowboy shows on television, and despite years without TV in Mexico and Egypt, he'd been obsessed with them, from *Wanted Dead or Alive* to *Have Gun Will Travel* to *Cheyenne*. The iconic pegged jeans, low-slung holster and cartridge belt, hat and vest and boots added up to an image that overshadowed plot and dialog and character. Dylan's new persona was equally powerful and fit precisely into the absence that the cowboys had left in Cole's imagination, the absence that the secret agents in their anonymous gray suits had never quite filled. Even more compelling was the lead guitarist at Dylan's left hand, pin-striped jacket and tie, black hair, guitar as blonde as the girl from the audience, half-smiling as he leaned into it, not so much creating the music as riding it the way a cowboy would, controlling it with flicks of the wrist, his body rippling with corollary motion.

As the song clattered to a close, Cole heard whistles and cheers over the applause and no boos at all. Cole clapped until his hands hurt. Dylan, more interested in his band than the audience, quickly started another song, "Baby Let Me Follow You Down," the Animals' rock version instead of the folk version from his first album, an album that hadn't moved Cole when Alex had played it for him.

He was moved now.

After that came "It Ain't Me, Babe," and what had at first been noise was full of melody, not as cheap and accessible as the Italian love songs that Cole had once listened to on KRLD's "Music Till Dawn," but all the more intense because of it. Then everything slowed and Dylan sang, "When you're lost in the rain in Juarez," and Cole snapped a mental picture to take with him for the rest of his life—blue lights washing the stage, the giant shadow of the head of the bass guitar on the white backdrop, the drummer and the piano player both hunched over, Dylan wide open to the microphone, the lead guitarist watching him, as everyone in the audience was watching him, leaning forward into the song, as Cole was, and all of them, together, surrendering.

After that "Like a Rolling Stone," and then "Maggie's Farm" as encore with Dylan on piano, not enough, but really, everything after that first electric onslaught had been overkill. The damage was done.

ON SATURDAY MORNINGS, Steve Cole liked to sleep late, put on his old brown corduroy bathrobe, nearly worn through in the elbows, and listen to Goodman at Carnegie Hall or Ellington at Newport. Betty would make French toast and then he would get dressed and maybe go out to the woodshop.

It was October 2, the first seriously cold morning of the fall. As he unfolded the newspaper at the dining room table, he heard the mower running in the front yard.

Betty brought him his first cup of coffee, and he said, "The kid's cutting the grass?"

"He said it needed one last trim before winter. He said to tell you he was lowering the blades to strip it."

Steve grunted in satisfaction. Nice not to have to remind the boy for once. "A little early, isn't it?" At this hour the lawn would still be damp with dew and the bag would get heavy fast.

"He's playing tennis later."

"With the Mexican kid."

"With his friend Alex, yes."

Betty went into the kitchen and a minute later he heard the bacon hiss and pop in the pan. The headline read, "Panel Ask Pay Boost, More Dallas Policemen." Steve nodded in silent agreement, wondering where the money would come from.

Betty brought in their plates and Steve poured syrup on the French toast. "Did he eat anything?"

"He had an Instant Breakfast."

"He'd take food pills if he could, like those astronauts of his." He cut the point off one of the triangles of bread and chewed it slowly. It was slightly underdone.

34

Betty said, "He brought up the guitar business again this morning."

"Why doesn't he talk to me about it?"

"Why do you think?"

Steve took another bite of French toast and then a bite of bacon that had been lying in the pool of syrup, salt and sweet together. "He'll get over it."

"I don't think so. Not this time."

"Well, he's going to have to talk to me directly. I don't want to hear any more about it from you. You can tell him that."

He reached for the sports page with his left hand and another piece of bacon with his right.

AFTER HE FINISHED the yard, the kid changed into tennis shorts and a sweater and then came and told Steve he needed to talk. Betty was hovering around the living room, pretending to dust and rearrange the magazines on the coffee table.

"I need to drive over to Centennial," Steve said. "Come with me and we can talk in the car."

The kid shrugged. "Sure, okay."

Dallas was a Baptist city, with antiquated and hypocritical Baptist laws. Blue laws kept most of the stores closed on Sunday, and liquor laws forced bars to resort to the "private club" dodge, like during Prohibition. North Dallas was dry, which meant you had to drive a couple of miles south and east to the island city of University Park to find a liquor store.

As soon as he backed onto the street, Steve said, "Do you think I like my job?"

He saw he'd thrown the kid for a loop. "Don't you?" he finally asked.

"As a matter of fact, I don't. Oil is filthy and I can't stand the smell of it. Most of the people I work with are ignorant and crude. Accounting is boring and I've hated most of the places we've had to live."

"Then why do you do it?"

"Life isn't about what I want to be. It's about making a good living in a job with security and a chance to get ahead. It's about making sure my kid gets opportunities I didn't have, to go to a first-rate college—"

"So I can get a job I hate?"

It stung, like the kid had snuck in a good right hand to the face. He took a second to clear his head. "No," he said. "So you have more choices than I did."

"What did you want to be?"

"What, you mean did I want to be a movie star or a big game hunter or pitch for the Dodgers? That's kid stuff. By the time I got out of the Army I was married to your mother and all I wanted was a job where I could make enough to get us a place of our own and get away from the foldout bed at your Grandpa Mac's."

"What about before you went in?"

Steve hesitated. He didn't like to talk about it. On the other hand, this was the first time the kid had attempted a real conversation since puberty. "I wanted to fly. I tried to volunteer before Pearl but I was too young. I turned eighteen in June of forty-two and they took me into the Air Corps. Then it came out that I'd had some epilepsy attacks when I was a kid. Nothing since I was three years old, but they had their rules and they washed me out before I got my wings. That's when they put me in accounting."

"How come you never told me?"

"It doesn't help to talk about it. There's different kinds of happiness. One kind is where you do your job well and take care of your family and people know they can count on you."

"I don't think that's a useful definition of happiness for a fifteen-year-old kid."

"You have to think about your future happiness, not just scratching whatever itch you have at the moment. If you don't think ahead, if you don't have a plan, you'll end up broke on some street corner with pencils and a tin cup."

"Or with a guitar?"

Steve looked over at him. No smirk, no challenge, no indication that he was smarting off. "Or with a guitar," he agreed. "Your mother told me. What do you want a guitar for?"

"Alex and I are going to start a combo."

"Who's Alex?" Something about the way the kid expected him to remember everybody's name made him contrary.

"I play tennis with him? Have eaten dinner over there? We went to the concert together?"

"Concert? Since when is some beatnik wailing a concert?"

The kid was struggling to keep his patience and Steve let him stew for a while. Finally the kid said, "I want this, Dad. I want it more than I've ever wanted anything."

"If you had one, how do you know you'd be able to play it? How do you know you won't get tired of it in two weeks and go on to something else?"

"I've played Alex's guitar. I can learn. It was like, like I already knew how and was just remembering it."

Steve let the silence unwind for a while before he said, "How much does it cost?"

"We went looking after school this week. We found just what I want at a pawn shop on Harry Hines. For everything—the guitar, a practice amp, a case, a 12-foot cord, a strap, an extra set of strings, and a half-dozen picks—it's..." He took a deep breath. "... a hundred and twenty-five dollars."

"Amp?"

"Yeah, a practice amplifier, it's about this big." He pantomimed a shape a bit larger than a shoebox.

"You're talking about an *electric* guitar?"

The kid was losing his temper, as he always did, though he tried to hide it. "Of course. To play in a group."

Steve shook his head. "Now, one of those Spanish guitars, I could maybe see that. But electric?"

The kid went quiet and Steve took another look. He had his jaw set and was wearing an expression of defiance that Steve had never seen before.

At that instant, Steve knew he was standing on the edge of a cliff. In the next thirty seconds he could lose his son, maybe for good. The thought made him so furious that he was tempted to press on, not only refuse the guitar, but ground him for picking one out before he had permission, for announcing that he was going to be in a combo with the Mexican kid like it was already

37

decided. Lock him in his room if he had to. If Steve had tried to blackmail his own father this way, even at age 15, he would have gotten a beating, probably with a razor strop. And if he'd fought back, his father would have gone after him with his fists and beaten hell out of him. He'd sworn he wouldn't be that kind of father. He'd also assumed his son would be like Steve was at that age, quiet, hard-working, obedient.

His window of opportunity to preserve his family was closing. He tried to clear the rage from his throat, found he couldn't, cleared it again. Looking straight at the road in front of him, he said, "Give me a minute to think about it."

They drove the rest of the way in silence. Steve parked and said, "Coming in?" and got only a surly shake of the head in reply.

He took his time. He picked up a fifth of Bacardi white rum for Betty and a fifth of Canadian Club for himself, then lingered for a while looking at the imported beers. This will pass, he told himself, like the kid's obsession with cowboy shows and toy six-shooters. And then he saw the way to turn this to his own advantage, and it was all he could do to keep from whistling as he walked out.

He drove back to Northwest Highway and said, "Okay, here's the deal. If you want this, it's going to cost you. I'll front you the money for the guitar, but you have to pay it back."

"Of course."

"Wait till I'm finished. You have to pay it back from what you'll earn in your summer job next year, working in the oil fields in Tyler."

"All summer?"

"Two months."

"Okay."

Steve was stunned. He'd underestimated how far the kid was willing to go.

"I'll draw up a contract, which you'll have to sign, so there's no misunderstanding. There are two other conditions. The first is, you have to keep up a B average at school. If that slips, you lose the guitar."

"Okay."

"The second one is this. You can play in this combo with your Mexican friend, but this is not going to be your career. I am not going to provide you with the tools to throw away your education and wind up using dope and living with Negroes and getting syphilis and dying at age thirty in some rathole. This is a hobby, and nothing more than that. Is that understood?"

It occurred to Steve that he might have pushed too far. So be it. He'd lived through the Depression and seen the despair in men's eyes who only wanted work, any kind of work, and couldn't find it. He'd been stationed in Europe for the last year of the war and seen how they lived over there, the bombed-out cities, people eating their own wallpaper. He, and every man he'd served with, had been determined to build a world where that would never happen to them, and they'd done it. Now that there was prosperity, maybe it was all too easy.

He didn't want to admit it, but it hurt him. Here is this gift, he'd said to his son. Here is the world I made for you. A world where you can be assured of a good job and a good living, your own home, your own car, enough money to raise a family. I worked all my life to make you this world.

And his son said no, I don't want that. It's worth nothing to me. What I want is an electric guitar.

They pulled up at a light and Steve turned to face him. "Well?"

"How long do I have? Since we're laying all this out. Do I have until I finish college to play in bands? And that has to include playing in public, because there's no point otherwise."

"Assuming you keep up your grades, I suppose so."

The kid licked his lips. "Okay, then."

"Not good enough. I need to hear you say, 'I agree.'"

"I agree," the kid said.

Steve bit back the words his own father had used so many times, about how it was for his own good. Take your bitter victory, he told himself, and show a little class.

"Good," Steve said. "Now where is this pawn shop?"

*

DAVE HAD TAGGED ALONG to San Francisco with Jake and the Spoonful, and what he'd found there was a city shedding its skin. The old city was North Beach, the tawdry burlesque joints and the Beat bookstores and coffeehouses, where the band was currently wrapping up a two-week residency at the hungry i, a folk and comedy club that was not remotely prepared to deal with their volume or the quantity of their recently converted fans.

The new thing was Haight-Ashbury, a Victorian neighborhood recently saved from the wrecking ball, now home to a cultural ferment so new that it didn't have a name. Their unofficial ambassador was one Luria Castell, a dark-haired entrepreneur in thrift-store couture and glasses, a founding member of something called The Family Dog, which had been involved in a rock dance scene that summer at the Red Dog Saloon in Virginia City. Luria had discovered the Spoonful at The Trip in LA, and during their previous San Francisco residency, at a club called Mother's, she had brought the Haight-Ashbury royalty to see them: her partner Chet Helms, a comedy ensemble called The Committee, and another theater group called the Mime Troupe, along with their loud and headstrong manager, a New Yorker named Bill Graham.

Now Luria had booked the Spoonful for a dance at the Longshoremen's Hall on the Sunday after the hungry i gig, touted as the sequel to a dance the previous Saturday, called "A Tribute to Dr. Strange," that the cognoscenti were still talking about. Those same scene-makers and dozens of hip, artsy, extroverted kids from the Haight had been showing up every night to shake hands and share a joint or two with the guys in the band. Because the guys already knew their way around—from Carol Doda's famous artillery-shell, silicone-injected breasts, on exhibit every night at the Condor, to the Roaring Twenties and its infamous Girl on the Swing routine—they dove headlong into the decadence. Everything they had worked so hard for was now theirs, not by the spoonful but by the truckload: adulation, sex, and at least the promise of wealth, though no actual money had yet arrived from the record label. What with the brazen availability of the girls in the audience, the seediness of the neighborhood, the excitement of the hit record, and the width of the continent between them and home, the boys were swept into a carnal frenzy that Dave was embarrassed to behold. Jake was no help. He'd loved the city since he'd attended a Jamboree there as a Boy Scout, and was out sightseeing all day in a rented car.

Dave had taken to roaming the streets of North Beach at night, browsing at City Lights or lingering over an espresso at Caffe Trieste. The hustle, the flashing neon, the loneliness of the commodified sex, all left him alienated and blue. Then, on the final Friday, he saw Hugh Romney's name on a flyer outside the Committee's theater on Broadway, a few doors down from the hungry i.

Dave had spoken to Romney a few times in the Village, fascinated by the dizzying wordplay that brought on intellectual and moral aftershocks. Lenny Bruce, who was managing Romney at the time, had carried him off to LA in 1962 and made him the first of a wave of defectors that eventually included Jim McGuinn and David Crosby.

Though the evening show was over, the doors of the theater were unlocked. The place had steeply raked seats and a big, open stage. A strange-looking guy with a long narrow face and an enormous nose asked him his business.

"My name is Dave Fisher. I was hoping to see Hugh."

"Wait here."

A minute later, Hugh appeared in dungarees and a sweater. Dave barely recognized him without his trademark finery. "Hey, I know you," Hugh said. "Dave, is it?"

"Yeah. I used to come see you at the Gaslight."

"Right! How you doing?"

Dave never felt awkward around Hugh, who radiated a fearless comfort with his own existence, and after a little small talk, Hugh consented to a cup of coffee.

"I'm just up from LA for a couple of days," Hugh said as they settled in at the counter of an all-night diner. "I'm trying to pick up a buck or two. I used to be a member of this outfit, so I guess I'm re-membering. I've got a day job teaching improv to actors at Columbia Pictures back home, but I'm part of this commune-type thing now and we go through a lot of money."

"A commune? For real?"

"Yeah, a bunch of the Pranksters got stranded in LA—you know about the Pranksters?"

"I guess I've heard of them."

"Buncha weirdos, do a lot of acid. Real LSD freaks. We're all living on this hog farm and doing crazy stuff on Sundays for anybody that comes up."

"I can't picture you on a hog farm. You were always so debonair."

"That's kitchen synchronicity for you. Always making you get a new set of plots and plans. There's change to spare these days and the Hog Farm is in the thicket of it. And the real epicenter is here in Frisco." Hugh waved one hand at their run-down surroundings. "Not *here* here, not in North Beach, but over in the Haight, or at these things they're doing at the Longshoremen's Hall."

Dave told him about the upcoming Spoonful gig.

"Aha! You'll see for yourself, then. I'd be there, but I've got to get back to LA, back to the Farm. I got married, you know." He seemed amazed. "She's an actress. She's smart and beautiful and sensible. We've got nothing in common." He smiled hugely. "Except empathy. We're having a mad, compassionate love affair."

"Congratulations," Dave said.

"I think the next thing that happens is that we take the show-and-tell on the road. We're preaching to the convertibles in LA. Can you imagine what they'll make of us in Peoria?"

When they stood up to leave, Hugh startled Dave by hugging him. "I've got to get back," he said. "I'm so glad to see you again. I love surprises. They're the proving ground for philosophy."

On Sunday afternoon, a young woman from the Family Dog arrived in a 1940s pickup to carry the Spoonful's equipment down to the Longshoremen's Hall. She was fresh-faced and auburn-haired, wearing a plaid shirt with the sleeves rolled up and battered Levis. Zal immediately claimed the passenger seat, leaving Dave to ride in the back with the gear.

The sun had finally broken through, raising the temperature into the 70s, and as they barreled downhill, Dave saw the Golden

Gate to his left and the Bay Bridge to his right. Straight ahead, across the deep blue of the bay, were the rugged hills of Marin County. This, then, was what Jake had fallen for, this supernatural beauty that grounded the weirdness and poetry and sexual license in an earthly paradise.

The hall itself was an octagonal concrete bunker with a high, domed roof. As the band attempted a sound check, Dave walked around the immense, echoing space without finding a single point where the acoustics were less than horrendous. They gave up and went their separate ways, Zally disappearing with the girl in the pickup.

When Dave returned at eight that night, banners painted on bed-sheets announced "A Tribute to Sparkle Plenty," with renderings of the ingénue from the Dick Tracy comic strip. What must have been a thousand kids filled the room, dressed as cowboys, soldiers, nineteenth-century aesthetes, hobos, knights, princesses, and deep-sea divers. In New York, rebel kids had hair that covered the tops of their ears and maybe spilled over their collars. Here, some of the boys had not cut their hair in years, letting it flow past their shoulders or corkscrew out in Caucasian Afros. These kids had none of the attitude that was mandatory in New York, the boasting, the strutting, the competing for attention. Instead they glided, wide-eyed and smiling, from one embrace to the next, passing around joints, wine, flowers, and fruit. The air was thick with pot and cigarette smoke, sandalwood incense, patchouli oil, English Leather.

Jake beamed as if he'd been airlifted to Valhalla. "Every one of these people," he announced, "is stoned or tripping or both. How fantastic is that?"

"I don't know, Jake," Dave said. "You tell me."

Jake had told him how he'd done acid after seeing Leary and Alpert in New York the year before, having bought some blotters in the lobby along with a copy of *The Psychedelic Experience*. He had gotten all he needed from a few trips, though he periodically urged Dave to try it so that he could work on the bardos of his own existence.

Jake was also excited about seeing the opening act, the Char-latans, who'd been the house band at the Red Dog in Nevada.

Luria Castell had brought him photos and a cassette at The Trip in LA, and Jake had been intrigued by the looks they affected—Victorian dandies, cowboys, riverboat gamblers—the kind of old-timey clothes that Jake himself loved, taken to the extreme, to the point of wearing loaded six-guns on stage.

Things got off to a slow start. First came shtick from a local DJ, followed by a lot of drug jokes from the long-faced Committee guy Dave had run into at the theater. The crowd got restless, wanting to dance, and the Committee guy got hustled off to make room for the Charlatans. Once they finally got going, their sound was so muddy that Dave couldn't tell much about them. They switched off lead vocals, and the songs were all over the place, from blues and jug band to folk and rock, none of them memorable.

The audience didn't share Dave's concerns. They began to dance at the first drumbeat, a whole different kind of dancing than Dave had ever seen, more sway than bounce, with no concern for pairing one woman with one man. The point was to make a personal statement, to do something nobody else was doing. One guy in pajamas did the backstroke across the floor, pushing himself forward with his legs. The other dancers, if they noticed him, gave him room.

Jake, grinning, waded out onto the floor. A blonde girl in an Indian headband, complete with feather, beckoned Dave to join her. Blushing, he waved her off. The last time he'd danced was the Hora at his bar mitzvah.

As he watched dancers attach and detach, forming singles and couples and groups, it gradually occurred to him that this was more than a new way of dancing. More than LSD, more than a new style of music, more than a few kids in an outpost of weirdness on the west coast. Change to spare, Hugh had said. By the time Hugh and his Prankster friends got to Peoria, Dave thought, it was going to be a tidal wave.

DAVE WAS PAGING THROUGH the in-flight magazine on the plane to New York when Jake said, "What did you think?"

"I think maybe I'm too old," Dave said. He had in fact turned thirty a few weeks before, the age at which he was no longer to be trusted, according to the radicals at Berkeley. He'd taken himself out for a solitary dinner to celebrate.

"Bullshit," Jake said. "You're just uptight. You need to work on your bardos of existence."

"You were into it."

"I was glad to see people loosen up. And, not to be cynical, there is money to be made with dances like that. Put them in a proper ballroom with decent acoustics, it could be gigantic." He spread Luria's photos of the Charlatans on his folding tray. "What did you think of these guys?"

"Not much," Dave said. In retrospect, something about them had put him off, a smugness that bordered on sarcasm.

"The gal, Luria Castell, she wants me to produce some demos on them."

Dave noted the first person singular. "Are you going to do it?"

"Something's happening out there," Jake said. "Yeah. Yeah, I think I am."

MADELYN TURNED AWAY from her locker to find two boys looming over her. One was Ed Wallingford, from her Civics class, and the other, whose name she didn't remember, played football. Ed had serious acne problems and a tendency to become tongue-tied when called upon; the football player did not appear to be emotionally engaged.

"We're supposed to give you this note," Ed said.

Madelyn, rattled, was reluctant to accept it. "Who's it from?"

"Billy Dixon," Ed said. He sounded irritable, as if Madelyn should somehow have already known.

"Billy Dixon?" Madelyn said. Billy was a track star and dreamily handsome. He was too good a student and too introverted to be in the first rank of popular boys, but he was high in the second tier. "What does he want with me?"

Ed thrust the note at her again. "Why don't you read it and find out?"

"Dear Madeline," the note read. She noted the misspelling and didn't take points off, being too used to it. "I think you're really cool, but I'm shy to talk to you in person. I think maybe you might think I'm just a dumb jock and not want to know me, which is OK I would understand. But if you would like to go to the Halloween Dance on Saturday maybe you could tell Ed and he would pass it on to me. I hope you will say yes. Billy."

Flattered, skeptical, and flummoxed, she read the note a second time and had started a third when Ed said, "Well?"

"Um, can I think about it?"

Ed looked at the football player incredulously. "Billy Dixon wants to go out with her and she has to think about it?"

Madelyn had no idea what to say, so she panicked and said the thing that was expected. "Well, then, yes, I suppose."

"You *suppose?*"

"Yes, then," Madelyn said. "Yes."

MADELYN'S PARENTS were skeptical too, though not nearly as much so as her sister Julia. Julia was two years younger and more conventionally pretty than Madelyn; she had short, nearly natural blonde hair where Madelyn's was red-gold and halfway down her back, breasts that had filled out much earlier and much further than Madelyn's, a pout that was more studied than spontaneous, and none of Madelyn's off-putting vocabulary. The boys in her freshman class were already chasing her, and Madelyn worried that Julia was not running nearly fast enough.

"Why would anybody popular want to go out with *you?*" Julia asked. "Does he need help with his homework?"

"He's pretty bright, actually," Madelyn said. "Which would also answer your first question."

"How far are you going to let him go?"

"What?"

Madelyn had spoken in shock; Julia took it, perhaps willfully, for ignorance. "On a first date, I don't think you should let him get past second base, outside your clothes. In any case, you need to make up your mind before, and stick to it."

Madelyn had not considered the issue. She was not completely without experience, although her prior dates had involved a parent or two as chauffeurs and chaperones, boys with bad posture and/ or glasses, a few sweaty and awkward dances in an echoing gym, and halting conversation in between. Whenever possible, she had double-dated with her best friend Hope, so she'd have someone to talk to.

The invitation had been extended on a Monday with the dance that Saturday; neither time nor money was available for an elaborate costume. Madelyn's mother helped her go through two trunks' worth of old clothes in the attic, where they turned up a blue, short-sleeved dress, a white apron, and a sufficiency of petticoats to produce a reasonable facsimile of the John Tenniel drawings of Alice. Madelyn already had the black Mary Janes, and she added a black domino mask for a hint of mystery.

"Dorothy, from *Wizard of Oz*?" Julia hazarded when she saw the finished product.

When Madelyn explained, Julia said, "Nobody is going to guess that. Not in a million years."

The arrangement, brokered by Ed, was that Billy would pick her up at eight at her parents' house. Only at 8:15 did Madelyn realize that she had no phone number for Billy, and no contingency plans. By 8:45 she understood that he wasn't coming.

They were all sitting in the living room pretending to watch NBC's *Saturday Night at the Movies*. Madelyn could not have said what the movie was. Now and then her parents exchanged a worried look or glanced at her. Finally Madelyn stood up and said, "Daddy, would you drive me to the dance?"

In preparation for meeting Billy, he was already dressed in a short-sleeved white shirt and black tie. At the gym, he retired to the parents' corner where cookies, ashtrays, and a pot of coffee had been provided.

Considerable effort had been expended to decorate the gym with fake cobwebs and cardboard ghosts. The band was on break, the dance floor empty. Madelyn knew that neither Hope, nor any of her other friends, were coming. She told herself the domino mask would provide her anonymity; in fact, she knew that she was already invisible in her plainness, in her failure to compete socially, in her perceived braininess.

She kept to the shadows until she saw Billy Dixon. He was with one of the cheerleaders, and they had circled up with other members of the track team and their dates. Madelyn watched him for ten minutes, while the band got up on the stacked risers and started to play again. Eventually Billy took his date's hand and moved toward the dance floor. Madelyn triangulated an interception point and contrived to bump into him as if by accident. From his utter lack of embarrassment, she saw that he was not party to the scheme. The notes, then, had been forged. She and Billy both apologized and Madelyn turned to go.

Ed and half a dozen members of various sports teams had lined up along the rear wall of the gym to watch. Ed was smirking and one of the others was straining so mightily to keep from laughing that his eyes bulged. Madelyn took care not to let her expression change as she walked by.

Driving home, her father said, "I'm sure I know the answer to this already, but I have to ask. You didn't do anything to Ed, even inadvertently, to trigger this incident?"

"No, Daddy." She paused, then said, "He's in my Civics class. He's... struggling."

"Ah." They drove for a while in silence, then he said, "I think you were very brave to show up at the dance. I'm proud of you."

"Thank you, Daddy." She stared out the window at the streetlit lawns of Highland Park, their dead leaves all raked and bagged and carted away, left with no cover for the coming winter. She was determined not to cry over having been deprived of something she hadn't wanted in the first place. There would be laughter at her expense on Monday, and that would be the hardest part. That much she had coming, she thought, for being so naïve.

As soon as they got home, she put on her pajamas and got into bed with the Andrew *Odyssey* and turned to Book One.

"Tell me, O muse," she read, and the rest of the world went away.

*

THE NEXT AFTERNOON, she borrowed the station wagon to drive to Hope's house. Hope had the twin afflictions of intelligence and excessive height. At five-eleven, she had learned that basketball players, the only boys who tolerated the latter, tended to be intimidated by the former.

"I'm through with boys," Hope announced, once they were in her room with the door closed. Madelyn, having told her on the phone about her humiliation, assumed this diatribe was at least partly in her honor. "I'm through playing dumb to get dates. I'm through having boys rub their hands on me like I was a towel."

"Well," Madelyn said, "nobody wiped his hands on me."

"They might as well have. They felt they had the right to play their stupid games with you. You remember that Lesley Gore song?"

Madelyn did. Nonetheless, Hope rummaged through a vinyl carrying case, pulled out a black-labeled 45 of "You Don't Own Me," and sang along at considerable volume and with a clenched-fist intensity that left Madelyn feeling as if her own suffering had been unfairly appropriated.

Afterward, Hope said, "It's true, you know. We are the property of our fathers, who loan us out to various boys until the official transfer of ownership, when they walk us down the aisle at our weddings."

"I don't think my father feels that way about me."

"No? What about all those reading lists and quizzes he gives you? You're like a..."

"Like a what?" Madelyn said frostily.

"Nothing."

"I hope you weren't going to say, 'like a trained dog.'"

"It *is* a little weird, that's all."

Madelyn stood up. "Thanks, Hope. I'll keep that in mind."

"Wait," Hope said. "I'm sorry. I love your dad, you know I do."

Eventually she let Hope talk her down, and they returned to Ed Wallingford and how Madelyn was going to deal with him. They agreed on silence and a confident smile, which Madelyn rehearsed in Hope's mirror until she had it pat.

Upon leaving Hope's house, however, the sting in Hope's insult returned. Was everything she did just to please her father? Where did that end and Madelyn's own desires begin? The truth was that she didn't know.

1966

ON A SUNDAY MORNING in the middle of June, Cole's parents dropped him off at the Tyler Motor Inn. Whitewash over a plywood exterior, a standard tourist court layout thrown together on the cheap for losers in transit. East Texas Crude, Inc., got a weekly rate.

Alex had warned him. "Talk about armpits," he'd said. "It's 1952 there. They're still crying about Hank Williams and waiting to see if Eisenhower got elected."

Cole had no option but to make the best of it. "No distractions," he'd said. "More time to practice."

Watching his parents drive away, he felt more elated than abandoned. His own place, for the first time in his life. A working air conditioner and maid service every Monday. As long as he kept the volume down, he could play guitar all night.

Or as long as he could stay awake. In his first full week on the job, that hadn't been much past nine PM. The work so far had been easy enough—he was too inexperienced to be on the drilling table with the roughnecks, the really dangerous job. Instead he cleaned up and carried and used his new driver's license to run errands in a pickup that was the same age as he was, held together with coat hanger wire and coats of battleship-gray Army-surplus paint. What left him light-headed and stumbling was the damp, choking heat, the noise of the drill, the long hours on his feet.

After a half-day on the rig Saturday morning, he was fresh out of the shower and looking forward to a steak and a few beers with two of his co-workers.

He sat up in bed with his guitar and opened a loose-leaf notebook that had the name "Chevelles" painstakingly lettered on the canvas cover. Alex had picked the name, and he'd invested in a Gibson EB-0 bass guitar and Fender Bassman amp. He'd also recruited a veteran rhythm guitar and keyboard player named Mike Moss from Richardson High. Mike had met with him and Alex just once, in late May, at Alex's house. They'd sat around with guitars and tried their voices together, and Alex had taught them the three-part harmony to "Look Through Any Window" by The Hollies, to see what they were capable of. The process took nearly an hour and when they were done they sounded so much like the record that it amazed them all.

It changed something in Cole. The way he held himself, the way he saw the world. He felt initiated, powerful. It happened again when he and Alex made it all the way through "The Last Time" by the Stones and Cole got all the lead parts note for note. All the songs in all the world were his to command.

He and Mike and Alex had put together the list that now made up the first four pages of the notebook—four 45-minute sets, totaling 60 songs. They'd started with Dylan, the reason the band existed. They'd quickly settled on "Mr. Tambourine Man," "It Ain't Me, Babe," and "Just Like Tom Thumb's Blues," which they knew they would have to shorten the way The Byrds had shortened "Mr. Tambourine Man." Then it had been a free-for-all, all three of them calling out titles faster than Alex could write them down. After that they'd gone over the initial list and filled in the gaps, coming up with break songs, slow songs, the obligatory songs like "Gloria" and "Land of 1000 Dances," relegating the Kinks and Beatles and Stones and Animals to no more than one song per set.

The one unexpected argument had been over Ritchie Valens' "La Bamba." Alex didn't want to do it.

"Are you kidding?" Cole had said. "When you and me both speak Spanish?"

«Y yo también,» Mike said.

"That's exactly the reason," Alex said. "I don't want us getting typecast."

"From one song?" Cole said.

"Every band in Texas does 'La Bamba,'" Mike said.

Eventually Alex had given in, but it reminded Cole that whenever he said something in Spanish, whether from habit or as a test, Alex always replied in English. Never making an issue of it, and never going along.

The rest of the book was lyrics and chords, some of which Cole was still figuring out. Alex was doing about half the lead vocals, Cole a third, and Mike the rest. By the time Cole got back in mid-August, Mike and Alex were supposed to have found a drummer and started rehearsals.

Cole sprinted through "Walk, Don't Run" and "House of the Rising Sun" to warm up, still not getting his arpeggios as smooth as he wanted. Then he skipped around the list, ignoring the easy ones like "Louie Louie" and "You Really Got Me," working his way up to "Do You Believe in Magic," where the guitar part was tricky enough even without the harmony part he had to sing behind it.

In the eight months he'd been playing, his hands had become the hands of a completely different person. Not just the calluses on the tips of the fingers of his left hand, not just the strength and flexibility. The intelligence behind his playing had moved from his conscious brain into the fingers themselves. He no longer had to listen to know how far to bend a note, rarely had to look down to find the right fret. Standing around at work, he would press his left thumbnail into the thick pads of callus, or bend his ring finger into a barred A against his thumb, the way a bodybuilder might flex and pose in front of a mirror.

His ears had changed, too. He could hear major sevenths on the radio, hear the I-IV-V progressions behind most of the songs, hear a note and put his finger on the guitar neck at the place where it lived. He begrudged the years he'd spent doing anything else.

He got in a couple of hours of solid practice before he had to get ready. Dress Levis and a brand-new green-plaid pearl-snap Western shirt he'd bought at Shepler's in Dallas for camouflage. His work boots were too muddy to wear, so he made do with his loafers.

A car honked outside. He checked himself in the mirror and was okay with it. The sun had dried out the two zits on his chin and no new ones had come up yet. His hair had started to grow out and the hard work had straightened his spine.

Jerry and Donald, he noted, wore variants of his shirt and jeans. They laughed and whistled, however, as he walked out to Jerry's black Ford Falcon.

"Where'd you get them shoes, college boy?" Donald said as Cole climbed in the back seat. Donald was the driller on Cole's rig, in his mid-twenties, a bit heavy and already losing his hair. "Jer, we got time to get this boy some proper footwear before dinner?"

"I don't see how we got much choice," Jerry said. Jerry was the same age as Donald, tall and lean and cooked by the sun. He kept a battered straw hat pulled low over his eyes and a Lucky Strike in the corner of his mouth. He was the derrickman, working high in the scaffolding when they took the pipe in and out of the hole, and monitoring the drilling mud the rest of the time. "You and me might could suffer for being seen with him in such a disgraceful condition."

They'd been paid in cash that morning, and Cole had over $50 in his pocket. "Let's do it," he said.

He resisted their efforts to get him into ostrich skin or caiman belly Luccheses and settled on a plain pair of Fryes with a walking heel. He felt like the bones in his feet were cracking when he put them on, though they felt fine once he was in them. They set him back $25, which the clerk said was an investment. "They'll last a lifetime, if you break 'em in right. Don't spend too many hours in 'em at first."

"What d'ya think, Jer?" Donald asked as they walked to the car.

"Better," Jerry said. "Needs a hat."

"Maybe next week," Cole said.

Gringo's Steakhouse was full of smoke, some from cigarettes, the rest from grilling meat. Cole ordered a rib-eye rare and took more kidding over that.

"Should have brung my sunglasses," Donald said when the platter arrived. "I never did like the sight of blood."

"Go easy with that knife," Jerry said. "I think I heard her moo."

Though Cole had never been much of an eater, he had no trouble putting away a 12-ounce rib-eye, home fries, salad, Texas toast, and a quart of iced tea. By the time he'd gotten on the outside of all that food, he was ready for a nap.

Donald had other ideas. "Wagon Wheel?" he said as he pushed back from the table.

"Wagon Wheel," Jerry said.

"What's a Wagon Wheel?" Cole asked.

The Wagon Wheel was a gigantic metal shed with tables salvaged from cable spools, rickety folding chairs, and a layer of peanut hulls over the concrete floor to catch the spills. The high ceiling made the level of tobacco smoke somewhat less toxic than at Gringo's. A row of carpet samples separated the tables from the dance floor that ran the length of the shed, and the dancers used it to wipe the peanut hulls off their feet.

Cole had never seen that kind of dancing before. The couples faced each other as they circled the outside of the floor, the man's right wrist on the woman's left shoulder, opposite hands clasped. The better dancers glided like they were on ice skates, the women spinning almost continuously. Both sexes wore cowboy hats and jeans and boots and Western shirts, though the jeans, Cole noticed immediately, fit one sex much more tightly than the other. A DJ provided the music from a long table at one end of the floor, alternating between two turntables and blasting the result out of a pair of Voice of the Theaters. The songs were vaguely familiar from Midland, where country music permeated the air as thoroughly as the smell of the refineries.

"If I was to buy you a beer," Donald said, having to shout over the music, "would you know what to do with it?"

Lone Star longnecks were what was available. "I believe the narrow end goes in my mouth," Cole said.

"See there, Jer? I told you the boy was edjamacated."

"College boy," Jerry nodded. Cole had given up his attempts to explain his actual academic status.

Donald bought the first round, two each for him and Jerry, one for Cole. Ice chips still clung to the bottles, and the beer was so cold that it tasted like nothing at all. Cole watched the women glide by. Some were overweight, overage, or both. Many were neither.

In the course of the next hour, a few roughnecks stopped by the table for shouted pleasantries that, between the background noise and the nearly consonant-free East Texas accents, Cole found unintelligible. He smiled and nodded, watched the dancers, and listened to what the guitar players did on the records.

Cole was looking the other way when a voice said, "Evening,

boys," followed immediately by the sound of two pairs of boots hitting the floor as Donald and Jerry straightened up in their chairs. The voice came from a dark-eyed blonde in a straw cowboy hat whose brim was curled as tight as Cole's toes at the sight of her. She wore a man's long-sleeved white shirt with the sleeves rolled up and the tails tied in a knot below her breasts, exposing a flat, tanned stomach and a pair of cutoff jeans that had frayed right up to the point where her long legs joined the rest of her body. She couldn't have been more than twenty, and was probably a good deal less. She had one hand on Donald's shoulder and the other on Jerry's and she was looking at Cole.

"I'm Corrina," she said.

"Cole," he said, standing up to reach across the table and take her hand. "Have a seat. I'll find us another one."

He held his chair for her while she walked around the table and sat down.

"Damn," Donald said. "Is that how they do it in college?"

It took him three tries to find a table with an empty chair. "Can I borrow this?" Cole asked. The three men at the table were huge, one with a heavy beard, another with a jagged scar on his lip.

"We're using it," said the bearded one.

The one with the scar tilted his head toward Cole's table. "Think the boy wants it for Corrina."

"Hell, take it then."

"Thanks," Cole said.

He set the chair down far enough from her not to crowd her. Not too much, anyway.

"What college you go to?" Corrina asked.

"UT," Cole said, and then, his conscience pricking him, "in about a year and three months."

That got a more convincing smile out of her. "You don't look like a roughneck. Summer job?"

He moved closer so as not to have to shout quite so loudly. "For another 57 days. Not that I'm counting. You don't look much like a roughneck either."

The ends of her mouth turned down in something between a grimace and a pout. "Thanks," she said. Cole figured her for smarter than she was letting on. She was alive in the moment, anyway, not on autopilot like most of the women in the room.

The DJ played a new song, one that Cole recognized. "Six Days on the Road," Dave Dudley.

"Do you dance?" Corrina asked.

"Not like this," he said.

She grabbed his hand and stood up. "First time for everything. It's not that hard."

"Go get 'er, college boy!" Donald called as Cole stood up. Torn between lust and the terror of humiliating himself, he let himself get drawn toward the dance floor.

She leaned in and talked into his ear. "Right hand here, hold my hand here with your left. Start on your left foot and just walk." She timed her words to the music. "Left-right-left. Right. Left-right-left." The floor was only half full. She pulled him into an opening and counted him in.

Cole did as he was told. In a few seconds he got the feel of it and tried to smooth it out, to not lift his feet so high. The song was not that fast and he could feel the beat. "Not bad," she said. "When I say 'now,' lift your left hand. Now."

He lifted his hand and she spun around twice. Watching her made him lose the rhythm, but when she was facing him again she was already mouthing the steps.

A few seconds later she picked his right hand off her shoulder and put it into her own right hand and turned herself one and a half times. Now her back was to him and she was wiggling the fingers of her left hand. Cole picked it up and they danced side by side, the length of her left upper arm pressing against his chest and abdomen, her hat poking him in the shoulder.

Chanting the steps under his breath, Cole watched the other leaders around him, and when she turned again, he changed hands on his own and got a big smile for it. He waited a few beats, then lifted his left hand and gave her a push with the right.

"I like the initiative," she said. "A little gentler next time, and wait for the second slow step."

They made it through the rest of the song without anyone getting hurt, and she said, "There. That wasn't so bad, was it?"

"No," he said. "But you did everything."

"That's okay, as long as you let me. You didn't fight me, and that's a good thing."

The DJ said, "And now a slow one for Corrina. How you doing, sugar?"

She blew an exaggerated kiss to the DJ and then said to Cole, "Now you get your reward."

The DJ played Eddy Arnold's "Make the World Go Away." This, Cole knew how to do. Corrina took her hat off and let it dangle from her left hand where it rested on his shoulder. She moved in until she was brushing gently against him, and Cole didn't pull her any closer than that. He couldn't remember why he'd disliked country music. The violins overflowed with emotion and the piano notes rang sweet and true. He swayed in place during the clean breaks at the start of every verse, where he could feel the breath move in and out of her.

By the time the song ended he'd lost all sense of time and space. "Maybe," he said, "we could, uh…"

"Yes?" She looked pleased with herself.

"Get a breath of fresh air? Talk for a minute without having to shout?"

She put her hat on. "All right."

As he walked toward the front door, he felt like every man in the room was watching him. In fact, he thought, they probably were.

The outside air was hot, but it moved around and it smelled of pine trees. A haze softened the stars and crickets creaked in the distance.

"New boots?" she asked.

"Nah, I've had 'em nearly four hours now. How old are you, anyway?"

"You should know better than to ask a lady her age."

"It's important. I'm trying to figure out if I should try to kiss you or not."

"If you have to ask, the answer is definitely 'no.'"

"What do you do, then? Maybe I can get a hint from your occupational status."

"I, it would seem, am a year ahead of you. I graduated from Robert E. Lee High School last month and am currently at loose ends. Living with my mama and hoping to get accepted into VISTA in the fall."

"VISTA?"

"It's like a domestic Peace Corps. I will be helping to fight the President's War on Poverty, though I am not far from that state myself. My mama can't afford to send me to college and I desperately need to get out of this place."

"I'm going to make a wild guess that your yearbook lists Drama Club under your activities."

"Why, however did you deduce that?" Her Deep South accent was credible. "Blanche DuBois in *Streetcar*, Ado Annie in *Oklahoma*."

"The girl who can't say no," Cole said. "I like you better by the minute."

They had arrived at Jerry's Falcon. The doors proved to be locked.

"Yours?" Corrina asked.

"Jerry's. We can sit on the hood and I can take a load off these boots."

"Can't live with 'em, can't two-step without 'em." She hopped up beside him.

He kissed her. Nothing fancy, and she kissed him back the same way, lips parted and soft. "Not bad," she said, when he finished. He put his arms around her and kissed her some more. He tried a little tongue and she responded, and he thought, is this finally going to be it? Here in the middle of the parking lot? But when he put a hand on her breast, she gently removed it and said, "Easy, college boy. No paw prints on the clean shirt."

"I could help you out of it," he said.

She turned her mouth down again. "I don't think so. Our acquaintance is not even as old as your boots, and your boots ain't half broke-in yet."

He made to kiss her again and she wriggled free. "I think we better work on those boots some more. Two more dances, then you go home and get them off before your feet swell up to where you have to sleep in them."

*

COLE ENDED UP with her phone number and a vague promise to see him again the next Saturday. "There's a two-step lesson at seven," she said.

"Will you be there?"

"I don't need lessons," she said.

On the drive to the Tyler Motor Inn he pressed for information. "How do you guys know her?"

"Everybody knows Corrina," Jerry said.

"Did either of you guys ever… you know."

"Fuck her?" Donald said. "In my dreams. If Jerry says he did, he's lying." All that beer had left Jerry contented and Donald irritable.

"As far as my personal experience goes," Jerry said, "she could be all flirt and no follow-through." He caught Cole's eye in the rear-view mirror. "I surely doubt it, though."

The boots were in fact a problem, and by the time he got the first one off he was afraid he might have done permanent damage to his foot in the process. He wrenched the other one off anyway. Then, after relieving the terrible pressure of his desire, he was awake for another hour calming down. It didn't help that the sound of highly vocal sex was coming through the thin plywood wall.

He tried Corrina's number throughout the day on Sunday. Between calls he practiced two-step and guitar, and walked in his new boots to the Silver Spoon Café—inevitably the Greasy Spoon to Donald and Jerry—for a late breakfast and then for an early supper. He finally caught her at 8:30. She seemed happy enough to hear from him. They were on the phone for close to an hour, talking about Shakespeare and country music and growing up in Tyler, Texas. Cole mostly listened.

At the end she told him he was "sweet" and said she would maybe see him on Saturday.

"Say you'll see me for sure on Saturday, so I can go to sleep happy."

"Maybe for sure," she said. "Good night, college boy."

★

DRUMMER NUMBER THREE was named Gary Travis, and Alex took a dislike to him at first sight. He was five-ten, skinny, and had his black hair slicked back in a style at least five years out of date. He wore khaki pants instead of jeans and a Madras shirt with a button-down collar.

He was Mike Moss's idea. Mike didn't know much about him beyond the fact that he played with the Richardson High Band. Mike had run into him at Preston Record Center after drummers one and two had washed out, and asked if he played rock. He'd shrugged and said, "Sure. Nothing much to it."

He had the smallest drum set Alex had ever seen, the bass drum not much bigger than the last drummer's floor tom. He'd spread a rug on the floor of Alex's garage before setting up, and he spent more time tuning his heads than he had putting the hardware together, holding his left stick in the crook of his thumb, jazz-style.

When he was ready, Alex handed him the song list and said, "The ones with the checkmarks we've worked on at least enough to get through." He'd already explained, on their initial phone call, about Cole.

Gary glanced over the list and said, "Why don't we start with 'Shake'? That'll give you a taste of what I can do."

They had already tuned Alex's bass and Mike's guitar to his Vox Continental organ. "Go ahead and count it off," Alex said, thinking, this shouldn't take long.

"Animals or Sam Cooke?"

The Animals version was the only one Alex knew. He looked at Mike, who said, "Uh, what's the difference?"

"Animals is faster. The drums are more interesting in the Cooke version."

Smart ass, Alex thought. "Cooke, then."

It took about five seconds for Alex to change his mind. Instead of playing through on the hi-hat and snare like the Animals drummer did, Gary played the bass line on his tom-toms. It wasn't fancy, no more than single notes in perfect time. Instead of driving, it swung. On the verses, that jazzy left hand hit with snap and authority. By the end of the song, Alex was wondering what they could offer him to get him to stay.

"On the Cooke version," Gary said, "it's just the drums the first time through. Bass and drums the second time, add guitar for the third, and on the last one he's got horns. I guess that's where your lead player would come in."

Maybe, Alex thought, putting up with Gary's shit was a high enough price to pay. "Let's try it again," he said.

Alex called "Look through Any Window" next because The Hollies had the best drummer in the business and Alex knew what the part should sound like. Gary counted it off and played a credible version, simpler here and there, always with the right feel, solid on the two and four.

Mike said, "I thought you said you'd never played in a rock band before."

"Never have," he said. "I listen to this stuff all day and night, though. This is cool. Can we do another one?"

They played for an hour, then went in the house for Cokes. "You're a secret weapon, man," Alex told him. "I would kill to have you in this band. I don't know if we're good enough for you."

"Depends on the lead player, I guess," Gary said. "You guys can both really sing, and I can't sing for doodley-squat."

"He can sing, too," Alex said. "We can do We Five, we can do Byrds, Beatles, everything."

Gary looked through the set list and said, "Okay, you've got 'Sloopy' on here, of course, but have you ever heard the original?"

"Original?" Alex said.

"It's a cover of 'My Girl Sloopy' by a colored group called The Vibrations. I brought a few records with me, if you want to hear it."

Alex reminded himself how good the guy's drumming was and bit back his irritation. "Yeah, sure, why not?"

In Alex's room, Gary took the lid off a cardboard pattern box from So-Fro Fabrics and pulled out a single on the red-and-black Atlantic label. Alex dropped the needle on it.

You could tell it was the same song, though the feel was different in the same way that Gary's version of "Shake" was different, that swing again, and much more. Conga drums rattled in the foreground and a cheesy organ fought to be heard in the back. Horns came in every now and then to kick everything in the ass. Through it all, a live audience shrieked and laughed and applauded.

Alex liked R&B the same as everybody did. Motown, Wilson Pickett, the Isleys, Chuck Berry, they were all on the song list. This was different, raw, sweaty, loose. It evoked a world of dark, gyrating women, spilled whiskey, and flashing razors that was completely alien to Alex's privileged existence, as alluring as it was frightening. "Where did you get this?" he said.

"I went to England with my folks last summer," Gary said. "The kids over there were crazy for American music. They kept asking me about all these people I'd never heard of, Arthur Alexander, Don Covay, Bobby 'Blue' Bland. They thought I was a moron not to know about this stuff that was right under my nose. So when I got back I started going to Goodwill and places like that, looking for old records. Here, listen to this."

He handed Alex another Atlantic single, Don Covay singing "Mercy Mercy," which the Stones had covered. After that, Doris Troy's "Just One Look." "Hear that rhythm?" Gary said. "That backbeat, one *and* two *and*? That's some kind of calypso thing out of Jamaica. The Hollies toned it down and sped it up, so it doesn't slam you in the gut like this does."

Alex was feverish. Suddenly, all of rock music looked like a paint-by-numbers imitation of something primal and vital and authentic, something Alex had no claim to because he was too light-skinned, too suburban, too rich. He felt like a phony for trying to start a band at all.

"Can I?" he said, pointing to the So-Fro box. Gary nodded and Alex slid out one record after another and eased it back, each in its paper sleeve with a hole for the label, each label bearing a name that at best he'd heard mentioned somewhere. "I need to…" Words failed him. "I have to…"

Gary looked at his watch. "I was going to hit a few stores this afternoon. You can come along if you like. I can point you to some stuff."

They both looked at Mike. "I have to get home," Mike said. "You guys go ahead."

"Yeah," Alex told Gary. "I would dig that."

AS THE MONTHS slipped by, Dave became increasingly desperate to find the act that would launch his production career. He worried that the boom was over already. Early in the year, Jake had recorded the Charlatans in one of the few decent studios in San Francisco, Coast Recorders on Folsum Street, and failed to get anything worthy of a record contract. They were not impressive as musicians, Jake said, couldn't agree on a sound or a direction, and were tense and wooden in the studio.

Meanwhile, trouble was brewing in the Spoonful. John had fallen for a woman who'd been with Zal first, and Zal, who had difficulty with the line between teasing and harassment, would not let him forget it.

Dave knew that side of Zal well. Late one night, as the two of them stood on 52nd Street outside the Columbia studios service elevator, waiting for a cab, Zal had said, "Your real name's not Dave Fisher. You're one of the tribe." Dave had told him the story, and Zal had called him Fischel ever since, usually in a mocking falsetto voice. Maybe it was all in good fun, though when it came from Zalman Yanovsky, who had never tried to hide his identity, who had lived on a kibbutz in Israel, for God's sake, it turned into an accusation that twisted Dave with shame, to Zal's neverending delight.

Then, on May 19, after a gig in Berkeley, Zal and Steve had driven over to Pacific Heights and bought a couple of lids from Bill Love of the Committee. Coming back, they'd attracted the attention of the cops with some crazy driving and ended up in jail. Zal, being a Canadian citizen, faced deportation and a permanent ban on reentering the US.

Nobody in band circles was talking about it. Dave suspected, without knowing any details, that they'd made some kind of deal with the cops. He only felt it as one more source of tension when they cut "Summer in the City," even as he started to come into his own in the studio, miking a garbage can and sending it through the speakers in the stairwell to get the boom for the opening, using the stairwell echo on Joe's snare, recording car horns on the street, making his mark on the record.

He'd put the word out among the local studio musicians that he was looking for an act to produce, and after a few bum steers, a sax player from Jersey told him about some Bayonne guys called the Meteors, real pros, supposedly. So on a Friday in late July he took a bus all the way down to Asbury Park to hear them play a place called Mrs. Jay's Beer Garden.

He got there at eight, after a cab ride through streets full of kids in beat-up cars. Mrs. Jay's was a white brick building on a corner lot, facing the ocean, dingy with soot, with Harleys and hot rod Fords, Dodge Darts and Volkswagen Beetles parked out front, rough kids in jeans and dirty white T-shirts and tattoos lounging against the walls, smoking and watching him suspiciously. If it hadn't meant another three-hour bus ride to get home, Dave might have chickened out then and there.

He also regretted wearing a suit, which had lost its press on the bus. He'd been afraid people might not take him seriously if he did end up handing out the new business cards he'd brought, the ones with the Columbia logo on them without Columbia's permission. Now he worried that they'd think he was a cop.

Hunger decided him. He pushed through the double glass doors into the end of the dinner rush. The interior was a gigantic sweat box where waitresses squeezed through the crowd with trays overhead, everybody was talking at the top of their lungs, and a blaring jukebox was barely audible in the background. He found an open stool at the bar and ordered the blue plate special: chicken-fried steak, mashed potatoes, green beans, roll, and iced tea for 89 cents. By the time he finished, the band was loading in their equipment.

At first Dave took them for older, maybe past their prime. On second glance they were just tough, working-class Italian kids, probably tired from schlepping their gear all the way from Bayonne, that gear including a full-sized Hammond B-3 and Leslie, two matching Vox Super Beatle amps, and the biggest drum set Dave had ever seen.

After the setup and a quick sound check, they disappeared for half an hour. Then, at 9:30 exactly, they hit the stage running, now dressed in matching black shirts and white ties, guitars tuned and strapped on, and they plugged in and counted off the first song before the audience had fully registered that they were there.

The first song was "Shotgun," the Junior Walker hit, and they blasted it out in four-part harmony, with blistering guitar fills and percussive riffs from the B-3 that sounded like a helicopter landing on the checkered linoleum floor and felt like a boxer pounding on Dave's solar plexus. No vestige remained of their earlier fatigue as they charged into the next song, and a crowd started to form in front of the stage.

By the time that second song was over, Dave knew he wanted to sign them, and by the third he was afraid someone was going to beat him to it.

The rest of the first set stuck mostly to R&B, soul, and blues standards: Bobby Bland, Smokey Robinson, Little Eva, Bo Diddley. The occasional curve balls included Elvis's "Don't Be Cruel" and the Rascals' arrangement of "Good Lovin'." Everybody except the drummer took turns singing lead, and they switched off between guitar-driven songs and organ-driven songs. They changed up the keys and the tempos and ended with a ten-minute workout on Ray Charles's "What'd I Say," going straight into "Green Onions" for the break.

Dave was petrified. All the lines he'd rehearsed deserted him. Only the fear of another scout being in the audience got him onto his feet. In a haze of fear, he followed the band and an entourage of girls into an overlit break room with a noisy refrigerator, a sink, a Formica table, and a collection of mismatched chairs.

The guys collapsed into the chairs and one of the girls went to the fridge and passed around bottles of beer. The rest of the girls seemed unsure what to do now that they were here. Dave felt much the same way. The guys had noticed him, however, so he had to say something.

"My name is Dave Fisher. I'm from Columbia Records and I think you guys are great."

They looked at each other and the sudden wonder, hope, and

excitement on their faces boosted Dave's confidence. He grabbed a chair and sat in it backwards. "Have any of the other labels talked to you yet?"

They had probably been imagining this moment for years, Dave thought. The drummer was the first to respond, a shake of the head.

"Have you got a manager? A booking agent?"

The organist spoke up. He'd recovered his wariness, and though he was hollow-cheeked skinny, he had a wiry menace. "To play dumps like this one, we don't need a manager."

"Bodyguards, maybe," the drummer said, and they all laughed.

"How about original material? Do you guys write any of your own songs?"

"We got a few," the organist said. "Maybe five."

"Six," the guitar player said, sitting up self-consciously, like he'd been called on in school. "We got 'Paradise,' remember?"

"Six," the organist said.

"Have you recorded any of them? Demo tape, singles, anything like that?" All but the bass player shook their heads. "Could you do me a favor, maybe play some of them tonight?"

"We'll play 'em all," the drummer said, then looked at the organist for confirmation.

"Sure," the organist said. "Not in a bunch, though. This crowd, they like stuff they know from the radio."

"That's the way of it, isn't it?" Dave said. "The clubs want covers, but you can't make that next step until you do originals." He was talking too much. "Listen, I can't promise anything. But I would maybe like to put together a showcase for you in the city, get some people from the label down to hear you, see what they think."

"Hell yes," the drummer said.

"Showcase?" the organist said.

"A club gig with some big shots in the audience. You'll want to pack the house, you know, get lots of girls there who'll scream and dance."

He glanced at the girls, who were watching with wide eyes. One of them said, "I can scream." She smiled and licked her lips.

The organist looked at her and said, "See me after the show."

"How can I get hold of you?" Dave asked.

The organist took a business card out of his wallet. Under the name THE METEORS was a drawing of a rock with speed lines, the names Sal, Tim, Rocky, and Mike, and two phone numbers.

"Who's Sal?"

"That's me," the organist said. "The first number on the card is me." Dave shook his hand and Sal said, "What was your name again?"

Blushing, and hating it, he said, "Dave. Dave Fisher." He remembered his own business cards and passed them around, shaking hands with the others: Tim on guitar, Rocky on bass, Mike on drums.

"Anybody under eighteen?" Dave asked.

The guys all shook their heads. One of the girls started to raise her hand and the girl next to her slapped it down and said, "Not you, stupid."

"Good, good, that'll make it easier if we get to the point of a contract." Time, he thought, to quit while he was ahead. "It was good meeting you guys. I hope to talk to you soon."

"You too," said Mike the drummer, and Tim the guitar player chimed in with, "Thanks." Sal was reading Dave's card like a cryptogram he was trying to solve. Rocky remained inscrutable.

Dave let himself out, and as soon as he closed the door, he heard the band let out a cheer. Dave felt like cheering, too.

He spent the rest of the night in a daze. He had tunnel vision and his brain kept flying to the four corners of the universe, already trying to picture the album cover, to decide which cover tunes to keep, how he would mike the instruments. Two of the band's originals sounded like hits, and two more were good enough for B-sides or album filler. Enough for a start.

He knew that word of who he was had spread through the club when people began to sneak looks at him. He was two parts embarrassed to one part pleased with himself. During the third break, a tall, skinny guy with the oversized jaw and forehead of acromegaly sat hunched and uninvited at Dave's table and explained that he was the next Dylan. To get rid of him, Dave traded one of his new business cards for the kid's address scrawled on the back of an envelope.

By 1:30, when the band finished, the club had emptied out except for a few old men passed out in the booths and a dozen or so girls. Dave said goodnight as the band was tearing down and promised to be in touch.

At the bar he asked where he might be able to find a room. "No chance," the bartender said. "On a Friday on the shore in July? Everything's booked up months ahead." He was dipping beer steins, two at a time, in a sink of gray suds.

"Can I get back to Manhattan?"

"First bus is six in the morning." He didn't meet Dave's eyes.

"What am I going to do?" Dave hated the desperation in his voice.

"Can't sleep here," the bartender said. "Try the bus station."

A female voice behind him said, "I can take you as far as Bayonne." He turned to see a blonde in her mid-twenties, a bit the worse for wear, dark roots, sympathetic eyes. "You can cab into the city from there."

Her name was Crystal and she had a blue-and-white Chevy Bel Air with a sizable dent in the rear bumper. As they got in, she said, "I imagine you're worn out, so if you want to sleep, that's okay. I'm a nurse, so I'm used to being awake at all hours."

"I may never sleep again," Dave said.

She smiled like she meant to collect that verbal IOU later, and put the car in gear. "My ex used to tell me I was to talking what a hurricane was to fresh air, so feel free to interrupt if I get on a streak."

"You're very generous to help me out." Trusting was the word he was thinking, which she seemed to pick up.

"Oh, you're safe, I can tell."

"I don't know if that's a compliment or not."

"Believe me, I had enough of the other with my ex." Contrary to her ex's warning, they cruised in companionable silence down Asbury Avenue, past the boardwalk and the weathered wood-frame shops and the last of the tourists.

"What's your connection with the band?" Dave finally asked, as they turned onto the Garden State Parkway.

"One of my girlfriends dated Sal for a while." She gave him

a sardonic look. "'Dated.' Yeah, right. Anyway, we followed the band around a little. I love music, I love to dance, and they're the best combo in Jersey, so I kept going after my girlfriend got tired of standing in line for a turn with Sal." She looked at him again. "I know what you're thinking. You're thinking, she's too old for this. Among other things."

"I'm way older than you are. And here I am."

"Yeah, but that's your job. Right? I mean, I heard you're a producer for Columbia?"

Already Dave liked her enough not to say yes. He explained the leap he was trying to make, which led to telling her stories about the studio and travelling with the Spoonful, whom she loved. She had a raucous laugh that matched her working-class Jersey accent, and Dave did his best to hear it again and again.

She pulled up in front of her apartment building a little after three AM. She turned sideways on the seat to face him. "I can call you a cab, or…"

"Or?" he said.

She smiled. "Or."

This was where, he thought, the old Dave would have been overcome by shyness and run away.

"'Or' sounds good," he said.

DAVE DIDN'T LEAVE her apartment until Sunday afternoon. It had been a long time for him. For her too. She made breakfast and lunch and ordered in the best delivery pizza Dave had ever eaten, and in between she told him about Bayonne.

"The whole town is in a time warp. You can still hear doo-wop groups practicing in the alleys where they can get a good echo. People who are born in Bayonne work in Bayonne and die in Bayonne. My mom is at the Maidenform factory up the street and my dad was at one of the refineries out on the Hook until they moved it down south to get away from the unions."

She told him about boarded-up store fronts and that the closest thing to parkland when she was a kid was vacant lots. Her older brother Tommy hated it and was always going over the bridge to Staten Island, where the drinking age was 18. Until the night eight years ago when his best friend's car crashed into the concrete abutment coming off the bridge onto the Boulevard. The other kids had gotten away with contusions and Tommy, riding shotgun, had gone through the windshield. Her parents found a way to blame each other and Crystal moved out as soon as she finished high school.

She played him her well-worn 45s, from the Church Street Five and the Dovells to Mitch Ryder and the Young Rascals. She'd gotten the music bug early, hypnotized by the juke box at the candy store where the kids all hung out, drinking fountain Cokes and working out jitterbug moves.

This is the world we're tearing down, Dave thought. Mitch Miller's world. The world of crew cuts and soda fountains and dead-end factory jobs.

When he finally got in the cab for Manhattan, he had a tentative promise that she would come into the city the next weekend, and he would take her to the Village and the Garden and the Park, anywhere she wanted to go.

On Monday he called Joe Marra at the Night Owl, who agreed to hire the band on Dave's recommendation and found him a Wednesday night slot two weeks away. He called Sal that afternoon to confirm the booking. Sal pushed for details: who would be there, what would the next steps be, what kind of advance was Dave thinking of. Dave tried in vain to scale down his expectations.

"You do like the band, right?" Sal said. "You do want to record us?"

"If everything works out," Dave said, "we'll see."

On Tuesday he made an appointment with Columbia's new head of A&R, Morgan Conrad, who had replaced Mitch Miller the year before. Although Dave barely knew him, Conrad was the one who would have to okay his move from engineering to production. Dave got 15 minutes before Conrad was scheduled for a working lunch.

He tried not to let himself think about how much was at stake. This was the way of things, after all. Bring the company a great band, get to produce them as your reward.

Conrad was running late. Dave lost the first ten minutes of his appointment, and Conrad looked at his watch as soon as they'd shaken hands. He was tanned and fit, his white hair was cut short, and a display handkerchief stuck out of the pocket of his Italian suit.

"I've been hearing good things about your work," Conrad said. "In *and* out of Columbia."

Dave ignored the implied reprimand. "Thank you, sir. I know you're in a hurry, so I'll get to the point. I've found a terrific young rock group and set up a showcase for them two weeks from tomorrow. If you think they're as commercial as I do, I'd like the chance to produce them."

"Whoa, slow down, Dave. Who gave you permission to scout acts?"

"I was showing initiative, sir. That's always the way it's been here, all of us on the lookout for talent that might bring the company a hit record."

"I appreciate the history lesson, but I'm not automatically persuaded that 'the way things have always been' is the best way to do business. Furthermore, there's no established career track from engineering to A and R. They're two very different professions." Conrad had produced a few stereo demonstration records in the late fifties for Audio Fidelity, then moved into entertainment law. He'd been at Columbia less than a year.

To his surprise, Dave's feelings of panic were manifesting as homicidal rage. He struggled to keep his voice even and reasonable. "I apologize if I was out of line. Regardless of how it happened, there's going to be a terrific group called the Meteors playing at the Night Owl on August 10, and Columbia has the inside track on signing them."

"What did you promise this group?"

"Nothing, sir. I told them I liked their sound and that I would like some other people at the company to hear them."

"And did you represent yourself in any way as having the authority to offer them a contract?"

"No, of course not. I just told them that I worked at Columbia."

"And I hope that continues to be the case." At that, Dave's

hands clenched the arms of the chair as if he had them around Conrad's throat. "I suggest you cancel this showcase and return to your assigned duties. In time, if your work remains solid, maybe we can let you co-produce one of the existing acts on our roster."

Dave was too livid to speak. He got up and started for the door.

"Dave?"

Dave hesitated with his hand on the knob.

"We're not cowboys here," Conrad said. "Not anymore. It's a new day."

Dave managed to not slam the door on his way out.

DAVE SPENT THE AFTERNOON waiting for callbacks from Jake, from Tom Dowd at Atlantic, and from Phil Ramone at A&R Studios. They were the only people in town that he trusted with the Meteors, and all three eventually phoned to say they would be there for the showcase. They all wanted to know why he wasn't signing them to Columbia, and he said, "Columbia has made it clear I don't have that authority."

He needed Dutch courage that night before he called Crystal. He hadn't eaten all day, and he wasn't used to drinking in the first place. He needed three tries to dial her number because of the shaking in his hands. She was completely tied up with the Meteors in his mind, and he knew that the longer he waited to call the harder it would get.

As soon as she heard his voice, she said, "What's wrong?"

He gave her the blow by blow. She was quiet for so long after that he finally said, "Are you there?"

"Why didn't you go to this Tom Dowd guy and say, 'If you like this band you have to hire me as producer'?"

"None of these guys are in a position to hire me, except maybe as an engineer."

"So are you going to engineer the record if they produce it?"

"That would be like... that would be like going to watch a woman I was in love with marry somebody else."

"Jesus and Mary, you're not even going to the club to see them, are you?"

"I doubt it."

After another excruciating silence, he said, "I'll talk to you later."

"Dave, wait," she said, but the blackness of his mood had swallowed him and he hung up the phone. A part of him hoped she would call him back, and when she didn't, he turned out the lights and got undressed. He lay on his back and listened to the noise of the street through the open window, the sirens and the horns and the squealing brakes.

THE NEXT AFTERNOON he called Sal. "Can we meet?" Dave said. "I have a couple of things to discuss with you."

"We're playing tonight," Sal said. His voice was still belligerent, as if that was how he always dealt with hope. "Can't we do it over the phone?"

"Yeah, okay. Listen, uh, there's a change in the lineup for the showcase."

"A change in the lineup? What the fuck does that mean?"

"Columbia's out, but I've got—"

"What do you mean, Columbia's out?"

"Columbia doesn't want to send anybody to the show. But I've got—"

"They don't want to *send* anybody? What the fuck, are you a producer there or not?"

"I never said I was a producer, I said—"

"You're not a producer? Then what the fuck are you doing handing out your business cards and setting up fucking showcases?"

"Sal—"

"What the fuck are you doing playing with us like this?"

"Sal, shut the fuck up. Shut the fuck up and listen to what I'm saying to you. I've got Tom Dowd, Phil Ramone, and Erik Jacobsen coming to see your *fucking* show, all right? That's the guys that produce fucking Ray Charles and the Rascals, John fucking Coltrane, and The Lovin' Spoonful, all right? So you are actually three times better off than you would have been if Columbia came, and I am not going to make a *fucking* penny out of this if you get a record deal. I did it because I didn't want to let you down. All right?"

He was shaking again, listening to silence over a phone line again. Finally, quietly, Sal said, "Tom Dowd? You got Tom Dowd to come hear us?"

"That's right. Don't fuck it up. Get to your originals right away, and if you want to write a couple more in the next two weeks, that might be a real good idea. Bring a lot of people and make sure they yell requests for the originals. Got it?"

"Dave, I'm sorry," Sal said. "We've been through a lot of disappointment, you know?"

"Yeah," Dave said. "Tell me about it."

DAVE STARTED TO DIAL Crystal's number twenty times over the next two weeks. Once he made it all the way through. He hung up after ten rings.

The day after the showcase, Tom Dowd called him. "I owe you one. I'm cutting a demo with them next week, and if it sounds as good as I think it will, we'll probably release it as a single."

"I hope they sell a million," Dave said.

"I still don't see what you're getting out of this."

"I'm not sure I do either," Dave said. "But *somebody* ought to get what they wanted out of this deal."

BY THE END of July, Cole's patience was gone.

His boots were broken in and he could glide across the dance floor with a reasonable amount of flair. If he only had a hat, Jerry told him, the women would be all over him.

The woman he wanted all over him had come back to the Tyler Motor Inn with him three times. He'd gotten her out of her bra, but the minute his hands went below her waist, she pulled away.

He'd played guitar and sung for her. "Not bad" was all she ever said, though he knew she was impressed. They'd spent hours on the phone, Cole searching for hidden meanings in everything she said, and everything she didn't.

She was not hard to figure. Father split when she was 5, mother's attempts at dating hadn't worked out. No female friends—other girls were either jealous or too "provincial." She was too smart and too ambitious for Tyler. Cole was "just a kid," as she never tired of reminding him, and she was looking for a lifeline to the Big City, whatever Big City was available.

As for work, the sum total he'd gained from his days on the rig was some muscle on his upper body and a farmer's tan. He couldn't imagine what it would be like to have that for his future, with nothing more to look forward to than a wife and kids spending his pay as fast as he earned it.

His alarm went off at six AM on Monday, August 1. He felt dazed, irritable, clumsy. The first day of his next-to-last week, and he didn't know how he was going to endure the next 12 days.

Corrina had been over the night before, and he'd played "Do You Believe in Magic" and the Contours' "Do You Love Me" because of the line about "now that I can dance." He'd finished with Ray Peterson's "Corrine Corrina," which he'd worked up especially for her. The usual mixture of making out and wrestling ensued. Corrina never got carried away with the heat of it the way Cole did. He'd asked her about it, and she'd said she liked the closeness. That he was "sweet," but what she may or may not have felt in the realm of passion was not something she intended to share with a kid like him. He hadn't gotten to sleep until nearly one.

He was sitting in his open doorway when Donald and Jerry pulled up at 6:25. Donald was already dipping his Wintergreen Copenhagen and the inside of the Falcon smelled like mint and rotting leaves. Cole's stomach wanted to turn inside out.

Jerry looked him over in the rear-view. "Looking a mite green this morning, College. Corrina keep you up last night?"

"Not the way I wanted her to," Cole said.

"You should talk to your daddy," Donald said, and spat into a paper cup. "Maybe he could pull some strings. I think all this frustration is beginning to interfere with your job performance." They both liked to kid him about his father having gotten him the job. Cole knew that if they had a real problem with it, the talk would have been behind his back.

At the Greasy Spoon, he was unable to finish his eggs or start his bacon, and Donald obligingly took care of both. "If your daddy could see you now," Donald said. "Hangover and blue balls. Not the summer he had in mind for you, I imagine."

At the rig, they found that the graveyard tour—which Cole had learned, in keeping with tradition, to rhyme with "hour"—had started tripping pipe at dawn. Every joint of pipe had to come out of the hole, be unscrewed from the string, and dropped in the rack, all 6,000 feet of it at this point, to get to the drill bit to replace it. Time spent tripping was money for no new footage, creating pressure to get it done as quickly as possible.

They changed clothes in the doghouse, each turning his back to the others in the quaint modesty of rural men that Cole studiously followed. He hated the first clammy touch of the sweaty, oil-stained jeans and T-shirt from the previous day. They put on their hard hats and went out onto the steel floor of the derrick, which stank of diesel and lubricating mud and vibrated constantly from the 1500 horsepower motor.

Elton, the driller on the daylight tour, was in his forties, his face as cracked and brown as drought-ravaged farmland. Stray salt-and-pepper whiskers where he'd missed shaving. Each of the three drillers was the lead man on his shift, and all three reported to the tool pusher, the boss of the rig. Though Elton was generally easygoing, every time they started a trip he ordered Cole off the rig, said he could get a closer look another time.

Today, as Jerry scampered up to the monkeyboard, 85 feet above the derrick floor, and the rest of the crew swarmed in to replace their graveyard tour counterparts, Elton finally said, "You can stay on the floor. But keep at least five feet away from the rotary, and don't get in nobody's way. Watch what they're doing and watch out for the fucking chain."

Elton went to the graveyard driller and took his place behind the big lever that controlled the throttle. Two roughnecks from the graveyard tour stood over the rotary while Elton hoisted a thribble, three connected joints of pipe, out of the hole. One of the roughnecks slapped a collar around the top of the fourth joint to hold it in place, while the other swung a four-foot pipe wrench onto the bottom of the thribble and gave it a full turn counter-clockwise. As soon as he pulled the wrench off, the first roughneck whipped one end of a heavy chain around the same spot, whistled at Elton, and then stepped away while the motor pulled the chain hard enough to spin the thribble free. The chain was barely off when Elton hoisted the pipe into the air, and the graveyard derrickman, high up in the lattice of the rig, wrapped his own chain around the top of it and pulled it toward the rack at the side of the derrick where another two dozen thribbles already stood, the roughnecks on the floor putting their shoulders into it to push from below.

Seeing the process up close was infinitely more alarming than watching from a distance. The roughnecks joked and pulled faces at the same time that each of their movements had a fierce concentration and precision. Things happened so fast that there was no leeway in the system, no room to take a breath.

Even as he thought that, some small anomalous sound or shadow made him look up and see the body falling toward him and a glint of metal in the air.

He reflexively lifted his right hand. Something brushed his glove and knocked his hand away, hard, before clanging into the metal floor, and then somebody yanked him backward, off his feet, and he heard, but didn't see, Jerry's body slam into the derrick floor a couple of feet away.

Cole tried to stand up. His legs refused to take his weight. He ended up on one knee, a noise like amplifier hum in his ears. Jerry lay with his neck twisted all wrong and blood leaking out of his hard hat. The life was gone from his face, like it was a rubber mask. Elton knelt next to him, hand to Jerry's throat. Feeling for a pulse, Cole thought, though there was clearly no point.

"Get that pipe in the rack," Elton yelled, "before somebody else gets hurt!"

Donald was standing over Jerry's body now, saying, "Oh Jesus, oh Jesus."

"Call an ambulance," Elton told him. "The number's on the phone."

Donald didn't hear. When Cole tried to get up and do it himself, everything tilted and he had to catch himself with his right hand, which was weirdly numb.

The graveyard derrickman was yelling as he came flying down the ladder. "What happened? I didn't even see him fall. Is he…"

The pipe banged into the rack and then both shifts gathered awkwardly around the body, some of the men pulling off their hard hats. A couple of them, including the graveyard derrickman, looked like they were about to cry.

"He come up onto the monkeyboard," the derrickman said, "giving me shit like he always done. I had my back to him, I was working the string. I never seen him, just out the corner of my eye when he was already falling…"

"Will somebody call a fucking ambulance?" Elton said.

Two of the men ran for the doghouse.

Cole was thirsty and he needed to lie down. His head felt fizzy. He didn't want to say anything because Jerry was dead and whatever was wrong with him was probably just him being a wimp and he didn't want the others to notice him in this condition.

He sat down heavily.

Somebody said, "Something's the matter with Cole."

"Look at his hand. He's bleeding."

Cole understood that they were talking about him. He didn't have the strength to respond.

Somebody had him by the shoulders. "Lean over," he said. "Lean your head between your legs. Hey, somebody get some water!"

Cole leaned forward and felt the blood rush into his brain. Somebody had a red plaid thermos of iced tea. He tried to reach for it with his right hand and a voice said, "Left hand. Use your left."

Somebody else said, "Get the glove off him. Gentle, now."

He took a drink with his left hand. Somebody knelt next to him and gripped his right arm tightly. Somebody else started pulling his glove and it stung his middle finger.

"Oh shit," somebody said.

"Is that ambulance coming?" said somebody else.

Cole looked at his hand. The end of his finger was a bloody ruin, blood dribbling out onto the derrick floor.

His peripheral vision went dark.

"Take it easy, man," somebody said, patting him on the shoulder.

There was something important he had to do. "Jerry?" he said.

"Just take 'er easy."

He heard a siren in the distance. There's an ambulance now, he thought. Maybe somebody could flag it down.

Elton helped him to his feet, putting Cole's left arm around his neck. "Lean on me," Elton said. "I got you."

Cole was able to make his legs move. His heavy work boots dragged against the textured steel floor. "That's it," Elton said. "Watch the stairs."

I'm never going to live this down, Cole thought, as Elton helped him stumble down the steps to ground level. Having to be carried off the rig like a baby. He felt something in the palm and wrist of his right hand, not pain yet, but an IOU for pain, and the numbers on it were high.

The ambulance backed up to within 50 feet of the rig. It looked like a station wagon his parents used to have, only the body was bright red, and the top of the back part was solid white and studded with lights. Two young guys in white coveralls came running, carrying a stretcher that looked like an oversized ironing board.

"Take this one first," Elton said. "It's too late for the other one."

They laid Cole out on the stretcher and strapped him down, then carried him to the ambulance, setting him on the ground by the open back door. One of them wrapped Cole's hand in gauze while the other gave him a shot in his left arm.

The one who'd wrapped his hand knelt down. He had red hair and freckles and was only a few years older than Cole. "If you feel weird, it's because you're in shock, okay? It's something your body does to keep you from feeling what happened to you. I want you to keep your right hand pointing up at the sky, like they're swearing you in on *Perry Mason*. You're going to be okay. We got to go get the other guy and we'll be right back."

As they grabbed another stretcher and sprinted away, the shot began to take effect.

Cole had never felt anything like it. The stretcher turned into a giant rubber raft and floated away into the ocean, bobbing gently to the rhythm of his pulse. A cool breeze touched his cheek and time stopped. Cole watched the clouds overhead. The sky was the exact blue of a colored pencil that he'd had in fifth grade.

They came back with Jerry on the other stretcher. A sheet, stained reddish brown, was pulled up over his face. They slotted Jerry's stretcher into the right side of the ambulance, then they lifted Cole. "You can put that arm down now," the redhead said.

As they slid Cole in next to Jerry, he was vaguely aware that he would have been claustrophobic if not for the drug. He didn't want to think about Jerry, lying so close by. He turned his head the other way and stared out through the window.

The ambulance started up and swayed heavily over the rutted road. Pines and scrub brush, finally giving way to farmland. They emerged onto blacktop and the driver hit the gas. The scream of the siren was comforting in its seriousness.

At the hospital, they transferred him to a gurney and left him in a hallway. He'd meant to thank them and now they were gone. A stark, office-style clock on the wall said that it was not yet 8:45.

A young guy in a short white coat took the gauze off and looked at Cole's finger. He had closely trimmed brown hair and a long nose and lots of lines at the ends of his mouth. A plastic tag on his coat said JECKYL. "Does it hurt?" he asked.

Cole had gotten a peek that didn't bode well. "Starting to," he said.

The guy waved a nurse over. "Get me a CC and a half of Demerol, would you?" He looked at Cole again. "Once we get some drugs in you, I'm going to debride this. That means clean it up. They've got a call out for an orthopod to sew this back together, but he's usually out drinking this time of day and they may have to sober him up." He squinted at Cole. "That's a joke, son."

Cole nodded. The nurse came with a hypo and a cotton ball that dripped alcohol. Cole had always hated getting shots before. He couldn't remember why.

The guy in the white coat dragged a cart over and turned his back on Cole, tucking the hand under his arm so Cole couldn't see what he was doing.

"Are you a doctor?" Cole asked.

"Intern," he said. "Almost a doctor, as Bill Cosby says. My name's Pete. What's yours?"

"Cole."

"Pleased to meet you. Forgive me if I don't shake hands. Nyuk nyuk nyuk. How old are you?"

"Sixteen."

"Well, my boy, I think you are definitely going to get laid out of this deal. The girls will melt with sympathy at the sight of your disfigurement. A touch of the melodrama, let them see how you're suffering inside, you'll be in like Flynn. Can you feel anything when I do this?"

Cole had a moment of panic. "No."

"That's good, because I'm not doing anything yet."

Somebody else, Cole thought, might have been amused. He couldn't stop thinking about the accident. Jerry must have dropped his chain before he fell, and that was what had hit Cole's hand. Why in God's name had he reached up like that? Then the second shot caught up with him and he drifted away.

The next time he looked up, he saw that Pete was gone and that the clock now showed a few minutes past 10. The time after that, the gurney was moving and doors flew open in front of him.

"What's happening?" he said.

"We're taking you to surgery," said a female voice. He was groggy enough, and her East Texas accent was thick enough, that he had to puzzle over the words.

They brought him to a room that was gray tile and shining steel, and they shifted him onto another, colder surface. His teeth chattered as they strapped him down. Three nurses, two men in white surgical gowns. One of the men put a heavy rubber mask over Cole's nose and mouth. "Wait," Cole said. Nobody was listening. The air inside the mask was cold and tasted like metal.

"Take some deep breaths for me," a male voice said.

Cole tried. It tasted bad and he was shaking with cold.

"I want you to count backwards, starting from a hundred."

"What are you going to do?" Cole said. Everything was moving too fast. What if they made a mistake? What if they amputated the entire finger?

Another male voice said, "Just be quiet and do what the man says. The sooner you stop arguing, the sooner we can get this over with."

The surgeon. The drunk, according to Pete. The kind of bullying authority figure that left Cole intimidated and resentful. "One hundred," Cole said bitterly. "Ninety-nine." He got into the lower eighties before he lost his concentration. Instead of drifting off to sleep, he found himself strapped to the side of a giant metal spiral hundreds of feet long. It turned slowly as it moved through the absolute cold of interstellar space. He saw himself as if from a great distance. His entire body was frozen, and he was terrified and alone. He tried to scream and nothing came out. The nightmare went on endlessly, the turning spiral, the deadly cold, the fear.

It seemed like hours before he floated free and rose upward into warmth. The warmer he got, the more nauseated he felt, and by the time he got his eyes open his stomach was heaving.

"Help," he said. "Throw up."

A nurse, from a chair beside the bed, handed him a beige plastic basin and said, "Take it with your left hand. No, the left. Now try to turn on your side." She was merely heavy above the waist, while her hips and thighs were gigantic. It cost her an effort to stand. She took Cole's right shoulder and gently pulled him toward her. The top half of the bed was cranked high, making it awkward. His stomach convulsed and he vomited into the basin, got a breath, and vomited some more, all viscous, sour liquid. The nurse wiped his mouth with a wet washcloth and put a sliver of ice into his mouth. "Suck on it, hon," she said. "It'll help."

She emptied the basin in the toilet and then took his pulse and blood pressure. Her nametag, Cole noted, said JACQUI. "Better now?" she asked.

Cole nodded, then shook his head and pointed at the basin again. Though he heaved repeatedly, only a trickle came up. His right hand burned, and his head spun and ached at the same time. Jacqui had him rinse his mouth and spit it out, then emptied the basin again. He lay back, the sweat cooling on his forehead. As long as he stayed completely still, the pain and the nausea were bearable.

Then it hit him. His hand. His right hand, his picking hand. Smashed. How was he going to play guitar?

He held his right hand in front of his face. Plaster from palm to elbow, Ace bandage and metal brace above that. The ends of his index and ring fingers purple with bruises and orange from disinfectant. Between them, a heavily bandaged stump. The first joint of his middle finger was gone. At the end of what was left was a button on the outside and, sticking out of the bandages on the inside, a long pair of wires as thin as high E strings. The wires appeared to go all the way through the remains of his finger. The thought of it made him dizzy and made the pain in his hand flare as if he'd held a match to it.

"You need something for the pain, hon?"

"Please."

She rang the nurses' station for more Demerol.

"I can't move my fingers," he said.

"You ain't supposed to move them yet, so don't be trying."

"I have to know how bad it is."

"Doctor'll discuss all that with you when he makes his rounds." Her tone was not unkind.

As soon as he started to relax, another thought hit him. "My parents. Somebody needs to tell my parents."

"They've been notified. They're on their way. Now settle down and put your hand on those pillows, fingers up, elbow down."

An orderly came in with the needle and Jacqui gave it to Cole in his hip. He felt it almost immediately, a warmth that spread into his gut and chest and out to the ends of his arms.

Two in the afternoon. The other bed was empty, and the big tinted window next to Cole's bed looked out onto a parking lot and a pine forest beyond. A black-and-white TV hung from the ceiling, and a bulletin came on, something about a sniper in the Tower at the University of Texas. Cole watched grainy footage of the Tower as a voice said that at least ten people were dead, dozens more wounded. They thought the police had killed the sniper.

The Demerol made it all unreal. He couldn't make an emotional connection to the fact that Susan was at UT. The idea was incomprehensible, in the same way that Kennedy's assassination had been. It was not something that could have happened in the world he'd known as a child, and it felt like a premonition.

He couldn't hold the thought. He turned away and within a few minutes he began to drift in and out of a light doze, watching the wind move the tops of the pine trees outside his window.

"Jeff?" His mother's voice.

He rolled onto his back. She had a bouquet of carnations and snapdragons in one hand and an old brown suitcase in the other. The reds and pinks and purples of the flowers clashed in a vaguely unpleasant way with the floral print of her dress. "They said it wasn't too serious, but then they said you lost part of a finger?"

Not my fault, he started to say, before he remembered that he didn't have to justify or excuse himself this time. "Is Dad here?"

"He went to the company office. He's going to find out what happened and who's responsible, don't worry."

"I'm not worried, Mother. It was an accident. It wasn't any-body's fault." After a second he said, "A man died out there this morning. One of my friends." I could have been killed too, he wanted to say. If some stranger hadn't yanked me out of the way.

"You saw it?"

"It happened right in front of me."

"Well, I..." She was clearly confounded. "I guess these things happen on oil rigs, don't they? That's why they're so dangerous..."

Cole saw that she only wanted the unpleasantness to stop. If she let herself feel too much empathy, it would only become more real. How wonderful to have all that Demerol inside him, and to not be emotionally involved with this conversation. To not be angry with his mother or devastated by Jerry's death. To not be worried about his hand or disappointed that his father had to be somewhere else.

"I brought your pajamas and toothbrush and some books that were by your bed, in case you wanted to read..."

"That's good, Mom, thanks."

"Did you talk to the doctor?"

"He hasn't come by yet."

"The nurse I talked to said he'd already left."

"Figures," Cole said.

"What, dear?"

"Nothing."

She put the flowers on the tray table and the suitcase on the floor and perched uncomfortably on the edge of the bed. "They certainly did a professional-looking job."

Cole hated to admit that a knot of anxiety in his chest had let go when his mother arrived. He sent her to the nurses' station to find him something to eat. She came back with two cups of orange sherbet, turned up the sound on the TV, and settled into a lounge chair to watch. Cole had to let the sherbet soften before he could manage it left-handed. Afterward his mother left the room while a new nurse helped him use the urinal, a humiliating and not entirely satisfactory experience that felt like wetting the bed. Those efforts wore him out, and he slept until 5:00, when his father arrived, right behind the nurse with Cole's dinner. He wore a white short-sleeved shirt, wilted from the heat, and a narrow tie. The first thing he said was, "I talked to the company, and they've agreed to cover all your hospital expenses."

And if they hadn't, Cole wondered, were you planning to hand me the bill?

The nurse, one he hadn't seen before, put a plastic tray on his rolling table. She was in her twenties, with brown hair and freckles. As she fussed with raising the angle of the bed and getting the table in position, his father said, "It doesn't look like there was negligence on the part of the company, though I've arranged to get a copy of the police report. We'll know more then."

The nurse took a metal cover off the tray. Roast beef, gravy, mashed potatoes, green beans. Red Jell-O for dessert. "I'll just cut this meat up for you," she said.

Cole thanked her and said, "There wasn't any negligence. It was an accident, is all."

When the nurse finished, Cole's father took her place and said, "Let me see your hand."

Cole held it out and speared a piece of meat with his left. It took two tries.

"This doesn't look so bad," his father said.

"The end of my finger is gone," Cole said.

86

The nurse said, "If you need anything, just ring."

"Thank you," Cole said.

"Compared to what could have happened," his father said. "You could have lost the entire hand, or a foot. That chain could have killed you."

"It also," Cole said, "could have missed me entirely." He saw it falling, sparkling in the sunlight, saw his hand reach out. Sweat broke on his forehead.

"You won't get far with an attitude like that," his father said.

"Now, you two," his mother said.

His father took a step back. "Are they treating you okay? The surgeon, does he seem like he knows what he's doing?"

Safe in his Demerol haze, Cole saw that he was on his own. That he always had been. He stood on top of a mountain. The air was cold and clear. He could see a long way.

"It's fine," Cole said. He'd lost his appetite, but he understood the need for show. He ate a couple of green beans and a bite of potato. The beans were overcooked and tasted of the can they came from.

"Good. I hope it's okay, because the company's insurance will only cover this if you stay here in Tyler until they discharge you. Now if there's a problem with the hospital, we'll pull you out and take you to Dallas…"

"No," Cole said. "No need."

His mother, Cole saw, had not heard this part of it. She looked hurt and confused. "Are we staying?"

"I have to be at work tomorrow," his father said. "You can stay if you want, I suppose. You won't have a car or a place to stay or a change of clothes."

She looked helplessly at Cole.

"Don't worry, Mom. I'll be fine. It's not that big a deal, right? Like Dad said." He thought he'd kept the bitterness out of his voice. He shoved another piece of meat in his mouth. The gravy was quickly losing its heat to the hospital air conditioning. "In fact," he said, "you've got an hour and a half drive back, and you'll need to get something to eat before you go. You should probably get started."

"Are you sure?" his mother said. "Are you sure you don't need anything?"

"You can call me in the morning and check on me. Now let me finish my dinner in peace before it gets cold."

His mother kissed him on the cheek and his father nodded stiffly. "I mean it about moving you to Dallas," he said.

"Try Gringo's Steakhouse," Cole said. "They can give you directions at the desk. I eat there... I ate there all the time. With Donald and... and Jerry." He managed a smile.

As soon as they left, Cole pushed the tray table away and curled onto his side and pushed the call button.

"Nurses' station."

"Can I get some Demerol in here?"

SECONAL KEPT HIM in a restless sleep all night, and in the morning an orderly walked him to the bathroom and back. He was shocked at how unsteady he was. After breakfast, he talked to his mother on the phone and then Pete the intern came by. Today his badge read CALIGARI. "Did Granbury ever come by yesterday?"

"Is that the surgeon?" Cole asked.

"Alleged surgeon, yes."

"No."

"Bastard."

Cole didn't know you could talk about surgeons that way. "Is he really a drunk?"

"No," Pete said. "Just an asshole."

Pete unwound the Ace bandage. When he saw Cole wince, he ordered more Demerol. Jacqui arrived with the needle, out of breath, and asked which cheek he wanted it in. "The last one was in the right," he said.

"How long ago?"

"I don't remember," Cole lied. "It's been a while." Almost two hours was a while, if you looked at it right. The warmth hit him as soon as the needle went in. Pavlovian reaction, he knew, a preview of the real thing to follow.

Pete touched the tip of Cole's right index finger with the cold metal bell of his stethoscope. "Can you feel that?"

"Yeah."

"Now?"

His ring finger. "Yeah."

"He didn't do too bad a job, for once," Pete said. "You got lucky."

"Listen, I play guitar."

"Right handed? With a flat pick?" Cole nodded. "You should be all right. There's a little hematoma on the fingers on either side—that's bruises, to you—but they'll heal pretty quick. You should give yourself four weeks. You won't, but that's what you *should* do."

"Is that button what I think it is?"

"The wire is holding your tendon in place." Pete gently wrapped the Ace bandage around his fingers. "And yeah, the button is holding the wire that holds the tendon that came from the house that Jack built. That's why you're not supposed to move your fingers yet. If that tendon pops loose, you'll need transplant surgery, and you don't want that. You especially don't want Granbury to do it."

The Demerol had been another double dose. Cole was sinking fast. "You got one of those name tags says MOREAU?"

"As a matter of fact."

"'M on to your game," Cole said.

"Too late, Mr. Holmes. That shot was drugged. I've eluded you again."

Granbury came at 1:20. Pete trailed him, carrying a clipboard. Cole was still flying. Granbury was probably forty, wire-rimmed glasses, long brown hair slicked back from his forehead. He took a cursory look at Cole's hand and said to Pete, "I want him up and moving around this afternoon. Between the drugs and the inactivity, his bowels will lock up. Get him Milk of Magnesia at bedtime, too."

"Yessir."

Cole said, "How long do you think I'll need to stay here?"

Granbury looked at him as if he'd disobeyed a direct order by speaking. "Until I decide you're healed enough to leave."

"Can you give me an estimate?"

"I'll let you know when you're ready."

Behind Granbury's back, Pete stuck the clipboard crisply under his left arm and stuck the right one out in a Nazi salute, left middle finger under his nose like a mustache. By the time Granbury turned back, Pete was writing on the clipboard as if nothing had happened.

"Keep up the antibiotics for at least another day or two," Granbury said. "That hand was filthy—oil and dirt and God knows what all else."

"Yessir." Pete followed Granbury out without another word.

DRUGS GAVE COLE a heightened appreciation of daytime television. He flipped idly between *Let's Make a Deal* and *As the World Turns* and an hour and a half of *Ben Casey* reruns. Pete showed up at three, wearing a name tag that said HACKENBUSH and towing an aluminum walker. They walked the halls, wheels squeaking on the pale, worn linoleum, Cole resting his cast on top of his head to keep the hand from swelling. Cole told him about The Chevelles and the drummer that Alex had described over the phone. Within ten minutes he was sweating, and after 20 he was exhausted and losing his high.

The nurse with the freckles gave him a sponge bath and a clean surgical gown and sheets. He'd barely gotten settled when Elton and Donald came in. They'd knocked off early for the occasion and they were still dirty from the rig.

It was awkward from the start. Cole told them the injury wasn't all that bad, and they all nodded. Elton said Jerry's funeral was the next day, Wednesday, and all three tours were getting the day off, with pay, if they went.

Donald said, "I reckon it ain't really gon' hit me till the weekend. Till I'm sitting at that there Wagon Wheel all by my lonesome." Cole saw that, despite his bloodshot eyes, Donald had been raised not to cry. Not as long as he was sober, anyway.

They were glancing toward the door. Cole said, "Somebody... when Jerry fell, somebody grabbed me and pulled me back. I could have died too."

"Weren't me," Donald said.

Elton shook his head. "Somebody from the graveyard tour, I think. I didn't see it." After a silence, he said, "You'll be headed on back to Dallas, I guess, when they let you out."

"Yeah. I'm not supposed to use this thing for four weeks."

"We'll try and get by again," Donald said. "But if we don't…"

"I understand. You guys were really good to me." Now Cole was choked up, and over a job he'd hated. "I appreciate all you did. Both you guys and Jerry too."

"No," Donald said, "that ain't what I meant. Whoever it was yanked you out of the way, they give you a second chance. You know? Don't fuck it up, that's what I was going to say." He nodded to Elton and they started toward the door. "And get a hat," Donald said. "Jerry always wanted you to get a hat."

SEVEN PM and Cole was still floating, thinking ahead to his next shot. The TV and the overhead lights were off and the daylight was fading.

Cole heard the door open and close. "Hello?" he said. No answer, just footsteps on the other side of the curtain that divided the room. He came fully alert.

"Turn the light off," a voice said.

"Corrina?" Cole put his book on the nightstand and turned off his reading light.

Corrina went to the window and closed the blinds, leaving the room in deep twilight. She held her finger to her lips and walked slowly to the edge of the bed, one foot directly in front of the other, making her hips sway. She was wearing a dark T-shirt and a light denim skirt and sandals. The cold hospital air made it clear she had nothing on under the shirt.

She picked up his cast and studied it. "Oh, my poor baby," she said. She kicked off her sandals and climbed carefully onto the bed, straddling him.

Like the sniper in the tower, Corrina seemed not quite real. When she kissed him, though, gently and repeatedly, and he felt himself getting hard, the drug let him relax with it, let him lie back and follow her lead.

"Your friend Pete?" Corrina whispered. "He's watching the door." She pulled the T-shirt up over her breasts without taking it off. Then, as Cole watched in amazement, she slowly pulled her skirt up around her waist and revealed that she was naked underneath. She dragged the sheet down around Cole's knees and lifted his surgical gown. "Oh, my," she said. "What have we here?"

She controlled everything, and Cole saw that she needed it that way. The weight of the cast bothered him, as did the need to hold it still, as did the angle of the back of the bed, and the fear that they might be interrupted. She shushed him when he tried to speak, put his left hand to her breast, kissed him on the neck and chest and stomach, and chose the moment when she finally guided him inside her. She waited for him to fully experience the heat and velvet smoothness of it before she began to move against him, only a little, before pausing to let him savor it again. She did what she could to make it last, but Cole had been waiting too long, and despite all the distractions, the urgency took him and he thrust his hips faster and faster until he exploded endlessly inside her.

They slowly rocked to a stop. Cole became aware of the noise of the bedsprings, wondered if it had been audible all the way out to the hall. His entire body had been so tense at the end that now his right hand throbbed. His ejaculation ran down between his legs and onto the sheets.

Corrina kissed him and said, "Did I hurt you?"

"You've got to be kidding."

"I meant your hand, dummy."

"No," he said.

She lifted herself away and plucked a couple of tissues from the nightstand, dabbing at herself and then at the sheets. "Your nurse is going to be suspicious."

All the while they were making love, he'd been able to believe that they were feeling the same thing. Now they were two separate creatures again and already he was losing her. She pulled her T-shirt down, and then her skirt.

"Wait," Cole said. He wanted her again, wanted to take it slower, with more kissing and touching, wanted her to come too. "Don't go."

She climbed out of the bed and put her sandals on. "Got to, sugar." She straightened his gown and pulled the sheet and blanket over him. "There."

"Corrina—"

"Hush, now," she said. She stood at the head of the bed and stroked his hair. In the near darkness, he couldn't tell whether she was about to cry or was just being theatrical. "Dream about me tonight," she said. She put her fingers to his lips and she was gone.

Eventually Cole pulled the sheet up over his face so that he could smell her on himself and in the bed. He curled on his side, remembering the feel of her body, and drifted until the freckled nurse brought his sleeping pill and Milk of Magnesia and a shot.

COLE DIALED Corrina's number a dozen times throughout the day on Wednesday and got no answer. Thursday was the same.

It wasn't just that he missed her and wanted her again and was sick with love for her. He had no idea what was in her head, whether she loved him too, what their future was going to be. He couldn't think about anything else. He replayed his memories of Tuesday night until they lost their sharpness, until they felt like they belonged to somebody else.

Even with Demerol, Cole's daily routines made him restless and left him too much time to brood. Morning phone calls with his mother, walking the halls with Pete twice a day, terse visits from Granbury, tasteless meals, bad TV.

On Friday Granbury said, "I've left orders for you to be discharged on Sunday."

Cole's relief was undermined by the knowledge that leaving the hospital meant going back to Dallas, an hour and a half from Corrina even if he had a car, every phone call racking up long-distance charges. And in four weeks school would start. He pictured himself housebound until then, his mother fussing over him, and he had an overwhelming desire to hold his guitar. To make the chords and finger the leads with his left hand, even though he couldn't use his right.

He rang the nurses' station and asked for a shot. The nurse put

Pete on the intercom. "Listen, bud, you've been taking a lot of that stuff. The pain should be starting to ease up. Do me a favor and just put some ice on it for now. If you still need the shot in an hour, you can have it."

Cole looked at the clock. Two-thirteen.

Jacqui brought a sandwich bag of ice and wrapped it in place with another Ace bandage. "It's hard being in here more'n a day or two, I know," she said, patting his shoulder.

The sympathy made Cole's throat close and his eyes sting. "Thank you," he said.

After she left, he dialed Corrina's number one more time. On the fourth ring, as he was about to give up, he heard a click on the other end.

"Hello?" Cole said. "Corrina?"

"This is her mother. Who is this?"

"It's Cole, Jeff Cole. We've never met—"

"Oh, hello, Cole. How's that hand doing?"

At least, he thought, Corrina had talked about him. "Coming along. It's going to take a while."

"You don't want to rush it, now."

"No, ma'am." After a pause, he said, "Listen, is Corrina—"

"I'm so sorry, Cole. She's gone."

"Gone?"

"Her VISTA application got accepted and she's gone to Philadelphia for training. She left yesterday morning. Said I shouldn't answer the phone, that she was going to write you, but every time it rang I thought of you in that hospital and I just had to let you know."

"Philadelphia?"

"After training they're going to assign her to some ghetto up there. Oh, Cole, I'm so scared for her, but she was always headstrong. Couldn't nobody talk her out of anything."

"How long has she known?"

"Two weeks. I asked her, did she tell you about it. She said she would take care of it. She was never good with telling people things they didn't want to hear. Never wanted to disappoint anybody, that was Corrina."

Cole noted the ominous past tense. "Do you have a phone number for her? Or an address or anything?"

"I can tell her you called. That's all I can do."

He tried for five minutes to break her down. It was as hopeless as trying to change Corrina's mind. He gave her his parents' phone number and the number at the hospital and hung up.

He couldn't stop picturing her on a grimy street corner in her cowboy hat and cutoffs, surrounded by tall, dark, leering strangers.

Two forty-one. He focused on the second hand as it clicked slowly around the dial and waited for 3:13.

ALEX CALLED the Tyler Motor Inn at noon on Saturday, their usual time. He called again at two and again at four. It was possible that Cole wasn't answering because he'd gotten lucky with Corrina on his last weekend in the piney woods. Alex would not have bet money on it.

He called Cole's parents. Cole's father answered, and he handed the phone off to Cole's mother as soon as Alex identified himself. By the time he got the whole story from her, Alex had to fight to control how pissed off he was. "Why didn't you call me? Why didn't you let me know? I would have gone up there."

"I'm sorry, I guess I wasn't thinking."

If it had been Alex in the hospital, his parents would have turned the place into party central to cheer him up. Cole's parents hadn't even been to see him since the day of the accident.

"You say he's coming home tomorrow?" Alex said. "Why don't you let me bring him back?"

She was reluctant, and he patiently demolished all her arguments until she agreed to talk to Cole's father and call Alex back.

While he waited for the call, Alex talked to his own father, who of course thought it was a great idea. A few minutes later Betty Cole called and admitted that Cole would probably be happier coming home with Alex.

He threw a change of clothes into an overnight bag and his mother put some leftover pot roast and fixings in an ice chest. "You give him our love, now," she said.

Alex made it to the hospital before seven and found his own way to the room. Cole was working the TV remote control, which made a noise like dropping a loaded garbage can onto concrete every time he changed the channel. He had a dazed look, which lit up when he saw Alex.

"Hey, Cole. I just found out this afternoon. Your fucking parents never told me, man."

Something passed across Cole's face that Alex hadn't seen there before, a look a convict might get at the mention of lawyers.

Alex kept going. "My mom sent food, and I talked your parents into letting me drive you home tomorrow."

"Shit, man, that's great. I am so glad to see you." Cole blinked and leaned forward. "What the hell happened to you?"

"Growth spurt," Alex said. "I've grown four inches since May. I've had to buy all new clothes. Twice."

"Holy shit."

"Yeah. My bones hurt. And I can't get enough to eat. At least I don't need my stump cushion to see over the steering wheel anymore." He shook his head. "Fuck that, let me see your hand."

You couldn't see much. The most disturbing thing was the absence. It was a hand like any other hand, only less so.

"Well," Alex said, "that's not going to keep you from playing. Good."

Cole didn't say anything. Alex broke out the food and Cole got one of the nurses to bring plates and silverware and a couple of Cokes.

"So," Cole finally asked. "How's the band?"

Alex was braced for the question. "Shaping up. We had practice number five last week. This drummer is amazing. Wait till you hear him."

Cole nodded. You could see how the accident had changed him. His cockiness had been hollowed out.

"Listen, man," Alex said, "we'll wait as long as we have to until you can play. Don't worry, all right?"

The truth was that Mike had been pushing to bring in another guitar player, "just temporarily," and Gary had said, more than once, "This guy must be great if we're waiting all summer for

96

him." Alex hadn't heard Cole play in two months, so he didn't know how good Cole was now, or how he would sound with a full band behind him, or how he would handle himself in front of an audience. And that was before he fucked up his hand.

Alex was gambling everything on friendship and a hunch. The Chevelles had the makings of a seriously commercial act, a much bigger deal than he'd first imagined on the night of the Dylan concert. They only had this one year before they all graduated. Mike was shooting for one of the West Coast schools like Reed or Berkeley, and Gary had his eyes on Juilliard, so they'd be scattered across the country. If Cole couldn't cut it, and cut it fast, Alex would have a tough call to make.

At the same time, he couldn't deny how empty the summer had seemed without Cole around. He'd had friends from school over to use the pool. He'd met a girl at a party and taken her to the Gemini to see *The Wild Angels*, where he'd gotten to second base in the back seat. He'd scored some vodka from the older brother of a guy from the tennis team and gotten loaded. None of it had felt like what he really wanted to be doing.

"What if I can't play anymore?" Cole said.

"Come on, Cole, cut the shit. If you'd lost that much off the end of your dick, you wouldn't even notice."

"The girls might have an easier time of it, it's true."

Alex heard the strain in the humor and asked the obvious question. "What's happening with Corrina?"

"Everything," Cole said. "And then nothing."

It took Alex a while to worm the story out of him. Cole answered in monosyllables and by the end he was in a worse funk than before. So, Alex thought, Cole is first to the pot of gold. And look at the joy it's brought him.

By nine o'clock he was exhausted from trying to cheer Cole up. He left with the key to Cole's room at the Tyler Motor Inn, since it was already paid for.

The place was a dump, plywood walls and threadbare carpets, third-hand furniture and no TV. Alex called home, collect, and gave his parents an update. After that he went through the closet and drawers to get an idea of how Cole had been living. The evidence was slim—western shirts and boots, a well-thumbed copy of *Playboy*, the guitar sitting out ready for use, a few paperbacks, a transistor radio, the funky green tape recorder, his Chevelles notebook, two warm beers in the ice chest. Alex packed the beers in fresh ice for later. No photos, no letters, no diary, nothing else to say who lived here. A few inches or a few seconds' difference and Cole could have been killed along with his friend Jerry, and this was all he would have left behind.

Alex picked up the guitar and sat on the bed, plucking idly through a blues progression. This could be five years from now, he thought. Me and Cole on the road with whatever band we're in by then. Cole next door with some chick he'd picked up at the gig. Maybe mine's in the bathroom getting ready. Tomorrow morning they'd be on a plane to the next stop.

That was all easy enough to imagine. The hard part was going to be the next four weeks.

FOR MADELYN, 1966 was the summer of *Marat/Sade*. Her father managed to put aside enough money to fly them both to New York in late June; to put them up for two nights at the Empire Hotel on Columbus Circle, where she passed Leslie Caron in the lobby; and to get them two mezzanine tickets for the show on Broadway.

How utterly like him. He had conceived a need to see the show and simply assumed that she would want the same thing. She did, of course, but because the idea was her father's, a price had to be paid. By means of the interlibrary loan system, he'd obtained a copy of the script in the original German and informed her that she was to give him a four-page, typed report that detailed the most significant differences between it and the English translation.

Not that it hadn't been worth it. From the minute she touched down at JFK, which she still thought of as Idlewild, she felt she was in the real world at last, to which Dallas was only the shadow on the wall of Plato's cave. They saw the Guggenheim, MOMA, and the Met while her father lectured the entire time. At the Met they accumulated a small crowd who thought he was a professional, and when he told them at the end that tips were accepted, he took in enough to pay for that night's dinner.

They ate bread and cheese lunches in Central Park the first day, and on the steps of St. Patrick's the second. Her one shopping trip was to the Drama Book Store on 7th Avenue in Times Square, where she spent thirty dollars of accumulated babysitting money and could easily have spent twice that. They did walk down 5th Avenue, "as an object lesson," her father said, like their brief glance into St. Patrick's.

And then there was the play. The theater was substantially smaller than the Inwood movie theater in Dallas, the velvet of the chairs threadbare, the aisles cramped. Not that it mattered. Nothing had prepared her for the intensity of the performance, which left her febrile and physically exhausted, eyes swollen from crying, unable to keep her hands from trembling when she remembered the chorus of voices singing, "We want our revolution... *now*!", so clearly a sham within a sham, neither about the French Revolution nor de Sade's anarchic disruptions of the asylum but about the Watts riots and the Kennedy assassination and the war in Vietnam, and because she was watching it in New York, which was so enchantingly real, the imminence of an authentic and violent revolution was that much more terrifyingly, excitingly real.

They stood for a while outside the theater afterward, her in a royal blue cotton jersey halter dress that skimmed her body, her father in his slightly shabby brown pinstripe suit, and for once he had nothing to say, instead merely stood with his hands in his pockets, a faint glow of satisfaction in his face. This, then, was the power of great art: it could even silence her father.

And the one other thing. For the first time in her life, for those two days in New York, men turned to look at her. And for the rest of the summer, in the Tom Thumb or the library or cruising Forest Lane with Hope, with increasingly frantic songs on the radio from Love and the Yardbirds and the 13th Floor Elevators, as the world accelerated into a strange and confrontational future, she saw that her own changes were also accelerating, from girl to woman, teenager to adult, and sometimes, in the middle of reading or eating or watching TV, she would catch herself holding her breath.

*

EIGHT DAYS OUT of the hospital, Cole had been exactly eight days with no sleep. During the day he was exhausted and stupid, clumsy and temperamental. At night he lay with eyes jammed open, legs twitching, hand throbbing, mind racing. Two or three times he drifted off and found himself on the rig, alone, in a weird yellow light. He would look up to see the bright chain writhing in mid-air like a snake, Jerry above it, spread-eagled, arms and legs moving in slow motion, his mouth working as he tried to tell Cole something terribly important.

Then Cole would jerk awake and lie panting, heart pounding, still trying to make sense of a message that was no message at all.

Or he would see Corrina in a crowd, walking away, and he would strain to chase after her with paralyzed muscles. Or it would be the spiral again in the vast, cold emptiness, and he would fight his way back to consciousness from that one, like pulling himself to the surface of a swimming pool with weights tied to his feet.

The hospital had sent him home with Demerol tablets, which did nothing at all. If he'd known where to get heroin, he would not have hesitated. But he was 16 years old, white, middle class, in Dallas, Texas. He might as well have been on the moon.

He'd had a couple of hours of relief on Saturday, when his parents had gone out to a company function and Cole had downed two shots of 100-proof vodka. He still hadn't slept, but for a while he didn't feel like his skin had been peeled off.

Monday, at last. Cole was sitting in an office in the Baylor Medical complex that looked like it had been slowly deteriorating since the 1920s. Green linoleum worn nearly through at the doorways, cracked brown leather exam tables, metal cabinets with outsize chrome handles.

Cole was uneasy about the doctor's name—"Skinner" was unfortunate for a surgeon. Skinner himself looked to be in his 70s. Long, thinning white hair and glasses so thick he could have burned ants with them. He used a tiny electric saw to cut the plaster cast off Cole's arm. A small cloud of white dust and gauzy threads floated above the dime-sized blade. When the cast finally dropped onto the table in two neat halves, Cole was shocked by how thin his forearm had become in only two weeks. Peeling patches of damp white skin gave off a corrupt, sweetish odor like spoiled hamburger.

Skinner wrinkled his nose. "Anhh, always it stinks a bit under there. A couple of weeks with no way to wash, no air circulating, it happens. Let me cut the rest of these bandages off." Cole looked away. "Now we clean." As Skinner wiped the skin with alcohol, Cole felt dangerously fragile, as if the weight of his hand could snap the radius bone like a toothpick.

"Better," Skinner said. "Now we get those stitches out."

"It's pretty tender," Cole said. "Could you give me a little something first?" He could feel the kiss of the needle, the wave of warmth washing over him. A light sweat broke on his forehead.

Skinner's glasses magnified his stare to grotesque extremes. Cole knew what he must look like—bloodshot eyes in deep, dark sockets, one leg nervously bouncing on the ball of the foot. At last Skinner said, "We can put on it some Lidocaine." He brushed a clear liquid onto the stitches. The pressure of the brush hurt. For the last week, every inch of his skin had hurt.

"You're not touching the button, right?" Cole said.

"Not for two more weeks. I want you to look at that chart over there on the wall. Can you see it?"

"The one that shows the arm bones?"

"Correct. Please read the labels on the chart, out loud."

"Greater tubercule," Cole said. It felt like Skinner was shoving big, glass-headed hatpins into his finger.

"Tubercle," Skinner corrected him. "Keep going."

"Lesser tubercle." Sweat ran down his face, and down the ribs under his arms. "Inter-tu-ber-cular sul-cus."

"We're done. Your stitches are out, and you now will always remember the geography of the upper humerus, I think."

Cole looked at his naked hand for the first time since the accident. Aside from the horrifying button and wire, this was what he would be living with for the rest of his life. It was ugly, deformed, and he couldn't imagine a desirable woman ever loving a man with a hand like that. No wonder Corrina had run away.

"Very carefully, I want you now to bend each of your fingers for me. We start with the index." Skinner held the other fingers lightly to restrain them. The fingers were swollen enough to make them stiff. Cole couldn't touch the end of his index finger to his palm, and the effort made his middle finger feel like he was shoving it into a cup of broken glass.

"And now the ring finger. Good. And the little finger. And now, very gently, the middle finger."

Cole took a breath and tried. The tip of the finger burned as the remaining joint in the middle bent, as instructed, a good half-inch.

The tension and the pain had left Cole exhausted. He sat passively while Skinner fitted him with a removable cast to wear at night or when he was in danger of banging the hand into something. "Otherwise you will leave it off and gently exercise the fingers during the day. Gently, you understand?" He wiggled his fingers to demonstrate.

In the car, Cole ignored his mother's attempts to talk about how well it had gone. Once they got home he went immediately to his room and locked the door. He lay on his bed and tried to conjure the feeling of a double dose of Demerol, from the nurse pinching up his flesh and the first prick to the fullest penetration of the drug into his toes and the follicles of his hair. The memories skittered out of reach. He had worn all the edges off them, like he had the memory of making love with Corrina.

Skinner had been disappointed in him, and Cole was disappointed in himself. The fictional spies that were his heroes were tortured routinely, and they egged their tormentors on with wisecracks. Cole had broken like a raw egg.

He peeled off the Ace bandage and the new cast and sat with the wounded hand in his lap. The whole balance of his hand was wrong, like a tennis racket with no strings.

Tennis. He'd been so obsessed with the guitar that he hadn't thought about tennis. Even when the finger healed, he would never have enough strength in his grip. The years of work, the way he'd defined his image with white jeans and a cable-knit sweater like Robert Culp in *I-Spy*, all gone.

Which left him nothing but the guitar. Eventually he took it out of its case and sat with it on the edge of the bed. He fitted the pick carefully into his right hand and hit an E chord. The pick slipped out of his fingers and through the strings and bounced on the carpeted floor.

He bent over to retrieve it and fatigue spun his brain so badly that he had to put the guitar aside and get carefully down on his hands and knees to find it.

He settled the curve of the guitar on his right thigh again and used both hands to get the pick in the right position. He squeezed it hard with his thumb and forefinger until the answering pain in his middle finger made him gasp. He relaxed the pressure to where he thought he could stand it and gently stroked the E chord again. Twice more, and then the pick turned sideways in his grip, blurring and muting the sound. In frustration he hit the strings again, and this time the stiff, swollen stub of his injured finger scraped against them.

"Shit!" he yelled. The pain was like an electric shock. He felt it in the backs of his knees, and flashbulbs popped in his vision. He wanted to hurl the guitar through the window. Instead he let it fall onto the floor and curled up on his bed on his left side, facing the wall, and pulled up his knees to shelter his throbbing hand against his chest.

A tentative knock at the door. "Jeff?" his mother said. "Are you all right?"

"Go away," he said.

He'd never talked to her like that before. He heard her try the knob and discover that it was locked. That had been an absolute rule, from the time he was big enough to reach a doorknob, that he was never, ever to lock his door. In the long pause that followed, Cole knew she was trying to decide what to do about it. The answer, it seemed, was nothing.

He closed his eyes and let his mind go where it wanted. His beautiful guitar, which he would never play again. His tennis racket, which he would never use again. Corrina, who he would never see again. His father, who had sent him to Tyler to be crippled. Alex, who would move on to a new best friend, a friend with two good hands, who could play guitar. His school, which bored him, Dallas, which he hated. The world, with its snipers in towers and Vietnam War. The wider the circles got, the more terminal and desperate everything seemed. Make it stop, he thought. Make it all stop.

He'd never thought seriously about killing himself before. A world without him in it—he had no vantage point to picture it from. Better to focus on his fucked-up, useless hand, and how he wouldn't have to live with that any longer.

He got up and waited for the dizziness to pass, one of the new habits he'd had to learn. He unlocked the door and opened it, and his mother, from the kitchen, said, "Jeff?"

"I'm all right," he said, and went into the bathroom. He took a leak and carefully washed his hands and got out his Schick injector razor. He slid in a new blade, wrapped the old one in a Kleenex, and held it loosely in his right hand as he opened the bathroom door. His mother stood at the end of the hallway, watching anxiously. Before she could say anything, he ducked into his bedroom and locked the door again.

He lay on the bed and took the blade in his left hand. When it came to it, he would do it in the bathtub, of course. Supposedly it hurt less as well as making less of mess. The question was whether he could bring himself to cut himself.

He turned his right hand over. A fat, blue-green vein ran from the base of his thumb diagonally across his wrist tendons and then all the way down his forearm. It was, he knew, the arteries he needed to cut, and they were deeper.

He touched the corner of the blade to the skin of his wrist. Above it was the coarse stump of his middle finger. A Frankenstein's monster of a hand. What difference would another cut or two make?

He pressed gently on the blade. It made a small indentation and then, finally, the skin gave way. He took the blade away and watched two tiny droplets of blood ooze their way out. He felt no more than a sting.

Okay, then, he thought. He put the blade on his nightstand and pressed the Kleenex against the cut and held it. All set.

His mother had kept the car that morning to drive Cole to his appointment. She would have to go downtown to get his father around four. That would leave Cole alone for at least an hour. Plenty of time.

His mother knocked on the door again. "What can I fix you for lunch?"

"Nothing," Cole said.

"How about a tuna fish sandwich?"

"I'm not hungry." He tried to soften the peevishness in his voice. "I'll fix something later."

Her footsteps receded down the hall.

Four hours to kill, he thought, and laughed at his pathetic little joke. He put on his shoes—loafers, since he could no longer tie laces—and put his guitar in its case and put the case in his closet. He put the razor blade under his alarm clock.

He stopped at the kitchen to say, "I'm going for a walk." His mother nodded, tried to find something to say, and gave up. Cole let himself out the front door. He hadn't put the removable cast back on. He wondered if his hand would frighten small children. When he tried to let it hang normally, it swelled up and began to throb, so he held it against his chest, like Boris Karloff as the Mummy.

High noon in suburbia. Cole was on a sidewalk that nobody used except the mailman. Nobody walked in Dallas. The streets were empty because everyone worked too far away to come home for lunch. There were four basic patterns of one-story ranch houses, not counting the mirror images and the ones turned 90 degrees. Mixed and matched with different colors of brick and trim and shingles, all built by the same developer, all between five and ten years old, all with parched lawns and the occasional low tree, all as alike as boxes of detergent on the Safeway shelf. His parents' house had cost $12,000, more or less what his father made in a year. Affordable, secure, clean, fundamentally the same as the neighbors'. Like the brown Buick sedan that had cost three months' pay. Both of his parents had lived through the Depression and this was their dream. A good house and a good job that no one was going to take away. Steak in the freezer and money in the bank. A kid they could brag about to their friends, private school, headed for college.

His mother would be devastated. And befuddled. Sorry, Mom, he thought. You should have had a spare kid, in case one broke.

As for his father, his disapproval would know no bounds. Cole pictured him finding the body, saying, "He always was a quitter."

Cole began to walk faster, as if he could outrun the thought. It dominated everything else he was feeling—exhaustion and pain, self-pity and self-loathing, love and lust for Corrina, depression and despair.

He'd nearly circled the block. Head down, not looking at anything but the sidewalk in front of him, he walked to his parents' house. He was sweating, and the air conditioning hit him like a snow bank. His mother looked up from her armchair and offered him a tentative smile, which he ignored. He washed his face and hands and used a strip of adhesive tape to bind the stump between the index and ring fingers. It hurt every bit as much as before, but this time he didn't care. "I hear you knockin'," he said out loud, "but you can't come in."

He locked his bedroom door and strapped on the guitar. The guy at the pawn shop had given him an assortment of picks, though Cole had quickly settled on a medium weight teardrop. Now he took out a thick, oversized triangle and wedged it into the first joint of his index finger.

Instead of starting with a chord, he picked the G string as his left middle finger slid up to the fourth fret. He carefully picked the third fret of the B string. G string again, slowly, then the fifth fret of the B string.

He breathed in and breathed out and let up on the vice grip that held the pick. He played the same four notes a little faster, a little more smoothly. Again. Then he finished the lick with the hammer-on and the slide down to the second fret. Again.

It didn't matter that his stump howled with pain. The fucking thing could fall off if it wanted to. Time for the E chord. Slowly. Then D, then A. This could be the last time, baby, the last time…

He played for forty minutes, slow fragments of 20 different songs, until his legs shook and the mixture of tears and sweat burned his eyes and soaked his T-shirt. When he was done, he wrapped his swollen hand in an ice pack and slept for three hours, waking only when his mother knocked and said she was leaving to pick up his father.

ALEX TOOK HIS CALENDAR off the wall and made some calculations. It was Sunday, August 21, and he hadn't seen Cole for two weeks, not since the drive from Tyler. They'd talked on the phone, where Cole had been distant and non-committal. You could tell he hadn't been sleeping, that his hand was hurting, that he was depressed about Corrina on top of everything else. He wouldn't leave the house, didn't want Alex to come over, and wouldn't talk about the band.

Alex's sympathy had hit its limit. The first day of school was two weeks away. If the band was not rehearsing by then, with some hope of playing gigs in the near future, then Cole would have to go.

Now all Alex had to do was tell him.

He put it off for an hour, then another, and then Cole called on his own and said he was ready to practice. "That's great, man," Alex said. "I'll call the other guys. You want to come over this afternoon, run through a few things?"

"Not today. I'll see you at rehearsal. Let me know when it's going to be."

"Cole?"

"Yeah?"

"Are you okay, man? Are you able to play and everything?"

"I guess we'll find out," Cole said, and hung up.

Alex stared at the phone. Man, he thought, enough is enough of this shit.

Mike and Gary were both able to make it the next day at noon. He called Cole back, and Cole sounded surprised that it was happening so quickly. "You said you were ready," Alex said, his patience gone. "Are you or aren't you?"

"Let's do it," Cole said.

★

ALEX HAD NO IDEA what to expect when he went to pick up Cole the next morning. The day was hot and clear, headed for 101. Cole waited in the driveway in a white T-shirt, wheat jeans, and cowboy boots. His right hand was wrapped in an Ace bandage, with some kind of metal support glittering through, and he held it against his chest like it was in an invisible sling.

Cole stowed his guitar and amp in the back seat and got in next to Alex without saying anything. Alex backed out and drove to Webb's Chapel Road. The longer the silence went on, the weirder it got, and the harder Alex struggled to find something natural to say. Finally he asked, "Have you been sleeping?"

"I'm up to four, maybe five hours a night."

Alex nodded. He didn't have another gambit, so they drove the rest of the way without talking.

The garage door was open as Alex pulled into the driveway. Gary already had his Indian rug down and his drum set mostly together. Mike was bolting the leg stand assembly to his Vox Continental. Mike looked up as they got out of the car and nodded to Cole. "Hey, Cole, how was Ty—" He saw the bandages on Cole's hand. He looked at Alex and said, "What the hell?"

Now Gary had seen it too. "You must be Gary," Cole said, raising his injured hand in a half-assed salute. "Pardon me if I don't shake hands."

Gary looked at Alex. Alex said, "Um, Cole had a little accident on the oil rig."

"What the fuck," Cole said. "You didn't tell them?"

"I didn't want anybody to freak out."

"Well," Mike said, "I am sure as shit freaking out now."

Gary straightened up and dropped his hex wrench on his snare with a clatter. You could hear the high buzz of cicadas in the distance as they shifted up a full step.

Alex closed the garage door and turned back to face them. "He can play," he said, as the sweat broke and ran down his forehead. "It's not a problem."

They stood looking at each other while Cole put his guitar down and made a second trip for his amp. Finally Gary said, "Can I see?"

"Sure," Cole said. He unwound the Ace bandage and Mike followed Gary over for a look.

Gary whistled through his teeth. "What happened?"

"Piece of chain fell from the monkeyboard up at the top of the derrick. I was a dumbass and didn't get out of the way."

Mike looked a little green as he walked to his organ. Gary nodded and watched with interest as Cole took a roll of adhesive tape out of his jeans pocket and bound three fingers together. Ignoring Gary, Cole looked at Alex and said, "Can I have a beer?"

It was not a precedent Alex wanted to set. As he hesitated, Cole shot him an impatient look and Alex gave in. "Yeah, I guess so."

Cole took a Bohemia out of the fridge and struggled for a while with the opener. Alex let him. When he got it open, Cole took a long swig and turned to the others. "Anybody else?"

Alex was relieved to see them shake their heads. "A bit early for me," Mike said pointedly.

Cole strapped on his guitar and plugged in the amp and hooked up his cord. He was taking deep breaths and his hands shook. He took another long pull on the beer bottle. It was like watching somebody on a ledge, sixteen stories up.

Gary finished setting up. Instead of his usual tapping and thumping, he sat in eerie silence and waited. Mike had his guitar on and was standing behind the organ. They both stared at Cole.

Alex put on his bass and asked Mike for an E. They all tuned up.

Alex said, "I've got the song list here. I put a check mark by the ones we've been working on."

"Did you do 'Last Time'?" Cole asked.

"Uh, no, not yet."

Mike said, "It's just E-D-A, right? I know it."

Gary shrugged. "You want me to count it off?"

In response, Cole played the opening riff and muffed it.

The old Cole, Alex thought, would have made a joke and laughed it off. He would have won Mike and Gary over and gotten them pulling for him. The new Cole squeezed his pick and started again. This time he got it close enough for Mike to fall in on rhythm guitar. Alex and Gary came in behind him and gradually, shakily, the song lifted off.

Instead of a proper PA, they had three microphones running through Mike and Alex's amps, carefully placed so they wouldn't feed back. Cole walked over to his mike and started to sing.

His voice had changed too. It had a rougher edge, and it was like he'd been thinking about the lyrics, like he wasn't just using them to hit notes with. He sounded like Lennon to Alex's McCartney. Alex stepped up and sang the harmony at the end of each line, and suddenly it was happening. In spite of being loose, of the drums being too loud in the confined space, of Cole missing notes and words here and there, the music had a power and momentum of its own, as if they had summoned it rather than created it. Alex felt a pure joy bubble up inside him.

Gary and Mike were both smiling, obviously feeling it too. They made it all the way to the end, Cole vamping somewhat unconvincingly on the "no no no no" before it broke down and rattled to a stop.

Alex let out an involuntary "Yeah!" and waited for Cole to join in, to bind up the wound he'd opened, to give up some word of praise or enthusiasm. Instead Cole said, "Hey, Mike, during the lead, could you play the chords up here?" He ran through the E, D, and A at the twelfth fret. "Just the top three strings."

"Sure," Mike said, and played the lick back. "Why don't we do that for the ending, too? Once to set it up, then the second time back to the low E to end?"

They tried the ending a couple of times, then played the whole thing through. Alex kept waiting for Cole to smile. Instead he finished his beer and said, "How about 'Daytripper'?"

Cole kicked it off and they all fell in, but after a few bars Alex waved them to a stop. Cole went through the riff one more time after everybody else had quit.

"The accents aren't right," Alex said to Cole. "It has to go, dah, dah da-da-dee DAH de DAH, harder on the DAH de DAH."

Cole stared at him for a second, then looked at the floor. "Yeah, okay." He started it again, still not perfect, but better. Alex let it go.

Cole blew the lead, stopped, and that slow fury came again, twisting up through his spine and his right hand. His eyes were dead, like those of an old man on a park bench staring into space.

"Take it from the bridge," Cole said. "The first B."

The second time was better but still not clean. Cole stopped them and said, "Again."

The third time he got it just like the record, the high A note ringing clear above the bent and released E. They cycled through the last coda a few times, then Cole raised his guitar neck and ended on the E chord.

Alex saw that Cole was impatient to move on. He stopped them anyway to work out the harmonies and play through the whole thing again from the top.

When they were done, Cole said, "You guys know 'Corrine, Corrina'?"

Alex said, "It's not on the list."

"Fuck the list," Cole said, with a casual contempt that made Alex's face burn.

Predictably, Gary said, "Big Joe Turner or Ray Peterson?"

Though Cole was being an asshole, Alex knew the mixture of embarrassment and irritation that he was feeling and his instinct was to diffuse it. "Cole, meet Gary. He does this all the time."

Cole said, "Turner, he did 'Shake, Rattle and Roll,' right?"

"Right."

"Peterson," Cole said.

Gary wasn't ready to let it go. "Have you heard Turner's version? It really swings. I can bring it next time."

Cole said, "Let's do the Peterson right now, okay?"

"Chords?" Mike asked.

"Same as 'Daytripper,'" Cole said. "E, A, B. It's just a blues."

"'*Just* a blues'?" Gary said.

Cole ignored him and played some arpeggiated chords with heavy vibrato in a kind of half-assed samba rhythm. What the hell are we doing? Alex wondered. He'd never liked Ray Peterson, a whiny wimp from an era that was over and done. Why would you want to play this song in the first place, other than to rub salt in your wounds?

Gary dutifully played straight 4/4 on his hi-hat while Mike lagged behind, working out his part. Alex played what he remembered from hearing the song on the radio. The parts all pulled in different directions. Cole plowed through two verses and the chorus, then tried to play the hokey string section melody as a lead before he shook his head and quit. "Well," he said, "that sucked."

"Maybe we can come back to it," Alex said.

"Yeah," Cole said. "What's next?"

Alex picked up the list. Before he could say anything, Gary said, "How about 'Sloopy'?"

"Fine," Cole said.

"Uh, listen," Alex said.

"Now what?"

"We're doing a kind of a different arrangement."

"Why?"

"Just try it, okay?" Alex nodded to Gary. "Count it."

Gary took them into their hybrid version, which now incorporated some of the grinding Vibrators heat. Alex had the lead vocal and Cole followed along, until the song went into a vocal break instead of a guitar lead. Finally he stood with his hands on his hips and watched, shaking his head at the end. "It's too slow."

"It's not really any slower," Gary said. "It's just got a different feel."

"Well, I don't like it."

Gary and Cole stared at each other. Gary smiled a nasty, superior kind of smile.

"Let's take a break," Alex said.

Cole took off his guitar and went out the side door and into the back yard.

Gary said, "We waited all summer for *this*?"

"I'll handle it," Alex said.

Cole stood at the edge of the pool, his back to Alex. Alex fought the urge to push him in.

"What the fuck is the matter with you?" Alex said.

Cole turned around. "With *me*? Whose band is this? This was supposed to be you and me, that was the idea from the start. Now it feels like I'm auditioning in there, and if you guys don't like it, then I'm out."

"You know what?" Alex said. "You *are* out. I'm sick of this shit. You've turned into a complete asshole and I don't want to do this with you. We'll find somebody else."

At first Alex thought Cole hadn't heard. Then Cole began to collapse in slow motion. He sank down onto one of the chaise lounges and folded his arms across his chest, the left protecting the right. Alex saw that he had taken away the last thing Cole had.

Cole's face went through a progression of emotions, from anger to despair. After what seemed like an hour, he said, "I'm sorry."

Alex waited.

"I don't know if I can do this," Cole said. "It hurts and I'm scared."

"You were doing it. There's nothing the matter with your guitar playing that a little practice won't fix. Your singing is great. The problem is that you're being a total prick."

"I'm sorry," Cole said. He had trouble getting the words out. "Give me another chance. Please."

"One," Alex said. "No more drinking when we're playing. Two. I run the practices. With suggestions from everybody, but I call the shots. Three. If you're enjoying this, act like it. If you're not, then get out."

Cole slowly nodded.

"Give me five minutes," Alex said, and went back in the garage.

"Is that the same guy I played with this spring?" Mike said. "Because I don't remember him being such a total asshole."

"He's been through some real shit lately. I'd like to give him another shot."

Mike grunted. "His singing's pretty good. The guitar playing, I don't know. He gets things right the second time. That's not going to cut it live."

"He's never played with a band before. And he's only a few days out of his cast. He'll come around." Alex sounded more sure than he felt.

"I guess we'll find out," Mike said.

"You all right?" he asked Gary.

Gary shrugged. "You don't expect to get along with everybody in a band. A little tension, not necessarily a bad thing. I will say,

I've never punched anybody with a crippled hand before. I would probably feel bad about that afterwards."

Alex considered his options. "Let's hope that doesn't become necessary," he said.

"We can hope," Gary said.

Alex went to the door and motioned to Cole to come inside. Cole was subdued. He put on his guitar and then said, "Look, I… I'm sorry, okay? I just… I'm sorry." He turned his back on Gary and Mike and checked his tuning.

"What's next?" Gary said.

Alex looked at the list. "How about 'Look Through Any Window'?"

They got through another half dozen songs. Cole turned on a few watts of his old charm and Gary backed off on the blues purist crap. Alex's mother came out to check on them and made sympathetic noises over Cole's hand. When it was over they agreed to do it again the next day.

As Alex drove him home, Cole said, "Maybe tomorrow morning we can go get me an amp."

"Are you serious?"

"If we're going to be doing gigs, I need something bigger."

"Your parents will spring for it?"

"I've got the money from Tyler."

"I thought that was supposed to be for college."

"They want me to go to college, they can fucking well pay for it. After what happened, they're not going to tell me how to spend that money."

Mr. Hyde had come out again. Alex changed the subject. "What are you going to get?"

"I don't know. You tell me."

"If you can afford it? Twin Reverb."

"I can afford it. I need to keep it at your place, though, all right?"

"All right."

Cole scrunched down in his seat. His right hand was in its splint and he cradled it chin-high with his left. "I wish it was tomorrow already."

Cole had his best night's sleep since leaving the hospital and
that allowed him to see what a mess he'd been at rehearsal. He
apologized again when Alex came for him at ten, and Cole saw
that Alex was going to let it go.

From Alex's house they called around for prices and Cole
watched in admiration as Alex negotiated him a great deal at
Brook Mays Music. They brought the new amp to Alex's garage,
and Alex helped him mount the casters he'd retrieved from the
junk box in his father's shop. The amp, the size of a big suitcase,
contained two 12-inch JBL speakers that weighed 20 pounds
apiece, making it a bitch to move around without the wheels.

He'd also sprung for a Gibson Maestro Fuzz-Tone like Keith
Richards used on "Satisfaction," a fat black doorstop that made
his beautiful clean Fender tone sound like it was coming through
a bag of broken glass and scrap metal.

They were fooling around with the amp and Alex was getting
on him about "Daytripper" again, so he started playing that one
section of the lick over and over again, and then suddenly he
heard something. He slowly picked out a descending version of
the same six notes and played it back-to-back with the original.
He punched in the fuzz-tone and tried again.

"Do you hear it?" he asked Alex.

"Hear what?"

"Our first single," Cole told him. He threw some chords against
the notes—D and F#, which he quickly changed to F# minor, for
the first half. He tried a few unexpected options from there, then
went with the obvious G to A for the second half. He got Alex to
switch to guitar and play the chords behind the lick.

"Yeah," Alex said. "It might work. You just need lyrics, a
chorus, and a bridge."

"That's the easy part," Cole said. As if I'd done it before, he
thought.

He was so excited about it that he couldn't stop himself from
playing the lick during practice.

"What's that?" Gary said.

"Just something I'm fooling around with," Cole said. He called out the chords to Mike as he went through the lick slowly. They played it a few times at tempo, Mike on rhythm, Alex on bass, Gary sitting out.

"Where's it go from there?" Mike said.

"D," Cole said, suddenly hearing it. "C, then A. Just a barred A moving down the neck. Hold that last A, then the lick comes in again."

"Nice," Mike said.

"Sounds like 'Daytripper,'" Gary said.

I should have kept it to myself, Cole thought.

"You should try it with a shuffle beat, it would sound more original," Gary said. He played a mid-tempo shuffle. "Come on, try it."

Cole, making an effort not to lose it, said, "I don't hear it with a shuffle beat. Can we do it the way I wrote it?"

"Maybe we should do it the way Lennon and McCartney wrote it."

"Fuck you," Cole said.

"Hey, man," Gary said. "Relax. I'm just giving you shit. Don't get all bent out of shape."

"You're really a prick, you know that?" Cole said.

Gary was smiling. "Well, any time you want to do something about it, let me know. You might want to wait until your hand heals up."

Cole looked at Alex and Alex looked back at him like it was up to Cole to get himself out of it. Cole hadn't left himself a lot of options. Either eat shit or quit the band. "Next song?" he said.

"How about 'Get Off My Cloud'?" Alex said.

"Good one," Gary said. "Let's go."

THAT NIGHT COLE sat on the edge of his bed, taking his mind off how much he hated Gary Travis by playing the lick from his song over and over, waiting for the notes to suggest something. After ten minutes he fell into a trance, and that was when he heard the words, "You never cared for me," and then the next time through he heard, "You let me take the fall."

He sang them and they fit, so he tried, "You brought me to my knees," and from there the last line was obvious, "You never cared at all."

He sang the whole thing through a couple of times. He couldn't tell if it was moronic garbage or if it was okay. It didn't seem any worse than the words to "The Last Time" or "Hang On Sloopy," though it obviously wasn't Bob Dylan. He would aim higher next time. He got out his Chevelles notebook and turned to a blank page and wrote them down.

He played the verse through again and then played the chords for the chorus and there it was, "You got me free fallin'…" And then, he thought, it should be a girl's name. "Laura Lynn," he sang. He'd never heard of anyone named Laura Lynn, but it fit, and because it was a name he'd never heard before, it added a bit of mystery.

By that point he'd figured out what the song was about and the second verse came as fast as he could write it down.

You never said goodbye
You left me hanging on
The phone just rang and rang
You were already gone

One more? he thought. He had to poke at it to make it come out.

You had us all lined up
You led us in a dance
You never stopped to think
I never had a chance

The phone was on a shelf in the hall, with a cord that was long enough for Cole to take it into the walk-in closet on the opposite wall. He huddled there with his guitar and notebook, the phone cradled in the crook of his neck, and played what he had for Alex. When he was done, Alex said, "Let me get my guitar." Not exactly the reaction Cole had wanted.

"I'm back," Alex said.

"What did you think?"

"I think it could work," Alex said, which was not what Cole wanted to hear either.

"Try this," Alex said. "After the second chorus, go to E minor seventh, then A. Then… G, then G minor. Then up to A on the fifth fret. From there back to D for the next verse."

They played it through together on the phone. "I don't know," Cole said. "It feels like part of a different song."

"It's a bridge," Alex said. "It's supposed to feel like that."

They took it from the top, played verse, chorus, verse, chorus, and into the bridge and by then it had already begun to feel inevitable. Even as he resented Alex moving in on his song, he couldn't hide his excitement. "Damn," he said.

"This free fall, this is some of your astronaut shit, right?" Alex said. "You should go with that. The bridge should just be imagery, clouds or something, as you look down at the Earth."

"Sure," Cole said. He'd looked out of too many airplane windows at a landscape of clouds and imagined walking around on them. "Clouds like a frozen/Field of snow/something something/ So far below."

"Blowing and drifting," Alex said.

"Yeah, that's it." Cole wrote it down.

"That's good," Alex said, "it's like a punchline, the clouds below instead of overhead."

"Yes. Oh man, this is so cool."

"The part about 'got me on my knees,' how about, 'I landed on my knees,' like as opposed to landing on your feet."

"Okay."

"Sing me the third verse again."

Cole sang it.

"Where you say, 'You never stopped to think,' what if… just a minute… what if it was 'You never reached for me,' back to the freefall thing."

"Yeah, that's good." And also true, Cole thought.

"One more thing. How stuck are you on the name Laura Lynn?"

"I don't know." He didn't want to admit that he wasn't entirely happy with it. Alex had already changed so much.

"Because you could turn it around and say, 'You got me falling free,' and that way you don't have to cheat to get it to fit the rhythm. And then the name could be Laura Lee."

"Which sounds like Lorelei, which is like some German legend or something."

"Marilyn Monroe in *Gentlemen Prefer Blondes*," Alex said. "Lorelei Lee was her name."

"Yeah, it works," Cole said. Reluctantly he added, "You should sing lead on the bridge. For contrast. And we should do harmony all the way through."

"From the top," Alex said.

They'd just gotten to the bridge when the body of the phone suddenly shot across the floor and slammed into the inside of the closet door, followed by his father shouting, "What the hell?"

"Talk to you tomorrow," Cole said, and put the receiver in the cradle a split-second before the closet door flew open.

"What the hell are you doing in here?" his father said. "I just tripped over that phone cord and damn near killed myself."

"I was talking to Alex," Cole said. "I didn't want to bother you—"

"Well, I'm sure as hell bothered now. What was so goddamned important that you had to call him at this hour?"

Cole nearly told him, he was so high from what they'd created. "Just talking about the band."

"Get it out of your system, because when school starts I don't want to see you unless your head is in a textbook. Did you manage to break the phone?"

"Me?" Cole said. "I wasn't the one who tripped over it."

His father had already squatted down and snatched the receiver. From three feet away, Cole heard the dial tone with relief. Then he saw his father's face.

"What did you say?"

Cole lost his nerve. "Nothing."

His father straightened up. "I don't care much for the attitude you've had around here lately."

Cole stared at him in disbelief. He had the nerve to criticize Cole's attitude? After sending him off to get crippled on his fucking oil rig?

"If you want to keep playing that guitar," his father said, "I'd better see some improvement, and fast."

He tossed the receiver onto the carpet and walked away, leaving the closet door open.

Cole had no room for coherent thought, only for white-hot rage. He hung up the phone and put it on its shelf. He gathered up his notebook and his guitar and carried them to his room. He locked the door, a small but vital act of provocation. He sat on the bed and slowly, gradually, let the memory of the song, *his* song, call him back from the edge.

Finally he picked up the guitar and played "Laura Lee." The first time through, he was still too angry to pay much attention. By the second time, his father started to fade. He played the song until he couldn't stand to hear it anymore, and then he copied the revised lyrics onto a fresh sheet of notebook paper and wrote the chords above the words. On a blank line under the title he wrote "(Cole" and then, with only a moment's hesitation, "/Montoya)".

COLE WENT INTO the next day's practice braced for another confrontation with Gary, only to find that Gary had thought up a drum part for the new song. He worked the toms during the verses, punching up the two big accents in each line, and it put the thing into overdrive.

They went through it three times, with Mike chiming in on harmony on the choruses. After the third time, which he wished he'd gotten on tape, Cole said, "Great drum part, Travis."

Gary seemed genuinely touched. "Thanks," he said. Then, reluctantly, "I stole it from 'Ticket to Ride.'"

"Well," Cole said, "at least we're robbing the same bank." Gary laughed, and as he turned back to the mike, Cole saw a look of approval on Alex's face.

Maybe, he thought, we can do this.

DR. SKINNER HAD WRITTEN a prescription for exactly three Valium. Cole took one the night before the appointment and the other two an hour before they went in, per instructions. Dr. Skinner sat him on the paper-covered exam table and Cole, sweating, said, "I can't do this without a shot. The Valium didn't do anything."

Skinner asked Cole's mother to leave the room. Then he said, "I think in Tyler they gave you too much Demerol. It is very addictive, Demerol, worse than heroin, some say. The first time I saw you, I thought, 'This young man is in withdrawal.' Today you are much better. I will not give you something that would start the cycle again."

"It hurts," Cole insisted. "You have no idea how much."

"Don't I?" Skinner said. He gently lifted Cole's hand in both of his own. He wheeled over a tray table like the one Cole ate from in the hospital and placed Cole's hand on a folded towel. "Here in this country there is not much hardship, I think, for a family like yours. I would guess you have never really known hunger, not the hunger that comes from not even the possibility of food. As for pain, pain is simply a warning system, like a fire alarm. And sometimes we must have fire drills, when we know it is coming and the warning is for nothing."

Skinner clipped the ends of the two wires that emerged from the inside of Cole's finger. His slightest touch on the wires ignited sparks of pain. Skinner turned the hand over. The button was glued to the skin with dried blood. He dabbed at the blood with a swab, and the chill of the alcohol traveled up Cole's arm into his chest and stomach. Skinner picked up a pair of needle-nose pliers with one hand and used the other, with surprising strength, to immobilize Cole's finger. Cole panicked and said, "Wait…" and Skinner ignored him. He gripped the loop of wire that protruded from the button, and a fireball of pain exploded down the right side of Cole's body as he passed out.

When he came to, Cole was lying on the exam table, a pillow under his head and his knees propped up. His hand lay on a towel on his chest, the finger lightly wrapped in gauze. A bright dot of blood stared at him from where the button had been.

His mother held his left hand and Skinner was saying, "… nerves only, nothing more. Ah, there he is now. Do you think you can sit up? Slowly, slowly."

Cole was only a little dizzy. His finger felt no worse than if he'd smashed it with a hammer while working in the shop.

Skinner gave a list of instructions to his mother. The bandage could come off tomorrow, no need for another appointment unless there were signs of infection. The boy should continue exercising it as soon as possible.

Cole's head felt clear enough. He got up and walked out and stood in the waiting room, holding his right hand shoulder-high. He heard his mother thank Skinner, then they walked out of the elevators.

"That was rude, to walk out without saying thank you," his mother said.

"He wouldn't listen to me. Do you think he was a Nazi in the war?"

"He's Jewish, dear."

Cole, embarrassed, couldn't make himself stop. "I thought suffering was supposed to make you more compassionate."

"Really?" his mother said, looking him in the eyes.

Cole turned away.

MADELYN'S FALL CLASSES were AP French, Calculus, AP Biology, and for her elective, Mrs. Plumlee's History and Culture of India. And of course AP English, where they would read *Hamlet*, *Great Expectations*, *Pride and Prejudice*, and Shakespeare's sonnets. No other poetry, no Tolstoy or Stendhal, though *The Charterhouse of Parma* and the unabridged Garnett translation of *War and Peace* were both on the list of "recreational" reading her father had given her. Drama club at school; ongoing art history at home, where they were up to the Impressionists. Not to mention the ongoing and less formal classical music quizzes, where she would be expected to identify whatever piece her father was listening to when she happened to walk into his study. Or, during dinner, be expected to match the Köchel number to the Mozart piece, or the date of the premiere to the Haydn symphony.

Her sister Julia had rebelled early on, seeing the enforced scholarship as a burden rather than a game, or, perhaps, not wanting to compete with Madelyn's two-year head start. Though he clearly loved Julia, and made intermittent attempts to find other ways to be close to her, erudition was the coin of her father's realm, and Julia resisted all his offers, as his favor increasingly became a wedge between her and Madelyn as well.

On the first Friday of the new school year, Hope and Madelyn walked out of History and Culture of India together. Hope said, "There's a party at Brad Potter's house tomorrow night. I'll pick you up at eight-thirty." Brad was a St. Mark's kid that Hope knew through a cousin's girlfriend's brother.

Madelyn had just looked at slides of untouchables standing in the filthy water of the Ganges at Benares, sorting through the ashes of freshly cremated bodies with fine-meshed nets, hoping to find a gold tooth or nose ring, and was not sure she was in the mood for St. Mark's boys.

"There's going to be a live band," Hope said. "Free food and probably beer. The boys will outnumber us two to one. If you don't come, you're crazy."

Thus Madelyn found herself looking down a rolling, grassy hill at a band playing on the patio of a house the size of a museum, set on grounds the size of a state park. Madelyn did not listen to a great deal of rock, given her father's distaste for it and her own passion for the subtlety and restraint of a good string quartet. However, she did appreciate the way a rock song could free her up and make her move—in the privacy of her own room.

This band was raw, but if the harmonies were loose here and there, the pitch and the emotions were all firmly in place. The drummer understood his job and she found herself swaying on her feet, risking the attention of predatory boys. She asked Hope, "Who's the cute guitar player?"

"The one on the left, or the one on the right?"

Madelyn sighed. The one on the left was playing bass, a distinction lost on some. "The right."

"I'll go find out," Hope said. "Don't wander too far."

A number of boys watched Hope make her Amazonian way down the slope, none with the height or the self-confidence to approach her. At the side of the stage, she engaged somebody in a conversation that involved her pointing to the guitar player in question.

The song stumbled to an end, and over an instrumental interlude, the cute bass player announced that they would be back in fifteen minutes. Madelyn noted, as the guitarist bent to put his instrument on a stand, that he had augmented the band uniform of jeans, white shirts, ties, and navy-blue blazers with a pair of cowboy boots, an uncommon affectation in the current crowd, at least among the younger generation.

Madelyn took a sip of her Tab and as she lowered the can, she locked eyes with a clean-cut young man with acne and a faint odor of whiskey on his breath who had somehow appeared in front of her. He nodded at the Tab can. "Maybe you'd like a taste of something stronger?"

Madelyn suppressed the urge to ask, "Than what?" and smiled sweetly. "No, thanks." She started downhill as Hope was coming up.

"They're called the Corvettes or some car name like that," Hope reported. "The ones on the ends are from St. Mark's, the other two from Richardson High. The one you like is Cole. I'm led to understand that this is the band's debut. I have also located the beer. There's a garbage can in the garage full of Coors and ice. The chaperones are not to know. Are you coming?"

"You go ahead."

Madelyn wandered into the house, pretending not to be looking for this Cole person, instead merely making herself available for some unspecified interesting thing to happen. Outside, the boys wore sport coats and ties, the girls mid-calf dresses from Neiman's. Here in the den it was mostly adults, the men in open collared dress shirts, the women in slacks and cashmere sweaters. Both generations had gravitated into same-gender clumps.

In the kitchen, which was large enough to serve a good-sized restaurant, the drummer stood in conversation with somebody's father, apparently about the stock market; a girl nearly as tall as Hope and wearing a cream-colored dress rummaged casually through the refrigerator.

A deserted formal living room contained furniture that appeared to have never been sat upon. Madelyn was vaguely tempted to wander down the hall and see what shenanigans might be going on in the bedrooms; instead she turned the other way and continued the half-hearted pursuit of her primary target.

A plain hollow-core door opened into the double garage, where at least a dozen young people leaned against either the Cadillac coupe or the Buick station wagon, beers in hand. Hope raised hers in salute, darted her eyes toward the far wall, then returned her attention to the football player whose shoulders curled toward her and threatened to split the seams of his jacket.

Madelyn followed the direction of Hope's glance to see Cole in conversation with someone next to a rack of lawn implements. She moved closer, keeping her eyes focused elsewhere in attempted misdirection, then risked a long look.

Cole's outstretched arm was planted against the wall, very close to the long, dark hair of a pretty girl who had tilted her head down in order to stare up at him through her thick eyelashes in a way Madelyn hoped she herself would never be caught at. And dear God, was that Tabu that she could smell a good five feet away? Cole seemed to be struggling not to look down the front of the girl's dress, despite the sizable incentives on offer there.

Madelyn decided she didn't care how the struggle turned out. She eased out of the garage, through the den, and up the hill. She took a handkerchief out of her purse, spread it on the grass, and settled into a funk, where Hope found her a half hour later.

"I'm ready when you are," Madelyn said.

"Sorry. From what I saw, he was quite charming."

"Evidently."

"Well, there's plenty more sharks in the sea."

"It's not just him. It's the whole sex. Superficial, opportunistic, gutter-minded, fickle, clumsy, obvious…"

"You could go on."

"I could go on."

Hope stretched out a hand and pulled Madelyn to her feet. "Good band, though," Hope said.

"If you like that sort of thing." Madelyn snatched up her handkerchief, tossed her empty Tab can at a trash barrel, and began the long walk to the car.

★

COLE, TO HIS SURPRISE, was not nervous on stage. The slight tremor in his hands came from excitement, not from fear. He was aware of the mistakes they made at that first gig at Potter's house, many of them his. They didn't matter compared to everything else. Alex meeting his gaze across the width of the patio and smiling with joy, Gary bouncing off his drum stool with manic energy, he and Mike and Alex all stepping forward at once to sing the chorus on "Mr. Tambourine Man" as if they had been choreographed. The surge of reckless confidence that hit him halfway through the second set when he saw the gorgeous brunette shaking like a go-go dancer on *Shindig* and staring right at him. Janet, her name turned out to be, Janet Nichols, with the intoxicating perfume and knowing looks. He already had her phone number in his pocket when, during the break before the last set, they wandered out onto the vast grounds until they found a secluded spot under a weeping willow and Cole pressed her against the trunk of the tree and kissed her with mounting passion until Alex's voice on the PA called him back. She blew him a kiss as she left, in the middle of "Poison Ivy," and he watched her until she disappeared in the darkness.

"Man," he said to Alex as they drove home, and then realized that he not only didn't have the words, he didn't want them.

"Yeah?" Alex said.

"Yeah," Cole said.

ALEX DIDN'T GET to sleep until sometime after 3:30, and when the band gathered at 1:00 Sunday afternoon for practice, the others were equally exhausted and sticky-eyed. Cole immediately started pushing for more gigs, playing for free or next to it to get exposure.

Gary, as usual, was skeptical. "We'll never pay off the PA that way."

"Once we get tight," Cole said, "we can raise our prices, start playing at the Studio Club or Louann's. Get a manager or something."

"You're dreaming," Gary said. "You need a big break to get to that level. I know guys in great bands who've played for years and never gotten noticed."

Mike cleared his throat. "Well. The Richardson Jaycees are holding a battle of the bands at the end of October. Johnny Hornet from KLIF is one of the judges. My old band played in one last year and my dad has some pull with them. But we'd have to get really good in the next month."

You could see the whole room light up, like the power coming back after a storm. "Oh, hell yeah," Cole said.

Alex felt it too. The air hummed and everything popped into sharp focus, the blood red of his bass guitar, the purplish chocolate of an oil stain on the concrete floor. The hot electronics in the amps gave off a sweet, resinous smell.

"Gentlemen," Alex said, "we have some work to do."

First they worked on the transitions, playing the end of one song and the start of the next. Then they went over the problem songs from the night before. Alex, like the others, had caught Cole's mood of urgency, and they quickly began to sweat in the muggy September afternoon. At five, when they called it quits from exhaustion, they agreed that the three singers would meet on Tuesday night to work on harmonies.

After Gary and Mike were gone, Alex said, "You want a swim?"

"Is there a beer that goes with it?"

"I suppose. Drink it in here. No glass by the pool."

"No problem." Cole got a Bohemia from the fridge and drained it in three long pulls.

They changed into swim trunks and Cole did a couple of racing laps before hanging by his arms next to Alex in the deep end. "My parents are going to some kind of party Saturday night and they're not going to let me have the car."

"Let me guess. This is about the brunette last night."

"I'm in love. I need to see her again."

He had the same desperate look as he'd had the month before when he talked about Corrina. "No more Rosaline, now it's Juliet, eh?"

"Rosaline took herself out of the running. Juliet is here and now. Can you get a date? We could all go to the Studio Club or something."

More chauffeuring, Alex thought. Oh, joy. "Yeah, all right, I'll figure something out."

"I wish… I wish I'd landed here three years ago. Then it could be us playing the Studio Club next week. I wasted so much time…"

"Yeah, yeah, yeah. In all those armpits of the world. Where you learned Spanish and Arabic and read more books than anybody I know."

"Big woo."

Cole was quiet for a minute and Alex contemplated how suddenly and how hard these black moods came down on him. For the first time he wondered if Cole might be genuinely crazy.

"If you had a window," Cole said, "and you could see yourself twenty years from now, would you look?"

"Of course. Anybody would."

"Not me," Cole said. "If I wasn't where I wanted to be, I couldn't stand it."

"And where is that?"

"Doing this, playing music. In the big leagues."

"You think there'll still be rock in twenty years? You think old guys will be playing it? Where's Benny Goodman now?"

"I don't know, but he's still playing music."

Alex shook his head. "I don't need a magic window. I can see me working for my father, married, couple of kids, big house, all that bullshit."

"Really? That's what you want?"

"Want it?" Alex said. "It's my worst nightmare."

"Then don't do it, man. Those days are over, following in your father's footsteps and all that. You can be whatever you want to be."

"Yeah," Alex said, feeling the edge of his own desperation. "That's the question, isn't it?"

IN LATE OCTOBER, the switchboard rang to tell Dave that he had an incoming call from Sal of the Meteors. Their first single,

"(You Take Me) Around the World," a none-too-subtle sexual innuendo, was in the top 20 in Billboard, top ten on WMCA, so he figured it was safe to pick up the phone.

In fact Sal, in gratitude, had called with a tip. "We had this guy and gal open for us last night, and you might want to check them out. The chick is, like, a fucking knockout, amazing tits, they've got great songs, bluesy, but trippy as shit at the same time. She said they were playing the Bitter End tonight. Her name's Sue Storm, you know, like in the comic book."

Dave didn't know, but he called the Bitter End and confirmed that she was in the eight o'clock opening slot, only a couple of blocks from his apartment.

He got there early. Though the Bitter End was slightly swankier than some of the competition, in the end it was another postage-stamp stage in front of a bare brick wall. His emotions were running high. He hadn't been out to the clubs since the whole verkakte thing with the Meteors. That disappointment still ate at him, and Crystal was part of it too. He didn't know whether to cry in his beer or turn tail and run. He ordered the beer just in case.

Then Sue Storm took the stage and he knew he wasn't going anywhere. She had long, reddish brown hair, a slightly turned up nose, a tiny gap between her front teeth, huge brown eyes that popped a little, like she had a secret she couldn't wait to tell you, and yes, beautifully shaped breasts above a small and undulating waist. All of which was secondary to the glow that came off of her, a slow, sinuous sexuality, frank without being lascivious, playful without losing its high seriousness. She wore folkie clothes: low cut peasant blouse, tight blue jeans, high boots. She carried a dreadnought 12-string guitar that might have dwarfed her had she not been 5 foot 10.

Dave glanced around the room. Every man in the place was staring at her, and that included the tall, skinny kid with the floppy brown hair and an actor's pretty face who got up on the stool next to hers with his own acoustic guitar.

"Hey there, everybody," she said, with a smile slightly brighter than the lights at Yankee Stadium, and she immediately swung into a medium tempo shuffle. Dave had heard it a million times before, and yet it was garden-fresh, with a contagious snap to the rhythm. The boy played a few passable blues licks, barely audible over that big, booming 12-string.

He was braced for a premature, whiskey-roughened contralto, and she fooled him with a clean soprano that she served up with no frills, though every so often she let him see a glimpse of the power she was holding back. The lyrics had been listening to Bob Dylan and reading Ferlinghetti and they tried too hard in places, though they could be fixed.

Still, something else was wrong, and it took Dave the rest of the thirty-minute set, where she mixed in a few more originals with covers of Billie Holiday, Edith Piaf, and Tampa Red, to put his finger on it.

He nearly didn't go backstage, because she was not fully formed, the way the Meteors had been. Between her and the recording studio lay sacrifices she was probably not prepared to make. He went anyway because he wanted to know what it would be like to stand only a couple of feet away from her, to feel that radiance direct from the source.

The green room turned out to be crowded with the rest of the night's lineup, changing clothes and tuning up and warming their vocal cords. He invited them to a table in the back of the club, leaning in so they could hear him over the music.

He kept it short. The first thing he told them was that he was an engineer at Columbia with no authority to sign anybody or produce anybody, but with friends in the business. He verified that Sue had written the songs, while Gene, her partner, insisted he'd contributed to the arrangements. Gene had hooked onto a jet plane with a fishing pole, Dave thought. Now the plane was taxiing for takeoff and he hadn't yet figured out that he was going to have to let go or get badly hurt.

"I'll be honest," Dave said. "I don't think the pure acoustic folk thing suits you. For one thing, it's not that hip anymore, and for another you need real power behind you to match the power of your voice. Have you ever thought about going electric?"

He'd thrown the question to Sue, and Gene intercepted it. "No. Absolutely not. We're serious about authenticity."

As he'd suspected, the kid was going to be a complete pain in the ass, as if that would help him hold on to her. Dave gave them each a card and said, "If you change your mind, give me a call."

He went back to his table long enough to finish his beer and settle up with the waitress. He overtipped her to prove that he wasn't taking out his disappointment on others. The singer on stage was attempting Josh White's "One Meatball" and failing to persuade. Dave waited for the end of the song and then quietly slipped away.

The wind cut through his jacket and rattled his teeth. He hunched his shoulders and turned up his collar, and had crossed Thompson Street before he realized that somebody had called his name.

"Mr. Fisher!" said the voice. "Wait up!"

He turned to see Sue, expensive hard-shell guitar case in hand. She had a sheepskin jacket over her peasant blouse and the cold had turned her cheeks bright red. She was out of breath from chasing him and had to set the guitar down and put her hands on her knees to get her breath. Finally she said, "Can we talk?"

"Sure," he said. "Where's Gene?"

"I departed the partnership."

Dave nodded, more pleased than he wanted to admit. "Let's get out of the cold."

They walked two blocks to the Kettle of Fish, Dylan's old hangout, which Dave chose for sentimental reasons. They shared a plate of French Fries while Dave laid out his ideas.

"The first thing I need is for you to sit down with a pro songwriter, like a Carole King or somebody, and have them work with you on two of your songs, that we will mutually agree on. Your songs are good, but I think they're just short of being hits.

"Then, based on what you learn from that, I'll want you to rewrite two more of your songs on your own. If we've then got four great songs, which I believe we will, we can move to Phase Two."

He gave her a minute to look at the tabletop and get her words in order. "This hurts a little," she said. "That you don't like my songs."

"I think your songs are terrific," he said. "If you want to record for Elektra or Folkways, you're ready to go. I'll call Jac Holzman tomorrow and put in a word for you. But if what you want is for Murray the K to play you on WINS—and only if that's what you want—then this is the quickest way I know to get you there."

She thought about it for another ten seconds and then she said, "Do you really know Carole King?"

"I've met her a few times. She's very nice, actually."

"What's Phase Two?"

"That's where I collect some favors and we get something on tape. Maybe just a song, maybe two or three. Then we shop the results around and get a deal where I get to produce."

"Not to sound ungrateful... do you know how to produce?"

He gave her the short version of his résumé, and her huge eyes got bigger and shinier as he talked. He had to look away to keep from falling in.

"How old are you?" he asked.

"'I'm just twenty-two and I don't mind dyin'.'"

"Now the truth."

She looked down again. "Nineteen."

Dave had turned 31 a month ago. Don't even think about her that way, he told himself. She's an artist, you're a producer, period. "And Sue Storm, that's not your real name."

"It was my little brother's idea. From the comic book, you know?" Dave shook his head. "The Fantastic Four? Invisible Girl?"

"Invisible is the last thing you are."

"I was born Sallie Krupheimer. Sallie with an I-E. I had my nose done when I was fourteen. I kind of feel bad about it now, but then again... I like what I see in the mirror and I used to hate it so much."

Dave flashed back to an old man in the Columbia accounting office. "What's your middle name?"

"Rachel. Why are you making a face? You're not anti-Semitic, are you?"

"I'm Jewish. That was my ex-wife's name. It could work. Sallie Rachel. The two first names thing, that's very rock and roll. Duane Eddy. Gene Vincent. Dick Clark."

"Brenda Lee," she said, smiling mischievously. "Aretha Franklin. Etta James."

"Dean Martin. Jerry Lewis."

"Minnie Pearl."

"Uncle," Dave said.

"Sallie Rachel," she said. "Sallie Rachel, Sallie Rachel."

SATURDAY, OCTOBER 29, cloudy and cold. A slow, steady drizzle had been falling all afternoon. Cole lay on his bed and watched the rain, trying not to let it bring him down.

The bands were supposed to arrive by six PM. They would draw lots for order of appearance, and the doors would open at seven. There would be a stage at either end of the Richardson High School gym, and as soon as one band wrapped up, the next would start. First band at 7:30, half-hour sets strictly enforced. Six bands, ending at 10:30. The judges would huddle, and at 11 Johnny Hornet would hand the winning band a check for 500 dollars.

It was absolutely essential that The Chevelles be the band he handed it to. Everything was riding on it, and Cole found that he liked the pressure just fine.

They'd played an even dozen gigs now, most of them in back yards with an audience of 20 or 30 people, failing as often as not to keep the volume low enough to prevent police intervention. As Cole had predicted, the routine of playing every weekend had tightened them up nicely, and they now rolled inexorably from song to song, building momentum as they went.

The biggest drawback was not having time for dating. His father refused to let him out of the house on school nights, and Janet had quickly tired of going to gigs. They were left with picnics and matinees on weekend afternoons, their make-out sessions inhibited by an excess of daylight.

She was a senior at Bryan Adams High in East Dallas and lived with her divorced mother on the far side of White Rock Lake, thirty minutes from Cole's house on the rare occasions when traffic wasn't an issue. She had her own car, a battered Volkswagen Beetle, though the sheer distance involved meant that they spent more time on the phone than in person.

Cole was still struggling to make sense of her contradictions. She was smart, but not interested in academia. She quoted from *The Feminine Mystique*, but read *Cosmo* and still liked Cole to open doors for her. She had powerful maternal instincts that rendered her incoherent around puppies and kittens, but couldn't see herself married or settled down or having any other restrictions on her independence. In fact she had a wild side, a taste for danger, symbolized by her ex-boyfriend Woody. Woody had graduated the year before and, as far as Cole could tell, was a borderline hood who rode a motorcycle, drank heavily, and had treated her badly. She and Woody had broken up in July after numerous infidelities on his part, though he still called her sometimes in late-night, alcohol-soaked depression. Her continued fascination with Woody seemed to be the main obstacle to her going all the way with Cole.

She was coming tonight, with a girlfriend from Bryan Adams that she thought Alex might like. In the victory celebration that was sure to ensue, anything might happen.

At 5:25 Mike's station wagon pulled into the driveway, and Cole ran out with his guitar and shoved it onto the pile of gear in the back. Nobody looked at him as he got in the back seat next to Alex. Something was clearly wrong.

"What?" he said. "What is it?"

Mike looked over his shoulder and carefully backed out of the driveway. "We don't have a lead singer," he said.

Cole looked at Alex, who was wearing a heavy coat and avoiding eye contact. "What are you talking about?"

"Alex woke up with the flu," Mike said. "He's got laryngitis. He's got no voice."

Cole collapsed into the seat. "Oh, shit," he said.

Gary handed him a sheet of notebook paper. "We redid the set list so it's all stuff you and Mike sing lead on."

"What about the harmonies?" Cole said.

"We think…" Alex started. It came out as a croak.

"Don't talk," Mike said. "Save what little you've got."

"We think," Gary said, "he may be able to do a few harmonies early on. He's got some stuff for his throat."

Alex looked miserable. Cole couldn't find it in his heart to tell him it was okay. It was not okay. It was the worst timing possible and on some level Cole was sure Alex had let it happen through a lack of moral fiber.

"We need to run through the new set," Cole said. "At least the transitions, so we're not fumbling around between songs."

"What difference does it make?" Mike said. Cole had never heard him sound so bitter. "We're fucked. I'm not sure we should get up on stage."

"What's eating you?" Gary said, tactful as ever.

"I promised my dad we were going to be really good and not embarrass him after he went out on limb to get us in this thing. Now he's going to look like an idiot."

"Do you want to back out?" Gary said. Mike didn't say anything. They were barreling north on Webb's Chapel now, hard rain turning the windshield to a kaleidoscope despite the wipers. "Well, do you?"

"I don't know," Mike said.

"What about the rest of you?"

"No," Cole said. "I want to play. Even if we suck."

Alex shook his head and croaked, "Play."

"Up to you, Moss," Gary said. "In or out?"

Mike sighed theatrically. "In. The performers have the boys' locker room for changing and stuff. We can hole up with the guitars and run through the transitions a couple of times."

"All right," Gary said. "You guys are such losers sometimes."

Cole pictured the car sliding off the rain-soaked road and a stop sign coming through the window and cutting Gary's head off neatly at the neck. In his imagination, the mouth was still working as the head landed at Cole's feet. "Nice team spirit, Travis," Cole said.

"Yeah, well, look at the team."

Cole slammed the flat of his hand against the front seat, making Gary's head snap forward.

"Cut it out!" Mike said. "Don't fuck up my mom's car."

Cole folded his arms across his chest. There would be five other drummers there tonight. Maybe one of them would be Gary's replacement.

*

COLE WATCHED 30 BOYS in various semblances of uniforms as they milled around the stage closest to the front doors, all of them wet from carrying their equipment in through the rain. The Chevelles in their usual blue blazers, a five-piece in matching Hawaiian shirts, one group in sweater vests. Everybody else in sport coats and ties.

Johnny Hornet had the running order for the bands, supposedly obtained by random drawing earlier. "If it was random," Gary said, "why didn't they do it in front of us?"

"Shut the fuck up, will you?" Mike said.

"Okay, people, listen up," Hornet said. He was shorter than Cole had pictured him, with dark blond hair, long sideburns, and black-framed sunglasses. Black corduroy pants, black turtleneck, long, oxblood leather coat. Cole gave him credit for not going in for a lot of his radio jive and for treating them like fellow professionals.

"The first two bands, when I call your names, get your gear and start setting up on stage. Band one here, band two at the other end. Bands three and four, get everything put together and have it ready at the side of the stage so we can do a quick changeover. Number three here, four over there. All right?"

He tore the end off a sealed envelope and took out a sheet of paper. "First band, the opening band for the night, is the Luaus." One of the guys in the Hawaiian shirts whispered, "Shit." Cole felt a twinge of pity. Opening was the kiss of death on a night like this. Not, Cole thought, that death had not already given The Chevelles a long, lingering one with lots of tongue.

They drew third position, not as late as they would have liked, but workable. Gary unpacked his drums and started unfolding metal stands. Cole had learned not to offer to help. They lined up the amps and the organ next to the stage and waited for Gary to finish.

Under other circumstances, Cole thought, this might have been fun. Checking out the other bands' equipment, talking shop, ogling their girlfriends in their miniskirts and tight blouses and eyeliner. If Alex had been healthy.

When Gary was done, they retreated to the locker room with the song list and talked their way through the set, moving a couple of songs around so that Mike only had to change from guitar to organ once, and then back to guitar for the last two songs. They tried "Look Through Any Window" with only two-part harmony and agreed they could live with it. They'd already had to scratch so many of their best songs—"You Were on My Mind" and "Liar Liar" because of the complex harmonies, "What'd I Say" because nobody but Alex could do the lead vocal. Cole burned with frustration.

Mike, who was a two-time veteran, hammered home the things he'd already warned them about. Keeping an eye on the time, better to go short than long. Keeping the volume down because the acoustics were muddy and the judges mostly old. Acting like they were having the time of their lives, no matter what.

A roar of noise from the gym floor. Cole's watch said 7:20. Johnny Hornet's voice boomed out in his radio persona, working up the crowd, plugging the sponsors, rehashing the rules. At 7:30 sharp he intro'd the Luaus, who should have blown in right on top of his voice, and instead let an awkward silence fall before they counted off a tired cover of "Walk, Don't Run."

"The order is rigged," Gary said. "They're throwing these guys to the wolves. We're fucked."

"We were fucked anyway," Mike said.

"Fourth or fifth band wins," Gary said. "Wait and see."

Cole took his guitar and walked out, afraid he would go berserk if he heard another word out of Gary's mouth. On the gym floor, the Luaus played to a nearly empty house, and lights flickered on and off around the room as the crew struggled to figure out what they were doing.

My father was right, Cole thought. This is no way to live.

The thought left him even more depressed. He put his guitar in its case, shoved his hands in his pockets, and walked over to the main doors to look at the rain.

Already kids were pouring in, wet but energized, and he was unable to hang on to his bad mood. Then he saw Janet come up the steps and forgot to breathe. A minute later she had him wrapped up in a huge hug and was kissing him all over his face.

"I'm so excited for you!" she whispered in his ear. "You're going to be so great tonight!"

When he didn't say anything, she pulled away. "What's wrong?" He told her.

"Aw, honey. You'll be great anyway."

The words rang hollow despite her best intentions. He could only nod feebly.

"This is Holly," Janet said, grabbing an immensely tall girl with bad skin and pulling her toward Cole. She must have been five-eleven in stocking feet, Cole thought, at least an inch taller than Alex after his growth spurt. Cole forced a smile and stuck out his hand.

"Hi," Holly said. She had orange hair that had frizzed in the humidity and she looked miserably uncomfortable.

Cole bought them all Cokes and they listened to the Luaus butcher "Wipe Out." This was one drummer, Cole noted, who would not be auditioning for Gary's slot. If only the other four bands were equally bad.

At 7:59 the Luaus were gathering themselves to start another song. Johnny Hornet moved quickly to the mike and said, "Let's hear it for the Luaus! Kowabunga! I can almost hear that mighty surf crashing when those guys play. And speaking of mighty, don't forget to tune in the Mighty Eleven Ninety, K-L-I-F, Monday afternoon and every weekday afternoon as the Blue Hornet spins the latest tracks, and that's the facts, Jack. And maybe one of these days we'll be hearing this next band on the Hornet show—please welcome... The Reverberations!"

The lights went up at the other end of the hall and a long, thunderous C chord crashed through the room. A guy in a frilled shirt and leather pants grabbed a mike off the stand and started to sing.

"Got to split," Cole said. "We're next."

Janet grabbed him by the ears and gave him a kiss that dislocated his brain. "For luck," she whispered.

He joined the others to watch the Luaus wrestle their equipment down the stairs behind the stage.

"I talked to the sound guy," Mike said. "He's going to push Alex's mike as high as he can."

Cole looked at Alex, who was shivering and drinking something out of a thermos. Mike said, "Hot tea and lemon juice."

The Luaus' drummer nodded to Cole. "Okay, we're off."

"Thanks," Cole said. "Good luck."

"Yeah," the drummer said. "Right."

The stage was bigger than they were used to, with a two-foot riser for the drums and two PA monitor columns that faced the band. They had to feel their way around in the near-darkness. When everything was in place, they tuned up to the organ, huddled by their amps to keep the noise down. Gary fluttered his sticks over the drums, never quite touching the heads.

The Reverberations, at the far end, were tight. The singer had a good voice and worked the crowd hard, though they didn't give him much in return. The songs were complicated and went off in weird directions.

"Who are those guys?" Cole asked.

Mike dismissed them with a flip of the head. "They do all originals. They're good, but the songs are nothing special. They come to all these things and never win."

It was 8:22 and they were as ready as they were going to get. Their amps were turned up and buzzing, set lists taped to the floor. The sweat poured off Alex's face as he gave Cole an unconvincing smile and mouthed, "Time of our lives!"

Cole had a brief and unaccustomed spasm of nerves, then remembered that they didn't have a chance. A great calm descended on him. He looked at the set list and pictured in his head the way the first three songs fit together. "Look Through Any Window" first, no need to count it, Cole would start it with a long, chiming arpeggio. After that, straight into "You Really Got Me," no countoff, Mike doing the opening riff on rhythm guitar and taking the lead vocal. After that Mike would say thank you and hi to the audience and Cole would come in on top of him with the opening to "The Last Time."

Eight twenty-five. Cole tapped his microphone to make sure it was live, and a blue spark popped as the shock stung his hand. He switched the ground on his amp and tested the mike again. He adjusted the stand a couple of times and looked over to make sure everybody else was ready. Eight twenty-seven. Alex sat on the edge of his Bassman cabinet, head in hands. Gary rocked back and forth on his stool. Mike, his guitar strapped on, played something on the organ with the volume off. The Reverberations lead singer said, "We're going to close out with a song we wrote a couple of years ago…"

Cole didn't know how he was going to wait the length of another song. He turned the volume off on his guitar and played all the way through "Look Through Any Window," and when he finished, the Reverberations still soldiered on. It was 8:31. Come on, he thought. Come on, come on.

Johnny Hornet got up on stage with the Reverberations and they worked around him. They built to a slow-motion climax, every note taking forever, then finally ended it, the drummer rolling the toms and then the cymbals and then the toms again as the singer said, "Thank you!" over and over again.

They're stealing our time, Cole thought.

Then he remembered that the volume was still off on his guitar, and the thought was like falling into a snowbank, snapping him to attention. He turned his guitar up and looked around to see if he'd forgotten anything else.

Johnny Hornet finally grabbed one of the mikes and said, curtly, "The Reverberations! And now a brand-new band with some seasoned players on board, please welcome—"

Before he could finish, Cole tore into the opening of the song. The notes rang like crystal as Hornet said, "The Chevelles!" and then Gary hit his stuttering lead-in and they were off. Cole was well into the chorus before he realized that the harmony was there, all three dovetailing parts, and he glanced over to see Alex looking back and grinning.

The crowd, who looked like they'd slept through the second half of the Reverberations' set, charged across the gym and packed the floor in front of the stage. Cole winked at Janet and sang his heart out. He dragged out the last minor chord at the end, and before the applause could top it, Mike was pounding out "You Really Got Me," and the kids were dancing and clapping wildly.

Holy shit, Cole thought. We're still in this.

Despite Alex going to his lemon tea after every song, his voice was fading by the end of "The Last Time." By then the crowd was already theirs. "This is a song," Mike said, out of breath, "by our lead guitar player, Jeff Cole. We're hoping it'll be our first single." Cheers came on top of the applause. Cole turned to Gary and they counted off "Laura Lee" together, nodding their heads in tempo, urging each other on all the way through the song. The time of our lives, Cole thought.

They sailed through "Heart Full of Soul" and "Kicks," and Cole checked his watch as Mike started singing "Sloopy." If they played all nine songs on the list, they would go past the top of the hour, thanks to the fucking Reverberations. Okay, he thought, time to score some brownie points. Cole walked around to each of them and yelled in their ears, "Skip 'Money' and go straight into 'Shake.'"

As the last chord faded, Gary pounded out his Sam Cooke drum part, solid, relentless, inevitable. Alex ran to the edge of the stage, hands over his head, and clapped along. Cole joined in and the crowd took it up. Some of the girls, including Janet, were dancing like they were possessed, and their sexual energy drove the boys into a frenzy. Cole himself was not immune.

Mike, who had left the talking to Alex at all the previous shows, suddenly turned glib. "On behalf of Alex, our bass player, who came out tonight in spite of bubonic plague, and all the rest of the Chevelles, we thank you from the bottom of our hearts, and have just one last favor to ask of you... do you think maybe... perhaps... you could... just possibly..."

"Shake!" they all yelled, the crowd yelling with them, and they ripped through the song and wrapped it up at 8:59.

Johnny Hornet hit the stage and worked the audience into a crescendo of applause and screams, then called the band out for a second bow before he finally introduced the next act, The Other Side, who opened with another version of "You Really Got Me."

"Outstanding," Hornet told them, flashing an OK sign and a smile as he rushed offstage. Cole looked around for Alex and saw him headed for the locker room at a fast shamble, right past Janet and Holly.

Cole and Gary and Mike hustled their gear off to a deserted corner and Gary started to break down his hardware. Cole was flying high and saw that the others were too. He wiped down his guitar strings, tucked the guitar in its case, and stowed his cords and Fuzz-Tone in the back of the amp. When he straightened up, Janet was watching him with an impatient look.

"Were we great?" he asked her. He lifted her off the ground in a hug that made her squeal and made Holly look away.

"Yes," Janet said, "yes, you were the best ever. What's with Alex?"

"He's sick, baby, I told you."

"He walked by us like he didn't see us."

"He probably didn't," Cole said.

A hand took him by the shoulder and spun him around. Alex, wobbly, smiling. He and Cole threw a few mock punches.

"Alex," Cole said, "this is Holly, who I was telling you about."

Alex mouthed "Hi" and held up one hand in a half-hearted wave. "Had to, uh, use the facilities," he said, sounding like one of those machines that people with throat cancer talked through. "All that tea."

Holly blushed.

Alex was barely audible over The Other Side playing "Nineteenth Nervous Breakdown." The band was competent and nothing more, with weak harmonies, though for some reason the crowd was going wild. So far, Cole thought, this is ours.

"Cole, are you listening to me?" Janet said.

"Sorry, baby, you know how important this is."

Holly said, "Janet said you guys, like, go to St. Mark's?"

"Uh, yeah," Alex croaked.

Cole to the rescue, he thought. "We are *from* St. Mark's, not *of* St. Mark's."

Janet tilted her head. "What's that supposed to mean?"

Holly, at least, was amused. "So you're not the idle rich?"

"He's rich," Cole said, hooking his thumb at Alex. "We are neither of us idle."

Alex pantomimed tossing a ball and reaching for a serve.

"Tennis?" Holly said.

"He does," Cole said, making with the thumb again. "I used to, until the accident."

"What accident?" Holly asked, wide-eyed.

Cole showed her his hand. She took it in both of hers, very gently. She was actually, Cole thought, not that bad looking at all. And Alex might not be taller than her, but Cole was.

Janet snatched Cole's hand away. "This one's taken," she said, then laughed as if she hadn't meant it.

"Gotta go," Alex said, holding up his hand again. "Later."

As he wandered off into the crowd, Janet said, "Cole, we need to talk. Please excuse us, Holly."

Cole led her to a comparatively quiet spot at the end of the bleachers.

"I can't believe Alex was so rude," she said, arms folded to warn Cole away. "What did you say to him?"

"I told him you were fixing him up. I'm sure if he wasn't sick—"

"And you! What were you doing flirting with her?"

"I wasn't flirting, I was trying to pull the conversation out of the ditch. Single handedly, I might—"

"I saw the way she was looking at you."

Cole moved in. "I can't help it if girls like me," he said. "You know it's you that I love." She was rigid in his arms. He kissed her neck, inhaling her perfume and thinking it was true, he was crazy for her. He moved up her jawline and nibbled on her ear.

"Cole, stop that," she said. She didn't pull away. And then she was kissing him back. "Cole, not here," she said in between, and then, "Oh, honey, you'll get in trouble," and finally, "Cole, we have to get back to Holly." With that she pushed him away and he staggered back, out of breath and transfixed by desire. "Come on," she said, and led him onto the gym floor.

The Other Side wrapped up their predictable set with "Louie Louie" and then "Gloria." Good-looking singer, promising guitarist, nothing there to justify the amount of yelling that came from the crowd.

Holly, standing to his left while Janet nestled under his right arm, quipped, "Songs chosen by Mrs. Miller's seventh grade class." Cole glanced at her and smiled. "Many of whom," she went on, still looking straight in front of her, "are attending tonight on stilts."

They crossed the room to hear the next band, who at least had a gimmick working for them. Baggy second-hand suits, wide ties, fedoras. They called themselves Night Train and had a sax player, and though they were all white guys, they did covers of R&B songs like Bo Diddley's "Who Do You Love" and the original "My Girl Sloopy." The lead singer had a strange, rough voice and the band had the kind of looseness that Gary was always on about.

The girls went off to powder their noses. Mike found him and watched for a while, and sure enough, Gary wandered by long enough to say, "Are you paying attention? That's what we should sound like."

A familiar-looking kid came up and said, "You guys were really terrific."

"Thanks," Cole said. "You're the guitar player with The Other Side, right?"

"Yeah. Eddie Yates." He stuck out his hand and Cole shook it.

Cole searched for something positive to say. "You're good, man. Some very nice solos."

The kid seemed genuinely embarrassed. "Thanks. We need to get some originals. That song of yours should be on the radio." The kid shook Mike's hand and faded into the crowd.

"Nice kid," Cole said.

"Yeah," Mike said. "Too bad we kicked their asses."

Holly and Janet came back. Cole introduced Mike to Holly and shortly afterward Mike moved on. "I have this effect on men," Holly said, as if talking to herself.

"Not all men," Cole said. Janet looked up to see what they were talking about and Cole shrugged.

The final band was The Zoo. "We love The Animals," the lead singer said. He'd cut his hair in short bangs to enhance his resemblance to Eric Burdon. "We *really* love The Animals." They went on to play ten songs, six of which were by the Animals. They did a good Animals imitation without straying into originality. Cole felt his confidence rise as they stumbled on Them's "Mystic Eyes."

As they wrapped it up with "Inside Looking Out," Cole saw that the rest of the Chevelles had formed up around him. Much of the crowd had gone home, leaving big patches of open floor. Johnny Hornet tried to work up some applause for The Zoo without much luck, then promised to be back in a minute with the results.

"We did it," Mike said. It was the first real silence in three hours and Mike's unamplified voice had to compete with the ringing in Cole's ears.

Alex stuck up his thumb and Gary said, "Much as I hate to admit it, they're not going to give it to Night Train, so I guess that leaves us."

In fact it did not take the judges long, though Hornet had to introduce them and then plug KLIF again. Finally he said, "And now, the moment you've been waiting for. The winner of tonight's contest, taking home five hundred crisp new simoleons, is... hey, c'mon, all these drummers here and I can't get a drum roll? The winner is... The Other Side!"

COLE LET GO of Janet and walked away. He wound up at the end of the bleachers where he'd been with Janet earlier. He squeezed in behind them and sat with his back against the wall.

"Cole?"

It was Janet.

"Cole, are you okay?"

"Sure," he said. Ridiculous answer for a stupid question. To his surprise, his voice sounded somewhat normal.

"Listen, I have to take Holly home. Her parents are really strict and she's all the way on the other side of R. L. Thornton."

He nodded.

"Call me tomorrow, okay?"

"Okay," he said.

She hesitated, clearly trying to think of something else to say, then turned and hurried away.

Thoughts slowly began to penetrate the fog in his head. Most of them were of the "what now?" variety, and the answer to that was easy. What was the point of going on? Of him continuing to play guitar, even? He could sell the guitar and the amp, and his father, at least, would be happy.

He knew that the rest of the guys were waiting on him. He finally got up and went to where their equipment was piled. Alex was pushing the Bassman cabinet toward the front door and Gary was loaded up with black fiberboard drum cases. "Mike's bringing the car around front," Gary said, and walked away. Cole grabbed his guitar case and wheeled his amp with his left hand, following Gary, but not too closely. They made one more trip for Mike's gear and the rest of the drums and stacked it all beside the station wagon as the rain continued to fall in fat, slow, cold drops.

"There's a lesson here," Gary said, setting his bass drum case on the tailgate where Mike, leaning over the back seat, could pull it all the way in. "We need a more authentic sound. More real. Night Train had the right idea—"

"Night Train lost too, you dumb shit," Cole said. "Why don't you just shut the fuck up for once?"

Gary grabbed him by the front of his jacket and threw him into the side of the car. Cole didn't see it coming, and the impact knocked the breath out of him. Before he could recover, Alex had Gary in a full nelson and Mike was out of the car and had a hand on Cole's chest.

From the darkness, Johnny Hornet's voice said, "Hey, fellas, it's supposed to be battle of the *bands*, not battle of the band *members*."

Hornet stepped into the light that spilled out the front doors of the gym. "If you guys can keep from killing each other, we need to talk."

THE WHOLE IDEA of the DJ was still new, and they were all of them making it up as they went along, not the least of them Mama Hardesty's favorite and only son Jack, who had stopped caring years ago where his allegedly real personality stopped and that of Johnny Hornet began.

Some of the older jocks bitched about the personal appearances and not getting to be with their families on weekends and the sheer inanity of the shit they talked and the products they plugged and the records they played. Not Jack. From the time he was getting beaten up by Cro-Magnons in grade school in Gladewater, capital of the Independent Duchy of East Texas, Jack had wanted to be a big shot, and he loved the free food and promo records, goofing around backstage with The Beatles and the Stones, getting recognized in the Piggly Wiggly. He loved breaking a new record that he knew was going to hit, and he loved sleeping late and staying up late and looking sharp. And the women. My God, the women.

A battle of the bands was not at the top of his list, though he was not ashamed to take pleasure in whipping up the crowd, urging them to "get a buzz on," and if the kids had no idea what the old blues guys had meant by that, neither did they mind filling the gym with his signature Hornet sound, music to his heart.

Then, while the Reverberations droned on, as he took a quick ciggie break under the front overhang, rain thundering down, who should appear but one of last year's chaperones, what was her name? The girls' basketball coach, he remembered that much, that and her long, lean, athletic body, although tonight her body language was not French or English or in fact any of the Romance languages, but strictly Greek to him.

"Well," she said frostily, "if it isn't Johnny Horndog."

"Hey, darlin', I was hoping I'd see you again this year."

"You might have seen me a lot sooner if you'd ever called me."

"I tore my place apart and couldn't find your number."

"Right. You could have called the school and asked for me. But to do that you would have to have remembered my name."

Like salvation from above it came to him—Phys ed, physical hygiene, hygiene, hi, Jean. "Jean," he said. He wondered why, in fact, he hadn't called her back. She was choice, and if memory served, highly responsive. He lowered his voice. "I didn't forget."

That luffed her sails for a second, then she heeled back on course. "Impressive trick. I bet you get lots of chances to use it."

"C'mon, Jean, give me a break here. At least let me take you out for a bite after the show. As an apology. No monkey business, I promise."

"No, thanks. I've almost got my self-respect back. I'd hate to lose it for good." She spun around and walked inside, heels ticking like a time bomb.

"Jean?" She didn't turn around.

Well, damn, he thought. It was no doubt his own fault that even his best friends couldn't tell when he was serious. He'd meant it about the no monkey business. He hated the image of him in her head, and he would have done anything, including not make a pass at her, to wipe it away.

Fine, then, he would call the school on Monday. She would talk to him eventually. And the Hornet charm would fix what it had broken.

Jean was still on his mind when the judges sat down for their vote, and maybe he didn't fight for The Chevelles as hard as he should have. His self-confidence was punctured and losing air. Still, when the vote went against him, he decided to take things into his own hands.

He found the band in a scuffle in the parking lot, having quaffed the lethal cocktail of testosterone and disappointment. Jack had seen the lead guitarist's girlfriend, ample cause for hormones to be running high, and a reminder of why Jack had made it an iron-clad rule to keep it 21 and over, even when it left *him* feeling iron-clad at the end of a long night like tonight.

They shaped up at the sight of him, looking properly cowed and respectful. "The Other Side packed the joint," he told them. "Most judges aren't sharp enough to tell when the crowd's been won over fair and square, like you guys did, and not bought and paid for. Next time you need to bring more friends."

The lead player, the broody one, said something under his breath, which Jack chose to ignore.

"You guys are really talented, and I can only imagine what you sound like with three healthy singers. And you, my man—" He pointed to the drummer. "—you've been listening to Earl Palmer, Benny Benjamin…"

The kid lit up like a pinball machine. "Bernard Purdie," the kid said.

"Al Jackson?"

"Oh yeah," the kid said. "Oh, definitely."

Jack knew exactly what it felt like to be a white boy bewitched with black music, black radio, black coolness. And this kid was able to suck it in through his ears and spit it out through his hands and feet, and Jack envied him that.

"You should think about working out your own arrangements of some of these tunes. It's cool that you can sound like The Hollies or the Stones, but you need to sound like *you*."

The lead player, who'd been squirming, finally spoke up. "We really appreciate your advice and all. But I'm not sure I understand why you're taking the trouble. We *lost* tonight. I don't know how much future we've got."

"Oh, I don't know," Jack said. "How serious were you about wanting that song of yours to be a single?"

It was what he needed to take away the sting of Jean's putdown, seeing them look at each other in disbelief, then look at him like he was Santa with the magic Clause.

"Here's the deal," he said. "I can't manage you guys, or put any of my own money into the recording session, because McLendon is a real tightass about conflict of interest at the station, you know, all that payola shit. What I *can* do is fix you up with a guy I know who'll bankroll a single, and once we get that on the radio, another guy I know can start booking you into the Studio Club and LouAnn's and probably on *Sump'n Else* too."

The others looked ready to jump up and down. The lead player was still searching for the dark lining. "What's this going to cost us?"

"The agent gets ten percent," Jack said. "Other than that, nothing." He handed out four of his bright yellow business cards and said, "Call me Monday. I'm off the air at seven. I'll try and set up a business meeting at the station for Tuesday night."

"What…" The bass player, the one with no voice, was trying to rasp out a question. "What do we call you? Mr. Hornet?"

"My friends call me Jack." He shook each of their hands, got their names, and by the time he got to the Hornetmobile he felt almost like himself again.

★

COLE CALLED JANET on Sunday morning. She was tentative at first. "I don't know how to deal with you when you're in those black moods like last night," she said. "It scares me."

"I know, baby, but I'm in anything but a black mood now." He gave her the rundown on meeting Johnny Hornet. She let out a muffled scream of excitement. "When can I see you?" he said.

She was quiet long enough to make Cole uneasy. Then she whispered, "My mother's going to Waco to see my grandmother. She's leaving now and she won't be back till late tonight."

"Hang on," he said.

Throat tight, hands shaking, he went into the front room and asked his father for the car. Without looking up from *Face the Nation*, his father said, "Is this more band business?"

"No," Cole said. "It's Janet."

His father looked up then. Cole's face must have shown what was happening, and he saw understanding in his father's eyes, maybe a trace of envy. His father reached into his pocket for the keys and his voice softened. "When will you be back?"

"After dinner?"

"Well," his father said, "at least we're saving money on food." He handed over the keys and looked at the TV. "I'll let your mother know."

Cole told Janet he was on his way. He brushed his teeth and put his sport coat on over his T-shirt and jeans. Outside it was overcast and cold, single drops of rain spattering the windshield here and there. Northwest Highway was full of church traffic. No music on the radio, just FCC-mandated public affairs programs. Silence made the drive interminable.

At Janet's apartment, he parked on the street and ran up the stairs. She let him in and locked the door, her own nervousness obvious in her tight smile. She kissed him hurriedly and then led him into the den by one hand. "Tell me again about Johnny Hornet," she said.

Her nerves, he understood, meant that her thoughts had gone to the same place as his. All he had to do, then, was take his time and not do anything stupid. He told her again what Hornet had said, exaggerated a little in saying that Hornet had broken up a fight between him and Gary, showed her the yellow card. "I'm so excited for you!" she said, and put her arms around him.

He kissed her then, and her eyes went serious. From there he was so filled with his own desire and the smell of her skin and the warmth of her mouth that time went sideways. Slowly, piece by piece, their clothes came off, and this time she didn't take his hands away or ask him to wait or pull away from him. When he took her jeans off, she was wearing only her panties and Cole was down to his jeans and underwear. "Let's go to your room," he said.

"It's messy in there."

"I don't care."

"It's *really* messy."

Cole stood up, lifted her to her feet, then picked her up in his arms and carried her down the hall. Clothes were scattered all over her bedroom carpet, school books and stuffed animals lay on her unmade single bed. Cole laid her down, took off the last of his clothes, and got in beside her. "I love you," he said.

"Oh, honey, I love you too."

He just wanted it to go okay. He was practically a virgin and she was experienced and he didn't want to disappoint her. She was as beautiful as a movie star or one of those women in *Playboy*, and she knew it, and she knew a million ways to drive him crazy. And this seemed real, she seemed to really want him, to want this.

And why not? he thought. He was about to record a song he'd written himself, he was on first name terms with Johnny Hornet, he was on his way. Why shouldn't she want him?

Once he was inside her, nothing else mattered. He moved in slow motion for a while, trying to make it last. Then Janet began to make small sounds in his ear, and her fingers were pulling at his hair, and as he moved faster it was like being caught in an avalanche, roaring downhill with no way to stop, and then suddenly Janet cried out and he felt a series of contractions go through her, squeezing him inside her, and that put him over the edge and he was spasming too, and he held onto her with all his strength as they rocked slowly to a stop.

He lay on top of her for a minute or so, trying to get his breath, as she gently stroked his neck and shoulders. Finally he started to feel claustrophobic and he reluctantly rolled onto his back, feeling the sweat on his chest and the juices on his groin turn cool.

"Don't go anywhere," she said, and slipped away to the bathroom. He heard something practiced in the way she said it, and he couldn't help but wonder if she'd said it in the same way to Woody.

Don't start, he told himself.

"I'm starving," she said when she crawled back into the crook of his arm. "I haven't eaten all day. Take me out?"

"We'd have to put our clothes on."

"If you're a good boy, I'll let you take them off me again when we get back."

She directed him to a pizza place in a shopping center near her apartment. Cole had never had pizza before he came to Dallas and now it was his favorite food. Sex had loosened Janet's tongue as well as giving her a ferocious appetite. She talked non-stop as she ate, even with her mouth full, about the miserable weather, about having resigned herself to going to UT Dallas, about whether she should try to get into vet school so that she could be around baby animals all day, about her ailing VW Beetle, which Woody used to keep running for her and Cole had little time to work on. Cole was content to sit and look across the table at her and think about what they'd just done, though he wished she had something to say about the band or about the two of them.

When he got an opportunity, he said, "Did Holly have a good time last night?"

"Oh, she liked *you*. She thinks you're wonderful. Alex didn't make a very good impression."

"But I *am* wonderful. Aren't I?"

She came around to his side of the booth, shoved him down to make room, sat next to him, and gave him a deep kiss. She smelled of perfume and sex and tomato sauce and Cole felt his eyes roll back in his head. "Silly boy," she said, and reached for the last slice of pizza.

*

1966

COLE LEFT AT 7:30 after having drifted off on Janet's couch, his head in her lap, the TV droning on, too many nights of not enough sleep finally catching up to him. His lips were raw as he kissed her one last time, his step light on the concrete stairs. "Walk Away Renee" came on the radio as he started the car. The rain had moved through and left the air damp and cool. He rolled the window down to wave to Janet, who watched him from the doorway, and left it down as he drove. He sang along as the radio played "Poor Side of Town" and "Bus Stop" and "You Can't Hurry Love." He could smell her on his hands. The streets were still wet, but nobody else was on the roads. Cole let the Buick unwind as he passed White Rock Lake, just to feel the world turn under him.

ALEX PARKED in an open lot in downtown Dallas and the four of them got out of the car. It was 6:50 PM, cold and dark. The KLIF studios were a block away, in a wedge-shaped building above a former gas station that now housed the KLIF News Cruiser vans when they weren't prowling the streets.

Alex's throat was still raw from Saturday's ordeal, and though the rest of the flu symptoms had passed and he was back at school, he felt like a cardboard cutout of himself.

Cole, for his part, had showed up at lunch on Monday fixing to burst. As they walked to class, he'd told Alex about scoring with Janet. Now, a day later, he was strutting to the meeting in his cowboy boots, which he normally only wore to gigs. Alex didn't know whether to be annoyed or jealous.

They entered through a glass door on Commerce Street and climbed the stairs to a reception area. Cole flashed Johnny Hornet's card and said they had an appointment. The girl at the desk couldn't have been more than 20 and had a hairdo shaped like the Greek letter omega. She got Hornet on the phone and then sent them up another flight of stairs.

Alex was the first to the studio door, where he hesitated in front of the small square of reinforced glass. Hornet faced him from the inside of a U-shaped table that held a mixing console, turntables on either side, racks of tape cartridges and players, a bulletin board, and a loose-leaf notebook. A boom mike hung overhead, and Hornet was on his feet, headphones on, spinning one of the turntables backward. He wore a short-sleeved white shirt and narrow black tie as if he worked in a bank. He glanced up and saw Alex at the window and waved him in.

Alex opened the door and saw another man lurking toward the back of the room, dark haired, with big bushy eyebrows.

"Come on in, fellas, I'll be off in a minute," Hornet said. "Watch out for that red light when the mike goes live. In the meantime, you can say hi to my uncle Mike Scott."

"Hi, there," Scott said.

Cole stepped up and shook his hand. "I enjoy your show."

"Thanks," Scott said, then pointed to the red light, which, as if by magic, blinked on.

Hornet said, "Coming up at the top of the hour, it's the Royal Order of the Night People, with Mike Scott. But to get there, we're going to have to wade in some water with Ramsey Lewis." He hit a button on the console and the turntable on the right spun to inaudible life. "See you all back here in the Hornet's Nest tomorrow afternoon at three, and till then, remember to keep your buzzzzz on!" The red light went out and he pulled off the headphones. "Got something cued up for you," he told Scott as he wrote in the notebook.

"I actually played what he cued up for me once," Scott said, as he rolled an office chair into the DJ station and pulled the boom mike lower. "Fortunately I faded it out before McLendon heard it."

Alex's numbness had worn off. He'd listened to KLIF since he was 9 years old and had gotten his first transistor radio for Christmas. Like most teenagers in Dallas, he had driven past the studios at night to see the on-air DJ through the smoked glass on the third floor, honking in the hope that he would look out or wave. And this, Alex thought, this is only the beginning.

"Gentlemen?" Hornet said.

At the end of the hall they filed into a carpeted room with an oblong wooden table and padded chairs, two of them occupied. The man on the near side was around sixty, balding, wearing glasses, an open-collared striped shirt, and a plaid jacket. The guy across from him was in his early thirties, with longish black hair and thick sideburns, a shiny blue-gray suit, and aviator sunglasses.

The older man stood up and held out his hand. "Julie Greene," he said, and they each shook hands with him and said their names.

Hornet pointed to the other man and said, "Sid Modesto, booking agent." Modesto lifted one hand as if the effort was more than they deserved, and Alex thought, who is he trying to impress?

They all sat down and Hornet said, "Julie is looking for business propositions, not a huge outlay, with the possibility of a decent return."

"Jack makes me sound like such a businessman," Greene said. "I just want to feel young again. Jack says you've got a song, you want to make a record."

Alex had a moment of doubt. They'd talked about it on the way back from Richardson on Friday night. Cole wanted to know why they had to get other people involved when Alex's father could easily front the money. Alex truly loved his father, and his father would happily have stepped up with the cash. And yet you knew there were emotional strings attached, at the very least the admission of need, an admission Alex hated to make. Yet here they were, making that same admission to a stranger.

"Yes, sir," Cole said to Greene. "We've got one original song and we're working on some more."

"Good for you," Greene said. "So let me hear it."

"Sir?"

"The song you want to record, sing it for me."

Alex had never seen Cole flustered before. "We don't have our instruments with us," Cole said, "not even an acoustic guitar…"

"Irving Berlin, George Gershwin, they didn't need guitars. A song is a song. If it hasn't got a melody, what good is it?"

"I—" Cole said, and looked to Hornet for help. Hornet smiled gentle encouragement at him. "Yeah, okay, give me a minute."

Cole looked at the floor for a good ten seconds, then looked up and started to sing. Alex gave him credit—he kept it simple, didn't try to hum the guitar lick or the solo, just sang the words and put enough feeling into it to sell it.

When he was done, Greene shrugged and looked at Hornet. "Cole Porter it isn't, but what is, these days? It's a real song, like you told me. You set up the recording thing, session, whatever it is, I'll put up the money we discussed."

Alex reached over and slapped Cole on the back. Mike lifted his clasped hands like a boxer, and even Gary gave up a smile and a thumbs-up.

Hornet looked at Modesto, who said, "There's an outfit in Arlington called Atlas Records. They've got a decent studio, they do quality work, they've gotten records on the radio from a couple of local groups. And they're straight. You pay up front, they don't own a piece of any of it."

"Once KLIF starts playing it," Hornet said, "KFJZ will have to get on it too. After that we wait and see, but there's a chance it could go national."

Cole said, "Don't we have to sign something?"

Hornet said, "I'll write all this up. You'll need a parent or guardian to sign for you. This is just for the one record, and it'll say that Julie gets twenty-five percent of the wholesale price after the initial recordings are paid off. He doesn't get any of the publishing, and if it goes on an album later, that's a completely separate deal. As for Sid, that's another contract, and your parents will have to sign that too."

"And what do you get?" Cole asked.

"I get to break the record on my show."

"Why do you want to break their record?" Greene asked. "I thought you liked it."

"He means he'll be the first one to play it," Modesto told him.

Julie shrugged again, using both hands. "Okay, so I'm learning."

"I've got a question," Alex said, his ravaged voice barely audible.

"Shoot," Hornet said.

Alex turned to Modesto. "What kind of suit is that?"

"Sharkskin," Modesto said. His smile showed a lot of teeth. "I like sharks."

★

156

NORMALLY ON A FRIDAY afternoon, Steve Cole tried to get out of the office early and beat the traffic. Today he'd worked late and settled for a plate of Dickey's barbeque instead of a home-cooked supper in order to meet the kid at a rock-and-roll radio station and sign a contract.

His father used to tell the old Arab story about the camel and the tent. First you let them stick their nose in, and then next thing you know, the camel's inside and you're out in the cold. That was the way this music business had turned out. Once he'd backed down on the guitar, it was one retreat after another. Letting the kid stay out until two AM when they had a job. Letting him have his own record player, and having to constantly tell him to turn it down or turn it off and do his homework. Letting him grow his hair and sideburns. Letting him miss meals without warning. Letting him spend the night again and again at a house Steve had never been in, with this kid Alex's family, whom he'd never met.

That, anyway, was finally going to change. Alex's father would be at the station, along with the fathers of the other two boys.

He checked his watch in the hallway outside the conference room. Ten past seven, ten minutes late. Not a very straightforward way to express his anger, he knew, and it made him a little ashamed.

The room was hazy with cigarette smoke, warm from holding 11 bodies where only six fit comfortably. The kid looked up as Steve came in, then immediately went back to talking to an older Mexican, obviously Alex's father. Betty claimed he was always provoking the kid, and this was a perfect example of how it cut both ways. Steve was tempted to turn around and walk out. Then where would they be?

Some 20-year-old hepcat in a black turtleneck and corduroy jacket introduced himself as Johnny Hornet, as if Steve was supposed to know who that was. At least Hornet had some manners and thanked him for coming. He led Steve around to an empty chair next to the kid. At that point the older Mexican stood up and said, "Al Montoya, Alex's father. So glad to meet you at last." He had a firm handshake and no apparent accent.

"Steve Cole."

"You must be so proud of your son."

"Why?"

Montoya flinched ever so slightly at that, then laughed as if Steve had been kidding. "Well, for one thing, this whole party is because of the song that he wrote."

The kid finally spoke up. "With Alex."

The kid hadn't mentioned writing it, and now Steve felt like he'd been made to look foolish. He laughed it off and said, "People write those things?"

"Some of it, I agree, it's hard to tell," Montoya said. His diplomacy seemed unforced. "Looks like we're getting started."

Hornet handed out copies of a mimeographed contract, two pages long. "Short and sweet," he said. "The terms are pretty generous—ten cents a copy artist royalties, five cents a song mechanicals. We'll press 500 copies, 50 of which are promos, on which no royalties are payable. Artist royalties go to recoup the recording costs, which are itemized, and the mechanicals pay from the get-go. Take a minute to read it over and then let me know if you have questions."

Montoya handed his copy to a skinny guy in wire-rimmed glasses and a rumpled suit. Brought his own lawyer, Steve thought. Smart, and also not so smart. This evening's billables would cost him more than the record would ever earn.

Steve read through the contract, most of which made little sense to him. What were mechanicals? What was normal in a case like this? The main thing, the thing he was looking for, was to make sure the kid wasn't obligating himself, or his parents, for anything beyond this one record, and that much looked okay.

Montoya's lawyer said, "Julie, did you write this?"

An old Jew at the end of the table grinned and said, "Maybe I did."

The lawyer said, "That's good enough for me." He handed the contract to Montoya and said, "Sign it quick, before he changes his mind."

The old Jew laughed and everybody around the table laughed and the mood shifted from wariness to good humor. The other fathers all got out their pens and started passing around copies and signing, so Steve did too, though he was still a long way from amused.

After all the copies had gone around the table, Steve said, "Is that it?"

"One more," Hornet said, and handed out another, longer set of mimeoed pages. "I think Sid wrote this one, so you better read it a couple of times." A shady-looking character in the corner barked a single laugh.

This was an agent's contract, and Montoya's lawyer had a few quibbles—the contract could be terminated by either party without obtaining mutual consent, artists could request an audit without notice, and so on. As each point was agreed to, they all wrote in the changes on their copies. Steve checked his watch. Finally the lawyer said, "That's all for me. I think it looks good. Anybody else?"

"I have a question," Steve said. "Who picked the record company?" He already knew the answer, because he'd asked the kid.

"That was me," said the guy Hornet referred to as Sid.

"Did you get a kickback?"

The room went quiet.

"A what?"

"Surely you know what a kickback is. A payoff, from the record company, for picking them."

He and Sid looked at each other for a few seconds. Steve had some practice staring down leasing agents who fancied themselves tough guys. Steve believed business was not a prizefight. It was business, and honest people shouldn't be afraid of honest questions.

Sid let out his breath. "I have an understanding with the company."

"That's good," Steve said, and made a show of signing his copy and initialing all the changes. "Because otherwise this didn't make a lot of sense. And I appreciate the fact that you didn't try to bull-shit me."

He passed his copy to Montoya and everybody else signed and initialed and passed, and then Steve said, "Are we done?"

Hornet said, "Don't you want your countersigned copies?"

"Send them home with the kid," he said, and stood up. He nodded to Montoya, ignored the kid, and walked out.

On the street the cold air sobered him up. He knew he'd been a horse's ass. The smart thing would have been to glad-hand all those North Dallas rich men and their rich sons, to act impressed by the flashy DJ and the rich Jew and the sleazy agent. To pretend that this was a real business, where real products were made by the sweat of men's hands and brows, and that it meant something and it was going to lead to something besides heartbreak. He might have done it, too, if the camel hadn't already pushed him more than halfway out of the tent, and if the desert night was not so terribly cold.

THE FOLLOWING WEEKEND, Cole made the transition from amateur to pro. Saturday morning, a two-hour photo session among the leafless trees of Lee Park and Turtle Creek, with the goal of an 8×10 publicity shot. The photographer was in his twenties, Fu Manchu mustache, yellow-tinted glasses. He had them in their blazers and ties at first, holding their instruments, cavorting Beatles-style around the Robert E. Lee equestrian statue, leaning, squatting, arms around each other's shoulders, all smiles. For round two they changed to black turtlenecks in the bitter cold and looked moody and intense and fought to keep from shivering.

Sunday six to eight PM was the recording studio, "off-peak" hours courtesy of Sid. Two hours to set up, get their levels, and record two songs. "Laura Lee" for the A-side, their abridged version of Dylan's "Just Like Tom Thumb's Blues" for the flip. Cole had them arrive half an hour early and they put everything together in the parking lot.

The sky was overcast and a cold wind whistled across the industrial wasteland of Arlington, a city that had yanked itself up out of nothing in the 1950s based on a GM plant and endless miles of warehouses and business parks.

At ten till, Cole rang the doorbell and got no answer. The building was a windowless cinderblock cube that could withstand a nuclear strike.

"If there's nobody here," Gary said, "and we did all this for nothing..."

Cole pounded on the hollow metal front door. Nothing. Alex said, "You know Friday the Thirteenth comes on a Sunday this month."

"There's two other cars out here," Cole said. "They have to belong to somebody. If they don't open up by six, we'll send Mike to look for a pay phone." Cole sat on the open tailgate of Mike's mother's station wagon and hugged himself for warmth. Mike and Alex sat in the front seat and Gary paced by the door.

At 6:01 the door opened and a guy in a white shirt and tie and heavy black-framed glasses stuck his head out. He looked about forty. Heavy jowls, dark hair slicked straight back. "Chevelles?"

"Yeah," Cole said. "Didn't you hear us knocking?"

"Sorry, it's just me here on the weekends. Looks like you're all set up. Great. Give me one second."

He went inside and closed the door. "Cheapskate," Gary said, "fly by night..."

"Fucking Sid," Cole said. "I'm going to kill the son of a bitch."

A minute later a big man in a brown suit came out. Behind him was the guy in glasses, carrying one end of a portable organ. On the other end was a large woman in her thirties with cat-eye glasses and a huge bouffant. As the three of them headed for a black Coupe de Ville, Cole grabbed his guitar and rolled his amp inside.

The cramped reception area was done up in cheap laminated paneling. Cole followed a hallway and ended up in the studio proper. He couldn't suppress an anticipatory thrill, though the place was a dump. The air smelled of stale cigarette smoke and sweat. Stained carpet on the floor, yellowed acoustical tile on the walls. Mike stands held together with gaffer's tape and coat hangers. An overhead fluorescent fixture that flickered in an epilepsy-inducing rhythm, and a spiderwebbed crack in one corner of the control room window. Still, it was a real studio, real records supposedly came out of it, and Cole was jazzed.

By the time the guy in glasses stuck his head in, they had all the gear in the center of the room. "I'm Vince," he said. "You guys want Cokes or anything?"

Cole said, "We'd like to get started, sir, if you'll tell us where you want everything. We've only got—" He looked at his watch. "—an hour and fifty minutes to do this."

"Relax," Vince said. "You guys are the last session of the night. I'm not going to bust your chops if we run a little long. You guys are with Sid, right?"

Cole and Gary looked at each other. "That's right," Cole said.

"Don't worry. I'll take care of you."

"In that case," Alex said, "I'll take a Coke."

In ten minutes Vince had handed cold Coke bottles around and positioned the instruments. Gary was in a corner, behind a cardboard screen cut out of a refrigerator box and padded with foam rubber, low enough to see over. A single microphone sat above his bass drum, pointed at his snare, and three more mikes were aimed more or less at their amps.

"What about vocal mikes?" Cole asked.

"Up to you," Vince said. "My idea was we'd get the instruments for both songs, then overdub the vocals. You want to do 'em live, that's jake with me."

"Overdubs are good," Cole said, looking at Alex, who nodded.

They all put on headphones, and Vince gave Cole a mike to do a guide vocal. "Let's hear what you got," Vince said.

They ran through a minute or so of "Laura Lee" while Vince, in the control room, pushed faders up and down, then waved them to stop.

"From the top again," he said. "Keep it simple."

They played the song through to the end and Vince said, "Okay, what's the other one?"

Mike said, "Shouldn't we, like, record this one before we move on?"

"You just did," Vince said. "What's the other one?"

Mike switched to organ for the Dylan song. Both Cole and Alex hit some bad notes. Vince reluctantly let them do a second take.

"Can we hear that back?" Cole asked when they finished.

"Later," Vince said. "Let's do the vocals." It was two minutes past seven, with an hour to go. "How many singers?"

He wheeled out a big boom mike like the one in the KLIF

studios and said, "Circle up. Lead singer stands this far away, harmony singers this far. Got it? You, the drummer. Come in the booth with me, we'll throw some handclaps on the A side. The rubes never get tired of handclaps."

The vocals for both songs were done by 7:30, and Vince finally played the songs back. He'd added enough reverb to the vocals to sweeten them up. The drums popped, the guitars sparkled, the bass hit right in the solar plexus.

"Holy cow," Gary said. "You're really good."

"Been doing this a few years," Vince said. "Laura what's her name, the one that sounds like 'Daytripper,' that's the A side, I assume. Want to juice it up a little more?"

"It sounds good now," Cole said.

"Up to you," Vince said. "We can ping those tracks onto another machine, throw some organ on there, where you can't hardly hear it, and double the guitar part, this time without the fuzz. While you two do that, we'll beef up the handclaps."

"Do it," Cole said.

THEY LOADED OUT at 8:30. Cole felt anxious walking away without a copy of the record in his hands. What if the studio burned down? What if they wrecked the song when they made the master?

Alex, on the other hand, was ecstatic. "Man, that sounded incredible," he said, when he and Cole had assumed their usual positions in the back seat. "That Vince guy, he's like Phil Spector or something."

Gary turned sideways in the front seat and said, "If Phil Spector was stuck in some cheapskate hole in the wall in Arlington, Texas." Then he relented and said, "It did sound pretty good."

"We need more songs," Cole said.

"Don't look at me," Mike said.

In fact Cole already had something in mind. It was called "Doesn't Anybody Know Your Name," and it was about a girl that nobody noticed at first glance, maybe a little too smart for her own good...

What was the matter with him? He was in love with Janet, she was perfect, he'd even wondered what it would be like to be married to her and spend the rest of his life with her. And yet he kept thinking about Holly. "She thinks you're wonderful," Janet had said. He could still feel the way she'd held his crippled hand in both of hers.

Stop it, he thought.

"What's happening with your old man?" Alex asked. "Is he still pissed off?"

"I don't know," Cole said. "We don't talk about it. It's the only way to get through dinner."

"If things ever get really bad, like if he gets, you know, violent or something, my dad said you can come stay with us."

"Are you serious?"

"My dad says sometimes when you're brewing beer the fermentation gets too hot and the pressure keeps building until the tank explodes. He thinks your dad is like that. He thinks he could go off any minute."

Cole pictured himself telling his father that he was going to stay at the Montoyas' for good. The thought chilled him. No going back from that, not ever, not as long as he lived.

He couldn't remember another adult ever criticizing his father before. Even as it confirmed his own sense of reality, it also suggested a frightening seriousness, an extremity.

"Hey," Gary said from the front seat. "Are we on the radio yet?"

FOR TWO AND A HALF WEEKS Cole thought of little else. Finally Alex got a call from Johnny Hornet and phoned Cole and the others to pass along the details. The single would debut the next night, Thursday, December 1, at 6:35.

Cole's intent was to keep his father from knowing that the record was out for as long as possible. They always ate at 5:30, which left Cole time enough to do the dishes and be sitting in the closet with Janet on the phone in one ear and the earplug from his transistor radio in the other.

At 6:30 Hornet played "Last Train to Clarksville" and followed it with the Supremes' "You Keep Me Hangin' On." Janet's radio came over the phone a fraction of a second behind Cole's.

As the Supremes wound down, Cole said, "Are you listening?"

"Shhhhhh! Yes!"

"The Marvelous Maidens of Motown," Hornet said, "new at number one this week on your KLIF Forty Star Survey, available at the Melody Shop and other fine marketers of musical merchandise in the metropolitan area. And speaking of the metropolis, all you KLIF listeners know that Dallas/Fort Worth is a motherlode of musical talent, and there's nothing in the world that warms this blue hornet's heart more than stumbling on a record by a brand new local combo that we think—"

The next second or two was drowned out by a stifled scream from Janet.

"—hit, and so, buzz cats and kittens, permit me to introduce you to—"

Cole's guitar lick echoed in both his ears.

"—The Chevelles!"

The main emotion Cole felt was relief. The record was real, it was a physical object, and it was on the air. As Cole listened, the song mutated from intimately familiar to as distant and strange as if he were hearing it for the first time, and then back again. He tried to hold on to it, to slow it down, to at least, for God's sake, have some sense of whether it was any good or not. The two minutes and 20 seconds slipped through his hands.

Over the fade Hornet said, "Great sounds from right here in our town—that was 'Laura Lee' by Dallas's own Chevelles. That's one we'll be hearing a lot more of in the coming weeks, I guarantee you. Stay tuned for KLIF 20/20 News at twenty before the hour, right after these words from your friends at Procter and Gamble."

He heard Janet's radio switch off. "I wish you were here," she said. She had dropped into the husky voice that drove Cole wild.

"Yeah? What would you do?"

"I would whisper something in your ear."

"Like what?"

"Wouldn't you like to know."

He did want to know, badly enough to consider begging his father for the car, despite there being no chance of his getting it on a school night.

"Can you hold that thought until tomorrow?"

"Maybe. As long as no reasonably attractive males happen to show up in my apartment tonight."

"Lock your door," he said, telling himself that she was only teasing him, only trying for a reaction. "I love you, but I have to go. Russian history test tomorrow."

"I love you too," she whispered. "See you tomorrow."

Cole kept the radio on while he studied. He was behind on his reading, he'd been having trouble concentrating in class, and if he didn't ace the test, he was in danger of losing the B average he'd contracted with his father to keep. The textbook was a fat, oversized paperback, George Vernadsky's *A History of Russia*, with tiny type that melted and ran as he tried to take it in.

Shortly after 8:00, Mike Scott played "Laura Lee" again and Cole was so focused on Vernadsky that he didn't recognize it at first, the beat making him tap his foot, the music filling him with a vague yet powerful sense of pleasure. Then his brain clicked in, and he was unable to find those stranger's ears again.

It was good, he thought. It sounded like a hit.

It sounded good again at 11:30, when it woke him from a dream that the band was playing for Catherine the Great at her new Winter Palace in St. Petersburg. Catherine, who looked like Holly, wore a low-cut gown and used an ornate fan to hide her smile.

ST. MARK'S SENIORS were allowed to leave campus during free periods, and though Cole had meant to finish studying for the exam, he ended up going out to lunch with Alex instead, to the pizza joint in Preston Royal by the Safeway. All morning, guys had come up to him, even the jocks that had never talked to him before, and said they'd heard the song on the radio and thought it was cool. Cole felt like he could sprint ten miles, and at the same time he was flooded with an immense contentment with the rightness of the world. Try as he might, he couldn't feel the urgency of Russian History.

"What did your folks think about you being on the radio?" Alex asked him.

"They don't know."

"For real? We had dinner early and then we all sat in the living room and listened together. Shit, man, you should have been there with us. Everybody was yelling so much you could hardly hear the radio."

"I was on the phone with Janet. It was pretty cool."

Out of nowhere, Alex asked, "What are you doing for Christmas?"

Cole gave him an inquiring look. "The usual, I suppose. My father will buy the cheapest tree he can find and my mother will hang too much stuff on it, including these embarrassing ornaments I made in kindergarten, and we'll exchange a few 'practical' gifts. Why?"

"You know we fly down to Guanajuato every year, all five of us, for like ten days or something. Jimmy didn't want to go this year and my father asked if maybe you wanted his plane ticket."

Cole stared.

"It's beautiful, man," Alex said. "It's in the mountains, in this natural bowl, hills on all sides, with these pastel stucco houses all over them. You have to go through a tunnel to get in, like a robber's roost, you know? And there's tunnels all under the city, and El Jardin de la Union, the central plaza, has this bandstand, and there's always something going on, dances and mariachis and military bands. We stay with my grandparents in this huge house with servants and everything. And the food... and the women..."

"Oh, man," Cole said. "There's no way in hell."

"Because of Janet?"

"No, she's going to be in Waco from Christmas to New Year's. Because of my fucking father."

"I was afraid of that. I mean, I don't get it. If he doesn't like being around you, why doesn't he just let go?"

"Let go? You've got to be kidding." Cole looked at his watch. "Shit. I'm going to be late for the exam."

*

IT DIDN'T GO WELL. Cole remembered Mr. Batchelor reviewing everything that was in the exam. He just couldn't remember what he'd said. Cole was able to bullshit his way through the essay questions based on what he'd read the night before. He knew that wasn't enough. As he labored over the short answer questions, his fingers felt cold and stiff. Sweat ran into his left ear. What had he been thinking? Why hadn't he studied instead of going out to eat? How was he going to get out of this?

AT 7:15 THAT NIGHT Cole heard the lawn-mower sound of Janet's VW in the driveway and ran to the door to let her in. She was unfailingly polite to Cole's parents and they were chilly and distant in return. Cole's mother complained in private about Janet's tight sweaters and short skirts, and Cole knew that it wasn't the clothes, it was the aura of sexuality that wafted around her as strongly as her perfume. As for Cole's father, it clearly disturbed him on a primal level to see his son involved with a girl that he himself found desirable.

Cole hurried her through a quick hello to both of them and then out to the car. They were headed to the Preston Royal Theater for a double-feature of *Our Man Flint* and *The Silencers*. Cole kept the radio tuned to KLIF, thinking, in vain, that any minute Mike Scott would play "Laura Lee" again. *Our Man Flint* disappointed him too, with its preposterous acronyms and cartoonish mad scientists and impossibly accomplished hero. He was more interested in Janet's body, though she moved his hands away when he tried to take a few liberties, and shrugged him off when he nuzzled her neck, saying, "I'm trying to watch the movie."

When it was over, Cole said, "Can we split?"

"There's another movie." Janet was big on getting her money's worth.

"Yeah, well, the Matt Helm novels are really great, and I don't think I could stand to watch them get turned into another 'spoof.'"

"Listen to you. You sound like your father."

A white phosphorus bomb went off inside Cole's skull. He stood up and squeezed past her to the aisle. Outside the theater, he sat on the curb and stuck his hands in his armpits. The temperature was in the forties, damp, not actively raining. He was only wearing a sport coat and dress shirt and jeans, and the heat was leaching out of his body. He checked his watch. 9:25. He would give her until 9:30, he decided. If she didn't come out, well, it was only five miles to his parents' house. A cold walk, but doable.

It should have been a great night. His song on the radio, their first Fort Worth gig on Saturday, a last-minute opening that Sid had gotten them at the Teen A Go-Go. And yet here he was, shivering on the street. He glanced over his shoulder at the meager line for the second show and thought, Fuck this. He stood up and hunched his shoulders and started down the sidewalk toward Royal Lane.

"Cole?"

He turned. Janet walked toward him, an anxious look on her face. He let her come to him. She put her arms around him and buried her head in his chest. "I'm sorry," she said. "I shouldn't have said that about your father."

"It's okay," he said. "I probably did sound like him."

They looked at each other and Cole saw that they both had harder things to say that they were both holding back. Janet kissed him lightly on the lips and said, "Let's go."

Their parking spot was an empty house on Talisman whose long driveway got lost in the shadows of trees. The VW was nearly impossible to make love in—the back seat was too short, and the best they could do was tilt the front passenger seat back as far as it would go.

Janet left the engine running because of the cold. A faint smell of exhaust came up through the floorboards. She set the parking brake and instead of kissing him she curled into his armpit and huddled there. "It's so cold," she said.

When he tried to kiss her, she turned away.

"What's wrong?"

"I don't know. Not in the mood, I guess."

"You were in the mood last night on the phone."

She didn't bother to answer. Panic and desire made him reach for her and kiss her repeatedly. She pushed him away. "Stop it!"

Cole slumped against the passenger door.

"It's cold," she said, "and we're going to get monoxide poisoning if we keep sitting here." She backed out and drove the block and a half to his parents' house in silence. She pulled up to the curb and sat staring straight ahead.

Cole sighed. "I'll call you," he said.

She nodded without looking at him. He got out and shut the door and watched her drive away.

HE WAITED UNTIL one o'clock Saturday afternoon to call. Her mother told him that she and Holly had gone shopping and wouldn't be home until after supper.

He couldn't think of anything else all afternoon. At the gig, on the high stage looking out at hundreds of dancing couples, he kept searching for her, picturing her suddenly emerging from the shadows to blow him kisses.

He dragged himself out of bed at ten on Sunday morning to call her and got only endless ringing. She finally answered at 11:30, sounding distant and artificially cheerful. He apologized again for Friday and told her how much he'd missed her Saturday night.

"Well, you know, I've seen you guys so many times now…"

"Are you tired of me?" Cole asked.

The pause went on too long. "No. But I think maybe we should try cooling it for a little while."

"'Cooling it'? What does that mean?"

"Well, I'm going away for Christmas anyway. Maybe we shouldn't see each other until after that."

"That's an entire month!"

"It would give us time to think."

"I don't need time to think."

"Maybe I do."

"Do you want to break up with me?" Cole hated the desperation in his voice.

"No. I love you. But this has all happened really fast. You've got your band, and then you're going away to college, and I need to think about what I want and what I'm going to do."

By the time they hung up, Cole was in tears. He could write her, she said, and she would write him back. No phone calls. Nothing she said made sense to him or explained why she'd changed or gave him a way to win her back.

He lay in bed for a while, nursing his misery, then bundled up and took a long walk. Weak sunshine, no wind. A good day for tennis, something he would never play again. His attempts to reassure himself—other fish in the sea, record on the radio—carried no weight.

That night he reread *Death of a Citizen*, the first Matt Helm book, and managed to lose himself for minutes at a time. Eventually he fell down the long, dark well of sleep.

Monday morning he told Alex about Janet. "She actually said she wanted to 'cool it for a while'? Man, where do girls come up with the stupid shit they say? Is there some kind of secret handbook or something?"

"I was hoping for a little sympathy here," Cole said.

"Either she'll come back in a couple of days wanting to make up, or she's an idiot. You're in a hot combo, you can sing, you're not too bad looking, you can have any girl you want."

"Apparently not," Cole said.

Monday afternoon Mr. Batchelor handed back the exams. Cole got a C- - -. A note at the end read, "This should have been a D, but I gave you the benefit of the doubt because I know you're a smart guy. If something's bugging you, please come talk to me. Your grade in this course is in serious jeopardy."

Monday night Cole listened to KLIF from 6:30 until close to midnight and they never played "Laura Lee." The phone rang once and Cole sprinted for it. It was somebody selling life insurance.

Tuesday, after school, he saw an envelope from St. Mark's on the dining room table. It was addressed to his parents, and it had been opened. His mother watched him from the kitchen. Trying to hide his panic, Cole said, "What's the letter from school?"

His mother said, "We'll talk about it when your father gets home."

He sat in his room and waited. When he heard his father pull into the garage, he began to shake. He heard his mother and father talking, then the sound of his father mixing himself a drink, something he rarely did. He was almost relieved when his mother knocked on his door and said, "Jeff? Come to the living room."

His father was in his recliner, the TV, ominously, off. His mother was in her overstuffed chair on the other side of the room. His father held a typed note on school stationery. "Sit down," he said.

Cole sat on the edge of the couch, hands clasped between his knees.

His father said, "This is exactly the kind of letter I was afraid of getting. It's from a Mr. Batchelor, and he tells me you're in trouble in Russian History class. He says you've been daydreaming in class, not completing your assignments, and that you didn't study for the exam last week."

"I, I wasn't feeling well last week—"

"You felt well enough to go on a date Friday night and stay out until three AM on Saturday."

His father had a faint smile on his face, like he'd had when he'd insulted Alex's father and gone after Sid at the contract signing. Like he'd had when he administered spankings when Cole was little, using a folded leather belt. Cole knew that it was involuntary and had no humor in it.

"I'm sorry," Cole said. "It got a little crazy there, but it's under control now. I promise it won't happen again."

"We had a contract," his father said. "The purpose of the contract was to make sure that things didn't get 'a little crazy' or 'out of control.' And it seems to me that they've gotten a lot out of control."

"I'm sorry," Cole said again. "Really. And I promise—"

"I'm sorry too. But we had a deal, and now it's up to me to make sure it won't happen again. Therefore as of now, tonight, this minute, you are out of the band. The guitar goes back to the pawn shop. You are grounded through the end of the year, meaning no dates, no spending the night with your Mexican friend, home here every night and all day on weekends."

"We've got gigs booked. You can't—"

"What?" his father said. The smile was still there, his tone mild, as if he couldn't possibly have heard what he thought he heard. "What did you say to me?"

"Nothing," Cole said.

"Do I make myself clear? Do you understand everything I've said?"

"Yes," Cole said. "I understand."

"You may go to your room. Your mother will have dinner ready in a few minutes."

Cole went to his room and locked the door. His hands trembled as much with excitement as with fear. The worst thing, he realized, would have been getting caught in some painful compromise or long, pitched battle. This, he thought, this was not even a choice.

He looked in his closet. A couple of plastic dry-cleaning bags on hangers, two good sized cardboard boxes full of old toys and books and letters. He put the contents of the boxes onto the shelves, then sealed the hanger holes in the bags with Scotch tape.

Nobody spoke during dinner. In the news, polio vaccination was now mandatory in Belgium. Mao's Little Red Book was being readied for international release, including in the US. The war in Vietnam was going badly, but General Westmoreland was still confident of victory by the end of 1967. Cole's father watched it all with an air of calm satisfaction, as if the new order in his own home had temporarily eased his anger with the growing chaos everywhere else.

Dinner was green bell peppers stuffed with ground beef and rice, a baked potato, a chunk of iceberg lettuce for salad. Cole, to his surprise, was able to eat. His body seemed to recognize that it needed fuel for a long night ahead.

After dinner he took the phone into the closet. He heard his parents discussing it as he dialed, his mother saying, "Let him at least have that much."

He got hold of Alex and said, "Is that offer still open? For political asylum?"

"I can barely hear you."

"I can't talk. Can you be waiting for me at the curb at midnight? Just sit there and wait."

"Yeah. Are you okay?"

"I'm not injured. Just be there, okay?"

"I'll be there."

Back in his room, the question was what to take and what to leave behind. The guitar had to come, obviously. Enough clothes for school and performing. Toothbrush, deodorant, razor. He didn't think he'd ever be back, so that meant the record player, which folded up into a suitcase-sized package, and his albums. Schoolbooks. A few other books he didn't want to leave behind, the Matt Helms and Joe Galls.

His father went to bed at 10:00, as always. Cole had the bags of clothes and the boxes of books and records lined up inside his closet. At 10:15 he heard a light tapping at his bedroom door. He opened it a crack and saw his mother in her chenille robe.

"Can I come in?" she whispered.

He shook his head.

"I'm so sorry about this," she said. "I'm going to work on him. I think I can talk him into letting you keep the guitar, at least, as long as you only play it at home."

He nodded stiffly.

"He does love you, you know. We both do. We want what's best for you, and school is so important—"

"What's all that whispering?" his father bellowed. The closed door of his parents' bedroom was directly across the hall. "I'm trying to go to sleep in here."

Cole's mother smiled sadly, kissed her fingers, and reached through the narrow opening to press them to Cole's cheek. Rocked by his sudden feelings of love for her, Cole held her fingers there and closed his eyes. "I'll be all right," he told her.

"Good night."

"Good night," Cole said. He closed the door as she turned away.

At 11:40 he couldn't wait any longer. He took the screen off the casement window above his desk and cranked it open. Freezing air gusted in. He knelt on top of the desk and passed his guitar case through, then leaned out and eased it to the flower bed outside. Next came the practice amp, then the stereo and the boxes and bags.

He closed the window, put the screen back in place, and took a quick look around by the light of the streetlight outside. He couldn't think of anything he'd missed. He put on his long black topcoat with the zipped in lining and his black high-topped tennis shoes. His cowboy boots were in one of the bags outside.

Ten minutes to midnight.

He opened his bedroom door and went to the bathroom. When he was done, he washed his hands and face. Still not too late to change your mind, he said to his reflection. But of course it was.

He heard his father snoring as he crept down the carpeted hallway. He went out the front door and eased it closed and locked it. The temperature outside was below freezing. He put gloves on and carried the bags and boxes to the curb. As he returned for the last load, he saw headlights in the distance. He ran to the house and crouched in the shadows until he saw Alex's Monza coast in to the curb. Then he grabbed the guitar and stereo and jogged down to the street.

Alex, in perfect secret agent style, was wearing a black turtleneck and jeans. He left the Monza idling and his door ajar as he ran to the front of the car and opened the trunk. He stowed the bags and boxes as Cole quietly opened the passenger door and put his gear in the back seat. Then they were both inside, holding their doors lightly in place as Alex eased down the street and around the block, then slamming them shut and accelerating toward Webb's Chapel Road.

Cole was giddy as he ran down the events of the evening for Alex. He kept looking over his shoulder for signs of pursuit. Like a convict in an old black-and-white movie, he'd made his break and he wasn't going to let them take him alive.

Alex was suitably appalled by Cole's father, yet at the end of the story, Cole saw he had something else on his mind. "Is there a problem with me staying at your place?" Cole asked.

"No, man, it's not that at all."

"Then what is it?"

"I didn't want to tell you tonight, with everything that's happened."

"Tell me what?"

Alex sighed. "I called Johnny Hornet tonight to see why they stopped playing the record."

"Uh oh."

"He said McLendon pulled it off the air. He said because Jack was involved it was a conflict of interest."

"But Jack isn't making any money off of it."

"That's what Jack told him. And McLendon said, 'That's why you've still got your job.'"

"What about the other stations?"

"Jack called up Mark Stevens over at KFJZ and asked him as a personal favor to play it. Stevens tried and management told him they weren't, quote, in the business of helping KLIF, end quote."

"So what are we supposed to do? Sail them into White Rock Lake?"

"Jack said he got a ton of calls on it. We can sell it at our gigs. Speaking of which, the airplay we got was enough for Sid to get us into the Studio Club at the end of January."

Cole sank deeper into the seat.

"Hey," Alex said. "You've got those other songs you're working on. We can try again. My dad would back us, if it came to that."

"KLIF will never touch us now. If we can't get on KLIF, we can't break nationally."

"Okay, so we don't break nationally. Look how far we've come already. From our first gig to the Studio Club in five months. If it wasn't for the band, you never would have gotten together with Janet—"

"Yeah, and look how that turned out."

"She still loves you, man, I know it."

Cole shook his head and stared out the window.

Alex's father was waiting up for them. He hugged Cole and said, "Are you okay physically?"

It was all Cole could do not to cry. "Yes, sir, I'm okay. He didn't hit me or starve me or anything like that."

"Good. Now, you're not seventeen yet, are you?"

"I will be on the twenty-third. In three weeks."

"Close enough. I checked with my lawyer, and once you're seventeen your father won't have any legal recourse. Did you leave a note?" Cole shook his head. "Good, that's probably best. I'll go see your father tomorrow and explain the situation."

Cole looked at him in wonder. "Are you sure you want to do that?"

"I flatter myself that I understand your father, maybe better than he understands me. I look forward to putting that theory to the test." He looked at his watch. "You and I also have a lot to talk about, which I'd rather not do tonight. I would like both you and Alex to go to school tomorrow. Is that possible?"

"Yes, sir."

"Do you need anything? Food or clothes or a toothbrush or anything at all?"

Cole would have loved a couple of beers but didn't want to push his luck. "No, sir, I think I've got everything. I've done a lot of packing in my life."

"You go on to bed, then. The guest room is made up for you." He squeezed Cole's shoulder. "You're home now, son. For as long as you need to be here."

Cole was able to get upstairs before the tears came.

STEVE COLE HEARD Betty knock on the kid's door like she did every morning. Except today he didn't answer, and Steve felt the first tug of unease. He finished putting his clothes on and was knotting his tie when she came back and knocked again. He heard her try the kid's door and heard it open. Then she gasped, and he had a heart-pounding moment of fear that made him grab the edge of the closet door.

"Steve!"

The little bastard cannot have killed himself, Steve thought. It's simply not possible.

When he saw the neatly-made bed, the gaps in the bookshelf, the missing clothes, he was more relieved than anything else. Then Betty turned on him, with a look on her face he had only seen a handful of times since he'd known her. "I hope you're pleased with yourself," she said, her voice barely audible, and very hard. "I hope you're just really, really pleased with yourself."

She pushed past him and Steve followed her into the living room. "He's at the Mexican kid's house, isn't he? Is that what you two were whispering about last night?"

"First of all," Betty said, "'the Mexican kid' has a name and you damned well know it. Secondly, unless you want to end up completely alone in this house, you will apologize to me right now for even thinking that I knew anything about this."

He was, in fact, ashamed. "I'm sorry, Betty. This is a shock for me too."

"Leave me alone for a minute. I don't want to talk to you right now."

Steve went to the bedroom and sat on the edge of the unmade bed. He felt strange and lightheaded. His stomach hurt and he thought maybe he should eat something. He wondered if he should go into work. What did people do in this type of situation? Should he call the police?

Sweat ran into his eyes and he saw damp spots darken his shirt. "Betty!" he yelled. He didn't hear her respond and so a few seconds later he called again. He couldn't get his breath.

She appeared in the doorway, looking put-upon. "What?"

"Can you get me something to eat? Maybe a banana and a glass of milk?"

She hesitated, like she was going to tell him to do it himself, then she went away and when she came back she had what he'd asked for. While she stood there, holding the milk, he tried to peel the half banana. His hands shook. He took a bite that didn't want to go down his throat.

Betty turned on the bedside light. "What's wrong?"

"I don't know. Had a really sharp hunger pain."

"You don't look right. I'm calling the doctor."

"I don't need a goddamned doctor."

She ignored him, and he heard her in the hallway, getting out the address book, dialing the number. "Can I speak to Dr. Gregory? I think it's an emergency… Yes, he's pale and sweating and he's got a pain in his stomach… Yes, as a matter of fact, why?… What do you… oh. Oh, I see… Should I do anything while we're waiting?… Okay. Yes, we'll see you there. Thank you."

She was standing in the doorway again. "Dr. Gregory thinks you might be having a heart attack. There's an ambulance on the way and he'll meet us at Parkland."

"If I were having a heart attack, do you think I would just be sitting here talking to you?"

"Yes," she said. "You always were stubborn."

She was still in her housecoat. He watched her gather up her underwear and a pair of slacks and a sweater and take them into the bathroom. She looked and acted normal, even as tears ran down her face.

He tried to take his pulse, first in his wrist, then in his neck, and couldn't find it. That was ridiculous. If he didn't have a pulse he'd be dead.

He noticed he still had the banana in his hand, but the idea of eating repelled him. He put the unfinished piece on his nightstand.

By the time Betty came out of the bathroom, he heard a siren in the distance. Why did they have to do that? It just made people nervous and afraid. In no time at all it was in the driveway, where all the neighbors could see, and Betty had let in two kids who looked like they should still be in high school. They insisted on putting him on a stretcher, and when he tried to argue, one of them gave him a shot that made him woozy. They put an oxygen mask over his face, and it was clear they were trying to scare him for some reason. He kept remembering Betty standing in the hall and saying, "I hope you're pleased with yourself."

In the back of the ambulance, he turned to the kid that was watching him and said, "Where's Betty?"

"Is that your wife? She's following us in your car."

At the hospital, lying on a gurney in a curtained-off section of the ER, they took an EKG. Curtains, Steve thought. Not a happy choice of décor. Was it going to be curtains for him? Betty arrived as they were peeling off the sensors and took his hand, for which he was as grateful as a child. When Dr. Gregory showed up fifteen minutes later, he said they were going to do bypass surgery.

"When?" Steve asked.

"Now," Gregory said. "Fortunately, you are a pretty tough buzzard. The cardiologist was a little surprised to see you still alive, given the looks of your EKG. I wasn't, but this operation is a different matter. It might take four to six hours, and there's a very real chance that you might not make it."

Steve's first thought was that this was the kid's fault. If he hadn't run away, this would never have happened. Then, ashamed, he looked at Betty as if she might have overheard. Her expression was unreadable.

"I'll give you two some privacy," Gregory said. He shook Steve's hand. "Good luck. If I know you at all, you'll pull through."

When they were alone, Betty stood over him and said, "I love you, Steve. I've stuck with you through bilharzia and dysentery and Midland, Texas. But if you die now, with things as they are…" She left the threat unfinished.

"I'm not going to die," he said.

Then the orderlies came and he only had time to whisper goodbye and feel her dry lips brush his cheek.

COLE WOKE UP tired and oddly peaceful on Wednesday morning. His possessions were piled on both sides of the bed in the Montoyas' guest room, where he'd finally managed to fall asleep after two AM.

At school, he apologized to Mr. Batchelor and offered to write a paper for extra credit. Batchelor, who had a taste for the grotesque, suggested he discuss how Ivan the Terrible had changed history by murdering his own son. Cole appreciated the unintended irony.

In PE, where he'd been exiled after his injury, he found a second wind that got him through the calisthenics, rope climbing, and laps. For once he was able to run past the tennis courts without the sound of rackets hitting balls causing him too much regret.

They drove home and walked in the door and Cole saw the look on Alex's mother's face. He listened numbly as she told him about the heart attack, the successful bypass surgery, the long recuperation ahead. "I can take you to the hospital. Frederica can finish dinner without me." She didn't seem to consider the possibility of Cole refusing, so he got in the blue Impala with her.

As she backed out of the driveway she asked, in Spanish, «Is it okay if we speak Spanish? I hardly ever get to around the house and I'm afraid I'm going to lose it.»

«Of course. Why is it you never speak it at home?»

«Adalberto thinks it's rude to speak Spanish in the US, that it makes people uncomfortable, so we shouldn't get in the habit. And when we're in Mexico, we don't speak any English. If it wasn't for that, he might not have let the kids learn Spanish at all. Bueno, I shouldn't be babbling on like this. I'm really sorry about your father.»

Cole noticed the way she'd turned the subject away from Mexico. Alex's father had mentioned the Guanajuato trip over breakfast, and Cole had said that he really wanted to go. Now they would take it for granted that he would stay in Dallas to be with his father.

He didn't know what to say to Alex's mother. Sorrow was not among the emotions ricocheting through him. Anger, pity, confusion, nasty slivers of triumph and guilt. He followed her lead and changed the subject again. «How did you meet your husband?»

«Adalberto, you mean?»

«Don't tell me you're not married.»

She smiled, Cole thought, rather wickedly. «No, but he's my second husband. I was married and working on the US advertising account for Cuautémoc when I met him. Very, very scandalous. I married much too young the first time, un ogro, you know that word?» Cole shook his head and she said, "A monster," in English.

"Ogre," Cole said.

«Esto. Adalberto was divorced himself and already excommunicated and going to hell anyway, so he had nothing to lose by marrying me.» She glanced at Cole. «That was Susana's mother, back in Guanajuato.»

«Alex never told me.»

«No, he wouldn't. Alejo, Adalberto, they don't talk about Susana's mother. They're ashamed of her.»

«But you *are* Alex's mother, right? In spite of not looking old enough for it?»

«Yes, I am. And you never stop, do you?»

«Stop what?»

She was easy to talk to, so Cole kept drawing her out. That and trying to think in Spanish helped distract him. She had majored in Spanish in college and was fresh out of school when she joined the ad agency and met Alex's father. She said the stork must have delivered her to the wrong family. She loved Mexico, loved mambo and *Don Quixote*, avocados and tacos al carbon.

Then Parkland Hospital loomed before them and the weight of the moment came down on Cole again. In the elevator, Alex's mother put her hand on his shoulder, the kind of gesture they didn't make in Cole's family. His longing for it made him resent his father even more.

His father was in a private room with tiled walls. A heart monitor on wheels was parked next to the bed, beeping steadily. On its screen, a green dot drew a sharp peak and two smaller bumps, over and over. His father lay on his back, eyes closed, sheets neatly folded beneath his collarbone, arms out straight at his sides. He had a breathing tube down his throat, a glucose drip in one wrist, and a catheter bag hanging near the foot of the bed.

Behind him, Alex's mother said, "Hi, I'm Linda Montoya. I'm so sorry we have to meet like this."

Then his mother's voice, less steady than he'd ever heard it. "Thank you for bringing him. Jeff...?"

He couldn't look away from his father. And as he watched, his father's eyes rolled open. Hooded, like the eyes of a predatory bird. They stared at him with a complete lack of emotion. Nothing else in his face changed, no turn of the mouth, no lift of the eyebrows, no sign of recognition, confusion, or acknowledgement. The eyes closed again. The monitor continued its steady beeping. The respirator made a sucking noise, a clank, a hiss, and then did it again.

Finally Cole turned his head to look at his mother. "Are you all right?" he asked.

She smiled weakly. It had been less than 24 hours since the last time he'd seen her, and she looked ten years older. "All things considered, I suppose so. After the first shock, there was something kind of inevitable about it. Like the other shoe had finally dropped."

"Listen," Alex's mother said, "I should probably go."

"No," Cole said.

They both looked at him.

"This doesn't change anything," he said. "Mother, I'm not coming back to your house. I'm sorry."

"Oh, Jeff…"

Now that the words were out, he felt a fierce, exultant sense of freedom. "I love you," he said. "I hate that you're going through this and I know it's going to be really hard to do it alone." He took a breath. "But I don't love *him*. And I'm not going to give up the other things I love just to be with him."

His mother looked down at her hands, folded in her lap.

"I'm sorry," he said again. "I'll call you." He walked into the hall.

Alex's mother came out a few seconds later and together they walked toward the elevators. Suddenly she stopped and leaned against the wall. She fumbled in her purse for Kleenex.

"You're disappointed in me," Cole said.

She dabbed at her eyes. "No. And I would never make you go back to that house, feeling the way you do."

"I can't," he said. "I just can't."

"I know," she said. "And it breaks my heart."

THAT NIGHT COLE called Janet. He let it ring ten times, hung up, and dialed again. On the third try, her mother picked up.

"It's Cole," he said.

"Somehow I guessed that. Janet asked you not to call her."

"She needs to know that I'm not at my parents' house anymore. It's a long story. If she wants to get hold of me, she can call me at my friend Alex's house." He gave her the number.

Janet's mother had always liked him. Girls' mothers always liked him, especially in comparison to guys like Woody. Her voice softened and she said, "What happened?"

"My father went crazy. I had to get away from him."

"Are you all right?"

"I'm fine. Physically, anyway." He was willing to go for the sympathy angle if it might change Janet's mind.

Her mother said, "I'm sorry, Cole," and said she would pass the message along.

Cole struggled with his homework until 10:00, most of his attention focused on the phone that failed to ring. Finally he gave up and plugged his guitar into the practice amp and turned it down low. "I did this for you, you know," he told it. Holding the familiar weight in his arms soothed him. He started a few songs and then settled into "Georgia on My Mind." He and Janet had danced to the Chessmen playing it at the Studio Club, the drummer singing like Ray Charles, Cole's body glued to Janet's by their mingled sweat. The song was all ninths and sevenths and minors, keening and hollow and sad.

He looked up to see Alex in the doorway, who disappeared and returned with his acoustic and sat cross-legged on the floor. He picked up the chords at the bridge and Cole filled in with snatches of melody and partial chords high on the neck.

They worked the song for five minutes, until it ran out of steam. Alex played a few random chords, marking time, and then Cole started into Floyd Cramer's "Last Date," one of the Chevelle's break songs. From there Alex took them into a slow blues in G, and after that E to B7 in an insistent rhythm that Cole didn't recognize until the chorus came around, and then he saw that it was "Cielito lindo."

The song had snuck up on him. Suddenly this stereotype of a Mexican ranchera, ubiquitous in Villahermosa to the point that Cole had sickened of it, flowered into something new, something heartfelt and apt. Canta y no llores, the refrain said. Sing to keep from crying.

So they did, barely above a whisper, Alex taking the verses, their voices interlocking on the chorus. When it was done, Alex stood up and said, "You okay?"

The immensity of Cole's gratitude closed his throat. He nodded, and Alex nodded back and closed the door gently as he left.

ON THE FOURTH DAY, Steve was sitting up in the hospital bed, having managed to escape all too briefly into the fat paperback of Michener's *Hawaii*. The phone rang and Betty answered it. She listened and then said, "Hold on." She looked at Steve and said, "Al Montoya's at the nurses' station. He wants to know if you feel up to talking."

Steve reluctantly marked his place and put the book down. "He's got his nerve, coming here."

"You don't have to see him if you don't want to."

Steve sighed. "Let him come in."

Montoya was dressed in a yellow shirt, slacks, and a brown V-neck sweater that looked like cashmere. He stood at the foot of the bed with his hands clasped beside him and said, "You're a remarkable man. They tell me most people would not have survived what you went through."

Steve grunted. "Have a chair, if you like."

Montoya sat down. "Will they keep you here much longer?"

"Another week," Steve said. "They've already got me up and walking around."

"A good sign," Montoya said.

"Look here, I appreciate the courtesy, but can we skip the small talk? You've somehow charmed my son away from me, and I want him back where he belongs."

Montoya nodded. "We're both businessmen, and plain speaking is fine with me. I'd like to offer you a deal. The problem is that, for whatever reason, Jeff is determined not to go back to living with you. You could get the police to drag him there against his will, but short of chaining him to the wall, there's no way to keep him from running away again. If he didn't run away to my house, he'd run somewhere else—if not to another friend's house, then out of town, out of state, maybe out of the country. If he does that, he'll never graduate from high school, let alone go to college. I know that's not how you want things to end up for him, not after all you've done to give him a head start. I'm sure you've thought all this through yourself, still, I wanted to get it on the table."

In fact Steve had not thought it through. The kid's Spanish was passable enough that he could disappear into Mexico and never surface again.

"If he's at my house," Montoya said, "he's agreed to finish St. Mark's and keep his grades up."

"That was exactly the promise he made me, and his inability to keep it was what started all of this."

"There's no guarantee, of course," Montoya said. "But you raised him well. He's a thoughtful, disciplined, resilient young man. Not to mention very talented. In any case, the thing I offer you is the knowledge of where he is and the confidence that he's being watched over by people who care about him. I think it's the best you can hope for at this point, and I don't know any other way you can be sure of it. That's just the reality of it."

"I suppose you know," Steve said, "that in a couple of weeks he can legally do whatever he wants."

"Yes."

"So the true reality of the situation is that I don't have any choice in the matter. While I appreciate your coming in here with a carrot instead of a stick, I can't stop you from doing whatever you want with my son, short of selling him into white slavery."

"You have the choice," Montoya said gently, "of making your peace with the situation, which is why I came."

"I'm afraid the only peace I'm going to find is of the eternal sort, and I hope that's still some ways off." He nodded slightly. "Thanks for stopping by."

Montoya, unruffled, stood up. "I wish you a complete and speedy recovery." He smiled at Betty, said, "Pleased to meet you," and left.

Betty said, "He seems like a good man."

"He's a charmer. The problem with men like that is once they're out of the room and you go over what they said, there's nothing of substance there. It's all fairy dust."

"Would it have killed you to be a little nicer to him? Considering everything he's doing for Jeff?"

"Yes," Steve said. "Quite possibly it could have."

AFTER SCHOOL ON MONDAY, Cole caught a ride with Alex to a small, well-kept house in Irving, ten minutes west of Dallas. There he paid $700 cash to an old man for a 1959 Cadillac Miller-Meteor hearse in fine condition. "Always wanted me a Caddy," the old man said, "and that were the only one I could afford. Used to belong to Restland, over there in Dallas. Still runs great, just a mite out of style these days."

Cole gave it a thorough inspection, then got behind the wheel. He felt weightless. For the first time in his life he could go wherever he wanted.

He'd found it in the *Times-Herald* want ads on Sunday. The Novas and the Chessmen and some of the other local bands had hearses to haul their equipment, and if it came to that, he could sleep in it. Alex's father had agreed to co-sign on the title and insurance. His only conditions were that Cole was not to stay out later than ten on a school night, and that he was to park it where the neighbors couldn't see it and become alarmed.

On Monday night, he pulled it into the Montoyas' garage and thoroughly vacuumed the interior. He ran the curtains from the back through the washer and dryer. Alex dug up a couple of old quilts from the attic and Cole spread them over the Formica and the hard rubber bumper strips in the back.

On Tuesday, as soon as he got out of the shower after gym, he drove to East Dallas in the falling darkness. He parked in front of Janet's apartment and ran up the stairs. He was sure he would think of something to say by the time he got there. Instead, when Janet opened the door, he could only stand there with his heart thudding and his cheeks burning from the cold. She was still in her DISD-approved calf-length skirt and a ribbed sweater that clung to her curves. She was beautiful and desirable beyond words and Cole struggled not to reach for her.

"I thought we had a deal," she said. She didn't sound angry.

"I had to see you," he said. "Even if it's only this much of you."

"What's so urgent about seeing me?"

"Can we just... can you come for a drive with me?"

"I'm almost out of gas."

"Not your car. My car."

She tilted her head in curiosity. "Just a minute," she said, and closed the door. When she came back, she was wearing a heavy jacket and gloves.

She laughed when she saw the hearse. "You've got to be kidding."

"You don't like it?"

"I guess it makes a statement."

He opened the door for her and then got in and started the engine. He turned the radio down low and said, "You want to get something to eat?"

"This isn't a date."

He pulled out of the parking lot. For want of a better idea, he headed for White Rock Lake. "Did your mother give you my message?"

"About you staying at Alex's?"

"I had a fight with my father and I moved out," he said.

"I can't imagine your father letting you do that."

"I didn't tell him before I did it. When he found out, he had a heart attack. He's in Parkland now."

She softened. "Oh, Cole, no. Is he going to be all right?"

"He'll live."

"What was the fight about?"

He gave her the details, including the disaster at KLIF and his brief visit to the hospital. As he talked, he drove around the deserted lake and finally pulled into the shadows under some trees.

"What are you doing?" she said.

"I wanted us to be able to talk in peace."

"The cops will see this thing from miles away."

"It's dark," he said. He saw that they had come to a crisis point. He turned toward her and put his arm on the back of the seat. "Come over here."

To his amazement, it worked. She scooted across the long bench seat and leaned her head on his shoulder. "Poor baby," she said. "What a week you've had."

That was all he needed. He tilted her face upward with his hand and kissed her. She kissed him back. They were both trembling. "Want to see the back?" he whispered.

COLE MANAGED TO SEE Janet three times in the last week before the holidays. She didn't mention the separation again. In between, the band played Christmas parties and Cole did his schoolwork. He was afraid, as he'd never been with his own father, to disappoint

Al Montoya. He got an A on his Russian History paper and he started to speak up in class. It was easier than he'd imagined.

Then, before dawn on December 23, the family took a taxi to Love Field and got on a plane for Mexico.

Nobody mentioned his birthday, and Cole assumed they'd forgotten in the excitement of the trip. He wasn't overly bothered. His birthday had always been overshadowed by Christmas. On the flight he had Alex on one side and Susan, who'd arrived from Austin late the previous night, on the other.

He hadn't seen Susan in over a year. She was cheerful in conversation, but in the silences, reading *Time* magazine, she seemed restless and vaguely unhappy, in a way that made Cole want to comfort her. She'd been sincerely concerned about his injured hand, and in the moments when they'd talked by themselves she'd made him feel like they shared a bond, like they were both just outside the line that defined the family.

They landed at the León airport, an hour from the city of Guanajuato. From the moment the plane touched down, Susan and Alex started talking across the aisle to their parents in Spanish. Cole, who was not completely fluent, had to shift gears. The airport had high ceilings and murals, and Cole remembered that it was Villahermosa that he had a problem with, not Mexico in general, which on the whole suited him well. Here was a guy in a yellow guayabera and dark blue pants, hunkered down on the floor with his son, playing with a toy car and laughing. A clerk at the Mexicana desk sang "She Loves You," massacring the lyrics. A bad muffler in the street made a machine-gun sound and Cole smelled tamales cooking. Christmas decorations everywhere, poinsettias on all the counters.

An old man waited for them at baggage claim. He hugged Al Montoya and shook hands with the others. Montoya introduced him as Octavio and said he ran the family house in Guanajuato. They collected their bags and followed Octavio to a cream-colored Ford Country Squire station wagon with fake wood-grain side panels. The luggage that didn't fit in the rear got tied to the roof rack with sisal rope. Alex and Cole squeezed into the third seat and they all rolled their windows down. Cole's watch said high noon and his stomach told him he was starving. The sport coat that hadn't been enough in Dallas was now too much. He wriggled out of it and threw it in the back.

Everything was familiar. Tiny old women mummified in black shawls, men in straw cowboy hats and low-rise boots, teenage girls with babies straddling their hips, gaudy peluquerias and fly infested carnicerias, smells of bus exhaust and frying food, dopplered accordion on passing car radios. Cole was happy to be so far from Dallas.

The road to Guanajuato took them over rolling hills dotted with cactus and mesquite, steadily climbing another thousand feet in the course of 50 miles. Alex nudged him as they came to a tunnel entrance. They emerged on the far side into an enclosed wonderland where stairstep rows of pastel houses climbed the sides of the natural bowl that held the city. At the bottom of the bowl he saw steeples and domes, red tiled roofs, expanses of blue and mustard yellow walls, and swatches of green parkland.

"Wow," Cole said.

Montoya had turned around in the front seat to gauge his reaction. «Beautiful, ¿no?»

Cole could only nod.

Before they got to the bottom of the hill, Octavio took them into another tunnel, lined with masonry and crowned with stone arches. The passageway was barely wider than the one-lane road and lit by intermittent floodlights. Other tunnels intersected theirs, and occasional flights of stairs led up to daylight.

«The legend is that these tunnels were part of the silver mines,» Montoya said, «but the truth is they were built to control flooding. They have dams for the water now, so they can use the tunnels to keep cars off the surface streets. That's the city center above us.»

They started to climb again. When they came out into daylight they were halfway up a hillside on a narrow street built out of closely set stone blocks. White stucco houses on either side, three stories high. Pocket size palm trees and brilliant red flowers tucked into crevices and balconies.

Five minutes later they pulled into a narrow driveway. Cole carried his suitcase up stone steps, moving from shadow to light and from heat to coolness and back again. The steps ended in a patio and fountain covered in glazed tiles of red and yellow and green. Louvered doors opened into a cool, dark living room filled with low bamboo furniture and Indian blankets on the tile floor. Alex's uncle and grandparents waited there, the grandfather thin and leaning on a cane, the woman heavier and evoking another era with her elaborately curled hair. The uncle was heavier still, his thinning hair worn long in the back. In the flurry of abrazos and kisses, Cole was introduced and told that their house was his.

Alex led him down a set of tiled stairs to a suite of guest rooms, each with French doors that faced a central sitting room with a TV, a wet bar, and a leather sofa and chairs. He and Alex shared a room with two twin beds, one of which was covered with five acoustic guitars. «That one's yours,» Alex said.

Cole turned in confusion. The others had followed them down and now were smiling at him. «A musician should choose his own instrument,» Al Montoya said. «Play each of these and see if one of them suits you. If not, there are others.»

Alex said, «My uncle Jesús makes guitars. He's very famous— he made guitars for Pedro Infante. He made the guitar I have at home. We wanted you to have one for your birthday.»

Cole was paralyzed by conflicting emotions. It was the electric guitar, not the acoustic, that he truly loved. On the other hand, it was the most expensive and thoughtful present anyone had ever given him. He didn't know how to react to generosity, except to wonder if he deserved it.

«I think we stunned him,» Linda Montoya said.

«Feliz cumpleaños, m'ijo,» Al Montoya said.

Then the grandfather began to sing, «Estas son las mañanitas...» and the others all joined him in the traditional Mexican birthday song. This is the morning song King David sang, we sing it to you on your birthday.

Being the center of attention when he was on stage playing and singing was one thing. To simply stand there while all these people sang to him was monumentally uncomfortable. He was in a country more foreign than Mexico, caught up in a transaction whose currency he didn't understand.

They all hugged him, Susan last of all, who kissed his cheek and whispered "Happy Birthday" in English, then pushed him toward the stairs. «He can pick out a guitar later. Right now we need to eat.»

DESPITE THE HARD SELL he'd given Cole, Alex's feelings toward Guanajuato had been mixed for years now. If your whole life was in Dallas, leaving town for two weeks put that life on hold. He felt that way every year until he got on the plane, when he remembered all over again what a relief it was to stop pushing—pushing the band, pushing at school, pushing to get somewhere with the girls he dated—and just let things happen.

Secret Agent Double-O Cole was thoroughly flipped out by the family's birthday surprise. He wanted so badly to belong, and then didn't know what to do when somebody gave him the chance. Sooner or later they would break him down.

In the meantime there was food. Guadalupe had made enchiladas mineras, miner's enchiladas, the signature Guanajuato dish, fried tortillas layered with potatoes, carrots, white cheese, and a mild red sauce. On the side she'd laid out black beans, guacamole, spaghetti, platters of ham and boiled shrimp, corn tortillas and sliced bread, and of course Bohemia all around.

After dinner, Tio Jesús came downstairs to talk guitars while everybody else took a siesta. They sat on the beds and Cole immediately picked up the plainest of the steel-string guitars. «Ah,» Jesús said, «La Pelirroja.» The Redhead. «That's basically the same design as the Martin D-35, only with better materials. Red spruce top and braces instead of Sitka spruce. Brazilian rosewood for everything else.»

«The top doesn't look red,» Cole said.

«That's because I didn't stain it, and I used clear varnish everywhere. That's the true color of the wood you're seeing.» He took the guitar and plucked a chord with all five fingers, then held out the guitar by the back of the neck so that Alex and Cole could hear the wood vibrate. «That's one of the nicest sounding guitars I ever made, and I didn't even put a lot of work into her. I got lucky with the wood.»

«Play something,» Alex said.

Jesús handed La Pelirroja to Cole and picked up a guitar that looked like a Mariachi outfit, black with pearl inlays. He started to play "Malagueña," then stopped after half a verse. «This is not a concert,» he said. «Play!»

Alex grabbed the only nylon string guitar and he and Cole joined in. For over an hour they played rancheras, Beatles hits, standards like "Stardust," Jesús faking the English when he sang, Alex and Cole doing what they could with the guitar parts.

Finally Jesús stood up. «Bueno, you like La Pelirroja?» You could see that Cole did. «I hope you choose her. She's a guitar that should be played.»

«Thank you,» Cole said. «From my heart.»

«Come by my shop tomorrow, both of you. I'll teach you some things, if you want. And now I have to go back to work, now that I've spoiled the siesta for everyone else.»

At dusk Alex and Cole walked down to the Jardín de la Unión in the center of the city. The plaza was triangular and shaded by Indian laurel trees whose branches had been pruned into continuous rectangular blocks. In the center of the triangle was a fountain and an elaborate wrought-iron bandstand. Restaurants, hotels, and shops made up two sides, and the third opened onto the baroque Catedral de San Diego, whose orange-brown walls and red domes you could see from most of the city.

They stood aside for a Posadas procession, where Joseph, played by a guy in a long robe, led a costumed Mary on a burro, followed by a crowd of angels and shepherds and giant plaster figures of Los Reyes, the three kings.

«They didn't do this in Villahermosa?» Alex asked an amazed Cole.

«It was pretty half-assed. Nothing like this.»

The procession moved up the street, stopped at a house, and Joseph began to sing.

«It's the whole 'no room at the inn' thing,» Alex explained. «You go around to various houses and get turned away. Come on.»

Alex led him under the trees and stopped outside the restaurant of the Hotel Posada Santa Fe, where a mariachi band in tan trajes with eagles on their jackets had surrounded one of the outdoor tables and was playing a sentimental ballad about Pancho Villa. The harmony was tight, the singing as powerful and irresistible as a hurricane, the instrumental solos passing from guitar to trumpet to violin. Birds in the laurel trees sang so loudly that they seemed part of the arrangement.

«Can we get a beer?» Cole asked.

«Sure. Anybody asks for your ID, show them a dollar bill. Unless it's a cop.»

«What do I do then?»

«I would recommend a five.»

If you owned a bar or restaurant in Mexico, you had an exclusive agreement with one cervecería or another. Out of family loyalty, Alex took him to a Cuautémoc restaurant next door to the mariachis, where you could sit outside and still hear the music.

At least two other mariachi outfits wandered through the Friday night crowd of local couples, students from the University, indios selling jewelry and shawls, little kids running any kind of hustle they could scrape together, from shining shoes to tap dancing. Tourists from the US were scarce, nowhere near as bad as San Miguel down the road.

Two gringas passed by, a year or two older than Alex, lingering to watch the mariachis for a while, laughing and tugging at each other, pointedly ignoring him and Cole. No one, apparently, had warned them not to wear jeans. Every male they met would assume they were either selling it or giving it away. «Now there's trouble waiting to happen.»

Cole said, «And I would love to be the trouble they find. In theory. I mean, I'm still in love with Janet and everything.»

Alex had no such qualms. Being in a band gave you opportunities, but so far he had failed to take any of them to the finish line. The ones who seemed willing hadn't held his interest, and the interesting ones had needed more cultivation than he had time or patience for. He'd sworn he would take advantage of any opportunity that might present itself in Guanajuato, where he wouldn't have to deal with consequences.

The waiter, who must have been in his sixties, responded to

Cole's hand signal with two more bottles of beer. «This is the life, no?» Cole said. «I'm having trouble remembering why I want to go back to Dallas.»

Thinking about women had left Alex discontented. He leaned forward, switched to English, and pitched his voice low. "What you see here is the cream that's floated to the tippy-top. This is pretty much as good as it gets, for rich people like my father, and all these students whose parents are rich like mine, and the lucky shop owners who get to make money off of us. Everything floats to the top here. Elections are a joke—el pri has won every election since 1928 by at least two to one. Did you know that they're technically part of the Socialist International? Even though Diaz Ordaz is busting unions, robbing the poor, sending armed police after anybody who complains. The whole system runs on bribery. La mordida is the single biggest expense on my father's budget for the Monterrey office. Whatever you're born as here, that's what you stay. If you're a farmer, there's nowhere else for you to go. If you're rich, your kids will be rich and so will their kids. And there's machine guns and helicopters and tanks to make sure it stays that way."

Cole looked down at his beer.

"Sorry," Alex said. "It's just… I love this country, but I wouldn't want to live here, not with the way things are."

"You surprised me, that's all. I didn't know you were so political."

"With Vietnam hanging over my head? How could I not be? All those Dylan songs, you think I didn't listen to the words?"

"I don't know. We've never talked about it."

"Maybe we should. You're what, apolitical?"

"I'm against the war. I'm for civil rights. But socialism? The government taking over the banks and the railroads and all that? That's going a little far for me."

"Cardenas did that here in the thirties. He saved the country. Woody Guthrie, Pete Seeger, they were both communists. John Steinbeck, that you like so much, he was a sympathizer."

You could see Cole pull back into himself, the way he did when he felt threatened.

"Look, man," Alex said, "I'm not criticizing you. All I'm saying is, the US is not that different than Mexico in some ways. Johnson's not going to give up the war. People like my father are not going to change voluntarily."

"What's so bad about your father?"

"I'm not saying he's not a good man. But he's invested in the system. Like I said, he delivers big envelopes of cash to los priistas, and he makes big political contributions in Texas. He fought to keep the union out of his factories and he's got money stashed in overseas accounts. You know how much he loves poker, and business is the same thing to him. He plays the game, you know? And he plays to win."

"When you take over, you'll change all that."

"Not happening, man. That life is not for me."

"For real? When did you decide that?"

"A while ago. It's going to break his heart."

"He'll get over it. He wants you to be happy. You can come be a star with me."

"Maybe," Alex said. "I don't know if I want it bad enough."

"That's okay," Cole said. "I want it enough for both of us."

COLE WOKE UP HUNGRY at seven AM and Guadalupe, the cook, insisted on fixing him whatever he wanted. That turned out to be three fried eggs smothered in a hot tomatillo sauce, with black beans and tortillas on the side.

«Not too spicy?» Guadalupe asked. Cole shook his head and she smiled. «Bueno. Hotter tomorrow.»

Alex took him to see the Pípila statue that looked down from a hilltop on the south side of the city. El Pípila was the local hero from the 1810 Revolution, a miner who strapped a slab of rock to his back to deflect bullets while he set fire to the Alhóndiga de Granaditas, the giant castle of a grain warehouse where the Spanish had made their last stand.

The altitude, some 6,000 feet higher than Dallas, got to Cole after the climb and he had to sit to rest his burning lungs. El Pípila towered over him, massively muscled, holding a torch in one hand. Deco-style letters on the base said, «Aún hay otras Alhóndigas por incendiar,» there are still more Alhóndigas to burn. The kind of threat that Alex would appreciate.

From the foot of the statue the view was spectacular, and Alex pointed out the landmarks. The red domes of the San Diego Cathedral, across from the Jardín de la Unión, were directly in front of them and almost straight down from where they stood. To the left were the orange walls of the Basílica de Nuestra Señora, and beyond that the pale blue serrated cliff of the Universidad de Guanajuato. To the right was a jumble of pastel colors, right angles, and the tiny black dots of windows.

After that they walked downtown, where Cole bought Christmas presents for the family. Silver earrings for Susan and Linda Montoya, a Mexican national fútbol team jersey for Al Montoya. For Alex, he found a recent songbook from the Trio Los Panchos in a used bookstore and managed to buy it without Alex seeing.

At noon they went to Jesús's shop, and between customers they spent two hours on fingerpicking and finding ways for Cole to work around his missing fingertip.

The afternoon meal was carne asada, potatoes, soup, beans, rice, and tortillas, and afterward Cole used the siesta time as it was intended, sleeping deeply under the humming ceiling fans.

That evening, Alex's father said, «Anybody want to look at some cards?» A poker game started up at the dining room table that included Cole and Alex, Alex's father and grandfather, and Susan. They used old wooden chips, no buy-in, and the whole family played with a joy and intensity that had nothing to do with money. Cole had learned the game from his paternal grandfather, a professional carpenter with a foul mouth and a photographic memory of every card that had been folded, and he quickly saw that he was out of his league. Alex folded early on most hands, yet steadily built up his winnings. Susan played with a careless bravado that none of the others were able to read.

At 11 PM they all walked downtown, including Octavio and Guadalupe and Jesús and his wife, Leticia. They waited in the street outside the Catedral de San Diego along with hundreds of others, all dressed in their church clothes. Little girls in white dresses ran wild in the streets while their brothers tugged at their collars and laughed until their faces glowed red. Tonight the forbidden became mandatory and they would be up until dawn, first at Mass, then at a late supper, then opening presents.

Cole had never been to a Mass before. Alex had dismissed it as a lot of standing and sitting and kneeling, but once inside the church, Cole was awed. The room was barely wide enough for two eight-foot pews, long enough for 15 or 20 rows, and was lit by hundreds of candles. The ceiling over the nave had to be at least 40 feet high and the dome above the transept rose even higher, with a walkway and circular windows that glowed with light from the street. Everything was tiled and painted and sculpted and inlaid with wood in shades of pink and yellow and ivory and white. Elaborate chandeliers hung halfway to the floor, glittering in the candlelight. A statue of Jesus presided over the altar from within a columned structure of white marble.

Hundreds of people crowded in, standing in the aisles and at the back. The family had two pews reserved toward the front, and Cole ended up between Susan and Al Montoya. Susan looked like a Hollywood vision of a beautiful peasant girl in a white cotton eyelet blouse, a long black skirt, and a black lace shawl over her head.

Religion had little foothold in Cole's family. His mother had grown up a low-church Episcopalian in rural Oklahoma, and his father, who possibly believed in some half-formed notion of God, was not interested enough to pursue the idea on Sunday mornings. When Cole was very young his mother had made intermittent attempts to take him to church, giving up after they moved to Villahermosa at the end of Cole's second grade year. Some of the Mexican kids told him he was going to hell because of all the Sunday school he'd missed. Cole had been upset for a few days, then figured it was too late to do anything about it. By the time puberty arrived he was in mostly Mohammedan Suez, and God, Allah, and Yahweh looked the same to him as Santa Claus and the Tooth Fairy.

And yet he felt something very like a divine presence in that cathedral in Guanajuato. The feeling only got stronger when an organ intro led them into an "Adeste Fideles" that was carried by three hundred voices with power enough to vibrate the granite floor. The priest and his retinue entered in a cloud of incense from a steaming metal censer, followed by a ritual exchange in Latin and a sermon in Spanish and then more singing. Though Cole didn't know the hymn, the effect was much the same, the crescendos of the organ, the huge aggregate of ordinary voices, the choir floating above them in gut-wrenching harmony.

The Mass went on like that for another hour and a half, and if it indeed involved a lot of standing and sitting and kneeling, it also included majesty and eloquence and transcendence enough to leave Cole shaken.

"Holy shit," he said to Alex as they walked out. "What happened in there?"

Alex gave him the single raised eyebrow that he'd recently affected. "Don't tell me you're getting religion."

"That was really intense."

"Got to put on a good show if you want the rubes to keep tithing ten percent of income they can barely live on."

"It was more than that."

Alex stopped and faced him. "It was the music, man. It talks directly to the body. Throw in a little razzle-dazzle to distract the brain and it's even more effective. Exactly like the Dylan concert, only Dylan was selling something real, and this is just a two-thousand-year-old scam."

Cole nodded, unconvinced, and gradually drifted away to walk next to Susan, whose silence and sad contentment better suited his mood.

THEY CHANGED CLOTHES and assembled again in the dining room, where Guadalupe brought in a ceramic pot filled with steaming pork tamales. They were the best Cole had ever tasted, tender, moist, with a hint of smoky darkness. Alex, in a voice low enough to exclude his grandparents, said, «Ask me what I believe in, and I'll say, 'I believe I'll have another tamale.'»

After the table was cleared they opened presents. The big gift-giving day was El Día de los Reyes, Three Kings' Day, on January 6, but it was a generous culture, so there were presents on Christmas morning, too. Cole got a guayabera, the pleated shirt that was standard casual attire for Latin men. Al Montoya laughed at his fútbol jersey and immediately put it on over his regular shirt. Susan and Linda Montoya both loved their earrings and took turns hugging him and kissing him on the cheek. Cole and Alex brought up their guitars and sang a few songs from Alex's new songbook.

They staggered off to bed as the sun crested the mountains that surrounded them. Alex was asleep in seconds. Cole lay awake and tried to imprint details and emotions in his memory. The power of the massed voices in the cathedral. The feeling of linking hands around the dining room table and the smell of tamales in the air. The warmth in Al Montoya's eyes as he looked at the family arrayed before him, which now included Cole.

COLE FELT A HAND on his foot and slowly opened his eyes. Susan stood at the end of the bed, a finger to her lips. She then beckoned to him with the same finger and backed into the hall.

One in the afternoon, Christmas Day. He'd slept seven restless hours. In the other bed, Alex slept with one arm hanging off the side, mouth slack.

Cole had to give himself a few moments for his morning erection to subside, then he brushed at his hair as he padded after her. She had dressed somberly in a long skirt, black turtleneck, vest, and high-heeled boots. She wore the new earrings Cole had given her. "Would you go somewhere with me?"

"You know I'd go anywhere with you," Cole said.

"Oh, Cole."

"Where are we going?"

"I'll tell you later. Can you get dressed without waking Alex up?"

Cole nodded, curious and flattered in equal parts. He put on his new guayabera, a blazer, and jeans, used the toilet and brushed his teeth, and found her waiting for him in the living room. "I'm going to see my mother," she said. "I thought maybe you'd want to come."

It regularly slipped his mind that Linda Montoya was not her mother. "I'd love to. You're not telling the rest of the family?"

"They know. There's no point in rubbing their noses in it."

«Bueno,» Cole said. «Vámonos.»

The sun shone fiercely despite the chill in the air, a dissonant sensation like standing in an icy spring on a summer's day. Susan, ever polite, made small talk about the Mass.

«So,» Cole asked her. «Do you really believe in all that stuff?»

«I believe in God, sure. It's too depressing to think we're just a cosmic accident. Heaven and hell, transubstantiation, the infallibility of the Pope, I don't know. I do know it's terrible to be alone.» She gave Cole a penetrating look.

Cole passed up the flirtatious comeback. He'd been alone most of his life, had come to depend on it in a masochistic kind of way. «Sí,» he said.

To the extent that he'd thought about it at all, Cole had imagined Susan's mother as one of those working-class women that sold vegetables on the streets, swaddled in black, overweight, and old before her time. He was surprised when Susan turned into the patio of a new, white stucco building and knocked on a door that was decorated with dried gourds and grasses.

The woman who opened it couldn't have been older than her late thirties. She was long-haired and slim, wearing a loose black top and long skirt. She had a good deal of makeup around her eyes, which were lit up by an alert intelligence. She ushered them into a high-ceilinged room, sparsely furnished in black leather and chrome. Susan hugged her, and her mother held on for a good long time.

«And this is Cole,» Susan said, when she finally stepped away.

Cole took her hand and held it. «Encantado,» he said. «It's easy to see where Susana got her great beauty.»

«You will call me Iliana,» she said, addressing him as «tu.» She tilted her head at Susan. «Your new boyfriend?»

«A friend of my brother's,» Susan said, and Cole winced.

«Es muy guapo. Don't be too hasty.»

«Mother, please. You're not funny.» She held out a package. «Feliz Navidad.»

«Gracias, m'ija.» She kissed Susan lightly and set the package on the bare coffee table without looking at it. «Come, sit down. Have you eaten yet?»

As Iliana threw together some huevos revueltos, Cole watched the conversation struggle to stay on course. The safe islands were linked by the narrowest of channels. Iliana asked about UT and Susan asked about Iliana's work. Cole, who didn't want to expose his ignorance by asking questions, gradually figured out that she was a law professor at the local university and was involved in legal actions against the government. The rest of the Montoya family was clearly off limits.

Cole's eggs were overdone and could have used some hot sauce for moisture, not to mention flavor.

«I don't cook much,» Iliana said. «I usually grab something along the way.»

«It's fine,» Cole said. «I was really hungry.»

«Cole is a musician, mama.»

«Really? What do you play?»

«Guitar. I'm in a rock and roll group.»

«Ah. So you're an enemy of the state, like me.»

«I'm doing what I can.»

«Are you famous? Are you on the radio?»

To relieve the awkwardness, Cole started to talk. He never said Alex's name or explicitly mentioned that Alex was in the band as he told the story of Johnny Hornet and "Laura Lee." From there he talked about being on scholarship at a rich kid's school. He gauged Susan's reaction as he went, and it looked like relief and approval and gratitude. Iliana laughed and continued to flirt with him, and if the flirtation was a bit perfunctory, Cole didn't mind.

«So you must have many girlfriends,» Iliana said.

«I have one serious girlfriend,» Cole said, «but of course it's Susana that I'm really in love with.»

«Of course,» Iliana said. «How could you not be?»

«You two,» Susan said. «Stop encouraging each other.»

They stayed an hour and a half. Iliana cried noiselessly when they left and didn't want to let Susan go. She hugged Cole, too, kissed his cheek, and gave him a wink that lacked conviction. As they walked back, Cole said, «I don't get it. Didn't you tell me once that your father left her because he was embarrassed by her?»

«You saw how she was. Flirting, saying whatever comes into her head. She's political. She doesn't cook or play the good little wife. No way Papá could take her to the US. And she'll never forgive him for that.»

«I liked her.»

«Of course you did. She flirted with you and laughed at your stories. Men always like her. That's part of the problem.»

Stung again, Cole didn't respond. Susan took his arm in both hands and said, «Thank you, by the way. For being so sweet to her. Seeing her like that can be really uncomfortable.»

«Do you not like her?»

«Of course I love her,» Susan said, which was not the question Cole had asked. «She's my mother.»

When Cole and Susan walked in, the rest of the family was at the dining room table. Nobody greeted them, and Cole sensed a distinct chill in the air. Susan went downstairs. Cole washed his hands and face and sat at an empty place next to Linda Montoya. She asked if he was hungry, which in fact he was. He helped himself to the platters of eggs and bacon and fruit and Guadalupe brought him a glass of fresh orange juice. Al Montoya, who was wearing his fútbol jersey, broke off his argument with his own father about the World Cup long enough to acknowledge Cole with a nod and pass him the tortillas.

Later, Cole went to the patio to watch night fall and listen to the fountain. Alex joined him a few minutes later and they stood at the railing watching lights flicker on in the city below.

"Is your dad pissed off at me?" Cole asked.

"Not pissed. Disappointed, maybe. So far you've seen the good side of the family. Time for the blinders to come off."

"What's he got against Iliana? I thought she was pretty cool."

"He doesn't like to be reminded of his mistakes. She's history that won't go away, and Susan won't let it go away. Your going to see her today, that could be perceived as taking sides. Just so you know."

"I didn't want to say no to Susan."

"Well, that's a skill you may need to develop." Having delivered his message, Alex visibly relaxed. "I'm going to grab a guitar and look at some of the songs in that book. Interested?"

They did it in the living room. Jesús, who had come for breakfast and stayed, joined them on guitar and made a few corrections to the printed chords. The room soon filled up with family, who sang along. Cole couldn't imagine anything like it ever happening at his house. "Malagueña" and "Cielito lindo," "Perfidia" and "Volver," "Bésame mucho" and "Quizás, quizás, quizás." Loose and spontaneous, with stops and starts and lots of crosstalk. They put their hearts into it where they were able, and pushed each other to flights of improvisation that sometimes, miraculously, succeeded. Their tiny audience clapped and whistled and cheered wildly.

That night, when they were both in bed with the lights out, Alex said, "That was good tonight. We should maybe do something with that."

At their lesson with Jesús the next day, they asked about playing in the Jardín de la Unión. «You have to be good,» Jesús said, «obviously. Like with anything else in this country, you have to be connected. And you have to give up la mordida. It's not the cops you have to worry about so much as the musicians who have waited and kissed ass and paid a lot of money for that territory, and it's not the musicians so much as the people the musicians are connected to.»

«Oh,» Cole said.

«However,» Jesús said, «if you wanted to sit on the steps of the Teatro Colón across the street, nobody is likely to fuck with you there. You can catch everybody coming and going from the plaza.»

«Will you come with us?» Alex said.

«Tempting,» Jesús said. «But I would get all the women, which would be a disappointment for you and more trouble than I could handle from Leticia. You guys will do all right.»

They spent the afternoon working up an hour's worth of material. Alex took the lead vocals on most of the Spanish songs because he already knew the words, and they filled out the set with quieter stuff from the Chevelles repertoire, including a sloweddown version of "Laura Lee."

Darkness was falling as they took their positions on the steps. The night had turned cool enough to wear jackets. The streets were crowded and two other young people plinked idly at guitars nearby. Alex rubbed his hands together and Cole checked his tuning. They hadn't brought a copy of their set list for fear of looking contrived, and Cole suddenly felt nervous in a way he never had with an amplifier behind him.

At that moment the two trouble-seeking gringo girls walked by and Cole did the only thing he could think of to get their attention, which was to stand up, hit an Am7, open his throat, and sing «Bésame» right at them. The girls stopped and turned around. He and Alex looked at each other and came in together on the D7, singing «Bésame mucho» in lingering harmony, and then they were off and running.

The girls stayed, and a knot of people quickly formed around them. Both girls were blushing and laughing, and Cole played to them shamelessly. The taller one had long, curly black hair, and a feral look that dared Cole to impress her. She overshadowed the other girl, whose long, thin fingers were always moving, touching her mouth, smoothing her hair, grabbing her friend by the arm. When they drifted away after half an hour, Cole was relieved. Teasing them had gotten his blood up and he wasn't sure how much restraint he was capable of.

As they closed in on the one-hour mark, Cole noticed a couple of mariachis lurking at the edges of the crowd, which had grown to respectable size. Short black jackets embroidered in silver, monstrous sombreros hanging down their backs. One of them, who kept staring at Alex, had a scraggly mustache and eyes that didn't track right. The other was short and thick, from his neck to his fingers to his legs. They both looked insensitive to physical pain.

«We should finish up," Cole said to Alex. "Let's do 'Last Time' and quit.»

«Órale,» Alex said.

They played the song and the crowd applauded and moved away, and Cole watched with increasing alarm as the mariachis began climbing the steps toward them. Just play the dumb gringo, he told himself. Sorry, we didn't know any better.

Before he could say anything, the one with the mustache charged Alex. It took Cole a full, panicked second to realize they were hugging, not fighting.

«Man, you guys were great,» the mariachi said. «I didn't even know you played guitar. Oye, this is Ernesto, Ernesto, mi primo Alejo.» He turned to Cole. «I'm Álvaro, ¿qué tal? I've known Alejo since we were this big, back in Monterrey.» He held his hand down as far as it would go.

«Cole. Mucho gusto.» They shook hands the normal way, then shifted to a soul grip, and then Cole shook with Ernesto too.

Alex suggested they get some beers and Álvaro said, «I've got a better idea. Follow me.»

He led the way through the plaza while Alex asked about people they'd known as kids. When they came out on the other side, they passed a convenience store and a bakery and then ducked into a narrow alley that smelled of rotting lettuce. Cole, already alarmed, became seriously afraid when he saw Álvaro pull a joint out of his traje jacket. He'd never seen marijuana in real life and suddenly his father was in his head, talking about musicians on dope and the long, downward spiral his life would take.

«Mira…» he said nervously.

«Don't worry,» Ernesto said. «It's the same thing as legal around here. Nobody cares.»

Alex was certainly eager enough. Álvaro lit the joint, took a lungful, and handed it off to Alex, who also took a deep drag. He passed it to Cole and said, in English, while holding his breath, "Just suck a little into your lungs and hold it."

Cole was more afraid of looking like a coward than he was of getting busted. He put it to his lips, puffed on it, and inhaled some stagnant alley air with the smoke. He held back the cough that was trying to escape his burning throat and gave the joint to Ernesto.

«First time?» Ernesto said, and Cole nodded. «¡Qué padre!» How cool.

By the time they'd smoked it down to the last quarter inch, Cole had gotten the hang of it. Álvaro extinguished it with a wet thumb and forefinger and swallowed it.

«Now it's our turn to play,» Álvaro said. «You want to come watch?»

«Absolutely,» Cole said.

They walked to the plaza, Cole and Alex carrying their guitars over their shoulders like hobos with their bindles on sticks.

«How'd you like la mota?» Ernesto asked.

«I don't think it did anything,» Cole said. «Listen, can we get something to eat where you're playing? I'm starving.»

Álvaro and Ernesto stopped on the sidewalk and shouted with laughter, and Alex was laughing too.

«What?» Cole said, hating being a laughing stock, hating Alex for going along. «What did I say?»

«I'll explain later,» Alex said. «We're all hungry too.»

The rest of the mariachis had assembled outside the Hotel de Santa Fe. The violinist, who was about 40, made a point of looking at his watch as they walked up. Cole's anxiety flared again. Living with his father had taught him to read moods, and this one was easy. Álvaro and Ernesto had let themselves get perceived as the fuckups, and the band was getting sick of them. The resentment had generational overtones, and Cole was sure they could all smell the marijuana smoke that hung like a fog over the four of them.

Álvaro played requinto, the small-scale, high-pitched lead guitar, and Ernesto played guitarrón, the oversized guitar that functioned as a bass. They picked up their instruments, failing to look as serious about it as they should have, and the violinist marched them onto the patio of the restaurant. They surrounded the nearest occupied table and immediately struck up "Allá en el Rancho Grande" with thunderous volume. Attitude problems aside, Álvaro and Ernesto were on the money with their playing, and Álvaro pulled off a great solo halfway through the song.

«Let's eat,» Alex said, and they took a table and put their guitars in the empty chairs. Alex's eyes were bloodshot and Cole wondered if his were too. They both ordered chicken in mole sauce and were well into it when the mariachis arrived at their table.

The violinist glanced at their guitars. «You are musicians also?»

Another easy read. «We're students of Jesús Montoya, that's all. Not good enough to play with a wonderful orquesta like yours.»

The name did its magic and the violinist's smile became genuine. «I didn't think he was teaching anymore.»

«Alejandro here,» Cole said, «is his nephew.»

The guy who played the full-sized guitar pointed to La Pelirroja. «That's one of his guitars, no?»

«They both are,» Cole said. He held out La Pelirroja. «Please, try it.»

They went a couple of rounds, the guitarist demurring, Cole insisting, and finally he took it and played a few chords. «Maravillosa,» he said.

Alex made a ten-dollar bill appear on the table in front of the violinist. «Maybe,» Alex said, «you could play something for us? Do you know 'Perfidia'?»

By the time they were done, Alex had tried out the guitarrón, Cole had acquitted himself respectably on the requinto, the manager of the restaurant had joined them, beer had been served to the mariachis on the house, all the other diners on the patio had turned their chairs toward their table, and the party had spilled out into the surrounding plaza. The musicians told stories between numbers and pulled out songs they'd never played together— Argentine tangos, sones jorochos from Veracruz, Bolivian música folclórica, polkas, Cuban habaneras. Plates of food arrived without explanation, followed by more beer. Then the tan-uniformed mariachis with the eagles on their backs showed up, and at one point Cole counted 23 musicians playing "De qué manera te olvido" at the same time, and at least that many more voices singing along, the loudest, most beautiful thing Cole had ever heard, louder and more beautiful than the Mass at the Cathedral de San Diego, than Dylan at Moody Coliseum, a noise that was surely keeping people awake all up and down the surrounding hills, and he hoped they were loving it as much as he did, and if they weren't, well, that was all right too.

At two AM he and Alex stumbled home, arms around each other's shoulders, guitars waving in their free hands, singing the chorus of "Cielito lindo" over and over again. The song was still playing in Cole's head when he finally passed out, fully dressed, in his bed.

THOUGH COLE WOULD RATHER have stayed in Guanajuato, he kept his feelings to himself when the whole family, three generations worth, took a bus to San Miguel de Allende the next afternoon. They checked in for two nights in the Hotel La Morada downtown, taking over most of a floor. The women spent hours in the market shopping for handcrafted jewelry, and the men sat around cafes and bars and got into conversations with the locals. Cole had brought La Pelirroja and spent most of his time on a bench at the edge of the Jardín Allende, the park in the center of town. Alex, restless, came and went, from the market to the bars to Cole's park bench.

The architecture was more Spanish than Guanajuato's, full of wrought iron and tile and arches. The landscape was flatter and drier and the colors ran to browns and tans. The streets and shops were full of expats from the US, painters and sculptors and poets in ragged clothes and long hair, hanging out with each other and speaking English in loud voices.

They returned to Guanajuato on the 28th, and Cole and Alex went out that evening with their guitars. It was a Wednesday and the town was hushed, as if recuperating from the excess of the holidays. Álvaro's mariachis were elsewhere, and Cole and Alex didn't get as much of a crowd when they played on the steps. When they finished and the rest of the audience moved on, the two gringo girls lingered expectantly. The one with the straight brown hair wore an embroidered sundress and the black-haired one wore a pleated dress in white cotton, very low cut. Cole, not wanting to be rude, and ignoring his better judgment, asked in Spanish if they wanted a beer.

"Cerveza?" said the one with black hair. "Sure. I mean, sí."

"Would you rather speak English?" Cole asked her.

"Only if you want us to understand you," she said, giving him that I-dare-you smile again. "Of course you lose your mysterious Latin charm when you do."

Cole nodded seriously. "It's a dilemma."

"Maybe," Alex said, "we could speak English with a really bad accent, and you could pretend." He was looking at the brown-haired girl, who laughed at him behind her long fingers, a trace of hysteria in her eyes. Just like that, Cole saw, they had paired off. The thought alarmed and enticed him in equal parts.

They sat at an outdoor table and Alex ordered Bohemia. The black-haired girl was named Sharon and the other was Debbie. Freshman roommates at Swarthmore, here by themselves, flying home the next day. "Our parents are all in Gstaad together," Sharon said, "so I wrote a check on Daddy's bank account. I don't imagine he'll notice."

Alex had taken the lead, and before Cole could stop him he'd spun an elaborate story where Cole was half Mexican and Alex was a Guanajuato native, cousins who'd known each other from birth. Cole, according to the story, had been supporting himself as a musician in Dallas since he graduated from high school two years before.

Cole was not sure that either girl fully believed it. The important thing was that it slotted into the fantasy that they were clearly in search of. They hadn't been at the table for an hour when Sharon looked at her watch and said, "Can you walk us to our hotel?"

«Claro que sí,» Alex said.

They stood up. Cole, despite his difficulty concentrating, knew that he should beg off. He also knew that if he did, and it ruined Alex's chances, Alex would never forgive him. The sight of Sharon's cleavage had scrambled his neurons.

Cole and Sharon took the lead. When Cole looked back, he saw that Alex had his arm around Debbie's waist.

At the hotel, Sharon said, "Can you walk us up? The light's out on the stairs." As they climbed, Cole heard Debbie giggle. At the end of the hall, Sharon unlocked the door and walked in, leaving the door open. Cole had no option but to follow.

The room was spacious, two oversized twin beds, illuminated

only by the light from the street. Cole saw a slip thrown on the dresser, a pair of panties on the floor, the tangle of unmade sheets, and his resistance began to boil away.

Sharon turned and faced him, smiling expectantly. Cole took a step toward her, then one more, watching her lips open and her head tilt back. Behind him, the door closed and the lock snapped shut.

He leaned his guitar against the wall and kissed her. The dark mass of her hair smelled of lavender. He'd always associated the scent with the elderly, though at the moment he found it over-whelmingly erotic. Her mouth opened under his and her hands moved over his body. Cole found buttons on the back of her dress and undid the top two without conscious intent. Then somehow he had undone them all and she stepped away to let the dress fall to the floor.

Underneath, she wore a sturdy bra and a girdle with legs that extended down her thighs. It was a garment that Cole had never had to contend with before. She unhooked the bra and cupped her breasts in her hands. "You like?" she said.

Cole nodded and stepped in again.

"What do you call them in Spanish?" she whispered, taking the lobe of his ear in her teeth.

Cole's brain was out of service. He was fifteen square feet of epidermis, acutely sensitive to anything that touched him, from his clothes to her lips to the pressure of her naked breasts against his shirt. Still he understood the fantasy she wanted. «Las pechugas,» he said, running his tongue over the nipples. «Tetas. Chichis.»

"Mmmmmmmm," she said, and pulled him toward the nearest bed. Cole began shedding his clothes as she squirmed out of her girdle and panties. He could hear Alex and Debbie in the other half of the room and he didn't care. He continued to murmur in Spanish, «Qué linda, qué guapa,» as he climbed into the bed.

She was a vigorous and athletic partner and Cole let her call the shots. He held out for a good long while, slowing things down when he had to, but finally he erupted inside her as she straddled him, pumping hard. She slowly collapsed on top of him, pinning him to the mattress.

As the floodtide of hormones slowly receded, guilt and

claustrophobia took their place. He gently rolled Sharon onto her side and stroked her hair. Inside he was in complete turmoil, unable to believe what he'd done. Alex was still going at it in the next bed. Cole didn't want to see. The smell of lavender was overwhelming, nauseous. He forced himself to smile and give Sharon a lingering kiss. «Qué rico, qué lindo,» he told her. She was still smiling, happily, he thought. She got up on one elbow and looked at what was going on in the other bed, her eyes crinkling with silent laughter. Cole wanted nothing more than to be out of that room so that he could begin to forget what he'd done. Alex grunted, a barely human sound, and the bedsprings slowed to a stop.

When Sharon had seen enough, she lay down next to Cole, with one hand resting lightly on his chest. They lay there in silence for a couple of minutes while Alex and Debbie disentangled themselves, then Sharon kissed Cole on the forehead and said, "We've got a very early day tomorrow. You boys need to run along now and let us get some sleep."

THEY WERE DRESSED and gone in ten minutes. Cole made a perfunctory effort to get last names or a phone number or address, to which Sharon said, "Maybe we'll meet again somewhere in the world. We'll leave it to fate." As she closed the door on them, Cole heard stifled laughter.

Disheveled, carrying their guitars under their arms, he and Alex descended the stairs and exited into the chilly streets of Guanajuato. "That," Alex said, "was my definition of a perfect evening." When Cole didn't answer, he said, "What the hell's eating you?"

"This didn't happen," Cole said.

"It sure felt like it happened to me. Hallelujah, at last. And don't tell me you weren't into it. We were watching you two after we finished. It looked like a stag movie over there. It got Irene so hot and bothered we had to do it again."

"Irene?"

"Yeah, she told me her real name, you know, in between. This whole thing was her friend's idea, the seduction, the fake names, kicking us out after."

1966

"Sharon's not her real name?"

"She wouldn't tell me what Sharon's real name was. Said she'd be pissed enough that Irene had told me her own name. What's wrong with you, Cole? You thinking about Janet? You sure didn't seem to be thinking about her half an hour ago."

"Well, I feel like shit now."

"Listen to me." Alex stopped in the street and Cole turned to look at him. "We've got talent. You more than me. Girls like those two tonight, they're just part of the reward for the long fucking hours we have worked at this. Hours when Janet was watching TV or trying on clothes or talking on the phone with her friends or whatever the hell she does. Entiendes? She doesn't have to know about it, any more than how much we get paid for a gig or whether we get free Cokes or not."

"You sound like Raskolnikov."

"And you sound like somebody's grandmother. Jesus Christ. Nobody got hurt, no consequences or entanglements. Those girls got to live out a harmless fantasy that they can tell all their friends about when they get back to Bryn Mawr—"

"Swarthmore. Or was that a lie too?"

"Swarthmore, Bryn Mawr, what's the difference? Everybody had a great time. Except you, apparently."

They walked on in silence. Cole felt at odds with Alex on top of a post-coital hollowness that he'd never experienced with Janet. Back at the house, Cole took a hot bath to get the smell of lavender out of his nose. To his shame, he was aroused by the lingering essence of sex on his genitals and the memory of the girl's wild stare in the twilit hotel room.

1967

"TELL THE TRUTH," Janet said. "Did the Mexican girls fall all over you?"

Their table was covered with a red-and-white checked cloth and a spattering of candlewax. The sign outside said The Egyptian Restaurant, though everybody called it Campesi's. Despite the unassuming façade in a strip of run-down businesses on Mockingbird Lane, it was famous throughout Texas for the quality of its Italian cuisine and the rumors that it was a mob hangout. Cole, in blazer and tie, was trying for a little class on his first night back.

"Au contraire," Cole said. "It's completely Catholic down there, and the girls are all vacuum-sealed until their wedding nights." So far his only lies had been of omission. He had filed Sharon, or whatever her name really was, in the category of lessons learned, a locked room from which she only escaped for occasional late-night guilty reminiscences. Tonight, with Janet pressing the length of her lower leg against his, in full makeup and perfume, the top three buttons of her blouse undone, Cole couldn't imagine ever wanting anyone else.

He talked about their triumphant night with the mariachis, high again in the telling, and skipped the slow decline of the rest of the trip. He'd kept his distance from Alex for a couple of days after the business with the girls, playing guitar by himself on the patio and taking walks on his own. Then on New Year's Eve they'd had another sing-along with Jesús and the family, and that had melted away the last of his annoyance. He and Alex had gone out on the town together the last two nights with their guitars and no further trouble had found them.

As Cole held the door for her on the way out, she looked up at him through her eyelashes and said, "We can skip the movie if you want."

Cole had fitted out the hearse with a double air mattress and blankets against the January cold. Once they were parked in their usual spot and had moved to the back, Cole took one last look past the curtains and then took a small foil package out of his jacket pocket. His hands had a slight tremor as he opened it and showed it to Janet.

"Is that what I think it is?"

"Direct from Mexico," Cole said, "at considerable personal risk."

The risk had been Alex's. Cole had known nothing until they were in Dallas and Alex had shown him a half-dozen joints that he'd bought from Álvaro on the sly. "Are you insane?" Cole had said. "They could have thrown us all in jail for the rest of our lives."

Alex had shrugged it off. "We're rich. They never look at our bags. And to tell you the truth, I dug bluffing my way through customs. It was a rush." He'd given the fattest one to Cole. "Turn Janet on with this."

Cole's initial reluctance had broken down when he thought about the load his conscience was carrying and how the dope might help.

"You ever done it before?" he asked Janet.

She shook her head, wide-eyed, the way she got when she was excited. This was bad boy stuff, like Woody's motorcycle, and Cole saw that he had scored major points.

They smoked it down, Cole taking small sips and letting Janet have the deeper hits. When it began to burn his fingers, he tried to snuff it the way Álvaro had and ended up with a hot coal stuck to his thumb. Janet wet her fingers and extinguished it before it did serious damage, and Cole swallowed the roach.

Once the evidence was gone, Cole's paranoia receded and he was able to concentrate on Janet's finger, which was still touching his right hand. It moved slowly around the edges of his forefinger, then traced the abbreviated contours of his scarred middle finger. In the near-darkness her eyes shone with concentration. "Wow," she said. "I like this."

Cole liked it too. The world had narrowed to a few cubic feet and each moment seemed bounded and discrete. In one of them, his finger touched the velvet skin over her collarbone. In another they both leaned forward, about to kiss.

★

THEIR FIRST Studio Club gig was January 27, a Friday. Cole parked the hearse on Sherry Lane in front of the club at 6:25.

Alex said, "Aren't we supposed to park in the alley?"

"I'll move it if they tell me to," Cole said. "I want everybody to see the name." He and Alex had painted the band logo across the rear window the previous weekend.

Mike and Gary had already arrived and they all began unloading the equipment. The club occupied a two-story space in Preston Center, the high-toned shopping village with Sanger-Harris and Preston Record Center, on the northern edge of University Park. University Park was where the rich SMU professors lived, and it merged into Highland Park, the old money part of Dallas. The Studio Club was appropriately ritzy. Red velvet curtains, a balcony, tiny tables around the edge of the dance floor. Jackets and ties required for boys, dresses for girls. The bar sold only Cokes, and the kids who did smuggle in a flask or an airline bottle knew to play it very cool.

Band morale was high. Wednesday had been their first rehearsal in nearly a month, and everything had clicked so well that they'd worked up a couple of brand new songs, the Buckinghams' "Kind of a Drag" and "Let's Spend the Night Together" by the Stones. The Studio Club was a top-forty place, and they'd packed the list with hits.

They'd updated their stage outfits, keeping only the blue blazers. Cole was in a black shirt with nickel-sized blue polka dots and a tie to match that he'd found at Penney's, and Alex had a red shirt and black tie that made him look diabolical. Mike had a paisley button down with no tie and Gary wore a black turtleneck.

They carried the gear through the foyer and across the dance floor to the long, narrow stage. Emptied out, with the high ceilings and the velvet and the chandeliers, the place looked like a whorehouse set from a Western movie. Cole was wearing his Fryes, as always, and they banged like gunshots on the hardwood dance floor.

Gary ended up front and center because the stage wasn't deep enough to put him in the back. The rest of them stood directly in front of their amps. Fortunately Cole's amp didn't come up past his knees, or he would have been deaf before the night was out.

They set their own levels, with the help of Alex listening from the middle of the room and playing through an extra-long patch cord, and when they were satisfied, Cole switched his amp to standby and put the guitar on its stand. Gary was still stamping on his bass drum. "Do you hear that?" he asked Cole.

"Sounds fine to me," Cole said.

"No, man, *listen*." He stomped again. "Listen to the sound of this room. The acoustics are amazing."

It was true. Cole's guitar sounded fuller, his vocals sweeter, than they'd ever sounded before.

Gary said, "I've been waiting a long time for this. I've been coming here since I was a sophomore and my parents had to drop me off and pick me up. Now... now kids are coming to see *me*."

He couldn't remember Gary ever making a speech of that length that didn't have some kind of implied criticism in it. "I can dig it," Cole said.

A tall, skinny blond guy came up to the stage. "Are these women yours?" He hooked his thumb toward the entrance where Janet and Holly had appeared. Cole hadn't known Holly was coming. The pleasure he felt contained the thrill of danger. "Well, one of them is," he said wistfully. The Studio Club was couples only, no stag, no drag, so all females had to be accounted for.

The guy waved them in, then offered his hand to Cole. Cole had to lean over to reach it. "Duncan Engler. I do the light show."

"I'm Cole." Cole's attention was impaired. Janet was in a yellow dress with white flowers, cut low enough to attract stares. Holly was in a knit dress with wide black and gray horizontal stripes that covered her from neck to below the knee, following her contours in a way that invited imitation. Her skirt was so tight that she had to place one high-heeled foot directly in front of the other, making her hips sway and reminding Cole of the Mexican piropo, «Si cocinas como caminas, me como hasta las miguitas.»

Cole vaulted down from the stage and crossed to the girls' table. Janet stood up to give him a hug and a kiss. He nodded awkwardly to Holly and she nodded back.

Janet did most of the talking while Cole tried not to stare at Holly. One of Janet's teachers had falsely accused her of talking in class and it had left Janet in a weird mood, unable to get past it. Cole told himself that trying to get Holly alone for two minutes was a lousy idea, yet every time he glanced at her she smiled and looked down in a way that made him think she might be interested.

At 7:30 the house lights dimmed and 20 minutes later the couples started to arrive. Cole's right leg began to bounce, like a runner's, waiting for the gun. He was turned inward, gathering himself, and could barely follow Janet's monologue. When she finally got to a stopping place, he stood up, kissed her, and said, "We're on in a minute. I'll see you at the break." He winked at Holly, a move that didn't feel as spontaneous as he'd hoped, and made his way toward the front of the room. The others were just getting up from the band table, and they quietly filed onto the darkened stage, switched their amps off standby, and gently touched their strings to make sure they were live.

The Studio Club, Cole thought. Holy fucking shit.

They all nodded to Alex, and Alex said, "Good evening, Studio Club!" Applause, whistling. "We are The Chevelles, and we are here to make you *dance*!"

Gary counted them into "Just Like Me" by the Raiders, organ and guitar hurling slow, descending chords against a ringing cymbal bell, then Cole's grinding, irresistible guitar line propelled the kids onto the dance floor. This early on the club was barely a quarter full, and most of the guys still had their jackets on, trying to look cool. Some of the women were already on fire. A stacked brunette rolled her hips like she was working a hula-hoop, one hand buried in her own hair. A tall, elegant blonde bent forward at the waist, bit her lower lip, and slowly closed both eyes. A skinny girl with light brown hair had both arms in the air, swaying like a houri. Cole wanted them all. His desire was boundless and indiscriminate and he poured that longing into his solo, stepping around the mike stand to put the toes of his boots off the lip of the stage.

At that point the light show cut in. Cole finished up his lead and turned to look. Random, scratchy home movies invaded by oily tendrils of green and yellow that pulsed in time to the music. Cole nearly forgot his guitar part, then the sheer weirdness and coolness of it seized him and took him even higher.

The gig was the standard four sets, eight to midnight, 15-minute break each hour except the last. By 9:30 the place was at capacity, dancers backed up against the stage, jackets off to reveal a sea of white shirts, the air musky with perfume and hairspray and Right Guard and sweat. The band was on, hitting the harmonies and keeping the rhythm tight, egging each other on, loving the moment, the lights, the crowd, the songs.

At the end of the second set, Cole, high on hormones and delusions of power, made his move. "You want some Cokes?" he asked the girls.

Holly shrugged and Janet said, "I suppose."

Cole swallowed his misgivings and said, "Holly, you want to help me carry them?"

Holly looked at Janet. Janet looked at Cole. Cole smiled and opened his hands like it was no big deal one way or the other. Janet finally shrugged and Holly got up uncertainly. Cole walked away, leaving her to follow or not. He got in line and Holly said, "What's the big secret?"

"I wanted to know... if I could call you some time."

Up close, her eyes were quite extraordinary. Cool, gray, intelligent, self-possessed.

"Why?" she said.

It was a bad start. Cole couldn't see any way other than forward. "I think about you a lot," he said. "There's just something about you, I don't know. I want to get to know you better."

"Intellectually speaking?"

Only two people in line ahead of them now. Cole panicked. "That too," he said.

"That too?" Holly said. "Oh wow, you're making a pass at me. Janet was afraid you might pull something like this."

Only one guy ahead of them. "I'm not pulling anything," Cole said.

"Janet's my best friend," Holly said. "She's in love with you, and I can't believe you're doing this."

"Three Cokes," Cole said to the girl at the bar. Sweat was pouring down his ribcage.

The girl waved away his money. "You're with the band."

Cole tried in vain to think of a way out. "Look, I'm sorry I said anything. I think you're fantastic, but I'll keep that to myself."

The girl at the bar passed over three paper cups full of crushed ice and Coke. Cole tried to hand one to Holly, who didn't want to take it. "What about Janet?"

"Excuse me," said the guy in line behind them, who looked like a lineman for the Highland Park football team. "Can y'all maybe settle this somewhere else?"

Cole fought down his urge to get in an argument with the guy and stepped out of line. "I don't really know where things are with Janet at the moment."

"Well, Janet seems to think *she* knows where things are, so maybe you need to enlighten her."

She took one of the cups and walked away. Cole hurried after her. At the table, Janet looked from Cole to Holly and back again. "Was it fun?" she asked. Cole had never heard her resort to sarcasm before.

"Less than you might think," Cole said. Before Janet could ask the next question, he said, "We sound good tonight, don't we? The acoustics here are amazing." It's come to this, he thought. I'm quoting Gary Travis for small talk.

Janet searched his face. He saw doubt and pain in her eyes and, against his will, he thought about Mexico and the smell of lavender. He vowed that he would not let her see his guilt and he banished everything from his head except the sight of her.

She was the first to look away. "Yeah. You sound good."

The conversation limped along. Cole dragged it forward, Janet grudgingly did her part, and Holly sat out. After ten agonizing minutes the time came to play again, and Cole practically bolted to the stage.

In the middle of the third song, Janet stood up and pushed her way through the dancers to stand in front of Cole. She was furious. She pointed one finger at him, ominously, then she and Holly walked out.

As she went through the door, Cole stepped up to the mike, right on cue, and sang, "This could be the last time…"

Had it been anywhere but the Studio Club, any night but their debut there, he might have gone after her. Five seconds later he told himself that it was better this way, that she would cool down overnight and apologize tomorrow.

The next song was the Temptations' "I'm Losing You," and Cole wondered if it was true, if his infidelity in Guanajuato was something he could never put right, even if Janet never found out.

Next up were The Byrds, and as he sang, "And I'll probably feel a whole lot better when you're gone," he watched the short brunette shimmying again with boundless energy, and he wondered what it would be like to not be tied down, to go from girl to girl like Alex did.

And so he tortured himself, song by song, as if he were a captured agent in some malarial prison, all the joy and swagger of the first two sets gone, his eyes stinging when they did "She's Not There."

At the break Alex asked, "You okay?"

"Yeah, I'm fine."

"What happened to Janet?"

"Holly had to get home."

He stepped out the back door into the alley. His sweat turned instantly to ice water and the shock brought him back to reality. Two guys he'd never seen before were standing with a girl who looked like she was about to burst out of a red prom dress, her makeup streaked and runny.

"Hey!" one of the guys said. "Y'all are outta sight. You're the best goddamned band in Dallas."

"Thanks," Cole said.

They all looked a little drunk, and his suspicions were confirmed when the girl handed him a silver flask. "Little something to warm you up?"

"Why thank you," Cole said. "I don't mind if I do."

He'd just taken a nip when the door banged open. He instinctively hid the flask under his jacket until he saw that it was Gary. He put the cap on the flask and handed it back.

"What are you doing?" Gary said.

"Nothing," Cole said.

"You stupid idiot, are you trying to get us fired?"

"Why don't you mind your own business?"

"This *is* my business. It's all of our business. If you screw this up, you dickhead, that's it for me. You can count me out." He slammed the door on his way inside.

"He always like that?" the girl asked.

"Pretty much," Cole said.

"He could use to loosen up some. You want another snort?"

"Nah," Cole said. "I better get back. Y'all take care, now."

He crowded into the men's room and threw some water on his face. Ignoring the other boys around him, he looked at his reflection and rapped on the mirror with one knuckle. "Anybody home?" he asked under his breath. Apparently not, not anybody with a mind of his own. Whatever other people thought of him was all that counted. If Janet was angry, even unreasonably, he felt like a shitheel. If Gary yelled at him, he felt guilty.

However, that small shot of whiskey had perked him up. I don't have to take shit from anybody, he thought. Not as long as I can make people dance.

The last set was mostly classics, "Shake" and "Shout," "Money" and "Louie, Louie," and "Land of a Thousand Dances." Through sheer willpower, he put everything else out of his mind and concentrated on the girls dancing, his only goal being to whip them into an even greater frenzy.

They played two encores and then the house lights came up, that moment of truth when the sweat stains and the liquefied mascara and the collapsed hairdos became glaringly obvious, when nothing remained to cover the ringing in the ears, when exhausted leg muscles had to find the strength to work the pedals for the drive home.

They tore down the equipment in ten minutes, by which time

the club was nearly empty. Alex's date du jour waited by the door and the stacked brunette nursed a cup of Coke at a table by herself.

Evidently Cole had not had enough trouble for one evening. "What happened to your date?"

She smiled tiredly. "We had a disagreement about what was going to happen after we left here." Her eyes were a little small, Cole thought, and her nose was a little large, but her mouth was just right. "I guess I'll call a cab. It's only a couple of miles down Preston."

Cole looked at Alex. "You going home with me?"

Alex pointed at his date.

"I can give you a lift," Cole said to the girl. "We need to load the equipment first."

Her smile got bigger. "I'm in no hurry." She stuck out her hand. "I'm Frances. Everybody calls me Frankie."

As Cole drove down Preston, she sat with her back against the passenger door, one leg folded on the seat, watching him.

"You go to Highland Park?" Cole asked.

"Until May. Then I'm off to nice, safe, conservative Duke. You?"

"St. Mark's. Then UT."

"I wish I was going to Texas. But Daddy doesn't want me to get corrupted. If he only knew."

"You're some kind of dancer."

"I can't help myself. I hear music and it just takes me over. You guys are really good, and your drummer—he's got a beat like a bad cold, you can't help but catch it."

Cole gave her a wry smile. "I'll let him know you liked him."

She kicked him gently with the leg that was on the seat. "Nothing against the rest of y'all. You play a hot guitar and you've got a great voice. But I suspect you've already got a girlfriend."

"That remains to be seen after tonight."

"What'd you do?"

"Flirted a little."

"Hell, nothing wrong with a little flirting. Long as it don't get out of hand."

"I'd ask you to explain that to her, but I expect that'd only make things worse. What about your boyfriend?"

"Patrick's so used to having everything his way, he forgets somebody else might have a way too. I'll probably forgive him, though, because he's got a sweet little GTO. Take a right at the next corner."

The huge houses had columns in front and long lawns that sloped down to the street. Frankie directed him to a cul de sac and said, "It's the second house, but don't pull in the driveway, or Daddy'll be out here with more questions than Dave Garroway."

Cole cut the lights and turned off the engine and coasted to the curb in neutral, to see what would happen. What happened was that Frankie straddled him, arms braced against the seat on either side of his neck. "Thanks for the ride home, cowboy."

Cole kissed her. Her mouth was, in fact, just right, soft and yielding, sweet from Cokes and Juicy Fruit. Her coat was open and he put his hands on her waist and then slowly moved them up until he was holding her breasts, and then he was rubbing his thumbs against where he hoped her nipples might be, somewhere beneath her extensive foundation garments.

She moved her lips to his ear and said, "Easy, cowboy, or I'm not going to want to stop."

Cole saw the future branch into two paths, and for once he chose the one without the oncoming bus. He shifted his hands to her waist and pulled his head back so he could see her face. "What if I wanted to call you sometime?" he said.

She took a lipstick out of her purse and wrote a number on his left hand. "Private line," she said, "so you don't have to talk to Daddy."

He kissed her again, more gently, and she opened the driver-side door. "You stay here," she said. "It's better that way for all concerned."

"G'night, Frankie."

"Sweet dreams, cowboy."

She ran up the long, curving driveway, heels clattering against the concrete, and Cole waited until she was inside and the porch light was off before he started the car.

As he drove away he called himself 17 kinds of idiot for not having her right there on the front seat. By the time he got home his feelings had changed to a kind of relief. Their differences would have been unavoidable after sex, and if he was doomed to see himself through other people's eyes, at least he'd ended the night with a beautiful girl feeling desire and wistful affection for him.

And if he changed his mind, he did have her phone number.

STARTING IN LATE MARCH, St. Mark's kept the chapel doors open for the morning assembly, leaving Cole unable to focus on the mandatory hymn singing for the noise of the birds and the smells of feverish growth—mimosa blossoms and cut grass and bright green cottonwood leaves.

He and Janet had weathered the Studio Club crisis, and in the aftermath the balance of power had shifted. Cole had maintained a wounded innocence. He felt the credit he'd earned by not having sex with Frankie was enough to cover his other sins, though he didn't attempt that argument with Janet. Within a week she'd called him and they'd had a passionate reconciliation in the hearse.

Both Cole and Alex had taken their senior option to drop athletics and leave every day at 3:10. They blew the bonus hour at Preston Record Center or cruising North Dallas. Once a week or so they took their acoustic guitars to Lee Park, where the changes that had swept London and New York and Amsterdam and San Francisco had finally begun to creep into Dallas. The marble steps in front of the Robert E. Lee statue had become the epicenter for the kids who designated themselves "freaks," boys with hair long enough to get them expelled from school and thrown out of Goff's Hamburgers, girls in Indian print dresses, the occasional furtive joint, guitars and bongos and wooden flutes. Cole and Alex, having changed into jeans and T-shirts in the hearse, would sit cross-legged in the grass and play a few Beatles songs. They'd draw a crowd of ten or fifteen people and sometimes the girls would dance. If anyone asked, they'd mention the band name and their next gig. Alex might collect a phone number or take one of the girls behind Arlington Hall for a quick make-out session, an "audition" as he called it. The girls who passed might get asked out a few times.

One of the kids in their class had surfed one summer in LA, and Cole kept thinking about the way he'd described it. It was like he and Alex had paddled out to where the big wave was building, and worked hard to stay in front of it, and now it was starting to pick them up and carry them. They didn't have time to look back to see how huge and powerful it was, they could only fight to stay upright and let it take them as far as it wanted to go.

WHEN HE AND ALEX got home on the second Monday in March, Cole made his usual beeline to the stack of mail on the hall table. He grabbed the two #10 envelopes from UT, handed one to Alex, and ripped open his own. He scanned it, and then he closed his eyes and let the tension ease out of his solar plexus. Not only accepted into UT, but into the Plan II Honors program. He'd had little to worry about—they were both Texas residents with good SATs and solid grades and the prestige of St. Mark's behind them—but anxiety was Cole's second nature.

He looked at Alex. "You?"

"Yes!" Alex said, and they did an Indian war dance in the hall.

They called Al Montoya at work, and he immediately proposed a trip to Austin for the three of them, to scout for apartments and give them a taste of the city.

They had a gig Saturday night, so the timing was tricky. Montoya arranged for them to get Friday off and they drove down in Montoya's Cadillac after school on Thursday. Interstate 35 was still not finished, leaving them with state highways and stoplights all through Waco, the halfway point. The landscape was as dull as any Cole had seen, flat and featureless except for prairie grass and stunted mesquite bushes. Cole nodded off after dinner at something called the Turkey Shop, and he woke up in darkness as they passed through a set of filling stations named Georgetown.

From there south, a giant hand had crumpled the flat surface of the earth, and by the time they arrived in Austin proper, the highway rose and fell with a pleasant regularity. They passed suburbs and shopping centers and the airport and, finally, the UT practice fields as they took the Manor Road exit. Alex, who'd learned his way around on trips to visit Susan, informed Cole that it was pronounced MAY-nor Road, one of a dozen idiosyncratic pronunciations intended to betray interlopers, including MAN-shack for Manchaca, GWAD-a-loop for Guadalupe, BURN-it for Burnet, and Miller for Mueller.

They turned under the freeway and into the parking lot of the Villa Capri Motor Hotel. Cole was charmed by the 1950s freestanding neon sign, the flying buttresses, the breezeways, the palm trees. The quintessence of every motel that he had longed for as a child and his parents had driven past, put off by the flash and expense.

By the time they checked in and unpacked, it was nine o'clock. Alex was tired but Cole was restless, and Montoya offered to drive him around. Cole was glad to have Montoya to himself. They cruised downtown with the windows open and the heater on, past the State Capitol and ten blocks of two-story office buildings and department stores, and then they took the Congress Avenue Bridge across Town Lake. Reflections of streetlights dancing across the dark water. A powerboat idling next to the bridge. Montoya parked on the south side and they walked back to look. Cole saw the lights of the Capitol and, above it, an airplane descending toward the airport.

Montoya explained that they were looking at the third in a chain of lakes on the Colorado River, fed by Lake Austin to the west of the city and Lake Travis to the north. Not far from where they stood was Barton Springs, a natural swimming pool that covered three acres. "It's like an oasis here," he said. "All this beautiful water."

They both had their hands in their pockets and their shoulders raised against the chill. Cole had no desire to move on. Being alone with Montoya made him feel grown up.

"I'm thinking of moving into Austin," Montoya said. "With the distributing company, I mean."

"Does that involve tommyguns and hijacked trucks and pay-offs to the cops, like on *The Untouchables*?"

Montoya laughed. "Not my style. This would be more about getting in on the ground floor. People graduate from UT but they don't go home, they stay in Austin. You kids, with all your groups and music, when you're twenty-one there's going to be nightclubs to play in and the nightclubs are going to sell beer."

"I would need somebody to be in charge of things down here. I've talked to Alex about it, about learning the business during the summers, and stepping in after he graduates. He's not sure if he's interested."

Not interested was an understatement, Cole thought. But he heard the disappointment in Montoya's voice and tried to protect him. "We're only in high school. We don't have all that stuff figured out."

"I know," Montoya said. "I mean, that's what we wanted for you kids, not to have to go to work full time as soon as you were sixteen, like I did. For you to go to college, to have the freedom to make your own lives." He considered his own words for a minute and said, "It's hard to live up to that in real life."

"Sure," Cole said. "Of course you want him to be part of your business." A hint, perhaps, for Cole to intercede. Not likely, Cole thought.

"What about you?" Montoya asked. "Still thinking about Russian for your major, not something in music?"

"Russian, I guess. It'd give me something to fall back on. Besides, they don't teach the kind of music we play in school."

"Something's happening, isn't it?" Montoya asked. Cole immediately thought of Dylan's Thin Man. "There were those motorcycle gangs in the fifties, but this is something brand new. That Human Be-In out in San Francisco, the music, the hippies, the drugs."

"That hippie thing, that's a stereotype the TV news came up with. The bare feet and fringed jackets and headbands and all that." Cole paused. Montoya had taken his words as reassurance, and now Cole had to let him down again. "But the rest of it, yeah. Something's happening. It's a brand-new world."

As he said the words, Cole realized for the first time that he wouldn't be able to last at UT. Wherever the world might be in four years, he would have to be out in the thick of it, not watching it happen from the distance of a college campus.

"Did you tell your parents you'd been accepted?" Montoya asked.

Cole shook his head. Montoya had brokered a deal whereby Cole's mother would call him on Sunday afternoons at 1:00. Cole had come to dread those conversational minefields, where every possible subject, from his father's health to Cole's life with the Montoyas to school or the band, had the potential to reduce his mother to a miserable silence. The calls made Cole feel heartless, yet the only alternatives were to cut her off entirely, or to go back to living with his father. "I'll call her when we get back."

Montoya didn't say anything, leaving Cole's guilt to do the rest. Montoya never held onto things the way Cole's father would have—within a few seconds the conversation had moved on. Still Cole felt left behind, unable to be the son his mother wanted, unable to be the student that Montoya was financing.

At the Villa Capri, Cole said, "It's early yet. Want to look at some cards?"

Montoya so loved poker that he was happy to simply deal out hands of seven card stud, no chips, verbal betting only, and Cole knew there would be a deck of Bicycles in Montoya's suitcase. "Are you sure?" he asked, a childlike happiness already spreading across his face.

"Of course," Cole said. It was the least he could do.

EARLY THE NEXT MORNING they drove to Susan's house, a tidy postwar bungalow full of sunlight a few blocks from campus. Susan fixed migas, eggs scrambled with cheese and tortilla strips and green onions, plenty of hot sauce on the side. Susan's roommate, petite and blonde and silent, joined them. Cole's attention was fully occupied by Susan, who seemed older and unexpectedly elegant as she presided over the table in jeans and a loose white Indian shirt.

After breakfast, Cole and the three Montoyas drove to UT and parked a couple of blocks off Guadalupe Street. Cole's first view of the campus was a cluster of yellow-white stone buildings with orange tile roofs, and, in the near distance, a high tower with a dome on top.

Suddenly the memory of that tower hit him hard enough to make him queasy. He remembered cameras pointing up toward a glint of metal where Charles Whitman stood on the observation deck, the pop of the rifle shots, the stretcher bearers hunkering down as they carried away a body. August 1, the day that Cole mangled his hand. He saw Jerry's body on the derrick floor, saw his own hand with the button sticking out of the bandages, felt a needle slide into his buttocks and the Demerol haze come down, saw Corrina's mouth say "Dream about me."

He was so unprepared for the vividness of it that he had to stop and grab a light pole. Susan, the first to notice, came to ask if he was all right.

"Just… a weird moment."

"Goose walk over your grave?"

"Something like that. I'm okay now."

He wasn't, quite. He'd popped out of the chronological continuity and now bits of him were scattered across the previous year. He tried to pull himself together as they crossed Guadalupe and Susan pointed out the student union and the Turtle Pond behind the biology lab. Under a cluster of trees, a bare-chested guy in jeans tossed a Frisbee with a girl in shorts and a bikini top. A dog wearing a bandanna leapt and sprinted between them. Another guy in jeans and tennis shoes and a faded red T-shirt sat in the grass and played "House of the Rising Sun" on an acoustic guitar. Cole remembered the SMU students at the Dylan concert in their white shirts and ties only a year and a half before, and his sense of time distorted even further. His past was present and his future was rocketing away.

They turned south at the Tower and walked down the South Mall, a paved walkway as wide as a four-lane highway. Live oaks lined both sides and beyond them were classrooms, housed in identical pale stone buildings with tiled roofs. The mall ended in steps that led down to Littlefield Fountain, where three bronze riders emerged from the water on creatures with the heads and forelegs of horses and the tails of fish, while a winged goddess and WWI soldiers looked on.

UT had 30,000 undergraduates, one of the highest enrollments in the country. Cole had expected giant multistory containment facilities for the students and was relieved to see the human scale of the campus. Of the entire city, for that matter, which lacked skyscrapers, or any tall buildings other than the Tower. A bell rang somewhere and within seconds a flood of students filled the mall, few of them in any great hurry. A succession of girls walked by that made Cole's heart ache.

They saw the library and the gym and saw Memorial Stadium from a distance. Cole began to understand that the campus was as large as a medium-size town, and that the shuttle buses they saw on every corner were not just to get students to and from off-campus housing, but from one end of the campus to the other.

They ate lunch at a hamburger joint named Dirty's, near where they'd parked. The food was greasy yet oddly compelling, and though the Lone Star longnecks they all ordered reminded Cole of Tyler, he thought he was mostly over his temporal vertigo.

"What do you think?" Montoya asked Cole when most of the food was gone. The question seemed more than casual.

"I like the vibrations," Cole said, which prompted Alex to make his "hippie bullshit" face. "If you're still willing to help me, yes, this is where I want to go to school."

Montoya visibly relaxed and his smile was radiant. "Good. Good. That's settled, then."

Cole felt like a liar, believing as he now did that he wouldn't last. He would give it a shot, he told himself. That was all, in his heart, that he'd agreed to.

Susan looked at her watch and stood up. "I have to get to class. Daddy, you can finish my burger." She kissed them all on the cheek. "'Ta luego."

As Cole watched her walk away, he wondered if he had the discipline to get up from a table of Dirty's hamburgers and long-necks to go to class. He supposed he would find out.

That afternoon they saw Barton Springs and the huge expanse

of Pease Park, full of dogs and college-age kids flying kites. The west side of the park bordered a high ridge with an actual castle on top. The neighborhood, Montoya said, was called Castle Hill in its honor. They drove up the steep incline of 12th Street and found the Castle at the singular address of 1111 West 11th Street. What they saw through the black wrought-iron gates looked like the corner of a medieval fort—one crenelated, three-story turret and an attached wall that extended 50 feet behind it. Montoya said it had started out in the late 1800s as the Texas Military Institute, a boy's school.

They checked out the neighborhood. Older, slightly run-down houses on small lots, many carved up into apartments or rented by the room. Cars parked on both sides of the narrow streets.

On Castle Hill Street, which overlooked Pease Park, Montoya pulled up in front of a two-story stone house, empty and starting to deteriorate, for sale according to the realtor's sign in front. Montoya told them to get out and look it over while he parked the car.

A cracked and buckled sidewalk led past blown dandelions and stalks of Johnson grass. The house looked to be from 1900 or so, oblong, with a wraparound porch and steeply pitched gables. One of the boards in the porch was broken and a front window was cracked. Cole saw wood floors and textured plaster walls inside, crumbling in places.

"Fixer upper," Cole said, glancing at Alex, who surprised him with a look of naked longing.

"Can you imagine?" Alex said. He looked up the street to the slice of Austin laid out below the cliff like an aerial photograph, then held out his hands, palms up.

Cole could indeed imagine. With some work it would be a party house for the ages, a house that would seduce women by their very presence in it, a place to stand from which they could lever the world. What Cole did not understand was how it had become a possibility so quickly. His father had never made an impulsive decision in his life, had never bought a house without the certainty of selling the one he was in. Yet Montoya was clearly thinking the same thing that he and Alex were.

Cole watched Montoya climb the sidewalk—alert, in his element, taking inventory and tabulating the results—and felt a helpless love for him. From their first handshake, Montoya had seen through Cole's bullshit and liked him anyway. Not merely liked him, had taken him in and taken on Cole's father to do it, and now was prepared to put him through college. It was more faith than Cole had in himself.

"How does it look?" Montoya asked.

"Looks like mostly superficial damage," Cole said, remembering the many houses he'd looked at with his father. "The foundation has shifted some." He pointed to a hairline separation between a massive piece of stone and the brownish mortar next to it.

"Good eyes," Montoya said, and squatted down with a characteristic tug at the knees of his slacks to preserve the crease. "Any house this old is going to move around. As long as the foundation itself is solid, it should be all right."

The three of them walked around to the back. Among the oak and sycamore trees and the brick barbeque pit and the dying St. Augustine grass, the yard held a stretch of sagging white plastic clothesline strung between two T-shaped metal poles. It gave Cole a pang of nostalgia, though he no longer remembered where the yard had been that had poles like these. The membrane between past and present was thin in Austin, and powerful emotions, sometimes unmoored from their origins, kept breaking through.

A flagstone patio, a low ornamental wall. Alex found a three-pronged outlet by the back door. "It's been rewired, and recently."

Montoya pointed to the massive air conditioner near the back door. "Window units look fairly new."

Alex tried the back door, then they all stood side by side and looked in the floor-to-ceiling windows, hands shading their eyes. A long, naturally lighted room and a pass-through into a big, tiled kitchen. Hardwood floors, dusty and scratched, a stain here, a cigarette burn there.

Montoya kept a poker face, but he wrote down the realtor's number from the sign, and later, as they drove around the small mansions north of campus, he stopped at a pay phone to set up an appointment for the next morning.

At four they picked Susan up at her house and she directed them up Mount Bonnell Road, two lanes of winding blacktop that took them north and west of the city, the scent of the furiously blooming oak and mimosa trees stoking Cole's already full-blown spring fever. Susan called out as they drove past a beat-up two-story beer joint that looked like a bait shop and turned out to be the Dry Creek Café and Boat Dock. Montoya parked on the side of the road and they walked back.

A middle-aged woman with badly dyed hair sat behind the bar watching TV. She wouldn't sell them more than two Lone Star longnecks, and that was only after scrutinizing Susan's ID. "Them boys ain't legal age. Y'all finish them two beers, bring the empties back, and I'll sell you two more."

The downstairs featured a pool table and a jukebox playing Jim Reeves' "Welcome to My World." The upstairs felt like a tree house, with screens for windows and sections of tree trunks holding up the roof. Round tables and odds and ends of chairs. A floor that a determined couple might dance on, if they were careful about where the linoleum was worn through. Susan led them onto a deck that faced the afternoon sun. Two distorted speakers relayed the music from the jukebox, and a weathered wooden railing provided dubious protection against a long fall down to Lake Austin.

Giving plenty of leeway to two men in tractor caps who were smoking at one of the tables, Cole approached the railing. The lake was little more than a wide spot in the river. A boat dock on the far side, possibly the one referenced in the Dry Creek sign, interrupted an otherwise unbroken wall of green.

Susan appeared next to him. She offered her longneck and Cole took a grateful swallow. "You like it here," she said. "Here, specifically, but Austin too."

"Yeah. I mean, this place has a great vibe, even if it is a dive. Peaceful. The whole town feels that way. It feels like home."

"I've seen that happen to more people than I can count."

"But not you."

"I'm a big city girl. I like Neiman Marcus and garden parties and charity balls."

Another obstacle between them. "Why didn't you go to SMU, then? Or Rice?"

"Too much money to waste on educating a girl. At least this girl, the daughter of the wrong wife."

"Your father said that?"

"He never had to."

The jukebox played Tammy Wynette. Cole knew these songs from Midland, and from Tyler, and from hearing them on KLIF and KBOX and KFJZ mixed in with the rock and soul and easy listening. Dancing with Corrina had given him a new appreciation for country music, and it suited his present mood as perfectly as it fit the surroundings.

"What does your girlfriend think about you leaving her behind?" Susan asked. Cole heard no condescension in her voice.

"She thinks we're somehow going to make it work, that I'll be coming up for weekends and vacations."

"And you don't think so."

"Once me and Alex get a band going, we'll be working weekends."

"Do you love her?"

Cole sensed an unspoken emotional investment in the question. He only wanted to steer the conversation away from Janet. "Well, there's love," he said, and looked at her, "and then there's love."

"Oh Cole. Sometimes I think you fall for your own nonsense. You're not in love with me." She was attempting, Cole thought, to be kind. "You're in love with your own illusions about this family, about how wonderful and perfect we all are. And some romantic notion about how you and I are the outsiders and how that gives us an affinity. Plenty of girls will love you for being such a romantic."

Cole's glib tongue failed him. "You shouldn't underestimate me," he said.

"Oh, I don't," Susan said. "Only myself. Always myself." She smiled a bright, artificial smile and said, "We need to get back to the table."

They shared two more beers and drove to Susan's house, where she made chicken in mole sauce, guacamole, and rice. Montoya and Alex watched TV while Susan cooked. She refused Cole's offers of help, so he got La Pelirroja out of the trunk where it had ridden all day and played on the back porch until dinner.

Montoya, who usually revealed his emotions sparingly, showed his pleasure that night. He'd successfully moved Alex and Cole two squares forward into contested territory and now the long game was on. More was at stake than the beer concessions in Austin, Cole knew. The prize was Alex's divided soul.

Being around so many young people had reset Montoya's internal clock, and over dinner he regaled them with stories of his exploits as a boy in Mexico. His father worked at Cuautémoc day and night, and his mother was distracted with cooking and cleaning, leaving him free to roam the streets. His first business was shining shoes while wearing sunglasses and pretending to be blind, asking his patrons to pick out the right color of polish, acting like he was working by touch. For a while he worked for a woman who sold fruit and vegetables in the city market that her husband had "liberated" from other people's farms the night before. From there he moved to collecting empty brand-name liquor bottles to sell to a bootlegger who would refill them with homemade imitations and seal them with a counterfeit stamp. "And," Montoya said, "I've been in the alcohol business ever since."

After dinner Cole washed the dishes while Susan dried. "Are all those stories true?" he asked.

"Probably, more or less. He doesn't tell them that often, and they never change."

"You knew this stuff when you were kids? And it didn't tempt you into a life of crime?"

"The thing is, he never did anything terribly wrong. He never told people he was blind, he let them draw their own conclusions. He didn't steal the fruit himself, he just moved it around. He did what he had to do without directly hurting anyone else." Once again Cole suspected that reefs lurked under the surface of the conversation. As if to confirm it, she said, "Let's sit outside. You can bring your guitar."

The evening chill felt good after the heat of the kitchen. Cole quietly played "Cielito lindo" with his fingers. Susan lit a Kool and puffed at it nervously. "I'm thinking about getting married," she said.

Cole stopped playing. It was like a stranger had vaulted the back fence. "Who to?"

"There's a guy in one of my classes. His name's Jesse. He's older. He was in Vietnam for two years and now he's finishing school on the GI Bill."

"Jesus, Susan, a Vietnam vet?"

"There's nothing wrong with serving your country."

Cole had nothing against Vietnam veterans other than the fact that he would never willingly be one in a million years. Now that turned out to be what Susan wanted to marry. "Does your father know?"

"I haven't told him anything yet."

Cole hesitated, then said, "Do you love him?"

"Tit for tat, eh, Cole? To quote a friend of the family, there's love... and there's love." She looked like she was about to cry.

"When?"

"Christmas. He graduates in December and he's already got a job lined up in Oklahoma City. We'll have the wedding in Guanajuato so he can meet all the relatives."

"So you won't graduate?"

"What's the point? Daddy only sent me here to find a husband, and I've found one."

"I don't believe that. You're at least as smart as Alex. You could do anything."

"I was brought up to cook and run a household and raise babies. Not to go to college for four years and law school for another three and then study to pass the bar and then fight my way into a law firm."

"Is that what you want to do? Go to law school?"

"Oh, Cole, I don't know. I think sometimes that if there is anything I truly care about, it's justice. That if I could, I would help other people, immigrants, maybe, or poor people. If I had the strength to push myself up that incredibly steep hill."

"Wait for me," Cole said, startling himself.

"What did you say?"

"You don't love this guy. Cut him loose and finish college. In a couple of years I'll be rich and famous and I'll put you through law school."

"Oh, Cole," she said, and ruffled his hair like she would a six-year-old's. "You're so sweet, and so full of it."

"I'm completely serious."

"I'm sure. I wish I had your faith in me. I wish Daddy did."

"Why don't we ask him? Right now. Ask him if he'll send you to law school. I know he'll say yes."

"Cole, don't you dare. He's not the problem, I am. I can't ask him for something like that if I'm not a hundred percent certain I can deliver."

"Will you think about not marrying this guy? Like, seriously think about it?"

"I'll think about it," she said. "And in the meantime, you have to promise not to say a word about any of it. Not law school, not Jesse. Not to Alex, not to my father, not to anybody. Promise me."

Cole slumped against the porch railing. "Oh, all right. I promise."

"Play 'Cielito lindo' again," she said. "That was beautiful."

NINE O'CLOCK Saturday morning. They had already checked out of the motel, and they met the realtor at the house. Blonde, late thirties, in a blazer with a logo on the pocket. Cole resisted the temptation to bring his guitar inside to test the acoustics. No point in freaking her out. He and Alex left Montoya to get the formal tour and explored on their own.

The top floor featured three bedrooms. The one on the north front corner had a spectacular view of the Tower and the tree-lined streets around it. "How do we decide who gets it?" Alex asked. "One hand of five-card stud?"

"It's yours," Cole said. "I want the one in back." He could see the old clothesline from there, and clusters of trees.

At the foot of the stairs, Cole opened a door and saw another flight leading down. "Alejo, check it out."

The basement had the same square footage as the upstairs,

with damp cinderblock walls and barely seven feet of clearance between the overhead joists and the unfinished concrete floor. "Oh man," Alex said. "Practice room."

"Egg cartons or blankets on the walls to deaden the sound. Except—" He pointed to a drain in the floor. "—that it obviously floods down here. We'll need a sump pump."

Minor cracks in the walls, nothing serious. A washer and dryer, in good condition, sat in one corner. "Two-twenty," Cole said. "No one-ten."

"Put it on the list," Alex said.

"Boys?" Montoya's voice came from the top of the stairs. "You ready?"

As they drove away, Montoya said, "It's pricey, but it looks like a good investment. I need to get an inspector in there that I can trust. If he likes it, I think we can make it happen."

"Fantastic," Cole said.

"Here's the deal. If you guys want to live there, it's a business proposition. You would each have a room, and there are two more bedrooms that need to be rented out. Alex, your job would be to find responsible young men to rent the rooms and to collect the rent every month. Cole, you would be in charge of maintenance. I would expect you to fix the stuff you can, and call in a professional for the stuff you can't, deducting the cost from the income that Alex collects. I would expect both of you to do that on top of your schoolwork, your social life, and any musical activities."

Cole, riding shotgun, looked over the seat to see how Alex was taking it. Not well, he thought. Montoya was single-minded and relentless, and the agenda at the core of the deal was not exactly hidden. Alex made his give-me-a-break face and stared out the window. "Yeah, okay," he said.

"Cole?"

"Sounds great," he said. "It's a beautiful house."

"We'll see," Montoya said, pleased with himself again. "We'll see."

★

IN APRIL, KVIL, which floated somewhere between easy listening and pop, started playing rock on its FM affiliate after the AM station went off the air at sunset. Cole had bought himself a Panasonic AM/FM portable the size of a kid's lunchbox to replace his pocket transistor radio, and one night he chanced upon a cheesy Farfisa organ, distorted guitar, and nasal voice singing about "sweet Loraine." The band turned out to be something called Country Joe and the Fish from San Francisco. The DJ was Ron David McCoy and the program was called The Psychedelic Hour. McCoy followed up with another San Francisco band called the Grateful Dead, with more cheesy organ and bubbling guitar and snappy drums and nasal singing. Cole felt like he'd tuned into a transmission from another dimension. His heart was beating fast. The music was dangerous, defiantly careless, willfully atonal, and it flaunted its shanghaied blues roots. Next was The West Coast Pop Art Experimental Band singing "If You Want This Love of Mine." Cole grabbed his guitar and figured out the song as it played.

He ignored his urge to run down the hall and tell Alex about it. He wasn't sure why. For the moment, he wanted this new music all to himself.

MAY WAS AP TESTING the first two weeks and finals the last week. The Chevelles played three and four nights a week for proms, private parties, and events like the Senior Follies Dance. Cole saw Janet for hurried sex on a Saturday afternoon while her mother was grocery shopping, or for a weeknight hamburger and a detour by White Rock Lake. Phone calls, movies, and walks in Lee Park had all fallen off the agenda.

Her frustration had started to show. "This summer is the last time we're going to have together for who knows how long. Is this what it's going to be like?"

"Of course not," Cole said. As long as he kept moving, he felt invulnerable. The band sounded as good as anybody on the radio. He was acing his tests. When he got the chance to sleep, he slept deeply and didn't remember his dreams. "It's graduation time. Every band in town is booked solid."

"I don't even feel like a person when we're together. I feel like an inflatable sex toy or something."

"Oh, you feel much better than that," Cole said.

"I can't tell you," Janet said, "how not funny that is."

The Final Assembly was at 11 AM on Memorial Day, a Tuesday, the end of the school year, other than graduation the following night. Cole had hated school since kindergarten, and he'd been waiting for this day ever since. He and Alex rode home together in the Monza, and they were both crazy with joy. The radio played "Somebody to Love" by the Jefferson Airplane and Cole reached over to turn it up. Alex grinned maniacally and turned it up some more. Cole cranked it all the way, until it was pounding inside his head, impossibly loud. They had the windows down and Cole stuck his head and shoulders out, then both arms. He turned and began to pound out the beat on the roof of the car. He and Alex screamed along in harmony, and drivers all around them pointed and laughed and Cole wondered if the rest of his life would be like this.

They were still singing along, now to "Friday on My Mind" by the Easybeats, Cole more or less back in the car and drumming on the dashboard instead of the roof, when they turned off Walnut Hill and Cole saw Janet's VW parked in front of the Montoyas' house. She was sitting on the hood, arms folded over her chest.

Alex turned the radio off. "Uh oh," he said.

"Let me out here," Cole said. "You go on inside."

"Yell if you need reinforcements."

Cole got out and watched Alex park behind the garage. He was suddenly conscious of his St. Mark's uniform, the blue, short-sleeved oxford shirt and gray slacks that had finally replaced Ban-Lon and khakis. Janet had never seen him in it and he was embarrassed by it.

He walked around to the front of the VW. She wore a long, flowered dress and a hippie headband that he'd never seen before. Her face was devoid of makeup. From her expression, he knew not to reach for her. "What's wrong?" he said.

"We need to talk."

"Okay." Standing in one place let his body complain about how tired he was, so he sat on the curb. "Talk to me."

She looked off into the distance and said, "I thought I could do this and now I don't know."

Cole knew then that it was going to be serious. "Did something happen?" he asked.

"Kind of. I guess, yes."

Cole shut up and waited her out. Eventually she said, "Woody called. A couple of weeks ago. At first I didn't want to talk to him, but he convinced me he'd changed."

Cole, who tended to jealous rage at the first mention of Woody's name, was strangely calm. Janet said that Woody had ridden out to San Francisco on his motorcycle and dropped acid and confronted his "negative self," which appeared to him like a color negative, all glowing oranges and blue-grays. After a long struggle, the negative Woody was banished and the positive Woody was cleansed and renewed. He'd come back to Dallas and gotten a custodial job at Timberlawn psychiatric hospital. He was going to study so that he could counsel people who'd OD'd or had bad trips. Along the way he'd realized that he was in love with Janet and wanted to be with her for the rest of his life. She had, reluctantly, taken acid with Woody on Sunday night. They had made love and she had seen that, like it or not, she was karmically linked to Woody in a way she never would be to Cole.

Cole, after resisting one sarcastic comment after another, found himself at the end with nothing to say. He searched Janet's face for the girl he had loved, at times to the point of desperation, for the last nine months. He hadn't known her at all. This other person, so easily swept away by a little crackpot spirituality, had been there all along. He could insult her by asking if she really intended to marry a janitor, or mock her drug-induced insights, or try to shame her for cheating on him. Or, he realized, he could accept that what she had wanted was to be loved wholeheartedly for who she really was, which Cole had managed intermittently at best.

"I'm sorry," Cole said at last. "I'm sorry I didn't treat you better."

"It doesn't matter. We both did the best we could."

Cole stood up, torn between feelings of liberation and terrible loss. Janet held out her arms and Cole lifted her down from the car. She moved in to hug him, and without Cole intending it, suddenly they were kissing, passionately, her tears running down into their mouths. Cole's emotions flipped again and he thought about the back of the hearse, only a few yards away.

Janet suddenly broke away and Cole let her go. She was smiling, a smile that Cole knew well. "Okay," she said. "Point taken." Then she was crying again. "This is hard," she said. "I'm going to miss you."

Cole took a step toward her and she held out her hands to stop him. She got in the car, backed up, and swerved around him as she drove away.

Eventually Cole went to the cabana and changed into swim trunks and began swimming laps. At some point he saw Alex standing by the shallow end and he stood up.

"What was that about?" Alex said.

"Woody's back," Cole said.

"You've got to be kidding me. She picked that loser over *you*?" Alex was genuinely affronted.

"It's better this way," Cole said.

They looked at each other. They were nearly men now. Questions that they didn't know to ask as boys were now off-limits. Alex was close to the line when he asked, "Are you all right?"

"I'm free now," Cole said. He lowered himself into the water and began to swim again.

THEY WERE IN DINNER JACKETS, seated in folding chairs on risers on the Memorial Auditorium stage, where the Beatles had played in September of 1964. The lights were in their eyes, preventing them from seeing the audience. Cole knew the Montoya family was out there, including Susan and Jimmy, and he knew this was important for Alex's father, so he tried to maintain his bearing when he felt the urge to jeer at the valedictory promises of how he would look back on his St. Mark's years as the best of his life.

He and Alex had shared a joint and then each had brought his own car downtown. Alex was going to a party at Brad Potter's house afterward, where The Chevelles had played their first gig and he'd kissed Janet for the first time. Cole had remained mysterious about his own plans.

The ceremony finally dragged itself to the end. Clutching their leather-bound diplomas, they began to file offstage in alphabetical order, one column down each of the two carpeted aisles, walking to the slow cadence of "Pomp and Circumstance" as it blared over the sound system.

And then Cole, as he hit the carpeted floor, saw his parents sitting in the tenth row. They were in aisle seats and he would have to walk right past them. His father looked impassive and his mother's eyes glittered. She held a box, wrapped in white paper and tied with a silver bow.

Their presence felt like a reproach. Cole broke into a run, passing the two boys in front of him, who immediately began to run after him. It turned into a stampede, the boys yelling over the nervous laughter of their parents. Cole slammed open the door to the lobby and ran out to the street, leaving the others to jump and shout and slap each other's backs. Cole never wanted to stop, not until St. Mark's and Janet and his parents and Susan and everyone else he'd ever known was so far behind him that even his memories of them had faded to sepia.

He ran until he got to the hearse, the stiff leather lace-up shoes burning his feet, his breath coming hard. He got in and started the engine and then, in the fullness of his freedom, realized that he had nowhere to go.

He drove through downtown and turned north on Central Expressway, windows down, radio cranked, holding a steady 5 miles an hour over the limit. Maybe his original intention had been to exit somewhere. He blew past the suburbs of Richardson and Plano and McKinney, finally reaching the open countryside of US 75 about the time the radio signal began to break up. He switched the radio off and watched the flat farmland and parched grass and heat-stunted trees flash by in the silent circle of his headlights. He had the road nearly to himself, the darkness broken only by a waning half-moon and a million stars.

He stopped for gas in Sherman, 15 miles from Lake Texoma and the Oklahoma border.

"You sure are dressed up," the attendant said. Lanky kid, greased-back hair, stained white T-shirt. "Where's the party at?"

"Dallas," Cole said. "I must have taken a wrong turn."

"Sure as hell did. Everything the way you're headed is Oklahoma."

Oklahoma. Susan's future home, his mother's birthplace. He'd turned four in Tulsa and had vague memories of prairie grass and tornado warnings. North of Oklahoma it only got worse. Kansas, Nebraska, the Dakotas. The Badlands. The guy was right. If he'd had any sense he'd have headed south. He'd have been halfway to Austin by now. San Antonio, Laredo, Mexico. He handed the guy a five. Easy enough to fill the gas tank, harder to recharge his motivation.

He checked his watch. Eleven-fifteen. He could make it to Potter's house in an hour, where things would just be getting interesting. If Janet didn't want him anymore, somebody else would. And if not, there was sure to be booze.

THE HIPPIES IN HAIGHT-ASHBURY were advertising it as the Summer of Love. As far as Dave could tell, no one had bothered to confirm that with Biafra, engaged in a bloody war of independence from Nigeria, or with the Arabs and Israelis, or with the Communist Chinese, who had exploded their first hydrogen bomb, or with the unemployed and desperate in Detroit or here in Spanish Harlem.

It was certainly not going to be the Summer of The Lovin' Spoonful. Word had gotten out that Zally had narked on Bill Love to keep from being deported, and the underground had lashed back. Flyers showed up telling people to boycott their records and concerts and asking girls not to have sex with them. Jake claimed that everything had been arranged, that the Spoonful had a lawyer who was going to get Love off, except that Love had gotten indignant and refused to cooperate. Then the band fired Zally, supposedly over the bust, but really because of the rift with Sebastian. When Jake complained, they fired him too. Dave turned down the chance to replace him, partly out of loyalty to

Jake and partly because a Spoonful without Zally, though it did mean no more Fischel jokes, was unthinkable.

It didn't look like it was going to be Dave's summer either. He'd quit Columbia at the end of 1966 to focus on Sallie Rachel, and he'd been unable to find the freelance engineering jobs that he'd been counting on. His savings were melting away.

It had taken three months to get from that table in the Kettle of Fish back in October to the half-dozen acetates of "Daughters of the Moon," co-written with Ellie Greenwich, that Dave had shopped to the majors. Tom Dowd had come through with a couple of hours with his best players: Bernard Purdie on drums, Chuck Rainey on bass, Cornell Dupree on guitar, Richard Tee on piano. Sallie had charmed them and Dave had let them follow their instincts, and the result was a cross between Ramsey Lewis jazz-funk, Julie London sensuality, and Judy Collins folk-art-rock. After Atlantic signed her, Dave hired the same guys to finish an album's worth of tunes, then dubbed in a horn section for added punch.

The "Daughters" single cracked the *Billboard* Top 40 and got Atlantic behind the LP, which hit the racks on the first day of spring, March 21, 1967. Atlantic had always been a singles house, and they were thrilled when the album sold well and kept on selling.

Sallie had never stopped flirting with him. There had been three AM cab rides after the studio, giddy with exhaustion and high on their own creative juices, when it had been all Dave could do not to call her bluff, not to lean in and kiss that amazing mouth from which such wondrous things emerged, not to put his hands all over that supple body. Mostly it was fear that held him back, fear that she was only teasing, or that she might give in for the wrong reasons. Most of all he was afraid it might jeopardize the work.

Albert Grossman had signed on to manage her, and he had her opening for Peter, Paul and Mary within a week of the album release. Dave took her to La Guardia, and at the gate she threw her arms around him. The last time she'd hugged him had been outside the Kettle of Fish on the night they'd met, and he told her not to do it again. Just as then, she smelled of shampoo and peppermint soap and her body was warm and soft.

"I'm scared," she said, holding on tight. "You made this whole thing happen for me and I don't know what I'm going to do without you."

"You'll be fine," he said. He had trouble breathing.

"Can I call you? And write you?"

"Any time you want."

"Thank you. Thank you for everything." One of her tears ran down his neck.

"You earned this," he said.

That had been three months ago. Now it was the end of June, and having not heard from her in those three months, he flew to Minneapolis to see her open for the Butterfield Blues Band. He thought he would surprise her after the show. The minute she came on stage with her 12-string and said, "Hey there, everybody," dressed in tight jeans and a low-cut spaghetti-strap top, glowing with relaxed energy and confidence and charisma, he realized, in quick succession, three things: that she didn't need him at all, that coming to see her was a terrible mistake, and that he was in love with her in the same desperate, hopeless way he'd been in love with the other Rachel when he first met her in high school. The largely male crowd went crazy for her and she egged them on while Dave, in agony, barely noticed what she sang. As soon as Sallie left the stage, Dave took a cab to the airport, changed his flight, and was home before dawn.

THE LAST HURRAH for The Chevelles was inscribed on the band calendar on Alex's bedroom wall, July 29, a Saturday night at the Studio Club, and Alex had been staring at it all month. Both Gary and Mike wanted time off before they went east to college. The band had gotten as far as you could go without a single on the radio that might hook you onto a package tour.

Lying beside the pool on the 24th, Alex put the thing he'd been thinking into words. "Let's go to San Francisco."

Cole, face-down on an aluminum lounge chair, said, "What, right now?"

"Next week, after the band breaks up."

Cole turned on his side to face him. "Are you serious?"

"Sure, why not? I want to drop acid. I want to see the Jefferson Airplane. I want to ball some hippie chicks. I want to be able to say I was there when it all went down."

"If it's been in *Life* magazine," Cole said, "it's already happened."

"What else are we going to do for the next four weeks? You going to just sit around and moon over Janet?"

"No," Cole said. "That's over."

Alex had learned when to back off. After a while Cole said, "Let me think about it."

THEY LEFT on Monday the 31st. Alex couldn't remember the last time he'd been so up for something. He'd convinced Cole to bring the hearse and their guitars and amps, which were crucial to the half-assed dream that he was nursing. Anything could happen, he'd told Cole. What if they got a chance to jam with fellow Marksmen Steve Miller and Boz Scaggs, who were in a band together out there? What if Grace Slick wanted to check them out?

Cole had built a plywood platform that fit over the gear when it was laid flat. The air mattress and blankets lay on top, so that from the outside it looked like there was nothing there you'd want to steal. They'd scraped the Chevelles' name from the back window and now it could pass for one more hippie wagon, nothing to see here, move on along.

In homage to the song and the TV show, they drove to Amarillo to pick up Route 66. In the middle of nowhere, you would suddenly find yourself on a stretch of Interstate 40 and then, as you approached a town, you'd be on 66 again. They stopped for the night at the Royal Palacio Motel in Tucumcari, a long, low expanse of floor to ceiling windows, overlooked by a juniper-studded butte. The man behind the desk explained, "It's the lawsuits. Towns along the highway are suing the federal government for bypassing them with this Interstate swindle. The only place they can do any construction is out in the middle of nowhere."

"Swindle?" Alex asked.

"You betcha." He was in his 60s, losing most of his white hair, his skin overcooked by the sun. He put his elbows on the counter and leaned forward, lowering his voice. "They got deals with all your big chains, your Howard Johnsons, your Best Westerns, to get the franchises on the exit ramps. You know they made some money on that one. Cut the local businesses right out of it. There's lawsuits over that too, not that it'll do any good. How far are you boys going?"

"All the way," Cole said. "California."

The man nodded. "Well, good for you. Enjoy it, because what you're seeing are the last days of the Mother Road. Another few years, won't be a mile of it left."

That night, as they watched TV, Cole noodling away on his Mexican acoustic, Alex said, "What about that guy at the desk? Flipped out over the Interstate Highway System."

"I don't know," Cole said. "I thought it was kind of sad. It's like getting old means watching everything you ever cared about get fucked up."

"That's us," Alex said. "We're the fucker-uppers." He switched to his Smokey Robinson falsetto and sang, "Get ready, 'cause here we come."

THEY DROVE ALL DAY Tuesday, spent the night in Flagstaff, and detoured Wednesday for a look at the Grand Canyon. By the time they were pointed west again, the sun was setting. They agreed to keep on through the night to Barstow, since the hearse's air conditioner didn't do much more than put a strain on the engine. Besides, the radio reception was better.

After Barstow, 66 turned south for 150 miles to San Bernardino. They followed it anyway, having already decided to take the scenic route, through Los Angeles and then up the Pacific Coast Highway to San Francisco.

They spent their single allotted day in LA at Disneyland. As hokey as the place was, as overrun with fat tourists in Madras shirts and Bermuda shorts and camera cases, Alex had grown up with the Mickey Mouse Club, Davy Crockett, Spin and Marty, and all the rest. If you didn't look too hard, you could ignore the chicken wire and stucco and still see the fantasy. The fantasies took another direction after they picked up a couple of local girls in New Orleans Square at lunchtime. They were both 16, with a tendency to giggle, lots of mascara, and short shorts and bikini tops. The four of them took the Submarine Voyage and rode the Skyway to Tomorrowland. They saw the House of the Future and drank Cokes and ate hamburgers and cotton candy. On Tom Sawyer Island at dusk, Alex got his date behind a tree for kisses and a handful of bikini, but then at 9:00 the girls suddenly said they had to meet their parents at the main exit.

The next morning Cole got them up at dawn and they didn't stop for breakfast until Oxnard. Afterward Cole dozed in the passenger seat while Alex followed the highway to the sea. The ocean was half-hidden in fog and the brownish-gray cliffs that towered over them were speckled with green-gray ice plant, stretching upward on his right as the land to his left fell away. The road had only two lanes, leading into one blind curve after another, in the midst of scenery too beautiful to ignore. Alex felt a wave of contentment so powerful that he knew his brain chemistry had been jazzed by something in the salt air that blew through the open windows. Which was perfectly fine with him.

In the course of the day, the stunted trees of southern California mutated into giant redwoods, the air turned appreciably colder every few miles, the red tile and stucco architecture gave way to wooden houses with shingled sides, and deserts gave way to moss and wildflowers. They stopped for dinner in Monterrey for Cole to see the original Cannery Row that his hero Steinbeck had written about. The literary history didn't matter to Alex, who was happy enough to be in a place that was nothing like anyplace he'd ever been in his life, all weathered wood and fish smells and row upon row of shacks rising uphill from the sea. They'd heard reports of an amazing music festival there in June, all traces of which were long gone.

They were both exhausted, so they cut inland from Monterrey to 101 for the last two hours of the trip. They already had a motel reservation, thanks to his father's AAA, at the Great Highway Inn, where Golden Gate Park met Ocean Beach, only three miles from the epicenter of Haight-Ashbury. Cole, paranoid as usual, made Alex help him carry in the amps and guitars before they crawled into their individual queen-size beds and slept for twelve hours.

ALEX WAS THE FIRST one up. He'd slept hard enough to be disoriented, then a faint tidepool smell reminded him where he was. Rather than open the drapes and risk waking Cole, he slipped behind them for a look. Through encrusted salt on the windows and heavy fog, he saw the Great Highway and 20-foot dunes on the far side. The ocean, he assumed, could be found from there.

He slipped into a pair of jeans and a T-shirt and eased the door open, then quickly closed it again. The air was cold and damp as a Texas November.

"Alex?" Cole said.

"Drop your rocks and grab your socks. You might want two pair."

They'd brought long sleeved dress shirts and sport coats just in case, and with those over T-shirts and jeans, and thick white athletic socks under their Jack Purcells, they were almost warm enough.

The woman at the office recommended a diner named Louis', a mile north on the Great Highway. As the road climbed uphill, they passed gray beach and gray ocean, and steep islands a few yards offshore that swarmed with seal and gulls. From their booth in the restaurant they looked down on broken concrete walls and flooded pools at the edge of the ocean. The ruins were part of the Sutro Baths, their waitress explained, the world's largest swimming pool complex back at the turn of the century. It had burned down only the year before. Alex visualized portly men in tank tops and women in ruffled skirts and leggings to their knees, passing around bootleg gin in monogrammed flasks, driving home in roadsters to heavy meals of stuffed grouse and beef Wellington. He was still high from yesterday's drive, from being in a city, unlike Dallas, that had an authentic history, from the Spanish conquest to the gold rush to the construction of the Golden Gate Bridge.

"Is it always this cold?" Cole asked the waitress. She was their age, with pigtails and freckles.

"Well, you know what Mark Twain said. 'The coldest winter I ever spent was a summer in San Francisco.'"

"Is there like a Goodwill or something where we can get some warmer clothes?"

"Everthing's picked over because of all the kids. And nothing's open on Sunday. If you go down to the Mission District tomorrow, there's some thrift stores there. Where're you from?"

"Dallas," Alex said.

She couldn't quite keep herself from recoiling. "Oh."

"We didn't actually kill Kennedy ourselves," Alex pointed out.

"I wasn't even there in sixty-three," Cole said.

"Sorry," she said. "I'm sure when you hear 'San Francisco' you think earthquake."

"Not anymore," Cole said. "Now it's 'wear some flowers in your hair.'"

"I appreciate that you didn't," she said. "Have you been to the Haight yet?"

"We're headed there now," Alex said.

"I don't imagine I can talk you out of it. But be careful. Leave your wallets locked in your car. Don't eat or drink anything anybody hands you on the street. Are either of you claustrophobic? Problems with crowds?"

Alex and Cole looked at each other. "Is it really that bad?" Alex asked.

"You'll see for yourselves. Also, there were two murders last week, both of them dealers. 'Shob' Carter and a guy they called 'Superspade.' They're all dealing speed now and it's getting ugly."

After a short, stunned silence, Cole said, "There's still music, right?"

"They passed an ordinance against music in the park. There's still, like, the Fillmore and the Avalon. Though they're not in the Haight."

"Is the Fillmore open tonight?" Alex asked.

"Every night except Monday, all summer long."

"Are you going to be there?" Cole asked.

She was not taking Cole's bait, Alex noted with pleasure. "Not a chance. My parents won't let me near the place. The drugs, for one thing, and any minute that whole neighborhood could go up like Detroit."

She left to put their order in. Cole collapsed in his seat. "Wow. Not what I was expecting."

"Wait and see, okay? She's pretty straight. She might be exaggerating."

On their AAA map, Golden Gate Park was a wide strip of green that ran due east from the beach to Haight-Ashbury, narrowing like a hypodermic needle to a block-wide extension called the Panhandle. Lincoln Way, the main drag that ran the length of the park, was bumper to bumper. Alex navigated while Cole drove, and finally he said, "We're pretty close. We can walk it from here." They circled the block to find a parking spot, stuck ten dollars apiece in their jeans pockets, and hid their wallets under the false bottom in the back.

They had barely stepped into the park itself when a kid who couldn't have been more than 15, cultivating the faint wisps of a future mustache, walked up to them and said, "Acid? Speed? STP?" Cole waved him away before Alex had the chance to consider the offer.

The park turned out to be a series of grassy fields broken up by walls of trees, mostly pines and cedars. The streets that cut through it were jammed with cars. On the grass, kids threw Frisbees, played guitars, made out, read, argued, slept. The fog had melted, leaving a gray sky and damp, chilly air. Some of the guys had taken off their shirts in an excess of optimism. A few were as young as 14 or 15, most were in their late teens or early twenties, four males for every female. For every hippie stereotype with long hair or a handlebar mustache you saw ten lost-looking runaways, their hair in the first stages of unkempt, wearing clothes their parents had bought them, their faces drawn, cold, and hungry.

Eventually they climbed a low hill and emerged into the chaos of the Haight.

Cars idled by, windows closed, faces pressed against the glass.

Mobs of people threaded through the traffic, kids crowded against middle-aged tourists slung with cameras. A Gray Line tour bus inched its way into the right lane, an amplified voice saying, "... far side of those pillars is the famous Hippie Hill, where the flower children can be found lighting up a 'joint' and 'grooving' on Mother Nature, or even 'tripping' on LSD, or 'acid' as they call it..." Human voices competed with car horns, motorcycle engines, and a cacophony of music from car radios, open windows, and street performers.

They stopped short and Cole stared at him incredulously. "It's a zoo."

"With no cages."

"Can we go back to Dallas now?"

Alex ignored him, taking in the sheer scale of it. He wished Cole would pull his head out of his own cynicism long enough to be curious about this thing that was exploding in front of them. What force had brought all these people here, what need, what longing? Runaways, acid-heads, and straights, the seekers, the believers, the gawkers, all responding to a desire that didn't have a name yet, a desire for more meaning, more connection, more experience.

It was a desire that Alex understood.

Cole, meanwhile, had stopped to stare at a girl dancing on a nearby strip of grass. She was maybe 20, some kind of Oriental, wearing a black silk kimono with nothing underneath. She swayed from side to side, disconnected at the hips, fast then slow, arms rising and falling, eyes closed. Her face was ecstatic, the music she was hearing entirely in her head.

"Yeah, okay," Cole said. "A little longer."

If it was girls you wanted, they were everywhere, in Granny dresses, in long skirts and sweaters, in jeans and T-shirts, in ponchos, in fatigues, in Greek fishermen's hats and cowboy hats and floppy newsboy caps, in headbands and with long hair blowing free. And Alex did want them, all of them.

He led the way between the cars and let the press of bodies carry them north and then east. Two- and three-story Victorian frame houses lined both sides of Haight Street. They had bay windows and intersecting gables and ornate trim, and most of them were in decay. The ground floors had been converted to shops, and Cole stopped at the first one and stared at a poster taped to the inside of the glass. "Holy shit," Cole said. "The Doors *and* the Yardbirds!"

"When?" Alex said. "Where?" You couldn't name two bands they wanted to see more. "Light My Fire" had been inescapable for the entire month of July and they'd both played the album constantly, second only to *Sgt. Pepper*. And Jimmy Page of the Yardbirds was Cole's guitar hero.

"The Fillmore," Cole said. "I'm trying to read this goddamn thing." The blue on green letters swayed and swirled into each other, drawing your eye down the page into melting orange peacock feathers. "Yardbirds Tuesday Wednesday Thursday only," Cole translated. "Doors Friday Saturday Sunday only. James Cotton and Richie Havens all week."

"July twenty-fifth to thirtieth," Alex said. "We missed it."

"Fuck," Cole said. His shoulders slumped.

They merged into the crowd, then immediately flattened themselves against the wall as a couple of Hell's Angels, complete with Nazi helmets, goggles, leather vests, and boots, idled their Harleys down the middle of the sidewalk. The one in the lead, skeletally thin, grinning with a mouthful of bad teeth, looked like something out of a fifties horror comic.

Across the street Alex saw an old movie palace, renamed, according to the marquee, from the Haight Theater to the Straight Theater. A list of apparent band names followed, though Alex had never heard of any of them—Clover, Melvin Q Watchpocket, Colours, Preston Webster. He pointed the sign out to Cole, who nodded, still clearly bummed about the Fillmore.

Half the storefronts sold hippie paraphernalia—handmade jewelry, roach clips, rolling papers, leather belts and hats, posters, plaid bedspreads from India. They were trying to sell it, anyway. The tourists weren't buying, and the street people couldn't afford the boutique prices. The rest of the stores predated the invasion and their days looked to be numbered—Sherman Williams Paint and Hardware, art supplies, ladies' dresses, a couple of liquor stores, a CPA, even, ironically, a barber shop.

By the time they'd gone four blocks down Haight, they'd been offered drugs five times, hit up for spare change seven times, and once asked if they were looking for "action" by a scrawny, jittery-eyed character who flashed them a Polaroid of two underage girls naked and unconscious on a bare mattress.

As they pushed past, Cole said, "Did you see that?"

"He probably found the photo in the trash, and now he's using it for some kind of ripoff."

"I don't know, man, this is seriously creeping me out." He turned in a full circle. "Where are the cops *now*?"

"The guy's gone," Alex said. "They'd never find him in this crowd."

They came to an expanse of plate glass below a hand-painted wooden sign that said, "The Psychedelic Shop." Alex recognized the name from something he'd read, and he pulled Cole inside. Along with the usual drug and fashion items, the shop carried records that Alex had never seen before—sitar players from India, folk guitarists from the UK, calypso singers from the Caribbean. In the rack next to them were singles and LPs by local bands with names like The Mystery Trend and The Serpent Power and The Chocolate Watchband. Cole's portable record player waited for them in the motel room and Alex wished he'd brought more money.

The shop also sold tickets to the Fillmore. Another ornate poster, this one featuring a round face surrounded by green and blue tendrils, promised them the Buffalo Springfield along with Muddy Waters and Richie Havens that very night. Starting Tuesday it would be Mike Bloomfield's new band, The Electric Flag, with Moby Grape and something called the Southside Sound System. That poster was, at least, less of a struggle to read—red and brown, incorporating a photo of the band and bunting and an eagle. They bought tickets for both shows, miniature versions of the posters, for three dollars each. If he'd had more money, Alex would have bought the posters too, to put up in his new room on Castle Hill in Austin. Assuming, of course, that nothing happened to derail his college plans in the next few days.

The guy selling the tickets looked to be 30, already losing his kinky, uncombed hair. Alex asked him, "Is there like a bulletin board around here for musicians to find each other?"

"Try Love Burger across the street. Or you can walk down to the Panhandle. There's so many musicians down there you couldn't fire a shotgun without hitting a couple of dozen. Which might not be a bad idea, now that I think of it."

As they walked away, Cole said, "What's this with the bulletin board?"

"I just thought musicians looking for a gig would be into jamming. I mean, that's why we brought our stuff, right?"

They crossed over to Love Burger, a lunch counter run by a woman with fiery red hair and some kind of Middle Eastern accent. The smell of frying meat was irresistible. They bought burgers for a quarter and Cokes for a dime and ate standing up in front of the bulletin board.

The board was hopeless. Hundreds of messages were stuck on with thumbtacks, paperclips, staples, or bits of tape, all overlapping, some merely stuffed between the layers. Loose cards and paper scraps fluttered to the floor whenever Alex touched anything. They offered a litany of sadness—parents looking for missing kids, kids looking for somewhere to crash, for any kind of job, for lost dogs and wallets and jewelry. So many musicians were looking for work that you couldn't narrow them down to a handful to call. "Maybe we should try the Panhandle," Alex said. Cole shrugged.

Alex's burger was tasty, if a little on the greasy side, reminiscent of the burgers at Dirty's in Austin. Underneath the cooking smells was the pungent odor of incense and aromatic oils. All the tables were full, the diners spilling over into the shared space of the Pall Mall Bar. A number of the customers looked like they'd been living on the street and were eating out on the change they'd collected that morning.

They jostled their way outside. The next intersection was Ashbury, where a cop leaned against the pole that supported the sign with the iconic Haight and Ashbury names on it. Tourists surrounded the sign, snapping photos relentlessly.

"Give the place credit for a sense of humor," Alex said. "Assigning a cop to have his picture taken."

"He's probably there to keep them from stealing the sign," Cole said.

Two blocks north, the street was broken in two by the Pan-handle. Giant cedars and conifers extended out over the pavement, and the overcast sky darkened the green of the grass. People slept on the few benches the city had provided. Suddenly Cole snapped to attention. He had clearly heard something other than the clusters of two or three kids playing acoustic guitars. As he followed Cole, Alex heard it too—bass first, the longest sound waves travelling the farthest, then the smash and rattle of drums, the hollow garble of amplified voices, the drone of electric guitars, and finally, filling the upper register, a police siren.

Past a stand of trees, they found the scene of the crime. Some enterprising musicians had run a couple of heavy-duty orange extension cords across Oak Street from one of the old houses, enough to power a couple of amps with vocal mikes plugged in next to the guitars. Four cops, one for each musician, waded in, making throat cutting gestures, and a kid with shoulder length hair and aspirations toward sideburns popped the strap on his cheap Harmony bass. The drummer was already tearing down his cymbals. The cops looked bored, the musicians aggrieved, and whatever audience they'd had was departing with casual haste.

Cole and Alex sat on the grass and waited while the cops stopped traffic to let the kids trundle their gear back across Oak Street and wind up the cords. According to the bass drum head, the band was called Paisley Octopus. The kids looked young, 16 or 17. After the cops left, Alex tilted his head toward where the kids now sat, instrument-free, on their front porch, and Cole shrugged.

The kids were laughing as Alex and Cole walked up. "Hey," Cole said. "What's happening?"

"We just set a new record," said one of the guitar players. His curly hair had mostly ended up on one side of his head. "We got in an hour and seventeen minutes before getting busted. Did you hear us?"

"Just missed it," Alex said. "What kind of stuff do you do?"

"Blues," the guitar player said. "Electric folk. Raga rock. You know. The usual."

As they talked, Alex let on that he and Cole played. They

adjourned to the living room and smoked a couple of joints, then instruments got passed around. The kids were not that far along, and when Alex and Cole did an impromptu version of "Laura Lee" on borrowed guitars, an uncomfortable silence ensued.

"Shit," the bass player said. "You guys are *good*."

They left shortly after and Alex saw that Cole's mood had lightened. It was after 3:30. "What do you want to do?" Alex asked.

"Fuck this scene," Cole said. "Let's go to the beach."

ALEX WAS USED TO the Gulf, which in the depth of winter was not as cold as the water off Ocean Beach in August. They both waded in and immediately waded out again. The afternoon was hazy, with a brisk wind off the water. Gulls glided into the face of it, making cryptic noises, as kids spilling over from the Haight wandered shivering up and down the dunes.

The hotel sent them to a Thai restaurant around the corner for dinner. Afterward they walked up to Geary and caught a number 38 eastbound bus crammed with kids headed for the Fillmore, decked out in scarves and top hats, tiaras and capes, vests and walking sticks and pith helmets.

As their waitress had said, the Fillmore neighborhood was a full-blown ghetto, the side streets dark in the last of the daylight, full of old men in undershirts sitting on stoops and drinking from bottles in paper sacks, junked cars, skinny dogs running in packs, barred and boarded windows.

The auditorium occupied half a city block, and the white kids shuffled slowly in from a line that stretched around the corner and downhill. Cole and Alex got on the end of it, in between a clutch of faux-Victorians and a threesome in Army surplus that smelled like it hadn't been washed in a while. Everybody talked too loudly and smoked too many cigarettes. The smoke was rich in pot, though the source was not obvious. Alex was excited too. He hadn't been to a concert since Dylan, mostly because there hadn't been any, nothing beyond the occasional teenybopper package tour.

Alex wanted to keep his ticket, and the guy at the top of the red-carpeted stairs refused. "You want the ticket, go back outside." The pressure of the crowd kept Alex from lingering in the entrance hall. He saw a barrel of apples, and glass cases with newspaper and magazine articles about musicians and "youth culture." Then he was through into the ballroom.

The room was so long, the ceiling so high, that you could have been outdoors. The tall, narrow stage took up most of the far wall, stacked with amplifiers and three different drum sets. The lights were low, the room less than a third full. White bedsheets hung on the walls, serving as screens for slides and home movies. In one corner, a bar served soft drinks and a grill sold hamburgers.

"So much for brown rice," Cole said, and Alex once again had to restrain an impulse to grab him by the shoulders and shake him out of his aloofness. The room quickly filled with smoke and incense and bodies. Everyone knew everyone else. They congregated by drug preference, wide-eyed here, giggling there, fast-talking over there. He and Cole were outsiders on any number of levels, straight among the stoned, dressed in their prep-school blazers for warmth, ignorant of half the conversational topics, from Diggers and com/co and a drug called FDA to the Flame and Dr. Sox. Did Blue Cheer refer to the detergent, a variety of acid, or a new band? Well, probably not the detergent. Alex kept his mouth shut and they moved on.

At eight the lights faded down. Cole grabbed his arm and pulled him to the front of the house. A short, older guy in a pork-pie hat stood at the center microphone, speaking in a low, modulated voice with a hint of an East Coast accent. "Ladies and gentlemen, will you please welcome a wonderful singer from New York City, Mr. Richie Havens."

A deep baritone voice said, "Thank you," and started to sing "San Francisco Bay Blues." At that same moment, the light show splashed color across the stage. Alex was surprised at how similar Duncan's show at the Studio Club had been—the film strips, the strobes, the vibrating blobs of dye, the spookiness of it.

Havens was a black man with a closely trimmed beard and wire-rimmed glasses, perched on a stool. He had a battered Guild acoustic in open tuning, which he chorded with his thumb while another black man played lead acoustic guitar.

People immediately began to dance and a wave of emotion rushed up Alex's spine and exploded in his brain. The amount of pot smoke in the air had to be a factor, and the rest was pure contact high, the ecstasy of being in the same room with over a thousand people who were, chemically or otherwise, lifting off together, in love with the moment they were in. He began to move without conscious intent, his feet somewhat restricted by the grip of his tennis shoes on the hardwood floor, his hips twitching to the beat, his hands rising on their own and pulling his arms after them. He was aware of Cole watching him with a mocking look, so he turned his back to avoid being brought down. A woman danced in front of him in a T-shirt dress that hugged her body from neck to knees. Her eyes were shut and her frizzy blonde hair whipped from side to side. She was older, maybe early thirties, with a long face and an inward smile. Alex dug the idea that they were dancing together without her knowing it. As the crowd shifted, he ended up dancing in front of a bearded guy in a lumberjack shirt, and that was all right too. He soon lost track of the individual songs, and eventually he found himself winding through the auditorium in a line a hundred people long, holding hands with a man in front of him and a woman behind, weaving intricate patterns that Alex could see like glowing contrails when he closed his eyes. Havens wrapped up his cover of "High Flying Bird" singing about the sit-down, can't-cry, gonna-die blues and a dozen of them collapsed on the floor, their feet pointing to a common center, and Alex imagined looking down from the ceiling and seeing the giant flower they formed, like the June Taylor Dancers on the *Jackie Gleason Show*.

A voice said, "Are you high?" It was the guy in the lumberjack shirt, sitting up now.

"Just on the music," Alex said.

"Do you want to trip out?" The guy held out a square of paper in the palm of his hand.

"Sure," Alex said, not giving himself time to think about it. He sat up and put the paper under his tongue. "Thanks."

"Have a good trip, brother," the man said. He got nimbly to his feet, extended a hand to Alex, and pulled him up as well.

Apparently Havens was finished. Recorded music came over the speakers, a heavily syncopated Cuban song from the fifties. Alex's father, who even then had been on his assimilation trip, had never played any Latin music in the house, and you never heard anything but trios and mariachis in Guanajuato. Alex felt like he was hearing the rhythm for the first time, and the complexity blew his mind, the way it pushed and pulled against itself, every measure speeding up and slowing down without losing its steady beat. A space opened up in the middle of the floor and Alex pushed his way over to see the guy in the pork-pie hat dancing with a tall, dark-skinned woman. He moved with confidence and style, a big, crooked smile on his face as he spun her two, three, four times at a crack, until she became a blur. He swung her out and in again, their hips undulating, her arms shooting straight up, sweat flying off their faces. Alex saw that Cole, on the far side of the circle, was into it too. When the song finished, the guy swooped her down almost to the floor and she threw her head and arms back in total surrender. The crowd applauded wildly. The guy set her on her feet, tipped his hat, and disappeared. Another song came on and some of the audience tried to replicate what they'd just seen, making a hash of it, laughing and bumping into each other. Alex made his way over to Cole.

"Where'd you go?" Cole asked.

Alex found that he didn't have the words. He held up his hands, looked around, made vague gestures. Cole would likely be pissed off when he found out about the acid, so Alex held the secret close for the moment, a private joke all his own.

Cole, always good at reading Alex's moods, turned away rather than pushing for a resolution. Alex wandered off, took a hit off a joint as it passed by, and then, as the Springfield was being announced, noticed something he'd never realized before, that the air was made up of small, intense dots of color, like the four-color lithography in comic books. If he focused on any one of the dots, it zoomed around like a firefly. The band started to play a song he knew well, though he couldn't think of the name. He knew it was the last song on side 2 of their album. A funny place to start, at the end. The notion struck him as quite profound. And the music. The music was made of discrete particles too, only much larger, each one like a flaming comet swooping through the room, making an audible whoosh as it passed. The world was far more intricate and connected and colorful and tactile than Alex had imagined and the knowledge turned him on.

THE FIRST THING Cole noticed about the Buffalo Springfield was that Neil Young wasn't with them. Instead some guy with heavy eyebrows and a dark mustache played guitar alongside Stills and Furay. One more disappointment. Young's shimmery lead guitar was one of his favorite things about their album, and the live sound was not the same. Though Cole had to admit that the PA sounded better than any he'd heard before, loud without being distorted or painful.

Next up was a new song by Furay, "Nobody's Fool," which had a country feel that Cole didn't like. They did a decent version of "Clancy," and then Stills announced a song off their forthcoming album, *Stampede*, called "Rock and Roll Woman." Cole looked around for Alex to see his reaction to the idea of a new Springfield album. In vain.

He would never have predicted that Alex would go native this way, and it made him anxious. So many things to go wrong this far from home, from bad drugs to cops to getting mugged. Cole knew he would be accountable to Al Montoya if anything happened to Alex. And something was eating him that he wouldn't talk to Cole about.

Somebody now stood next to Cole where Alex had been earlier, a girl with ragged-cut brown hair and dark, smudged eyes. Short, thin, in loose jeans and a white T-shirt that had seen better days, a man's shirt over it like a jacket. She looked up at him and smiled and he said, "Hi," then looked back at the stage.

The new song had a hook like Muhammad Ali and built up to a big three guitar climax. Cole swayed to the music and so did the girl next to him, their shoulders or hips touching from time to time. What had started as accident turned to flirtation, the contact lasting longer each time.

The band played three more songs, ending with a ten-minute workout on their recent single, "Bluebird." The house lights came up halfway and the girl put her hand on Cole's shoulder. "Sorry," she said. "I'm a little unsteady. Haven't eaten in a while."

Cole, who recognized a hint and an opportunity, bought her a hamburger. They sat against a wall near the grill while she wolfed it down.

Her name was Becky and she'd grown up in Mobile, Alabama. She had the strongest southern accent Cole had heard outside of TV. She was "almost 17" and she'd hitched across the country to get away from her stepfather, only to be robbed within two hours of arriving in San Francisco. Her oversize purse had held her ID, her money, a change of clothes and extra underwear, and the list of people to call that she'd put together before she hit the road. She'd spent the night before in the doorway of one of the Haight Street shops. She'd come to the show with some people she'd met that afternoon, who she didn't entirely trust. She'd been drawn to Cole because he looked like "a gentleman."

The room darkened and Muddy Waters began to play. Cole, who'd always been indifferent to the blues, stayed put, listening to Becky. She was more than pretty, she was brave and vulnerable, looking down with genteel shyness one minute, and the next staring into his eyes and touching him on the arm or the leg.

All the while, as he was drawn to this girl and feeling serious possibilities, Cole was aware of the music too. The loose-jointed way the bass and drums framed the piano and guitars, the way the vocals and harmonica fit into the rhythm like gears in a machine, rickety at first listen, then too powerful to resist. Becky heard it too, swaying as she talked, finally saying, "I like this song. Can we dance?"

Cole looked at the dancers around him, waving their arms like they were giant underwater plants, or swooping and diving like birds. "I don't know if I can dance like that."

"Not like that," she said. She got up and so he did too. She came into his arms and slowly moved from side to side. "Like this." She smelled a little of sweat and smoke, of public restroom soap, of some distant, lingering sweetness. Cole, who hadn't danced since his two-stepping days in Tyler, let the music move his feet. He knew where a 12-bar blues was going, where it wanted to stop and start. With her holding on, the guitars burned into his brain. Muddy finished "Rock Me Baby" and went straight into "I Just Want to Make Love to You." Becky didn't let go, so they danced into the next song, her head burrowed into his chest, her breath warm against his skin.

Later they sat against the wall again, holding hands, Becky's head on Cole's shoulder. Alex walked up, eyes as big as saucers, like the dog in the fairy tale. "Oh, man," Cole said. "What did you do?"

Muddy was playing "Got My Mojo Working" for an encore and Cole barely heard Alex's response, except for the occasional "fantastic" and "amazing." He looked childlike and highly pleased with himself. Cole saw that it was useless to lecture him in his current state.

"This is Becky," Cole said. "Becky, this is my best friend Alex." Becky jumped up and wrapped Alex in a powerful hug. Alex stood with arms and eyes wide, still smiling, looking to Cole for a clue as to how he should react. Cole didn't know either.

Muddy finished, reminding people that he would be back for a second set later. Cole had other things on his mind. It seemed to be understood that Becky was coming to the motel with them. She and Cole walked downstairs with their arms around each other, Cole keeping his other hand ready to grab Alex if he started to wander off.

During the ride back, Alex tried to explain something about how so many people on the bus were tripping that they were no longer traveling through conventional space-time. It looked to Cole much like the reverse of the previous ride, only in darkness now, and with a different sense of anticipation.

At the motel, Alex asked Cole to play *Surrealistic Pillow* and then sprawled out across his bed. Cole got the stereo going and then stood in front of Becky. He was about to kiss her when she said, "Can I, like, borrow a toothbrush and use the shower? I want to be nice for you." Cole showed her which toothbrush was his and where the towels were. He started to back out and she said, "Hey, where you going?"

Cole hesitated.

"You don't have to be *that* much of a gentleman," she said.

They showered together, soaping each other's bodies and giggling like kids, Cole becoming so aroused that they started making love standing up in the shower and finished on a pile of towels on the bathroom floor. By the time they'd dried each other off and gotten into bed he was ready to go again and this time it took forever. She had a hunger in the way she kissed, in the ribs and pelvic bones that showed so plainly beneath her skin. She was literally hungry too—when they were done, Cole got into their road supplies to fix her a peanut butter and jelly sandwich and some potato chips.

He kept the music going for Alex, who had undressed and gotten under the covers, signifying his presence with an occasional "wow" when Cole changed the album side. At three AM, Cole put on the Grateful Dead, volume low, and crawled into bed with Becky. He was exhausted and happy, thinking about how he had never been able to spend the night with Janet, and how much he was looking forward to falling asleep with Becky tucked under his arm.

"Hey," she said, just as he'd faded into sleep. "Do you think your friend would want to ball?"

"What?" Cole said. "Alex?"

"I don't want him to feel left out. Only if you don't mind."

Cole saw then how wrong he'd gotten everything.

"You *do* mind, don't you." A trace of disappointment in her voice.

"No, man," he said. "It's cool. Whatever you want."

"You're sweet," she said, and kissed him on the corner of the mouth. She got up and padded naked over to the other bed.

"Hi," Cole heard her say to Alex.

"Hi," Alex said, sounding sleepy and pleasantly surprised.

"Want some company?"

Alex could say no, Cole thought. Cole would, if the situation was reversed.

Alex didn't say anything. Rustling noises. "Oh wow," Alex said.

Cole turned his back to them and put a pillow over his head. He could barely hear the Dead and Becky's and Alex's voices were no more than wordless murmurs, his rising, hers falling.

At some point he fell asleep. He woke up at dawn, and Becky was in bed with him again, curled against his back. It gave him a warm feeling at first, then he remembered what had happened.

When he woke again, she was standing over him, fully dressed. "I'm going to split now," she said. "Thanks for everything."

"Wait," Cole said. "Where are you going to go?"

"I'll be all right," she said.

"You don't have any money, or anyplace to stay." He got up, shivering in the morning chill, and found his pants on a chair. He took a couple of tens out of his wallet and crumpled them into her hand.

"I'm not a whore," she said.

"It's a loan. Till you get on your feet. You know where to find us."

She put her arms around him and kissed him. Cole resisted at first, then gave in to the warmth, becoming aroused again despite himself. "Such a gentleman," she said, and let herself out, a tentacle of chill fog snaking in as the door opened and closed.

Cole, still freezing, checked on Alex. Tucked in, deeply asleep, mouth open, snoring quietly. Suddenly paranoid, Cole did a quick inventory and verified that all their stuff was there.

And yet he still felt like he'd been ripped off.

ALEX WAS TORN between the need to proselytize and the inadequacy of language. Acid had changed him, and he couldn't explain that to Cole.

"I don't know," Cole said. "I don't think I can let myself get that out of control, not here. I don't feel safe here."

They were in their booth at Louis', eating breakfast at one in the afternoon, watching the seagulls glide into the murky pools below.

"You felt safe enough to bring a total stranger to our room."

"You didn't have any complaints last night."

"What, are you pissed that I got it on with her?"

Cole looked out the window. No doubt about it, he'd been assuming romance when all the girl wanted was a place to crash and a little hedonistic thrill. Cole needed perspective. This, Alex thought, was why you dosed your unsuspecting friends. The temptation was strong.

"We should have stayed in Los Angeles," Cole said. "It was nice and warm, we could go swimming, there's plenty of great bands there."

"Yeah, if you like the Mamas and Papas."

"I *do* like the Mamas and Papas."

"So do I, but you know what I'm saying. LA is plastic. This is where it's happening now."

"What exactly is it that's happening? Scrounging for spare change and freezing to death and getting so fucked up you don't know where you are? I'll pass."

"Last night a bunch of complete strangers got me high, took care of me, welcomed me into their thing. There was no judgment, no violence, no manipulation, no expectations. I was living in the moment, and it was fucking beautiful, man."

"I was living in the moment too last night. The real moment, not a hallucinated moment."

"I think you were hallucinating as much as I was," Alex said. "Maybe more."

For once Cole didn't have a comeback, which pleased Alex no end.

The next order of business was clothes. They took the hearse down to the Mission and hit a couple of Goodwill stores, coming away with sweaters, flannel shirts, and windbreakers. When they walked out of the second store, the sky had cleared and it was 70 degrees, golden sunlight sparkling off the buildings. They drove uphill to Twin Peaks, and from there you could see the Golden Gate and the headlands of Marin County, the whitecaps and the freighters steaming toward the Pier. Golden Gate Park was a green carpet that unrolled from the center of the city to the ocean.

The previous night's LSD paid Alex a return visit, giving him a momentary sense that he was not sitting on a hillside, but instead gliding through the slow afternoon, looking down on a peaceful world. The beauty of the view was so obvious and overwhelming that it didn't bear discussion. Even Cole had enough sense to see that.

Eventually they drove downhill toward the Marina. In places the grade was so steep that when you crossed an intersection, it looked like you were driving off a cliff. Cole inched his way forward, as always unable to trust his common sense or the example of the car in front of him, while Alex grooved on the roller-coaster thrill.

They took the first parking place the hearse fit into and spent the afternoon walking around. The freshly painted row houses of the rich, their pricey shops and outdoor cafés, made a potent contrast to the poverty of the Haight. They worked their way downhill to the circular Palace of Fine Arts, with its arches and friezes and pure-white dome, and through the surrounding parkland to a gravel path that led past grassy fields and marshes right up to the foot of the Golden Gate Bridge. Alex thought it all so fucking majestic and iconic and breathtaking and perfect, gulls flying overhead, fresh breeze off the bay, light that made everything seem like a painting.

On their way back, Alex spied a knot of hippies on the grass, pretending they weren't passing a joint. He walked over, leaving Cole on the path, and said, "Hi. We're new here. Is there any music happening tonight?"

The five of them looked at each other instead of him. Finally one of them, in a cowboy hat and mustache, said, "There's always music at the Fillmore."

Another one, with a big head of kinky hair, said, "Not on Mondays."

The cowboy said, "Oh, right, except Mondays. What about the Avalon?"

"Weekends only," said the guy with kinky hair, amused.

A girl, wearing a pea coat despite the warmth of the afternoon, said, "What about the Matrix?"

The kinky haired guy said, "I think there's a jam session there tonight."

The girl gave Alex directions, and the cowboy, his suspicions lulled, produced a joint from behind his back. It had gone out, however, and he seemed uncertain as to what to do about it. Alex thanked them and ran over to Cole.

"I found us a jam session," Alex said. "It's just up the street."

"Were we looking for one?"

"That's why we brought our equipment, remember?"

"Our equipment is back at the motel."

"We can use somebody else's equipment tonight, if we get to play."

"So we didn't need to bring our equipment."

"We'll need it if anything comes of it."

"What are you expecting to come of it?"

"I don't know, what's with the third degree all of a sudden?"

"What's with you, is the question. What's going on in your head?"

"I'm curious, that's all."

"About what?"

"About how good we really are. Are we good enough to play in the big leagues."

"And if we are?"

"Well," Alex said, relieved to finally get the words out, "I guess that would be the question."

"Would you do it? Would you blow off college and move out here and go for it?"

Alex chewed his lower lip. "I don't know."

"This is about your old man, right? About the house in Austin and going into the beer business?"

"I don't know. Maybe."

"You can tell him no, you know. He would do anything for you. If you want to live in a dorm, if you want to transfer to some big Eastern school next year, if you want to take a year off and bum around Europe. You don't have to drop out and move to San Francisco to be your own man."

"Maybe you don't. You've already split from your family."

"My family sucks and yours doesn't."

"You don't get it. I love my father. That's the problem. I wouldn't care about disappointing him if I didn't love him so much. Your father made it easy for you."

Cole preferred hearing that he had a monopoly on problems. You could see him wrestle with his emotions and then finally put them aside. "Okay, then. Let's go find out."

They ate fresh seafood at a café on Marina Boulevard and got to the Matrix at 8:30. It was bigger inside than it looked from the street, maybe 50 feet by 80, with a few widely scattered tables. The bar was by the door, and the stage, barely higher than the floor, ran along the wall to the left. At the moment, a guy who might have been a weathered 30 pounded away on a 12-string that was in dubious tune. He had a big nose, big lips, and big curly dark hair that he shook from side to side as he sang, making his voice fade in and out on the PA. His audience was almost entirely female, most of them very young. An enormous guy in a loud shirt, blazer, and dark beard sat next to the stage, evidently enjoying himself.

Alex had expected more, somehow. He looked at Cole, but Cole was scanning the faces in the club, no doubt searching for the girl from the night before, whatever her name was.

The woman behind the bar said, "Can I help you guys?" Her blonde hair was cut short and she wore a lot of eye makeup. She had on a man's white shirt, sleeves rolled to the elbows.

"We heard there was a jam session," Alex said.

"Yeah, well, it kind of got hijacked. You guys know Dino? Dino Valente? He wrote 'Get Together' on the first Airplane album?"

"Yeah, okay," Cole said.

"Once he gets going, that's usually it for anybody else. And his little harem there will sit and listen to him all night."

"You don't sound like one of the converted," Alex said. He pulled up a stool and so did Cole.

"I don't swing that way myself, and if I did, I hope I'd have better taste."

"Who's the big guy?" Cole said.

"I see you guys are new around here. That's 'Big Daddy' Tom Donahue from KMPX. He's Dino's biggest fan."

"Is it usually this slow?" Alex asked.

"You picked the wrong week. We usually get a few big names on Monday because the auditoriums are all closed. But the Airplane and the Dead just played the Expo up in Montreal. Big Brother is on their way to Denver. Quicksilver is probably over in Marin, lying in the sunshine. Hey, did you hear about George Harrison?"

"Did something happen to him?" Cole asked.

"No, nothing like that. He just showed up in the Haight around six o'clock."

"Holy shit," Alex said. "Is he still there?"

"Nah, he walked around a little and then split."

"I don't believe it," Cole groaned.

"He was in LA taking sitar lessons with Ravi Shankar and flew up to check us out. A chick I know was there, said it got a little freaky. This huge crowd following him around, you know. Trying to get him to play guitar and everything."

"'Summer of Love,'" Cole said bitterly.

"You should have been here a year ago," she said. "There were so many positive vibes, it felt like we could do anything. Stop the war, feed the world, stay high all the time."

"What happened?" Alex said.

"I guess we turned out to be a fad. Peace and love, the hula hoops of 1967."

AT THE HOTEL, Cole sat on the floor and leaned against the bed. He had his Twin next to him, turned low, and his Strat plugged in. He thought about the way Muddy Waters had played, the slap and sting of his guitar parts. Across the room, Alex turned on the TV and collapsed on the other bed. Cole ignored him, trying various two- and three-string grips. Playing the notes he remembered, and not getting the same sound. Muddy's guitar had a brittle quality that wasn't a matter of bridge pickup or treble boost. It was in his hands and in the life he'd lived.

COLE PUSHED to go back to the Psychedelic Shop on Tuesday, this time with more cash. The crowds had shrunk to half the size of Sunday's. Fewer tourists meant fewer panhandlers and fewer cops and less of a sense of desperation. Monday's warmth and sunshine had proved to be an aberration, however, and cold and hungry runaways still huddled on every block. Cole kept thinking he would see Becky among them, though he wasn't sure what he'd say if he did.

As they walked in the store, a record full of African conga drums was playing, and a chorus of voices was singing "Jin-Go-Lo-Ba" over and over. The same balding guy was behind the counter and he showed Cole the album cover. *Olatunji! Drums of Passion.*

"What are you guys looking for?" he asked.

"I don't know yet," Cole said. "Something I've never heard before."

He and Alex went through the racks. Most of the records were obscure folk recordings on Folkways or Elektra or Vanguard, or they were Indian sitar music, which didn't do much for Cole, or they were some other kind of foreign music from Africa or Asia. The rest were from local psychedelic bands.

"What's this?" Cole asked, holding up *The Guitar Player* by somebody named Davy Graham. They had multiple copies of several of his records.

The guy reached over the counter and flipped through the albums, pulling up an open copy of Graham's *Folk, Blues, and Beyond*. "This is the one you should start with," he said, putting it on the turntable. "Check it out."

Two hours later, Alex had bought a dozen albums, mostly blues, and a red, white, and blue diaphanous flowered shirt with a long, pointy collar. Cole had the Olatunji, the Graham, *Tim Hardin 1*, and a six-album set that the guy had forced him to buy called *The Anthology of American Folk Music*. "You're into Dylan? This is what Dylan is into." He had a "lightly used" copy that had the original cover art and notes, which he insisted were important.

They took it all to the motel and started listening, Cole with unplugged guitar in hand. He skipped around the folk anthology, liking a few of the "Ballads," not much of the "Social Music," and mostly intrigued by the "Songs." The thing was a puzzle that he didn't have the patience to solve at the moment.

Alex played a record by Robert Johnson called *King of the Delta Blues Singers*. Supposedly Johnson had met the Devil at the crossroads and the Devil had tuned his guitar for him. Johnson, who had been a mediocre guitarist at best, could suddenly play better than anybody in Mississippi. The record was nothing but Johnson and his guitar recorded live in a hotel room. Old and strange, like the *Anthology*, except that his playing had an irresistible rhythm, like two guitars at once, and he had the voice of a much older man.

That night they took the bus to the Fillmore again. Alex kept after him to drop acid, and Cole put him off. Clearly Alex meant to take it again, and Cole didn't want both of them high at the same time.

The Southside Sound System was a bunch of white guys from Chicago that Cole had seen on various liner notes—Charlie Musselwhite on harp, Harvey Mandel on guitar, Barry Goldberg on keyboards. They led off with "Wade in the Water," which Cole knew from the Ramsey Lewis version. Before the song was half over, Alex had disappeared, dancing away with his arms in the air. Cole focused on Mandel, who had some serious guitar chops, and told himself as often as necessary that he didn't need to go looking for Becky.

Except between bands, he decided during the break. As he walked around, most of the people he saw made him uneasy. Hippie had become a style choice, a role anybody could play, like the pirate he'd been for Halloween as a kid. Eye patch, bandana on his head, oversized white shirt, plastic sword. Anybody who saw him knew immediately what he was supposed to be.

More disturbing were the people who didn't have to play at being weird. LSD had harvested a bumper crop of nutcases from the fertile soil of the repressive fifties. Here was a guy spinning faster and faster until he fell down, then getting up and doing it again. Here was a guy with glazed eyes talking to himself under his breath. Tripping, needy, or schizo? Cole didn't intend to find out. He did worry about it happening to Alex, that acid might flip some switch in his head from "conflicted" to "crazy."

He was on the verge of a black mood, and not looking forward to Moby Grape, whose debut had failed to impress him when he'd listened to it at the Melody Shop in Dallas. But then the lights went down and the band hit the stage singing, "What a difference a day has made," and it knocked the air out of Cole's lungs. Three guitar players—a pretty one, a manic one, and one tearing off incredible licks with great tone and sustain. A first-rate bass player and drummer. All five of them singing, all of them on fire. The manic guitar player ran in place and waved his arms and sang alternate lines on the verses, splitting them with the bass player. Then they all exploded on the chorus. The audience, in turn, went wild at the end of the song, Cole yelling and applauding along with everybody else.

As the set progressed, Cole felt like he'd woken up after a troubled sleep. This was exactly what it was all about, these disparate parts fused into a relentless force, these multiple voices welded into a single instrument, this living proof that together was better, that we were none of us alone, that everything was irrelevant that was not music.

At the end of the forty-minute set, he leaned against a wall and closed his eyes and replayed what he'd just heard and seen, no longer looking for Becky or Alex, his sense of purpose renewed.

In comparison, the Electric Flag let him down. Neither the singer nor the material did much for him, though the horns had a nice punch and the rhythm section was tight. He studied Bloomfield's playing as if he were in class, admiring his technique without being moved emotionally. When the band finished with a long version of "Killing Floor," he considered waiting around for the second Moby Grape set, then decided he was ready to go home.

Alex was not.

He was tripping massively, pupils wide and shining, feet barely touching the ground. "These guys I met are going to a party in the Haight. You want to come along?"

"I just want to go back to the motel," Cole said.

"Go ahead, then. I'll catch up with you tomorrow."

Cole pictured Al Montoya staring at him as he tried to explain why he'd let Alex, out of his mind on LSD, go off with a pack of hippies, never to be seen again. "No," Cole said. "I'll come along."

Alex took a plastic envelope out of his pocket that held a dozen half-inch squares of construction paper. "You want to turn on first?"

Cole shook his head. Alex gave him a sad, condescending smile and led him to a foursome near the front door. Alex was having trouble remembering names, so they all introduced themselves. Chris, tall and bearded, top hat and cape. Guy, frizzy red hair and acne. Ben, short and round-faced, straight cut bangs like a medieval page. Deb, tall and rangy, tortoise-shell glasses, sharp nose, aloof expression.

Two blocks up Geary they turned into a side street. A black teenager in stained coveralls watched with narrowed eyes as they stopped in front of a light-green vw microbus. Chris patted his pockets and came up with a set of keys. "If you're not tripping," he said to Cole, "do you mind driving? It might work out better."

Cole considered the poverty of the two choices and finally held out his hand for the keys.

"Oh... can you drive a stick?"

"Sure," Cole said. Between the truck in Tyler, Janet's bug, and Alex's four-on-the-floor Monza, he'd had practice enough. Chris took the shotgun seat and the four others squeezed side-by-side into the back.

"You know where Buena Vista Park is?" Chris asked.

"Sorry," Cole said. "We're new."

Chris directed him down Fillmore Street to Haight Street. The brakes were grabby and the weight of six passengers made it hard to get moving on an uphill slope. Cole feared a cop would see him struggling to drive a busload of costumed freaks and take it as an invitation for a bust. The LSD in Alex's pocket had been illegal in California since the previous fall, and God knew what the others were holding. Sweat broke across his forehead.

A steep, tree-covered hill rose precipitously on his left. "Turn left past the park," Chris said. "Deb, do you remember the address?"

"How should I know? I never talked to the guy."

"Just drive around, maybe I'll recognize it," Chris said.

"Have you been there before?" Cole asked.

"No," Chris said.

Deb said, "He's going to try to pick up the vibe." The weary sarcasm in her tone confirmed Cole's guess that they were a couple.

Cole made a complete circle around the park, a mile in circumference, while Chris's internal radar remained mute. Cole saw that he could be driving all night. "Maybe we should park somewhere," he said, as they started the second circuit. A space appeared and Cole took it without waiting for a consensus. Despite the unfamiliar vehicle, despite two of the tripping hippies trying to give him directions, despite the narrowness of the space, he eventually got parallel parked and handed the keys to Chris with relief.

The buildings alternated between extravagant mansions and decaying or refurbished row houses. Up the street, the upstairs door of a duplex opened and light and party noises spilled out.

"Bingo," Deb said, with little enthusiasm.

It took five minutes to traverse the 100 yards to the party. Everybody had a lot of difficulty deciding what to leave in the car and what to bring with them. Once they got moving, they stopped to stare at the glowing cloud cover overhead or something on the sidewalk. At one point Alex lay face down on somebody's lawn and ran a single blade of grass between his thumb and index finger, over and over.

Inside the house, the lights were all off in the living room. Bodies sprawled on worn couches and overstuffed chairs and the threadbare Oriental carpet on the floor. The stereo played some kind of faux country music, guitar and banjo and fiddle and a nasal vocal that couldn't decide if it was mocking or not. They were butchering "The Cuckoo," one of the songs Cole had liked on the folk music anthology. In the brightly-lit kitchen, more conversations seemed to be happening than there were people. Cole helped himself to a beer from the fridge and pushed through the bead curtain to the living room.

Chris came up to him and said, "This isn't the right party. I don't know anybody here."

"Does it matter?" Cole said.

Chris's eyes lost focus. "Oh, wow. I hadn't thought about it that way."

Leaving Chris in contemplation, Cole explored the rest of the apartment. In the first of two bedrooms, a joint went around a circle while lit candles dripped wax on all the furniture. The second bedroom was dark. As he hesitated in the open doorway, he heard snoring, and what sounded like sex. It was not a mystery he cared to unravel.

In the living room, Alex sat cross-legged on the floor, talking earnestly to Chris. Deb had pulled an Indian bedspread aside and sprung a few Venetian blinds to look outside.

"Having fun?" Cole asked.

She dropped the blinds. "Chris says this isn't even the right party. But here we are, so…"

Cole offered his beer. She took a sip and handed it back. "Want one of your own?" She shook her head. He made one last try. "Want to sit outside for a while?"

She shrugged and followed him out, where they settled on the top step. The air wasn't significantly colder than it had been during the day. "How did you end up in San Francisco?" he asked.

"I was born in Ojai, came up last fall to go to San Francisco State. Tuned in, turned on, dropped out."

"You don't seem—how can I put this delicately?—very stoned."

"It affects everybody differently. Chris becomes one with the universe. I get a nice light show."

She expressed no curiosity about him, which left him with all the work. "What were you studying before you went the Tim Leary route?"

"The usual freshman shit. I was thinking of doing pre-med. But it all seemed so wrong-headed. Trying to pretend we're all mechanisms."

She was wearing only an oversize T-shirt and a pair of Capri pants, and she suddenly shivered with the cold. Cole put his arm around her for warmth, and she turned to look at him, as if to check his motivation. He leaned in to try a kiss and she jerked her head away. "Don't!"

He dropped his arm and looked away. "Sorry."

"I mean, good grief, can't we just have a friendly conversation?"

"Sure, but you could help a little. I feel like I'm pushing this thing uphill by myself."

"So since the conversation wasn't going well, you thought you'd jump my bones?"

Cole didn't intend to spend the rest of the night apologizing. "They are pretty nice bones."

"Well, I'm not into it."

"I divined that."

"I'm not mad or anything, I just..."

"Just what?"

"Is that what we do now? We drop acid, we go see some groups, we fuck somebody we don't know or maybe don't even particularly like, and then tomorrow we go out and do it again?"

"I don't know," Cole said. "I just got here."

"You and a hundred thousand other people. They all came looking for the party, for the drugs and the free love."

"So what is it we should have come for?"

She shook her head. "There isn't a name for it yet. I wish you could have been here in January and seen what it was supposed to be."

"You're talking about the Be-In?"

"Yeah. You know in all the old war movies, before they go into battle, they always synchronize their watches? That's what it was. The hippies, the politicos, the poets, the Diggers, the musicians, everybody, we all got in one place and we synchronized. We all understood what had to be done. Stop the war, stop discrimination, legalize psychedelics, end capitalism, free our minds, change the culture, change the world. You should have seen it. You know the Polo Fields?"

Cole shook his head.

"It's at the far end of Golden Gate Park, this giant outdoor grassy arena. Full to overflowing, tens of thousands of us. Leary, Ginsberg, Ferlinghetti, Dick Gregory, all the bands—the Dead, the Airplane, Big Brother, Quicksilver, as an equal part of the one big thing. We had so much energy there, you could light up a city with it. We did light up a city."

"What went wrong?"

She was quiet for a while. "What always goes wrong? It was all supposed to be free. Free love. Free music. Free everything. Only it's not. The food's not free and the rent's not free and love is not that free either. You know who Bill Graham is, right?"

"The guy who runs the Fillmore."

"There are people who hate him because he doesn't fit in. He charges three dollars a ticket, and he's inflated the prices the bands charge, and he's fucked over his competition. If you're late, you're fired, and nobody gets in for free, and he's always screaming at people because everything is supposed to be exactly the way he wants it. But you know what? If he didn't make a profit, there wouldn't be anyplace for these bands to play, and a lot of them would probably never have formed in the first place. So because he's a particular kind of obnoxious asshole, you can go to the Fillmore any night of the week and see a great show. You don't have to ask who's playing, you just go. You go to the Avalon, who knows when the show will start, whether the bands will show up, whether they'll be in tune or not. The bands don't know if they'll get paid and neither does the landlord. That's the hippie dream in action. That's where we are six months after everybody walked away from the Human Be-In and tried to make it stick. We're going to the Fillmore and not the Avalon, which is not even open on weeknights. We're seeing a show and dropping acid and getting laid." She gave Cole a wry, apologetic smile. "Present company excepted."

"I'm not sure I understand. Are you saying we all should be assholes like Bill Graham?"

"I don't know what the fuck I'm saying. What was your name again?"

"Cole."

"Well, Cole, you were right. It *was* nice to talk to you, once I helped. And now I'm going to toddle off to bed." She stood up and started down the stairs.

"Where are you going?"

"It's only a few blocks."

"Aren't you telling Chris?"

"He wouldn't remember if I did."

"Let me walk you." She raised her eyebrows. "No bone jumping," Cole said. "I'm from Texas, where chivalry ain't dead yet."

"All right," she said.

Cole stuck his head in the door and got Alex's attention. "I'll be back in half an hour," Cole said, and Alex nodded distractedly.

He and Deb crossed Haight and walked up to Page in companionable silence. "Do you like music?" Cole asked.

"I like to dance. If you asked me who played what in any of the bands we saw tonight, I couldn't tell you." She gave him another wry smile. "I've disappointed you again."

Page Street consisted of more Victorian row houses, mostly run down, and at three AM on a weekday people were out strolling in their hippie garb or sitting on their front steps playing guitars. One couple stood necking in a doorway.

"The bands here," Deb said, "they're not into making the individual musicians into stars. They're like little communes. The Dead have a house over on Ashbury. Quicksilver has a ranch in Marin. Big Brother used to live in a house down the street. That's part of what made this all so special. Only that's changing too. All the runaways trying to get a little piece of it, all the TV networks trying to put it in a frozen TV dinner package, all the record companies coming up from LA and throwing cash around."

She was quiet for a while, and then she said, very softly, "We thought it was the beginning, but it was already the end."

She stopped in front of a narrow three-story house with peeling gray paint. "I'll be safe now," she said. "Go back to the party. Thanks for walking me."

Cole took a step back and said, "I enjoyed it. Sleep well."

She gave him one more wry smile before she climbed the stairs and disappeared inside.

THE PARTY HAD THINNED considerably by the time Cole got back. He found a cheap Harmony acoustic guitar leaning against the wall and took it out on the steps, got it in tune, and played quietly for a while, pausing a couple of times for a fresh beer.

Around five o'clock Chris and Alex, Guy and Ben, and half a dozen others emerged in a cloud of marijuana smoke. "We're going to walk down to the beach and watch the sun come up," Chris said.

Cole put the guitar inside and followed along. He saw no reason to point out that the beach was nearly five miles away and that the sun was scheduled to rise in the east.

They paraded down Haight Street, past bodies huddled in doorways, past blowing scraps of paper and cigarette butts and puddles where people had urinated against the side of buildings, past an open second floor window from which Country Joe and the Fish's slow, dreamy "Bass Strings" floated out. One of the three women in the party, wearing a long, flowing dress and wire bracelets on both arms and both ankles, periodically spun around in a jingling, billowing tornado of color and Indian spices. Another noodled on a plastic Tonette. Chris had his top hat and cape on again and occasionally mimed a baton as he led the procession.

The dew was condensing on the grass as they entered Golden Gate Park. Cole's tennis shoes were quickly soaked. He let himself drift toward the third girl, with neither bracelets nor Tonette. She was dark-haired and compact, wearing black-framed glasses and well-worn jeans that dragged on the ground.

"Where are we?" Cole asked.

"San Francisco," she said. "Western hemisphere, planet Earth, Sol system, Orion arm of the Milky Way galaxy."

"I'm not tripping," Cole said. "I'm just new here. Looking for something more specific."

"In that case, we're on Hippie Hill. This is where George Harrison was yesterday. Or, to be precise, two days ago, since it's technically Wednesday now."

"Science major?" Cole asked.

"Journalism."

Her name was Valerie and she was a junior at San Francisco State. She'd tried acid and didn't like feeling out of control. She'd grown up outside Springfield, Oregon, where her parents grew hazelnuts. "Filbert farmers," she said. "Not how I saw myself."

As they walked she pointed out the sights. Kezar Stadium to the left, home to occasional NFL games. Carousel to the right. Japanese Tea Garden and Stow Lake. Speedway Meadow, named for a nineteenth-century horse track.

By the time they got to the Polo Fields, the sky had lightened behind them. The long night and the long hike had turned the parade into a trudge. The fields themselves were vast, the size of three football fields, sunken fifteen feet below the surrounding land and encircled by rough wooden bleachers. Kids huddled in the stands or lay in sleeping bags on the short grass, curled up with their backs against the horse barns north of the stadium. Cole wondered if Becky was one of them.

Eventually they emerged onto the Great Highway and a tired cheer rose up. They shambled toward the beach, Valerie running ahead of the others. Morning had fully arrived, foggy and cold, the gray of the ocean blending seamlessly into the gray of the sky. Up the beach a bonfire blazed, surrounded by bodies, most of them asleep in the sand. Cole sat on the edge of a dune and watched as the others ran and skipped along the firm stretch of beach where the tide had receded. Valerie joined hands with the woman in bracelets and the two of them danced in a circle, leaning further and further away from each other until they let go and tumbled backward, shrieking with pleasure, into the wet sand. The air smelled of fish and salt and, faintly, of exhaust from the highway.

Cole's eyes closed and he must have fallen asleep. When he opened them again, Alex was walking toward him. It took a long time. Finally Alex stood in front of him, smiling peacefully. "Let's go," he said.

As they crossed the highway to the motel, Alex said, "Did you manage to have any fun at all?"

"Something like that," Cole said.

ALEX DIDN'T WAKE UP until late in the afternoon on Wednesday. The first thing he saw was Cole sitting up in bed, playing his unplugged Strat. They went out to eat, then came back to the room, Cole to his guitar, Alex to the two underground papers he'd picked up the day before at the Psychedelic Shop.

The Oracle had evidently started out as a regular underground paper and then gone astray, evolving into a psychedelic literary magazine with themed issues, this one on American Indians.

It featured dizzying color art, complicated layouts that kept you from reading it in order, and rambling philosophical arguments. Along the way it had shed its sense of timeliness and community function—the current issue was dated June. The few want ads were selling something or looking for missing kids or lost property.

The Berkeley Barb was more like Dallas's *Notes from the Underground*, except the last third was ads for nude models and massage parlors, stag films and erotic toys, mixed with explicit personal ads. A few of the ads were from musicians, and Alex made some calls.

He eliminated the kid still living with his parents, the drummer who was so stoned he sounded like a stroke victim, and the organist who'd never played in public before. He was left with somebody named Frank who was staying at a ranch in Marin County and who'd been in a couple of bands as a rhythm guitarist and backup singer. He already had a bass player, but was willing to see what Alex could do. He had a line on a drummer and was mostly looking for a lead singer and a lead guitarist. Alex pitched it to Cole, who was willing to give it a shot. He called Frank back and made a date for the next afternoon.

The drive took them across the Golden Gate Bridge under bright sunshine and fast-moving white clouds. Alex was high again from being in a place that he'd seen in a million photographs and TV shows. The two supporting towers were like giant orange ladders into the sky, the suspension cables like monumental bass strings. The Bay was a pure, cold blue and the Marin hills ahead of them alternated pale rock faces with dense patches of vegetation.

Once on the Marin side, you were in the country, surrounded by redwoods and high grass. You'd see the occasional gas station or feed store on the roadside, built of unfinished lumber, with old metal or carved wooden signs. Traffic eased as you got further north, and Alex stuck his head out the window to suck in a lungful of the sweet, cool air. They turned off before San Rafael and drove west through San Anselmo, a Disneyland version of a 1950s small town. From there they skirted the edge of the mountain range that included Mount Tamalpais, and the road turned into a roller coaster flanked by massive trees.

Frank's directions were precise and got them slowed down before they turned in at his mailbox. They took a rutted dirt road into the forest for a painfully long mile and a half and eventually emerged into a clearing. On one side, a long, two-story house was in the process of slowly falling down, and on the other a barn looked out on a corral with a few horses in it. In between were three pickup trucks, from brand new to thirty years old, and a tractor. Next to the tractor was a bearded guy in a Hoss Cartwright hat, hair past his shoulders, with a Winchester lever-action rifle cradled in one arm.

Cole drove up to him and put on his best Texas accent. "We're lookin' for a fella name of Frank?"

"Barn," the man said.

Cole drove through the open barn doors and parked next to a beat-up station wagon. At the far end of the ramshackle building was a raised wooden platform with a double bass drum set. Next to it was a Marshall, the monster British amp that Alex had heard about but never seen, and a beautiful flame maple top Les Paul resting on a stand. Sitting in front of the improvised stage was a husky guy with long dark hair and a beard. Next to him was a skinny kid with lank brown hair, long enough in front to fall over one eye, putting a joint to his lips.

"Frank here?" Cole asked, and the skinny kid, in mid-toke, raised one hand and nodded. With the other hand he held out the joint, and Alex took it gratefully. It was the strongest dope he had ever tasted and he was immediately high. He offered it to Cole, who took a minimal sip and passed it on.

Frank finally exhaled and said, "How you guys doing?"

"It's beautiful out here," Cole said. "It's like paradise."

Frank smiled proprietarily. "Ain't it though? This is Doug, the drummer I told you about. I decided not to call the bass player today."

They unloaded and set up. After two more hits, Alex was floating so high that he saw acid-flashback sparkles at the edges of his vision. When he tuned up, he not only heard the notes beat against each other, he saw the ripples they made in the air. "That is amazing shit," he said.

"Home grown," Frank said. "That's what paid for the gear."

Alex realized that the guy outside with the Winchester was not just playing cowboy.

Cole, who hadn't had any more dope after the first sociable hit, said, "Want to try something?"

Frank tuned to them and kicked off a mid-tempo shuffle in A. The drummer was steady and simple, not touching his array of toms and cymbals. Frank had the goods—a nice touch, fat tone, tasty embellishments. His amp was so loud that both Alex and Cole had to turn up. When Cole punched his treble boost and started a lead, Frank went with him, playing fewer notes and lagging half a beat behind, weaving in and out of Cole's melody. Alex dug the spacey effect and closed his eyes to get caught up in it. When he opened them again, Frank was looking at him, nodding him toward a vocal mike.

The riff was close enough to "Rock Me Baby," so that's what Alex sang. Frank nodded his approval, and Cole started playing the lick from the Animals version behind him. Frank immediately played a tight harmony version of the part a third higher.

They dragged the song out for probably ten minutes and it began to get weird. Cole would drop back and comp some chords to let Frank solo, and Frank would comp along with him. As soon as Cole began a solo, Frank would play over him.

Finally Cole brought it to an end, looking more puzzled than annoyed, and the drummer did a big finish.

"Neat," Frank said. "Very nice."

"What songs do you know?" Cole asked.

"Songs?"

"You know," Cole said. "Beatles or Stones or Yardbirds, anything like that?"

"You mean, like, top forty shit?"

"Album cuts, whatever. What we don't know we can probably fake."

"That's not really what I had in mind. I'm not interested in doing anything anybody else has already done." He fished another joint out of his shirt pocket, lit up, and took a gigantic hit. As he held it in, he said, "My vision is of something organic, built up bit by bit by bit." There were no takers when he offered the joint. "Each note grows out of the note before it, through trial and error."

Alex saw that it was time to step in. "That's great for the long term. How about something we can play today? You're a really good player, you said you'd been in other bands, what'd you do with them?"

"Blues, long jams. The blues is like the soil that the music grows out of, dig? Endlessly fertile." He took a bottleneck off the top of his amp and played the Elmore James "Dust My Broom" lick, the joint hanging out of the corner of his mouth. "See what I mean?" He played the lick again and the drummer fell into the same shuffle rhythm as before. Alex had to give him credit, he was steady.

They stuck it out for an hour. When Cole tried to teach Frank one of their originals, Frank had trouble remembering the changes. They did a slow, 12-bar blues and then a weird jam that sounded like Butterfield's "East-West" where Frank retuned his guitar to all Ds and As. At one point Cole gently suggested that they take turns soloing. Frank shook his head and said, "That's not my vision, man. The guitars should intertwine, like two vines growing around each other."

Before they left, Alex bought two ounces of the incredible weed, which he hid inside the speaker cabinet of his Bassman. They hadn't been able to score any dope in the city, and having a stash again made the afternoon seem like less of a waste.

Cole, to Alex's surprise, was more amused than anything else. Once they were back on 101, Alex said, "Can we look for someplace to eat? That dope gave me some serious munchies."

"Sorry," Cole said. "That's not my vision, man."

THAT NIGHT THEY WALKED around the Haight after dark. The place made Alex edgy and you could see that Cole was close to freaking. Most of the stores had closed by eight PM, leaving the street people to take over. Clusters of men huddled in the shadows, throwing paranoid glances over their shoulders. Hollow-cheeked girls sat in doorways, smoking tiredly, probably available for the price of a meal and a place to crash overnight, not unlike Cole's friend Becky. Now and then Alex heard a few bars of distant music before the wind shifted and took it away.

"Let's get out of here," Cole said, "before something bad happens."

"And go where?"

"I don't know. Back to the motel?"

"We came a long way just to sit around a motel room. How about if we go back, you drop acid?" When Cole didn't immediately refuse, Alex said, "You'll never have a better opportunity. No parents to wander in, nobody to call the cops on you. Hell, I'll stay straight if it makes you feel more secure. I'll spin records for you, we can walk around in the park."

Cole was thinking about it.

"You have to try it at least once. If you don't try it, you'll never know."

"Okay," Cole said.

COLE FELT RECKLESS, exhilarated. Alex, clearly afraid he would change his mind, wanted to dose him then and there. Cole shrugged and put the scrap of paper under his tongue and handed over the keys to the hearse.

By the time they got to the motel, Cole was feeling precarious. An odd, formless anxiety, as if only the force of his will kept the ground solid under his feet and his body upright. Then he noticed that his hand left afterimages as it moved. He stopped on the walkway outside their room and waved his hand in front of his face slowly, then quickly. "Hey," Cole said. "This feels great."

"Told you," Alex said.

Inside, Alex put on a table lamp and threw a pink T-shirt over it. He stacked some pillows on the carpet in front of the stereo and said, "Make yourself comfortable." He cued up the first Grateful Dead album while Cole arranged himself and the pillows against the end of the bed. The objects in the room had haloes and the glow from the lamp spread through the room, turning everything a warm, friendly pink.

He felt a sudden rush of warmth for Alex. This Cole, sitting here in this motel room, this guitar-playing, hearse-driving, separated-from-his-parents, no-longer-a-virgin Cole was somebody that Alex had willed into existence. An irresistible impulse brought him to his feet and took him to where Alex was flipping through the stack of records against the wall. He pulled Alex up by his armpits and hugged him. Alex hugged back, and surprised Cole by kissing him gently on the cheek. Then Cole got distracted by the idea of human bodies, how stuffed they were with organs and blood and muscle, all of which were inhabited by bacteria and other organisms, using humans as transportation. We are all clown cars, he thought, and couldn't stop himself from laughing.

Alex took half a step back and held him by the elbows. "You're feeling it."

"Oh yeah," Cole said.

"I'm jealous. I wish I was tripping with you."

"Next time."

"Yeah," Alex said. "Next time."

Cole made for the pile of pillows. The carpet felt like high grass and made swishing sounds as he walked, so he took his shoes and socks off to feel it more clearly. They'd had a thick, lush lawn in Mountain Lakes, New Jersey, when he was 8 years old, and it made him happy to think that he still carried that lawn with him, verdant in memory despite the deserts of Egypt and West Texas.

When he sat down, the music hit him hard. He closed his eyes and fell into an infinite space, a space very different from the one where he'd been trapped by the anesthetic, a warm and happy space. Garcia's guitar flowed like a yellow-white waterfall of light over the mossy rocks of the bass and drums. The coals of Pigpen's organ, on the other side of the universe, warmed from orange to bright red as the wind of the music blew over them. Golden bubbles frothed up from another direction, releasing snatches of lyrics as they burst. The rhythm guitar wound through the other instruments like the copper-colored ash from a pharaoh's serpent on the Fourth of July. Farmer Frank's dream of intertwining melodies had now, literally, become Cole's vision too. The thought made him laugh again, a laugh that went inward rather than out.

Alex said something and the individual moments of time lost

their cohesion and scattered like playing cards from a botched shuffle. In one of them, Alex was asking if he was okay. Cole was confused, and didn't know where that moment belonged. Was it from an hour ago? Had it even happened yet? Here was a moment where the record side was over and he was listening to the textures of the silence, and here was another moment with music in it, maybe from before the record ended, or maybe from the other side. And here was a moment where Alex was saying, "Cole, say something, man, you're making me nervous."

I should say something, Cole thought. But what?

Here was Alex's hand on his shoulder. "Cole? Can you nod your head or something?"

Over there was Cole nodding. And a moment where he said, "I'm good. Listening to the music."

And another where he said, "Can you turn the record over?"

At some point Alex suggested a walk on the beach. At first Cole loved the waves that exploded into purple fireballs, the salt air that tasted of Cambrian, arthropod-filled seas, but soon the immensity of the water began to weigh on him. They crossed over to the park and lay down in a field. Half a moon glowed feebly behind the wall of cloud overhead.

"Remember in Texas how you could see the stars?" Cole asked.

Alex sang, "The stars at night/Are big and bright—"

Cole joined in. "Deep in the heart of Texas!"

"Da da da dee, da da da dee, shit, that's all I know of the goddamn thing."

"Me too." Without conscious intent, Cole said, "I'm homesick."

Alex was quiet a long time, and then he said, "Yeah. We can talk about it tomorrow."

Later, Cole got out his Japanese reel-to-reel and plugged in his guitar and played through one 30-minute side of tape, reverb on full, letting the music lead him through one change after another. He felt like he understood reverb for the first time. The music made a space in your head, and then the reverb gave that space a vast, echoing size, a dimension large enough to get lost in. He was reasonably sure he had the makings of at least three new songs in what he'd recorded.

His energy began to fade after that. Alex shared a joint of Farmer Frank's dope to take the edge off. Cole saw that he was coming down. His kidneys hurt, he was physically exhausted, and his emotions sank into a mire of deathly ordinariness that seemed to go on for hours. He and Alex lay side by side in Alex's bed, talking fitfully. Alex fell asleep before Cole did. Eventually, as morning lightened the drapes, Cole turned away from Alex and let go.

LATE FRIDAY AFTERNOON. Cole finally admitted that he was awake to stay. He rolled onto his back. Alex opened his eyes and gave him a sleepy smile. Cole, uncomfortable with the intimacy, got out of bed and said, "Need to take a shower."

Alex shrugged and Cole took clean clothes into the bathroom. He stood motionless under the hot water, feeling the pressure of Alex's expectations.

When they were both dressed and ready to go out, Cole knew he had to say something. "Thanks for babysitting me last night. It was... intense."

"Yeah?"

"I mean, it was really weird and interesting and... intense."

"But...?"

Cole made himself go on. "But I don't know how soon I need to do it again."

"That's cool," Alex said, a little stiffly.

"That's not a put-down, it's just..."

"Not your thing."

"It's not even that. It's like going to Disneyland or something. It's fun, but I wouldn't want to live there."

"To me?" Alex said. He was standing next to the dresser, and he spread his hand out on the mirror as if any second his fingers might dip below the surface. "*This* is not real. What I felt when I was tripping, what I felt from *you* when you were tripping, that's reality."

Cole suddenly remembered Alex kissing him on the cheek. Had that been a hallucination? "I'm not arguing with you, man. I'm not saying I'm right and you're wrong or anything."

"No," Alex said. "It's just about feelings, about your not feeling the same way I do."

When had Alex developed such a fierce stare? Had he looked like that before LSD? "It's not that big a deal, man."

"To you, obviously, it isn't."

"What do you want me to say? Do you want me to lie and say it was the greatest experience of my life?"

Finally Alex looked away. "No," he said. "I don't want you to lie." He took his hand off the mirror. "Let's go eat."

OVER FOOD, in an attempt to ease the strain, Cole said, "What do you want to do tonight? Last night was mine, tonight is yours."

"Let's find some women and get laid. It's supposed to be free love around here, right? Let's hold 'em to it."

They took their acoustic guitars to the park and did the same act they'd done in Mexico, substituting English lyrics where available. In an hour they drew thirty kids, sitting, standing, and dancing. After they wrapped up, Alex ventured into the crowd and cut out a pair of adequately attractive girls, one with short, sandy hair and the other full-figured with henna-red curls. Cole watched from a distance as Alex got the blonde laughing, then waved Cole over. Her name was Jennifer and the redhead was Doris.

Later, after a couple of joints of Farmer Frank's finest, after the lights went out and Alex and Jennifer began giggling under the covers of Alex's bed, Doris said that she had a yeast infection that made penetration unbearably painful. Instead, she gave Cole his first blow job, and if his heart was not entirely in it, other parts were.

Saturday morning they took the girls to a late breakfast, after which Alex coolly asked, "Where can we drop you?" The answer turned out to be a crumbling Victorian on the border between the Haight and the Fillmore ghetto. As Cole drove away, Alex folded his hands behind his head and said, "My friend, we could do that every night for the rest of our lives."

Cole didn't know about Jennifer, but Doris had been tough sledding in the conversation department. She didn't have much of a sense of humor, and her main pastime in her home town of Smyrna, Delaware, had been TV. She seemed as disappointed in Cole as he was in her, and he could not imagine spending the rest of his life that way.

The silence dragged on. Finally Alex said, "Yeah, okay, we're spinning our wheels here. When do you want to leave?"

"We could pack up and be out of here in an hour," Cole said.

Alex sighed. "Fuck it. Let's go home."

THEY PULLED UP at the house on Castle Hill on a Friday after-noon, August 18, a week and some before registration. When Alex saw that the remodeling was not done, his mood went to shit. He stayed in his car and left it to Cole to confront the contractor.

He'd enjoyed the drive down well enough, him in the Monza, Cole in the hearse, trading off the lead, goofing on each other when they passed. Whenever one of them found one of their favorite songs on the radio, he would honk and the other would search until he found the same station, so it had been "The Letter" and "Carrie Ann" and "Light My Fire" and "Higher and Higher" for the whole three and a half hours.

But now the future had arrived. What should have been four reasonably carefree years were tainted by the landlord gig his father had laid on him. The San Francisco trip, instead of giving him a ticket out, had only put a thin, invisible barrier between him and Cole over the LSD thing.

Cole came out of the house and bent over Alex's window. "He says he can wrap it up over the weekend, which is bullshit. He hasn't even started refinishing the floors. I'd say a week to ten days, minimum."

Alex would have to show the place anyway. By the time school started it would be too late. One more major pain in the ass.

"Which means," Cole said, "that on top of everything else, we've got no place to stay."

"Villa Capri?"

"Órale."

They scored the last available room at the motel, unloaded the hearse, put on swim trunks, and hit the pool. Alex let Cole swim his laps, then they stretched out side by side on aluminum lounge chairs.

"My dad is going to kill that fucking contractor, and then hang around here until everything is the way he wants it."

"No he's not," Cole said, "because you're going to call him up and tell him the situation and tell him you're handling it. You're going to tell him that you've assigned me to the work crew and instructed me to ride those guys until they get it done."

"You're volunteering for that?"

"Oh, hell yeah. I haven't gotten to do any carpentry since, you know. Since I moved in with you."

Alex looked to see if Cole was going to cop to missing his father. Apparently not.

"That's giving him exactly what he wants."

"You're going to end up there anyhow. This way it's a preemptive strike."

"I hate it that you're better at psyching out my father than I am."

"I've got some distance."

Alex didn't want to think about it anymore. "What are we doing tonight?"

"We could go hear some music. If we knew where to go."

"Susan'll know."

Alex went to the room to call her, leaving Cole to guard their lounge chairs. "Austin is not exactly the live music capital of the universe," she said. "There's the Jade Room, which is top-40 combos. The New Orleans Club, which is the same thing with an older crowd. That's pretty much it, except for private parties. You know, since it's Friday, what you really ought to do is go to Charlie's Playhouse. It's a Negro club on the East Side. They've got a great band on weekends."

"Are you serious? Is it safe?"

"The weekend crowd is mostly white. Don't worry. Jesse and I'll go with you."

Susan had brought Jesse to Dallas a couple of times since she'd officially announced the engagement. Alex's father liked him, and even Cole, instead of turning jealous and sulky, played gin rummy with him for hours at a time, a penny a point, invariably losing. Alex didn't trust him, didn't trust anyone who would volunteer for Vietnam. He had an urge to dose him with LSD at Charlie's Playhouse, and only the fear of blood-drenched headlines held him back.

"We can eat at the Hoffbrau first," Susan said, "if we beat the rush. We'll pick you up at six-thirty."

THE HOFFBRAU had been in the same location west of downtown since the 1930s. The wood paneling and the sheet metal grill and half the patrons looked to Cole like they'd been there since it first opened. The place was an artifact, Susan explained, of the collision of German immigrant and native Mexican cultures in Central Texas, the same collision that brought accordions to rancheras and put place names like Pflugerville on the map.

Susan wore a sleeveless minidress, white with yellow daisies, matching yellow hairband, and yellow Keds. She was energetic and happy to see them, and Cole couldn't take his eyes off her. She leaned forward in her seat and Jesse leaned back in his, a proprietary arm draped over her shoulders.

Cole had not managed to dislike Jesse, despite his best intentions. He'd been home from Nam for a year now and had let his reddish-brown hair grow over his ears and collar. Unlike Susan's previous boyfriends, he played only touch football and was an inch shorter than Cole, with a strong, wiry build. He was laid-back, confident, handsome, and he treated Cole and Alex like favorite younger brothers.

Susan paid cash for the steaks and afterward Jesse drove her T-bird east on 11th Street, over I-35, and into a different city. Tufts of grass growing out of the cracks in the sidewalk, windows with plywood instead of glass, houses with paint that had blistered and peeled to the gray boards underneath. Jesse drove four blocks, turned into a side street, and parked.

"You're not going to put the top up?" Alex asked.

"We come here all the time," Susan said. "It'll be fine."

On the sidewalk outside the club, a black man in a white suit and Panama hat was telling a story that involved a lot of large gestures to a uniformed white cop, who had his hands in his back pockets, laughing.

Two-thirds of the people inside were white, all crowded on one side of the room. It was not yet 8:00 and the band was nowhere in sight. Jesse grabbed one of the last tables on the white side and they all sat down. "Just so you know," Susan said, "there's no mixing allowed. White people can't share a table or dance with colored."

"I thought segregation was illegal," Cole said, and Susan shook her head and smiled like he was simpleminded.

Once the tables filled, people lined up along the walls and then around the edges of the dance floor. The band was called Blues Boy Hubbard and the Jets and they came on shortly after nine. Seven of them, counting trumpet and sax and a lead singer, all dressed in tuxedos. Hubbard, the guitar player, had a cream-colored ES-335 that he wore high on his chest. He came out swinging, playing a fast shuffle with stinging single notes, choppy chords, and flurries of speed picking. The band was tight without being dry, the horn men hitting the ensemble sections in lockstep and throwing out solo riffs with casual ease.

Cole felt like he'd muscled his way in on his white privilege. As much as he admired the musicians, the music itself tasted of bootleg gin and flop houses, pig's feet and back alleys, dusty overalls and hoodoo, a life and a culture completely alien to his experience.

Alex, on the other hand, was transfixed, clearly not suffering the same doubts as Cole. Gary from The Chevelles would have been in hog heaven, Cole thought.

Couples moved onto the dance floor, mostly black at first, doing a modified jitterbug that didn't take up much room, the couples revolving in tight circles or the women turning under their partner's arms. If Cole let his eyes go out of focus it was like clothes in a washing machine, the couples surging toward each other and away again in a rhythmic pulse.

The next number was a mid-tempo blues and Jesse and Susan squeezed their way onto the floor. They slow-danced the way the other white couples did, the way the kids at the Studio Club did, mostly standing in one place and swaying. Some of the black dancers, however, did things Cole had never seen in public before, women grinding against a man's leg thrust between their legs, men's hands traveling down the hourglass of armpits to waist to hips and coming to rest on the buttocks, women being dipped within inches of the floor. Cole found it disconcerting to watch, especially the lascivious looks on the men's faces.

A few songs later another slow one came around and Susan leaned across the table. "Come on, Cole, let's dance." Cole looked at Jesse, who shrugged and smiled, the picture of self-assurance.

Cole, nervous as a feral cat, was not about to miss this chance. They found a few square inches of floor and Cole put his arms around her. She smelled like a summer garden, heady like flowers, with a damp, earthy scent underneath. He couldn't get enough of it. "I don't know how to do this," he said in her ear.

"Sure you do." He felt the heat of her body against his chest. She put her right foot between his feet, rested her forearms lightly on his shoulders, tickled his chin with her hair. He had one hand all the way around her back to her shoulder blade, the other half-way to her waist. The song was "Stormy Monday" and he felt the chord modulations coming, tried to shift his weight with them, one-two-three pause, one-two-three pause. All their contact was above the waist and Susan moved with him easily. He turned as he stepped in double-time at the end of the verse, following the guitar as it hammered away on the V chord.

Was she aware of what she was doing to him? Was she flirting or only trying to make him feel included? If she was flirting, was it all a shuck, or was there something real behind it? Deep in Hubbard's guitar solo he tried a move several of the black dancers were doing, slowly bending his knees as he rocked back and forth, taking Susan with him until she was straddling his right leg. She gently slapped the back of his neck and said, "Cole? Cut it out." He straightened up instantly, feeling the heat in his face.

For the rest of the dance he was terrified that he'd gone too far, only to have her slip out of his arms at the end, pat his cheek, and say, "That was nice."

Over the course of the evening he worked up his nerve and danced a few more times, once with a girl who was an entering freshman like him, freckled and innocent-seeming, there with her future sorority sisters, and once with a woman who must have been close to thirty, with dark roots and a gravel voice, who called him "hon" and talked him through dipping her until he got it. After that he danced with Susan again, and dipped her, allowing himself to fantasize briefly about what it would be like to go home with her to her trim little white-shuttered house.

By 11:00 Susan was yawning and the noise level in the club was climbing, the band cranking their volume to cover the noise of the shouted conversations. The air was thick with smoke and humid with sweat and Cole was relieved to get out into the hot night air.

At the Villa Capri, Susan got out and hugged Alex, then Cole. "Welcome to Austin," she said, and kissed his cheek. Then she got in the car with her husband-to-be and drove away.

REGISTRATION AT THE ancient, unairconditioned Gregory Gym was every bit as hellish as Susan had warned them. Cole was assigned a one PM slot on the first day and arrived to find a line that stretched out of the gym and down the block. He'd brought the latest Joe Gall novel, *The Star Ruby Contract*, to read while standing in line.

Gradually they moved out of the blazing sun, up the stairs, through the three massive doors, down another set of stairs, and up another set to the top of the bleachers. One row at a time moved down to the gym floor, and the other rows shifted down behind them. Sections of wooden fence, held in place by sandbags, corralled off the basketball court, with hundreds of students lined up at the various tables. For the first time, Cole began to comprehend the magnitude of thirty thousand students on one campus.

By the time he reached the third row, he was halfway through the book. Gall had been captured by a renegade Chinese regiment in Burma. After a lavish dinner, he was forced, at gunpoint, to watch a Kachin sword dance. Suddenly he was pinned to his chair, hands immobilized on the tabletop. One of the sword dancers darted in. "And there I was. Staring at my left index finger, parted neatly from my hand."

Cole shut the book. The bleachers tilted and he couldn't find his breath.

"You all right?" a deep-southern voice asked. It belonged to a compact guy with a Hawaiian shirt and blond sideburns that flared out past his earlobes.

"Yeah, I just… It's a long story."

"You need a drink of water or something, I'll hold your place."

Cole nodded, stood up confusedly.

"There's a fountain over yonder."

"Thanks," Cole said, and wove his way through the lines. He splashed water on his face and down the back of his neck. The temperature had to be close to a hundred, and the air smelled like old gym shoes. He stared at the stump of his middle finger, the horror of that morning returning in snatches—the ambulance, Jerry's body, the post-surgical nausea, the pain. The memory of the pain burned its way from finger to elbow, making him squeeze his wrist with his left hand.

He ran cold fountain water on the phantom pain until it stopped, and then he took a long drink. He dried his hands on his jeans and went back to the bleachers and introduced himself.

"Joe Maynard," the blond guy said. "Tupelo, Mississippi."

By the time they got called down to the basketball court, Cole had the rough outlines of Joe's story. His father was a lawyer and Joe was the youngest of four kids. His sisters had opted for community college and his brother for Ole Miss. Joe was more ambitious. He'd gotten good grades and done well enough in what he called "throwing events"—discus, shot put, javelin, and hammer—to have his pick of non-Ivy League universities. His father had wanted him in a conservative southern school like Vanderbilt, Duke, or Emory, and Joe had fought for UT instead. Fewer restrictions, a strong and modern English department. More women. Like Cole and Alex, Joe had made it into Plan II.

Joe was excited about being away from home, about starting

what he called his "real" life. Cole chose not to burden him with his own misgivings, which the registration process was only making worse. He felt like a tree being fed into the sawmill of the university, destined to emerge in four years as uniform pieces of lumber suitable for shoring up the decaying structure of society.

They made their way past the barricades to the English table, and found the tray of computer cards for the World Literature course. Joe reached for the cards and the irritable grad student behind the table snapped, "Don't! Lesson One, freshman, is do not touch the trays."

"May we have two cards, please?" Joe said, feigning contrition as Cole wondered how often fist fights broke out in the lines.

They both had to show their Plan II acceptance letters to get the cards. "Don't sweat on them," the grad student said, "or the computer'll spit them out. Then you'll really be in for it."

Holding their cards by the edges, they hit the other tables together. The 101 Algebra course Cole had signed up for was already out of cards. "They may open another section later," the math grad student said. "Or they may not. You can always try your luck at adds and drops next week." Joe had placed into an advanced course that Cole wanted no part of, so he took a Geometry card instead. They split up at the end so that Cole could sign up for Russian and Joe for German.

Cole understood that they were lucky to have gotten most of the classes they'd asked for. A day later, Susan had warned them, and they wouldn't have had it so easy. At the end of the maze they took their stacks of cards to another hostile grad student, who fed them into the computer and handed them their course schedules on sheets of 11 x 14 paper with pale green horizontal stripes.

He took Joe to Dirty's to celebrate. Over cheeseburgers he explained why the book had freaked him out and showed off his mangled finger. Joe had a few scars of his own from weekends spent fishing and camping. As they finished, Joe mentioned that his next job was to find a place to live, and Cole smiled. "This is your lucky day."

*

BY FIVE PM the outside temperature had finally started to drop. As far as Alex could tell, it was hotter than ever inside the house on Castle Hill. He'd opened all the windows and set up a couple of box fans to help get rid of the resinous smell of the tung oil that the workmen had used to finish the floors. He stood in front of the downstairs fan and let his sweat dry while he checked his watch again.

As Cole had predicted, the floors had only finished curing the day before. The contractor had hooked up the electricity and gas, but due to the crush of students, the phones had only been working for two hours. Haverty's was scheduled to deliver the furniture any minute, and Cole was still not back from registration. Alex wondered if he'd met some chick in line and was having his way with her in air-conditioned comfort.

At that moment the screen door banged and Cole walked in with a redneck in a loud shirt and ridiculous sideburns.

"Alex," he said, "meet our first tenant. This is Tupelo Joe."

Much as Alex wanted the whole renting business over with, he was not at all sure that this rube was somebody he wanted to share a house with. Nor was he thrilled with Cole having made a unilateral decision. As he searched for a polite way to say all that, the Haverty's truck pulled up at the curb and suddenly Cole and Tupelo Joe were helping to unload it and Alex was standing by the stairs directing traffic.

They'd picked out the furniture at a Haverty's in Dallas in July, Cole and Alex and his father, and Alex had watched in wonder as Cole talked his father into double beds for each of the rooms, solid wood desks and chests of drawers, and a foldout couch in the living room for his father's own use.

"Which one is my room?" Tupelo asked from the back of a box spring headed up the stairs.

"The middle one upstairs," Cole answered from the other end. "Between me and Alex."

They were done in less than an hour. Alex tipped the Haverty's guys then went inside, shut all the windows, turned on all the air conditioners upstairs and down, then sprawled in the middle of the living room with his arms outstretched. Tupelo lay down companionably a few feet away and Cole sat on the bottom of the stairs.

"This is a beautiful house," Tupelo said. "How'd y'all come by it?"

Alex had to admit, now that it had some furniture, it lived up to his first impressions, and then some—high ceilings, lots of light from the oversize windows, and the glossy oak floors.

"Alex's father bought it," Cole said. "It's his Austin beachhead for his crime empire."

"Y'all are pulling my leg now, right?"

"You never heard of the Mexican Mafia?" Alex asked. "La eMe? That's us. Drugs, prostitution, murder. Cole there is our top hit man."

"I wouldn't mind some drugs, now that you mention it," Tupelo said. "We can maybe bring in some of them prostitutes later on."

MADELYN'S FIRST TASK for the so-called Summer of Love had been to dispose of her virginity with the least fuss possible. She'd been on the Pill for three months and was as ready as she'd ever be. A number of boys had made clear their willingness to provide the service; she chose the sweetest of them. When the moment came, he was surprised at her lack of resistance, all the more so when she told him it was her first time. The act itself had been fun and exciting and only slightly painful, though it didn't end with the fireworks she'd hoped for, at least on her part. Apparently it was more than satisfying for her partner, who proceeded to fall in love with her. She hadn't anticipated that, and though she tried to break up with him as gently as possible, it was gruesome for both of them in the end. She saw that she'd been naïve to think it could be a simple, friendly transaction; she would remember that going forward.

She filled the rest of the summer with a minimum wage job at Skillern's Drugs and plans for UT. Her father had insisted on a private dorm for the first semester, until she "got her bearings." The contract specified a ten-PM curfew on weeknights, midnight on Saturday and Sunday. She supposed she could put up with it for four months. Even more iniquitous was the university policy that forbade coeds to wear pants or shorts to class; only dresses and skirts were permitted. The length of the hemline was not specified, and Madelyn planned to put that oversight to the test without delay.

As a Plan II student, she also had few options for her courses. She couldn't afford a car, and after paying for her dorm, her father would not have a lot left for an allowance. She suspected she might have to get a part-time job, despite her father's opposition to any interference with her studies.

With her dreams of freedom being smothered in the cradle, she put up only token resistance when he vetoed her idea of studying Arabic and pushed her toward Russian instead. "The Arabs," he said, "would regard an unveiled Western woman who spoke Arabic with the same lack of seriousness that they would a talking camel. Whereas the Soviet Union has transcended gender."

"Yes, Daddy," she said.

IN THE HALLWAY before her first Russian class, Madelyn recognized someone from her dorm, a petite girl from Denton named Denise Glover. Unlike most of her dorm mates, who sported items from the fall Neiman-Marcus catalog, Denise's appearance was subtly off, her hemlines in a no-man's land between ankle and knee, her palette too dark, her black, frizzy hair always out of control. This had already endeared her to Madelyn, so she took the opportunity to get her talking as they found two seats together near the front of the room.

Denise admitted that she was taking Russian from a purely practical viewpoint. "I can work as a translator until I can make a living doing what I really want to do."

"Which is?"

"I have no idea," Denise said, and put back her head and laughed.

That was when Madelyn had her second recognition of the morning. Three rows behind them sat a skinny guy with longish, wavy brown hair that she knew from somewhere. The Chicano boy next to him was also familiar.

The feeling nagged her through the first five minutes of class and finally drove her to a second look. This time she noticed his boots, which activated her memory of the St. Mark's party. Unfortunately, he caught her looking and offered her a cocky grin, which went on to remind her of the garage and his predatory stance over the perfumed brunette with the breasts.

She gave him her best I'm-here-to-make-a-return-not-a-purchase smile and faced the professor again. Interesting coincidence, she thought.

When the class ended, he blocked the aisle. "I'm Cole," he said, holding out his hand.

She pretended not to see it. "Oh, I know who you are. Lead guitar." She pointed to his friend. "Bass guitar."

"You have the advantage of me," he said, startled.

"Yes, it appears that I do, doesn't it?" She flashed her most dazzling smile. "If you'll excuse us?"

He stood aside and she and Denise made their exit. Denise, she was pleased to note, did not spoil the effect by looking back.

"Gracious," Denise said. "Who are they?"

Madelyn wondered if she'd ever heard anyone her age say "gracious" before. "A couple of private school boys from Dallas. A bit full of themselves."

"I think the tall one was interested in you."

"I suspect he's even more interested now. He needs a little air let out of his tires. He'll be able to grip the road better that way."

FIRST ALEX HAD TO go through Adds and Drops to get into the World Literature class he needed for Plan II. He barely pulled that off, and he was unable to trade his Economics class for Introductory Accounting like his father wanted. It was like a microcosm of the Soviet Union—shortages, lines, uncertainty, delays, bureaucrats, senseless rules.

Then there was the ordeal of the fourth roommate. Having confirmed that Tupelo Joe smoked dope, Alex didn't want to bring in a straight. His father was putting on the pressure and couldn't understand why he'd turned down three applicants in a row, one of them an ROTC cadet.

Last-minute salvation arrived in the form of Sunny, from Pakistan via Fort Worth. His father was a doctor, and Sunny himself was worldly to the verge of arrogance, dark-skinned and handsome, with a voice as mellifluous as a TV anchorman's and long hair that he flipped out of his eyes with a toss of the head. He'd missed registration because he'd been visiting Pakistan with his parents, a "minor issue" that was "being taken care of." He found the downstairs suite "suitable" and they negotiated a few specifics. Sunny was vegetarian and would use his own cookware, which he would keep in his room. Alex explained that there would be band rehearsals downstairs, that the basement was soundproofed, that they would never go past midnight. Sunny wrote a check for the first and last months' rent.

The next day, as Alex made the rounds of bulletin boards to remove his flyers, he found a hand-lettered notice on bright yellow paper: "Experienced drummer and organist seek singing guitar and bass players for top 40 combo with intent to pull down heavy bread on Fraternity Row." Alex copied down the phone number and brought it up with Cole that night.

"It's like fate or something," Alex said. "The exact pieces we're missing."

"Frat parties?" Cole said.

Alex had hoped for more enthusiasm. "That's where the big money is. Why, what were you thinking?"

"I guess I hadn't thought about it. Sure, what the hell, let's give 'em a try."

Alex made the call and set up an audition for the next afternoon, Saturday.

ALEX WAS DISMAYED to discover that the organ in question was a Hammond B-3, weighing over 300 pounds. Getting it down the basement stairs was an ordeal of another sort, costing strained backs and multiple bruises. This better work out, Alex thought.

Nolan, the drummer, had a double bass set, four toms, and five cymbals in addition to the hi-hat. By the time they were set up next to the organ and the cases were piled in a corner, the basement was smaller than Alex had hoped.

A dehumidifier had taken care of the dampness. The remodeling crew had turned them on to some salvaged acoustical ceiling tiles, which Cole had mounted on the walls, and they'd pieced together scraps of industrial carpet on the floor. Still, once you turned the instruments high enough to cover the drums, it got loud fast. It also got very hot, and with no windows, the box fans didn't help much.

Ron, the organist, had a sweet tenor that complimented Cole's and Alex's voices. Nolan's drumming was steady and he knew all the parts. Substituting organ for rhythm guitar changed the sound of a few songs like "Daytripper"—not, Alex thought, necessarily for the worse.

It came out fairly quickly that their band in Houston had been named The Other Side, and when Cole made a disgusted sound, Alex jumped in to cover for him. "We had a, uh, rivalry with a band called The Other Side in Dallas."

Ron had a long, shiny mane of blond hair that Alex suspected might be dyed. He smiled and said, "If you can't beat 'em, join 'em."

The Other Side and The Chevelles overlapped on two thirds of their song lists, though The Other Side did the white arrangements of songs like "Sloopy" and "Shake" and Ron preferred to keep it that way. "Give 'em what they know and love," he said.

They ran through "Good Lovin'" and "Land of 1000 Dances" and "Gloria," and then Ron said, "I don't know about y'all, but this sounds good to me. If we worked hard for a couple–three weeks, I think we'd be ready to get out and make some money."

Alex, expecting grief from Cole, said, "We should probably talk it over, maybe sleep on it."

To his surprise, Cole jerked his head to summon him into the corner. "I'm up for it if you are," he said.

Ron discreetly played ice-skating music to cover their voices and Nolan, in the way of all drummers, couldn't keep from playing along.

"Are you sure?" Alex said.

"Sure, why not? These guys are pros, that Hammond sounds boss, even if it is a bitch to move."

"Well, shit. Okay, then."

The four of them sat at the dining room table and hashed out the particulars. Sunny was in the kitchen and weird bean and curry powder smells wafted out of the pass-through.

"I can build a ramp," Cole said, "to help get that B-3 in and out. Maybe put a pulley inside the door."

Ron nodded. "Great idea."

"What about originals?" Alex said. "We've got a few from before."

Ron made a face. "We can do one or two if it's important to you. Basically we should give 'em—"

"—what they know and love," Cole finished for him.

"Hey," Ron said. "It worked for us."

"After they've heard our songs a couple of times," Alex said, "they'll know and love them."

"It's all right," Cole said, surprising Alex again. "Let it go."

"What about uniforms?" Ron asked.

"No uniforms," Cole said. "That's history. We should dress sharp, but not alike."

Nolan spoke up for the first time. "He's right. Uniforms are so 'Meet The Beatles.'"

"All right," Ron said. "Now somebody needs to handle bookings. I did it in Houston, and I know the game. I would want ten percent off the top if I'm going to do the extra work."

"I'm willing to try it," Cole said. "If it doesn't work out, we can switch to a pro."

"Fair enough. And the name? Are you guys all right with The Other Side?"

Cole laughed. Something sarcastic in it turned Alex off. "Sure," Cole said. "Why not?"

After Ron and Nolan left, Alex tried to get Cole to open up. Cole denied that he was acting weirdly. "We sound good together. We can get up and running in no time. Why shop around? Maybe it's like you said. Maybe it's destiny."

"I guess," Alex said. He was straddling Cole's desk chair while Cole lay in bed, playing "Laura Lee" on his unplugged Strat.

"Let's talk about something else," Cole said. "Let's talk about that strawberry blonde in Russian class. Miss Brooks." The instructor took roll by last name only.

"I don't know what the big deal is. I think she's stuck on herself. Her little friend is cute, though. Laughing all the time? Girls that laugh like that can be had."

"Perfect," Cole said. "You go after her friend on a second front. Your victory will open the way for me, like the Schlieffen Plan." He made a scissors with the index and middle fingers of his left hand.

"The Scheisskopf Plan. Look, it's Saturday night. You couldn't find your blonde girlfriend if you had to. We need some action, here." He ran down every option you could think of—a freshman mixer at the Union, Blues Boy Hubbard on the East Side, the dollar theater, even offered to take him dancing at the Broken Spoke, a country joint in South Austin that Susan had mentioned. Cole was uninterested.

Alex stood up. "Suit yourself, man. I'm going to get something to eat and see what I can promote at the mixer."

"Careful what you bring home. We could end up with your one-night stands camped out in the yard, throwing themselves at you every time you go in and out."

"Cole, what the hell is eating you?"

"Nothing, man, it was just a joke. Are you OTR tonight or something?"

"Ah, fuck you, Cole. I'll see you later."

"Good luck!" Cole said as Alex closed the door on him.

If anybody was on the rag, it was Cole—moody, secretive, tossing out those little backhanded cutdowns. Alex had never been with a woman who could piss him off as much as Cole.

He stopped by Tupelo's room, and Tupelo was up for the mixer. They grabbed a pizza on the Drag and then headed up to the Ballroom on the second floor of the Union. They showed their freshman IDs at the door and entered a huge, wood-floored hall. The outside wall had French doors down its entire length that opened onto a balcony. Massive chandeliers hung from the arched ceiling and overlit the room. A couple of tables against the long inside wall held a vat of pink punch and bowls of Fritos and dip.

At the far end was a band in matching jackets, missing the point of Wilson Pickett's "Funky Broadway." The drummer twirled his sticks like twin propellers, the organist kept raking one hand across the keys and throwing it in the air, the singer crouched and lunged all over the front of the stage, the guitarist hopped up and down, and the bass player, for contrast, stood motionless and stared over the heads of the crowd. All of their faces were stretched into fake smiles.

Is this what I got us into? Alex wondered. It was like a minstrel show without the blackface, a performance so artificial and stylized that it reminded Alex of the animatronics robots at Disneyland. He had a feeling that the old Houston Other Side had looked quite a lot like this, and that the new, improved Other Side might turn into more of the same.

The other thousand or so people in the room also looked like they had escaped from a previous decade. Most of the girls were in dresses that had been starched into suits of armor, the boys in slacks and button-down shirts and flat-top haircuts. When they danced, nothing moved below the waist. Though the boys out-numbered the girls two to one, Alex saw girls dancing alone or with each other.

"What's wrong?" Tupelo said.

"I don't know, man, this is not looking like my scene."

"You want to split?"

"Kind of."

"Don't worry about me. I'll catch a shuttle, or I can walk back."

"You sure?"

"Absolutely."

Alex toured the perimeter while the band went into a version of "My Girl" that involved a lot of shouting at the audience. Tupelo was on the dance floor with a short girl whose mouse-brown hair had been combed and sprayed into a perfect sphere. They slow-danced with virtually no points of contact.

On his way to the exit, Alex caught a familiar head-tossing gesture. Sunny had two girls with him, both knockouts, a blonde in bangs and a brunette in a ponytail. Both wore low heels, skirts above the knee, and form-fitting tops.

Sunny beckoned him over. "This is Alex, the capitalist tool who overcharges me for rent," he said without a smile. "This is Rhonda and Natalie."

Sunny had not indicated which was which. Alex shook hands with the blonde and said, "Rhonda?"

She didn't correct him, and the brunette waved. Sunny picked up where he'd evidently left off in a lecture about Islam. He seemed to have both girls hypnotized. When he came up for air, Alex said, "Where are you guys from?"

"Waxahachie," said the blonde. Waxahachie was the first city far enough south of Dallas on I-35 that it had not yet been absorbed. It had likewise failed to absorb any of Dallas's sophistication or pretentions.

"We came down together," the brunette said. "How long have you known Sunny?"

"I only got my capitalist tentacles around him on Thursday."

Neither of them cracked a smile. "Well," said the blonde, "that's two days longer than us."

Then Sunny was off again, starting with the medical career he had mapped out for himself, veering into the health benefits of vegetarianism, and ending up with an argument that vegetarian-tolerant Sufism was superior to the rest of meat-eating Islam. It was the last thing Alex would have dreamed of as a come-on, but, miraculously, it appeared to be working.

He made one last effort to cut one of the women out for himself. "What are you girls doing at UT? Shouldn't you be in Hollywood becoming movie stars?" Cole always got away with lines like that, yet it fell flat for Alex.

"We're here," the blonde said, "to make acquaintances that will be important to us all our lives."

The brunette's etiquette kicked in as if by reflex. "What are you studying?"

Say accounting, he told himself. Tell her you'll be taking over your daddy's multi-million-dollar company. "English, probably," he said. "I'm a musician."

Alex watched the last shreds of interest fade from both their eyes.

"Well, nice meeting you," he said. "I hope we continue to be important to each other." He put a hand on Sunny's back. "See you at the Castle."

As he walked away, he heard the blonde ask Sunny, breathlessly, "You live in a castle?"

The Varsity Theater, across the street, was showing *The Trip*, with Peter Fonda, so he wasted an hour and a half watching Hollywood anti-drug propaganda. He did get a few laughs out of the "trip" scene, as did a few others in the audience who obviously knew more about LSD than the writers did. Mostly the Mike Bloomfield soundtrack made him remember seeing Bloomfield on acid at the Fillmore, half a continent and a lifetime away. He felt old and sad.

He got home after eleven. The front of the house was dark except for faint purple light leaking past the blinds in Sunny's room. As he walked in, he saw that Sunny's door was ajar and heard a muted string quartet. Another faint light came from the kitchen, where the brunette stood in front of the open refrigerator door. She had nothing on but her knit top. A dark thicket of pubic hair was visible below the bottom of the shirt and the cold had stiffened her nipples. She smelled of incense and marijuana. Her eyes were bloodshot and dull.

"Natalie?" Alex asked.

"I'm Rhonda," she said. "Natalie's in the bedroom."

"Both of you?" Alex said. He failed to keep the amazement out of his voice.

Rhonda giggled. "Isn't it decadent? Oh, are those donuts?"

They were Tupelo's. "Those aren't for—"

He was too late. She'd already taken a bite out of one and speared a second with a long, red-tipped finger. She finished the first and licked her fingers, then her full lips. "The other's for later," she said, closing the fridge. "'Scuse me." She squeezed past him and walked unsteadily to Sunny's room and closed the door.

It's like I'm the hired help, Alex thought. It wasn't like he'd connected with her, emotionally or intellectually. It shouldn't have mattered. Yet it did. He went upstairs, rolled a fat joint from the diminishing stash of Farmer Frank's pot, and hoped for a mercifully swift end to the day.

MADELYN ARRIVED in Russian class Monday morning to find two long-stemmed roses on her desk, one red, one white. She glanced at Cole, who stared at the ceiling and pretended to be whistling innocently.

She confronted him after class. "What's this supposed to be, Lancaster and York?"

He tried, with mixed success, to maintain a grave expression. "Ah, Miss Brooks. The roses are a gift to you, free and clear. If you want to know about my thought processes, however, we're going to have to open some communication channels. I would need, at a minimum, your first name and phone number."

He still had his three-ring binder open. Juggling the roses and her books, she picked up his Bic pen and wrote the requested information in large letters across the bottom of his class notes.

"Excellent, uh, Madelyn. Can I call you tonight?"

"Tomorrow would be better." In fact she had no conflicts; his extortion scheme had merely left her feeling perverse.

He offered his hand to Denise. "I'm Cole."

"That's what I hear." She pumped his hand brusquely. "Denise. How come you don't have a first name?"

"My parents were too poor to afford one. This is my bass player, Alex."

They both shook Alex's hand, then Madelyn hustled Denise away.

"Alex is cute," Denise said. "Is he Mexican or something?"

"I fear we're going to get the opportunity to find out."

"What is it you have against these guys? They're cute and funny and if they went to private school they must be rich."

"And that would be the problem."

"How is that a problem?"

How to sum it up? She struggled for words and finally said, "I'm not... I'm not somebody's privilege."

"Gracious! Well, neither am I."

"I know that, dear. The problem is communicating it to *them*."

Cole, of course, called that night, as she'd known he would. Hope had often complained about this very thing; so much enthusiasm in the beginning, so quick to fade. She let her roommate answer the phone and then left the room so that it could truly be said that Madelyn was out. She didn't enjoy playing games, but she wanted Cole to listen to her.

He called again Tuesday night at 8:00 sharp. She liked to think that he had set himself that arbitrary target and then forced himself to wait for it. He was glib and funny, tossing off compliments that had a hall of mirrors quality, too smooth to be entirely believed, yet so extravagant as to resemble Trojan horses with real feelings hidden inside them.

"I believe you owe me an explanation," she said at last, "for the roses."

"Ah. Yes." For the first time he seemed uncomfortable. "Okay, well, to make it brief, the red rose is passion, the white rose is purity. The red rose is fire, the white rose is ice. You come on like the white rose, and I think you're really red."

It was as if, having charmed her defenses away, he had reached through the telephone to touch her under her clothes. His impertinence shocked her even as she caught herself wondering how he knew. A ploy, she told herself, a parlor trick. She tried to get her thoughts in order. "I guess I shouldn't tell you," she said, "that I kept the white rose and gave the red one to Denise?" In fact both roses sat on her nightstand in a Coke bottle full of water.

Very quietly Cole said, "You shouldn't tell me that if it's not the truth."

If white was ice, the ice was melting under her feet. "I take it," she said, equally quietly, "you intend to propose some sort of experiment to test your hypothesis?"

"A preliminary fact-finding session on neutral ground, with observers. You, me, Denise, Alex, dinner and a movie Saturday night. They're showing *Blow-Up* on campus and I've never seen it."

"I, for one, would not want to hold back the progress of science, but I can only speak for myself. I think Alex should submit his own agenda to Denise."

"Is she there now? We could put together the entire grant proposal tonight."

"Hold on, I'll see."

"Wait. You'll get back on with me after? To iron out the specifics?"

"Assuming the other principal investigators are on board."

Madelyn found Denise and brought her to the room. Alex kept her on the phone for ten minutes, most of which she spent laughing. When she was done, she handed the phone to Madelyn with an OK sign. Madelyn explained to Cole the arcane process by which he and Alex were to call for them at the downstairs desk on Saturday and they said goodnight.

"Well!" Denise said. "Did a tornado just blow through here?"

"Don't know yet," Madelyn said. "Wait till the casualty reports come in."

THE AWKWARD MOMENT always came, Madelyn thought, when you left the theater and found out how far your date's reaction to the movie varied from your own.

So far it had been an unexpectedly pleasant evening. The boys had arrived in, of all things, a Cadillac hearse, with Cole at the wheel. "I lost the toss," was all he would say. In the absence of a back seat, Alex and Denise sat on pallbearer's chairs that folded down from the sides. Alex explained to Denise that they used it to move the band's equipment; he failed to explain the double air mattress and blankets covering the floor, as ominous in their way as the hearse itself.

In a fit of nerves, Madelyn heard herself say, "I'm more of a sports car person. Austin-Healey, Triumph, MG? Not that I've ever owned one."

"I could see you in a sports car," Cole said.

"Maybe someday."

The evening, fortunately, improved steadily. Dinner was at

Matt's El Rancho, a Mexican place near Town Lake. The owner had decorated the red-painted walls with posters and other memorabilia from his previous life as a boxer. He escorted them to their table while Cole and Alex showed off their Spanish, asking him questions about his career. Her own Spanish was sufficient to get the gist and to thank Matt politely for holding her chair, which prompted Denise to complain that she didn't understand a word anyone was saying. The food was delicious, qualitatively different from the El Chico's fare that her parents occasionally sprang for in Dallas. The only uncomfortable moment came when Madelyn noticed the missing joint on Cole's right middle finger and asked about it. "Another time," he'd said, and she'd backed off.

As for the movie, Cole had been completely focused on the screen and, other than putting one arm on the back of her seat, had kept his hands to himself. She especially appreciated his silence during the scene where the photographer had not-entirely-consensual sex with two aspiring models.

Once they were outside, Denise took the lead. "Well," she said, "that went completely over *my* head."

"I liked the Yardbirds," Alex said. "Beck and Page both, did you see that, Cole? Otherwise, I'm with Denise. Pretentious, pseudo-intellectual, art-house drivel."

"Took the words right out of my mouth," Denise said, and laughed loudly.

Madelyn looked at Cole. He was in thrall to powerful emotions.

"Come on, Cole," Alex said. "You didn't like it, did you?"

"What did *you* think?" Cole asked her.

"Some of the symbolism was heavy handed," she said, "but the way it undermined its own mystery plot, and used that to make a statement about society, I thought that was pretty profound."

The approval in Cole's eyes was quite heady. "Yeah," he said. "Profound and really sad."

"It certainly choked *me* up," Alex said, putting his finger down his throat. Denise was predictably amused.

"Mock on, mock on, Voltaire, Rousseau," Cole said. "Anybody for dessert?"

It was 11:00. "We'd better head home," Madelyn said. "If we're not back by midnight, not only do we turn into pumpkins, both of you will be turned into rats."

"Would you be able to tell the difference?" Alex asked, and Denise laughed again.

Once they got into the hearse, Madelyn overheard Alex telling Denise the floor was more comfortable than the seats; giggling ensued, then nothing audible over the sound of the engine. Madelyn felt more nervous than the situation seemed to warrant. Worst case, the streets were well lighted and the dorm within walking distance.

With the dorm in sight, Cole pulled to the curb and turned off the engine and the lights. "You're not out of gas," Madelyn said. Her breath came raggedly and she was tense from neck to heels. "I checked the gauge."

"No," Cole said. He put his arm on the seat behind her and moved slowly across the seat toward her. Wit failed her, followed by basic motor skills. She closed her eyes a moment before he kissed her, then a wave of dizziness passed over her. His lips were gentle, slightly parted, sealing themselves to hers. When he pulled away, she saw her own feelings in his face: surprise and longing and a momentary loss of all guile and cleverness and pretense.

The next kiss was more intense, not threatening and yet not entirely under control; his left hand touched her face along the jawline. She was now seriously disoriented. Her own right hand went to his neck and buried itself in his hair, seeking a lifeline. She lost her sense of time, and when Cole pulled away again she whispered, "Oh, shit."

Cole smiled, his eyes glistening. "What?"

She put a hand on his chest and gently pushed him away. He smelled of Right Guard and warmth and Mexican food and shaving cream and clean cotton shirts and God only knew what else, and she knew she was in real trouble and had to clear her head while she was still able.

"We've got to go. Be gentlemen and walk us to our door."

"Coming!" Denise called brightly. "Give me a sec."

Alex's voice came over various rustling noises. "Can I help?"

Denise laughed. "You've done quite enough already, thank you very much. Okay, let's go."

At the door Cole kissed her one more time and said, "I'll call you."

"Okay," Madelyn said. She pulled Denise out of Alex's embrace and hustled them both inside.

Denise collapsed against the wall, fanning herself. "Tornado," she said, laughing. "No doubt about it."

MADELYN, HAVING FINISHED her class assignments, was reading a library copy of John Fowles' *The Magus* when Cole called on Sunday afternoon. "Can you help me with my Russian homework?"

"What kind of help?" she asked.

"I can't concentrate on it because all I can think about is you."

"And your proposed solution to this problem?"

"I thought if we walked around for an hour, that would hold me for a while. Like giving a heroin addict a Darvon."

"Shouldn't a heroin addict be going cold turkey?"

"You'll note that I haven't made any red rose references despite last night. The least you can do is not pick at my metaphors."

"I do admire a graceful winner."

"Would now be a good time?"

He picked her up in the hearse and drove her to Pease Park, west of campus, pointing out where he and Alex lived on the hill that loomed above them with the hint of an invitation. "Another time," she said.

She loved Texas in September. The heat, so oppressive in the summer, had a transience in the fall that stole its power, with occasional days as cold and clear as spring water. That afternoon lay in between, warm in the sun and cool in the shade. Boys with footballs and girls with dogs filled the park, running with an abandon fueled by the season.

Cole took her hand as they walked, and she asked him again about his finger. One question followed another, so much to learn and tell to catch their rational brains up to where their emotions had already gone. She told him about her father and her love for Shakespeare and Pinter and Anouilh. She admitted to seeing The

Chevelles at what she learned was their first performance. He told her about his accident and, adding gasoline to the fire, his middle class, itinerant youth and his split from his parents. It appeared that he was neither spoiled nor rich; his spending money came from playing with the band.

The walk ended, as she'd known it would, with them kissing, him leaning against a tree, pulling her into him. He seemed to know how far she was willing to go and to stop there. Well. She hadn't meant to let him put his hand on her breast, though he did stay on the outside of her blouse. That left him well behind Alex, who, according to Denise, had his mouth on both of her bare breasts Saturday night. Madelyn believed that Cole was not simply looking to take advantage, though she no longer trusted her judgment. She was as tyrannized by the literature of romance as she was awash in hormones.

The one-hour Darvon turned into a four-hour fix, as Cole took her to dinner at Nau's Enfield Drug, where they ate hamburgers at a soda fountain out of *Ozzie and Harriet*. She insisted that she had to get home, yet they ended up parked across the street from the dorm, kissing some more.

She was not prepared for how urgent it all felt. Cole had band practice on Monday, Wednesday, and Thursday, and he called her in the few minutes he had beforehand on all three nights. On Tuesday she'd agreed to dinner on the condition that they go to the library afterward. Between the music and the time they spent together, she worried that he would get behind in his schoolwork; yet when they weren't on the phone or in physical contact, she was anxious. What did he think, what did he feel, when she wasn't there? Was he indeed as obsessed with her as he claimed? Maybe his ardor had already started to cool. Maybe he was still hung up on somebody from high school. Maybe he was playing her for a fool. No matter how hard she tried to focus on her studies, her thoughts always came back to Cole.

Russian class was hardest of all. She knew he was ten feet away from her, watching her all through class, and she could barely concentrate.

On Friday she and Cole saw *You Only Live Twice*. Cole, it

developed, was obsessed with secret agents. "It doesn't pay to be the spy's girlfriend," Madelyn observed afterward. "They keep getting killed."

"That's true," Cole said, and looked over at her with a raised eyebrow. In a passable imitation of Connery's Scots burr, he said, "Best watch your step, lass."

On Saturday the four of them went to an East Austin Negro club, and she and Cole danced all the slow songs, leaving her so dizzy and stimulated that if she hadn't been having her period, and if the back seat of Alex's car were not so small, something drastic might have happened on the way home.

They both knew where they were headed. Denise had already provided Alex with what she referred to as "oral gratification." "Makes them docile as babies," she said. "Just be sure you have Kleenex handy."

Madelyn had a more romantic consummation in mind. She didn't want it to be devoid of spontaneity, nor did she want it to be rushed. Between the band and her curfew and both their home-work she didn't know how it was going to work out.

On Tuesday Cole brought her to the Castle for the first time. He'd already made spaghetti sauce, and the dining room table held a vase of red roses and a bottle of red wine. The house was mysteriously deserted, except for the Pakistani lodger in the downstairs bedroom who could be heard moving around, and who didn't come out to be introduced. She understood then that the time had come.

In her nervousness she babbled about the beauty of the house, and she was relieved to see that Cole was nervous too. He opened the wine and she forced herself to go easy. Then the pasta was done and they ate spaghetti and salad and a plain baguette with no garlic to spoil their breath. They neither one ate much, though she assured Cole that the meal was delicious. Afterward, they piled their dishes in the sink and Cole said, "You need to see the rest of the place."

She realized he hadn't touched her, other than a first quick kiss when she came down from her dorm room. The skin of her hands and her throat and her inner thighs tingled with anticipation.

OUTSIDE THE GATES OF EDEN

She led the way upstairs. Cole showed her into Alex's room, and
even as she admired the view of Austin spread out before her,
she was equally aware of the heat of Cole's body where he stood
behind her.

He pointed out the closed door to Tupelo Joe's room, and then
led her into the back bedroom. She stood in the middle of the
floor and took in the bookshelf, the acoustic guitar on its stand,
the closed blinds, the neatly stacked books on the desk, the double
bed with the single red rose on one of the pillows.

Cole closed the door and pointed to the clock on the bedside
table. "It's now six forty-five. The alarm is set for nine-thirty.
Plenty of time to get you home for your curfew. So you don't have
to think about it. Okay?"

"Okay," she said. Her chest was tight and she could barely speak.

He took her face in both his hands and began to kiss her with
the slow, steady determination of a man who does not intend to
stop.

"HE SET AN *alarm*?" Denise said.

"You don't get it. He did it because he understands how my
brain works. He understood that I would be worried about the
time, so he made that go away. He showed me that he'd thought
of everything, so I didn't have to think. He knew what a relief
that would be for me."

"Well, Alex certainly didn't need an alarm clock, if you know
what I mean." Apparently after Madelyn and Cole had shut themselves in Cole's room, Alex and Denise had come back from their
dinner and repaired to Alex's room for similar purposes.

"Uh, no?"

"Let's just say he's more of a sprinter than a distance man.
Which is perfectly fine with me."

Madelyn took a deep breath. "Speaking of which. There's something I've been meaning to ask you about."

Denise's eyes twinkled. "Ask away, my sister."

Madelyn was so humiliated, she had to simply spit the word
out. "Orgasms."

Denise put her head back and laughed.

"Please don't laugh at me. I know you're very experienced at all this and I'm not, but—"

"You're wondering why you're not having earth-shattering, life-changing, nuclear bombs of pleasure exploding up and down your spine because some guy stuck his big ol' protuberance inside you and spewed? Honey, why on earth should you? The vaginal orgasm is a myth. If you want a climax, you have to do it for yourself. You *do* know how to do that, right? I see by the sudden redness of your complexion that you do."

"Sex does feel good. Really good. But Cole is sensitive and I think he feels bad because I didn't... I didn't..."

"Come? Honey, you have to do like I do, and every other sensible woman does. Fake it!"

She shook her head. "No. Not with Cole."

"Suit yourself," Denise said, and gave her a quick hug. "Don't say I didn't warn you."

A HEAVY THREE-RING BINDER with five dividers, each with a brightly colored tab. Two hundred sheets of college-ruled three-hole notebook paper. Three new Bic medium-point blue pens in a zip-up plastic envelope that was three-hole punched for the binder. Textbooks stacked on top with their slick white pages and plastic smell.

To Cole they felt like a ball and chain that anchored him to his childhood. The idea that he was back in school, four long years still ahead of him, the same interminable sentence that he'd served in high school now to be served all over again, filled him with despair.

Susan had agreed to buy him a case of beer a week, and he rationed himself to three a night. Theoretically that left him a few extras for the weekend, though he always came up short. The problem was that Sunny, who didn't drink, kept bringing home women who got stoned on his hash and then raided the refrigerator and threw the returnable longneck bottles in the trash.

He thought music might help, so he'd signed on with the band that Alex found. Though they began to sound professional within a few rehearsals, Cole was just going through the motions with them, like he was going through the motions in his classes.

Like he'd been going through the motions, at first, with the blonde in his Russian class. A game to get her attention, maybe get her into bed. Then he'd kissed her and he'd seen something in her eyes, something that he must have already suspected, a willingness, a need, even, to be utterly serious, the capacity to raise the stakes to the limit and beyond. It had knocked Cole sideways.

She made him want to live up to her image of what he could be. When he went to Susan to ask her to buy them a bottle of wine, he saw how childish his infatuation with Susan had been, and how his feelings for Madelyn were entirely his own and not tangled up with his envy of the Montoya family bond.

And when he finally saw Madelyn naked, nipples as dark red as rose petals, hips as curved as Earth from space, the arc of her instep, the down of her belly, he knew he would never grow tired of looking at her, or of the smell of her skin or the taste of her mouth, or of her husky voice that bent upward here and there with a hint of Texas drawl. He wanted to drown in her. He was crazy in love.

Which only made the rest of his life more onerous. The night after he first made love to Madelyn, band practice seemed endless, despite their breaking off at 9:00. Cole immediately grabbed La Pelirroja, rounded up Alex and his guitar, and drove to Madelyn's dorm, where they stood under her window and Cole led him through the most love-drunk Spanish songs in their repertoire: "Obsesión," "Copa rota," "Bésame mucho," "Malagueña." Girls began appearing at open windows immediately, laughing and cheering. Cole sang only to Madelyn, whose goofy, crooked grin was exactly the thing he needed to see. Alex hammed it up, orbiting Cole, occasionally leaning against him for a bit of tight harmony. By the time they got halfway through "Malagueña," where Alex went into his falsetto, the girls were screaming like he and Cole were the second coming of The Beatles. That was when a campus cop car pulled up, lights flashing, and Cole and Alex took it on the lam, running around the block to crawl into the hearse and escape into the night.

That Saturday afternoon, using a rented recorder, the band laid down two four-minute medleys that showcased their best songs. On Monday Ron took the tape to Sonobeat, a local record company, and ordered 50 copies, which he planned to hand out to the social directors of all the frats.

Tuesday afternoon was the photo session for their requisite 8×10 glossy. Cole had the idea of inviting Madelyn and Denise to bring every good-looking girl they could find to the session. With Sunny reluctantly opening his black book, they ended up with a dozen beauties looking up adoringly as the band posed with their instruments on the lawn at Zilker Park. Ron congratulated Cole on his grasp of the fraternity mindset, and Madelyn told him not to get used to the idea of having her at his feet.

Getting Madelyn home for her curfew got increasingly hard. Classes, fortunately, were easy. Even so, he might have been in trouble without Madelyn riding herd on him and without the constant fear of Montoya's disappointment. He made mostly Bs on his exams and papers. Except for Russian, where, between a lack of natural aptitude and the distraction of Madelyn's presence, he barely kept a C average.

Any day now, he told himself, he was going to have to get himself in gear.

THE BAND'S DEBUT was set for October 21 at the Sigma house, a frat that was legendary for their alcohol consumption. Cole asked if they could bring dates and Ron said, "We did a lot of these things in Houston and I would advise against it. A frat house on a Saturday night, especially this frat… it's a war zone."

Madelyn wanted to come anyway. "I only saw your old band once. I haven't seen your new band at all." They were in Cole's room on the Tuesday before the gig. They'd had dinner with Alex and Denise at Susan's house, and Cole was in a pleasant stupor from their lovemaking.

"I don't think you understand how wild these things get."

"My roommate is dating a KA. I've heard stories. Is there something you're not telling me? Are there going to be orgies? Is the band being fixed up with floozies as part of your pay? What is it you're covering up?" This facet of Madelyn's personality had only surfaced recently. Her over-analytic brain would suddenly refuse to accept Cole's perfectly reasonable explanations and insist on answers that would hurt her more deeply. Even now, as she pretended to tease, Cole sensed her lurking insecurity.

"If I brought you," Cole said, "I wouldn't be able to leave in the middle to take you home. We're playing until one AM, after which we have to load out the stuff. That's way past your curfew."

Cole's complaints about her curfew had become a sore point. "The curfew is not my fault. If you really wanted me there, you'd find a way."

"That's just it. I don't want you there. It's our first gig, and if you were there I'd be worried sick about you the entire time. I wouldn't be able to concentrate."

"I'm not a child who has to be supervised every minute." She leaned over him to look at the clock. "And speaking of curfew, we'd better get dressed."

When he pulled up in front of her dorm, she kissed him perfunctorily and said, "You don't have to walk me to the door."

He didn't insist, and she didn't look back.

THE SIGMA PARTY ROOM had gray paint on the walls and checkerboard linoleum tile underfoot. The windows, Cole noted, were made of Plexiglas, scratched and fogged to obscurity, which struck him as odd. Other than a big kitchen, several bathrooms, the stage, and a few tables and chairs, the ground floor was empty. The stage was five feet high, two feet higher than the one at the Fillmore. Cole heard shouting upstairs where the brothers watched the UT-Arkansas football game on TV.

"Hope they win," Ron said.

"You're a football fan?" Cole asked.

"I prefer happy drunks to mean drunks." Cole imagined he

might see the same nervous cheer in a gung-ho Marine about to go into a firefight.

They loaded in the gear, set up the PA, tuned up, and were ready to go by 7:30. Some of the brothers had begun to roam the bottom floor, and Cole called out to one of them, "How'd we do?"

"Twenty-one twelve!" he said happily, extending his index and little finger in the Hook 'em Horns gesture.

"We need one of us to go fetch some burgers," Ron said. "The rest stay here to watch the stuff."

"That bad?" Cole said.

Nolan laughed and said, "Just you wait. I'll go." He held up one hand and Ron tossed him the keys to his truck.

While Nolan was gone, Ron reviewed the ground rules. "These guys may be drunks, but they're sticklers for contracts. We start on time, we don't take more than fifteen-minute breaks, and above all, we keep the music flowing nice and steady, like the booze. This audience doesn't want a lot of stage patter. If the music stops for anything other than a scheduled break, the mood in here could shift and it could get ugly."

Alex said, "It sounds like we should be getting combat pay."

With complete seriousness, Ron said, "We are."

After dinner they changed, one at a time, into their gig clothes. Cole wore his blue polka dot shirt and tie with a new pair of jeans and his boots. Ron wore a black turtleneck and brown leather jacket. Alex wore his flowered shirt from San Francisco, and Nolan wore a plain black shirt and tie and black chinos, saying, "I like to disappear."

Cole thought about calling Madelyn. They'd had an awkward phone call on Thursday, not mentioning the gig, that had ended with her breaking their date for Friday, saying she might be coming down with something. The obvious lie had infuriated Cole, so he'd wished her goodnight, said he hoped she felt better, and hung up. He missed her excruciatingly every minute, had tossed and turned the last two nights, and wondered if this was going to be the end, with both of them too stubborn to back down. He wanted to say all those things to her, and yet he didn't make the call because a part of him feared she'd take advantage of his weakness to reopen the argument.

They started at 9:00 sharp with "I Ain't Gonna Eat Out My Heart Anymore," Ron on lead vocals, Cole playing the guitar part straight off the record. At the first notes of music, the lights went out except for two spots over the stage. Despite the fact that he *was* eating his heart out, Cole was glad to be on stage in front of an audience, playing loud. It had been two months. From the Rascals they shifted immediately to "Funky Broadway," Alex on vocals, and then to their rather odd rendition of "Sunshine of Your Love," where the organ did the second guitar part.

By their first break, the room had filled up. Almost all the men were dressed up in slacks, blazers, and ties. Their hair was short and their cheeks were shaved and they were ready to step into the boardrooms of America. Their dates were in high heels and dresses with hemlines above the knee, their hair sprayed into immobility and their makeup impeccable.

Sixteen-ounce plastic cups made their way around the room containing the Sigmas' legendary "knockout punch," consisting of various hard liquors, Everclear, and cheap champagne. Ron had warned them away from it, so Cole stuck with the free beer provided for the band. As they took the stage for the second set, Ron's predictions of chaos seemed highly inflated.

Yet, as the set wore on, Cole felt a slow, creeping unease. First the dancers strayed farther and farther from the beat. Then he noticed that a number of the women on the dance floor were no longer moving under their own power. The makeup that had been perfect an hour before was now runny and smeared. Some of them were draped over their partners like sacks of produce. As Cole watched, one of the older brothers shifted a semi-conscious woman into a fireman's carry and staggered up the stairs with her.

Suddenly Madelyn and Denise were standing in front of the stage. Cole blinked to make sure he wasn't hallucinating. They both grinned and Madelyn waggled her fingers at him. Cole stared in shock.

The band was in the middle of "Hit the Road, Jack" and Cole had missed his vocal cue. Alex, in falsetto, stared at him and sang, "I *said*, you ain't got no money and you ain't no good *what*soever."

Cole jumped back in. "I guess if you say so…"

They finished the song. Madelyn and Denise had retreated to an empty table near the stage, and they applauded enthusiastically. Cole looked at Alex, who shook his head, no, this was a surprise to him too. Before he had time to say or do anything, Ron started the lead-in to "Money." Keep it flowing, Ron had said, or there could be trouble. Cole and Alex fell in behind Nolan, Cole playing stiffly now, fearing imminent disaster.

During the instrumental break, he looked at the girls and saw a drunk couple making out on the far side of the table. Denise was pointing to them and saying something in Madelyn's ear when the woman turned and casually vomited onto the tabletop. Madelyn and Denise both jumped to their feet, though the tide stopped short of their side of the table. The man raised one hand in the air and shouted, "Pledge!", the word barely audible over the music. A freshman in a maid's uniform and a turban ran up. The man pointed to the vomit and the freshman saluted and ran off again. Denise was laughing and Madelyn was horrified.

Two younger frat brothers, in ties and without dates, approached the girls, offering cups of the anesthetic punch. Both girls refused. The boys kept talking. One of the boys put his arm around Madelyn's waist. Cole, barely able to concentrate on the song, was torn between the need to rescue them and an angry desire to see them get taught a lesson—as long as it didn't go too far. He wondered what Joe Gall would do.

Before he had to make up his mind, the man with the vomiting date stepped in and sent the boys away. The freshman in the maid's uniform reappeared with a bucket and towels and cleaned the table, then was summoned to the other side of the room. The appearance of order was restored for the moment, but Cole now saw how fragile that order was, that the rules of society had been suspended in this place, and while there might be consequences later, that threat wouldn't prevent anything from happening tonight. Denise was no longer laughing and Cole saw naked fear on Madelyn's face.

Two more songs in the set, "Jenny Take a Ride" and then "Walk, Don't Run" as a break song.

Next to the kitchen, a circle of brothers chanted "Chug! Chug!" as the man in the center upended a can of beer over his mouth, nearly strangling on it, the beer overflowing and running down his shirt, before he recovered and showered everyone around him with the last drops. A handful of brothers converged on a shoving match in the doorway and pushed it outside, where Cole heard angry voices and the crash of a garbage can falling over.

Cole plowed through the song and didn't look at the girls. Then, as he started "Walk, Don't Run," somebody began pounding on the door of one of the bathrooms. Cole glanced up and saw a drunk yank open the door. In the brightly lit interior, a woman straddled the lavatory, head against the wall and face turned away, skirt hiked up to her waist, panties dangling from one foot. He couldn't tell whether she was conscious or not. A man was taking her from behind, his pants around his ankles, and he shouted at the drunk, "Wait your fucking turn!" He had one arm around the woman's waist and with the other he reached out and slammed the door.

Cole looked for Madelyn. She and Denise had backed against the wall, faces grim.

Cole finished the song, jerked his strap loose, switched his amp to standby, and propped his guitar against it. Alex was already walking toward him. Everybody in the room seemed to be talking at the top of their voices, the noise level nearly the same as when the band had been playing.

"I'm getting them out of here," Cole shouted to Alex.

Ron was on his feet. "Cole!"

"I'll be back in ten minutes!" Cole called to him, and vaulted down to the floor. Frat brothers grabbed at him and pounded his back, saying, "Y'all are fantastic!" Cole smiled and thanked them and pushed his way past.

He grabbed one of Madelyn's hands and one of Denise's and began to drag them toward the outside door. One of the frat brothers asked what he was doing and another called out, "Don't be greedy, man, share the wealth!" Everyone in the room was so drunk that they swayed in currents and eddies. Cole ignored his anger and fear and rode the waves onto the lawn and the street.

The hearse was parked at the end of the driveway so that no one could block him in. He hustled the meek, silent girls into the front seat as, up and down 26th Street, voices rose in drunken ecstasy, in anger and confusion, in sheer hormonal excess. Live music clashed against records, glass broke, primitive rhythms were pounded out on trash cans and car hoods. Cole had to stop repeatedly as crowds surged into the street without looking. Once he got past Rio Grande he was able to speed up, and he circled around to the dorm on Pearl.

He squealed to a stop in front of the dorm. Madelyn broke the silence. "Cole…"

Cole stared straight ahead. "I have to get back. Now."

"Cole, I'm so sorry."

He looked at her and felt one eye twitch. "I'll call you tomorrow."

As soon as they were both out and Madelyn had closed the passenger door, he hit the gas. He managed not to run anyone over as he careened through Fraternity Row. Miraculously, his parking spot was still there. An officious drunk tried to tell him he couldn't park there and Cole held up a strand of his polka-dot tie like a badge. "I'm in the band."

He'd been gone for 16 minutes. "Shit," he said under his breath as he pushed his way toward the stage. "Shit, shit, shit." The band had already started "Green Onions," their designated string break song. Cole ran up the steps and strapped on his guitar, easing into the lead guitar part.

Ron summoned him over to the B-3 with a jerk of the head. Cole leaned in and Ron, off-mike, said, "This is why I said no bimbos at the gig."

Cole, his bloodstream awash with the chemicals of rage and panic, chose not to add still more regret to the mixture. "It won't happen again," he said.

Ron nodded once, dismissing him.

They had only begun the third set of four. Cole wondered how it could possibly get any worse. Gang rape in the middle of the floor? Gunplay? Instead the crowd became increasingly loud and increasingly incapacitated. Many of the women had either been dragged upstairs or returned to their sorority houses and dorms to make curfew. The increasingly male crowd began to focus more and more on the band, singing along, swaying glassy-eyed in front of the stage. Nolan occasionally threw drumsticks into the audience, far more of them than he could have broken with his mild playing. The brothers used the sticks to pound on empty whiskey bottles, cowbells, the mike stands, the stage.

Halfway through the fourth set, only a handful of women were left, and the brothers without dates had devolved into monsters from the Id, lurching, baboon-like incarnations of pure lust, howling and hooting and screaming. They no longer had any hope of sex, or of a kiss or a caress or so much as a friendly word. In their despair, they now strove only to make these last unattainable women look at them, if only in disgust, to force some kind of acknowledgement of their wretched existence. In turn the women were determined not to give them even that satisfaction as they chatted with their dates, sipped the last of the punch, shuffled to the music.

As Cole watched, one of these primate brothers picked up a chair and, taking a running start, hurled it at a window. Neither the chair nor the window was damaged, though the boy slid headlong into the wall. Cole now understood the reason for the Plexiglas.

"Ladies and gentlemen," Ron said, "we have been The Other Side, and we thank you for coming out tonight. We're going to leave you with one last song." Nolan counted them down into "Light My Fire" as another of the brothers methodically hammered one chair with another until he managed to break it. He stacked the wooden parts together, doused them with a cup of punch, and, kneeling before the pyre, threw a match on it. The chair erupted in blue flame and in its sudden light, Cole saw that the boy's face was wet with tears.

Somebody walked over unhurriedly with a fire extinguisher and sprayed the burning chair with foam, and, as an afterthought, doused the boy as well. The boy toppled over and lay still.

Cole turned to Ron, who was in the middle of his solo, and raised his eyebrows, asking if they should do anything. Ron looked up, shook his head, and resumed playing.

The thirty or so people who were left made enough noise that Ron brought them back onstage to do "Johnny B. Goode" as an encore, and then, at last, it was over. The harsh fluorescent overhead lights came on. The boy was still stretched out on the floor next to his extinguished fire, and Cole was relieved to see his chest rise and fall. They walked around him as they carried the equipment out to the hearse, except for the B-3, which rode in Ron's custom trailer. Then they made a last pass around the room and collected drumsticks, for Nolan to throw again another night.

They turned a table right side up and had one last beer while Ron collected their pre-signed check from the social director, and then sat down and wrote them all checks on his personal account for $180 each. It was the most money Cole had ever made in a night.

"This is just the beginning," Ron said. "Once word gets around, we should be making two-fifty apiece, maybe three hundred. Despite a few… *distractions*…" He smiled indulgently at Cole. "… it was pretty damned good for a first gig. I believe we're on our way."

Nolan rode to the Castle with them to pick up his car. Lights were on all across Fraternity Row and cars weaved drunkenly down the street. The neighborhood did indeed look like a battle zone, with unconscious bodies strewn across the lawns and smoke rising from half a dozen small fires.

On Castle Hill, they piled Nolan's drums next to the amps on the basement floor, and Nolan waved as he drove away. Cole watched him from the front steps, smelling the smoke and alcohol fumes and sweat that saturated his clothes, listening to the crickets, and watching the traffic down on Lamar Boulevard.

Alex sat down next to him. "Well," he said, eventually, "that was interesting."

"I don't know if I can do this," Cole said.

"Maybe we'll get used to it. It's a fuck of a lot of money."

"It is that."

"Did the girls say anything?"

Cole shook his head. "I don't think they'll be attending any more frat parties." After a minute he said, "How's it going with Denise?"

"Well. It's not Romeo and Juliet, like you and Madelyn. She's fun. She's up for anything, and I like that."

"I don't know where me and Madelyn are after tonight."

"I've seen the way she looks at you, pal. You've got nothing to worry about." Another pause. "Me and Denise, we're going to do acid together. I've got enough for you and Madelyn to join us if you want."

"I'll think about it," Cole said. He knew, and Alex knew, that it wasn't going to happen.

"It's nearly three," Alex said. "I'm going to hit the rack."

"I'll be up in a minute," Cole said.

Alex went in. From where he stood, Cole could see 26th Street, dark and silent at last. If he were to drop acid at that moment, he thought, he would see an entire world populated by drunken, desperate boys, with needs so overwhelming that nothing could satisfy them.

Satisfy us, he admitted.

Maybe he was just exhausted. He undressed in the basement and left his reeking clothes in the hamper by the washing machine, then, naked, climbed two flights of stairs and stood under steaming hot water until he felt almost clean.

COLE WOKE UP at noon, starving. He washed the crud out of his eyes, brushed his teeth, and dressed in old jeans, a white T-shirt, and a plaid flannel shirt. As he came down the stairs he saw that the front door was wide open. He went to close it and saw a body on the couch, wrapped in the multicolored afghan they left there. His first thought was that she was somebody Sunny had kicked out of bed. Then he saw the strawberry-blonde hair hanging to the floor.

He knelt gently beside her and inhaled the sweet smell of her neck. She woke slowly, saw him, and started to cry. She had no makeup on, and her eyes were swollen and bloodshot. How beautiful she is, he thought.

"Cole," she said. "Oh, Cole, I'm so sorry."

"Shhhh," he said. "It's okay."

"Oh, Cole, that horrible place. Those horrible men. I was so scared. And then you were so angry at me…" She broke down in sobs. "I couldn't sleep for missing you and I got up at six and walked here…"

Cole was crying too. "I'm sorry too. I love you, Madelyn."

"Oh, Cole, I love you too."

They'd never said it to each other before, and the words were a powerful aphrodisiac. He kissed her, tasting both of their tears, and she threw both arms around his neck. "Can we go upstairs?" she whispered. "Oh God, Cole, please, can we?"

In Cole's bed, their naked bodies wrapped around each other, they generated an intensity beyond anything Cole had felt before. Nothing existed in the universe beyond the two of them. He seemed to move inside her for hours, and when he finally came, he still wanted her. He was all hunger.

He grabbed some tissues and mopped up the wet spot, and then, still drunk on desire for her, he began to trace the edges of her labia with one finger. She shivered. "Oh God," she said, "please don't stop."

"Okay," he said, and smiled at her. She put a hand on his cheek and fixed him with her serious look, the look that drove him crazy.

"I need you to keep doing that," she said, "and I need to know that you won't get tired or bored or give up on me before I'm done."

He understood then what she was asking. "I promise," he said, looking into her eyes. "I won't stop unless you tell me."

"Right there," she said, and sighed, and he felt the warmth of her breath on his mouth, getting him aroused again. He kissed her and said, "Is that okay?"

"Yes."

He kissed her nipples.

"Oh yes," she said.

She took a long time, long enough that he would have stopped if he hadn't promised. Then again, it excited him to watch her eyes close, and her hips slowly begin to move, and her breathing grow ragged, until finally she stopped breathing altogether, and then she gasped, and he felt her contractions in his hand, and by that time he was out of his mind and had to be inside her again.

At the end they were holding each other with all their strength. Madelyn's legs were wrapped around his, and as they slowly rocked themselves to stillness, he felt tears stream down her face again. He understood that the tears came from gratitude and physical release and the helpless vulnerability of being so completely naked in front of someone you loved. The knowledge that having been utterly joined to one another, they were inevitably drifting back into the broken halves of their separate bodies.

MADELYN INSISTED on making breakfast. She was overflowing with love and needed new ways to say it. At 2:30 in the afternoon she piled the dining room table with bacon and scrambled eggs and toast and orange juice for the two of them.

"How did you like the band?" Cole asked her.

She kissed the top of his head on the way to her chair. "I liked your old drummer better."

"This one's a lot easier to get along with."

"You're very sexy on stage, you know."

"Am I?" He gave her a teasing look. "You didn't seem to think so when you saw me before."

"Oh, I did."

"You didn't come up to me and fling yourself at me."

"Actually I did go looking for you, only somebody got there first."

"Janet," he said, and she sensed some unfinished business. "You really looked for me? So we almost met a year ago? We could have been together all this time."

She reached across the table and took his hand. He was so easily hurt. How had he survived this long? "We're happy now. That's all that matters. There's no point in second-guessing the past."

He looked at his injured finger. "It's practically all I do. But speaking of being happy in the present, we have to get you out of your dorm."

"We've been over this. They won't refund the money, and my father can't afford to lose it. We can't both live in your little bedroom."

"We'll find you a room close by and I'll pay for it."

"With the money from playing frat parties?"

"One or two more and I'll be able to pay for the rest of the semester. I want to go to sleep with you, and wake up with you in the morning."

She pictured herself telling her father. He loved her; he would have to understand. "All right," she said.

The surprise on Cole's face made her laugh out loud. "What?" he said. "Did you just say yes?"

"Yes," she said. She got up and walked around the table and got in his lap and kissed him. "Yes. Yes. Yes."

MADELYN TOOK CHARGE of their Thanksgiving schedule. Her parents would have Cole to Thanksgiving dinner; she would eat Friday at the Montoyas'. They drove up together on the Wednesday before, Madelyn, Cole, Alex, their suitcases, and two acoustic guitars all in Alex's little car, Alex having lost the toss. Holiday traffic stretched what should have been a three-and-a-half-hour drive into more than five hours of excruciating stop and go, which Madelyn spent imagining the ways the dinner could go wrong.

Madelyn picked Cole up at noon the next day in the family station wagon. Cole wore a blue checked shirt, khakis, blazer, and tie. And real shoes, for a change. As soon as they got in the car, Cole was all over her and she had to gently push him away. "I am far too nervous for this right now."

"Why?" Cole said. "What do you think is going to happen?"

"That's just it. I have no idea."

Compared to the Montoya mansion, her parents' house was a shoebox, the neighborhood in decline, the yard a sump of unraked leaves. But Cole had not grown up in the Montoya house, and money would not be the issue. The problem was that no one could possibly live up to her father's expectations for her. Because she'd moved out of the dorm, her father knew that she and Cole were sleeping together. All he'd said on the phone was, "I hope you're being careful."

Her father reacted warily when she introduced him to Cole. He wore the baggy brown cardigan with the leather elbow patches that her mother hated, and under it he wore one of the identical white, no-iron, short-sleeved, button-down dress shirts that he wore seven days a week. He'd married late because of the very fastidiousness that she now feared he would deploy against Cole; his age showed in the curvature of his spine and his thinning hair. Her mother, plump, aproned, a sheen of sweat on her forehead, shook hands and retreated to the kitchen.

For his part, Cole was relaxed, deferential, dropping sirs and ma'ams with no hint of artifice. He asked twice if he could help in the kitchen and twice her father refused him, herding him instead into the living room. Cole took one end of the sofa and Madelyn sat chastely in the middle, leaving a couple of feet of clearance. Cole immediately asked about the integrated circuits that her father had helped invent at Texas Instruments, and kept him talking for the 45 minutes until dinner was served.

As soon as her mother told them to come to the table, her father said, "Go see what's keeping your sister, will you?"

Julia's room was awash with perfume, and Julia was admiring herself in the mirror. She wore a perilously low-cut ivory cashmere sweater, belted tightly at the waist, and a miniskirt the approximate size of a paper cupcake liner. Her eyelashes were as long as butterfly wings, her lips as soft and shiny as a sateen pillowcase. She might as well have been wearing a Zsa Zsa Gabor Halloween costume.

"Julia, what in God's name...?"

Julia turned on her with a smile as realistic as her makeup. "I wanted to look nice for your boyfriend."

No way to win this, Madelyn thought. Let Daddy deal with it. "Mother wants us at the table."

Julia made her entrance at the same time as the turkey. Cole stood up politely and Madelyn said, "Cole, this is Julia." Then, unable to restrain herself, she said, "As you can see, she's adopted."

"Madelyn!" her mother said. "You apologize to your sister."

"Sorry!" Madelyn said cheerfully. Cole gave her an inquiring look that might have meant, "Has your sister always been insane?" or "What's the matter with you?" but probably represented the typical male reaction, "Why didn't you tell me she was good-looking and easy?"

"I understand," her father said, as he began to carve the bird, "that you're in a musical group."

Uh oh, Madelyn thought. Now it begins.

"At the moment," Cole said, "it's strictly a commercial proposition. We play top-forty hits, rock, and soul music."

"I love soul music," Julia said huskily.

"However," Cole said, "I'm about to make a change. The atmosphere at those fraternity parties is pretty... hedonistic. I don't care for it. I'm looking for something where I can express myself more. Something more in the folk and blues sort of vein."

Cole had talked about the possibility of a new band; now he sounded like it was a fait accompli. She didn't know whether to believe him or not.

"Which would inherently be less commercial," her father said.

"In the short term, yes, sir. In the long term it would be more conducive to original material, a record contract, national exposure."

"Is that where you see yourself in ten years? Touring nationally?"

Madelyn knew her father couldn't help himself. Still she wished he sounded less like a cross-examination.

"It's hard to say, sir. It's a fickle business. That's why I'm in college, so I'll have a Plan B."

Her father nodded and Madelyn saw that Cole had scored points: vocabulary, common sense, respectful demeanor. She wondered how much was conscious and how much was Cole's need to make people like him. And she wondered if it was enough to overcome his deficits: long hair, musician, screwing his daughter.

In turn they passed their plates to the head of the table for her father to serve them. Julia, sitting across from Cole, leaned forward unnecessarily to hand off her plate, causing her décolletage to swell like two pale pink water balloons. "Breast, please," she said.

Madelyn saw Cole struggle to keep from choking. "Julia!" Madelyn said.

Julia's innocence lacked all credibility. "What?"

"It's Thanksgiving," her mother said. "Can't you two be nice?"

A year ago, her parents would not have allowed Julia at the table dressed for a *Playboy* cover shoot, would not have tolerated risqué remarks, would have taken Madelyn's side against Julia's outrages. Were they punishing her for leaving home? For sleeping with Cole?

Cole must have seen how abandoned she felt. He covered her hand where it lay on the table and gave it a comforting squeeze. Madelyn looked up as her father saw the gesture, and his reaction was instantaneous and heartbreaking. She read their entire history in his face: him teaching her how to hold a violin at age 7, explaining Van Gogh to her at 12, standing outside *Marat/Sade* with her only the summer before last, all those moments now slipping through his fingers and into the hands of another man.

"What's everybody so glum about all of a sudden?" Julia said. "Are we going to open the wine or not?"

AFTER DINNER, COLE disappeared into the den with her father. Madelyn and her mother did the dishes and Julia camped out in the living room with the TV, perhaps hoping to ambush Cole when he emerged.

"He seems like a very nice young man," was all her mother offered. "Well spoken, nice manners. Tell me what your new dorm is like."

When Cole and her father finally came out, Madelyn saw no signs of violence. They all sat around the living room and fought off the soporific effects of the big meal for another hour or so, Julia unsuccessfully, and then Madelyn drove Cole home.

"What did you two talk about in there?" Madelyn asked.

"He wanted to know how many times a week we were having

sex, whether we were doing anything kinky, and whether you were having orgasms."

"I hope you told him yes."

"Yes." He knelt on the bench seat and pushed the hair away from her ear and began kissing her neck.

"Cole, stop it, not while I'm driving."

"Can you pull over?"

"No. Now about my father. Seriously."

"He started with some Haydn and Schubert quartets. Maybe he thought if I heard some of that stuff on a great stereo I would give up the evils of rock and roll. Then after that he played some Josh White and Odetta and The Weavers, and it was pretty cool, actually. And that really is an amazing stereo. Do you have any idea how hard it was to sit next to you all afternoon and not jump on you?"

"Was it me that got you so worked up, or was it my sister?"

"Wow, she's a case, isn't she? I'd hate to be her boyfriend."

Sincere or not, she was grateful for the words. Her shoulders eased a couple of inches downward. "You're one of the few males in Dallas who feels that way."

"She's your exact opposite. Lancaster on the outside, York inside." They had turned onto the Montoyas' street. "Speaking of which, park in front of the house next door. I want to show you something."

Cole led her across the neighbors' lawn, down the Montoyas' driveway, and into a cabana next to the pool. He was in secret agent mode, flattening himself along all vertical surfaces, and her pulse picked up despite her better judgment. The cabana held pool cleaning equipment, lounge chairs, plastic bags of chemicals. Louvered doors let in stripes of daylight and the air smelled faintly of chlorine. Cole began to kiss her heatedly.

"Cole... what if somebody sees us?"

"It's November. Nobody even looks at the back yard in November."

He had her bra unfastened and was massaging her breasts. The sensation was not unpleasant, but she was entirely too self-conscious and her family was too much on her mind for her to feel sexy. The same clearly could not be said for Cole, who now had her stretched out on one of the lounge chairs, panties off, and was dutifully attempting to get her aroused.

He had been wonderful with her parents and deserved a reward. "Sweetheart," she whispered, "it's not going to happen for me right now. You go ahead."

ALEX HAD BEEN THINKING of breaking it off with Denise after Thanksgiving, but Cole had been sneaking around putting it to Madelyn every chance he got all weekend long, and by the time they got to Austin on Sunday afternoon, Alex was in the mood for some easy action. Denise was up for it too. She now shared a room with Madelyn at the new co-op dorm, so it was no longer strictly necessary to get her home by ten, but she had Russian homework and was cool with an early night. When Alex got back from dropping her off, he saw the light was still on under Cole's door.

He knocked and stuck his head in. Cole had the new Albert King record on the stereo and was following along on guitar.

"Madelyn's not here?" Alex said.

"Doing laundry in the basement."

Alex turned the stereo down a decibel or two and straddled the desk chair. "Denise said that Madelyn said that you said that you're quitting the band."

"Thinking pretty hard about it. You?"

"I'm ready. I'd say it's no fun anymore, only it never was."

"I don't think it's going to come as a big surprise to Ron. Let's talk to him tomorrow."

"Okay."

"You been thinking about what's next?"

"Yeah," Alex said. "I have."

Cole pointed to the stereo. "Steve Cropper, Duck Dunn, they're white guys, and they're playing some serious-ass blues on this record. We could do that. Not fraternity-ready black pop songs, the real thing."

"You want to be in a *blues* band?"

"What's wrong with that?"

"I'm remembering all the shit you gave Gary when he wanted to do 'My Girl Sloopy' or the Joe Turner version of 'Corrina.'"

You could see that Cole was still pissed at Gary. He was about to come out with a lot of defensive bullshit, and then his better nature took hold. "Well, shit. Even assholes can be right some of the time. Seeing Muddy at the Fillmore, that really changed things for me. And hearing what Hendrix and Cream and those guys did with it. I almost wish Gary was here. He'd be perfect for the new band."

"Cole, we have to talk about that. I'm thinking I may take some time off."

Alex had hoped he could casually drop the news into some conversation or other and not make a big deal about it. Apparently not.

"You mean... quit playing bass?"

"Yeah, for a while, anyway. I'm a little burned out." He saw Cole's brain working, reading between the lines. "Look, man," Alex said, "I just don't need it the way you do. To be a star."

"That's not it," Cole said. "That's not it at all. I don't care about being famous and I sure as hell don't care about the money. All I want is to be able to do this all day." He held the guitar up off his stomach like Alex had any question about what "this" was. "If I'm not playing music, I want to be listening to it. If I'm not listening to it, I want to be talking about it, or reading about it, or daydreaming about it. I don't want to have to study or have a day job or tend bar or grow vegetables or do anything except play music until I die."

Alex turned his palms up. "I don't feel it like that. And the music's changing. When we started out it was Paul Revere and the Spoonful, 'Daytripper' and 'Satisfaction.' Now it's weird stuff like the Doors and the Airplane, or virtuoso shit like Hendrix and Cream. Even Motown has wah-wahs now. It's not about parties and girls anymore, it's serious. I love to listen to it and dance to it, but playing it? I don't want to have to work that hard. I don't want to be onstage at the Fillmore, I want to be in the audience, tripping."

Cole looked devastated. "I just thought... you and me..."

"What?"

Cole shook his head. "What about El Mariachi Montoya?"

"I will always be up for El Mariachi Montoya. Especially when there's pussy involved."

Madelyn picked that moment to walk in with a plastic laundry basket full of neatly folded clothes. If she'd overheard him, she had too much class to show it.

"Cole, can you run me home with these... oh, hey, Alex. Am I interrupting?"

"No, it's cool," Alex said, getting up. "We're done."

COLE WAS RELIEVED at how easily it went. Ron already had a list of substitute players—"including keyboard players" he made sure to point out—and he promised to start auditions right away. Nolan had a friend in the Longhorn Band who'd once offered them the band room for practices. Cole promised that he and Alex would fulfill their commitments until their replacements could take over. All very civilized.

Within the week Ron had a new bass player and called for a series of crash rehearsals in the Castle basement to work him in. The new guy was six-two, with a big belly and a short beard. He played bass like Nolan played drums, without danger of attracting attention to himself, and he could do high harmony vocals. With his arrival, Cole lost any last pleasure he might have taken in the band. The new configuration played the next two weekends and then, just before Christmas break, Ron phoned to say they'd found a guitarist and they would be by at Cole's convenience to pick up the gear.

The following Friday, he and Alex and Madelyn drove to Dallas. The next day, Cole's birthday, the extended Montoya family, sans Madelyn, flew to Guanajuato.

Cole would have preferred to stay in Austin with Madelyn, or even Dallas with Madelyn, but Susan was getting married in Guanajuato on the 30th and he and Alex and Jesús—the full version of El Mariachi Montoya—were scheduled to provide the music.

On their last night together in Austin, Madelyn had said, "It'll do us good to be apart for a few days. 'Absence doth sharpen love,' as the poet said."

"Shakespeare?"

"Thomas Overbury."

"You're tired of me," Cole said, "because I don't know a fraction of what you do. That's why you don't want to be around me anymore."

"Thomas Overbury never gave me an orgasm," she said, kissing him, and then she hesitated. "He may have come close a couple of times."

They'd heard rumors that UT was considering a change to the school calendar, starting classes in August and having finals before Christmas. Until that happened, the threat of exams still hung over the holidays, so Cole took his books to Mexico. Between Madelyn and The Other Side, his grades had slipped. He needed to ace his finals to keep his promise to Montoya.

Cole had sacrificed his birthday celebration to the greater good of Susan's wedding. Montoya promised a belated party after finals and Jesse's graduation. In the meantime, Susan had brought two bridesmaids and Jesse had brought his best man, and while they all went to the Hotel Santa Fe to sleep, the Montoya house was full of frantic activity and the harsh sound of English from afternoon until late at night.

By Christmas night, Cole was desperate to get away, and he let Alex talk him into taking their guitars to El Jardín de la Unión. Cole's biggest worry was that the girls from Swarthmore or Bryn Mawr or wherever the hell they came from would show up again. Strong as it was, he preferred to not have his resolve tested by the lavender scent and generous proportions of the body that still appeared periodically in his fantasies.

Being on the streets cured his nerves. He felt at home there in a way he never had in the US—the smells of flowers and decay, of car exhaust and fried onions and mop water on warm pavement, the distant sound of fútbol on TV and laughter and music, always music somewhere.

A gang of students in black academic robes had set up at the foot of the Teatro Colón, playing guitars and singing. «They'll move on in a minute,» Alex said, and eventually they did. He and Cole stepped up behind them and went into their act. Most of the fifty-odd tourists on the steps stayed put, and a few new ones showed up. Despite himself, Cole noticed a pair of Mexican girls in eyeliner and jeans and big hoop earrings. One of them had a ragged hairstyle in the peculiar shade of orange that Peroxide produced in naturally black hair. Catholic girls gone bad, ripe for the picking.

Alex had seen them too and he began to target them with his attention. Cole played along for Alex's sake, leaning back to back with him on the chorus of "Copa rota," adding wolf howls to "Bésame mucho," improvising Motown-style dance steps to "Quizás, quizás, quizás." The audience ate it up, and sure enough, the girls hung around awkwardly as people came up to shake their hands and congratulate them.

Alex went over to talk to them and a minute later called out, «Órale, Cole, we're going to have a beer. Are you coming?»

«I don't think so.»

«You sure?»

«I'm sure.»

Alex turned to the orange-haired girl and said, «I apologize. My friend had a terrible accident and now his pinga doesn't work anymore.»

She didn't know whether to be shocked, sympathetic, or amused. «What happened?»

«A tragedy,» Alex said. «He fell in love.»

Alex disappeared into El Jardín de la Unión with the girls and Cole walked home. He sat on the patio and played through some blues changes, missing Madelyn, feeling distant from Alex. Three and a half more years of classes and cramming and exams bordered on the unthinkable. Madelyn, on the other hand, thrived on it and would be crazy not to go for a doctorate and end up as a professor herself. He couldn't get those two pictures into the same frame.

He smelled smoke and looked up to see Susan sitting ten feet away with a cigarette. "Don't stop," she said. "You have completely picked up on my mood."

Cole kept playing. "What's wrong?" He had a good idea—Jesse's real estate job in Oklahoma City meant leaving her family and all her friends behind.

She sighed dramatically. "I suppose all brides get cold feet before the wedding. Are you still prepared to run away with me?"

Before he could respond, she said, "I'm sorry. I shouldn't tease you. Madelyn is wonderful and I'm truly happy for you."

"I like Jesse too," Cole said.

"Everybody likes Jesse. Even *I* like Jesse."

"You didn't let me finish. I like Jesse, but he's not right for you. He's perfect for the person you pretend to be, not the person you really are."

After a shocked silence, Susan said, "You say the most outrageous things to me sometimes. I don't know why I put up with it. What made you such an expert on the human heart?"

"Not all hearts."

"You never give up."

"I can be in love with Madelyn and still care about you. I don't know where they come from exactly, but you've got some inner demons. Jesse's got some too, and I don't think your demons are going to get along."

Eventually she said, "Speaking of inner demons, where's my brother?"

"We, uh, met a couple of girls and Alex went to have a beer with them."

"So he and Denise aren't…"

"No. I think she likes *him* well enough, but she's not, like, The One or anything."

"He doesn't seem to care that much about anything lately. I'm worried about him."

"Yeah," Cole said. "Me too."

"This family… I know we look like some kind of sitcom perfection to you. You don't see the pressure underneath. Daddy doesn't mean to do it, but the weight of his expectations, the immensity of his disappointment, it can crush you, or warp your personality."

"So the only reason you're marrying Jesse is to please your

father?" She didn't answer, so he said, "You can call it off, you know. Better that than be unhappy for the rest of your life."

"Just play the guitar, will you? Play 'Cielito lindo.'"

THE WEDDING TOOK PLACE at La Catedral de San Diego, where they'd spent Christmas Eve. Cole sat with Alex and Jesús on high stools to the side of the front pews, all of them in dark suits. Susan had stuck with the obvious for the music—the "Here Comes the Bride" processional from Wagner's *Lohengrin*, Mendelssohn's "Wedding March" for the recessional. Before and after, he and Alex played a few simple chords and left Jesús to do the heavy lifting. What with his musical duties and holding various mental snapshots of Madelyn in his mind, Cole managed to keep from getting over his head emotionally.

The heat and pressure Susan had talked about on Christmas night had metamorphosed her into marble. Her face was pale and immobile with makeup, and Cole guessed she'd also taken Valium. She'd always been small-boned, and in her old-fashioned white-corseted wedding dress she was greyhound thin. Her tense smile never varied during the ceremony, which involved a good deal of praying and one hymn that Jesús handled solo. Jesse managed to look both smitten and cocky, and Montoya had to wipe away a tear as he watched Susan and Jesse walk out of the church.

Back at the house, El Mariachi Montoya did their thing, to much dancing and applause. They were less ragged than the year before, while still some distance from professional. A good deal of cerveza Cuautémoc was on hand to make up the difference. Alex had invited his girlfriends from Christmas night, who blended without incident among the fifty or so other guests—guests that did not include, Cole noted with disappointment, Susan's mother.

By two AM Alex had disappeared with his women. Jesse and Susan had long ago departed for their hotel and were headed to Acapulco in the morning. Cole, who had played a set of US top 40 hits with Alex in addition to the mariachi material, was worn out and had retired to the patio alone, leaving Jesús to hold the fort.

1967

The night was cold after the crush of bodies indoors, and the stars glittered like pellets of ice in a vast emptiness. A dog yelped in the distance, high-pitched, desperate. Madelyn seemed like a figment of his imagination, and the new year ahead was a math problem he couldn't solve. He'd been drinking all night and it hadn't helped. Maybe, he thought, one more beer would do the trick.

1968

THE FIRST DAY of the new year came up gray and bitter cold, and the latest snowfall lay heaped on the sides of the streets, turning black from the exhaust fumes of the eternally honking cars.

San Francisco, Dave thought.

Why not?

Jake had moved earlier that winter. He'd been spending more and more time there and then one day he simply failed to come back. "You should come out," he told Dave over the phone. "This is where it's happening now. LA and New York are done."

Dave still loved New York and always would. What he wanted to leave behind was the person he'd been here, the loser who gave up The Meteors to Tom Dowd, who'd run away from Crystal and from Sallie Rachel, who'd been bullied by Mitch Miller and Morgan Conrad and even the Columbia accountant who'd stripped him of his name.

If he moved to San Francisco he would be the Dave Fisher of the album cover credits: engineer, producer, maker of hit records.

Two things worried him. The first was the lack of career session musicians in San Francisco, which itself was due to his second concern, the lack of modern studios. Despite the fact that Ampex already had a prototype 16-track recorder, expected to be generally available by mid-year, San Francisco had only a single 8-track machine in the entire city.

For homework, Dave listened to records from the best of the San Francisco studios. From Golden State came the first Beau Brummels album and the Charlatans single that Jake had produced. From Coast, the Mojo Men and Jack Jones's *Dear Heart*. From Columbia, the great We Five single and the final Kingston Trio albums. He strained to filter out the production and the performance and to hear only the quality of the equipment and the sound of the rooms.

On Sunday the 7th he flew out to listen for himself.

The three-hour time difference meant he was able to check into his hotel, change out of his suit, and make it out to the Fillmore Auditorium he'd heard so much about. A benefit was in progress for "Stop the Draft Week," Phil Ochs headlining. The place was mobbed, and at first Dave wondered if somebody had put out a casting call for people dressed as hippies. The mad, dizzying variety of costumes he'd seen at the Longshoremen's Hall two years ago had turned to formula: flowing hair past the shoulders, headbands and love beads, bell-bottomed jeans and sandals.

Bill Graham himself stood at the door taking tickets, and Dave took a second to introduce himself. "Dave Fisher!" Graham said. "I thought you were in New York."

"I'm considering a change," Dave said.

"Can you come by my office tomorrow afternoon? It's downstairs here. We should talk."

"Sure," Dave said. "Absolutely."

Inside the cavernous auditorium, Dave was assaulted by the loudest band he'd ever heard. They had only one guitar, a bass, and a drum set, yet the massive distortion, screaming feedback, and pounding double bass drums was the soundtrack to a relentless air raid. Dave retreated to a corner with his hands over his ears. He really wanted to see Phil Ochs, whom he remembered from the early days in the Village. He wasn't sure he could hold out long enough. Before he quite made up his mind to leave, the band wrapped up their set to enthusiastic applause. Their name, they said, was Blue Cheer. Dave thought they shouldn't spread it around.

Next up was a mediocre white R&B outfit called the Loading Zone. The competence of their horn section didn't make up for their shortage of original material. They did get the dancers on their feet, reinforcing how different the local culture was from that of New York, down to the very way that the people moved.

Finally Ochs took the stage. He looked good, handsome and mischievous as ever. He had only his acoustic guitar for accompaniment, though his last album had featured complex arrangements that included strings and rock instruments. Ochs had ambitions as all-devouring as Dylan's or Elvis's, but the same lightning had never struck him. The failure was eating at him, Dave thought. He would play the opening chords to a song and then stop to talk, making with the self-deprecating humor, quoting from his bad reviews, throwing out despairing political quips. He talked about his love for John Wayne, even as he called him a "right-wing reactionary," and Dave had sudden vision of Ochs in a cowboy outfit, his back to a dusty Utah cliff, firing pistols in both hands at the hordes of savage conformists, only to be turned away in the end from the supper table of chart success.

Dave left under a cloud of memories. Folk-rock was something that he understood, that he knew how to produce, and he wondered if, at the age of 32, he was already sliding from the cutting edge back onto the flat of the blade.

LATE THE NEXT MORNING, Dave met Frank Werber at Columbia Recorders, home of the only 8-track in town. Werber had dark curly hair and a beard, a deep tan, and what Dave could only describe as a powerful life force. He wore a white turtleneck and a herringbone jacket with a flower in the lapel. The studio, as well as the entire flatiron-shaped Columbus Tower that sat above it, were only a part of the investments that Werber had made with the money that poured in from the Kingston Trio, whom he'd managed until their breakup the previous June. Another one was the Trident Restaurant across the bay in Sausalito, and he insisted on driving Dave there in his Mercedes 300SL, with the doors that lifted straight up like wings. Werber smoked a joint while he drove at reckless speed, talking Eastern philosophy and investments, race horses and pop music. He told Dave he thought Sallie Rachel's record was "brilliant." Then he said he was moving away from production because he was "tired of wiping musician's asses."

The Trident was immense and multileveled. A continuous, curving, wood-paneled interior with potted palms and ferns gradually stepped down to a dock with outdoor tables, which was where Dave and Werber ended up. The temperature had climbed into the upper sixties and a cool breeze lifted Dave's thinning hair. A parade of stunning waitresses came by the table to say hi, one in full costume as a leftover Christmas elf, some in jeans and T-shirts, one in a sari and glitter, one in a gauzy white muslin shift. None of them, Dave noticed, were wearing bras.

"I hire them all myself," Werber said. "We don't have uniforms here, and we encourage the girls to go with the vibes, to be themselves. We get lots of applicants." He smiled in a way that made Dave uncomfortable. Dave nodded and looked at the menu, whose heading read, "Positive energy projection is the trip."

Werber also made it his duty to hire the chef, and the food turned out to be superb. Cooking was among Werber's many skills, along with gold mining, scuba diving, commercial art, driving a cab, operating a ski lift, and untold others. He said that he'd learned to cook from his father, who'd used it to keep them alive in a concentration camp in Vichy France. Just as Dave's credulity was feeling strained, Werber, unbidden, pushed back his sleeve to show Dave the number tattooed on his forearm.

Dave had seen his share of those numbers as a kid in Yonkers. He could never get used to the sight, and seeing it here on this clear, sunny day, in a fabulous restaurant full of sensual women, reminded him that comfort and safety and well-being were never more than provisional, subject to revocation without warning, and he decided he didn't begrudge Werber his auditions of waitresses after all.

Werber picked up the check without ever making a sales pitch for the studio, and dropped Dave off at the Fillmore at three in the afternoon.

FOR DAVE, sitting with Bill Graham was like being back in New York. Graham had a New York face, meaty, with a New York hard stare. Everything about him said that he was an intense, play-for-keeps kind of guy who happened, at the moment, to be on his best behavior. They talked for a few minutes about New York, about Sallie Rachel, about Phil Ochs, and then Graham got to the point.

"People are pushing me to expand the business. Start a record label, open a recording studio, get serious about artist management.

I don't know. For me, it's always been about producing the live event. I don't think I have the patience for the other stuff. But whether I like it or not, it's going to happen, and soon. Top-notch recording studios, big name producers, record company offices. Only it's going to happen with a San Francisco twist. They don't want hit factories here, no Brill Buildings, no studio musicians. What they want is artistic freedom. They're not interested in three-minute singles, they're writing entire albums. The guy who can understand that, and still ride herd on them, bring a professional sensibility to bear on all this meandering self-expression, he's going to be able to write his own ticket."

"I don't know if I'm that guy."

"I think you could be. I remember you from when you were here with the Spoonful, the Sparkle Plenty show. I've been seeing your name. You're a good engineer, you know how to make records sound good. And you're a good producer. Your records all sound different, because you're serving the artist. If I end up doing this label thing, you're the kind of guy I'm going to hire."

"And if you don't do it?"

"Somebody else will. You're thinking about moving out here? I wouldn't hesitate."

THAT NIGHT DAVE stayed in and watched TV. Between Blue Cheer and Frank Werber and the surrealistic humor of *The Monkees*, he felt old and out of place. He was crazy, no matter what Graham said, to even think about leaving New York.

His Tuesday appointment was Don Geis, the engineer at Coast Recorders. Coast was owned by Bill Putnam, a legend for the way he'd outfitted other studios, including Western in LA. The room was spacious and lively, with a stage at one end where they liked to put the drummer for a big, booming sound. Dave put it on his list as "possible."

He spent the afternoon at Fisherman's Wharf, watching boats sail out past the Golden Gate and into the great unknown world, wondering if he had maybe outgrown the record business, if he should look for something else to do with the rest of his life.

After an early dinner he took a cab to the hungry i, where the Spoonful had played the week before Sparkle Plenty. The owner, Enrico Banducci, in trademark beret and walrus mustache, remembered him and showed him to a table down front.

He was in time for the opener, a kid named Skip Shaw, and within five minutes his palms were sweating with the desire to sign him.

Shaw looked all of 16, crouched over his acoustic guitar like a vulture over a rabbit carcass. He was skinny and sickly-looking and chain-smoked Luckies that he kept in an ashtray on a second stool next to his own. His dreamy eyes closed when he sang, and his bruised and husky voice reminded Dave of Timmy Hardin. His original songs also bore the Hardin influence in their extended metaphors or open-hearted confessions, though they were all good enough to stand on their own merits. His covers showed taste and expertise, picked from Hardin, Fred Neil, Tim Buckley, even Phil Ochs, to whose "There but for Fortune" he gave a spare, wrenching reading. Clearly the audience loved him, especially the female contingent, and after his encore, Dave sought out Enrico at the bar.

"Has this kid got a record contract?"

"Hmmmm. Not an easy question. Has he made a record? No. Is he actively recording one? No. Are there people who think he owes them a record? Most certainly."

"Oh."

"He's unreliable, I'm afraid. I always have a last-minute substitute available when I book him. And I keep booking him because he makes me cry."

"I want to meet him."

"I'll bring him out. Don't say I didn't warn you."

Dave sat at the bar with Shaw, who sipped steadily at a double Jack Daniels and didn't talk much. He bowed his head at Dave's praise and they exchanged business cards and Dave walked away without a real sense of the guy other than his inscrutability.

Which didn't stop him, first thing in the morning, from calling the manager listed on the card, a fast-talking former DJ named Wes. Wes assured him that Shaw was 19 years old and no longer encumbered by a previous record contract that "hadn't panned out." They closed the call with a verbal agreement that Dave would pay for a recording session within the month and shop the resulting demo.

With Shaw in mind, Dave's enthusiasm revived for his appointment with Leo "The Baron" Kulka, owner and chief engineer at Golden State. Kulka was six feet tall and balding, wearing thick glasses and a white shirt and ascot tie, whose formality didn't match his easy, joking manner and big voice. He let Dave sit in on a session for a gospel group from Oakland that he was recording live: four singers, guitar, bass, drums, and piano.

"Is that going through the echo chamber?" Dave asked during a slow piano and bass break.

"It's the room!" Kulka said. "It's the room!"

The room was not as perfect sonically as Columbia's "church" or their Studio A, but it had that big room sound, and it *was* a big room, over 50 feet on a side, with a high, arched ceiling. Dave had a vision of what Skip Shaw would sound like in there, letting the acoustic guitar ring from wall to wall, backing him with a small combo, string bass, quiet drummer, piano, some sonic coloration like cello or muted trumpet, an accordion here, an electric guitar there.

"Let's talk," he said to Kulka, "about what dates you've got open."

Back at the hotel, he checked his answering service. Sallie Rachel was looking for him and had left a Denver number.

He sat on the bed with the slip of paper and stared at the phone, nervous as a high-school kid. It took him three tries to punch in his credit card number correctly. Maybe she'd already left for sound check. After three rings she snatched up the phone, out of breath and charged with the energy of youth and success. Dave was paralyzed with longing. What was the word for nostalgia for something you'd never had?

"Sallie, it's Dave, I got your—"

"Dave! Where are you?"

"San Francisco. I—"

"I love San Francisco! What are you doing out there?"

The more he said, the more she drew him out, until he'd told her everything, from Blue Cheer to Skip Shaw. When he was done, she said, "Why don't we make my next record there too?"

She was overdue for her sophomore album and Dave had assumed she'd already started it with somebody else. "Wouldn't it make more sense to do it where Cornell and Bernard and those guys live instead of flying them all the way across the continent?"

"Actually," Sallie said, and after a long pause her voice got very quiet, "I've got my own band now."

He'd read in *Billboard* that she was now headlining theater-sized venues on the strength of two pretty successful singles, steady album sales, and a couple of hits she'd written for other people. Of course she would have her own band now.

"I know what you're going to say," she said. "You're going to tell me the studio is not the road, different set of skills, every mistake costs hundreds of dollars. Am I right?"

He'd been taking in the breath to say those very words. "Yes."

"You see? I really was paying attention all this time. Everybody in the band has studio experience. They're all fantastic. Wait till you hear them."

"What if you fly them to San Francisco and put them in a hotel and we get them in the studio and it doesn't work?" He remembered her crying in the airport before the Peter, Paul and Mary tour, afraid to be without him. The power had shifted. She was a star.

"Don't worry," she said. "You'll love them."

DAVE BOOKED THEM back to back at Golden State, the first two days in February for Shaw, the next two weeks for Sallie. He cancelled his return flight to New York, rented a spartan furnished apartment in the South of Market neighborhood a few blocks from the studio, and went to work.

Leo Kulka gave him a list of jazz musicians he'd worked with and the clubs where he might find them. He met with Shaw and they settled on three original songs for the demo: "Tender Hours," "Orchids for Your Smile," and "South of the Line." Skip shook his head at the notion of a jazz combo. "That's great for a Tim

Hardin or a Sallie Rachel. I want something with balls. I'm not asking for Keith Moon on drums, but I want a solid two and four. And an electric bass and electric lead guitar. I can play the leads."

In one ear Dave heard Enrico tell him, "Don't say I didn't warn you," and in the other Bill Graham said, "You serve the artist." Dave said, "Okay, we'll try it. We've only got two days in the studio, so it's got to come together fast."

"Don't worry," Shaw said, and then, after a second, "There's one problem. My electric's in hock."

They took a cab to the pawn shop, where Dave paid $150 to reclaim the guitar. It was a cherry-red Gibson ES-335, and when the clerk brought it from the back, Shaw opened the case and sat on the floor and cradled it like a baby. "Never again," he said to the guitar, "I promise." He looked up at Dave with misty eyes and said, "Thank you," and Dave could only nod and look away in embarrassment.

"I don't suppose you have an amp?"

"I'm between amps at the moment," Shaw said.

That next morning, he called Ahmet Ertegun and told him Sallie wanted to record in San Francisco with her own band.

"That's a lot of unknowns," Ertegun said.

"I don't disagree," Dave said.

"That first record did well for us. I'd be glad to have another one like it. Are you sure you can take control of the situation if you have to?"

"I'm sure," Dave lied.

With some reluctance, he called Bill Graham and asked his advice on bass and drums for Shaw. Graham was flattered and happy to help. "You're not going to get the Airplane or the Dead for session work. I would try the Sons of Champlin."

"Who?"

"Exactly. That's why you stand a chance of getting them. Good players, and they're hungry."

Dave took a cab to Oakland to see the band, wondering if he was going to have to buy a car and learn to drive it. The band turned out to be another R&B flavored horn band, with better material than the Loading Zone, but, in Dave's opinion, lacking a certain magic. The drummer and bass player, however, were as solid as Graham had promised and were willing to do the session.

He spent a couple of hours on the phone with Sallie. She played him half a dozen new songs, and they sounded to Dave like the road had sharpened her commercial sense without dulling the things that made her unique.

On Thursday, February 1, Dave arrived at Golden State Recorders ready to go to work, and all his careful preparation began to fall apart before Shaw even walked in the door.

First of all, he was an hour late. His face showed the flattened affect of terminal nerves. Dave had already miked the drums, had set up the rented Fender Deluxe amp that Shaw had requested, and had a tentative sound for the bass. The first words out of Shaw's mouth were, "You put me on the wrong side of the drummer."

After they switched the amps around, Shaw taught Al, the bass player, the part for "South of the Line," note for note, while Dave adjusted the mikes and set levels, Kulka assisting from the control room. Al made a couple of suggestions for improvements, which Shaw instantly vetoed. When it happened a third time, Dave stepped in. "Al's right. He was right the other two times as well. We're paying him to play bass. Let him do his job."

Shaw put his guitar down and walked out. Al exchanged a look with Bill, the drummer, and Dave held out both hands in a plea for patience.

Shaw came back two minutes later and they began running through the song. Shaw had a lot of instructions for both players, but after half an hour Dave was starting to hear potential.

They took a lunch break and Dave ordered in Chinese. Shaw came and went the whole time. At two they tried a couple of takes.

The playback sounded thin. "What about doing the basic track with your acoustic?" Dave said.

"The bass and drums'll overwhelm it."

"We'll close mike it and punch it up in the mix. It'll sound fine in the headphones."

"I don't know. Let me think about it." Shaw disappeared for five minutes, and when he came back they tried the acoustic. Getting the balance right took time, and Shaw's patience began to slip.

By the time they tried a take, Shaw was slurring the guide vocal and botching the rhythm. The next time he walked out, Dave gave him a minute and then followed him into the men's room. Shaw stood in front of the sink, draining the last of a pint of Old Overholt.

"You're drunk," Dave said.

Shaw dropped the bottle, which shattered on the tile floor. Then he gripped the edges of the sink with both hands.

"I'm paying for this out of my own pocket," Dave said. "Every time you fuck up, it costs me money. Money that I'm spending because I believed in you."

"I know," Shaw said. "You think I don't know? I'm scared out of my gourd. This is my last chance. Nineteen years old, and I'm on the edge of being washed up."

"Go home," Dave said. "Get some sleep. Come in here tomorrow sober, on time, and ready to work, or we're done. Do you understand me?"

Shaw nodded glumly and Dave followed him into the studio. While he packed up his guitars, Dave took Al and Bill aside. "I'm paying you both for a full day. You have my word that this bullshit will not happen again tomorrow. I'm counting on you guys to stick with me and help me wrap this up."

"We'll be here," Al said.

SALLIE AND HER BAND had hit town at about the time that Shaw's whiskey bottle broke. Dave took a long, scalding shower before meeting her for dinner, trying to shake the sense of doom that Shaw had left him with and to settle his own love-struck nerves.

She was waiting outside Sears Fine Food on Powell Street when his cab pulled up. She looked the same as ever, the lighter-than-air red-brown hair, the bottomless eyes, the devastating smile, the tight jeans, the ribbed sweater that clung to her the way Dave longed to. She ran to him as he got out of the cab and hugged him quickly, nothing much behind it.

They both had the roast turkey and dressing blue plate special and the famous Swedish pancakes for dessert. As he knew she would, she coaxed the complete story of his horrible day from him, and when it came time for her to reciprocate and talk about her last nine months on the road, he knew she was holding something back. To his shame, he found himself unwilling to push to find out what it was.

Standing on the street afterward, she said, "Can I come by the studio tomorrow? To check the place out?"

"And see my enfant terrible?"

"Yes."

"Okay. Try not to spook him."

"Me? How could I spook anyone?"

TRUE TO HIS WORD, Shaw arrived on time and sober on Friday morning. His hands trembled and his concentration was poor. After three blown tries at "South of the Line," Dave took him outside. "What's the problem?"

"I'm a mess," Shaw said, unnecessarily. "Nerves. I keep thinking about what this is costing you."

There should be a word, Dave thought, for causing something by the very act of trying to prevent it. "What's it going to take to get you calmed down and ready to work?"

Shaw gave the answer Dave expected. "A drink. Just one. Just the hair of the dog."

"Did you bring any?"

Shaw nodded, then turned defensive. "You said I had to turn up sober. You didn't say I couldn't bring anything."

"Where is it?"

"In my gear bag."

"Bring the bag into the control room. I don't want Bill and Al to know about this."

Dave confiscated the bottle and gave him a jigger's worth in a paper cup, mixed with Coke. Shaw knocked it back, and a half hour later they had a clean backing track for "South of the Line." By seven that night, thanks to two more medicinal doses of whiskey, they had instrumental tracks for the other two songs. No vocals. No lead guitar. He'd used up all the time he'd allotted to Shaw, with Sallie ready to come in the next morning.

Sallie herself had dropped by in the middle of the afternoon and he'd played her what he had. "Beautiful," she said. "It's... vibrant."

Kulka, who was listening in, said, "It's the room!"

"The kid is cute, too," Sallie said, giving Dave his one-millionth pang of jealousy.

"The kid is a complete pain in the ass," Dave said. "It's going to be such a pleasure to work with you."

On Saturday morning the band assembled at the studio: keyboards, bass, and drums, the keyboard player doubling on sax. Dave spent a couple of hours getting the mikes positioned and listening to the sonic qualities of the instruments. He was not a fan of the saxophone, preferring the shiny sound of a trumpet where horns were concerned. But the saxophone was not the problem. The problem was Ted, the drummer, who was overly busy and tended to lose time on his fills.

After a run-through of the first song, "Breaking the Ice," Dave checked it against a metronome and then brought Sallie into the control room to listen.

"Maybe he just needs to warm up?" she said.

"We've only got two weeks to make an album of sufficient quality to satisfy Ahmet Ertegun."

"What are we talking about, here? Are you talking about replacing Ted?"

"If he doesn't come around..."

"We can't do that."

"It happens all the time. Somebody can be perfectly fine on stage—"

"I know, I know, different skill set, we've been through that. These guys are all friends, it would mess with their morale—"

"You said they were pros. Pros are used to this kind of thing."

Sallie didn't answer. She looked at her hands, knotted in her lap.

"Sallie, what is it you're not telling me?"

Her voice was barely audible. "Ted and I are... we have a... a personal relationship."

You have no reason, Dave told himself, to feel devastated. What did you think, she was going to be celibate?

"The rest of the band doesn't know," Sallie said.

Dave doubted that. In the studio the three men, dressed in khaki slacks and sport shirts, were laughing, smoking, tossing a few progressions back and forth. Ted was tall and thin. A lock of brown hair fell over one eye in a way that struck Dave as vain.

He congratulated himself for not expressing dismay or disapproval. He stayed calm and practical. "Either you need to talk to him or I do. I'm going to put a click track in his headphones, and I want him to stay on it. He can shift the accents, as long as he cuts back on the fills. Anything he does I want short, sharp, staccato."

"I'll talk to him," she said. Her eyes shone. "Thank you. We'll make this work."

THEY KNOCKED OFF at 7:00. With some splicing, Dave was confident that they had a couple of acceptable basic tracks. Sallie wanted him to go to dinner with the band, and he had to beg off. He got a quick bite to eat and then went back to the studio to start overdubs with Skip Shaw.

Kulka was long gone and the two of them had the place to themselves. The studio lights lacked dimmers, so Dave killed them all and lit a few candles that he'd brought for the purpose. Shaw was relaxed and talkative, telling Dave about hunting rattlesnakes in the Sierra Nevada as a kid and running away to Mexico his sophomore year in high school, the inspiration for "South of the Line." The stories were self-deprecating and genuinely funny, and Dave let him take all the time he needed.

Dave still had a question in his mind about whether they would need a session guitarist. Shaw quickly laid it to rest, putting thoughtful, melodic leads on all three tracks by 11:30. Skip wanted to keep going, so Dave made a pot of coffee and pressed on for the sake of getting the ordeal over with. At three AM Dave and Skip stood at a boom mike and added harmony vocals and handclaps to "South of the Line" and they were done.

"I'll mix it down next week," Dave said. "But I think this is a salable product."

"Can we mix it tomorrow?"

"No," Dave said. "Monday."

Shaw turned solemn and shook Dave's hand. "I don't ever want to work with another producer than you."

My God, Dave thought, what have I done?

HIS NAME WAS LENNY. Taller than Cole, six-three and skinny, two years older, reddish brown hair, mutton-chop sideburns, big, tortoise-shell rectangular glasses. If Lenny had been female, Cole would have described his feelings as love at first sight. Nothing sexual about it, just an instantaneous pleasure in Lenny's company that felt immediately reciprocated, a recognition of a common sense of humor before the first joke was told.

Without that sudden and mysterious bond, things might have been awkward. The spidery lettering on the index card had read, "THE AUSTIN BLUES GROUP. Up-and-coming Chicago-style blues outfit seeks competent rhythm guitarist and outstanding lead singer."

Cole had talked to Marc, the bass player, on the phone, mentioning only that he sang, played guitar, and had his own gear. Marc had thrown him a couple of questions to make sure he actually knew something about the blues—what was the name of Howlin' Wolf's guitar player, who did Robert Johnson meet at the crossroads—and then they'd set up an audition for the next night in a communal dorm across from Eastwoods Park.

At the audition, Cole sang, "So Many Roads, So Many Trains" by Otis Rush, sticking to the chords while Lenny played a searing lead on his gold-top Les Paul. Marc was not as creative a bassist as Alex, but he played low on the neck, with no treble, to produce a booming tone that Cole liked a lot, more of a presence than a set of notes. Tommy, the drummer, had a kind of loose, rattling style à la Ginger Baker, busy and musical.

Cole suggested they stretch out on "Stormy Monday." He sang two verses and let Lenny do a nice, trebly lead in the T-Bone Walker style. Then, for kicks, he turned and made eye contact with the drummer, who quickly figured out that Cole had taken the volume down and began to do something quiet with only the snare, floor tom, and bass drum. Cole opened with a few soft trills and slowly built up to a nice frenzy. Lenny, grinning by this point, waited for Cole to nod him in, then switched from chords to lead and proceeded to weave their parts in a way that Farmer Frank would have envied. Probably nine-tenths of it didn't work. The tenth that did made Cole's heart beat fast.

They tortured the song for thirty minutes before they finally put it out of its misery in a big finish. Cole and Lenny were laughing with the pleasure of it even as Marc looked troubled. He was the earnest sort, blue work shirt and round, wire-rimmed glasses, and he told Cole, "You're a great guitarist. But... we've already got a lead player, and I don't know..."

"Cole, is it?" Lenny interrupted. Cole nodded. "Can you give us five minutes?"

Cole sat outside on the steps. February 19th. The day had been a preview of spring, even now, at eight in the evening, hovering in the high 50s. Winter was on the run, and Cole knew he was on the brink of something. When Lenny came out and sat next to him, Cole wondered if he'd misread the signs.

Lenny lit a Marlboro and said, "We've been together a year. We lost our lead singer over Christmas. He'd been out of school since last summer and he got drafted, poor bastard. Anyway, we had the idea that we were going to get another singer and keep doing what we were doing, a poor man's Butterfield. Marc, he's got good traction, but he doesn't corner all that well. Whereas I can see some real possibilities here."

"Me too," Cole said.

"Most of what we just played was crap," Lenny said.

"Yep."

Lenny laughed and it infected Cole. "Why don't we go back in there," Lenny said, "and see where this goes?"

MADELYN HAD WATCHED as the Castle evolved a communal spirit over the course of the winter. The boys took turns cooking for the whole house, and even Sunny came out to sit with them most nights, though of course he refused anything with meat in it. On Friday nights they gathered in the living room to watch *Star Trek* together. The stray orange cat that Joe had been feeding ended up with the name Spock and the run of the house. Cole put up a blackboard next to the kitchen phone for messages, which was quickly subverted for insults, running jokes, and amateur art.

Lenny dropped into the scene in late February without a ripple; Madelyn got used to finding him on the foldout sofa, fully clothed under a blanket, curled up against his guitar. As likeable as Lenny was, something about him made Madelyn anxious from the first. She wanted to believe that she wasn't jealous of the private jokes between him and Cole that she didn't get, or the complete absence of tension between the two of them, even when Cole was tense with her and everyone else. Most of all she wanted to believe she wasn't jealous of the new band. She hadn't believed, after all, that his leaving The Other Side was the end of his musical ambitions. Cole was not to blame if she'd gotten used to having him around, used to their schedule of sleeping apart most Monday through Thursday nights and being together all weekend—making love, studying, going to movies or live music, driving to San Antonio one Thursday in mid-February to see Jimi Hendrix, which had made her reevaluate what electric music could be.

Before Lenny, everything had been perfect. She felt at home at the university in a way she never had at high school, loved the challenge of Russian, took pride in her straight As, was grateful for the way her personal life dovetailed so seamlessly with school. After Lenny, her perfect life began to slip through her fingers.

For a couple of months they'd been going to a new place called The Vulcan Gas Company, and that had added to her anxiety. Only a year before, she'd been at the Studio Club, with its dress codes and tightly rehearsed bands playing three-minute pop songs. At the Vulcan, the Thirteenth Floor Elevators featured an electric jug hiccupping behind lyrics about transcendent mental states and a singer so intense he looked like he might break down on stage; Shiva's Headband put an electric violin to sprawling songs that twisted the blues together with country-western and disdained any pretense of commerciality. This, Alex and Cole both assured her, was exactly what was happening in San Francisco, a city they both claimed to dislike, and whose spell they could not seem to escape.

The audience for those shows mixed UT students with members of the growing street culture, former students who had graduated or dropped out and remained in Austin working at menial jobs or no jobs at all, panhandling, selling drugs, showing up for occasional shifts at Manpower. And while these people—the men often bearded or with finger-in-the-socket hair, the women often braless, matriarchal in muumuus or waiflike in jeans—were interesting from a sociological point of view, something in them frightened her, a sense of idealism without a clear agenda, the feeling that they had not merely dropped out of straight society but also cut themselves adrift from common sense.

The drugs scared her too. Cole had taken LSD once and suffered no apparent harm. Alex still took it on occasion and now Denise was joining him. Madelyn couldn't help but wonder if the acid had contributed to Alex's emotional distance.

As for Denise, she'd initially been part of the communal scene in the role of Alex's girlfriend; between Thanksgiving and Christmas, as Alex had increasingly withdrawn from her, she had ended up in the living room watching TV with Tupelo Joe or practicing Russian with Madelyn at the dining room table. After Alex finally dumped her over Christmas, Madelyn only saw her at the dorm. That lasted a month or so and then, to everyone's surprise, and with Alex's presumed blessing, she was back, this time under the auspices of Tupelo Joe.

As weird as the situation appeared to Madelyn, none of the principals seemed to mind. "He's sweet," Denise told her. "He's so *grateful* for sex. It's nice not to be taken for granted."

They had created, Madelyn thought, a haven from a world that was growing increasingly chaotic.

In January the Viet Cong launched a surprise offensive across South Vietnam. In response, strikes and protests ramped up in Poland and France and the UK as well as the US. LBJ pulled out of the presidential race because of the war and Bobby Kennedy jumped in.

Then, last week, Martin Luther King had been murdered in

Memphis, and Madelyn had stayed on the phone with her father, who was inconsolable, until after midnight. She woke up the next day to news of riots across the country and around the world.

Cole was not insensitive, exactly. He understood the tragedy and injustice of it; he understood why Madelyn felt the way she did. He just didn't feel it himself.

He was focused on the band's debut at the Vulcan, Friday, April 12, which had somehow suddenly arrived. She spent the day trying to replace her anxiety and mourning with feelings more appropriate to the excesses of the spring erupting outside, dogwoods and redbuds dropping their blossoms to reveal tender new leaves, dandelions blowing, cloud shadows racing across warm lawns.

Cole and the rest of the band had left early for sound check. Madelyn caught a ride with Alex and Joe and Denise. It was the first night of a two-weekend run, at the bottom of a bill with Shiva's, Rubaiyat, and Conqueroo.

The club occupied an empty retail space on Congress Avenue downtown, three blocks from the river. Painted mandalas filled the display windows, and the glass front door was papered over with handbills for the show. Inside, church pews and crude benches provided the only seating; the high stage was at the opposite end of the long, narrow room from the entrance. Exposed pipes criss-crossed the high ceiling, barely visible in the gloom.

Cole, wearing his gig clothes, wandered out from the side of the stage. He enveloped her in a hug and kissed her enthusiastically. She tried to remember the last time she'd seen him this radiant. With one arm still around Madelyn, he put the other around Alex's neck. "I wish it was you up there with us tonight. Don't you miss it?"

"Nah, man, it's cool. I'd rather dance."

The place had no liquor license, part of an ongoing struggle with the Austin political establishment that was symptomatic of the birth struggles of the new culture. That same conflict had led to the owners pleading with the audience not to smoke pot on the premises. So people brought their own drinks, from bottles of Coke to surreptitious beer and wine and flasks of hard liquor, all of which they freely shared. And, because LSD was technically no longer in one's possession once it was in the bloodstream, a substantial portion of the crowd had chosen that option.

The Austin Blues Group hit the stage at 8:15. Madelyn realized that she was seeing Cole on stage for only the third time; despite her meager statistical sample, she saw immediately that this band was of another order of magnitude than The Chevelles or The Other Side.

They started with something that Cole had taught her was called a shuffle, syncopated 4/4 with a triplet feel. The energy was ferocious and was augmented by the dizzying light show. Cole looked like he'd been waiting his entire life for this moment, only to discover that it was more fun than he'd imagined. After a couple of minutes of rising tension, Cole took the microphone and sang about Automatic Slim and Fast-Talking Fanny, and then Lenny and the bass player came in on harmony and threatened to pitch a Wang Dang Doodle all night long.

A couple of minutes further into the song, it became unstable, apparently on purpose, and began to shake itself apart. Lenny, who seemed nervous, especially compared to Cole and the other two, faced the drummer and together they steadied the music into a straight 4/4 beat, and Cole sang "Get Out of My Life, Woman." From there they segued into "Sunshine of Your Love," to Lenny's apparent surprise, though he'd been the first to throw out the guitar line. When the lead came around, he and Cole played it together, Lenny off the record, Cole straying into harmony. The audience loved it, waving their arms as they danced, reacting, Madelyn thought, as much to the joy that poured off the stage as to the music. Lenny's awkwardness notwithstanding, it reminded her of The Beatles on Ed Sullivan, charm and enthusiasm and finely-honed technique, minus the innocence.

She'd been standing with Alex since the set began, watching him sway and shift his feet, and finally he said, "C'mon, let's dance." She followed him into the growing throng in front of the stage, surprised, as she had been on previous Vulcan trips, at the way this poised, well-scrubbed young man, shaped by money and prep school in a way Cole had not been, was able to lose himself so completely in movement, undulating, spinning Durga-armed, bending and leaning and weaving. Madelyn tried to follow, knowing she was stiff and self-conscious, trying to relax into it as Alex smiled encouragement.

The music from the stage never stopped, instead shifting in form like the spheres of colored oil projected onto the musicians, speeding and slowing, dropping into one song or another and then moving on. Half an hour into their set they gradually quieted until Madelyn could hear the bodies around her, their breath slowing, footsteps slowing, along with the music. The drummer barely touched his cymbal; Lenny held one long note. Madelyn turned to look as Cole stepped up to the microphone and said, "This is for somebody special." He started to sing a song she'd never heard before:

> Golden light comes streaming in
> On golden hair and molten skin
> Gold can't buy the gift she brings
> A love that glides on golden wings

She saw that he'd written it for her. She didn't doubt that he loved her and that he meant every word he sang. But now, in the midst of her country coming apart, the fact that the band was this good meant another coming apart, and the tears that she'd been holding back broke and ran down her face, not because the music tore at her heart, though it did, but because she knew he was telling her goodbye.

THE CROWD DIDN'T WANT to let them go. Madelyn didn't either. She clapped and screamed along. The band charged back onstage and Cole said, "Just one more," and they played a breakneck reading of "Fire" from the Jimi Hendrix album that Cole had played until he wore it out. After that came the anticlimax of clearing their equipment off the stage, and then Cole was pushing through the crowd to get to her, and she wondered if she could survive the heartbreak of looking at him.

He swept her up in an embrace, crushing her to his sweat-soaked shirt and saying, "Did you like your song?"

"Yes, baby, of course I loved it, you idiot, it's beautiful."

"Why are you crying?"

"Just shut up and hold me."

Over the next four hours, Cole came and went, sometimes standing with her to watch the band onstage, an arm around her waist, then excusing himself to talk with Lenny or guys from the other bands, or disappearing backstage for half an hour, always returning to her with love shining in his eyes.

Sometime after one, after Shiva's was well into their headline set, Alex caught up with her and said, "We're going to blow. Are you coming?"

"Give me a minute," she said.

She found Cole and Lenny in a comparatively quiet corner by the front door. "Am I going home with you or with Alex?"

He kissed her and said, "You should probably go with Alex. I don't know how long we'll be."

She tried to hide her disappointment. "Okay."

"But you'll stay with me tonight, right? You'll be there when I get home?"

"Okay," she said, wanting to make some gesture of independence, unable to find the will.

Though it was terribly late when she got back, she needed to shower; she ended up in bed with her hair still damp. She lay for an endless time with the entire world inside her head, too numb to sort it out, and only realized she'd fallen asleep when Cole woke her.

He was on fire. He'd brushed his teeth, though she could still taste the beer and marijuana on his breath. His skin smelled of smoke and sweat, not altogether unpleasantly, and he was lobotomized by desire, hands all over her, capable of only minimally coherent speech, telling her how beautiful she was, how much he loved her. The magnitude of his desire was exciting, and also impersonal in its urgency. When he was done, he made a halfhearted effort to pleasure her as he kept nodding off. "Shhh," she told him. "Go to sleep now. It's been a big day for you."

"I love you," he said, and then he was asleep.

She was up before him in the morning. She got dressed and made coffee. Though she was hungry, her stomach was in turmoil and she couldn't imagine keeping food down. She pretended to read the Sunday *Statesman* while Denise, then Alex, then Joe, then finally Cole wandered downstairs, fixed something to eat, and sat down with a section of the paper. She waited until Cole had finished eating and then, as unobtrusively as possible, she slipped upstairs.

Cole joined her a few minutes later. "Are you okay? I'm sorry I passed out on you last night, I was just…"

"I know, sweetie."

He sat on the edge of the bed and took her hand. "Something's wrong."

Having been handed the opportunity, she couldn't find the words. Eventually she let him worm it out of her. "You've gotten too good for Austin. You're going to have to go on the road."

"Where did you get that idea?"

"Are you going to tell me you haven't talked about it?"

He looked guilty. "It's… come up."

"And what did you decide?"

"We haven't decided anything yet. But we were talking last night—it was so cool." The embarrassment vanished. "Guys from Shiva's and Conqueroo. Jim Franklin—he's the guy that draws all the posters with the armadillos on them, he's one of the owners. Powell St. John, you know who he is? He wrote songs with the Elevators and started Conqueroo. All anybody could talk about was San Francisco. Jim went to art school there. Powell is there now, playing with Mother Earth. Conqueroo is moving out there, like, this summer. Shiva's and the Elevators are talking about it too."

Madelyn didn't know where to begin. Hysterics seemed a poor choice. There was only one question: What about us? To be reduced to asking it meant she had already lost. She didn't intend petulance either, though a trace still showed when she said, "I thought you hated San Francisco."

"I didn't love it. The thing is, it's where this kind of music is happening."

"When do you leave?"

Cole hesitated too long for plausible denial. "Lenny wants to go as soon as classes are over."

Well, there it was. Quite nearly the worst possible answer. All that Madelyn saw to salvage was the remnants of her dignity, which meant not crying in front of Cole.

"Look," he said, "as soon as we get out there and get settled, you can come out."

"What, for my summer vacation?"

"No, come out to stay. Powell knows somebody at San Francisco State, he says the residence requirement is only a year. Then you'd be eligible for in-state tuition. See, I asked. I know what college means to you."

"San Francisco State?"

"Okay, Stanford. I know it's expensive, but with your SATs and grades, you could get a full ride."

She scooted off the foot of the bed, put her shoes on, and gathered up her books and last night's clothes.

"Madelyn?"

"I need some time to think about this," she said, quite calmly, she thought. "I'll walk home, it'll help clear my head." She managed to hug and kiss him. "We'll talk," she said, and escaped out the door.

She passed Denise on the stairs. "Madelyn?" Denise said.

What must I look like? Madelyn thought. "Later," she said.

She rushed out the front door, ran as far as Enfield Road, and then caught her breath.

She was in shock, as surely as if she'd looked down to see one of her arms lying severed on the ground. The thought of staying on in Austin without Cole was as utterly unacceptable as the idea of giving up everything she'd worked for and moving to California, where she was not even sure she was wanted.

She had walked this route dozens of times, feeling like royalty as she descended from her castle on the hill and looked upon her kingdom spread before her, an orderly world where she knew exactly what was expected of her and knew that she was more than equal to the task. That now seemed like a child's simplistic universe of Santa Claus and Easter Bunnies, a sand castle eaten away by the rising tide of the grown-up world, where good choices didn't exist, and certainly not easy ones, where every road dead-ended in loneliness and futility.

Once she was in her dorm room, she kicked off her shoes and threw her sweater at her desk chair. She pulled the covers over her head to shut out all thoughts and feelings, willing time to pass. When the phone rang, she barely heard it, and later, when Denise came in and whispered her name, she didn't respond.

Eventually she had to use the bathroom, and when she came back to the room, Denise wormed the story out of her.

"The bastard," Denise said.

"He's not a bastard," Madelyn said. "This is his dream. What if he stayed in Austin and he never got a chance like this again?"

"Does he love you? No, don't answer that, I've seen him with you. So if he loves you and you love him and he has to go to San Francisco, what does that leave?"

"Giving up *my* dream."

"Which is what, exactly?"

"I want a life where I go to dinner parties and drink pinot grigio while a Brahms string quartet plays in the background and people argue about Matisse and Virginia Woolf."

"Better you than me!" Denise laughed.

"Not a roach infested apartment with people smoking dope and drinking Pagan Pink Ripple and mumbling incoherently about how stoned they are."

"And how was Cole ever supposed to fit into your dream?"

"He's in boots and a corduroy jacket, and he compares Dylan with Emily Dickinson and Wallace Stevens and every woman there and half the men are sick with envy." She started to cry. "I'm an idiot, right?"

"Idiot is a little strong. Naïve is certainly not out of the question. You said he brought up Stanford."

"I'm months too late to apply."

"Start next spring."

"What if I didn't get in? What if I didn't get a scholarship?" She was suspended halfway between hysteria and despair. "What would my daddy say about any of these harebrained ideas?"

"If Cole drops out…" Denise began, then didn't want to finish.

"What?"

"He'll lose his student deferment."

"Oh, Jesus."

They sat in silence. Eventually Madelyn picked up a page of Denise's Russian homework and stared at it without seeing it.

"How am I supposed to go to Russian class on Monday?"

"Don't. I'll turn in your homework, you can copy my notes."

The phone rang.

"It's him," Madelyn said.

Denise, with a sangfroid that moved Madelyn to both envy and discomfort, cheerfully told Cole that Madelyn wasn't there, that she hadn't seen her, and yes, she would tell her to call.

"Now what?"

"Finish your homework. I'll fetch us some burgers."

MADELYN WANDERED THROUGH her Monday classes like a mental patient, unable to concentrate, constantly looking behind her. That night Denise reported that Cole, visibly distraught, had been waiting outside class. "I told him you had strep throat and couldn't talk."

"Did he believe you?"

"Why, was he supposed to?"

"I should call him."

"He is currently six blocks away. He wants to be two thousand miles away? Let him stew for a while."

When the phone rang that night, Denise didn't pick up. "What if it's Joe?" Madelyn asked.

She laughed raucously. "He can stew too."

MADELYN WASN'T COMPLETELY surprised when she saw Cole sitting on the grass outside Batts Hall. He knew her schedule as well as she did. Panic dried her mouth and made her heart race. His shoulders drooped and his eyes were sunken, and there was a split second before he saw her when she considered running away. Then it was too late and he was loping up to her and taking her by the shoulders.

"So you're not sick," he said. "I've been so worried."

She tried to imagine she was someone else. Denise, she decided, would give Cole a quick kiss, on the lips, not negotiable into anything more highly charged. That was what she did. "'The report of my illness was an exaggeration,' to misquote Mr. Clemens. I'm fine."

"You're avoiding me."

"I told you. I need time to think."

Her casualness confounded him. "I miss you."

She couldn't resist. "Just think how much you'll miss me when you're in San Francisco." She smiled. "I'm going to be late for class." With his stunned, tragic look burned into her memory, she stepped around him and hurried into the building where, for the next hour and a half, she replayed the scene over and over, oblivious to the Sociology class around her.

MADELYN CUT RUSSIAN again on Wednesday. She was sleeping poorly and looking as haggard as Cole.

"How long am I supposed to keep this up?" she asked Denise.

"Have you decided what to do?"

"How can I decide?"

"Then you've got a ways to go."

WHEN MADELYN CAME OUT of Sociology on Thursday, Cole was waiting for her. "Cole," she said, "I told you I—"

He didn't say anything. He slid one arm around her back and had her off balance before she knew what was happening. She threw one arm instinctively around his neck and her books scattered on the path. Cole scooped her up and began to carry her toward Littlefield Fountain.

"Cole, my books."

He didn't answer. He had a look of grim determination that frightened her.

"Cole, if you don't go back for my books, I'll scream."

He stopped. "And if I do go back you won't?"

"No," she whispered. It had been days since he'd held her and she was overwhelmed by his heat and smell and lean muscularity.

Clumsily, he set her on her feet next to her spilled books, and as soon as she had them in her arms, she let him pick her up again. She had been so confused, so torn, and what a relief it was to surrender to someone else's clear and simple vision. His hearse was parked on the street near the fountain and he set her down on the hot vinyl seat cover. They drove to the Castle in silence. Cole gently pulled her out of the car by her wrists and then hesitated, as if trying to decide whether to attempt to carry her up the stairs. "I'll come quietly," she said, "but I have to pee."

What a scene from a tawdry romance novel it would have been, she thought, if she hadn't spoiled it with dropped books and a full bladder.

In the bedroom he was more passionate than she'd ever seen him, telling her over and over that he loved her and couldn't live without her.

Afterward they lay side by side, Madelyn stroking his back with the tips of her fingers.

"I meant what I said," he told her. "I don't want to live without you. If that means staying in Austin, then that's what I'll do. I want to be with you. Forever."

"Oh, Cole, you can't stay here. We both know that."

"I won't leave unless you come with me."

She looked into his eyes, dark blue-green and sunken deep into his skull, bloodshot and leaking hot tears, and a reckless calm came over her, a certainty that defied reason and pushed aside the unfairness of it all. "Then we'll go together," she said.

He closed his eyes and kissed her neck and face. "Really?" he said. "Do you swear?"

"I swear."

Abruptly he rolled away and opened the drawer of his night-stand. He took out a small red velvet box and held it out to her. "It's just from the Co-op," he said, "but it's real gold. Denise told me the size, so it should fit."

She flipped back the top of the box to reveal a thin gold wedding band.

"Cole, this is a wedding ring."

"I want you to marry me, right here, right now. Texas is a common-law state. If we say we're married, then legally we are."

She blurted out the first thing that came into her head. "I'm naked."

"All the better. Try it on."

Slowly she reached for the ring, waiting for her better judgment to kick in. Her thoughts refused to cohere. She took the ring out of the box and slid it onto her left hand. It did indeed fit, though she couldn't escape the sense that it was looser than it actually was, that it could too easily come off.

Cole held both her hands with both of his. "I now pronounce us man and wife," he said. "I may kiss the bride."

The kiss was so soft, so warm, that Madelyn felt herself melting, as if she herself were molten gold, like in Cole's song, a pool of hot liquid flowing over his skin, her form becoming his, shining, beautiful, inseparable.

COLE DROVE TO DALLAS the weekend after their decision so that he could tell Montoya the news in person. He brought Madelyn along to break it to her father. They were mostly quiet for the three and a half hours, listening to "It's a Beautiful Morning" by the Rascals and "Dock of the Bay" by Otis, "Dance to the Music" by Sly and "Lady Madonna" by The Beatles. Cole thought about everything he was leaving behind.

He dropped Madelyn off and arrived at the Montoyas' in time for dinner. Jimmy was at a friend's house, leaving only Al and Linda, though as always there was plenty of food. Cole tried to help with the dishes afterward, wanting to put off the discussion as long as possible. Frederica scolded him and sent him back to the table.

Linda had quietly disappeared. Cole sat at a right angle to Montoya, beers in their hands. "There's been," Cole said, "a change in plans."

He told Montoya everything. The band, the move to San Francisco, the common-law marriage. Through it all Montoya stared at his hands clasped around the Bohemia bottle, nodding from time to time. His high seriousness made it easy for Cole to keep talking.

"My only regret," Cole finished, "is that I feel like I'm betraying your trust in me. You invested in my education with the understanding that I would follow through with it. And I'm letting you down."

Montoya was quiet for a long time before he said, "You're not letting me down. My hope for you has always been that you would turn out to be a good man, and the fact that you're here, telling me this face to face, says a lot for that hope." Finally he looked Cole in the eye. "But I have to ask some questions, because I care about you."

"Sure. I mean, I want you to care."

"Going to San Francisco, that couldn't wait until you finish school? Alex said the band is doing really well in Austin."

"Something's happening," Cole said. "The idea of what music can do, of what it means, it's changing so fast. Like, every day almost. In three years, the world is going to be so completely different... this is my chance, right now. I have to take it."

"What about the draft?"

"It's a gamble," Cole said. "I'm hoping my finger will get me out if I get called up."

"And Madelyn? She's okay with this?"

"It's not ideal. But we love each other."

"Forgive my asking this, but she's not..."

"Pregnant? No, we're careful."

"And Alex didn't want to be part of this?"

"No. It's weird. The band was his idea in the first place. Now he seems to have lost interest. Outgrown it or something."

"I almost wish he hadn't. I worry about him."

"You shouldn't," Cole said, not entirely believing it. "He's finding his own way. That's what college is for, right? He might even find his way back to the family business."

"God willing. One last question. Are you going to see your parents before you go?"

Cole shook his head.

"Not even to let them meet their daughter-in-law? If you could find a way..."

"Sorry," Cole said. "It wasn't me who closed that door. I won't go back in that house." He still talked to his mother every couple of weeks on the phone. He hadn't managed to tell her about the marriage yet.

"Okay." Montoya drained his beer and stood up. "It's late. Thank you for the respect you showed me tonight."

"Thank you for understanding. And for... everything."

Cole hugged him and found it hard to let go.

"You'll always have a home here, my son. Your room is ready for you upstairs."

MADELYN LOVED SAN FRANCISCO from the moment she first saw it. That moment came as Interstate 80, rolling into Berkeley from the north, intersected the shores of the Bay. Misty and mysterious, a sprawl of white buildings climbed back into green hills, triangulated by the Bay Bridge, the Golden Gate, and the deep blue water of the Bay itself. It was the most beautiful city she'd ever seen. The late afternoon light had a unique muted quality, a softness, as if the buildings themselves glowed with the pleasure of the day.

The journey that had started in Cole's bed with a wedding ring, that had taken weeks of preparation and days of driving and covered two thousand miles, had reached its conclusion here in the second week of June. She felt like Percival outside Camelot, Pip come to London, Katherine Hepburn arriving in New York. It was the kind of city where destinies were forged.

The hardest part had been her father. She knew the wedding ring would give it away, yet she couldn't bring herself to take it off. Her father noticed it immediately and said, "You're not pregnant, are you?"

When she'd imagined the conversation, she was alone with her father in his study. The reality was all four of them in the den, her father wounded and distant, her mother in shocked silence, Julia, unexpectedly, in tears.

"Julia," her father said at last, "what in God's name is the matter with you?"

"She's going to be so happy," Julia said. "I wish it was me." She ran from the room.

Julia's words touched her father in a way that Madelyn's had failed to. "She's right, isn't she?" he said. "This is your happiness we're talking about."

"Yes, Daddy. I love him."

He sighed. "I know the kind of person you are. That means I have to trust you. Can you promise me one thing? Promise me you'll finish out the semester, and get decent marks, so if you do go back you'll have that much done."

"*When* I go back. And I'm going to make straight As this year, I promise." Her heart was full of love for him in that moment, and love for Cole, with enough left over to even feel sorry for Julia.

She delivered her As, and Cole, thanks to her nagging, finished with a B average. It didn't stop her nightmares of driving off a cliff or being pulled out to sea in an undertow; it did, however, reassure her that her will power was still intact.

They drove two cars to San Francisco; Madelyn rode with Cole in the hearse and Lenny followed in his pale blue Mustang, taking turns at the wheel with Tommy, the drummer. Their bass player had elected to stay in Austin, a situation that the others shrugged off. "There's a million bass players in San Francisco," he said. "We'll get one in the first week."

Of all the things she feared, Cole's optimism was high on the list. That was her role, and too much confidence looked unconvincing on him. He was equally sure that they could find a cheap place to stay in the Haight, and be able to practice there, and that they would be playing at the Fillmore within a few weeks.

Yet now, as they passed weird, scrap-lumber sculptures of humanoids and animals that stood in the mudflats at the edge of the Bay; as they crossed the Bay Bridge and made landfall to the pungent aroma of roasting coffee from the Folgers building; as they navigated the forest of signs for South Beach and Rincon Hill and the Embarcadero; as she bounced around the front seat, excitedly taking in everything she could see and hear and smell;

as all this magic unfolded, she was willing to believe six impossible things before dinner and no end of unlikelihoods.

Cole pointed out the sights as they drove across the peninsula: Buena Vista Park, the Haight, Golden Gate Park, and finally, as they made a short circle before pulling into the motel, the vastness of the Pacific. Gradually her excitement subsided into calm delight. She gave herself credit for making the right choice; she saw that already she was more sophisticated than she'd been the night before; she knew that no books or classrooms could replace the richness of immediate experience.

At the motel, she signed the registration card "Mrs. Madelyn Cole," the "Mrs." and the "Cole" so unpracticed as to look fraudulent.

Over dinner at a Thai restaurant that Cole knew, Lenny was the only one whose feelings approximated hers. He'd never been out of Texas before and the trip had been one revelation after another, with San Francisco as the somewhat unnerving climax. "Freaks everywhere!" he said. "It's like a sci-fi movie where the revolution is over and we won. I mean, I'm fucking terrified, but I love it already."

Cole, who had let Madelyn spell him for no more than short stretches over the last three days, was exhausted. "It's even colder than I remembered."

Madelyn, having heard Cole's complaints about San Francisco weather on too many prior occasions, had dressed for winter in jeans, boots, and a bulky sweater and was perfectly comfortable. "I refuse to be brought down by the likes of you," she told him, and raised her glass of Tab to Lenny. "Here's to new beginnings."

ON MONDAY, August 5, near the end of their second month in San Francisco, Cole woke up once again at four AM, consumed by regrets and recriminations, ready to give up.

He'd been an idiot to come back to this city that he hated. Blind to think that they could simply find a bass player when, without a bass player, they couldn't even perform in public and get a reputation that would get them the quality performer they needed.

He'd begun to obsess over increasingly desperate schemes.

Was there some way to get himself and Madelyn enrolled for the fall semester at UT and crawl back to Texas, his tail between his legs? Could he talk Alex into coming out for two weeks, long enough to learn an hour's worth of tunes, play a few gigs, and attract enough attention to find a replacement? What if he or Lenny switched to bass and they worked for a while as a power trio? What if he just ran away, got up right now and put on his clothes and hitchhiked to Mexico and left Madelyn and Lenny and Tommy to fend for themselves?

He looked at Madelyn, snoring softly next to him. For the last month, she'd been working at an art gallery at the Marina, hired for her looks and her brains, making enough to pay the rent on their dilapidated two-bedroom apartment, not in the Haight where he'd wanted to be, but over the line in the Fillmore district, where racial tensions still sat on a lit burner, ready to boil over on a moment's notice, and where Madelyn got hassled nearly every day, though Cole walked her to her streetcar stop every morning and met her there every evening.

Cole had looked for a steady day job, as had Lenny and Tommy, and all the unskilled jobs were taken for miles around. Cole found a contractor who would give him occasional construction work, when there was enough to go around, which was not often. Bands were moving out of the Haight, which had lost its cool and turned increasingly dangerous as speed and heroin continued to take the place of LSD and pot.

The Fillmore Auditorium had closed after the July 4 show, and Graham had moved his operation to the old Carousel Ballroom and reopened there the next night. The hall was bigger, and an easy walk from the apartment, but they'd only been once, to see Jeff Beck open for Moby Grape a week ago. Cole had become leery of spending money on anything beyond food, and Madelyn was still not that deeply into rock, especially when it was live and loud. The show had been vaguely disappointing. Skip Spence, the crazy Moby Grape guitarist, had gone literally crazy in New York and been committed to Belleview, taking much of the band's life force with him. Beck was distracted and out of sorts. Even the room lacked the magic the old Fillmore had.

The Matrix was still the only organized jam session he knew of, and his best shot at finding an unattached bass player. So far it had been a waste of time. The Avalon was rumored to be in danger of losing its lease, and, only the night before, the Straight Theater had presented its last regular live music show. The whole scene was imploding.

To her credit, Madelyn didn't blame him for the mess he'd made of their lives, not out loud, anyway. Still, on those nights when she came home exhausted from work and Lenny and Tommy were laughing at some sitcom on Lenny's portable black and white TV, and Cole hadn't started their dinner yet, and the kitchen faucet was dripping again, and the light switch had shorted out in the bedroom, he knew she was wondering what exactly she had given up her dreams for. He felt her reluctance to complain about her job, and he knew how ungrateful he would sound if he ranted against San Francisco. They went days at a time without making love, without even talking much, gritting their teeth and putting one foot in front of the other to get from morning to night.

At six he gave up and slipped out of bed and got dressed. As he brushed his teeth he realized he'd forgotten to call his mother the day before and knew he would have to add that to his list of chores for the day. He sat in the living room with the Strat and played it unamplified until Madelyn's alarm went off at 7:30. He made coffee and oatmeal for the two of them while she showered. She ate in her terrycloth robe, her hair wrapped in a towel, offering him a sad smile in thanks.

He checked the hearse as he walked Madelyn to the streetcar. No signs of trouble. He'd taken to leaving the doors unlocked after the second time the driver's window had been smashed. Nothing to steal anyway.

In the beginning, Madelyn had said goodbye every morning with the promise, "Good things will happen for you today." Lately she kissed him perfunctorily and got on the trolley. Cole saw her off with a raised hand and shuffled back to the apartment.

He smelled cigarettes when he opened the door, which meant that Lenny was awake. He sat on the couch with his Strat and picked up where he'd left off. A few minutes later Lenny himself appeared, shirtless and barefoot in bell-bottom jeans from the Army Navy store, Marlboro dangling from his mouth. He helped himself to the coffee and sat down across from Cole with his Les Paul, picking up Cole's mood and playing it back to him, a reassurance and a reminder of why they were there.

In the afternoon, Cole and Lenny walked over to the Haight to check the bulletin boards. Tommy, who was sliding deeper into depression by the day, stayed home, allegedly to practice, more likely to smoke dope and watch TV.

The Haight had changed from the summer before. The crushing overpopulation had subsided, and along with it the last traces of glamour, leaving it no more than a hippie slum. When the occasional tourist bus came through, the lectures were in past tense. Career dope dealers had run the amateurs off and at least a dozen prime storefronts were boarded up. Cole reflexively looked for Becky among the street population, hoping she'd gone back to Mobile, that nothing worse had befallen her.

Nothing new on the Purple Unicorn board, nothing at the Pall Mall Bar, former home of Love Burgers. Cole collapsed in a chair at the Pall Mall and said, "This is starting to get me down."

"What's the hurry?" Lenny said. "We've barely been here two months."

Cole envied Lenny his easygoing nature. "Two months where we haven't played a single gig."

"It'll pick up when school starts. We're fermenting, man. Like fine wine. We're paying our dues."

"Well, Madelyn's paying them, anyway."

"If I could find a job..."

"Yeah, I know. I know. Me too."

Cole looked up to see a familiar face at the bulletin board. Brad, his name was, the bass player from Paisley Octopus. Cole had run into them a few times, and heard them recently in the Panhandle. A year of practice hadn't made them click.

"Hi, Cole. Hi, Lenny."

"Brad," Cole said. "What's happening?"

"We're losing our lead player." They'd been through several in the past year. "I don't suppose either of you guys...?"

"Sorry," Cole said. "We're still trying to get our thing going."

"Still looking for a bass player? Because I'm thinking…"

Brad's time-keeping was just iffy enough to sap the power from the band. "Next time we have an audition, we'll let you know."

"Don't tell the other guys, okay?"

Cole nodded.

"Say," Brad said, easing out of the awkward moment, "did you hear there's a party at the Airplane house tonight?" In defiance of the exodus from the Haight, the Airplane had bought a three-story mansion across from the northeast corner of Golden Gate Park. "Like, an open house kind of thing. Starts around eight or nine."

Cole looked at Lenny, who was starstruck. "Really?" Lenny said.

"You should see that fucking place," Brad said. "It is unbelievable."

"We *will* see that place," Cole said. "Nothing could keep me away."

He called Madelyn from the apartment and told her about the party. "What time are you coming home?" he said. "You don't want to miss this."

"Oh, sweetheart, I think I do want to miss it. I'm going to be working late, and I have to be in early tomorrow."

Cole's disappointment was the edge of something deeper. For all the things they had in common, a fundamental gap remained in the heart of their relationship. He'd been kidding himself to believe that rock music would ever touch her the way it did him.

"Cole? I'm sorry. I know this is a big deal for you. You need to be able to go and stay there as long as you want."

"Don't apologize. You're the one that's actually working."

"That'll change. Maybe tonight you'll find your bass player."

Maybe tonight I'll meet Grace Slick, he thought, then immediately regretted it. "Yeah," he said. "Maybe."

"Cheer up, for God's sake. This should be a big adventure for you."

"You make it sound like a toddler's first day at kindergarten."

"That's in your head, not mine."

He'd managed to push her into the very corner they'd been avoiding for weeks. If he kept it up, there would be bloodletting. "I'm sorry," he said. "I love you."

"I love you too. Have fun tonight."

"Okay. Hope you don't have to stay too late."

"It's okay. The new artist is here and it's interesting for a change."

He tried to remember what she'd told him about the new show she was working on and drew a blank. "Then you have fun too."

He hung up and wondered if he should have pushed it. An ugly fight, both of them letting out the bile they'd been accumulating, phones slammed down, him staying home so they could have a painful discussion until early morning, ending in tearful sex and reconciliation.

Another time, he thought. Tonight he was going to the Airplane house.

TOMMY WAS AS EXCITED as Cole had seen him in weeks. Lenny was nervous and almost bailed. By the time they found a parking place, it was after nine and the noise from the party was audible from Stanyan Street, a long block away. Live music clashing with records, voices shouting to be heard over the chaos.

The mansion sat on a corner lot, tall, white, narrow in front, massive Ionic columns holding up the top floor. The wrought iron gate was open, and a half-dozen steps led up to the front door, also open. A small crowd milled around on the sidewalk, and Cole led the way through them as if he were expected inside.

The contrast between the long-haired, freakishly dressed party-goers and the stately Victorian setting got stranger as they pushed their way in. Thick Persian carpets on the floors, chandeliers over-head, mahogany paneling and wainscoting, patterned wallpaper, massive furniture, high ceilings, vast rooms. The dining room alone would easily seat 100. The tables were covered in Madras bedspreads, loaded with cut veggies, exotic breads and cheeses, imported crackers, ham, turkey. A pot of brown rice for the macrobiotic crowd. In the middle of the table sat a bowl of ice with a smaller bowl inside that held tiny black beads. A crowd spooned them onto little pancakes, among them the enormous figure of Tom Donahue, the DJ Cole had last seen at the Matrix the year before.

"Is that what I think it is?" Cole asked.

"Caviar," Donahue said with his mouth full. "Get some now, it's not going to last long." Donahue pointed with his plastic spoon at the platter of pancakes. "Blini, crème fraiche, caviar on top."

Cole tried it. The taste was slightly salty and incredibly rich. "Wow," he said.

"Yeah," Donahue said. "Caviar is the reason people go to the trouble of making vast amounts of money."

Cole squeezed his way in for the last spoonful of eggs. He could get used to this.

Another table was set up as a do-it-yourself bar. Wine, Jack Daniel's, Southern Comfort, Smirnoff vodka. Garbage cans full of ice and beer. "Hey, check this out," Lenny said. "Bottled water! How crazy is that?" Cole nodded and helped himself to a Heineken, using an opener that hung on a piece of twine.

Other than Donahue, Cole didn't recognize any of the fifty people in the dining room. Lots of cowboy hats and leather vests, women in tight jeans and high-heeled boots. Lenny and Tommy looked like it was all they could do to keep their mouths from hanging open. Cole, who liked being out of his league, felt sharp and ready for anything.

They wandered through the first-floor rooms, which were quickly filling up with smoke, both tobacco and cannabis. A fire blazed in the parlor fireplace, and a crowd of acid heads watched it as if it were a Bergman film. A library, an industrial-sized kitchen, a music room where a guy in full American Indian getup played show tunes on a grand piano, a sitting room with wicker furniture, orchids, and a view of the gardens.

Back at the stairway at the front of the house, Lenny said, "Up or down?"

Loud rock music came from the basement. "Down," Cole said.

The basement was the size of the entire ground floor, which was to say, huge. Amps, drums, keyboards, and a few floor lamps at one end of the room. A few dozen folding chairs in a random arrangement in front of the makeshift stage. The song was a mid-tempo, 4/4 blues, "Get Out of My Life, Woman" or something like it. Jorma Kaukonen was on lead, easily recognizable by his massive forehead and hawklike nose. Another guitar player, who Cole didn't recognize, stood behind him. Grace Slick, wearing a tunic top over Capri pants, played something dissonant on a Farfisa organ, exuding a chilly sensuality. Cole hiked his shoulders back and tried for a believable smile. Spenser Dryden was on drums, in his trademark cowboy hat and Fu Manchu mustache, looking bored. As Cole walked the length of the room, Dryden noodled briefly on his hi-hat, then got up and wandered off to the side, talking to a man in coveralls.

Tommy, eyes blazing, pushed forward. "Gentlemen," he said, "I believe this is what they call the chance of a lifetime." He made his way over to Dryden and said something in his ear. Dryden shrugged and Tommy got behind the drums.

Cole was pleased for him, but his attention belonged to the guy playing bass. Six-foot-three, built like a football player. Hair cut so short that Cole could see the shine of his scalp underneath. He was playing Jack Casady's brown Guild Starfire bass and he had Casady's style down pat—subsonic low notes, midrange and high notes that were unexpectedly perfect in retrospect, melodic and propulsive at the same time.

Casady himself sat in the front row in his tiny round sunglasses, a thin headband holding back his stringy blond hair. Cole sat down next to him while Lenny retreated to the shadows. "Who is that guy?" he asked.

"Says his name's Gordo," Casady said. "I never saw him before."

"He's so good, I thought he was you."

"He's phenomenal," Casady said. "Am I hallucinating, or is he *dancing*?"

"I think it's Motown footwork," Cole said. "Like the Temps or the Four Tops."

"I believe you're right."

They sat and watched together for a minute or two, Cole thinking, I just had a conversation with Jack Casady. Holy fucking shit.

He worked up his nerve and said, "I need to get up there and play guitar."

Casady looked at him over the top of his glasses. "Are you any good?"

"That's my drummer up there now. We're pros."

Casady considered the idea.

"Look," Cole said, "if I couldn't play, I wouldn't dream of getting up there and making an idiot out of myself in front of Jorma and Grace."

"That's Jorma's little brother Peter on the sg," Casady said. "I'll ask him to give you five minutes. If you stink up the joint, he'll ask for it back and you have to give it to him. Deal?"

"Deal," Cole said.

Casady got up and talked to Peter, who had dark blond hair and glasses and didn't look much like his brother. They went back and forth and then Peter shrugged and smiled and held the guitar out to Cole. Cole jumped up and took it in one hand and put the other on Peter's shoulder. "Thanks. I need that bass player."

"Good luck," Peter said.

Cole had played a couple of sgs. They were heavy and tended to go out of tune easily. This one had lightweight strings that would only make the problem worse. He turned the volume knob all the way down and closed his eyes and listened. When he felt Jorma come to the end of a phrase, he plucked a note and slowly turned up the volume. He faced the amp and let the note decay into feedback, then tried a simple riff or two. The guitar had nice tone. It boosted his confidence and he stepped out to the front of the stage. Jorma had reverted to playing chords and was watching him with an encouraging smile. Cole played a fairly simple eight bar lead and then focused on Gordo, the bass player. He squeezed off two quick notes and then choked them, so they fell in between the notes Gordo was playing. On the next measure he did it again, and this time Gordo answered him. Tommy was on it immediately, and now they were all stopping and starting together in a stuttering rhythm, including Grace. Cole nodded to Jorma and Jorma began to bounce off the stops, building momentum until he rocketed free. Cole caught Tommy's eye and went back to the progression, and after eight bars of that, he wove a second lead around Jorma's. They built to a nice climax and tied it off and got a solid round of applause from the hundred or so spectators in the room.

Grace walked over to him and Cole held his breath. The camera loved her, he saw, and she was not perhaps as perfect in the flesh as she seemed when fully made up and dramatically lit. She was still astonishingly beautiful, and the cynical intelligence in her gray eyes was unmistakable. "That was pretty good, kid," she said. She glanced at Gordo and Tommy. "Are you guys in a band or something?"

"Yeah, we are," Cole said. "Only Gordo there doesn't know it yet."

"What?" Gordo said. "Band? What?"

Cole said to Grace, "I've been in love with you since the first time I heard your voice."

Grace didn't even blink. "That's nice. How old are you, seventeen?"

Cole felt himself flush. "Eighteen."

"Uh huh." She started to turn away, then said, "What's the name of the band?"

"We don't have one yet."

"Quirky. You'll need one to play the Fillmore." She walked over to Spenser Dryden and kissed him on the mouth, rather showily, Cole thought.

Cole looked at Jorma, who laughed and shook his head. "Shouldn't have told her you were in love with her. Do you know 'Good Morning, Blues?'"

AFTER WORKING OUT on 'Good Morning, Blues' for twenty minutes, Cole opted not to wear out his welcome. He handed the guitar to Peter and thanked him. Then he thanked Jorma, who shook his hand and said, "Come back sometime when it's not so crazy. What's your name?"

"Cole."

"I'm Jorma. I guess you knew that. Take it easy, Cole."

Gordo gave the bass to Casady, thanked him nicely, and then he and Casady started to talk. Cole hovered nearby, waiting for his chance.

A voice said, "Nice guitar playing," and Cole turned to see

dark eyes in a round face with heavy black eyebrows, black beard, disheveled black hair.

"Uh, thanks. Jerry Garcia, right?"

"Yeah. What happened to your hand?" He held up his own right hand and Cole saw that most of his middle finger was missing.

"Accident on an oil rig. What happened to yours?"

"My brother cut it off with an axe." Garcia laughed at the expression on Cole's face. "It was an accident, I was four, we were chopping wood. Were you already playing when it happened?"

"Yeah."

"Wow, that must have been a trip. Obviously you got over it. You play really nice now." Garcia saluted him with his right hand. "Brothers of the mangled finger!" He smiled and walked away.

Cole was still recovering his wits when Gordo found him. "What was that about a band?"

"Uh, yeah, we need to talk." He beckoned Lenny over. "Did you see that? Jerry Garcia's got a fucked up middle finger too!"

"Where?" Lenny said.

Garcia had vanished. "Maybe I dreamed it." Tommy didn't look like he wanted to stop for a band meeting, so Cole decided to proceed without him. "Step into my office."

With fresh beers, they found a stone bench in one of the gardens outside. Cole was too hyped to sit. "To cut to the chase, yeah, we're a band. Lenny here is also on lead guitar—we do double lead stuff like I was doing with Jorma. The guy on drums, that's our drummer, Tommy. We do a mix of originals and old blues stuff that we've hot-rodded into something new. We lost our bass player when we left Texas two months ago."

"Texas?" Gordo said. "Where in Texas?"

"Austin," Lenny said.

"No shit," Gordo said. "I'm from Laredo."

«¡Órale!» Cole said. «¿Hablas español?»

«¿Es el papa católico?» Gordo said. He gave Cole a high five.

"English, please," Lenny said.

Gordo, born Steve Gordon, was 19. He'd left Laredo at 15, he told them, the summer after The Beatles were on Ed Sullivan. He wanted to play bass just like Paul. Even then he was big for his age, so he hitched to New Orleans and worked on a shrimper until he had enough money to get a Hofner bass like McCartney's. Then he worked another year while he learned how to play. After that he made his living in bar bands, cranking out blues and R&B in places where he wasn't old enough to get in the front door.

Then he heard "Somebody to Love" and it was like The Beatles all over again. Casady's bass playing, the edgy guitars, the aggressive lyrics, they were part of something new, something that felt like it belonged to him personally. "It was like I'd been wearing hand-me-downs all my life and suddenly I had a brand-new suit, tailor-made for me."

People thought he was crazy when he tried to put together a psychedelic band in New Orleans. After a year of trying, he sold everything he had except his bass and hitchhiked to the coast. He'd been busted for vagrancy in Flagstaff and they'd shaved his head. He could have gotten off if he'd showed the cash he had hidden in his shoe, only he was afraid the cops would steal it. He'd been in San Francisco less than a week.

Lenny said, "This means you don't have an amp?"

Gordo shrugged. "I can put some money down on something. Right now I don't even have a way to bring it home."

"The thing is," Cole said, "we need you to audition, and pronto. Como ahorita, en este momento, ¡ándale, muchacho!"

A voice came out of the darkness, speaking Spanish. «Did I hear the voice of mi gente?»

«Órale,» Gordo said.

"I'm getting a beer," Lenny said, and walked off.

A slight Latin guy in his twenties, short dark hair and a moustache, jeans and a white guayabera, emerged from the shadows and offered his hand. "Carlos," he said.

"I'm Cole, that's Gordo, and Lenny, el que no habla español, will be back in a minute."

"Are you guys in a band?" Carlos asked.

"About to be," Cole said. "We just have to convince this guy. What about you?"

"Yeah. I play guitar."

"Me too," Cole said, and pointed at Gordo. "Bass."

"'All we need is a drummer,'" Carlos sang.

"Our drummer's inside, jamming with Jorma and Jack."

"There's a jam?"

"In the basement."

"Qué padre. Con permiso, I'm going to go check it out."

«Disfrútelo,» Cole said, and Carlos waved as he walked away.

"I wonder," Gordo said, "how many people at this thing are musicians."

"I don't know," Cole said, "but before any of the others get to you, can we set up a date for an audition?"

COLE DIDN'T LOOK at his watch until they got home. Two-thirty in the morning. Tommy couldn't stop talking about this guy Carlos and how he played like nobody he'd ever seen. They'd brought Gordo back to sleep on the couch since by that point he was too wasted to clearly articulate where he'd been crashing.

Cole's head was buzzing too, from excitement and not from the beer and the occasional hit of dope he'd taken. Despite his best efforts to get into bed quietly, Madelyn turned to face him and said, without opening her eyes, "I hear the elephants have returned to the circus. How was it?"

"Unbelievable. I jammed with Jorma Kaukonen and Jerry Garcia liked my playing and we found our bass player and I met Grace Slick, and by the way the bass player is sleeping on the couch and I think this is it. I think we're on our way."

Madelyn opened one eye. "You didn't shoot speed, did you?"

"One hundred percent natural energy." She had one arm wrapped around her pillow and the armhole of the sleeveless sweatshirt that she slept in had slipped down to reveal the curve of one breast. Cole's throat went dry. "I don't suppose there's, like, any chance you could call in sick tomorrow? Or go in a couple of hours late...?"

She closed her eye again. "No, honey, I told you, we've got that opening Thursday, remember?"

"Yeah, you told me."

"Stop vibrating and go to sleep. I'm very happy for you. Really."

*

IN THE EARLY AFTERNOON, Cole drove a badly hung-over Gordo by his rented room in the Haight. His bass turned out to be a Guild Starfire like Jack Casady's, except for the color, which was red.

"What happened to the Hofner?" Cole asked.

"I got rid of that piece of shit years ago. I used Fenders until I found out what Jack played."

The next stop was Sunset Music, west of the Haight, near the park. Gordo didn't like any of the rentals and Cole, losing patience, asked the clerk if they had anything used. "As a matter of fact," he said, "we got this in yesterday…"

He rolled out a Kustom 200-watt head on top of a cabinet with two 15-inch JBLs, both pieces upholstered in black Naugahyde, looking brand-new. Gordo said, "Oh, man," and plugged in.

For 15 minutes Cole watched him work out on the amp. At one point the clerk came to check on them. "Does he always do that?" the clerk asked.

"The dancing?" Cole said. "As long as I've known him."

Gordo paid with a wad of soiled and crumpled bills from his front jeans pocket. "This is my lucky day," he said.

"Just wait. You haven't even heard Lenny yet."

THEY PLAYED FOR two hours, pausing once when the chords for one of Cole's originals got a little tricky, and a second time so that Gordo could show Lenny his footwork. "It's just a cumbia step," Gordo said, "backstep with the left, then with the right. Then sometimes I travel with the molinete, you know, the grapevine. Step in front, open up, step behind, open up." What the hell, Cole thought, and on the next instrumental break they all three did it together.

"Well," Cole asked when they finally took a breather. "What do you think?"

"About what?" Gordo said.

"The band, pendejo. Are you in?"

"Of course I'm in," Gordo said. "Are you chiflado?"

"Aren't you going to consult the rest of us?" Lenny said.

"Oh," Cole said. "Uh, Gordo, maybe you could..."

"You dumb shit," Lenny said. "Yes, I want him."

"Uh, Tommy?" Cole said.

"Fuck yeah," Tommy said. "Do I look—" He glanced at Gordo. "—chifla whatever it is?"

"Chiflado," Gordo said. "What's the name of this band, anyway?"

"We don't have one yet," Cole said.

"Really," Gordo said.

"Yeah, that's what Gracie—" He pulled up short.

"What?" Gordo said.

"The Quirq," Cole said. "Q-U-I-R-Q. Qs at both ends."

Lenny looked at Tommy and Tommy looked at Gordo.

"Let's sleep on it," Gordo said.

THAT FRIDAY AFTERNOON, Cole drove to the Paisley Octopus house. Despite the fact that he had yet to play a gig in San Francisco, the guys looked up to him, and when he proposed that their two bands do a free gig together the next afternoon in the Panhandle, the Octopus providing the extension cords, they went for it.

"I guess this means you found a bass player," Brad said.

"Yeah, at that Airplane party Monday night. I owe you for that. You guys find a new guitarist yet?"

"Not yet," Brad said. "And Don's gone after next week." Brad was in the same despairing place that Cole had been Monday morning, with less reason for hope.

"Sorry, man. Listen, you guys have done the Fillmore audition thing, right?"

"Yeah, three times. Every time we break in a new guitarist. Graham just says, 'Come back in a couple of months.' He's switched it to Tuesday nights at the new place. Supposedly all you have to do is show up. I would drop by a day or two ahead of time and schmooze Graham a little. Give him a business card, band photo, something like that. Get him interested without pissing him off. That's the hard part. And right now he's the only game in town."

MADELYN HAD NOT STOPPED loving San Francisco, and she hadn't stopped loving Cole, or given up on the idea of going back to school. She was swimming for her life, and the niceties could wait.

She'd answered a want ad from Benjamin Kindred Galleries wearing her blue halter dress from New York. She'd put her hair up, worn more makeup than ever before in her life, and stared at Kindred during the entire interview as if he were the most fascinating man on the planet. If she felt guilty for prostituting herself, she got over it; the pay was good and somebody had to cover the rent on the damp, dingy, dangerous apartment she was living in.

Kindred was 30, dark, TV-handsome, and operating on a trust fund of substantial proportions. He was the embodiment of a kind of privilege that made the typical St. Mark's boy look like Jo the Crossing Sweeper from *Bleak House*. Without question he had given Madelyn the job with the expectation that she would be sexually available, despite her wedding ring, and by the time he discovered his mistake, she'd made herself indispensable— sweet-talking his blue-haired lady clients, flattering his artists, getting discounts from his suppliers, scoring press coverage in the *Chronicle* society pages.

The business catered to extremely wealthy trophy hunters in search of the status conveyed by big-name artists. The majority of the paintings that Kindred sold never saw his gallery walls; instead he negotiated the back-room acquisition of a de Kooning here, a Pollock there. More and more of his clients wanted a Warhol or a Rauschenberg or a Lichtenstein or an Oldenberg without caring which Warhol or which Oldenberg, or even which artist as long as it was someone hip and happening.

The show that had just closed featured a local painter obsessed with German expressionism who placed angular, abstracted, allegorical figures into sexually charged tableaus that threatened imminent mayhem. The artist himself was short, red-bearded, and rather jovial. Madelyn had coached him into a more sullen persona that played better in the press, with the result that he managed to sell a couple of his larger canvasses.

The new show was something else again. The artist was Italian, Michelangelo Pistoletto, and at first Madelyn had dismissed him as another stunt artist, like Warhol. The paintings consisted of oblongs of thin, polished steel mounted on canvas, to which Pistoletto had affixed life-size figures painted on tissue paper, paint-side down. As she studied photographs of the work, she appreciated the cleverness of what Pistoletto had done. The steel "canvas" reflected its surroundings, incorporating them, and the viewer, into the art. Set the piece in an old chair on a dusty street and it was a completely different piece than it was in the pristine setting of the gallery.

Pistoletto himself arrived to supervise the placement of the paintings on the Monday of Cole's adventure at the Airplane House. Normally Madelyn worked Tuesday through Saturday, but she'd agreed to come in for the occasion. She'd bought a copy of *See It and Say It in Italian* to refresh her meager skills and, when Kindred led Pistoletto in, she managed to go back and forth for more than a minute of pleasantries before having to admit her limits.

Pistoletto was not what she expected from a major figure of the Arte Povera movement, whose tenets included a rejection of corporate materialism. He still looked like the commercial artist he'd once been; though only 35, his hair was thinning and his body appeared well-fed inside his beautifully cut suit. His eyes, however, had real warmth as well as intelligence, and her attempts at Italian made a good impression. Kindred noticed as well, and when Pistoletto specifically asked that Madelyn be included in their dinner plans, Kindred agreed.

Thus she found herself at Alioto's, looking out over Fisherman's Wharf and the rows of fishing boats, drinking an expensive California Chardonnay and discussing art and politics with two powerful, attractive, and exquisitely dressed men. Cole, despite a bit of snippiness, had shown no jealousy when she called to tell him she'd be late. He'd never been short of self-confidence; this felt more like a lack of interest in her life. Trouble lurked over that horizon, waiting for her to have the time to deal with it.

"What does your husband do?" Pistoletto asked.

He had apparently noticed the ring. She felt oddly embarrassed to talk about Cole. "He's... a musician."

"Ah. A rock musician?"

"Yes, a guitarist. His band was very popular in Texas, so we came out here to..."

"Make it big?"

Madelyn blushed. "Yes."

"Good, good. Rock music, rebellion, all of this is very good. You heard about the riots in Paris in May?"

"There wasn't a lot in the news here."

"Very important, I think. There have always been riots because of hunger or physical oppression, or like you had here because of the assassination of your Reverend King. In France they had riots about philosophy. 'Ne travaillez jamais,' the Situationists say, 'Never work.' This was painted on the walls of buildings. Not because they were lazy, but because the time is here to talk about the way we live our lives. There is a book you should read, but it's not in English yet I don't think. *La Société du spectacle* by Guy Debord."

"I read French," Madelyn said.

"Very impressive." He looked at Kindred. "You must hang on to this one."

"Trying to," Kindred said, with an ambiguous smile.

"The book explains the way capitalism makes us passive consumers and turns everything into commodities. Here, I write it down for you." He took a matchbook from the ashtray and wrote the name inside.

The talk drifted to contemporary art, where Kindred was more comfortable than in the realms of Marxism and revolution. Madelyn found herself wrenched by sudden sorrow, and it took her a minute to figure out the reason. She had missed this kind of talk. The intellectual world of the moment was a conflagration in a firecracker factory, and every new idea that exploded set off another dozen around it. The frenetic pace couldn't last forever, and she longed to be in the thick of it now.

Cole, she knew, was close to admitting defeat. He hadn't said as much out loud, and she was afraid to bring it up. Still, for all her pleasure in doing her job well, for all her anticipation of the Pistoletto show, the thing that got her out of bed every morning was the hope that today would be the day that Cole put his arms around her and said, "Let's go home."

And so, when Cole woke her up that night brimming over with excitement about his party, her first, selfish reaction was disappointment. Her second was to keep the details of her own evening to herself, to hold inside her a while longer the memory of Pistoletto's attention and approval.

On Tuesday they put up the descriptions and the prices for the paintings. Wednesday was an exclusive preview with a lecture by Pistoletto, and Thursday was the opening. Madelyn was not sure that Cole had registered her absence, being fully occupied as he was with the bulky stranger now sleeping on her couch, whom she understood to be a bass player of heretofore unrecognized genius. Every night Pistoletto offered to drive her home in his rented Cadillac, and every night she refused, less from fear that Pistoletto might harbor ulterior motives than from shame. Every night the streetcar ride meant leaving Oz for the pigsty on a black-and-white Kansas farm.

Friday afternoon was Pistoletto's flight to New York and from there back to Turin. He stopped off at the gallery to say goodbye. For Kindred he had a firm, US-style handshake; Madelyn he hugged and kissed on both cheeks, then, before she realized what was happening, he kissed her lightly on the lips. He gave her his business card and said, "Next time you're in Europe, call me."

She watched in a daze as he got in the Cadillac and drove away.

"You made quite a hit," Kindred said.

"I liked him," Madelyn said. "Can I have tomorrow off?"

"My charms are not enough to bring you in, now that Michelangelo's gone?"

"My husband's playing his first local show. He just found out."

"Sure, what the hell. You've earned it."

Cole seemed truly pleased that she was going to be there. After dinner she went to bed and slept for 12 hours straight.

MADELYN WAITED in the park as the band set up, impressed by the near military precision. One of the octopi stopped traffic while Tommy ran across the street with his bass drum, the other octopi unrolled extension cords, and the rest of the band rolled their amps across. Everything else came in a second wave. Five minutes later Cole stood at a microphone saying, "Ladies and gentlemen, we are The Quirq."

Lenny, laughing at Cole, stepped up to his own mike and said, "Maybe."

Tommy counted them off and they started into "Born Under a Bad Sign," from the Albert King album that Cole had played a million times.

For once the sky was an endless blue, the temperature warm enough for short sleeves. The park was full of kids and dogs and Madelyn thought that if she squinted hard enough she could see the ghost of the Summer of Love hovering overhead in star-shaped sunglasses and buckskin fringe, touching smiles onto lips with glitter-painted fingernails.

Good as the band had been in Austin, she saw that something had been missing, and Gordo was the magic ingredient. Just as Cole had told her. Fifteen minutes into the show, a girl at the front of the crowd peeled off her sweatshirt, revealing titanic breasts that wobbled crazily as she danced with her arms over her head. Most of the audience was dancing, and the few that weren't watched Cole and Lenny with rapt fascination.

The premonition Madelyn had felt in Austin returned, stronger than ever, Cole on the road, topless women offering themselves to him, money, drugs, adulation. And now, instead of her being left behind in Austin to finish her degree, she would be left behind in San Francisco with a slum apartment and a job with no future.

She tried to remind herself that she was only 19, young yet. She didn't feel young at all.

*

ON THE NIGHT of August 28, Dave sat in front of his TV and watched his country come apart at the Democratic National Convention in Chicago. Fighting on the convention floor, blue-helmeted Chicago police dragging delegates into the chaos outside. Searchlights, screams, teargas exploding, wave after wave of police chasing kids and beating them with nightsticks, bodies bleeding in the streets while the whole world watched.

It was the climax to the strangest year of Dave's life.

Columbia had beaten out Capitol and Atlantic to sign Skip Shaw, and in late March Dave had taken him into Golden State Recorders to finish the LP. They completed work on Wednesday, April 3, and Dave sent the master tapes to New York by messenger that afternoon. The next day he got two phone calls within an hour of each other.

The first was from Tom Dowd, saying that Martin Luther King had been shot. Dave, like Dowd, lived in a secluded corner of the world that was, if not free from racism, freer than most. He worked alongside black artists every day, to the point that he'd begun to take it for granted that the change Sam Cooke sang about had already come. To have his face pushed into the reality of the anger and hatred on the streets made him despair.

He was reeling when the second call came, from a lawyer at Columbia Records. He informed Dave that Warner Brothers had filed suit against Columbia, claiming that Skip Shaw owed them an album under a contract signed the year before.

In the days that followed, Columbia sued Shaw, including Dave in the suit, and Dave, on his lawyer's advice, sued Wes, Shaw's manager. Shaw used his signing advance to countersue everyone, including, with epic ingratitude, Dave. Eventually the lawyers all got together and hammered out a deal where Columbia got its money back, Warners scheduled the *Tender Hours* LP for mid-summer, and Dave lost every penny he'd earned in producer's fees, plus his out-of-pocket expenses for the demos, to lawyers and settlements.

Billboard deemed Sallie Rachel's second album a "sophomore slump" due to "lack of electricity," though label mates the Meteors hit the top ten with their cover of "Breaking the Ice."

Dave, who had never paid attention to politics when he lived in New York, suddenly found himself engrossed in the Presidential race. He understood that he was doing it to distract himself from his career. Even so, the campaign was unlike any other in history. As the Tet Offensive in January had turned the Vietnam War into a bloodbath, so the war for the soul of the US had escalated in violence. George Wallace had entered the race in February, threatening to "get rid" of all anarchists, while his running mate, Curtis LeMay, promised to use nuclear weapons in Southeast Asia. Then the King assassination, then Bobby Kennedy's murder in Los Angeles in June, and now rioting police in Chicago.

Sickened, Dave turned off the TV and stood at the window, looking out at San Francisco. He'd moved into a nice apartment on Nob Hill when Columbia signed Shaw. If something didn't shake loose soon, he wouldn't be able to stay.

He put Sallie's new album on the stereo. Maybe it did lack electricity, but that voice... it took all the lonely nights he'd ever spent and refined them into a pure essence that he inhaled and held in his chest until it burned.

ON SEPTEMBER 12, a Thursday afternoon, Cole went to make his pitch to Bill Graham. He was perfectly calm right up to the minute he arrived in the hall outside Graham's office. When he heard Graham yelling, his nerve failed. The voice had a relentless quality, the volume slowly and steadily rising, the words rhythmic as a drumbeat, no pauses, no opening for anyone else.

"... asking that when the *fucking* phone rings that somebody pick it *up*, this is supposed to be *business*, when the phone rings at a *business*, somebody is supposed to fucking *answer* it so the person on the other end knows that *yes*, this is in *fact* a business—"

Cole was about to hightail it when a thin woman with short brown hair hurried out of Graham's office, glanced at Cole and shook her head, and went into another office down the hall. Now Graham was standing in the doorway, still going strong. "—one that manages to *give* a shit about the people who call—" He had seen Cole, and without a pause was yelling at him. "—and what the fuck do *you* want?"

Graham had a coarse look about him, Cole thought. Dark eyes, big nose, thick lips. Like a second-string henchman in a gangster movie. "Uh, maybe I should come back another day," Cole said.

"I got enough problems in my life, I don't need *you* hanging over my head like the Sword of fucking Damocles. Get in here and get it over with." He turned his back on Cole and retreated into his office.

Cole had done his homework. Though the prevailing opinion was that Graham was simply a bad-tempered asshole, the people who'd studied him believed he didn't take his own act seriously, that he merely used it to bully people into giving him his way. Cole hoped they were right.

He followed Graham into his office. The room was immense, windowless, covered on three walls and part of the ceiling with concert posters from the Fillmore. Graham picked up a stack of invoices and moved them to the center of his desk and stared at them intently. "Yes?" he said.

Cole couldn't remember the speech he'd carefully prepared. "Mr. Graham, I've got a band—"

"Auditions are on Tuesday. Be upstairs at six with the entire band and your equipment, ready to play."

"We're from Austin. Uh, Texas. We used to play at the Vulcan Gas Company with the Thirteenth Floor Elevators, Shiva's Headband, the Conqueroo."

Graham didn't look up. "Auditions are Tuesday. Be there at six."

"Yes, sir. I brought a photo and a business card to help you remember us."

Still focused on the invoices, Graham said, "At this point you'd be better off if I forgot you. And nobody calls me 'Mr. Graham.'"

"Yes, sir." Graham looked up, glaring, and suddenly Cole was overwhelmed by the ridiculousness of the moment. He laughed and held up the publicity shot that Madelyn had taken with the gallery's camera. "Here's that photo, Mr. Graham."

Graham, in spite of himself, cracked a smile. He held out his hand and Cole put the photo in it. Graham said, "The Quirq? What the hell kind of a name is that?"

"It'll grow on you," Cole said. "Just like me. Here's our card."

Graham took the card and said, "Now get the hell out of here and don't let me see you before Tuesday."

A FILLMORE WEST BANNER hung above the old marquee for the Carousel Ballroom, which said, TUESDAY NIGHT DOLLAR NIGHT. Graham, never one to miss an opportunity, charged admission to the auditions and got an evening's worth of performers for free. Below the marquee was the awning for the Buick dealership that had formerly occupied the ground floor, the letters crudely painted over.

Cole got them there at five minutes to five and parked the hearse by the fire escape stairs at the back of the hall. He left the keys with Lenny and walked around to the front and up the stairs to the auditorium. A basketball game was in progress, the players in numbered Fillmore West jerseys, mostly guys with long hair in braids or ponytails or held back with headbands. Graham, at 5 foot 8, moved through them like a wolverine in a pack of sled dogs, as if everyone else was playing for fun and Graham was playing for his very life. As Cole watched, Graham pursued an opposing player all the way to the basket and fouled him in mid-air, then heckled him during his free throws. Once he got his hands on the ball, he easily faked out the man guarding him and drove in for the layup.

The woman he'd seen fleeing Graham's office the week before was standing a few feet from Cole. "Can I help you?" she asked.

"We're here to audition. The Quirq? I'm Cole."

"Marushka." She offered him a long, thin hand. "You're early."

"It's part of our charm," Cole said. "Which is the best slot to go on?"

"It shouldn't matter if you're good. But... you don't want to be first, and you don't want to go on too late, after everyone is tired. Second or third, maybe?"

"Can you help us with that?"

She smiled. "Maybe."

She unlocked the back door for them and they brought up their gear. Other bands were arriving, some young, some with ratty equipment, all of them wearing whatever they'd happened to put on that day. Cole, on the other hand, was in his lucky polka-dot shirt and tie, Lenny in a black turtleneck, Gordo in leather pants he'd saved from his New Orleans days, Tommy in black T-shirt, chinos, and Converse All Stars.

Missing was Madelyn, who was exhausted and unwilling to stay up late. Cole had tried to convince her to come for a while and leave whenever she wanted, and she was equally unwilling to walk home alone after dark.

The Quirq were in fact third on the bill, scheduled to start at ten PM sharp. Graham, who'd been personally supervising every aspect of the show—taking tickets, visiting the dressing room, introducing the bands on stage, prowling around drinking one canned 7-Up after another—watched as Cole plugged in and checked his tuning. "Okay, hot shot," Graham said. In the indistinct light, Cole couldn't tell if he was smiling or not. "Impress me."

Cole smiled back anyway. "Yes, sir."

The hall had giant curtained arches across the back and a high, draped velour ceiling. A raised platform opposite the stage held the bar and the command center for the light show. Capacity was three thousand and so far fewer than a third that many people had showed up—still the largest crowd Cole had ever played for.

Lenny walked over from his usual spot at stage right. "Nervous?" he asked.

"Excited," Cole said.

"I'm fucking petrified. Whose idea was it to come to San Francisco?"

"Yours," Cole said. Reflexively he scanned the crowd in the hope that Madelyn had changed her mind.

"Ladies and gentlemen," Graham said into the mike, "formerly of Austin, Texas, now making their home here in the Bay Area, please give a warm welcome to... The Quirq!"

As a precaution, they'd worked out the first ten minutes in

some detail. Tommy counted them into "Wang Dang Doodle," but the energy was low and the changes felt stiff. They got through it and had begun the modulation that would take them into one of Cole's new songs when Cole decided to take over. Lenny was staring fixedly at his picking hand, and Cole had to walk right up to him to get his attention. They were riffing on E minor and Cole started throwing in a D chord. That finally snapped Lenny to attention and Cole felt the band come to life. He held the D longer and longer, and once the others were with him, he played the riff to "Laura Lee" and went back to the mike. Halfway through the song he felt a burst of energy from the audience and looked back to see Gordo dancing. Lenny saw it too and finally broke into a smile.

Their booster rockets fired and took them into orbit. Toward the end, as they played "Sunshine of Your Love" and had the audience completely enamored, he saw Bill Graham standing at the front of the crowd, digging it. An impulse seized him and he played the melody line to "Perfidia" instead of the Clapton lead. He turned to face the band and raised his guitar neck, then, after two bars, dropped it to cut the song off short. The silence was absolute, perfect. He let it hang for an agonizing four counts, then he started playing the "Perfidia" chords so that Lenny could see them and called them out as he played, "C, E minor, D minor, G." Gordo was on it immediately and Tommy came in with him, doing an improvised cha-cha-cha rhythm on the snare and toms. Lenny got it the second time through, and Cole walked to the mike and looked at Graham while he started a verse in Spanish. Graham immediately grabbed a woman and led her into cha-cha-cha footwork while the crowd around him cheered.

Cole had no way to teach the band the bridge, so after the second verse he played the melody again with a lot of sustain, and then took them into "Walk Don't Run," which they *had* rehearsed. Lenny played double lead with him and the crowd loved it all, especially when Cole and Lenny started dancing along with Gordo. They got called back for an encore, and after that, as they moved their equipment offstage, Graham beckoned Cole over. "I want to talk to you." He looked unhappy.

Cole followed him backstage. Standing next to the fire door, a bee-bop record echoing over the PA, surrounded by coils of rope and sandbags and a couple of broken chairs, Graham turned on him. "Where did you learn to sing 'Perfidia' like that?"

"Guanajuato, Mexico. Me and my high school bass player, we used to do a mariachi act."

"I fucking love Latin jazz."

"I know. I saw you dancing last summer at the Fillmore."

"I won a dance contest at the Palladium once. That was one of the proudest moments of my life. Do you even know what the Palladium is?"

"In New York? Yes, sir. My father has a record of Tito Rodriguez playing there."

"I was probably in the audience when they recorded it. Have you heard Santana?"

"Heard the name. Haven't heard the band yet."

"You should check them out. In the meantime, what are you doing the weekend of October 24 through 26?"

Cole's throat closed up. "Playing at the Fillmore West?"

Graham nodded. "You're opening for the Airplane and a Haitian dance company. That all right with you?"

"Yes, sir."

"Have you got management?"

"No, sir."

"You need to get some. But talk to me before you sign with anybody, because some of these guys are complete assholes and they'll rip you off."

"Yes, sir. Thank you, sir."

"Don't thank me yet. The pay is shit for opening acts. Though if you keep playing like you did tonight, you won't be stuck with opening for long. Come by the office tomorrow and we'll work out the details."

"Yes, sir."

Graham hesitated, like he was going to tell him again to knock off the "sir" business, and then he shook his head and laughed and walked away.

Cole, to his surprise, didn't feel like yelling for joy or throwing a huge party or calling everyone he knew. Instead he felt an immense calm where he hadn't realized he'd been afraid, because until that moment he hadn't been able to put a name to it. When he was 7 and 8 years old in New Jersey, he'd been friends with a boy named Glen, whose father worked the night shift in a steel mill. When he was at Glen's house in the daytime they had to whisper and walk on tiptoe so as not to wake his father. His father got up at four in the afternoon and watched TV and ate dinner and left for the mill. He had massive, reinforced shoes and he carried a dented black lunch pail with a domed lid that held a thermos. He was friendly to Cole and Glen loved him, but he seemed haunted, a man serving a sentence rather than living a life. Cole came away with the idea that most jobs were like that. A couple of missteps and there he'd be, kids, a mortgage, a meaningless job, no escape. For the first time, standing there backstage at the Fillmore West, Cole was sure that he was not going to end up like Glen's father. He closed his eyes and listened to himself take a long, deep breath.

THE FIRST NIGHT of their run. A clear, warm October evening after a sunny day. Cole got the band to the ballroom early for a 6:00 sound check. The Airplane had been and gone, and Ballet Afro-Haiti was setting up. They had three hand drummers playing congas and djembes along with two other percussionists on stage. More than a dozen singers and dancers worked a cleared area in front of the stage, picked up by a pair of boom mikes.

When The Quirq got their turn it went quickly, then they were backstage with the Haitians. Cole was intimidated by their blackness, by their brightly-colored African robes and flat, round caps, by the indecipherable patois he overheard, by the overall voodoo menace that surrounded them. Gordo, on the other hand, had worked and played with Haitians in New Orleans and started talking to them. Cole drifted over. It turned out that they were actually named the Danny Duncan Company of Dancers and Musicians and that Ballet Afro-Haiti was the title of this particular show. They were based in San Francisco and included musicians from all over the Caribbean and US. A couple of joints magically appeared and a common bond was forged.

By the time they took the stage for their first set, Madelyn was there. She'd hitched a ride with Gordo's new girlfriend, an aspiring poet named Irene who wore tight black T-shirts, tight jeans, motorcycle boots, and, according to Gordo, had a tattoo on her ass of a knife piercing a heart. Cole didn't know what he thought about a woman with a tattoo. He did know that it was none of his business and he was glad that she and Madelyn got along. They waved from the side of the stage and Cole blew Madelyn a kiss.

Eight o'clock on a Thursday, the hall mostly empty. A few hundred people milled around, buying drinks, talking instead of dancing. The band opened with "Good Rockin' Tonight" by Roy Brown and His Mighty Men, then moved through some of the usual originals. By the time they got to the new stuff they'd worked up for the gig, the room was half full, and "Tighten Up" by Archie Bell and the Drells got them moving. They slowed the rhythm to a cha-cha-cha and swung into a full-blown "Perfidia," Gordo singing high harmony, and seconds later a clearing materialized with Graham dancing at the center. From there they worked their way into a new song that Cole and Lenny had written together, a spacey, echoing number inspired by their shared love of NASA, Pink Floyd, and Jimi Hendrix. It was called "Mariner" and it had vague lyrics about voyaging into the unknown that could mean whatever anyone wanted them to. The crowd loved it and brought them back to do a medley of "Wang Dang Doodle" and "Laura Lee," and then Cole went out to watch Ballet Afro-Haiti with Madelyn.

They were emerging from their rough patch, Cole thought, with everything intact. They stood with their arms around each other and watched the dance, which was intense and frightening, the drums loping along at a pace that Cole's heartbeat involuntarily tried to match. According to what he'd learned that afternoon, the dancers' movements, though stylized, represented surrender to rapacious gods. Madelyn was captivated, and when it was over she looked at him with shining eyes. "That was wonderful!"

"You want to go backstage and meet them? They're nice."

"No! Way too scary."

The Airplane came on and he felt her attention flag. In person they were more chaotic than on record, the tempos faster, Marty and Grace improvising furious vocals as the band attacked the songs.

"I'm going to dance," she said during the second song. "Join me?"

Cole shook his head. Even if he'd been able to let loose enough to dance like that, he was a performer tonight and not a spectator. That distinction had less force in San Francisco than anywhere, but still meant something to him.

She smiled and said something to Irene, standing a few feet away, and led her into the mass of moving bodies. Cole tried to focus on the Airplane, telling himself it was nothing, despite the chill on his left side where she'd been standing.

GORDO WANTED TO ask one of the conga players from Afro-Haiti to sit in on their second set, and Cole said, "Sure, why not?"

"What's wrong? We sound great tonight."

"Nothing," Cole said. "I'm cool."

Taking a page from Richie Havens, they opened the second set with "San Francisco Bay Blues." The audience clapped and cheered and loved everything they did afterward. The band did a few more cover songs than the first set and managed to not repeat anything. Samson, the conga player, paid close attention and laid out during most of the transitions, playing great solos on "Third Stone from the Sun" and "All Your Love."

Cole kept one eye on Madelyn the whole time. She was either dancing or watching him with a big smile. So what's wrong, he asked himself, with her liking me more than the Jefferson Airplane?

In the break before the second Afro-Haiti set, she said, "It's late, we're going to go on home. You were wonderful." She kissed him passionately and looked back to wave one more time as she walked away.

Jorma found him as he was fishing a beer out of the mostly

melted ice backstage. "I thought you were going to come around and play sometime," Jorma said.

"I didn't think you were serious," Cole said. "I didn't want to impose."

"Well, now I've invited you again, so clearly I'm serious. Hey, after we do our encore tonight, why don't you come out and jam with us?"

"Oh, man," Cole said. "I would love that. But I wouldn't want to leave Lenny out, our other lead player."

"Bring him too. And that guy Samson, the conga player. You guys were really good tonight."

"Thanks," Cole said, embarrassed into silence.

"Uh oh," Jorma said. "Here comes Bill. See ya."

Graham beckoned Cole over. "Did you get hooked up with a manager?"

"We asked around," Cole said. "This guy Matthew Katz called, but I'm not sure I liked the sound of him."

"Pronounced 'Kates,'" Graham said. "He's bad, bad news. A total rip-off artist. Ask the Airplane about him. I've got half a mind to take you on myself."

"I'd have to talk to the guys, but I can tell you what they'd say. They'd say, 'Yes. Yes, please, sir.'"

"You talk to them about it, and call me tomorrow. I'll want to do a written contract and get you guys down to the office to sign it. Are you all over eighteen?" Cole nodded. "Any day jobs or any other reason you can't go on the road straight away? There's a big outdoor show November ninth at Long Beach State that we can probably get you on."

"No, sir. We're ready."

"Okay." He handed Cole an envelope with cash inside. "Take this now, because if you end up with Shady Management, I'll be taking a cut from that point on."

"Shady Management?"

"That's the name of my management company. And my booking agency is the Millard Agency. That okay with you?"

"Yes, sir. That's fine with us. And we'll be sure not to sign until after Saturday's show."

1968

Graham laughed, and then got serious again. "You guys are just kids, but you act professional. You dress up, you're here on time, you don't get so fucked up you can't play. I like that, and you can go a long way on that. I take a lot of shit for being a tight ass, but I'll tell you something. These kids want a fucking revolution? It's not going to happen. You don't win a war by letting everybody do their own thing." He poked Cole in the chest. "Call me tomorrow."

MADELYN WOKE to the sounds of a stoned and drunken band trying to carry their equipment back into the apartment quietly; the alarm clock showed eight minutes before seven AM. Early morning was never her finest hour, and her first thought was, where in God's name had they been all night? She rolled onto her back and listened to the second load come up the stairs, accompanied by thuds and shushing. Then the bedroom door creaked open and Cole stepped into a shaft of sunlight from a gap in the blinds that lit him up from the inside out. He was already radiant from his triumphant night, and as he smiled down on her, Madelyn found her irritation subverted by desire. She sat up and pulled off her long-sleeved T-shirt, the chill air giving her gooseflesh. Cole needed no further incentive. He struggled to get out of his clothes and his boots all at once until Madelyn, laughing, pulled him into bed so she could help.

"You'll be late to work," Cole said afterward, as they lay wrapped up in each other under the sheets and blankets.

"Special occasion. Where were you?"

His exhaustion was now complete, and he was barely coherent as he offered fragments of the story, nodding out in between. Bill Graham wanted to manage them. They'd gone to the Airplane house and jammed with the Haitian drummers. There had been booze and dope...

"And groupies?" Madelyn asked.

"I didn't notice," Cole said, and if she didn't quite believe him, she gave him points for the attempt.

She left him there asleep and hurried through a shower and a cold breakfast. The October morning was fresh and clear as she walked to her streetcar stop, the morning fogs gone since September. San Francisco was a never-never land, spring all year round, timeless and all-embracing. That Peter Pan quality appealed to Cole, and he was finally falling for the place, even as her own love for it began to dim. Last weekend her father had told her on the phone that the leaves had all turned and were starting to fall, and she'd found herself nearly in tears for a season she'd never cared about before.

She arrived at the gallery at 9:30, only half an hour late, with plenty of time before they officially opened at ten. No sooner had Madelyn locked the door than Kindred emerged from his office in the back and said, "I need to talk to you."

"I told you yesterday I might be late this—"

"It's not about that. Come in and sit down."

She sat in one of the Eames chairs that faced his desk. He struck one of his dramatic poses, swiveled sideways and staring into the nonexistent distance. Finally he said, "Where do you see yourself in ten years?"

"Realistically, or in my dreams?"

"Best-case real-world scenario."

"With a PhD in English literature, teaching at a good university."

"How do your chances look for that at the moment?"

She sighed. "Lousy."

"Would you be willing to consider the idea of a PhD in Art History from Stanford instead?"

Her mood lurched dizzyingly from apprehensive to wildly hopeful. "I'd certainly be willing to talk about it."

"In ten years I picture myself with a business partner, somebody who can run this gallery profitably while I do other things. The person I have in mind would be intelligent, charming, organized, and have the credentials to be taken seriously in the international art community. You are three for four."

She nodded for him to go on.

"From what you've told me, you shouldn't have any problem getting into Stanford or getting financial aid. As it happens, my family has some influence there, should that be necessary. What

I'd offer you is a flexible schedule and all the hours you wanted to work while you were getting your PhD, plus a modest stipend so you wouldn't have to worry about where your next meal was coming from."

"And in return?"

"You commit to at least five years as my partner at the Kindred/ Brooks Galleries once you have your degree."

"I apologize, but I have to say this. I *am* married, and in love with my husband, and if there are any strings attached—"

"No strings. There are plenty of beautiful women in this town who *are* available. What you have to offer is harder to find."

"I'll need to think about it."

"Of course. Take your time."

"Whatever I decide... thank you. For believing in me."

"What I'm asking for is a hell of a commitment. Probably fifteen years at the very least. I know you won't take that lightly. I can promise you you'll end up making a very good living. What I need to know is that you'll be happy doing it."

No, was what she was thinking. Not completely happy, because this is not what I had planned.

She reminded herself that neither had she planned to be married at 19, or living in San Francisco, or out of college after a single year.

"My head is spinning," she said.

Kindred nodded. "Maybe you could make us some coffee while it's settling down."

BY THE TIME Madelyn got home, Cole had already left for his gig. She would have to tell him eventually, like she would have to tell her father. At the moment what she wanted was a girlfriend to talk it out with face to face, and the closest she had to that was her fellow band widow, Irene.

Irene took her down to the Mission District in her battered black Falcon, to a crowded, noisy, cafeteria-style taco joint. Irene was 21 and happy to buy beers for both of them with Madelyn's money. Once they got a table, Madelyn laid out Kindred's offer.

"This isn't about whether going back to college is what you

should be doing, right?" Irene said. "Because we can, like, take it as understood that the university, especially *that* university, is the last bastion of the bourgeoisie. Ivy-covered ivory towers and all that shit, and speaking purely for myself, it's the last fucking place a poet should be, but we're not talking about me, right? We're talking about you, and what *you* want, in which case, hell *yes* you should do it. It's like if all you want is to be a millionaire in Gstaad, and what you are is flat broke in Des Moines, and then somebody offers you the chance to be a millionaire in Zurich instead, and you want to fucking *quibble* about it?"

"Well, when you put it that way... but why is it okay for me and not for you?"

"Because you're a change-from-within kind of a person, and I'm a tear-down-the-fucking-walls kind of a person. If *I* do it it's hypocrisy. Since you actually believe in all that shit, you might even do some good."

"You wouldn't want your poems to be taught in a university someday?"

"I want the academy to be too fucking terrified of my poems to admit they exist. I want the US government to make my poems illegal. I want people to throw rocks through the windows of bookstores that carry my poems. The point of this exercise is the end of the world as we know it."

"Do you really think it's going to come to that?"

"It already has. Did you see what went down in Chicago?"

Later that night, her mind cartwheeling from three beers, Madelyn tried to decide whether Irene had, intentionally or not, been putting her down as part of the perceived establishment. Was it wrong to want anything less than the complete destruction of western civilization? Did it all have to go, John Donne along with Tricky Dick, *Mrs. Dalloway* with Richard Daley?

She woke up, in any case, with the knowledge that she would tell Kindred yes. She couldn't do it until she told Cole, and Cole was dead to the world in the bed next to her. Saturday was her late day at the gallery, ten until seven, so Cole was gone again by the time she got home. It was Sunday afternoon before they were both awake at the same time in the same place, and over scrambled eggs and bacon that she'd cooked, he told her that they'd signed a management contract with Graham and that they would be going on the road, starting with a show in Long Beach in two weeks.

"What's wrong?" he asked, when she didn't say anything.

Tommy was ten feet away, sprawled on the couch watching football. Lenny was at the other end of the dining room table with the Sunday comics, coffee, cigarette, and guitar. She thought Cole might have discussed it with her before he signed on to a whole new career path, even as she was walking around, bursting to agree to Kindred's proposal before he changed his mind, and holding back for Cole's sake. She was unwilling to throw that particular gauntlet with Lenny and Tommy practically in their laps, so she swallowed her disappointment and said, "I guess I hadn't thought it through, about your being on the road. It's going to be lonely here without you."

"Aw," Cole said, and came around the table to pull her head into his chest. "You'll be fine, I know you will."

Irene, Madelyn thought, would be so ashamed of me. She was ashamed of herself.

Later, she coaxed him out for a walk and told him about Kindred's offer.

"That's fantastic," Cole said. "That's exactly what you wanted."

"Not *exactly*." They were walking north on Laguna Street, vaguely in the direction of Jefferson Square Park. Houses and businesses were shuttered because of urban renewal. Knots of sullen young black men languished on the corners, which didn't help Madelyn's feelings of alienation. "What I wanted to study was literature."

"Do a double major. If you're still not sold on Art History after your BA, you can renegotiate. Besides, we'll be rich by then and you can do whatever you want."

His utter confidence should have been charming, and she couldn't explain why it had the opposite effect. "So between you and Kindred, you guys are going to make sure that I get to play at being an intellectual."

"I don't know where that bullshit is coming from, but it's not from me. I'm not condescending to you about college. Your brain amazes me. You're already at least twice as smart as I am, and by the time you get a PhD you're not going to want to talk to an illiterate dropout like me."

"You're not illiterate. You read Matt Helm novels." The joke, if she'd meant it as one, backfired, and she saw him withdraw into himself. "I'm sorry. That was not worthy of me. I don't know what's gotten into me today."

"We're growing apart," Cole said.

It was like she'd fallen through a crack in the ice into freezing water. She was too stunned to keep walking. "Is that what you really think?" she said softly.

"You're not that crazy about rock music. You've seen us what, twice since Gordo joined? I feel like you're waiting for me to grow out of it. There's no way that I've got any more college in my immediate future, maybe ever. The more successful the band gets, the more we'll be away, and the more successful you get, the more tied you are to San Francisco."

"We knew that from the start. And talked about it."

"It's different when it plays out in real life, though, isn't it? You can't pretend anymore that it's not going to happen. You can't keep putting off how you feel about it."

Emotion was dialing up Cole's volume. Madelyn awarded herself points for keeping her own voice down. "How do *you* feel about it?"

"I'm scared to death. I don't want to lose you."

"Oh, Cole." Her mood broke and she moved into the circle of his arms, burying her face in his neck. "I will never leave you."

His arms tightened around her, and in his silence she heard the other, unspoken possibility, that he could be the one to leave and still blame her for it, and now she was scared too, holding on, like he did, to escape the curse of self-consciousness and to be no more than two bodies in the October sunshine.

WHEN THE PHONE RANG on the morning of Friday, the 13th of December, Dave seriously considered not answering. He'd been awake for an hour and a half and unable to get out of bed. He didn't think he could bear any more bad luck.

He gave in on the fourth ring.

"I was wrong, okay?" the voice said. "Let's get that out of the way to start with."

"Hi, Sallie," Dave said. "Nice to hear your voice."

"Can we do it your way? Get all the guys from the first record, record it in New York, the same room, even, the whole megillah?"

"Me? Oh, I'm fine. An opening for you? Yes, I imagine I can find an opening for you."

That got her to apologize and they spent the next half hour catching up. Her drummer boyfriend had been relieved of both positions. She blamed the failure of her second album on "too many upbeat songs" and assured him that would not be a problem this time. He told her about the Skip Shaw debacle, about scrounging for work even as the industry was exploding all around him.

"We need each other, Dave." He didn't say anything, just put his hand on his chest to try and make his heart slow down. "I want to be on the radio again. Can you get me on the radio again, Dave? Please?"

"You bring the songs," he said, "I'll bring the hit-making magic."

He had barely calmed himself when Bill Graham called. "I'm not ready to do the Fillmore Records thing yet," he said. "But I've got a band I think you should hear. They're at the Fillmore West tonight, eight o'clock."

BEING BILL GRAHAM, he made Dave pay for his own ticket. The band was called The Quirq, though Graham said they were trying to come up with something better. Dave liked what he heard. The problem was that their live show depended on a gimmick, a kind of musical high wire that they walked between the songs, apparently reinventing the path from one to the next every night. Dave didn't see how to capture that drama on record.

He felt conflicted enough that he didn't approach the band that night. He went home to bed, only to lie there with the melody to "Mariner" going through his head.

He went back for another listen on Saturday and then, while Terry Reid's raspy voice filled the hall, he talked to the band backstage. The main singer went by the name of Cole and the others deferred to him in small but noticeable ways. He was handsome in a baby-faced, tragic way that *Tiger Beat* would have loved, if the band had been courting a different audience. Dave handed out his cards and was gratified that they knew his name.

"Here's what I'm thinking," Dave told them. "If I produce you, I'm not going to try to recreate your stage show. I think you've got an album's worth of solid, hummable songs, and that's what I would want to get out there. Then when people see you live, and those songs that they know from the record start to emerge from the jams, they're going to go crazy."

"Do you see us as a singles band?" Cole asked.

Dave shook his head. "What is it with you San Francisco types? What's so wrong with having a hit single?"

"We're from Texas," Cole said, "and we'd love to have a hit single."

THE SUMMER AFTER Cole and Madelyn moved to San Francisco, Alex took a job loading trucks at the 7-Up bottling plant in Austin. The idea was his father's—you needed to be 21 to work at a beer company, and a lot of the soft-drink logistics were the same. The work was brutal, mindless, leaving you too exhausted to think. Which was probably for the best.

Sunny was in Fort Worth, Joe was in Tupelo, Denise was in Denton, and Alex had the house to himself. He kept thinking that he heard music from Cole's room, a couple of times so distinctly that he had to open the door and look in to prove himself wrong.

On weekends he'd go to Barton Springs, lie in the sun, and read *The Brothers Karamazov*, the Russian angst a good match for his mood.

In the fall he took second year Russian grammar, Russian conversation, and Russian literature in translation, along with Economics and Accounting. He rented Cole's room to a bookish senior English major.

1968

At first Cole phoned every week or two. Then, as things started to take off for him, every three weeks, then once a month. He didn't blame Cole. Cole was the one with something to talk about: going to the Airplane Mansion, playing at the Fillmore, getting a record deal. Alex hated his own side of the conversation, how trivial it was, how utterly mundane. He didn't want to trade places with Cole, he just wanted...

He didn't know what he wanted.

As SOON As Cole saw the envelope, he knew what it was. The return address was "US Selective Service Administration" and it was addressed to him at his parents' house. His mother had enclosed it, unopened, inside a larger manila envelope. Madelyn, across the table from him, must have read it in his face. "What's wrong?"

Cole opened it. He was to report for his pre-induction physical in downtown Dallas on Monday, December 23, at 8 in the morning. It would be his 19th birthday.

He handed the letter to Madelyn and watched her face go slack. "Dear God," she said. "What are you going to do?"

"You wanted to go back to Dallas for Christmas. I guess we're going."

She came around the table to hold him. "They can't take you," she said. "You're mine."

"They take guys like me every day."

They'd talked about it. Rumor had it that the government was about to institute a lottery system that would standardize the selection process. At the moment it was shrouded in mystery. Cole had not notified anyone that he'd dropped out, so he assumed UT had. He'd known the risk, and he'd put off dealing with it.

He woke up at three AM with his mind racing. If he did pass the physical, crippled finger and all, it surely meant Vietnam. Since the Tet Offensive had begun in January, the war had burned through young soldiers' lives like cord wood. Surely, he thought, with his brains and education they wouldn't put him on the front lines.

Maybe he would live through it and come home and write about it. Songs, maybe a novel. Maybe Susan would finally be impressed with him.

Or, like Country Joe said, maybe he would come home in a box. Or missing an arm, and never play guitar again. Or paralyzed, impotent, deaf.

Once in Midland he'd found some partially incinerated frogs from the biology lab. The skin had burned away, leaving muscles and bones that had turned hard and brown. A napalmed body would look like that, he thought, and smell of cooked meat and gasoline.

He never made it back to sleep.

THEY FLEW TO DALLAS on the 21st. Cole had burrowed so deeply into himself that the outside world barely registered. Alex picked them up at Love Field and Cole recognized that he was happy to see them both. As for his own emotions, Cole couldn't locate them.

Alex was driving his father's Cadillac. Cole got in the back seat and they took Madelyn to her parents' house. Cole carried her suitcase in and he and Alex said hello to her parents. Everyone was about as relaxed as if he had terminal cancer. When he kissed her goodbye, Madelyn gave him a worried look and he said, "It'll be okay."

At the Montoyas' everyone gathered at the dinner table. Susan and Jesse were there, both parents, and Jimmy, who would start high school the next fall. Cole regaled them with stories of his budding fame, meeting Gordo at the Airplane mansion, playing the Fillmore West, traveling up and down the coast with the Dead, Moby Grape, and Country Joe, getting ready to go into Pacific Recorders in January to cut a demo with the guy who produced Sallie Rachel and Skip Shaw.

When he laid it out like that, he even impressed himself. Had he really come so far in six months? At the same time, he knew he was making an inventory of everything he stood to lose.

Later, as everyone headed off to bed, Jesse put a hand on his shoulder and said, "Let's take a walk."

The night was clear enough to see stars, the temperature in the forties. Despite his thrift-store pea coat, Cole couldn't warm up. They headed toward the school playground down the street and Jesse lit a joint and handed it to Cole. "You haven't been eating much, have you?"

"No," Cole said.

"You trying for 1-Y?"

"What's that?"

"Deferment for non-disabling medical condition. Underweight, overweight, high blood pressure."

"I hadn't really thought about it."

Jesse stopped and faced him. "Think about it. You don't want to go over there. Believe me on this."

Cole had to look away from the intensity of his eyes. "I don't want to go."

"Your physical is Monday?" Cole nodded. "Don't eat again between now and then. Drink a big glass of water before bed tonight and don't drink again. Starting tomorrow afternoon, spit."

"Spit?"

"Every time you think of it. When you're in the bathroom, when you're outside, keep spitting. You'll dehydrate yourself."

They got to the playground and sat on the merry-go-round. The green painted wood creaked when they sat and the cold burned through Cole's jeans. They finished the joint in silence and then Cole said, "How bad was it?"

"I generally don't talk about it. Talking about it makes it more real, you know? But I will say this. That fear you've been living with since you got the notice? You don't have to say anything, I could see it the minute you walked in the door. It's like that, only worse, and it never goes away. You can't live like that, not without it changing you. It changes you into the kind of person who can function while being afraid a hundred percent of the time, and when you become that person, you can never stop being afraid again, because now being afraid is part of who you are. Down at the cellular level, down in your DNA.

"When you're scared all the time, you're not really there. The way you haven't really been here tonight. You learn to fake it.

People think you're normal, you're hanging loose, you're having fun, and inside your head you're on point with an M-16, listening for a rustle in the grass or the snap of a twig."

Jesse was quiet for half a minute, then he stood up. "Let's go get you that glass of water."

COLE LET MADELYN drive him to the Selective Service office downtown. A tall gray building in a block of buildings just like it. He felt like an automaton. He kissed Madelyn without feeling. She said, "Call me as soon as you know anything," and clung to him briefly. He got out and took the elevator upstairs.

A big room from another era, worn linoleum floor, plastic chairs. Thirty or forty other young men waited there for their names to be read out. Most of them were black, which struck Cole as odd, because he'd hardly seen any black people in Dallas in the time he'd lived there.

In another dingy room they stripped to their underwear and put their clothes in wire baskets, like at the swimming pool. A hippie with shoulder-length brown hair and drooping mustache had to explain to the sergeant that he wasn't wearing underwear and was allowed to keep his bell-bottoms on. Blood pressure test, short arm and anal inspection, height and weight, urinalysis. Cole was so dehydrated that he couldn't piss. Eventually he squeezed out a couple of drops and left the cup where he was told. Nobody said anything about it.

At one point a doctor said, "Ever have any problem with those feet?" Cole shook his head and the doctor walked on. Only later did he remember something about high insteps when he was a kid, and having to pick up marbles with his toes. Wait, he wanted to say, I do have problems, but it was too late.

Later they were lined up in a hallway, still in their underwear, the hippie standing next to him. "I'm on speed," the hippie whispered. "My blood pressure is through the roof. I'm already as good as out of here." He shifted from leg to leg with nervous energy. Cole stared at him. A few minutes later two men in uniform came and took the hippie away.

Finally he was alone in an office with a doctor who was reading from a clipboard. He had white hair and a lined face. "Jeffery Cole?"

Cole nodded.

"Height five-ten, weight one hundred and twenty-two pounds." He looked Cole over.

"I'm six feet."

The doctor said, "We measured you today at five-ten." They had lied, Cole realized, because they knew what he was trying to do. "That's still seriously underweight," the doctor said. "High arches, injury to right middle finger. Let me see your hand." Cole reached across the desk. The doctor put on a pair of glasses and gently examined Cole's finger. He nodded, took the glasses off, and looked at Cole and smiled. "Yeah," he said, "I think we can get you out."

COLE DRESSED and rejoined his group and they were led to a room with elementary-school-style desks where he was given a written test to complete. He felt a grudging admiration for the way the test was put together. No matter how little education you had, it would be difficult not to pass. Along with basic math, the questions drew from auto mechanics, from farming, from gambling. As they finished, they handed their tests to a sergeant at a desk at the front of the room, who graded them while they waited. The room was overly warm, and Cole dozed until his name was called.

The desk sergeant handed Cole a piece of paper with the status of 1-Y stamped on it. He pointed to the door and said, "You're free to go." Then he paused and shook his head regretfully. "Outstanding intelligence test, I have to say."

It was one in the afternoon. Cole went down to the street and found a pay phone. He called Madelyn and she screamed with joy when she heard the news. He felt like screaming too. He was only beginning to realize how completely his emotions had shut down.

He called the Montoya house and told Alex's mother. "Thank God," she said. "Are you on your way home?"

"Madelyn's coming for me."

"See you soon."

He crossed the street to Dickey's, where he got a sliced brisket sandwich and potato chips and a big Coke and a wedge of cheddar cheese. He sat by the window to watch for Madelyn, and forced himself to eat slowly. Even so, his stomach had shrunken to where he couldn't finish and he felt queasy.

Vietnam only accounted for part of his fear. Hiding under his desk in primary school, rehearsing for a nuclear attack. Living in Suez during the Cuban missile crisis, seeing a bomber flying low overhead and believing he was about to die. Hearing the news of the JFK assassination as a freshman in high school and realizing nobody was safe. He'd spent his entire life under the shadow of annihilation. How could he not have loved Bob Dylan, picked up a guitar, moved to San Francisco?

He was waiting at the curb when Madelyn pulled up in her parents' station wagon. She jumped out of the car and ran to him and cried as she hugged him. "I was so scared," she said.

"Me too," Cole said. "Me too."

The Montoyas, despite preparations to leave for Guanajuato the next day, had thrown together a surprise birthday party. A homemade banner said, SORRY ARMY YOU CAN'T HAVE HIM. Susan held him tightly and said in his ear, "I'm so glad we didn't have to have the Plan B party."

"Was there a theme?" Cole asked.

"O Canada."

Alex hugged him too. "Would have served you right, you fucking idiot, but I'm glad you got out."

Jesse gave him a thumbs-up with one hand and flashed a peace sign with the other.

Much Bohemia was consumed, and Cole, dehydrated and undernourished, got drunk very quickly. No one seemed to mind, and he had little trouble convincing Madelyn to stay the night. They retired early, leaving the party to continue downstairs without them, and made love with exquisite tenderness.

"I was never lucky before," Cole said, holding her in the dark, his hands amazed all over again by the softness and contours of her skin, his nose full of her scents. "I'm making up for it now."

"Hold that thought," Madelyn said. But he was too exhausted and the world slipped away.

THE NEXT MORNING, as Cole helped load the Montoyas' luggage, Alex's mother took him aside. "I hope you won't be mad. I told your mother you were staying with us. You don't have to see her if you don't want to…"

"If it was just her, it wouldn't be a problem."

"She understands that." She hesitated. "I know it's hard for you. But if you could find your way clear to letting her come over and see you… not so much for her sake as for yours. Hardening your heart can get to be a habit."

"I'll think about it," Cole said.

His mother called in the early afternoon. "Steve thinks I'm at a party with my bridge club. I don't have long. Can I come over? Or I could meet you somewhere. And I want to meet Madelyn."

She rang the doorbell ten minutes later. When Cole hugged her, he found it hard to let go. He introduced Madelyn, and his mother took Madelyn's hands in both of her own and started to cry.

The three of them sat in the living room, Cole and Madelyn together on the couch, as Cole had arranged it, his mother in an armchair facing them. Cole didn't have a lot to say that they hadn't already covered in their Sunday phone calls. The conversation was more of an excuse to make eye contact and read each other's body language.

After half an hour, the pitch that Cole dreaded finally came. "You know how your father is. He would never admit how much he misses you. He does, though. If you could just come by the house for ten minutes, make the first move, I know it would mean so much to him."

The warmth Cole had been feeling dissipated and his defenses locked back into place, with a sound in his head like a trunk slamming shut. He shook his head.

"You're both so stubborn," his mother said. "If you would only give a little."

Madelyn, who'd been mostly silent until then, said, "Mrs. Cole, with all due respect, I don't think this is a case of my husband being stubborn. I think, given any chance at all, kids grow up loving their fathers and wanting to be around them. I think this is a case of his having been repeatedly hurt to the point that he couldn't take it anymore. And I don't think blaming him is a productive avenue of conversation."

His mother bristled at first, in spite of Madelyn's quiet, reasonable tone, then looked down at her hands, where they lay knotted in her lap. "I'm sorry," she said.

Cole squeezed Madelyn's hand.

His mother stood up. "I should go. I don't want Steve to get suspicious."

They walked her out to her car, Cole shivering in the chill. "Thank you for seeing me," she said. It was a terribly sad thing for her to say. Cole hugged her and he and Madelyn watched her drive away.

Cole said, "I don't think anybody ever stood up for me like that before. Thank you."

"Get used to it," Madelyn said. "Nobody messes with my man. Now come inside. It's freezing out here."

1969

MADELYN'S FIRST DAY at Stanford was January 13. She had
an hour bus ride from San Francisco south to Palo Alto
and another hour back, which she spent reading. With the help of
a phone call from Kindred, she'd managed to get all her classes
scheduled on MWF, leaving her free to work six-hour shifts at the
gallery on Tuesday, Thursday, and Saturday. Cole worried that it
was too much; he still failed to comprehend what it meant to be
a lifelong overachiever.

She'd been to the campus for interviews, placement testing,
and orientation, but on that first day of classes it dazzled her
all over again with its arched and porticoed Spanish architecture
and red tile roofs, its palm trees and ordered gardens and pristine
lawns, where she felt completely safe for the first time since she'd
fallen in love with Cole. And though she hated to admit it, a part
of her was reassured by the relative conservatism of the students,
the boys in button-down shirts and V-neck sweaters, the girls in
pleated skirts and Mary Janes.

In each of her five classes she sat in the front row and asked
questions and took careful notes. She wondered if Cole felt the
same way when he took the stage, excited and confident, filled
with a sense of rightness, of doing what she'd been placed on
Earth to do.

THAT SAME MONDAY, Cole and the band went into Pacific
Recorders in San Mateo with Dave Fisher. Though it was halfway
to Palo Alto and had only been open for four months, Pacific had
already become the studio of choice for local bands. The owner
had cut a deal with somebody at the nearby Ampex headquarters
and had scored only the third MM1000 16-track recorder in any
studio in the world.

Studio 1 was 50 feet long and half that wide, with a 20-foot
ceiling. Everything had a fresh-out-of-the-box smell of paint and

camphor and rosin and plastic. The mike stands all worked without gaffer's tape or pieces of coat hangers, and the carpet was free of stains. Dave expressed some concern about the room being small, the ceiling being too low and acoustically dead. Cole only knew that it was twice the size of the room where he'd recorded "Laura Lee."

Cole and Lenny had taken their guitars to Dave's apartment a couple of times to pick the songs for the demo. Dave was 15 years older than Cole. He'd listened to big band radio broadcasts as a child, been in grade school during World War II. He was very much a New Yorker, from his accent to a hint of aggression in his manner. He told great, self-deprecating stories, had been at ground zero for Dylan, had recorded the Spoonful and Tim Hardin. Cole was smitten.

In the studio, Dave spread them out, isolated them with waist-high rolling partitions, and put microphones right up on the speakers of their amps. He put mikes on each of Tommy's drums, plus one for the hi-hat and two overhead to catch the cymbals in stereo, painstakingly mixing them down to four separate tracks in the control room. He'd warned them that he'd never worked with 16 tracks before, but then hardly anyone had, and it looked to Cole like he knew what he was doing.

As they said goodnight outside the studio, Dave intoned, "And the placing of the mikes and the setting of the levels were the morning and the evening of the first day." Cole was too tired to be appropriately amused.

In the late morning and early afternoon of the second day they did four full takes and twice that many broken ones of "Mariner." Dave ordered in some tacos and they sat in a circle on the studio floor. "It's like an operating room or something in here," Cole said. "I'm not feeling the mood."

"What this place gives us," Dave said, "is the freedom to make mistakes. You can get your fingers stuck in the strings, and we can still come away with good tracks from the rest of the band. So I want all of you guys to loosen up. If you screw up, keep playing. Or wait a couple of seconds and get your head right before you come in again. Have fun with it. Fool around a little if that's what you have to do. What I need is a performance that feels good. We can fix the technical stuff later."

After lunch they found a compromise on the lighting between too harsh and too dark to see. The next take was a complete fiasco, yet they played it all the way through as ordered, goofing on it, all of them laughing by the end. Over the squeal of the rewinding tape, Dave said, "That's the stuff. That sounded like real human beings out there. From the top now, don't think about it. Take fourteen."

Take fourteen was a keeper, and they moved immediately to "Doesn't Anybody Know Your Name," one of Cole's early numbers whose storyline he and Lenny had updated from a teenage crush to an identity crisis, with a mild guitar freakout in the middle. They had a good basic take in two hours, broke for dinner, and came back to nail the last of the demo songs, their cover of "Wang Dang Doodle," on the first try.

On the third day they started overdubs. Listening to "Mariner," Lenny said, "I'm not crazy about my part on the double lead."

"What's wrong with it?" Cole asked. During one of their road trips supporting the Airplane, Jorma had explained recoupment. Which meant that you didn't collect any royalties until the record company had been reimbursed for all your recording costs. Even though they hadn't signed with anyone yet, Cole knew that every hour in the studio would eventually cost them money.

"I can't explain it. I've just got a better idea. Can I try it?" Lenny was asking Dave, not Cole.

"Sure," Dave said.

"I like the one he did yesterday," Cole said. Gordo and Tommy ignored the opportunity to back him up.

"We'll keep that one too, for now," Dave said. "Don't worry."

An hour and three tries later, Lenny had laid down a new harmony lead. "Nice," Dave said when they played it back.

Lenny looked at Cole. "Well?"

"It's a better part, I agree."

"But…?"

"Something's missing. A spark. Passion. Spontaneity. Something. I don't know."

"You're jealous because my guitar part now kicks your guitar part's ass."

He and Lenny had always kept up a certain amount of mock-aggressive banter, but Cole missed the fun in this one. He bit back his own automatic "fuck you" because he wasn't sure how it would come out.

"Play it again," Lenny said to Dave. Dave did, and Lenny nodded along. "Perfect," Lenny said at the end. "I love sixteen tracks. How often in life do you get to make perfection?"

They had moved on, Cole saw.

"Speaking of perfection," Gordo said, "there's a bad bass note in the bridge. Can I fix that too?"

"Be my guest," Dave said.

Cole looked at Tommy. "Et tu, Tommy?"

"What?"

"You want to do the drums over?"

"Why, is there something wrong with them?"

"Forget it," Cole said.

At least Gordo was quick. After he patched his bass part, Dave said, "What would you think about a single sustained feedback note behind the double lead? A ton of reverb on it. We could maybe pan it back and forth between the channels."

While Cole tried to imagine it, Lenny said, "A harmonic, decaying into feedback. Let's try it."

Cole sat and watched for another half-hour while Lenny worked out the part and dubbed it in. After that Tommy chipped in the idea of a slowly rising roll with mallets on the floor tom, building with the feedback, and then everybody except Cole was having ideas. Dave vetoed most of them, keeping three or four that took another two hours to build into the track, including a few high notes on the grand piano in the far corner of the studio.

They went out for lunch before starting the vocals, and as they walked, Lenny fell into step with Cole and said, "What's eating you, man?"

Cole thought it should have been obvious. Eventually he took a breath and said, "Feeling left out, I guess."

"That's by your choice if you are. Everybody else is getting into it." When Cole didn't answer, he said, "I think you're pissed off because it's not the Cole Show in there today. I think you kind of forgot there's four people in this band, and two of us were in it a long time before you were."

"How long have you been sitting on that little grievance?"

"A while now. Who gives a shit? That song sounds great. That's what matters. We did that, the four of us, especially you and me, who wrote it. I'm so proud I can hardly stand it, and I wish you'd stop being a pain in the ass and be proud with me."

What if he's right? Cole thought. What if the song *is* better with the overdubs and the careful, calculated harmony guitar part?

In the five years since The Beatles had reinvented rock music, one standard after another had been washed away, from the Brill Building professional tunesmiths to the three-minute single. Now there was FM radio and the concept album, and new technologies from stereo LPs to 8-track cartridges to 16-track recorders, from fuzz tones to wah-wah pedals to electric sitars. Until today, Cole had happily ridden the tidal wave that had drowned Patti Page and Perry Como and Arthur Godfrey. Now he saw that the wave had grown too big to stop, that before long it would wash away "Liar, Liar" by the Castaways and "Shout" by the Isley Brothers and even Cole himself, 19 years old and already clinging to a past that hadn't had a proper chance to be over with yet.

COLE SURRENDERED to the inevitable and joined in the sanding and detailing and shellacking of their three demo tunes. He didn't have the gift for it that Lenny had discovered in himself, but when he looked on it as a game, he was able to play it with a modicum of grace.

At midnight on Thursday, Dave finished a rough mix and dubbed it down to audio cassettes for each of them. Cole drove the band home in the hearse and then, too keyed up to sleep, got into bed next to Madelyn and tried to hold still.

"How'd it go?" she said into her pillow.

He hadn't had a chance to talk to her since they'd been recording. "I've got a cassette."

She sat up. "Play it."

He had a Radio Shack cassette machine the size of a fat paper-back book that he used to record song ideas. He brought it into bed and put in the tape. "The quality is not going to be that great, I mean, it's a crappy little player…"

"Hush," she said.

When it was over, she made him play it again.

"Oh, Cole, it's beautiful. It's so… finished and professional. It sounds like a million dollars." She squinted at him. "What's wrong?"

"I don't know. It doesn't sound quite… human."

"Neither does *Sergeant Pepper*." She kissed him on the fore-head. "Stop fretting. It's wonderful. I am so proud of you." She glanced at the clock and shook her head. "If I didn't have to get up in four hours, I would show you how much." She turned her back to him and, as Cole listened, her breathing evened out and she was asleep again.

COLE WAS STARSTRUCK when Dave announced that he would send the tape to Ahmet Ertegun first. After that, he found it hard to think about anything else, and pestered Dave every few days for news. When the call came, however, it came from Bill Graham, in his Shady Management guise. "I just talked with a contract guy at Cotillion Records. They want to sign you."

"Cotillion? Who's that?"

"Specialty imprint at Atlantic. Mostly southern R&B acts, but they want to diversify, they tell me. Don't sweat it, it's the same dis-tribution as Atlantic or Atco. They offered forty thousand advance. I talked them up to fifty, to cover my cut, and I think that's as high as they'll go."

Cole had to sit down. "Fifty thousand dollars? For real?"

"For real. Dave Fisher to produce, of course."

"They liked the demo?"

"What the fuck do you think, they pay fifty grand for a band they don't like? Talk to the other guys, call me back, let me know you're all good with this, so I don't have to make you find a new manager."

1969

*

IF IT WAS GOOD ENOUGH for Ahmet Ertegun, Cole thought, it was good enough. When the band went into the studio in March, he no longer fought the 16-track perfectionism, and when the time came to bring out La Pelirroja for "Gold," his song to Madelyn, and for their cover of "Cielito lindo" that ended the album, he did the endless retakes Dave wanted until the notes shimmered like diamonds on black velvet.

BY MID-APRIL, with the end of the semester in sight, Madelyn wanted nothing more than to sleep. Not for a night or two, but for at least a week where she only got out of bed to eat and use the bathroom. She longed to read a book that no one had assigned her, to sit in the sand at Ocean Beach and watch the waves curl and break without reviewing a mental checklist. She wanted to see the band when they were in town, to go to the Airplane mansion and meet Grace Slick, to make love and not have one or the other of them immediately pass out from exhaustion. Lately there had been too little time to see to her own satisfaction, or too much pressure for her to get there, despite Cole's attempts.

The band was on the road half the time, enough that when they were around, Cole no longer fit into her routine. She talked to him more on long distance than she did when they were in the same apartment. So when she got home from class to find him waiting, failing to completely hide a cocky grin, she knew something was up.

"Let's walk," he said.

She'd walked the length of the campus twice already that day. "Can't we talk in the bedroom? I'm beat."

"We don't have to go far," he said. He was already on his feet, not to be denied. Madelyn dropped her books on the dining room table and let him take her hand.

"Cole, what is going on?"

"Nothing," he said. "Can't a guy take a walk with his wife?" Despite the grin, his voice had an edge that hadn't been there six months ago.

She went along in silence as they descended the stairs and turned onto Oak Street. Cole suddenly stopped. "Hey, check it out," he said.

An MGB, lavender-gray, top down, was parked between a beat-up Dodge Dart and a rusting vw microbus. "It's gorgeous," Madelyn said, "but whoever owns it is an idiot to leave it sitting out like that."

Cole had dropped her hand and walked into the street to peer into the passenger side. The car was set up for the US, with left hand drive, she noted. Probably a '66, just before the Mark II, and in perfect shape.

"I mean," Cole said, "this is pretty much your dream car, right?"

"I suppose. If I had time for dreams."

"We ought to steal it."

Cole had his hands on the passenger door. "Come on, Cole, get away from there. You're going to get in serious trouble."

"Don't you want to at least sit in it? See how it feels? Who knows when you'll get another chance like this?"

He opened the passenger door and got in.

"Cole, are you insane? Get out of that car!"

Cole stared straight in front of him. He slowly raised his left fist in the air and then, one at a time, opened his fingers until the thumb and forefinger were left holding a dangling car key.

Madelyn screamed.

Cole turned around in the seat and said, "Madelyn, will you please get in the fucking car?"

Her hands were shaking so badly that Cole had to reach over and open the door for her. She got in and moved the seat forward until she could reach the pedals. She took the key and started the engine. It purred like a leopard. She revved it, looked at the tachometer, and realized she couldn't see for the tears in her eyes. "How...?" she said. "What... when...?"

"The Cotillion advance finally came in last week. The check cleared our bank account today. I found this a month ago and gave the guy a big deposit to hold it for me."

"But... but..."

"I don't want you taking the bus to school anymore. You can

434

get there in half the time in this. I've rented you a space in a garage two blocks from here. And we might want to think about moving into a place of our own."

"Oh, Cole," she said, and reached for him.

He hugged her and kissed her lightly and pointed forward. "Drive."

BY LATE APRIL, Alex could see that something was not right with Denise and Tupelo. Denise had been a more or less constant presence in the Castle since classes had started again in September, her raucous laugh part of the ongoing soundtrack. When the laughter stopped, the tension began.

Being around somebody you were no longer having sex with was weird enough. Alex had handled it okay when she and Tupelo were going through the first obsessive phase of their relationship. Being apart for the summer had brought things back to a boil in the fall, but by Christmas Denise was down to room temperature and Alex had caught her looking at him a time or two with memories on her mind. Alex was not without memories of his own.

The tension came to a head on a Wednesday. Tupelo had a language lab Wednesday afternoons and was typically gone from eight AM until suppertime. Alex was fixing himself a grilled cheese sandwich for lunch when Denise came in and perched on the kitchen counter.

"Aren't you supposed to be in class?" Alex said.

"I'm having my period and I'm cramping like nobody's business."

Denise's desire, Alex knew all too well, ran especially high during her period. And, Denise being Denise, Alex knew that Tupelo had an old-fashioned repugnance toward menstrual blood. Whereas Alex had always been happy to throw an old towel over the sheets.

It had been a while for Alex. What was it about sex with an ex? The combination of the forbidden and the familiar was nearly irresistible.

"Joe asked me to marry him," Denise said.

Alex turned to look at her. "What did you say?"

"I told him I needed to think about it."

"Do you?"

"No, not really. It's not a question of thinking. It's about feeling, and…"

"You're not feeling it."

"Not marriage, no. He's a wonderful guy and I really care for him, but… I'm not the girl he thinks I am."

The very air in the kitchen was combustible. The slightest spark could set it off. Alex turned off the burner under his sandwich. "What kind of girl are you?"

Denise bounced her legs on the counter. "I'm bad," she said. "I have bad thoughts."

They looked at each other.

Alex told himself that he was not going to take Denise to bed. He'd never been as close to Tupelo as Cole had been, but they were all living under one roof. He wanted to believe that he was not capable of that kind of betrayal.

He was, however, capable of kissing her. Just to see. Just to find out if she was feeling what he was feeling.

He took a step toward her. She stopped jiggling her legs and slowly opened them. Alex stepped in and kissed her and her arms went around his back. She moved her lips across his cheek and then giggled in his ear. "This is a really bad idea," she said, and bit his earlobe.

"Yeah," he said. He was going to pull away, or at least he was starting to think about pulling away, when Denise said, "Oh, shit," and suddenly let him go.

Alex turned to see Tupelo Joe in the doorway of the kitchen. He still had the remnants of a smile on his face, fading fast. He backed away, nodding, as if somebody had answered a question. Alex supposed that in a way they had.

"Wait," Alex said. "It's not what you think."

"Really?" Joe said. He turned and ran lightly up the stairs.

"I'll talk to him," Denise said.

Denise followed Joe upstairs and Alex gripped the edge of the counter, staring at the sandwich in the frying pan, slowly oozing orange cheese, for which he had lost all appetite.

Joe's bedroom was above the kitchen. Alex heard the floorboards creak as Joe moved around, heard Denise outside his door, pleading, then ordering him to let her in. Alex stood paralyzed with self-hatred.

Ten minutes later he heard Joe on the stairs and went to intercept him. Joe had a suitcase and his eyes were distant. "Get out of my way," he said to Alex, and something in his voice made Alex step aside.

Denise, on the landing, slid her back down the wall and started to cry.

Alex watched Joe gently close the front door behind him. He felt nine years old again, staring down at the shattered hand mirror that his mother had inherited from her grandmother and that Alex had been pretending was a tennis racket. This time there was nobody to spank him and send him to his room. He would have to find his punishment on his own.

ALEX GOT A CALL from Denise on Saturday. She'd got hold of Joe's mother, who told her Joe had flown home on Wednesday night, and on Thursday morning he'd volunteered for the Marine Corps. He'd left a few hours ago on a bus for Parris Island, South Carolina. His father was upset, and his mother was terribly proud.

In the silence, Alex tried to think of consoling words. Sooner or later Denise would have broken it off. Joe would have reacted the same way. Maybe the words were even true. But the words he kept hearing in his head were, "We've killed him."

In the end he didn't say anything except to thank her and tell her goodbye.

COLE TOOK DOWN his wall calendar and wrote down the dates as Graham gave them to him over the phone. The album was scheduled to hit the streets on Tuesday, July 1. They had in-store appearances that day in New York City, radio interviews that evening, a gig Wednesday at the Bitter End, then shows Friday and

Saturday at the Fillmore East, second on the bill to Iron Butterfly. On Thursday night, Graham promised to take them backstage to meet Jeff Beck—after they bought their own tickets, of course.

For reasons Cole didn't entirely understand, he was reluctant to tell Madelyn about the trip. After a day of sitting on it, he forced himself. They'd finished dinner and for once the other guys were not around. Cole laid out the order of events and, to his profound disappointment, she said she couldn't come.

"It's the second week of the summer session. And Kindred has an opening that weekend."

This, Cole saw, was what he'd been afraid of.

"I'm sorry," she said. "I know this is a big deal for you."

"It's not just a big deal 'for me.' It's a big deal period. It's an album on a major label, a showcase at a famous club, and our first Fillmore show where we're not the opening act."

"If there were any way…"

"Where there's a will," Cole said, "there's a way."

"I'd just be underfoot. None of the other guys is bringing a girl-friend, right?"

"The other guys are planning to take advantage of the more than abundant local resources."

"I see." Cole recognized this phrase as an amber warning light. Not an indicator, yet, of mortal danger, but definitely a sign of thin ice. "That's what this is really about, isn't it? There's going to be a lot of ego stroking going on and you want to make sure you get laid at the end of the day."

"I had assumed," Cole said, "you would prefer that it be you I'm getting laid by."

As soon as the words were out, Cole wanted to take them back. Madelyn's face turned hard. "So that's the choice now? Either I fuck or somebody else will?"

"That's not what I meant," Cole said.

"It's damn well what you said."

"I was counterpunching. I didn't mean it. What I'm trying to say—"

"I think it was the truth slipping out in an unguarded moment."

"What I'm trying to say," he repeated, talking over her, "is that there are only so many pivotal moments in a person's life. This is one of them. I want you there because you're my wife and I love you."

"You know what I wish? I wish that in this new, hip, egalitarian, psychedelic world you guys are building that there was a place for women that wasn't flat on their backs with their knees in the air."

She must have known she'd now gone too far herself because she pushed her chair back violently and retreated to the bedroom and banged the door.

Cole went downstairs and headed on foot into the sunset, toward the Haight and Golden Gate Park and the Pacific Ocean. A full moon hung in the darkening sky behind him. He wondered if he and Madelyn were coming to the end of their road together. She didn't want to be a sex object, but she still wanted him to desire her and her alone. And sex was one of the few things they had in common.

He thought about the lavender-scented girl in Guanajuato, and how miserable he felt afterward. Yet the thought of leaving Madelyn was equally intolerable. As was the thought of more and more fights like the one they'd just had.

The thing that he wanted most in life was to feel wholehearted. To give himself to the people and things he loved without being undercut by doubts and second thoughts. Apparently even that small thing was too much to ask.

Their fights usually ended with tears, apologies, and especially satisfying sex. The bedroom door was still closed when Cole got home, light showing through the crack underneath. If she was waiting for him, it was with a textbook in hand. He did not feel invited. He got out La Pelirroja and played a few Mexican songs, songs he'd once played to a laughing girl with dark, scented hair.

WHEN THE BAND arrived in New York, Cole found himself in a restless, dangerous mood. He and Madelyn had gone through the motions for the last month, everything normal on the surface, tensions still pulling at them underneath. They'd kissed, even made love a couple of times, without anything being resolved.

As he carried his guitar through LaGuardia and out to the limo that Cotillion Records had sent, Cole felt himself being watched. Some of the attention was from women—curious, possibly interested—and some was from envious men. By the time they got to the Warwick Hotel on 54th, Cole had fully accepted the role of rising star on the brink of fame. He'd been waiting all his life to play it. If anything, it made him feel more dangerous, more capable of something drastic.

Not so the others. Tommy was awed, craning his neck to look up at the buildings. Gordo was acting out, swaggering and talking too loudly. Lenny's nervousness was the worst Cole had seen it, walling him off from the world. And so it fell to Cole to make small talk with Ahmet Ertegun when they toured the Atlantic offices on Tuesday morning, to make a connection with the promo man who took them to the record stores, to do most of the talking in the radio interviews, to push "Easy Go," the first single from the album.

He and Lenny were sharing a room, so Cole sat in the bar downstairs Wednesday night while Lenny had his way with a woman he'd met at the highly successful Bitter End show. An elegant blonde in her thirties in a skin-tight knit dress brought her drink to Cole's table and started talking to him, and he took ten minutes to realize that she was a professional. He was mildly curious as to what it might be like with her, but sex, like rock and roll, was not something where he valued a detached and polished performance. He explained that he was married and not in the market, and she raised her glass to him and moved on. Maybe, he thought, he was going to make it through the whole trip without seriously being tempted. The idea left him vaguely sad.

Meeting Jeff Beck was also a letdown. The band was coming apart, Beck and Rod Stewart not speaking to each other, and the live show featured mostly music from their new *Beck-Ola* album, which Cole thought inferior to *Truth*. Beck himself was nice enough, though Cole found they had little to talk about.

And so, on Friday night, after a terrific first set, Cole was into his second beer before his sweat dried. Unlike the San Francisco halls, the Fillmore East was a former theater, with seats still in place. They'd gotten most of the audience on their feet, a few of them dancing in the aisles, yet the vibe was distinctly different.

One more night, he thought, then he would be home, waiting for the next fight to start. Then what?

He was leaning against a brick wall outside the dressing room, looking down at the beer bottle. When he looked up, he was staring into a pair of enormous, heavy-lidded brown eyes. They were set in a narrow face with a longish nose and wide, swollen lips that were turned up in an easy smile. Her dark brown hair was disheveled and her breasts were on the verge of spilling out of her low-cut black T-shirt.

"I don't know how many times I came while I was watching you play," she said. "I think I lost track around eight or nine."

"Now that," Cole said, "is what I call an opening line." She wore an intoxicatingly musky scent. She was at least Cole's age, Italian or Jewish, a classic New York tough chick.

"I'd like to return the favor," she said. "A quickie in the bathroom if that's what gets you off. Or I would really like to go back to your hotel and fuck you all night long."

Cole, going under, made one last attempt to grab a lifeline. "I should tell you, I'm married."

"I should tell you, I don't really give a shit." She stepped into him, put both hands in his hair, and pulled his mouth down onto hers. The kiss was soft, and her lips and tongue fully enveloped him and moved with a slow hunger. He felt her breasts and pubic ridge press against him, and if they'd been alone in a room with a bed, he would have already been tearing at her clothes. They were in public, however, and that thought made him break the kiss and look up to see Bill Graham watching him with a big grin on his face.

"I don't want to interrupt," Graham said. "I'll catch you later."

"Wait," Cole said. He looked at the girl. "I got to go."

"I'll be around," she smiled.

Graham walked him toward his office. "I see you met Sandy. Did she tell you about her orgasms?"

Cole blushed and nodded.

"I can't speak from personal experience," Graham said, "but she comes highly recommended."

Cole, hating himself for it, suddenly visualized what Madelyn would think of Sandy, what she would think of Cole if he had sex with her. As much as he tried to tell himself that Madelyn's opinion didn't matter, in the end it did. "I think maybe I better pass. What's happening?"

"I wanted you to meet this guy, John Morris, who works for me. I got you into this festival he's part of." He opened the door to an empty office. "Looks like he's already split."

"Festival?" Cole asked.

"Yeah, middle of August, upstate. It's called the Woodstock Music and Arts Fair."

MADELYN SLOWLY SLIPPED from hair-trigger anger into a deep depression. The emotions felt like someone else's, as if she'd gotten lost inside a John O'Hara novel. Not that there was time in her life for fiction; she'd been without the consolations of literature since January. It was the thing she missed most.

On a Wednesday afternoon, August 6, she agreed to go to dinner after her Early Renaissance Drawings class with a boy named Gregory Baxter. Baxter, sandy-haired, freckled, full of moneyed confidence, had made his interest clear since the start of the summer semester; Madelyn had diverted his previous invitations by holding up her left hand and letting the light catch her wedding ring. That Wednesday she only wanted to delay going home as long as possible because she knew Cole would be there.

Baxter's goal in life was to become, by means of his father's money, the sort of art collector whose name was whispered at Christie's and Sotheby's. Irene would have thought him a parasite; Madelyn noted that he was amusing, well read, and had lovely manners.

Even so, she failed to be fully present during dinner. She was distracted by the thought that, having admitted that she was happier away from Cole than with him, she would now have to deal with the consequences.

Baxter finally dropped her off at her car at 8:00. They were alone in the parking garage and Baxter got out to open her car door for her. She knew what was coming and yet somehow failed to entirely avoid his kiss. She did then gently push him away, and Baxter said good night and waited while she backed out.

On 101 North, the chilly night air swirling inside the car, she came to her senses. Women were raped in parking garages every day, often by privileged boys like Gregory Baxter. She was lucky that Baxter was in fact a gentleman, or it could have gone another way. What in God's name had she been thinking?

Cole and Lenny were laughing on the couch when she got home; the minute she came through the door, the laughter died. In the ominous silence that followed, she walked straight into the bedroom and closed the door.

She woke in the night to Cole's lips on the back of her neck and his hand gently stroking her belly. Half asleep, she let herself respond and rolled over. Then, once he was inside her, her last shred of involvement evaporated and she felt herself go inert. Cole immediately sensed it and froze. "Madelyn?" She was too far away to answer. Her head was turned toward the wall and her eyes were closed, so she didn't see as he slowly pulled away, then got out of bed. She heard a rustling of clothes and the sound of the bedroom door.

When she left for work in the morning, he was asleep on the couch. By the time she got home that afternoon, he and Lenny were both gone, along with their guitars and amps. She looked at Cole's wall calendar and saw, with relief, that they were in Eugene and Seattle that weekend and wouldn't return until Tuesday. He would be home two nights and then leave on Thursday for New York again. He'd written the word "Woodstock" and drawn an arrow through to the following Monday.

He didn't call from the road.

She knew Cole was having problems of his own. Reviews of the Quirq album were mostly tepid and radio stations were not playing the single. She also understood that their issues as a couple could not wait for happier times.

On Monday Baxter asked her to dinner again and she refused. Tuesday at work she rehearsed her arguments and tried to envision Cole's responses. She nearly rear-ended a Cadillac on the drive home, and when she walked in the apartment she felt as if she'd swallowed an icicle; she shook from the cold of it.

Once she got Cole alone in the bedroom, she didn't know where to start. She sat on the edge of the bed, elbows on her knees. "We have to talk," she said. "We've been putting it off, both of us, and I can't stand it any longer. We're neither one of us happy. You said it yourself, a year ago. We're growing apart, more and more. We hardly see each other anymore, and when we do, we fight. I hate the fights and I know you do too, but they keep happening..." She stopped, breathed in, breathed out again. "I think we need to take a break."

Cole stood against the door, arms folded, shoulders hunched up toward his ears. "A break?"

"I'm thinking about getting my own place for a while. Let things cool off, see where we are."

Cole stared at her, his face expressionless. The silence sucked more and more words out of her. "Not tonight, not this week, I've got finals coming up. Maybe after you get back from this next trip, before the fall semester starts..."

"So that's it?" Cole said. "This is the end?"

"All I'm asking for is, like, a trial separation. If it doesn't work out, we could, we could always, we could..."

Cole's eyes were red. "Tell the truth. It's over for you."

Seeing Cole so vulnerable had always undone her before. This time she had sworn she would be strong. "I think," she said, "it's been over for a while for both of us."

Cole walked out and closed the door.

She didn't go after him. She took more deep breaths and sat quietly for a while, then she got out *Drawing Lessons from the Great Masters*. She turned to page 165, a skinless man by Vesalius, and attempted to recite the muscle groups as she sketched them, not letting herself think, pausing only when she had to dry her eyes in order to see.

COLE SPENT TWO NIGHTS on Gordo's couch, numbing himself with grass and beer so he could sleep. Gordo assured him that Madelyn would change her mind. Irene acted like whatever happened had been Cole's fault, and Cole didn't disagree. His own emotions rattled around like the last wooden match in a box. One minute he knew that Madelyn was right, that they were only torturing each other. The next his need for her was so desperate that he wanted to throw himself at her feet.

He went to the apartment on Thursday afternoon to shower and change and pack. He'd prepared a speech. The speech said that he loved her and he would honor her request for a separation and that he would be waiting for her if she changed her mind. He sat until time to leave for the airport and she still had not come home. By then he was on the emotional roller coaster again and didn't trust himself to write a note.

FRIDAY MORNING, August 15, JFK airport. A guy in a beard and mirrored sunglasses met them when they got off the redeye from San Francisco, holding a sign that said QUIRQ. When Cole asked him if he was their limo driver, the guy laughed as if it was the funniest thing he'd heard in days. He hustled them into a golf cart and drove them to a helipad at the far end of the airport.

Once they were in the air, Cole got the joke. The main freeway headed north from New York City was a parking lot, and when they banked to the left and followed a smaller road, it was also at a standstill. Soon Cole saw cars abandoned by the side of the road and a continuous stream of human beings trudging northwest on foot.

The scene was eerily familiar, and Cole flashed on a nightmare from his childhood, refugees from a nuclear war lining the roads as they fled their irradiated cities. That thought, in turn, made him realize that everything he had assumed about the festival was wrong. Even the most wild-eyed predictions of a hundred thousand people were clearly and hopelessly low. Something that had been building since the Beatles set fire to the Ed Sullivan Show in 1964 had reached critical mass, and if it wasn't an atom bomb, it looked to be nearly as devastating.

This, Cole thought, is bigger than Madelyn. Bigger than The Quirq, bigger than a music festival.

They veered off from the traffic route and headed north to the town of Liberty. There they landed in the parking lot of the Holiday Inn, where the promoters had booked rooms for the bands. Cole was still giddy when he stepped off onto the asphalt with his guitar and his suitcase. He looked at Lenny, who rolled his eyes and shouted, "Un-fucking-believable."

The front desk was in chaos as the staff tried to deal with Janis Joplin, her new band, and her ever-expanding entourage. A couple of straight families with kids looked on in horror and wonder at this invasion force from Planet San Francisco, fringe and denim and scraggly hair, patchouli and cigarettes and cannabis resins, feathered boas and cowboy hats, guitars and saxophones. Meanwhile hotel employees in green smocks raced around the lobby in a frenzy. When Cole and the band finally got to the head of the line they agreed to help with the housing crisis by taking only one room with two double beds and two rollaways. The clerk gave them their backstage passes, business-card sized, featuring the guitar neck and dove logo in black and white, their names and the band name scrawled by hand.

They descended a sloping corridor to their room and helped themselves to a couple of rollaways that were lined up along the wall. They were all exhausted from the overnight flight, Cole the worst, thanks to Gordo's couch. He volunteered to take one of the rollaways, thinking he could sleep anywhere, then regretted it five hours later when he came completely awake. The room was in near darkness and his back hurt.

He lay for a while with his mind churning, unable to get comfortable. Madelyn seemed impossibly distant—emotionally, geographically, even temporally. As she burrowed deeper into the Renaissance, Cole had just flown over the future. She'd made her choice, and, Cole realized with some finality, he had made his.

He brushed his teeth and shaved and when he came out of the bathroom, Lenny was sitting up on the other rollaway. "I'm going to look around," Cole said. "Want to come?"

Lenny groped his way toward the bathroom. "Piss," he said. "Then more sleep."

Cole took his guitar to the lobby, which was full of Country Joe and the Fish and the Grateful Dead. Jerry Garcia held up his right hand to Cole, calling out, "Hail, brother of the mangled finger!" Cole flashed him a crippled peace sign and Garcia laughed. A harried older woman in a green smock directed him to the lounge, down the hall to the right of the registration desk, through the double doors under the awning.

Joplin was already in residence at one of the green banquettes across from the bar, and a couple of extra tables had been stuck on to accommodate the crowd. Marty Balin and Jack Casady sat in the next booth over with two black men that Cole didn't recognize. "Hey Jude" wound down on the jukebox, and as soon as it finished it started again.

A small parquet dance floor. A second room with a pool table and a scattering of tables set up for meal service. All of them deserted. Unsure what to do, Cole set down his guitar and perched on one of the low-backed bar stools. A brass rail ran around the edge of the bar, supported by the trunks of brass elephant heads, a touch of bizarre elegance that Cole would not have expected at a Holiday Inn.

Richie Havens came in, tall, orange dashiki, jutting beard, and walked over to the Airplane table. "Michael wants us to go on first. We're supposed to be *fifth*! And Eric's not here... I can't do it, man." The two black guys murmured something reassuring and Havens said, "Anyway, we should probably get over there."

The three of them left to a chorus of good wishes, and Cole turned to the bar. Drinking age in New York State, he remembered from his previous trip, was 18. He asked for a Carta Blanca, the only Mexican beer they had. The festival, it seemed, was picking up the tab for all the performers. Cole dug out some change for a tip and left it on the bar.

A shrill female voice cried out, "Who's the cute guitar player?"

Cole looked around to see who she was talking about and found Janis looking at him. Her photos had not prepared him for the hypnotic openness of her face. She had bad skin and her eyes were small, yet they shone with a light that was more than hunger and a readiness for fun. She radiated a childlike trust that was as endearing as it was sad.

He pointed at himself and mouthed the word, "Me?"

"Yes, you, you cute little devil. Come over here and introduce yourself."

Cole picked up his beer and somebody found an extra chair and managed to squeeze it in close to Janis. Cole said his name and a few of the others reciprocated. The only one he registered was a Chicano named Luis. When it came out that he'd moved to San Francisco from Austin, Janis leaned across an intervening person to hug him, nearly knocking over the open fifth of Jack Daniel's in the middle of the table. She asked if he ever went to Threadgill's, her old stomping ground. He hadn't, but she knew East Austin well and they bonded over Blues Boy Hubbard and the Jets.

Half an hour later, as Cole was feeling a distinct buzz from two beers and a couple of shots of the whiskey, somebody let out a loud whistle. Cole turned to see a paunchy middle-aged guy in slacks who looked like an off-duty cop. "I've got a chopper headed over to the fair and I got space for one more."

Impulsively Cole raised his hand. "Hey Jude" had been repeating the entire time he'd been there and he didn't think he could stand much more.

"Got any carry on?" Cole pointed to his guitar case and the pilot said, "You'll have to put it in your lap."

Janis grabbed his shirt and pulled him down for a kiss on the lips and a bawdy wink. Cole grinned and waved to the others and followed the pilot out to the parking lot. Unlike the copter he'd ridden in that morning, this one had a spherical glass front, like the one in the *Whirlybirds* TV show from Cole's youth. The seat next to the pilot was open. Country Joe sat in back, wearing a sergeant's green military fatigues, his dark, shoulder-length hair held by a headband.

The combination of Joe's uniform and the sound of the idling rotors gave Cole a jolt of Vietnam terror at the base of his spine. He thought of Tupelo Joe, who could at that very moment be in a helicopter over a burning jungle with tracer bullets arcing toward him. The last time he'd talked to Alex on the phone, Joe's mother hadn't had any news in weeks.

Cole strapped in and set the guitar case on end in front of him. It blocked at least part of the disorienting view through the Plexiglas floor.

"Hey, Cole," Country Joe said, and Cole reached through the gap between the seats to shake his hand, movement style. Most of the musicians that Cole knew were searching for something. Joe seemed to have found it and tired of it and given it away a long time ago. He'd been a red-diaper baby, had spent three years in the Navy, was highly literate and political and always kept a level head, even when he was tripping, which was a good deal of the time. He had the best deadpan comic delivery of anyone Cole had ever met, and as with so many truly funny people, the humor was fed by a wellspring of bitterness.

Joe gestured vaguely at their surroundings. "It's like being in the fucking USO, isn't it?"

"Luckily," Cole said, "you're already dressed for the part."

The helicopter lurched and lifted off and Cole watched the motel and the city fall away, replaced by a landscape of rolling hills, lakes, and trees. Straight lines and pale olive colors where the land was cultivated, a darker, textured green for the woods. Narrow roads cut the abstract canvas into interlocking pieces. These were working farms with tractors that needed to be moved around and produce that needed to get to market. Even from hundreds of feet in the air, Cole sensed something peaceful that emanated from the countryside itself.

The helicopter banked downward and Cole felt a rush of excitement. In a matter of seconds they began to see barns and fences and abandoned cars and then, all at once, throngs of people. In the distance a half-finished stage, a giant framework of raw white pine and a flapping sail of white canvas strung above it. Everywhere else it was a pointillist painting in daubs of pink and white and tan that Cole understood to be a continuous sea of human flesh.

"Incredible," Country Joe said. "They're saying three hundred thousand by tonight."

The number was meaningless to Cole. What he saw was an area the size of a small town that consisted of nothing but one person sitting or standing next to another, and another, and another, in all directions. When he thought there couldn't be any more, thousands more rolled into view, and thousands after that.

The helicopter circled the site. Pale green canvas tents clustered at the far end of the field, next to a board fence that extended from both sides of the stage. Half a dozen towers of metal scaffolding held spotlights and speakers. A row of portable toilets, not nearly enough. Behind the stage, trailers and a giant tepee. Mostly he saw kids, mostly male, mostly white, mostly teenaged.

Cole remembered the crowds at the Haight two years before. At least three times that many kids had come for the fair, all at once instead of over a period of months. His earlier vision of refugees was wrong. They were here as an affirmation, not a denial. He thought of the way Dylan's songs, more than anyone else's, had created an "us" and a "them," and that he was looking at the culmination of all the songs like them. Hundreds of thousands of kids who saw themselves as part of that "us" had answered the call that they read between the lines of the festival posters. The revolution had happened, invisibly and bloodlessly, in the endlessly repeated acts of packing a knapsack or grabbing a sleeping bag and hitting the road.

"Joe?" Cole said. "I think we just won."

"You think? That would be nice. We've still got a war to end and a few details like that."

"Look at all those people," Cole said. "They can't ignore us now."

DAVE UNDERSTOOD that whenever Bill Graham was involved, multiple layers of reality would come into play. His best guess was that Bill had gotten involved with Woodstock because of territorial issues. A lot of the big names he'd booked for the summer at the Fillmore East were also playing at the fair, and he didn't want his New York audience to skip his shows and go to Woodstock instead. Being Bill, he then inflated this not unreasonable complaint into a towering, screaming fit of rage and drastic threats, to make sure he got everything possible out of it.

1969

Mike Lang, the curly-haired kid who had taken charge of the festival, was smart enough to not back down or go to war. He gave Bill a few concessions and flattered him by asking for his help in picking bands and then convincing them to sign on. Bill helped, but he kept upping the price. First he wanted Santana in the lineup. When he got away with that, he asked for The Quirq. He demanded helicopter transport to the festival and back, for himself and then for Dave too.

Thus Dave, who had both Sallie Rachel and The Quirq on the schedule, had answered Bill's summons and arrived at the festival site early on Friday afternoon as things were coming apart.

The helicopter landed in an empty field, fenced off from the overflowing crowd. The pilot pointed to a trailer and said, "Command center," and then to a wooden ramp and said, "stage." He smiled. "Don't lose your backstage pass, or you're fucked." Dave thanked him, carefully stepped down onto the grass, and watched the copter take off again. What in God's name had he gotten himself into? And why was he wearing dress shoes?

The ramp consisted of half-sheets of plywood and a wooden railing, running up and over the road behind the stage and then down again to the stage itself. Dave didn't see anyone checking credentials, so he climbed the ramp and crossed the bridge. And froze.

Eventually a voice behind him said, "Excuse me." Dave apologized and got out of the way of a skinny, long-haired guy in a straw cowboy hat and mustache and no shirt who was carrying a load of lumber on his shoulders. Dave wondered how long he'd been standing there in shock, staring out across the vast, bare plywood stage at the mass of humanity that stretched from the foot of the stage to the horizon and beyond.

He heard a familiar voice and turned to see a man in a dirty white coverall and a torn and battered ten-gallon hat. The man's eyes were little more than slits and the front teeth were missing from his wide grin. He was talking to a good-looking guy with big sideburns and brown hair to his shoulders, and it took Dave several seconds to recognize that the last place he'd seen this demented-looking cowboy was in a San Francisco coffee shop.

"Hugh?" Dave said.

"Dave!" Romney excused himself from his conversation and came over to give Dave a hug that lifted him off his feet. "What are you doing here?"

"I was going to ask you the same thing."

"I'm head of security!" Romney laughed so hard it flirted with hysteria. "No kidding. The Police Commissioner of New York City pulled the plug on the off-duty cops they'd arranged for. So we're going to have a Please Force instead." He pulled a strip of yellow cloth from his pocket that featured a crude version of the dove from the concert poster in red ink. "We made these ourselves with a potato stamp. Ken Babbs had the idea. If we're walking around and we see somebody doing a good deed, we give him ten armbands and tell him to hand 'em out. If we work it right, we'll deputize the whole crowd before it's over. Want one?"

"No, thanks," Dave said, "I'm trying to quit." What was the word for a society where everyone was in charge? "How are you taking tickets?"

Romney laughed again. "There were twenty thousand people here this morning. They wanted me and my buddy Tom Law from the Hog Farm to clear them off the field and make them line up to show their tickets. Tom knew they'd made a big-money deal for the film rights and so he said, 'You want a good movie or a bad movie?'"

"Are you saying there's no fences?"

"They had to change the venue at the last minute, and they ran out of time. They could either finish the stage or finish the fences. No stage, no music, there would have been riots. No fences, no money, the investors take a bath. Some choice, huh? Fortunately they made the right one."

Dave looked out at the crowd and was suddenly, deeply afraid. "Are you sure this is safe?"

"Compared to what? Crossing the street in New York City? Being in Vietnam? Close your eyes."

Romney waited, apparently meaning it literally. Dave reluctantly closed them.

"Can you feel it?" Romney said. "Just feel the vibe. It's very mellow. All we have to do is keep reinforcing that."

Dave opened his eyes, not convinced. "The Hog Farm, that's that commune you were in back in LA?"

"Yeah, only we're in New Mexico now, when we're not on the road. First they hired us to set up some camp sites, blaze some trails and stuff, and we talked them into letting us do a free kitchen. Then this whole security thing happened."

"I can't get over how different you look."

"When you knew me, I was a comedian. Now I'm a clown. I found out it was a much safer identity if you're going head-to-head with the cops. It tends to defuse the violence."

A dark-haired, slender woman in a halter top and shorts took Romney aside to ask him something, and when he came back he said, "I got to go. It appears we need to set up a tent for acid casualties. If you want to find me later, we're directly over that-away." He pointed off stage right. "On the other side of the trees. Just ask anybody for the Hog Farm."

Romney hugged him again and walked away. Dave felt precarious. He was too old to believe in vibes and karma and auras and the rest, yet he feared his mental turmoil would communicate itself to the mob beyond the stage, toppling their emotional balance and turning the field into the last reel of *Lord of the Flies*. He fled down the wooden bridge to the performer's compound.

Almost immediately he saw another familiar face. Tim Hardin, strapped to an acoustic guitar, staggered around the field in a long-sleeved shirt and corduroy trousers. Dave had heard that Hardin was on methadone, but at the moment he looked to have fallen off the wagon. He was playing snatches of song and calling out to the various clumps of people who passed him by, hurrying to some emergency or another. Dave had decided to turn away and avoid him if possible when Hardin recognized him.

"Dave! Fancy meeting you here."

Dave barely heard him over the helicopters, the motorcycles, the members of the crew shouting to each other, the Crosby, Stills & Nash album blasting over the PA. Hardin started toward him, tripped, recovered, and stumbled on again.

"Hi, Timmy."

"They wanted me to open the show. I said, 'You've got to be kidding.' Did you see them?" He flung one arm out in the general direction of the audience. His stage fright was legendary, and if ever a crowd was going to provoke it, this was the one. No wonder he'd gotten high.

"It's unbelievable," Hardin said. His eyes clouded over. "What are they all doing here? Where did they come from? I mean, I used to play for a hundred, two hundred people, maybe sometimes for a thousand, two thousand. But this, this is crazy."

"What are they doing here?" Dave said, in anger and despair. "These are all the Black Sheep Boys, who grew up on Desolation Row. They're here searching for the dolphins, because that's what you guys told them to do, and they listened to you. And what are you going to tell them now? Now that you called them and they came? Nothing. You're not going to tell them anything because you're too fucked up."

Hardin's mood turned penitent. "You're right," he nodded. "I *am* fucked up. I'm always fucked up or fucking up." He looked like he might start pummeling himself and once again, against his better judgment, Dave felt sorry for him.

"No, Timmy," Dave said. "You're one of the greatest singers and songwriters that ever lived. I wish that was enough for you."

Dave walked away. Hardin, after a moment of silence, struck a minor chord and sang, "I'm the family's unowned boy..."

A massive white helicopter settled on the grass and Richie Havens climbed out, carrying the open-tuned guitar whose top he'd nearly worn through with the violence of his strumming. Dave knew him from their days in the Village and Havens paused to wave and give him a gap-toothed smile as he headed toward the stage.

It occurred to Dave that most of the opening night acts came from those Village folk days—Hardin, Havens, Sallie Rachel, Joan Baez, Arlo Guthrie—as if to remind people where this thing, this movement, this quest had started.

If it was a quest, he thought, it had so far failed to find any answers. All it had found was more and more people asking the same questions in louder and louder voices. Now he was at the epicenter and all he wanted was to get out before it fell apart.

COLE'S HELICOPTER landed in a clearing behind the stage and a guy with a long braid down his back ran over to meet them. "Michael's got a kind of command post off stage right, check in with him when you get a chance. Do you guys need anything?"

Hoping to impress Joe, Cole said, "An end to capitalist imperialism?"

"Working on it," the guy said, and turned to Joe. "How about you?"

"A sandwich would be nice," Joe said.

Cole realized the hotel booze was sloshing around in an empty stomach. The guy with the braid pointed to the giant tepee and Joe, ever polite, thanked him.

Apparently the organizers had prevailed on Richie Havens to open. His voice blasted through the PA, singing "Strawberry Fields Forever." Over the top of the board fence, a crush of humanity extended to infinity, and Cole wondered how much the ones at the back could see and hear of the stage.

The sides of the tepee were open and the floor was a layer of shredded bark. The inside might have held 80 people. Oblong tables, covered with paper tablecloths, were scattered randomly and each had a complement of wooden folding chairs. A banquet table was stacked with paper plates and Dixie cups alongside the standard backstage food—fruit and cheese and lunchmeat, bread and pork and beans and iceberg lettuce salad, Fritos and potato chips, a pot of brown rice and a lentil stew. Bottles of fruit juice stood next to a bowl of punch. At one end of the table were trash cans that kept beer, sodas, and wine on ice.

They filled their plates and as Cole looked for somewhere to sit he saw Dave Fisher at a table with John Sebastian and a very tall, stunning woman with auburn hair. Dave caught his eye and waved him over.

"My producer," Cole said to Joe. "Come join us."

"Thanks, I'll catch you later."

Cole left his guitar and his plate of food at an empty place next to Dave and returned to the punchbowl. He drank two cups of it standing by the bowl because it tasted so good.

The woman turned out to be Sallie Rachel, whose songs he'd heard on the radio and liked well enough, but had not taken seriously. He saw that he would have to reconsider. She smoldered like coals in a fireplace, full of light and heat and positive energy.

Dave said to Sebastian, "I didn't know you were on the bill."

"I'm not!" Sebastian said, and laughed. "Paul Rothchild told me I absolutely should not miss this, so I went to the Albany airport, where I happened to see Walter Grundy—you remember him, Dave, he was a Spoonful roadie—loading the Incredible String Band's instruments into a helicopter. He said if I wanted to go to Woodstock, he was my only chance."

Cole assembled the ingredients on his plate into a bologna and cheese sandwich, cut it into triangles with a plastic knife, and offered it around before he dove in.

"They wanted to put the instruments in this yellow Volkswagen bus tent," Sebastian said, "and they couldn't quite figure it out. Now, it happens that I have been living in an identical tent in California, so I ended up in charge. Which means," he said to Cole, "if you get tired of schlepping that guitar around, I can take care of it for you."

"Thanks," Cole said. Sebastian's easy affability had immediately disarmed him.

"Dave was telling us about your band," Sallie said. "He says you're really good."

"The record doesn't do them justice," Dave said. "They're a great live act, and I got carried away in the studio doing overdubs and potchkying around when I should have left it alone. Which is what Cole wanted to do all along."

Though Cole appreciated Dave's apology, it sounded like he was writing the album off, after they'd put so much work into it. He looked down at his food, unable to summon a witty response.

"They're first up tomorrow," Dave said. "Once people see how good they are live, it could break them wide open."

Havens finished to huge applause and Sallie said, "Listen to that. It's like thunder. You can feel the earth shake. I have to go up in front of that?"

"You'll be wonderful," Dave said, and Cole suddenly saw that Dave was in love with her. And why not? With the slightest encouragement, Cole thought that he could fall in love with her too. She and Sebastian both projected a tremendous warmth and accessibility that made Cole feel like they'd been his friends for years. This, Cole thought, is what real stars have.

And I don't.

Somebody was making announcements on stage, apologizing for the noise of the helicopters.

It's why they call them stars, he thought. Because of the way they shine. The thought seemed terribly profound, and it made him see constellations in the way the sunlight glinted on the cars parked alongside the tepee.

The announcer said it was a free festival now, that the promoters were going to take a bath. His voice began to echo strangely, like it was getting sucked down a hole into caves under the earth.

"Oh, shit," Cole said. "I've been dosed." The others turned to look at him. Their faces had swollen like balloons, turned waxy and unconvincing. "They spiked the punch with LSD."

"Sorry, man," Sebastian said. "Are you okay?"

"Yeah, fine," Cole said. He stood up. "I just need to walk around." Mostly he didn't want to do something stupid in front of Sallie. "Can you take care of my guitar? I really love it a lot."

"Don't worry," Sebastian said. "I've got it."

"At least you don't have to play tonight," Sallie said. She sounded sympathetic, though he could no longer read her puffed-up features.

He felt like a kid who'd pissed his pants in front of the grown-ups. His need to escape became urgent. "It was nice to meet you guys," he managed. "I'll check you later."

As the drug continued to come on, he felt himself pop in and out of reality, like in the *Superman* comics where people got sent to the Phantom Zone, only the Phantom Zone was inside his own head. The next time he was back in the world, there was a Swami with an Indian-from-India accent on the PA, talking about how sound energy was the most powerful energy in the world and how the sacred art of music would lead to peace that would "pervade all over the globe."

Really? Cole thought. Maybe it was possible. It certainly felt peaceful where he was, still in the backstage area, behind the organizers' trailers and out of sight of the performers' pavilion. The sun was pleasantly warm and in the distance the clumps of forest were cool and inviting, leafy green and flickering, thanks to the acid, with a deep and calming blue. The countryside did feel magical, nurturing, timeless, resistant to ambition and possessiveness. He shifted into a cross-legged posture and pushed his hands against the dirt, imagining his fingers rooting deep in the soil. His annoyance at having been dosed melted away and he decided that fate had led him to this moment, to be tripping here at this event that was already taking on historic and symbolic weight like a ship taking on water.

He heard a band playing, flute and electric piano and a sassy chick singer. Not the music, he thought, that would bring world peace like the Swami had predicted. Restless and uncomfortable, he got up and made his way to a gate that opened onto the road behind the stage. A guy in a yellow armband verified that Cole had his performer's pass and said, "I'd think twice about going out there if I was you. There's half a million people out there."

"I'll be okay," Cole said, surprised to find that he believed it. He tucked the pass into his pants pocket and went out the gate. He made his way to the main north-south road, where people were continuing to arrive by the thousands. To his left was the stage. Ahead of him, at the top of the gentle rise that faced the stage, stood the M-shaped awnings of the concession stands. To his right was the official information booth and the woods and the main campground.

As Cole circled around toward the front of the stage he saw that any idea he had of walking out into the audience and sitting down was hopeless. Down front they had squeezed themselves in as tightly as possible, their knees planted in the backs of the people in front of them, their backs resting on the knees of the people behind. What happens when somebody has to take a leak? he wondered.

He realized that he needed to go himself. Long lines had already formed for the portable toilets, so he made his way into the woods and pissed against a tree. After that he wandered for a while, sometimes forgetting where he was, fascinated by the intricacy of the layers of leaves, branch after branch and tree after tree. Eventually he stumbled onto a trail and followed it toward a cluster of booths selling hippie crafts. Candles, tie-dyed T-shirts, jewelry. Beyond them was a clearing full of tents and school buses painted in wild colors and slogans. One of them was the famous Merry Pranksters bus with the destination "Further" above the windshield. He wondered if Ken Kesey was around. Madelyn loved both of his novels...

The memory of Madelyn was not bearable in his present state.

Next to the Prankster bus sat a bare wooden stage, three lengths of plywood across by three widths of plywood deep, no higher off the ground than the 2×6s that supported it. A commotion was going on at the side of the stage, and Joan Baez emerged from it in jeans and a patchwork jacket, carrying a guitar and conspicuously pregnant, trailing a small entourage. Cole had never liked the polish and vibrato in her voice, but at the moment he badly needed to put Madelyn out of his thoughts. He sat in the short grass with a few dozen others as Baez adjusted the microphones and then started to sing "Poor Wayfaring Stranger."

Cole managed to make his Daliesque watch solidify long enough to figure out that it was around seven PM. The sun, retreating down the sky, had turned the trees blue. Or maybe that was the acid. The guy next to him, early thirties, ragged beard, leather hat and no shirt, tapped Cole on the arm and offered him a lit joint. "You tripping?" the man asked. Cole nodded and the man said, "Your pupils are as big as a deer's." He laughed, and together they smoked the joint down to the roach.

The guy called himself Sugarfoot. He was from Champaign-Urbana, where he'd spent the last ten years failing to write his dissertation at the University of Illinois Agriculture school. He was "custodian" of a giant tepee, and he, and the people who were crashing in it, were going to start a commune on 50 acres near Wytheville, Virginia. Cole, for his part, admitted to being a performer and Sugarfoot politely pretended he'd heard of The Quirq.

Baez was charming and had a dry, self-effacing humor that melted Cole's resistance. She played "House of the Rising Sun" and "Man of Constant Sorrow" and "There but for Fortune," along with some ballads that sounded like the American Folk Music records. At one point a skinny, bearded, naked man got up on the stage and danced. He didn't approach Baez and she didn't acknowledge him, and after a while he wandered away again.

"Did you see that?" Cole asked.

"You mean the naked guy on stage?" Sugarfoot said. "Nope, you must have hallucinated it."

When Baez was done and the applause died down, a long discussion ensued. At the end of it, some more guys with no shirts filled the stage with amps and a drum set and began to play a meandering blues. Sugarfoot had disappeared and twilight had arrived. The air looked misty, maybe from fog, maybe from campfire smoke, maybe from Cole's altered perceptions. Cole's emotions always ran high at sunset, and he was feeling lost and lonely. He was afraid he wouldn't be able to find his way to the main stage in the dark, so he got unsteadily to his feet and followed Baez and her entourage as far as the main road. Then he turned right and climbed toward the top of the hill.

They were between acts on the main stage. The MC read the names of people who needed to call home, of somebody with a broken arm, of somebody proposing to his girlfriend. By the time Cole got to the concession area, the sky was completely dark and his stomach was rumbling. The islands of light inside the hamburger stands were yellow, the rest of the world deep brown, creating a stark and depressing contrast that Madelyn would have called chiaroscuro. The thought of Madelyn kindled feelings of desperation that he fought to push aside. Even if he could find a phone, he was in no state to talk to her. He bought a hamburger and ate it standing up, licking his fingers when he was done, and then the MC said, "Tim Hardin!"

Cole moved closer, picking his way between clusters of people in the near darkness. He could make out the stage and the people on it, but no faces. Apparently they hadn't had time to set up overhead stage lights and were trying to get by with follow spots mounted on the speaker towers. Hardin sat hunched at the piano, alone in a pool of deep blue light. He played a few random-sounding arpeggios and partial chords, then, suddenly, he broke into the opening notes to "How Can We Hang on to a Dream," Cole's favorite song from *Tim Hardin 1*.

A girl's voice behind Cole said, "Hey, man, would you sit the fuck down, please?"

Cole sat, and the people on either side made room. Against the haunting minor chords in 3/4 time, Hardin sang about his lover walking away from all they had. He wasn't fooling anybody. The loss was bigger than one relationship, one life. It was written all over his cracked, vulnerable voice and his precarious piano playing, both of which threatened to tumble at any moment into the abyss. The question was purely rhetorical. There was no way to hang on, it was already slipping away. Cole remembered standing outside a Victorian mansion in the Haight, listening to a woman named Deb tell him, "We thought it was the beginning, but it was already the end."

FROM THE SIDE of the stage, Dave watched Tim Hardin, vastly the worse for drug wear, wander through the chords of "Hang on to a Dream" on the piano. His band looked on with no attempt to follow.

Sallie sat with him, gripping his hand in an excess of nerves. "My God," she whispered in his ear, "was he like this in the studio?"

"On a good day," Dave whispered back. He knew she didn't mean anything by holding his hand. Timmy had that effect on people. It was like watching a runaway roller coaster ride.

After *Tim Hardin 1*, Timmy had gone to Los Angeles for good, taking the demos he'd recorded for Jake with him. Jake's erstwhile partners, Charles Koppelman and Don Rubin, who Zally always called Koppelthief and Robberman, recorded a few more songs, overdubbed some instruments, and took production credit for *Tim Hardin 2*. And that, in terms of legacy, was it for Timmy Hardin.

Since then he'd released a live album, a set of early demos on Atlantic, a selection—incredibly—of the Columbia sessions that Dave had worked on a lifetime ago, and a "Best of" package that took songs from *Tim Hardin 1* and *2* only. Those were the songs he was now singing at Woodstock, his band struggling to follow his pauses and odd phrasing and turnarounds.

If Timmy had stayed with Jake, could Jake have saved him, kept the songs flowing? Most likely not. Timmy had been stuffed head to toe with combustible material and it had all gone up at once. It left Dave wondering whether Sallie was destined to burn out too. If so, did he have the power to delay it, to coax a few more songs out of her that might not otherwise have existed? The responsibility was crushing.

Timmy was winding down. He started "Simple Song of Freedom," a song Bobby Darin gave him as payback for Bobby's huge success with "Carpenter." It had gotten enough airplay to provoke a smattering of applause as the band fell in. Sallie kissed his cheek and said, "I can't take any more of this. I'm on in an hour and I need to get my head in a better place."

"Knock 'em dead," Dave said. And, as she had so many times before, she walked away and left him to watch her go.

COLE SAT MOTIONLESS as Hardin managed to walk a tightrope through an entire short set. The emotion he provoked was as much nervousness as melancholy. "Reason to Believe" and the encore, "Misty Roses," both had the ring of stammered confessions under torture.

As soon as Hardin left the stage, a cool, steady drizzle began to fall. It was pleasant enough at first, coming after the dry heat of the day, but it showed no sign of letting up. Cole briefly considered catching a ride to the motel on one of the helicopters that continuously rattled over the site, but the Holiday Inn and even the performers' pavilion seemed unreal to him. He had passed through a one-way membrane when he left backstage. The thought of being on that stage tomorrow, the stage that Tim Hardin had just vacated, felt absurd.

He found himself walking back to the free stage. Somebody had strung Christmas lights in the trees along the path, and he saw that the lights were no more than lights now, that the acid had peaked and faded, leaving him achy and dissatisfied.

At the campsite, he was drawn to a glowing tepee. He hunkered outside the door and saw that a fire was burning inside, with an opening at the top that pulled at least some of the sweet smoke up and out. A hand reached out to him. Cole blinked and saw that it belonged to Sugarfoot, the guy from the Baez performance. He took it and let Sugarfoot pull him in.

The space inside was larger than he had imagined, holding twenty people, some of them sprawled on sleeping bags, some roasting hot dogs and marshmallows. Cole found a spot where he could feel the warmth of the fire. He declined the food, but did accept a warm beer, and when a Sears Silvertone acoustic guitar made its way to him, he tuned it up and sang "Cielito lindo." The act of playing anchored him to the moment, let him accept that Alex was no longer there to sing with him, that Madelyn was not waiting for him to return. Nothing existed beyond the here and the now.

He carried on into "Bésame mucho." Most everybody sang along, at least on the choruses, humming where they didn't know the words, and he threw in some fancy guitar work that earned him a few indrawn breaths.

Ten feet away, a brown-eyed blonde watched him fixedly. An inch or so of dark roots, a white T-shirt with nothing underneath, green Chinese vest with gold embroidery, low-slung jeans. He knew he was at a turning point. He'd resisted more temptations than a dozen Buddhist monks, and holding the high moral ground had earned him nothing. He was ready to let it go, let everything go. The decision left him sad and reckless.

He made eye contact with the blonde as he sang the word "Bésame" and gave her a smile to go with it. She squirmed with pleasure and smiled back.

He let the tide pick him up and take him out to sea.

★

DAVE HAD ALWAYS admired grace under pressure. As the rain came down, Sallie quietly made half a million people fall in love with her. Alone on stage with her guitar, she sang every song of hers that had rain in the lyrics, and where there was no rain she added it, or riffed on wet clothes or wet kisses and generally made it clear that nobody could possibly want to be anywhere in the world other than there in the rain with Sallie Rachel. The construction crew had hung a couple of tarps from the girders over the stage that didn't do much. Every gust of wind blew rain in her face and on her guitar, and throughout the entire set he had a sick fear in his gut that she would touch her lip to the vocal mike and be electrocuted.

Counting her encore, she played ten songs and left them wanting more. A small crowd formed around her at the bridge, everyone talking at once, happy and excited. Somebody handed her a towel and she saw to her 12-string first, getting it dried and in its case before she patted quickly at her face and hair. Dave hung back and followed her across the bridge to the performers' tepee, where she dug a can of ginger ale out of the ice and turned and saw him and waved.

"I did good, huh?" she said.

"You did fantastic."

"Hopefully I can catch a chopper to the hotel tonight."

"I'll come with."

"Really?" she said, tilting her head flirtatiously.

Dave was too tired to kid around. "Are you coming back tomorrow?"

She shook her head. "I want to get home to New York. I'm too old for this."

"Tell me about it. I was too old for this ten years ago."

"It's weird, though, isn't it? All these kids. They have some kind of built-in sense of belonging. You do have to wonder if this really is the start of something."

Did he? Dave thought. He couldn't pinpoint why he was in such a lousy mood. He was certainly tired of hearing how wonderful these kids were. What had they accomplished, after all, other than to show up for a weekend-long party so woefully unprepared that they turned it into a disaster area? This was not heroism, it was middle-class privilege, the belief that somebody would surely take care of them because they were so precious and special. That the somebody had turned out to be hundreds of struggling local farmers, the financially ruined festival promoters, and the US Army did not, to Dave's mind, speak well of them. "It's a spoiled generation. They had everything handed to them."

"Including assassinations of their heroes, the threat of nuclear annihilation, and one-way tickets to Vietnam. I don't think I'd want to be one of them." She touched his arm to soften the slap. "What about you, are you coming back tomorrow?"

"Yeah, I've got The Quirq opening the show. As soon as they're done, I'll be on the next flight to San Francisco."

After a silence she said, "Are you doing okay out there?"

He shrugged. "It's not the Village in sixty-four..."

"... but what is, right? And you've got an endless supply of hippie chicks to see to your needs."

"Yeah," he said. "Right." He took a step backward. "I'll go see what I can find for transport."

"Dave? I'm sorry for teasing you. It's only because I love you, you know."

It was one more thing to blame the hippies for, the way love had become such a devalued currency. "I love you too," he said, putting the words on the tracks without hooking up the emotional freight cars that went with them.

"Seeing all those kids tonight, I feel like my time has come and gone."

"What are you talking about? They went nuts for you."

"That was just... the chemistry of the moment. Long term, I'm scared that I'm about to be a relic."

"Not going to happen. Your voice is for real, not some Vegas caricature. You write great songs with great hooks. That never goes out of date."

She hugged him and pressed her head against his shirt. "You're always there for me," she said.

"That's right," he said, and as soon as her arms loosened he stepped away. "And now I'm going to go get us a helicopter."

HER PARENTS HAD named her Laramie, she told Cole, in honor of the town where she was conceived. She had quit dyeing her hair after her first acid trip in June, and at the moment it felt right to be carrying her old life and her new life together growing out of her head, though eventually the time would come to cut the old life off. She had decided not to go back for her senior year at Northwestern, and instead to throw in with the commune people, who had picked her up near Toledo as she was hitching her way east to the fair.

She wanted to know where Cole had learned to play guitar like that, and said, "You should be on the main stage," and he told her that he would be, in the morning. "You are bullshitting me," she said, and she made him pinky swear. He used their linked fingers to draw her forward into a kiss and she kissed him back with eager intent. Then they were lying on top of her sleeping bag and then he was pulling his boots off and crawling inside it with her. Cole was shaking with excitement. Her mouth tasted of hot dogs and mustard, her neck of salt and woodsmoke. He couldn't get enough. When she started to unbutton his shirt, he said, "Uh, you don't care about all these other people?"

"In Japan," she said, "you're never alone. So you have to make your own privacy. In your head."

"How do you know about Japan?"

"Army brat," she said, and bit his nipple. He had no further questions.

They worked their way out of most of their clothes and then he was inside her. It made her crazy. She writhed against him and made little noises in his ear, clawed at his back, and came repeatedly. Cole hoped the rest of the tent understood Japanese privacy. At the moment he was past caring. He held out as long as he could and then the force of his climax felt like it was turning him inside out. As his last spasms finished, she was panting as if she'd run a mile.

1969

Cole lay on top of her, still connected. In a moment of post-coital clarity, he realized he'd done something irrevocable, and he felt a premonition of guilt to come. To drive the feeling back into the darkness, he kissed Laramie again, and kept kissing her and touching her skin and her hair and then they were moving together again, more slowly this time, and she came twice more, arms and legs wrapped around him tight, and he thought, how could I not accept this gift, this sublime pleasure, what in this world is better than this?

Despite Cole's exhaustion they stayed up past two AM, when the music from the main stage, which had faded in an out like a radio playing in another room, finally stopped.

Cole was smitten and felt jealous and protective of her in a way he knew he wasn't entitled to feel. She asked him about the band and apologized for not having heard of them. She said she wanted to know everything there was to know about him, and he told her that he too had been around the world against his will, that he had seen Dylan and been transformed, that he had left home at sixteen and college after a year. She asked if he had somebody in San Francisco, which made him think she was more than a little smitten herself. He told her he was married but separated, the first time he'd spoken those words. They were deceptively easy to say.

"It's cool," she said. "Eskimos, when they travel, they expect to receive sexual hospitality wherever they stay."

"Eskimos," he said fuzzily, and that was the last thing he remembered.

When he woke, desperately needing to pee, the sun was well up. His watch said it was a few minutes past nine. He found his jeans and underwear stuffed down in the bottom of the sleeping bag and managed to extricate them and himself without waking Laramie. The tent smelled of wet ashes and, from the contents of some of the sleeping bags, he surmised that he and Laramie were not the only ones to have counted on Japanese privacy.

Outside he found a drizzly Saturday morning. The badly scuffed ground had turned to mud, and puddles of rain water dotted the clearing, reflecting the clouds overhead. His hands smelled of sex.

Probably his whole body did. Thinking about it made him want
Laramie again, at the same time that he thought briefly and guiltily
of Madelyn.

At the moment he had more urgent needs. He considered making for the woods again, then multiplied that by half a million
and decided to do the responsible thing and find a portable toilet.
The line was mercifully short. Despite the smell and mess inside, it
did function, and there was toilet paper, and a makeshift hydrant
nearby where he could wash his hands and face.

The next order of business was to find out when he was supposed to play, and maybe score some breakfast. He walked back to
the tepee, where the first thing he saw was Laramie sitting hunched
over in the sleeping bag. Her face lit up at the sight of him and
she held out her arms. He knelt beside her and she embraced him
fiercely. "I thought you'd gone," she said, her breath hot against
his neck.

She loaned him her toothbrush and made her own trip to the
toilet and then they headed out together for the main stage. The
rain had finally let up. Laramie walked with one arm around Cole's
waist, leaning into him as if they were in a three-legged race, intoxicating Cole with her touch.

Most of the crowd had spent the night in the same place they'd
spent the previous day, some with blankets or sleeping bags, many
of them without and curled up together for warmth, many of
them still asleep. The concave field, while making a perfect natural
amphitheater, also collected rainwater. The individual differences
between the audience members were fading as they all began to
take on the color of dried mud. An acrid urine smell hovered in
the air, telling Cole that some had not bothered to go as far as the
woods to relieve themselves.

They arrived at the gate to the backstage area at 9:45. Once
they were inside, Cole saw the MC from the night before at the
back of the stage and crossed the wooden bridge to him.

"I'm Jeff Cole with The Quirq. Do you know when we're supposed to go on?"

"John Morris," the guy said, and they did the soul brother
handshake. "There's a chopper on the way with the rest of your

guys. You're on first, it's just that we're not too sure right now when that's going to be. It might surprise you to learn we're a little disorganized this morning."

"It's cool," Cole said. "I'll be down at the performers' tent."

As they walked back down the bridge, Laramie squeezed his arm with both hands and said, "This is so amazing." Her excitement made Cole realize how blasé he'd let himself become. He tried to picture himself four years ago, listening to Dylan for the first time in Alex's room.

The performers' pavilion was crowded. A cluster of British guys sat off by themselves, one of them in an old-west-style flat-brimmed hat over long brown hair and a beard. Another group took up two tables, talking excitedly. Cole recognized one of them, a skinny Chicano who'd been at the Airplane house the night they found Gordo. Carlos, his name was, supposedly a guitar player. John Sebastian was at a table with a couple of girls. Paul and Grace from the Airplane were at the buffet table and Laramie said, "Oh my God, is that...?"

"Yep," Cole said. He led her over and said, "Hey, Grace, how's it going?"

"Morning, Cole." Then, living up to her name as she occasionally did, Grace smiled at the sight of Laramie, mouth half-open and eyes as wide as if she'd had a bad shock. "Who's your friend?"

"Grace, this is Laramie." Laramie stared at Grace's extended hand for several seconds before gingerly reaching out to shake it.

Cole said, "The punch was spiked yesterday, so you might want to be careful."

"Was it good stuff, at least?" Grace asked.

"Distinctly mediocre."

"We've got some Orange Sunshine that's outstanding," Paul said. "If you're interested."

"Maybe later," Cole said. "We're on first this morning."

"All the more reason," Grace said.

The food was the same as the day before. Cole was starving and not inclined to be fussy. Neither, evidently, was Laramie, who was eating with both hands as she filled her plate. Cole had just built an exact replica of the previous day's bologna and cheese sandwich when he heard Lenny say, "Well, well, look who's here."

Cole turned to see Lenny with his hands on his hips, wearing an artificial smile. Gordo and Tommy were a few yards away, talking to Carlos. "Hey, Lenny," Cole said. "This is Laramie. Lenny's the other lead player in the band."

"Oh, yeah," Lenny said, "that's right. We've got *two* guitar players. I kind of forgot there for a bit."

"Want some food?" Cole said.

"We had breakfast at the hotel. Fresh eggs. *Really* fresh." Lenny looked at Laramie, then Cole. "Like they'd just been *laid*."

"Something troubling you, Lenny?" Cole asked.

"Nah, not really. I like getting a phone call that we're about to be on, asking me where the hell you were."

"I'm right here, Lenny."

"It's just that this is a pretty important gig. Half a million people, for Christ's sake. Movie cameras."

"You'll have to excuse my friend Lenny," Cole said to Laramie. "He's not usually this much of an asshole."

"How much of an asshole am I?" Lenny asked. "Usually?"

"Tell you what," Cole said, "let's finish this conversation later. I'd really like to eat before we go on." He turned his back on Lenny and fished around for a Coke in the mostly melted ice. The closer he let someone get, the more power they had to piss him off. His stomach had clenched up and now he wasn't sure he would be able to eat.

Lenny was gone when he turned around again. Cole and Laramie sat at a table by themselves. "I apologize for Lenny," he said. "I don't know what's bugging him."

"Nerves, I bet," Laramie said. "I'm terrified, and I'm not even going on stage."

"Maybe he's jealous," Cole said, and leaned over to kiss her. She sighed into the kiss and put her arms around his neck. He'd never been with a woman before who was so deeply into sex. He knew intellectually that sex was not the only thing he wanted out of life, though at the moment everything else seemed trivial. He offered her half his sandwich, and she scarfed it down eagerly.

On stage, a guy led the crowd in something he called "Breath of Fire" that was like rapid panting, through the nose instead of the mouth. The crazy Hog Farm guy, Hugh something, had also been making announcements, calling this "the first free city of the world in the Aquarian Age." Cole was unable to say why he found the words so moving and why he was unable to laugh them off as hippie bullshit, the way he would have 24 hours before. He felt like he was in an after-the-bomb science fiction novel where the human race, reduced to savagery, tried to make sense of the technology that had been left behind, a technology consisting of guitars and amplifiers and microphones.

He drained his Coke and said, "Come on, let's go introduce you to John Sebastian."

Sebastian was decked out in an orange tie-dyed jacket and blue and white tie-dyed jeans. He kissed Laramie on the cheek and escorted Cole to the vw camper. His Strat, Cole was relieved to see, was not only there but clean and dry. Sebastian was radiant. He waved off Cole's thanks and said, "We're all doing for each other now. That's how it's supposed to be."

Cole carried the guitar over the bridge, Laramie tucked under his other arm. She paused at the back of the stage and said, "I can't go out there."

"Why not?" Lenny was already moving their amps around with one of the stage crew, a guy in a crumpled cowboy hat with dark hair hanging down his shirtless back. Tommy pulled drums and chrome-plated stands out of black fiberboard cases and piled them up. The yoga guy, also bare-chested, with a dark blond braid, finished and raised his hand as he walked away, accompanied by whistles and applause. Another dozen or so groupies, stagehands, and performers milled around the stage.

"You're not nervous?" she asked.

"I wish they had another million of them out there."

"You go on. I'll stay here."

Cole found his amp among the drum cases. A guy in a ragged Hawaiian shirt, sporting a horseshoe mustache with long, dangling ends, said, "You with The Quirq?"

"That's me. We supposed to load up this giant turntable thing?"

"Don't bother, just put it wherever the fuck you want it to end up. I don't know how much life the cheap-ass casters on that motherfucker got left in 'em. Like everything else around here, good idea, execution entirely for shit. You need anything?"

"Nah," Cole said, pushing his amp in the direction of the audience. "The casters on *this* motherfucker are still good."

The guy laughed and went to help Tommy.

The front of the stage, Cole saw as he got closer, did not drop ten feet straight down to ground level, but only four feet to a ledge where the film crews and still photographers were setting up for the day's shooting. On the far side of the ledge, a board fence separated them from the crowd. The top of the fence was festooned with clothes drying out from the rain of the night before.

The sky had cleared to a deep blue with a few puffy clouds, temperature around 70, the sun warm on his skin. Once again Cole felt a benevolence that emanated from the very landscape, unlike the deserts he'd known in Mexico and Egypt and West Texas. He closed his eyes and drank in a sense of calm and rightness. As he stood there, somebody put side one of *Music from Big Pink* on the PA system, the slow moan of "Tears of Rage."

When he opened his eyes again, he saw a stack of equipment at the back of stage left that included a Hammond B-3 and so many conga drums that they were lined up like bowling pins. Laramie had wandered over to investigate and a couple of rough-looking guys had come to check her out, one a short Chicano in high-heeled boots, the other a gringo in a sleeveless black T-shirt, both with huge Afros. Cole felt a pang of jealousy until she said something to the short one, pointed to Cole, and smiled and blew him a kiss.

Cole waved back and set to work. He plugged his amp into the AC supply, then laid out his pedals and patched them all in line. When he switched his amp on and tried an experimental chord, a small cheer went up from the crowd. It was good, Cole thought, to be the first band of the day, to catch the audience when it was hungry.

He saw that Lenny had set up at the other end of the stage, 50 feet away, far enough for the sound from his amp to be delayed. Tommy, meanwhile, had placed his bass drum to stage right of

Cole's amp and was nailing the pedal to the stage. "What's up with Lenny?" Cole asked him.

"Fuck if I know. On the rag for some reason."

Gordo pushed his tuck-and-rolled Kustom cabinet to the other side of the drums, far enough back for Tommy to be able to hear him. "You guys discussing la cabrona?" He tilted his head toward Lenny, whose back was to them, playing his Les Paul with the sound off. Cole couldn't remember Gordo showing hostility toward anyone before, certainly not calling anyone a bitch.

"I've never seen him like this before," Cole said.

"Yes you have," Gordo said. "Every time there's an important gig, he freaks out, directly proportional to how important it is. Half a million people, he's mega-freaking. I been feeling like I was gonna echar la pota myself, ever since I got up."

"If that means what I think it means," Tommy said, "please do it off the back of the stage."

Two stagehands converged on Lenny. One of them, with glasses, blond muttonchop sideburns, and handlebar mustache, squatted in front of him and pointed to the crowd, to the towers that held the speakers, to the rest of the band. Finally he smiled and squeezed Lenny's shoulder and together they rolled his Marshall stack to within a few feet of Gordo's Kustom.

The guy with the sideburns came over and shook hands all around. "I'm Chip Monck," he said in a deep baritone.

"Oh, hey," Cole said. "You work with Bill Graham."

"Yeah, some carpentry, some lights, some this and that. I think your friend is experiencing an episode of nerves."

"Thanks for talking to him," Cole said, though in truth he was out of patience. Neither Gordo nor Tommy seemed particularly sympathetic either.

"Glad to help," Chip said. "Have a good show."

Cole bit the bullet and walked over to Lenny. "You want to tune up?"

"You must think I'm an idiot," Lenny said.

"I've always known you were an idiot," Cole said, "but I don't see what that has to do with tuning guitars."

In terms of lightening the mood, Cole's quip was about as

successful as LBJ's Vietnam policy. "Fuck you," Lenny said, and started to take off his guitar.

"Hey, take it easy." Cole felt the first thrill of panic. He searched for an idea that Lenny could relate to. "Do you have any idea how many women out there are going to want to fuck you after you get offstage? Thousands. You have never had odds like this in your life. Let's tune up, let them make their announcements, play for forty minutes, and the rest is sex. Okay?"

"Yeah, yeah, fine, let's get it over with." Between his nerves and the Band blasting through the speakers, Lenny's perfect pitch had shorted out. Cole fetched the miniature tuning fork from his guitar case and waved Gordo over, and between the three of them they managed a rough consensus.

"Oh, man," Lenny said, "this is really going to suck."

They put their amps on standby and their guitars on stands and Tommy put his sticks in one of the tension rods of his bass drum. Cole collected Laramie, getting a "who the fuck are you?" look from the short guy in heels, and they all went back to the performers' tent.

Eleven-fifteen. Cole, ready to go, watched the minutes drag by in awkward silence or fumbling conversation. Lenny wandered off again and Cole decided that somebody else could go after him this time. No one did.

The constant drone of helicopters reached a fever pitch around noon. John Morris announced from the stage that the US Army was flying in medical teams. "They are with us, man!"

Chip Monck stuck his head in the tent and made eye contact with Cole. "Quirq? You guys are on." Cole couldn't get over his buttery smooth voice. "Aren't you missing a guitar player?"

"Evidently," Cole said.

They all crossed the bridge again, Cole wondering if the flimsy railing would last all three days. Lenny sat with his legs hanging off the back of the stage, looking at a 20 foot drop to the road below and leaning against another flimsy 2×4 railing. "Órale, cabrona," Gordo said. "Let's go play."

Lenny got miserably to his feet. Cole wanted to slap him. Laramie grabbed Cole by the hair and kissed him thoroughly.

As she ran to the side of the stage, Cole saw a grand piano there, covered in green oilcloth, with Dave Fisher sitting on the bench and smiling at him. Dave, who'd been to dinner with him and Madelyn in San Francisco, and who couldn't have missed that kiss. Cole felt himself blush.

"I'm proud of you guys," Dave said, getting up to put one hand on Lenny's shoulder. "You've come so far in such a short time. This is going to put you on the map."

The words hit the band's negative energy and fizzled out. "Thanks," Cole said.

John Morris was still talking as they strapped on their guitars, the audience already whistling and clapping for them. "Insulin and all other drugs are available in the medical centers. If you need something, for God's sake don't sit there. You can always come back, we're going to be here."

Cole switched his amp off standby and heard a nasty 60-cycle hum, followed by radio transmissions from a nearby airport. Switching the ground made no difference. Oh well, he thought, nothing to do about it now. He touched the switch on his mike to make sure it was on. A blue spark flashed and knocked Cole back a step, the electric shock numbing his hand and traveling all the way up his arm to his jaw. "Fuck!" he said reflexively, and the mike picked it up, blasting it from the speaker towers. The crowd laughed.

Cole, his temper about to boil over, switched the ground on his amp again. Then, gingerly, he touched the mike like he would a burner on a stove. It still hummed with ungrounded power, not quite as badly.

He looked at Morris. "Can you do anything about that?"

Morris shrugged. "We're working on it."

He glanced to make sure Lenny had seen. Lenny was staring at his feet. Fuck it, Cole thought, let him get shocked.

Off mike, Morris said, "You guys ready?"

Tommy and Gordo were watching Cole. Cole nodded.

Morris got back on the microphone. "Okay, I guess the reason we're here is music. So let's have some music."

Suddenly Cole felt like he'd stepped on ice and his feet had flown out from under him. He'd been thinking about Laramie and then pissed off at Lenny and embarrassed for Dave, and then the shock had wiped his brain. He'd missed his chance to stop and get his bearings.

"Ladies and gentlemen… The Quirq."

Tommy counted off "Wang Dang Doodle," and three out of four of them started the song. Lenny was lost somewhere in his own brain. Cole had had enough. He crossed the stage, and at the end of a measure, he kicked Lenny in the ass, hard. Lenny jumped forward a couple of feet and turned on Cole with an enraged expression while the kids near the front of the stage laughed.

"Play, cabrona," Cole said.

"Quit calling me that," Lenny said, as he turned up the volume on his guitar and fell in.

Back on his side of the stage, Cole started to sing, keeping a respectful distance from the spherical head of the mike. This was where they always won the crowd over, at the top of the set, hitting them with a burst of joyous energy, and today the notes fluttered off the stage and lay twitching in the dirt. Everything that was supposed to feel relaxed and spontaneous came out forced and artificial. Cole struck a few poses when his leads came around and managed to coax a little audience response that way. He got them all clapping along for "Get Out of My Life, Woman," but when he got up next to Gordo and got him to dance a few steps, Gordo stepped on his own cord and unplugged the bass.

They were almost at the end, having built some momentum in spite of themselves, about to go into their final medley, when John Morris came on stage and held up one hand. For a terrible moment Cole thought they were about to get the hook. Morris said, "Hold it just a second," and then took the mike. "I apologize to all of you for doing this, but Hugh has something he's got to talk to us about, so let Hugh talk."

Hugh was the clown guy with the missing teeth and the white jumpsuit and trashed cowboy hat. He took the mike and said, "Listen, we are all different parts of the same revolution." Cole looked at Lenny, who stared back at him. Was this really the reason they'd interrupted the set? Hugh said something about people trying to get violent, and if that happened, "let's all just jump up and kiss 'em. And lick 'em." Then, in what was apparently the real issue, he asked for someone named Patty's asthma medicine to be brought to the information booth near stage right because she was having an attack.

As soon as he finished, Cole started the riff to "Smokestack Lightning." It was too late. The energy they'd manage to build had evaporated. They struggled through the usual segue to "Cielito lindo" and back without it ever catching fire, wrapped it up, and unplugged and huddled at the rear of the stage.

Laramie was ten feet away, leaning forward in a folding chair, squeezing her arms between her thighs, looking at Cole with awe. Cole was disappointed that she could be so easily impressed. He gave her a flash of a smile and held up one finger for her to stay put.

To Cole's surprise, they got a decent amount of applause. Chip had taken over for John Morris and his mellow voice was saying, "Ladies and Gentlemen, The Quirq. I don't think you've convinced them. Come on, you'll have to do better than that."

"We going with 'Mariner' for the encore?" Tommy said.

"Too slow," Cole said. "'Seventh Son.'"

"We hardly did any originals," Lenny complained. "We need to do 'Mariner.'"

"Listen," Cole said, "we sucked so bad, we're lucky they didn't kick us off the stage. This is our last chance to make some kind of positive impression."

Chip was waving them back on stage.

"I say 'Mariner,'" Lenny said.

"Gordo?" Cole said.

"Fuck, I don't know. 'Mariner,' I guess."

"Fine," Cole said. "For Christ's sake keep it short."

"Fuck you," Lenny said.

The spacey, echoing guitars and moody lyrics were, as Cole anticipated, exactly the wrong tone, and when they faded it out after five minutes the applause was barely polite.

As they walked off stage, Gordo said, "Okay, bad idea. You were right."

Cole wiped down his guitar and put it in its case. "Can you do me a favor? Can you make sure my gear gets back to San Francisco?"

Gordo looked at Laramie, loitering by the bridge. "Give her one for me, primo."

"Gracias, vato," Cole said. He started toward Laramie and she ran across the stage and climbed him like a ladder, wrapping her legs around his waist and putting her tongue deep in his mouth. "You have no idea," she said, when she came up for air, "how sexy it was to watch you."

"We were terrible," Cole said, though at that moment he couldn't remember why. He couldn't think of anything, in fact, beyond the girl in his arms.

"I don't care," she said. "The rest of the band was messing up, but you were fantastic. I want you. Now."

"Here? On stage?"

"Come with me."

She led him over the bridge, then through a gap in the chain link fence where a guy checked his performer's pass, across the road behind the stage, and then under the stage itself.

"One of the girls told me about this," Laramie said.

"The girls?"

"You know. One of the ones that goes with musicians."

The underside of the stage was remarkably crowded. Piles of lighting instruments that never got used because the roof of the stage never got built. Women changing 16 mm film reels. Stagehands sharing a joint. Somebody had hung blankets on the scaffolding to create four cubicles with at least the illusion of privacy. Cole heard voices from behind one of the blankets as Laramie pulled him toward a vacant space next to it. He was as aroused as he could ever remember being, reduced to a brainstem and a few square yards of eroticized skin. Laramie pulled the blanket in place behind them and went to her knees, unbuckling Cole's pants and tugging them to his ankles. She took him in her mouth and worked him with her tongue and Cole heard himself make a lowing sound like a cow. She kissed his stomach and pushed up his shirt and said, "You taste like us." They undressed each other and spread their clothes out on the grass to make a pallet. Laramie pushed him onto his back and straddled him. At first Cole was aware of the roughness of the ground under him and then he wasn't.

At some point music came on above them, Country Joe playing an acoustic guitar. Joe was finished before Cole and Laramie were, when Cole, after coming twice, finally collapsed in exhaustion.

Cole lay on his back, Laramie tucked into one armpit, stroking his chest. The air felt cool now, without his internal fires raging, and he pulled her close for warmth. Desire had filled his entire world, and now that he had emptied himself of desire, the world was empty too, devoid of meaning. Laramie's face was pressed against his neck and he felt her tears run down his collarbone, as if she'd read his thoughts. "Hey," he said. "What's wrong?"

"Nothing," she said, nuzzling him. "Everything is groovy and wonderful and amazing."

"You're crying," he pointed out.

"It's all a little too much," she said. "All these feelings. Leaving school, changing my life, meeting you. I don't know who I am anymore."

Cole had heard the expression countless times and never understood it. "How can you not know who you are?"

"I don't have anything like your guitar. I just have all these things I know I'm not. I'm not grocery lists and polyester dresses from Sears and hospital corners like my mother. I'm not one of the eager-beaver kids headed for J-school who are going to rip the lid off the maggot-ridden Daley administration. I'm not a back-to-the-land visionary who's going to build a utopia with her calloused hands. I'm not your wife or your girlfriend, I'm just some crazy chick who balled your brains out at a festival."

"You're more than that," Cole said, hugging her. "Way more than that."

After a few seconds she pulled away. "It's chilly down here. We should get dressed."

A HAZE OF CLOUDS had lightened the early afternoon sky to the palest of blues. As she and Cole stumbled blinking into daylight,

Laramie said, "I need to go to the tepee for a while. If I don't shower and clean up, I'm going to get a yeast infection."

"That's cool. I could use a shower too."

She shook her head. "I'll meet you here in a couple of hours. Okay?"

"You'll need a pass to get in."

She smiled. "No I won't. And if they give me any trouble, I'll have them come get you."

"Laramie..." He didn't like the sudden darkness that had come over her mood and he didn't want them to separate. At the same time, if she needed space, he had to give it to her.

She leaned into him and kissed him sweetly. "I'll see you in a while."

As she walked away, he waited for her to turn and look at him one more time, telling himself that if she did, everything would be okay. She just kept walking, past the guard at the fence, disappearing into the crowd at the side of the stage.

Cole wandered over to the performers' pavilion and froze when he saw Lenny fishing out a Coke by the buffet table. Lenny saw him and waved him over.

Lenny was like Cole, verbal and not a fighter, but the day had already proved that all bets were off. Cole approached him warily.

"I was looking for you," Lenny said.

Cole nodded.

"I don't know what happened out there this morning," Lenny said. "I only know that I hated being up there, as much as I ever hated anything. Small clubs are okay, but even at the Fillmore I was really scared. I've been fighting this for a long time and today... today it blew up in my face."

Cole had no idea what to say, so he nodded again.

"Being in the studio, man, that was great. If I fucked up, I could do it over, I could make it perfect. I loved that. It only made it worse playing for big crowds. So..." He took a deep breath. "So I'm sorry."

"I'm sorry too," Cole said. "I was really shitty to you out there."

"It doesn't matter. Because I've been thinking, and I need to quit the group."

"You can't quit," Cole said. "There is no group without you." During the set, the idea of firing Lenny had passed through Cole's head and he had immediately dismissed it. Lenny had started the band, Lenny was the better guitarist, Lenny was the one who never lost his cool. "You don't want to make this kind of decision on the spur of the moment anyway. When we get back, we'll talk it over—"

Lenny shook his head. "As soon as I decided, it was like one minute I was drowning and the next I was standing up on dry land and I could breathe again. I know it's right." Unexpectedly, Lenny hugged him. "I'm sorry," he said again, and he walked, almost running, toward the helicopter landing zone.

Cole took one step after him, then another, and then a devastating weakness took hold of him and he sat in a folding chair. He looked down at his stomach, expecting to see himself sliced open and gushing blood onto the bark floor. Instead there was only himself, physically and emotionally exhausted, alone in a crowd of half a million.

A BAND STARTED up onstage. Conga drums and a bass, nothing else. The sound was riveting, the drums simultaneously primitive and melodic. As the music poured into Cole's empty head, it sounded familiar and brand new, sounded like it was being played for him alone. It sounded like the Olatunji album he'd bought in San Francisco and the mambo and cha-cha-cha records his father had played in the fifties.

The music drew him over the bridge and into a chair on stage right. The organ and guitar and trap set had joined in by then, playing a series of descending chords that gave way to bursts of furious guitar work. The guitarist, he saw, was the guy Carlos that he'd met at the Airplane house. The organist and the shorter of the two conga players were the two guys who'd hit on Laramie that morning. Finally Cole realized that this was the Santana band that Bill Graham had pushed him to see.

They went from the conga piece into a smooth cha-cha-cha, the short conga player moving to timbales. The organ player sang lead and Carlos sang harmony and the rock instruments fused perfectly with the Latin rhythms. The band was set up in a semicircle instead of a line, able to watch and listen to each other, to push each other to take risks, and to watch each other's backs in case somebody slipped.

Cole was devastated. He'd held all the pieces of what they were doing in his hands and failed to see the possibilities. Instead he'd opted for the same whey-faced versions of black blues that half the bands at Woodstock traded in, from Canned Heat to Joplin to Johnny Winter to Keef Hartley to Ten Years After. He wanted Carlos's job, though he knew he was not guitarist enough to fill it. More than that, he wanted to go back in time, to the fall of his freshman year at UT, to forget about The Other Side and The Austin Blues Group, to instead invent electric mariachi music with Alex and take it to the Vulcan, where the crowd would have eaten it up.

Two songs later, as Santana swung into "Jingo" from the Olatunji album, Cole felt even worse. He was an idiot, inspiration-deaf, a failure before he turned 20. And the audience loved it. Most of them had never heard of Santana before, yet they were on their feet, dancing and clapping along. Sitting through the rest of the set was torture for Cole, and he stayed there to teach himself a lesson. As his father would have said.

When it was over, the crowd still screaming for them after their encore, Carlos saw him and came over to shake hands. "Hey," Carlos said, "I saw you at the Airplane house that time. You guys were good this morning. I love that you did 'Cielito lindo.'"

"We were terrible," Cole said. "But you guys were amazing. I never heard you before today. I couldn't believe how good you were."

"Really?" Carlos said. "They lied to us about when we were going to go on, said it was going to be like two in the morning, so I took some mescaline. I was so high when we got up there, I had no idea what I was playing."

"It was one of the best performances I've ever seen." Cole was afraid he was going to cry.

"Aw, thanks, man. Hey, you guys are with Graham too, right? He should put us on tour together or something."

"Sure," Cole said, unwilling to say out loud that The Quirq was done. "That would be cool."

"I got to split. I'll catch you around, okay?"

"Okay," Cole said.

As soon as Carlos walked away, John Morris came over and crouched in front of him. "Uh, listen, man, I'm afraid I have some bad news."

Cole stared, wondering how things could get any worse.

"It appears that the film people had some kind of problem," Morris said. "I'm not an expert or anything, but apparently they use the eighth track of the sound recording to sync up with the film, and somehow that track didn't get recorded during your set. They found the problem and fixed it before Joe came on, but…"

"But we're not going to be in the movie."

"Yeah, I'm afraid not. I'm really sorry. With everything else we're dealing with, it's pretty amazing that we haven't had more fuckups than that."

"Yeah," Cole said. "Thanks for telling me."

Morris nodded and touched him gently on the shoulder as he straightened up.

Cole waited a couple of minutes and then went to the performers' pavilion and chugged a Budweiser. He didn't want to get falling-down drunk in case Laramie came back, still, a second can was required to get any anesthetic effect at all. He sat down at an empty table to finish it, where exhaustion and an empty stomach let him doze off.

When he roused himself, it was 3:30. Chip Monck was saying something not quite intelligible onstage. Cole's head hurt and his mouth tasted bad. He was still tired and the pain of the day lurked in easy reach, threatening to knock him down again if he stuck his head up too far.

He ate some cheese and vegetables and washed them down with club soda. When he looked outside, he saw that it had rained again, turning more of the ground to mud. He used one of the somewhat less foul portable toilets reserved for the performers, then washed his face with a double handful of ice water from the soft drink barrel.

There, he thought. I'm a new man.

He wandered onto the side of the stage, where the crew swept standing water off the plywood with push brooms and John Sebastian had come to the microphone. "I don't know if you can really tell how amazing you look," he told the crowd. He was still in his tie-dyed suit of lights, stoned and immensely peaceful. "But you're truly amazing, you're a whole city. And somehow you're something that an awful lot of us talked about, eight and ten years ago, in little living rooms…" He trailed off as he got his guitar in tune. "I have a song for you."

He began to sing something Cole had never heard, about bringing back odd mementos from all over the world, and went on to play for half an hour, a handful of gentle songs with great melodies. He charmed the crowd and made them feel good about themselves, as Cole struggled to get on their wavelength.

Before his encore, Sebastian said, "Just love everybody all around you and clean up a little garbage on your way out and everything gonna be all right." In spite of himself, Cole found himself choked up. Could it really be as simple as that?

Laramie had been gone two hours. Not long enough for him to go after her. He was restless and anxious and wished he hadn't sent his guitar away with Gordo. Backstage again, he paced the cage of six-foot-high chain-link fences, past the helicopter landing zone, past the portable toilets, past the U-Haul and Ryder trucks, finally along a deserted stretch that looked into the woods, some other farmer's land where only a few reckless tents had been pitched. He sat for a while on a damp, grassy mound and watched branches move in the wind.

Eventually the sound of music lured him to the stage. He watched Keef Hartley for a while, a basic blues three-piece with a trumpet and sax added that gave them a sweet, jazzy sound. The drummer was the guy he'd seen earlier, with the reddish beard and flat cowboy hat. Tight and melodic as they were, in the end it was more white-boy blues and Cole was not in the mood.

At five he gave up and headed for the tepee, anxious and excited in equal parts. Maybe it was a test. Maybe she'd just wanted to know if he would come looking for her.

At the free stage, some guy had set up dozens of cymbals and gongs and walked around from one to another, creating tidal waves of sound that crashed and ebbed and swelled again. Cole hurried past and arrived at the tepee out of breath. He paused for a second outside the door and then ducked inside.

Before his eyes fully adjusted to the dimness, he knew Laramie wasn't there. The interior was practically deserted and her sleeping bag lay empty where they'd left it that morning. Three young guys passed a joint near the ashes of the fire.

"You guys seen Laramie?"

"Who?" one of them said.

"What about Sugarfoot?"

One of the others said, "Free kitchen."

Cole followed the smoke to a big orange and yellow striped awning where giant pots of food simmered. A long line snaked away from the serving area. Cole followed it until he found Sugarfoot, standing on one leg with his eyes closed.

"Sugarfoot," Cole said.

A man behind him said, "No cutting in line, asshole."

Cole wondered if he would ever grasp the fine points of Yankee hospitality. "I'm not cutting," he said. "I just need to talk to my friend for a second."

"I'm watching you," the guy said. He was short and thick and looked like an ex-sailor.

"What's up, Cole?" Sugarfoot said, opening his eyes and settling on both feet.

"Have you seen Laramie?"

"She was around earlier. We all took a shower in the downpour, passed around some Dr. Bronner's. It was amazing."

Cole felt a stab of jealousy, involuntarily imagining her naked body in the rain. "You didn't see her after that?"

"Sorry, man."

The ex-sailor said, "You done?"

Sugarfoot turned to the guy and said, "Be cool, man, we're not messing with your trip."

"I been waiting in this line for an hour and I'm not going to wait even longer because of assholes cutting in. I'm fucking starving."

"Maybe you should bring your own food next time," Cole said, and walked away.

"Fuck you!" the guy yelled after him. "Come back here and say that, motherfucker!"

Peace and love, the cowboy clown had said. Cole was trembling from anger and the sick panic of not knowing where Laramie was. He took a detour into the forest to try and calm down. He had known Laramie less than 24 hours. He had no claims on her. He could find another band, or start something new from the ashes of The Quirq. And would anyone pay to see a movie of what he'd witnessed here so far? He looked at his watch. Maybe he and Laramie had passed each other. Maybe she was waiting for him at the main stage even now.

Over the next hour he made the circuit twice more, from stage to tepee and back, his feet beginning to seriously ache. On his last trip to the stage he thought, okay, this is it. She'd stood him up, for reasons beyond his understanding. He would get some food backstage, drink a couple of beers, maybe go back to the hotel for a hot shower and some sleep in a real bed.

That was when a voice behind him said, "Jeff!" His parents were the only ones who had called him that in years. He didn't fully register it until the voice said, "Jeff! Jeff Cole!"

A shirtless guy around Cole's age, six-two and beefy, with shaggy brown hair and a patchy beard, grinned at him. "You don't have the vaguest idea who the fuck I am, do you?"

Cole smiled reflexively. "Sorry, no."

"It's Pauley, man. Pauley from Mountain Lakes."

Cole shook his head a couple of times to clear it and looked again. The last time he'd seen Pauley, Cole had been 9 years old. It was the summer after third grade and the moving van had already taken all their furniture off to storage and a man in overalls had bought their high-mileage station wagon and driven it away. He and his parents would spend the night in a motel, and in the morning they would fly out of Idlewild Airport to Villahermosa.

Cole's best friend Glen had held a desultory going away party, and Pauley had been there, along with Glen's little sister Sharon and a couple of the other neighborhood kids. The party was Glen's parents' idea, and it had ended with everyone out on the lawn to watch Cole's parents take him away in a taxi. Cole remembered standing awkwardly in the grassy ground between his friends and his parents, feeling like he didn't belong to either one. "Hurry up!" his father had yelled. "The meter's running."

"Holy shit," Cole said. He could see faint traces of a skinny, belligerent little kid in the older Pauley's eyes and the angle of his head.

Pauley laughed and gave him a bear hug that knocked the wind out of him. "Glen's here too, and Sharon and Tony. Come on, we got some blankets and some cheap Chianti and some dope." "Chianti" rhymed with "panty," taking Cole back to 1950s New Jersey.

They began to pick their way through the bodies on the hillside that faced the stage. The air was thick with the odors of sweat, urine, mud and smoke.

"I can't believe this," Cole said. "How did you recognize me?"

"We seen you on stage this morning. When that Quirq record came out, Sharon figured out it was you and we told everybody we know. Then somebody saw you was going to be here, and we thought, what the fuck. See Jimi, see Janis, see Jeff, what have we got better to do?"

Up ahead, Cole saw three people sitting on green garbage bags on top of wet, muddy blankets. He would never have recognized them without Pauley's warning. Tony now had a massive forelock of black hair that eclipsed the upper-right third of his face. Glen's reddish-brown hair had gone frizzy and was receding at the temples above his fighter-pilot shades. And Sharon had simply grown up. She was only a year younger than Cole and she had gone tall and willowy, flashing a white-toothed smile when they made eye contact.

"Look what the cat drug in," Pauley said.

Tony, whom he hadn't known that well, stuck out a hand to shake. Glen got up to give him a one-armed hug, the other hand holding a cigarette, and Sharon, turned shy, looked down at her lap and said, "Hi, Jeff."

Cole sat down and accepted a swig of wine from a jug in a

straw basket. As soon as he passed the wine on, a fat joint arrived from the kids next to them. Cole took a substantial hit and sent it on its way. Tony sat on the sidelines as Pauley and Glen caught him up on the last 11 years. Sharon contributed a word here and there, hugging her knees, watching all of them, looking away and blushing whenever Cole met her gaze.

Pauley was at CCM, County College of Morris, trying to keep his 11-s deferment without giving up nightly parties. Glen was home for the summer from Rutgers in Newark, and Sharon, who'd just graduated high school, would join him there in the fall. Both had jobs to help pay for school, Glen at a construction site, Sharon in a hospital. Glen and Sharon's dad had finally made it to the day shift. Tony had gone straight from high school to working in his father's chain of pizza parlors. "Which I fucking hate," he said, the first words he'd spoken since Cole arrived. "My father makes me wear a fucking hair net." Two kids Cole knew had been drafted right out of high school and sent to Vietnam, both still alive as of last report. Phil Donleavy, who had lived down the street, had been struck by lightning while on a Boy Scout camping trip to Pyramid Mountain. The scoutmaster had revived him with artificial respiration, but his brain was damaged and he was now stuck at a fourth-grade level. Cindy Roper, whom Cole had had a crush on in third grade, had been high school valedictorian and gone off to Radcliffe.

Cole couldn't explain why it seemed so odd that all of these people had gone on in his absence to grow up and have their own lives. The world became impossibly complex because of it, three and a half billion people, all of them with pasts and aspirations, struggling forward in the darkness toward their own individual ideas of dawn.

Beneath the constant roar of the helicopters, someone on stage was reading a poem: "I make a pact with you... I make peace with you..." The wind and helicopters carried most of the rest away. Odd music followed, plucking and tinkling and singing not quite in key, and Pauley said, "Ah, the Unlistenable String Band. Whose genius idea was this?"

Cole remembered something he'd heard backstage. "They didn't want to play in the rain yesterday."

"Pussies," Pauley said, and the others laughed.

"When did you start playing guitar?" Sharon asked politely, and Cole told his story, zigzagging to pick up Villahermosa and Midland and Suez. In third grade, Cole had been picked last and exiled to right field. He'd been teased about his jeans, bought extra-large to keep up with his growth spurts, and the iron-on patches on their knees. He'd been tolerated more than liked, though Glen had eventually warmed to his ability to make wooden toy guns in his father's shop. Now Glen and Pauley looked at each other in disbelief when he talked about touring with the Airplane, playing the Fillmore, getting wined and dined by Atlantic Records.

"Man," Pauley said, "you must be getting more ass than a toilet seat."

Cole felt Sharon's eyes on him. "No, it's not like that. I mean, there are opportunities, sure, but being married and all…"

"What are you," Pauley said, "fucking nuts?"

No, Cole thought, just a hypocrite.

"We've got some peanut butter," Sharon said, breaking the tension, "and some jelly and a loaf of bread. If you're hungry."

"You guys go ahead," Cole said. "There's food backstage whenever I want it."

She made sandwiches and cut them into triangles, then handed them off to Glen and Pauley and Tony and put one aside for herself. Then she made four more and passed them to their immediate neighbors. A steady stream of food, drink, and drugs had passed through their hands as they talked, a hip recreation of the loaves and fishes that included a bag of Fritos, a bottle of Pagan Pink Ripple, a paper cup of cream of tomato soup, two joints, some cold French fries, and a quart of warm beer.

The Incredible String Band had taken some heckling, and at the end of one song the guitar player abruptly said, "We have to leave now. I'd like to say goodbye to you and thank you very much. Goodbye."

"Good riddance!" Pauley shouted toward the stage and a few people around them applauded him.

Cole shifted around until he was leaning back on his elbows, his legs stretched out partway into a neighbor's blanket, who looked around at Cole and nodded an okay. Sharon, after cleaning up, ended up on his left, facing him instead of the stage. Glen had turned toward him too, leaving Pauley and Tony symbolically cut off on the far edge of the blanket.

"When I graduated high school," Glen said, "I still thought one hit of marijuana would instantly make you a heroin addict. When *Sergeant Pepper* came out, I thought it was scary. Now look at us." He held both arms straight out. Due to the curvature of the ground, Cole couldn't see anything but other people in all directions. "Everybody smokes dope. Everybody digs the same music. Being here all in one place like this, we can all see that. It's going to change the world."

Cole remembered having the same thought as the helicopter brought him in. The Quirq's lame performance and subsequent demise had cost him that feeling of consensus and put him on the outside looking in. As failure had a way of doing.

"Well," Cole said, not wanting to spoil the mood, "the world is ripe for changing."

In the silence, Sharon said, "I need to use the toilets. Jeff, would you walk over there with me?"

"Sure," Cole said. "I'll take you backstage. They're not as gross."

When they stood up, Pauley said, "Glen, you going to let your sister go off with this pervert guitar player?"

"Shut up, Pauley," Sharon said tiredly.

As they walked away, Pauley shouted, "For God's sake, wear a rubber!"

"Jealous, is he?" Cole asked.

"He thinks because he's Glen's friend and we all grew up together that he's got dibs on me. I try to put up with him for Glen's sake, only sometimes I wish... I don't think he's a good influence on Glen. He got him smoking dope, and now they're both taking LSD too."

"Glen'll be all right."

"Glen's all excited about the way everything's changing. He thinks we're going to end the war and impeach Nixon and legalize drugs and it's going to be one long party after that."

"And you don't?"

"I just want a normal life. I want to meet a nice guy and get married and have a couple of kids. A nice house and a big yard and a dog."

As they approached the backstage fence, Sharon picked up on Cole's anxiety. "Looking for somebody?"

"I, uh, was supposed to meet a friend earlier, and they didn't show up."

"Female friend?" Cole's discomfort answered the question for him. "Don't worry, Jeff. Your secret is safe with me."

While Sharon used the facilities, Cole grabbed a plate of lunch meat and a cold six-pack. The sun had just set as they started back. Darkness settled in and candles began to sparkle on the hillside. Canned Heat played one loud, distorted blues shuffle after another, to Pauley's evident satisfaction, as he periodically cupped his hands around his mouth and shouted, "Boogie!" at the stage.

Cole's usual sunset melancholy was particularly acute. He made a point of drinking from every wine bottle and taking a hit of every joint that came his way. Canned Heat gave way to Mountain, then the rain started to fall again. He ended up huddled under an umbrella with Sharon. He was pretty sure she wanted him to kiss her, an idea that struck Cole as bad in more ways than he could count.

The Grateful Dead came on, then stopped after two songs to completely rewire the stage, which seemed to take forever as various band members babbled into the microphones. They noodled at "Dark Star" for a while, then went into an interminable "Turn on Your Love Light." Cole had begun to nod off. He came to in the middle of Creedence playing "Proud Mary." It was one in the morning and surely, Cole thought, Laramie would be at the tepee.

He stood up and said, "It was great seeing you guys. Maybe I'll come by tomorrow."

"No you won't," Sharon said softly.

They all hugged him except Tony, who was passed out cold. Glen said, "We'll always remember our brush with fame."

"Cut it out," Cole said.

Sharon held him tightly and kissed his cheek and whispered, "I hope you find her."

He made his slow, careful way through the sprawled bodies to the road, then hurried through the woods to the campground. Despite his best efforts, he discovered that he had not adequately prepared himself for the disappointment of finding Laramie's empty sleeping bag. He pulled his boots off and got inside, and, with the smell of their lovemaking in his nose, he fled from unhappiness into sleep.

He woke up each time a new band took the stage, and around four in the morning some acoustic anomaly brought him the sound of Sly Stone exhorting the audience to sing "Higher" with him. By the time the Airplane came on at eight AM, every lump under the tent floor had a matching bruise on his body. He dragged himself onto his feet and watched the Airplane from the top of the hill by the concession stands, two of which had apparently burned down during the night.

He went backstage to find some breakfast and saw Grace sitting at one of the tables. "Great set," he said as he passed.

"Cole?" she said sternly. He turned back. "Cole, you have clearly gone native and lost your mind. You smell even worse than you look. You are going to the hotel, where you will dispose of those clothes and clean yourself. You do have a room there, yes?"

"Yes," Cole said.

"Do you need me to find you a helicopter, or are you capable of doing that on your own?"

"I'll do it," Cole said.

He wandered out to the landing zone and caught a ride. The lobby of the Holiday Inn could have been on another planet— clean, dry, and comparatively quiet, though he could hear the party still going on in the lounge. He went to his room and saw that the others had checked out and the rollaway beds were gone. He took a long, hot shower and lay down for a few minutes to get his strength back.

When he woke up it was two in the afternoon. He dressed in fresh blue jeans, a clean white T-shirt, and a plaid flannel shirt. He'd adopted the uniform in Mountain Lakes because of the

Hardy Boys serials on the Mickey Mouse Club. He cleaned the worst of the mud off his boots and put two pairs of socks on underneath.

The kitchen was still serving breakfast, so Cole had three eggs and hash browns and toast and coffee and juice. The plastic bag in his room that held his filthy clothes was the only evidence that what he'd lived through for the past two days was real. He could easily get a ride into the city and exchange his plane ticket and be on a flight to San Francisco by that evening.

The idea filled him with despair.

Whatever it was that had hold of him, it was more than Laramie, more than the music, more than just another gig, more than mud and cold and bad smells and crowds.

He went to his room, brushed his teeth, and put the toothbrush and travel size toothpaste in his jeans pocket. He packed his suitcase, checked it at the front desk, and told them he was through with the room.

Outside the skies had gone black and the trees at the edge of the parking lot whipped from side to side. He saw a pilot tying down the rotors of his helicopter. "You're not going back to the fair?" Cole asked. He had to shout over the wind.

"Are you crazy?" the pilot said, and pointed at the sky. At that moment lightning flickered nearby, followed immediately by booming thunder and the first drops of rain.

Cole waited out the storm in the lounge. It lasted more than two hours, a relentless, pounding deluge, with curtains of water like tidal waves slamming into the windows of the dining room. At one point a balding guy in a Holiday Inn green staff smock came in and talked to Hendrix, who was holed up in a corner with his entourage. "They may cancel the rest of the fair," the man said, and Cole felt a surge of helpless panic. "They want you to stay put for a while longer while they decide."

"Oh, man," Hendrix said. "God does not love this festival."

By 5:30 the rain had slacked off and the guy in the smock returned. "They're going ahead, but everything's delayed. You're going to come on late. Like really, really late."

"How late?"

"They don't know yet. There's like seven or eight acts still to go before you."

At the desk Cole learned that thousands and thousands of people had left during the rain and that the roads were negotiable again. Shortly after six he caught a ride in a limo with guys from the Butterfield band, none of whom had played on the first two records that Cole owned.

The limo dropped them off at the performers' pavilion. Crew members were once again sweeping water off the stage. Small lakes had formed in every concavity, and everything glistened and shone in the setting sun. The crowd near the stage looked the same, but high on the hillside it had thinned considerably. At the edges, kids had made the most of the situation and were sliding in the mud while bystanders beat out rhythms on cans and bottles. Dozens, maybe hundreds of people had turned completely brown with mud from head to foot.

Below stage right, Cole saw a bearded guy in a straw cowboy hat, white shirt, and vest. Embarrassed, unable to stop himself, he said, "Levon? Levon Helm?"

"That's right."

Cole introduced himself and they shook hands. Levon introduced him to the man next to him, who turned out to be Richard Manuel. Cole registered little more than bad posture and a lot of black curly hair. Cole said, "I saw you guys back in 1965 in Dallas, touring with Dylan."

"Some kind of basketball arena, wasn't it?" Levon said. "That was a good show. Bob always said y'all in Texas were the only ones that understood what he was trying to do."

"It changed my life," Cole said. "I started playing guitar because of you guys."

That flustered Levon as much as it did Cole. "Y'all on tonight?" Levon finally asked.

"We were yesterday morning," Cole said. "We were terrible."

Levon and Manuel both laughed and Manuel said, "I know what *that's* like."

"Amen," Levon said. "It happens to the best of us."

Cole went out the gate and struck off for the free stage area. The roads were full of people leaving and Cole heard them complain in tired voices, "... be so glad to get home...", "... what a fucking disaster...", "... believe I have to be at work in the morning?" Cole wanted to plead with them not to go, not to give up, that it wasn't over yet.

He had nowhere to walk where the ground didn't suck at his boots. The trees were soaked and dripping, and the open areas were strewn with bottles and shoes and bits of paper and plastic wrap and blankets and sleeping bags, all coated in homogenous brown mud.

When he got to the site where the tepee had been, he tried to convince himself that he was in the wrong place. But the circle it had left behind was the only visible grass in a sea of mud, and Cole recognized the stones that had held the campfire.

He had not, he realized, had much hope of finding her. No point now in his last ditch plan to have Chip page her from the stage.

He retraced his steps toward the main stage for what felt like the hundredth time. A drummer began playing rapid cut time over the PA and Chip introduced Country Joe and the Fish. Cole had retreated into numbness, like a man who had gambled away his life savings yet was unable to leave the casino. He was no longer hungry or thirsty, sleepy or angry or anything else. He only wanted the music to keep going, because when it finally stopped he would have nowhere to go.

He sat on the side of the stage through the Fish show, and, after sunset, through more blues from Ten Years After. Levon gave him a thumbs-up as the Band took their places around ten PM. Robbie Robertson's guitar was high in the mix and Cole admired the complexity of his work at the same time that the very idea of guitar playing laid him low, as if The Quirq's failure and Laramie's disappearance were part of the same loss.

Crosby, Stills, Nash and Young finished around four AM. During the lull afterward, Cole slept for a while on his corner of the stage. The Butterfield Blues Band woke him at dawn. His muscles ached from sleeping on the bare wood floor, so he walked out into the audience. A steady exodus through the night had left only a few thousand people to hear Sha Na Na and the opening of Hendrix's set.

Cole found an abandoned camp stool and set it up at the edge of the crowd where he wasn't blocking anyone's view. It was nine in the morning by the time Hendrix came out, dressed in a red scarf, white fringed jacket, blue jeans. He had two conga players, a second guitarist, a bass player Cole didn't know, and Mitch Mitchell from the Experience on drums. He remembered seeing Hendrix in San Antonio with Madelyn and Denise and Alex, only a year and a half ago in calendar time.

Hendrix himself radiated the same melancholy that pulled at Cole. He played a few of the expected hits, some new material, and a couple of slow numbers where his new guitarist sang lead, including Curtis Mayfield's "Gypsy Woman." The new songs lacked the verve and wit of Hendrix's early albums, as if he'd emptied himself in one sustained burst of pyrotechnics.

After an hour and a half, and an extended version of "Voodoo Child," he stepped up to the mike and said, "Thank you again, you can leave if you want to, we're just jamming, that's all, okay? You can leave or you can..." The rest was inaudible as Hendrix turned to his guitar. The jam wrapped up and out of the chaos Hendrix began to play "The Star-Spangled Banner," an unaccompanied, exploding, blood-soaked version straight out of Vietnam and Watts. From there he played a perfunctory "Purple Haze" that ended with Hendrix alone on guitar again for five solid minutes of tortured screams and howls, and Cole saw that Hendrix didn't have any answers either, that he was tired and frustrated and maybe disappointed that the new band hadn't changed things.

The solo guitar rampage ended with a slow, quiet instrumental of such transcendent beauty that Cole found himself, though he'd thought himself past all that, in tears. The set was nearly over, and with it the fair and whatever hope for transcendence and meaning it had held.

The song ended on a haunting A minor seventh. Hendrix said, "Thank you," and walked away. Of course the crowd called him back, and after some indecision he made an uninspired pass at "Hey Joe," his first UK hit from early '67, so long ago now. When he sang, "Where you gonna run to now?" Cole felt like he'd been shoved up against a wall, and when he answered himself, "way down south, way down to Mexico way," Cole thought he might do that too.

When Hendrix was gone, Chip Monck came on the PA one last time, with a plea for people to fill up a garbage bag on the way out. Then he said, "May we wish you anything that the person next to you wishes for you—good wishes, good day, and a good life. Thank you."

After a few more announcements the only sound was the clanking of cans and bottles as people tossed them into bags, and the muted roar of the last few helicopters carrying away the survivors.

Cole stood up. The first step was always the hardest. He got a garbage bag from the stage and found an abandoned pup-tent pole to stir with. He quickly mastered a technique by which he could flip trash into the open bag without having to put his hands in the foul-smelling mud. Though he took his time, all too soon the bag was full. He tied the corners together and left it and began to slowly shuffle toward the road.

"Cole!"

He was sure the voice was a hallucination, so he didn't bother to respond.

"Cole? Cole, wait up."

Finally he turned, and there she was, running toward him over the muddy ground, and then she was in his arms, and he still was not ready to believe she was real.

"Laramie?" he said.

"I went to the tepee and they were packing to go and Sugarfoot said you'd been looking for me and looking for me and I thought you'd gone and I was so sorry I ran away and I—"

"Shhhh," Cole said. He felt the heat of her tears on his neck. "It's okay now. Everything's okay now."

PART TWO

1971

COMMENCEMENT FELL on June 13, a cool, sunny Sunday. Madelyn's parents had flown in from Dallas and brought Julia along. They were staying at the Creekside Inn on the other side of campus from Madelyn's apartment; they would pick her up for breakfast in a matter of minutes. She had her cap and gown in a neat pile next to the door, and she waited on the balcony with a cup of black coffee, trying to find a celebratory mood.

Most days she was fine. Between schoolwork and the gallery her life was full; she'd made new friends who'd never met or even heard of Cole. For special occasions, like their anniversary, her birthday, and Christmas, she protected herself with vigilance and scheduled activity. The unexpected was what invariably tripped her up, like today's utterly unreasonable fear that he might show up to see her graduate.

Nearly two years had passed since Lenny came back from Woodstock, exhausted and forlorn, dragging Cole's equipment behind him. Madelyn, who'd finished her last final for the summer session the day before, had been celebrating by rereading *East of Eden* in her bathrobe on the couch. Lenny told her that the festival had been a disaster, their performance a shambles, that it was all Lenny's fault and that he'd broken up the band. She asked about Cole and Lenny grudgingly admitted that he'd taken up with some groupie, an act for which Madelyn could hardly blame him. What she wasn't prepared for was Lenny swearing to her that it was the first time, that Cole, despite Madelyn's refusal to believe it, had been faithful to her until then.

Cole's subsequent failure to return had brought her months of turmoil. She had a recurring vision of his undiscovered corpse rotting in the Mexican jungle, and on some days she hoped it was true; he deserved it for not having the decency to at least send her a postcard. On other days she tortured herself with the idea that she could have prevented his disappearance, that against all logic and common sense she could have kept the marriage together;

after all, Cole had clearly not given up on it, not until she drove him away.

In time she chose to see the breakup as inevitable. Cole's reaction to it had been his own decision. She only hoped that he hadn't killed himself, and that he was all right, wherever he was.

Having learned that there was no common-law divorce for a common-law marriage, she made a serious and expensive effort to locate him over the course of a year, mostly to make sure he hadn't ended up in a hospital somewhere. As part of that effort, she had forced herself to sit through the newly released *Woodstock* movie in March of 1970, straining her eyes for a glimpse of Cole that never came. Finally, on August 18, 1970, she had boxed up Cole's belongings, including his guitars and amplifier, and shipped them to Alex in Austin, who'd agreed to store them in the basement of the Castle. Then she'd taken an Affidavit of Diligent Search to a judge and filed for Divorce by Publication. Six months after Cole's deadline to respond to the published summonses, she was granted a Default Dissolution of Marriage. That had been two and a half months ago, on April 1, a Thursday, a day she had spent waiting for someone to leap up and cry, "April Fool."

In the meantime, her life had gone on. She'd made straight As every semester, and would graduate with Distinction, the Stanford version of cum laude. She had never accepted Greg Baxter's advances, but she had accepted others, with pleasure. Experimentation was the fashion, all over the world, and despite waking up alone some nights and missing Cole profoundly, she was grateful for her freedom. She'd found that on the whole she preferred clarity of thought to intoxication, though she was not averse to a joint or a glass of wine when appropriate, as it would certainly be tonight.

Her doorbell rang and her cat, Egon, bolted for the bedroom, claws skittering on the hardwood. She stood up, carefully assembled an approximation of a smile, and went to answer it.

THE MAIN COMMENCEMENT ceremony was in Stanford Stadium, to be followed by endless diploma ceremonies. The speaker was

Eric Sevareid, who did the two-minute editorial segments on the *CBS Evening News*. His speech was less inspiring than alarming, as he talked about unrest, dissent, repression, and the rest of "America's present ills, so many of which are obvious to every one of you." He ended by extolling middle-class virtues and wishing them luck.

The effect on Madelyn was both powerful and, she was sure, unintended. She hadn't realized things were so dire. Admittedly, Stanford was an island of privileged calm, but she was aware of the marches and strikes at UC Berkeley and SF State. On those few occasions when she had time to watch TV, scenes of mayhem in Vietnam were unavoidable. Nixon was a thug; his hatchet man Agnew, with his corny alliterations and stunt vocabulary, beneath contempt. Still and all, these were merely friction points as the world moved into the new frontier that Kennedy had promised. Civil rights, Medicare, man on the moon, all checked off, with an end to the war and the passage of the ERA now seeming inevitable. As inevitable as her own passage into grad school, and after that into her career with Kindred's gallery.

When she stepped up to receive her diploma, she thought she heard yelling in the stands, which she dismissed as coincidence. But no; the truth was revealed when she met her parents outside the stadium and two familiar figures came shouting and capering toward her.

"Dear God," she said. "Denise? Alex?"

Alex got there first and wrapped her up in a hug that lifted her out of her shoes. Denise piled on from behind, both of them yelling, "Surprise!"

Eventually breath was recovered, shoes reattached, Denise introduced. Denise looked the same except for bell-bottoms, peasant blouse, and lots of beads and bracelets. Alex could have passed for a Chicano revolutionary in jeans, chambray work shirt, and black curly hair to his shoulders. He'd gone from skinny to well-built, and Julia's face registered the impression he'd made.

They all crammed into her parents' rent-a-car and went for drinks, during which only the most superficial news was available for discussion. Alex and Denise had graduated a month earlier.

Denise had gone home to Denton, where she planned to get a Teacher's Certificate at North Texas State in the fall and "do something with disadvantaged kids or something."

Alex remained in the house in Austin for the moment. Even as she had to fight off her own memories of the room she'd shared there with Cole, she understood that this was not the place or time for Alex to talk about his future.

Her parents had heard a good deal about Alex and Denise during Madelyn's freshman year and little since, so they had to be caught up with three years' worth of events that Madelyn knew about from their letters and phone calls. When they got to Alex's senior thesis, however, dealing with the Situationist International and the May 1968 insurrections in Paris, her father paid unequivocal attention.

"It was all because of Madelyn," Alex said. "One of her artists told her to read *Society of the Spectacle*. This was three years ago, and when she told me about it, I flipped. Only it wasn't in English yet. So I switched from Russian to French so I could learn to read it."

«Avez-vous lu Vaneigem?» her father asked. «*Traité de savoir-vivre à l'usage des jeunes générations?*»

«Bien sûr,» Alex said. «Bien que ça n'existe toujours pas en anglais.»

Denise turned to Madelyn and launched a separate conversation. "Are you still going through with it? All the way to PhD and then to work for this guy, what's his name…"

"Kindred," Madelyn said. She wanted to hear what Alex was saying to her father, but it was hopeless. She reassured Denise that yes, it was what she wanted, art and the occasional class in literature, that in the fall she would start her Teaching Assistantship, and within a year be teaching her own classes.

For her part, Denise had been seduced by the times. She was a work in progress, she said, and before she could change the world she had to perfect herself. "I don't want some meaningless office job. I don't want to be a housewife. But what am I good for?"

"You can translate Russian."

"Not in Denton, Texas, I can't! Maybe if I moved to New York. Or Moscow."

"Maybe you should," Madelyn said.

"Sure I will!" she said, and put her head back and laughed, the way she did when she'd given up on herself.

Her father ordered dinner in stages, an hour's worth of hors d'oeuvres followed by leisurely entrees, so that it was nine PM by the time they finished dessert and a bottle of cheap champagne. "It's eleven in Texas," her father said. "We should turn in."

"You'll come over to my place," Madelyn said to Alex and Denise, and her father agreed to drop the three of them at Alex's own rental car.

"Can I come too?" Julia said. "Alex can bring me home after."

"Julia!" her mother said. "You can't just invite yourself—"

"It's fine, Mrs. Brooks," Alex said. "I can bring her back."

Madelyn kicked him sharply under the table and he pretended not to notice, though with her pointed shoes it must have hurt. Then he fought with her father over the check, her father's pride easily winning out over the Montoya family money. As they all stood up, her father hugged her and said, "I'm so proud of you."

"I know," Madelyn said. "I know you are."

FOR ALEX, it was like he'd spent his life in purgatory, standing motionless in a crowd of millions, shifting his weight from one leg to the other, waiting. Then a voice said, "Alex? Alex Montoya?" and a path opened up, and at the end of it was Guy Debord, who put one arm around his shoulders and talked to him earnestly about the «degradation of *being* into *having*,» followed by the sliding of «*having* into *appearing*.» We've become isolated and alienated, Debord said. We've given up our authentic lives to watch representations and buy commodities we don't need.

Alex saw his life, and his father's entire world, in everything Debord said. The more you studied the revolution that the Situationists had helped to inspire, the more moving it became. «Under the paving stones, the beach,» they wrote on the walls of Paris, a slogan that took on new poignancy when you understood that the sand they were talking about was exposed when they dug up cobblestones to hurl at the police.

In the fall of 1969, Alex's junior year, as he took his first French class and struggled through *La Société du spectacle*, the Revolution began to seriously take hold on the UT campus. Alex's connection was a guy named James Landon, who had taken over Cole's room in the Castle. Landon had been to the national SDS convention in Chicago, where the organization shattered into splinter groups: Weathermen, the Revolutionary Youth Movement, the Progressive Labor Party, the Worker Student Alliance, Yippies, Motherfuckers, and more. He'd returned full of activist fervor, determined to prove the former SDS leaders wrong when they said that students were not a revolutionary force in the US.

Landon's arch-enemy was Frank Erwin, Chairman of the UT Board of Regents, the most powerful man in the UT system, and a right-wing asshole who had become famous for threatening mass expulsions and saying, "We don't need 27,000 students at this university." In October, a week after the biggest fall mobilization ever against the war, Erwin sent bulldozers to take down a stand of old-growth trees near Waller Creek on campus. Landon and other protesters climbed the trees to save them, and Erwin responded by calling in the city cops to pull the students down, beat them, and arrest them. As the bulldozing proceeded, Erwin, with hardhat and bullhorn, applauded each tree that fell.

Alex got drawn in when Landon called him after his Waller Creek arrest and Alex drove downtown to bail him out. They got back in time for a demonstration on the Main Mall where hundreds of students had dragged limbs from the creek to block the steps to the main Tower entrance. It was Alex's first protest and he was surprised at how much he got off on the cocktail of nerves, righteous anger, and community.

Landon's temper had not begun to cool down when the Student Union Board voted, in the first week of November, to ban non-students from the Union's Chuckwagon Café. The move was clearly aimed at the political groups who used the café for meetings, and a confrontation broke out when the police came in and hauled away a runaway girl, with one of the cops waving a gun.

A mix of enraged students and street people threw rocks and bottles at the squad car as it drove away.

"Erwin wanted a riot," Landon said. "He deliberately provoked it so he could take back the Union." He talked Alex into coming to the protest the next Monday at noon.

It started with speeches on the West Mall outside the Union, then quickly escalated into an occupation of the Chuckwagon, as hundreds of students barged in without showing IDs. The University called the city cops, who surrounded the building and gave the protesters until four PM to exit peacefully.

Alex had gotten separated from Landon and ended up sitting on the floor next to a table full of radicals. In chairs on either side of him were a light-skinned black man with a limp afro and a poised white woman in heavy black-framed glasses and hair pulled back in a bun. He was ashamed to admit to either one of them that he wanted to get out before the deadline, and so he stayed.

Scouts returned from the outside with increasingly ominous reports. Dozens of cops were lined up in full riot gear, wearing helmets with Plexiglass visors and gas masks, armed with Mace and teargas and billy clubs. Rows of regular uniformed cops massed behind them. An ominously unmarked panel truck sat at the curb ready to haul away bodies.

Alex tried to reassure himself that things wouldn't turn violent. The place was full of students, and the old hands among the leadership had gone over the passive resistance tactics they'd used in their civil rights days. Still he found himself paralyzed with fear.

At 4:00 the demonstrators who'd chosen not to get arrested started for the doors. Alex couldn't see what happened next. He heard an eruption of voices, screaming and cursing, and the sounds of scuffling in the hall. He stood up, along with the others at the table, and was trapped by the crush of bodies around him. He heard the glass doors of the Chuckwagon shatter and then he heard shots. A few agonizing seconds later, pale gray smoke began to fill the room.

The woman next to him said, "Teargas. Cover up." She got a bandana out of her bag, poured a glass of water on it, and tied it over the bottom of her face like a Western outlaw. Alex did what he saw some of the others doing and pulled his T-shirt up over his mouth and nose.

The riot cops were inside the café now and kids were panicking, throwing chairs and turning over tables. Alex was immobilized by the mob as the cops drove them away from the doors. He smelled something bitter at the same moment that his eyes puffed up and began to water and snot began running from his nose. He couldn't breathe. At the same time he was afraid to suck more gas into his lungs. His bare arms, the exposed skin of his face, and the newly revealed skin of his stomach burned. He had lost all orientation and let himself be carried along as the crowd surged through the kitchen. The floor underfoot was slippery with tears and mucus, drool and vomit, and as they stumbled into the cold outside air, Alex saw people all around him on their hands and knees, throwing up.

He was still half-blind from the gas, coughing though his throat felt shredded. Common sense kept him from rubbing his eyes with his hands, which, like all of his exposed skin, felt scorched. He staggered to a tree and leaned against it until his breath came somewhat normally and his vision mostly cleared.

In front of the Union, protesters had gone on the attack. Regular uniformed cops tried to push the bystanders aside while riot cops dragged struggling kids toward the van on Guadalupe Street. A second line of riot cops stood with their arms folded, doing nothing as enraged students screamed at them and threw anything they could find—rocks, bottles, fruit, fallen tree branches. Knots of protesters struggled with the first wave of cops, pulling victims free and hustling them away. The air was full of angry voices, and Alex heard a woman's voice nearby cry out, "Fuck you, you fucking pig!" followed by a long scream. Alex smelled the hot pepper odor of Mace, saw a riot cop knock a kid to the sidewalk with his club, saw another cop take a blow to the helmet from a thrown Coke bottle and shrug it off. Some of the students had moved into the street, trying to slash the tires of the van.

A crazed anger boiled up inside him, and he kept it down only by imagining himself in a wheelchair, brain-damaged and paralyzed from a nightstick beating. He stayed away from the front lines, part of him amazed and terrified by what he saw, part of him so consumed by rage that he wanted the riot to spread until the entire city, the entire unjust country, was torched to the ground.

The cops finally managed to get a few token prisoners into the van, and they retreated down Guadalupe, sirens blaring, as the mob ran after them, grabbing at door handles, yelling, throwing bottles and rocks.

Alex found a patch of grass to sit on. He was still unable to completely get his breath, and when he coughed it tore at his ravaged throat. A long-haired guy with a full beard knelt beside him at some point, touched him on the shoulder, and asked if he was okay. Alex nodded. Eventually he made his way to his car and drove to the Castle.

Landon was already there, and helped him wash his eyes with saline solution. Landon was jazzed, convinced the Revolution was underway. Alex took a lukewarm shower—his teargassed skin couldn't bear the touch of hot water—and it was only then that he connected what he'd just been through to the Paris riots of the year before. It gave him a surge of excitement and a new, romantic image of himself: Jean-Paul Montoya, Situationist philosopher and revolutionary.

A rally the next day drew two thousand people, Alex among them, to demand the release of the prisoners and the prohibition of city police on campus. The protest was in vain. By the end of the week, the Student Association and the students themselves had sold them out, voting to ban non-students from not only the Chuckwagon but from the entire Union building.

Alex was bitter and Landon unfazed. Revolution was a process, Landon said, and loaned him Lenin's *What Is to Be Done*.

Throughout the winter and spring the protests came faster and faster. Alex was at most of them, prepared for teargas with long sleeves and a plastic sandwich bag that held a bandana soaked in lemon juice. The rallies protested the war, the travesties at the Chicago Seven conspiracy trial, the felony indictments of 22 Chuckwagon protesters. In April, the radical Ying-Yang Conspiracy candidate was elected president of the Student Association. Then, on May 1, 1970, in complete contempt of the growing opposition to the war, despite a year of gradual troop withdrawals and so-called "Vietnamization," Nixon ordered US soldiers into Cambodia.

Landon was ecstatic, saying, "This is going to do it. The whole country is coming down." Over the weekend he went out to pay phones and used bogus credit card numbers to coordinate with activists on other campuses, and on Monday, May 4, the demonstrations began.

Alex didn't hear the news from Kent State until that night, the four unarmed students shot dead by the Ohio National Guard. "It's a declaration of war," Landon said with a grim smile. "And if that's what they want..."

Nixon's reaction was blunt. "When dissent turns to violence," he said, "it invites tragedy," blaming the protesters and promising more bloodshed to come. Alex, in fury and disbelief, understood that Nixon had just personally threatened to kill him.

With eight thousand others he was on the Main Mall the next day at noon, ready for anything. The rally organizers began by asking the crowd to endorse a set of demands that Landon had helped draft over the weekend. The first demand was that the university stop feeding the war machine with their ROTC program and "defense" research. Other demands included punishment for the killers at Kent State, justice for Bobby Seale and the Black Panthers, and an end to repression in Austin, all of which the audience approved by acclamation.

The rally turned into a march and Alex let himself be swept up in it, shouting until his voice was gone. Any semblance of a plan was abandoned and the mob, still numbering in the thousands, paraded down the middle of Guadalupe Street, headed for the State Capitol. They evaded police attempts to stop them until they got to the capitol grounds, where a full complement of police in riot gear tried to turn them back. More teargas was fired, some of it inside the Capitol building. Marchers pulled off their shirts and wet them in the sprinklers on the lawn, tying them over their mouths and noses and attacking the cops with their fists. Even with his lemon-soaked bandana, Alex was blinded by the gas and was wildly flailing his arms when friendly hands took hold of him and guided him back toward campus.

That night Alex lay in bed and shook.

The more violently the police tried to crush them, the harder the students fought back, and the more police came out to suppress them. It was Vietnam come home, escalation leading to more violence, more violence leading to more escalation. In a moment of clarity he saw how his own helplessness and fear was expressing itself as anger and defiance, feeding the cycle, and how the same thing was true for the other side, adults terrified that their children had become monsters, seduced by communism and drugs into tearing down everything America represented.

He'd been reading about the Paris Commune of 1871, where for over two months the city became an independent socialist workers' state, only to be violently overrun by the regular French Army during "La Semaine sanglante," the bloody week of May 21. How strong would the US students have to be to stand up to the local cops and the Army and the National Guard? How many more would die?

Imagining defeat was easy, imagining winning, for whatever meaning you gave the word, was vastly more difficult. Worker-owned businesses, communal farming, mandatory work assignments, like in Cuba? Corrupt party officials and long lines for everything, like in the Soviet Union? Where was the model for what they were trying to build?

He couldn't see the way forward, couldn't bear to retreat. He curled up and hugged his knees and waited for dawn.

After two days of recruiting and rallies and votes, with classes cancelled and 25,000 people mobilized, with rumors flying of National Guard intervention and police armed with shotguns, the Friday demonstration was an anticlimax. At the last possible moment, as protesters were already on the street, law students convinced the city to let them march. Official approval robbed the day of its fury. Marchers stayed on the sidewalk and police stood by in silence. Red flags were waved, coffins were carried, signs held high. NAPALM: BETTER KILLING THROUGH CHEMISTRY. NO MORE BOYS IN BOXES. They chanted, "One, two, three, four, we don't want your fucking war!" and "Hey, hey, USA, how many kids did you kill today?" The 13-block-long column of students and faculty and sympathetic locals wound harmlessly through downtown and back to campus, where a party ensued. Wine and dope and guitars passed from hand to hand. Couples retreated to empty classrooms to make love, not war.

Alex climbed a tree on the South Mall and watched the dancing and listened to the excited voices and asked himself what, exactly, they'd gained. The university had not agreed to any of their demands. The successful march had defused the mounting tension. The self-congratulation marked, he thought, the end of something that had barely gotten off the ground.

The next Tuesday, following Landon's instructions, he went to a barber shop and got his hair cut short, put on a white shirt and tie, and roamed downtown with a clipboard and a pocket full of pens, trying to get signatures on a petition to end the war. The air was muggy, the sun relentless. At one point a police car followed him for thirty minutes, trying to rattle him. It worked. He had started the day with a warm smile, asking, "Would you care to sign a petition for peace?" After hundreds of refusals he was simply asking, "Peace?" and still getting "no" for an answer. In the early afternoon, a convertible pulled up with four college-age boys in it. The one in the front passenger seat asked to sign. When Alex handed over the clipboard, with the paltry 27 signatures that represented his entire day's work, they drove away with it, laughing and giving him the finger.

That night he got very drunk and the next day he went back to class.

In Paris, at the end of May of 1968, with millions of workers on strike and thousands of students celebrating in the streets, de Gaulle dissolved the National Assembly and called for new elections in June. It sounded like victory and the strikers returned to work. De Gaulle's party won a landslide victory and the revolution was over.

Landon was graduating and headed for the Salinas Valley in California to help Cesar Chavez's United Farm Workers in their struggle against the Teamsters. As a farewell present, he gave Alex a copy of Marx's *Capital*. On the flyleaf he wrote, "The true revolutionary is never discouraged and never satisfied. He is always vigilant for the moment of opportunity." As he drove away in his battered Ford Falcon, he saluted Alex with a clenched fist held high out the car window.

The week after finals, his father drove down alone and Alex put him up in Cole's newly empty room. They went to the Hoffbrau for dinner, and Alex didn't have to wait long for the question he'd been dreading.

"Tell me," his father said, "what happened to your grades."

He'd managed an A in French, the rest Bs and Cs. Every semester before, all the way back through high school, he'd made As with only the occasional B. His father's voice held more concern than accusation, and Alex was more embarrassed than militant. "It won't happen again," he said.

"Was it a girl?" his father asked. "Or..."

Alex supposed that drugs were at the top of his father's list of suspects. "Politics," Alex said. "I was demonstrating against the war."

His father nodded. They both had Carta Blanca longnecks, and Alex watched the sweat on his father's bottle break and run down the label. "Like the kids at Kent State."

"And because of them."

"The war is wrong," his father said. "We've got no business in Vietnam. And I don't want you to end up over there."

"But...?"

His father looked over Alex's shoulder, the way he did when he was about to say something he wasn't proud of. "But your job right now is to get a diploma. I'm naturally going to worry about anything that endangers that."

"I thought my job was to learn. I've learned more in the last nine months than in the rest of my life put together."

"Did you learn anything you can use in the real world?"

For his father, the only real world was business. Alex longed to say that business meant nothing to him. All of his confrontations with police in riot gear had not taught him how to say those words to his father, whom he loved.

That summer he was back at the 7-Up plant, this time helping with the books and making bank runs, including cashing checks for the men without bank accounts, some of whom were undocumented workers from Latin America. When he could, he talked to them, in Spanish where appropriate, about their working conditions and made some suggestions about what a union might do to help.

July 3 was a Friday, a paid holiday for the clerical staff. Late Thursday afternoon, the plant manager, a graying ex-football player that everyone called Bud, walked up to Alex's desk and said, "My office. Now."

Alex followed him, hating his automatic fear response. Bud sat behind his cluttered desk and said, "Close the door."

As soon as the door shut, Bud said, "I owe your father a lot, which is why you're not out on your ass right now. Texas is a right-to-work state, which, if you don't know, means nobody has to put up with the extortion, corruption, bullying, and general bullshit that goes on up north because of gangster unions. There's not going to be a union in my shop, and that's not just because I want it that way, it's because the employees don't want to be pushed around by a lot of fat-ass parasites."

Alex was about to politely dispute that characterization when Bud said, "I don't want to hear a word out of you. There will be no more union talk in this building, is that clear? You can nod your head and come back on Monday, or you can shake your head or open your mouth and clean out your desk. Your call."

Alex was so infuriated that his eyes wouldn't focus. He clenched his teeth and swallowed and forced his head to move stiffly up and down.

"You jackass college kids read a few books and think you're qualified to tell people how to run their business, people who've spent their entire lives doing real work and sweating decisions with real consequences. And you know what? After a few years down here in the trenches, most of you come to realize we weren't so goddamn stupid after all."

He paused to see if Alex wanted to defy him. Alex doubted he could relax his jaw to talk if he had to.

"Go home," Bud said. "Come in on Monday ready to work and I won't say anything to your father about this. He's a good man and deserves better than this from you."

Alex stood in silence and Bud said, "That's all. Get out of here. Leave the door open when you go."

In the fall, Frank Erwin fired a number of UT administrators, apparently in retaliation for the chaos on campus in May. Students protested, and an anti-war march was called for Halloween that drew a few thousand supporters.

Alex stayed home, reading in Vaneigem's *Traité de savoir-vivre* how Power turned everything into commodities, which were dead things, and that life as a commodity was no more than mere survival, «to the point that the forces of death threaten to overwhelm human survival itself. Unless, of course, the passion for destruction is replaced by the passion for life.»

For Vaneigem the antidote was art, poetry, and sex. Poetry, he said, came from «the impulse to change the world to meet the demands of radical subjectivity,» which he defined as «an indomitable will to create a passionate life.» Poetry, he said, «is the act that engenders new realities, the consummation of radical theory, the revolutionary act par excellence.»

Alex was not sure that Vaneigem was not copping out, though the students in Paris in '68, inspired by Vaneigem, had turned their revolution into art, maintaining a sense of humor that Alex had lost from the get-go.

Marx was harder. Though his edition of *Capital Volume 1* was ostensibly in English, Alex could rarely manage more than a page or two without falling asleep. Fortunately he found plenty of secondary sources for his quotes for Marx.

He titled his thesis *The Descent of Philosophy, the Philosophy of Dissent*, playing on the kind of turnarounds that peppered Vaneigem's book. His advisor, Dr. Sobel from the French department, had been one of the striking professors that spring. She was thirty, with a Parisian father and a mother from Barcelona. She had golden skin and short hair dyed bright orange. She dressed in men's clothes, either big sweaters or oversize jackets and neckties. She was fluent in French, Spanish, and English, and had a street knowledge of Arabic and Russian. She had a lilt to her voice that was not quite an accent. From their first meeting, Alex was powerfully attracted, and equally intimidated by her age and worldliness. He also had no idea whether she was even into men.

The deeper Alex got into the thesis, the more Sobel's enthusiasm grew. At a meeting in late October, she urged him to go on to graduate school in history, spend a semester in France doing interviews, and turn it into a book. She had a way of looking at him with a fixed intensity that made him want to believe her interest was more than intellectual.

"Maybe we should talk about it over dinner," he said, and only after the words were out and she'd stared at him with a knowing smile did he consider the damage you could do to your academic career if you pissed off your thesis advisor.

She let him sweat for a while, then said, "You know the GM Steakhouse, downtown?"

It was a blue-collar joint on Congress Avenue. "Yes."

"You have a way to get there? A car or something?"

"Yes."

"I like to eat early. Meet me there at 6:30."

"Okay."

She picked up her pen and looked at an open folder on her desk. "See you then."

She was 15 minutes late. Once he saw her, Alex was disinclined to complain. She wore high heels, tight jeans, a tight black turtleneck with no bra, and a tight navy-blue blazer. He stood up as she got to the table, which made her laugh. She told him to call her Vivienne as long as they were not on campus.

They both ordered the $2.07 sirloin with fries and salad. As they ate, they gave each other the short versions of their life stories. Hers included several years in Algeria and a couple of stepfathers. When Alex mentioned his bands, she said, "Ah. This gave you a lot of women, I think. This is where you get your confidence."

"I don't feel very confident at the moment," Alex said.

"Nor should you. As it happens, I don't fuck my students, and I like older men anyway." She popped the last bite of meat in her mouth and looked up at him through her lashes. "Do I shock you?"

"No," Alex lied. He forced himself to eat a blood-soaked French fry. "I guess I'm wondering what we're doing here. And... why you're dressed like that."

"First, this is the way I dress when I'm not at work. And what we're doing here is that I am toying with you."

"I don't get it."

"Of course you don't. You are a man, or nearly one. You have a great sense of entitlement. You are not to be toyed with. Especially by a woman that you desire. Your desire is a categorical imperative right out of Kant."

Vivienne was greatly amused. Alex wondered if he would jeopardize his degree by walking out.

"Let me ask you a question," Vivienne said. "Do you have any women friends? By that I mean, women that you spend time with but haven't had sex with and are not trying to have sex with?"

"I don't understand. If I like a woman, and enjoy being with her, and she's attractive, and attracted to me, why would I not want to have sex with her?"

"I have a gift for you," Vivienne said. She burrowed into her purse and came up with a paperback of Simone de Beauvoir's *The Second Sex*, an English translation with a sexy naked blonde on the cover. Alex knew the name because she was Sartre's mistress. Vivienne pushed it toward him. "It's a lousy translation, and it's abridged, though it says it isn't, and that cover... but it's what there is in English. If you try to read it in French it will take you a year and I want you to read it now, right away."

He felt petulant, like Vivienne had pulled a bait-and-switch on him. He reluctantly picked up the book and flipped through it.

"You're a brilliant student," she said. "You have great insight and great compassion. But your insight and your compassion are, what is the word?" She cupped her hands to the sides of her head. "Blinkered. Reading this book will help your thesis. And it will make you a better person."

Alex started the book that night in anger. His intent to skim it as quickly as possible was thwarted by the dense and circuitous prose. The book had been published in 1949 and much of what Beauvoir had to say was now old hat. She overreached herself on some points and belabored others. He quibbled and quarreled with her all the way through the book, even as he recognized the connections to Debord and Vaneigem and saw how women themselves had been commodified. In the end he found himself changed, if for no other reason than for having spent so much time in the head of a brilliant, uncompromising human being who was so proudly female. The feeling was intimate, even sexy. Alex spent a couple of hours in the library looking at photos, reading about her affair with Nelson Algren. It would be a trip, he thought, to stay up late in cafés with her, drinking and arguing. He didn't think that he wanted to be her lover.

When he told all that to Vivienne, she said, "We are very lucky, you and I, because for us the act of reading can be revolutionary. It can change who we are. My wish for you is that you never lose that ability."

That same fall of 1970 he took his first film class, on the French Nouvelle Vague. His initial motivation had been to see Truffaut's *Baisers volés*, which included scenes shot during the '68 riots. The class opened with Goddard's *À bout de souffle*, and Alex loved the combination of trivial, realistic dialog with heavy-handed portentousness, the relentlessly long takes, followed by weird jump cuts, Belmundo's rubber-faced charisma and Seberg's androgynous sexiness and American-accented French. Best of all was the voice in his head that said, "*I* can do this."

He was able to add the Intro course for the Radio-TV-Film program to his fall load, and, with Vivienne pulling a few strings, that allowed him to get into Film 1 in the spring. There he put together a series of still photos with an audio track, like *La Jetée*, and then an actual short Super 8 film.

It all added up to a single thing in his head, the New Wave films and the Situationists and the French protesters and the teargas in Austin in the wake of Kent State, and even after he turned in his thesis he felt like he wasn't finished.

The Saturday before the last week of classes had arrived. His undergraduate career was all but over. Lonely, horny, thinking of Vivienne, he found himself in danger of drowning in regret. He'd only had a couple of chance encounters with Denise since he switched to French from Russian, momentary, but friendly enough. He dialed the last number he had for her and was surprised to find her home. "It's Alex," he said. "Want to get a pizza or something?"

"What is this, a desperate bid for easy sex after striking out everywhere else?"

Alex thought it over. "I think what I want is to apologize."

"Interesting," Denise said. "Pick me up in half an hour."

Under the distinctly unromantic fluorescent lights of Mr. Gatti's, Alex undertook his first self-criticism session. He told Denise that he'd been callous and selfish, that even though he had genuinely cared for her, he had nonetheless taken advantage of her and disregarded her own feelings.

Denise didn't answer right away. She looked out the front window, then looked down at her hands. "Well. Since you brought it up. I was in love with you pretty much from the start. But I was smart enough to see that you were too self-centered and too judgmental to reciprocate. So I kept it to myself and eventually it went away."

"I'm sorry," Alex said. This was proving to be even less fun than he'd imagined. Struggle sessions, he remembered, were used in Mao's China as torture. He let Denise talk, didn't interrupt when she began to repeat herself, and didn't try to justify himself, just tried to understand what it was he was apologizing for. Neither of them, he thought, was getting a lot of relief from the conversation, yet when it finally ran out of gas, Denise put her hand on top of his. "Thanks. I appreciate that you did this."

On the drive to her dorm, Denise brought up Tupelo Joe. "You know he's home, right?"

"No," Alex said. "Is he okay?"

"As far as I can tell. I hear from his mother every once in a while, on the sly. He still won't talk to me. I sent him a couple of letters and they came back refused."

"I was so sure he was going to get himself blown up."

"Tell me about it."

"Maybe," Alex said, "if I drove down there. He wouldn't refuse to see me if I was on his doorstep."

"From what his mother says, I think he would."

Alex brought her up to date on Cole and Madelyn, and by that time they were parked on the street in front of her dorm. "She doesn't graduate till June," he said, without thinking it through in advance. "Why don't we go out there for it? My treat."

"Separate hotel rooms?" Denise asked.

"Whatever terms you're comfortable with," Alex said, his throat tightening. "I'm still not in love with you. But I'm not going to pretend I don't want you, either."

"And I'm still over you. But we actually talked tonight, and honestly, that's left me a little hot and bothered. I don't want to do anything tonight, because I don't want to wake up and question your motives for calling me. But yes, I would love to see Madelyn, and I imagine two rooms would be a needless expense."

She got out of the car and blew him a kiss. "I'll call you."

MADELYN GOT EVERYONE settled and put out glasses and a couple of half-finished bottles of wine. They'd no sooner drunk a toast to old friends than Julia shocked her by pulling out a pair of joints and a book of matches. Without asking, she lit one and passed it to Alex, whom she'd somehow ended up next to on the couch. Alex took a long hit and then passed it to Denise, sitting cross-legged on the shag carpet.

Madelyn, reluctant to speak frankly in front of Julia, decided that Alex was the one who had invited her and so it was on his head. "Straight up this time," she said. "What happens to you now? You said you were, quote, accepted into the MBA program at UT, endquote, which is not the same as 'I'm going to get an MBA.'"

Alex laughed. "Smart, aren't you?"

"No," Madelyn said, "but I've developed a pretty good ear for bullshit."

"Okay, the truth is I have also been accepted into a fast-track Bachelor of Science program in RTF, which is Radio-TV-Film for those of you who are not at UT. Since I've got all my university requirements already, I'll finish in two years. Madelyn, your mouth is open."

"I'm remembering the three of us walking out of *Blow-Up* and you saying the only thing good about it was the Yardbirds." Neither Alex nor Denise, she noted with gratitude, saw the need to remind her that there had been four of them.

"I still basically think that," Alex said. "Antonioni's early stuff is okay, I guess. *Blow-Up* is like a Hollywood blockbuster compared to what I'm into."

"What does your father think of all this?" Madelyn asked.

"Yeah, well," Alex said. "That's the problem, isn't it? I haven't told him yet."

"Oh lord," Madelyn said.

"Exactly. This is not a good time to drop any bombshells on him, either. Jimmy's having to go to summer school because of bad grades—due to 'attitude problems,' apparently. And Susan's getting divorced."

"You're kidding. I thought she was seriously Catholic."

"More or less. But Jesse got heavy into cocaine up in Oke City, and after he went through all of their money he started dealing, and one night Susan woke up and found him in the living room on the tail end of a three-day binge, cleaning his .45 service automatic. She waited until he crashed and took a cab to the airport and flew home. She's been living there for the last month."

Madelyn shook her head. "Your poor father."

"It's not what he had in mind," Alex said, "for any of us. But it's not like I haven't been trying to tell him my whole life that I don't want to be J. Paul Getty. And now with this film thing, I've found what I really want to do."

Julia fired up the second joint and passed it around. "I'm in Broadcast/Film too," she said. "I'm studying acting at SMU."

As usual, Julia displayed prodigious amounts of cleavage, though she was leaner in the face than she'd been at Christmas, older than her years, a little hard.

"Cool," Alex said politely. "That's a good school."

Madelyn went to the kitchen to see what she could scare up for snacks. She had leftovers from an opening a few days before—

brie, grapes, some fancy Swiss crackers. As she put it on plates, Denise came in to help.

"What's with you and Alex?" Madelyn asked in a whisper. "Are you two an item again?"

"Definitely not an item. A matter of convenience. After this trip, who knows when we'll see each other again?"

"Just be careful, okay?"

"Don't worry. I can handle it."

Madelyn nodded, unconvinced.

"What about you?" Denise said. "Any affairs of the heart?"

Madelyn shrugged. "Matters of convenience for me too. And not a lot of them. Most of my social life is gallery parties, and the straight guys are all off limits. They're either our artists or somebody else's artists, or they're critics or patrons, and despite the fact that other people do it, I refuse to be gossiped about or accused of conflict of interest."

"This sounds much too serious."

Madelyn sighed. "I never was big on fun."

She brought out more wine, also left over from the opening, all of it quality stock from a Kindred family winery in Napa Valley. Before Madelyn quite realized what was happening, the dope had subverted her resistance to the wine, and then she was too drunk to want to stop drinking.

They'd successfully walked a high wire over the past all night, and now alcohol threatened their balance. Julia inadvertently destabilized the conversation when she said, "Wow, I'm pretty drunk. Though this is nothing like the punch I had one night at this frat party? One glass and all kinds of terrible things were happening to me."

Madelyn, desperate to change the subject, said to Denise, "Remember that frat party we crashed, so we could hear the guys play? We were like a couple of pieces of raw meat in a shark tank."

"Oh, my word," Denise said. "I didn't know if we were going to get out of there alive."

"That was profoundly dumb," Alex said.

"Cole was so pissed off," Madelyn said, and the memories piled up in a chain-reaction collision: walking heartsick up to the

Castle at dawn, falling asleep on the couch, Cole finding her there and taking her upstairs…

Rushing to change the subject again, she looked at Alex and said the first thing that came into her head. "Or the time you guys did your mariachi act under our dorm windows?"

"My roommate was so jealous," Denise said. "She said, 'If you don't want him, I do.'"

"El Mariachi Montoya," Alex said, "separating girls from their underwear since 1966."

"Alex!" Denise said. "Shame on you!"

"I never heard Cole's record," Julia said. She got unsteadily to her feet and made her way to the albums lined up on the floor next to the stereo. "Is it in here?"

Before Madelyn could say no, Alex got up. "You're drunk," he said. "I'll do it." Julia pretended to push him away and lost her balance. When Alex reached out to steady her, she managed to press her breasts against his forearm. Alex guided her to the couch and then began to flip through the records. Stop, Madelyn wanted to say. The word failed to come out.

"Ah, here it is." A moment of hiss was followed by two guitars chasing each other around the melody of "Wang Dang Doodle."

"Louder," Julia said.

"The neighbors," Madelyn said, in vain.

She'd only listened to it once since Cole disappeared. That had been a year and some ago, in the grip of spring fever and a couple of glasses of wine. It sounded good, she thought, and here they were, like grownups, able to sit and appreciate it simply as a pleasing collection of songs.

Yet somehow the conversation had gotten derailed and they were unable to get it back on track. Denise tried to talk about some movie she'd just seen called *Billy Jack*, where the hippies were the heroes, and Alex kept disparaging the Hollywood "machine," though Denise tried to explain that it wasn't Hollywood, it was independent, and at that point Madelyn realized that everybody else was pretty blasted as well, and that it wasn't really a movie that Alex and Denise were at odds over. That made Madelyn pull away from the conversation and into the music, and about that time "Gold" came on, and then all she could think of was the first time Cole played the song for her at the Vulcan.

She wondered why on earth she had ever thought she could listen to the record objectively. She got up quietly and went into the kitchen, where the first thing she saw was a pair of wine bottles, one white, one red, Lancaster and York, two roses on her desk in Russian class, and she stood over the sink and listened to her big, fat tears thud into the stainless steel.

She felt a hand on her shoulder, and when she turned around, Alex pulled her into an enveloping embrace and she surrendered to it. "He really loved you," Alex said. "Like nobody else, ever, in his life. Don't ever forget that."

Oddly, it was exactly what she needed to hear, and she let herself have a good minute and a half of crying her eyes out.

That ended the party. Madelyn made a half-hearted offer to put everyone up on the couch and the floor. Alex insisted he was perfectly fine to drive and Madelyn chose to believe him.

After they were gone, she opened the balcony doors to clear out the odors of dope, wine, and Julia's perfume. She refilled her wine glass, got a box of Kleenex, turned the stereo down, and started the Quirq album again from the beginning.

ALEX HAD PLANNED his return trip to include an overnight layover in Dallas. Denise had left her car in long term parking and dropped him at his parents' house on her way to Denton.

That night he took his father to Tupinamba's by Bachman Lake, the best Mexican restaurant in Dallas. He stumbled through the lines he'd rehearsed on the plane, explaining what he wanted, that he was determined to get the RTF degree, whether his father supported him or not. The sight of his father's disappointment hurt him worse than he'd imagined.

They ate in silence for a while, then his father said, "When Jesús was eighteen, he'd already been working for Cuauhtémoc for two years, and I knew he hated it. We were still in Monterrey then. I was sixteen and was running errands at the plant after school. One day Jesús made me come with him when he went to talk to our father, for protection. You look at your grandfather now, skinny and old and dignified, you can't imagine how afraid of him we were. Jesús says he's got a chance to apprentice to this guy who makes guitars and violins and that he would never be happy working in the factory. And our father says, 'Happy?' This was late 1945. Mexico had been through the Revolution, the Cristeros, the Depression, one hard time after another. The war was over but there were still a lot of shortages, and inflation was bad because the US had invested a lot in Mexico so they could take our oil and resources for their manufacturing, and we were drowning in debt. So our father says, 'To think that following your own selfish desires is the path to happiness is the stupidity of a child. Marrying for "love," chasing daydreams, setting yourself against God and tradition and family, where is the happiness in that?' Jesús was determined and he left the house and moved in with the violin maker and married his daughter and we didn't see him anymore, and my father put the whole weight of his expectations on me. He was very, very Catholic and he hated the US, and the day came when I knew I had to get divorced and move to the States and start my own import/export business, and I had to go to my father and tell him, knowing he would disown me too. I was never so afraid in my life. To my surprise he got very sad and said, 'I miss Jesús every day. I know what you're doing is wrong and you'll be sorry in the end, and I also know you're not going to listen to me, and I don't want to lose you too.' So he gave me his blessing, more or less, and helped talk Cuauhtémoc into investing in my business, and I made so much money that I was able to bring him in as a partner and he was able to buy the house in Guanajuato and move Susan's mother and Jesús and his family there too. And to this day he doesn't treat your mother with the respect she's due, and if the subject comes up he will tell you without blinking that I'm going to burn in hell for getting divorced, and that we should never have split off from Cuauhtémoc, and that Jesús never grew up and is wasting his time making guitars, though people play them all over the world."

Through the whole speech Alex had felt his hopes rising. "Does this mean you'll help?"

"What it means is that I have more sympathy for my father than I ever had before." Alex wished his father had smiled when he said that. "It means that even with the example of my father in front of me, I still think you're making a terrible mistake."

"But you and Jesús were both right."

"Which has nothing to do with whether *you're* right."

"It has to do with your being against anything I want that isn't part of your plan for me. Like your father was with you."

Alex had never said anything like that to his father before, and his father's eyes went wide and his head jerked back a fraction of an inch. For a couple of long seconds, Alex thought he'd blown it. His blood was up and he didn't care.

His father must have seen that. He looked away and thought for a while and then he said, "I'll agree to the two years for this new Bachelor's degree, if you'll continue to manage the house. After that we'll have to see where we are."

"Thank you, Papa."

"My father used to say, 'The entire world has lost its mind.' That was nothing compared to now."

"No," Alex said. "For the first time in history, the world is trying to get sane."

MADELYN KNEW that there were creatures called "morning people." Clearly they existed and were able to function with the disorder; all the same, she had never understood them.

Benjamin Kindred was one. When she got to the gallery that November Saturday at nine AM, Kindred had already run four miles, showered, and had a big breakfast while he read the *Chronicle*. Madelyn herself had stumbled out of bed only an hour before, thrown a cup of instant coffee down her throat, and eaten a cold croissant as she drove up from Palo Alto, the top up on her MG because of a light drizzle and a temperature in the fifties.

Kindred wanted to see her in his office—immediately, of course. Repeated hints that she preferred some quiet time when she first got in had been as incomprehensible to him as jogging before dawn in the rain was to her.

"I've put off talking to you about this until I was more certain about what's going to happen," he said.

"Ben, it's nine in the morning and I haven't had any real coffee yet. Please come out and tell me if this is going to be bad news."

"That depends on you."

"Oh dear."

"You know that business has been good. As it happens, it's been good enough that I've been weighing my options for a second location. I think I've found it."

Refusing to encourage his tendencies toward drama, Madelyn held herself very still.

"This is a pretty exciting time," he said. "The picture dealers on Fifty-Seventh Street have had a stranglehold on the New York gallery scene for decades, and that's breaking wide open. You've heard of SoHo?"

Madelyn realized she'd stopped breathing. She forced herself to inhale and scrubbed any trace of enthusiasm from her voice. "I've read about it in *Artforum*."

"They finally changed the zoning laws in January, so the artists can legally live and work in the lofts there. The scene is going crazy. Giant canvasses, huge sculptures. Happenings. Film and dance. They're redefining art."

Madelyn, who was reasonably satisfied with the old definition, nodded along.

"A couple of galleries have already opened there and—"

"Yes," she said.

"Yes what?"

"Am I willing to move to New York and manage the new gallery? Yes. I assume I'd finish up the PhD at NYU, since it's around the corner."

"Actually I was hoping to manage the New York location myself and leave you in charge here."

"Oh." She knew she was losing the battle to keep her emotions from showing.

Kindred gave her a few seconds to suffer for her presumption, then said, "Unfortunately, my roots here are too deep and it doesn't look like it's going to be practical for me to move. So yes, that's the offer. Relocate to one of the most dangerous cities in America, which Mayor Lindsay has spent into insurmountable debt, take on the responsibility of a storefront in an area recently known as 'Hell's Hundred Acres,' and somehow continue your education at the same time."

Broadway, Madelyn thought. Brentano's and the Drama Book Store. Greenwich Village and Washington Square. Columbia University and MOMA and the Guggenheim and the Met. "When do I start?"

"Madelyn, are you absolutely sure about this? You should take a few days to think about it, maybe talk to your parents..."

"My father trained me my entire life for this."

"Work on the space is absolutely, positively supposed to be finished in March. I'm hoping they'll be done by June, which is when I want to open. At the end of your spring semester, in other words. We should fly up and take a look before then, try and find you a place to live. My realtor can help."

"Thank you," Madelyn said.

"We'll see if you still say that a year from now."

She was unable to concentrate for the rest of the day. She called Gordo's now ex-girlfriend Irene, with whom she kept in sporadic touch, and made a date for dinner.

Irene, unsurprisingly, knew quite a bit about SoHo. "Christ, I am so jealous," she said. They were splitting a plate of Ethiopian lentils, green beans, and cabbage. "It's the fucking Revolution up there. Guys like George Maciunas and Fluxus, they're tearing the whole thing down to the sidewalks. Are you sure you're up for this?"

"That's what Kindred asked me. Why would I not be?"

"Well, aside from your being comparatively conservative politically and artistically, there's the whole issue of how a gallery is going to make money off this scene. I mean, most of the hard-core guys are anti-capitalist and anti-art. They're out to fuck over people like you. They're doing all this shit that can't be commodified, like performance art and film. How does John Q. Collector take that home and hang it over his sofa?"

"I guess if I figure that out I'll be rich. Then I can see how firm these guys' anti-capitalist convictions are, once there's real money on the table."

"Or," Irene said, "just maybe, they'll win you over and you'll put that amazing intellect in the service of truth, justice, and anarchy. Wouldn't that be something?"

1973

D AVE FOUND OUT about it when a manila envelope showed up at his office in late February, bearing the return address of a friend who worked at *Billboard*. Inside were page proofs of an interview with Sallie Rachel about her upcoming album, *Sallie Rachel Krupheimer*, which she'd recorded in LA with Bones Howe "captaining the console."

Asked about her name change, she said, "It's all about being honest, being who I really am. From day one the music business crams you into their one-size-fits-all boxes. Giving you a new name, picking your backing musicians, crafting your 'image.' I've finally fought my way to a place where I don't have to do that anymore. It's the seventies now, people want to get real, and that's what this album is. Real."

Dave crumpled the pages into a ball and threw them across the office. He went out into the hall and had a long drink at the water fountain and then bent forward and played the cold water over his face, imagining the heat of his anger vaporizing the water into clouds that floated above his steaming head.

It wouldn't have hurt so much if he hadn't been in love with her so very long.

He was doing so well otherwise. Two gold records in the last two years, a nice house in Ingleside Terraces, and maybe the start of a relationship with a marine biologist at the Exploratorium. He was getting offered more interesting projects than he could take on, and Judy, the biologist, had him walking every day and losing some weight. Until five minutes ago he'd felt better than he had in a long time.

He returned to his office and flattened out the interview, needing to know if she'd insulted him by name. He didn't have to read far. The interviewer said, "Dave Fisher is one of the better respected producers in the business. What does Bones Howe give you that Fisher can't?"

"The sense that I'm the one in control," Sallie had answered.

She rattled off a list of first-call LA session men: Jim Gordon on drums, Lee Sklar on bass, Leon Russel on piano, James Burton on guitar. "It felt like a real band when I was in the studio with them."

The songs included a couple of remakes of previous album cuts alongside new versions of songs she'd written for the Meteors, the Fifth Dimension, and Johnny Rivers. She'd done a couple of cover tunes and only two new originals. "It's a new beginning and a coming to grips with my past," she said. The photo showed she'd cut her hair, turning it into a wild mass of curls. Dave conceded the distant possibility that, despite its studied artlessness, her hair might have looked that way on its own and not been the result of hard work by an LA stylist.

He locked the article in his desk, telling himself he would not think about it again. He had a date with Judy and hoped that she might be ready to spend the night.

He kept refilling his wine glass at dinner. He was not a drinker, rarely had more than a single beer or glass of wine. Judy sensed immediately that something was wrong, but it took his third glass of wine before he would tell her the outlines of the story.

"'It felt like a real band,'" he mocked, after finishing the bottle. "That's like picking up an aging hooker and telling yourself it's love."

Judy had tried sympathy and making excuses for Sallie and she had clearly tired of the subject. "Dave, you need to let this go."

"Besides which," Dave said, "I let her record with her actual real band that she was touring with and they were lousy and the record bombed."

"Dave…"

"Which she pressured me into because she was screwing the drummer."

"Can we change the subject? There's some interesting stuff happening with plankton in the Baltic Sea. They just found eight species there that they've never seen before…"

Dave managed to get the bill paid. Judy insisted on driving his car back to his place. He showed her around and she was suitably impressed. She declined a drink and at first Dave did too. They sat on the couch and Judy said, "Are you working tomorrow?"

"No, I'm in between. I'm supposed to do something with Quick-silver in a couple of weeks. Unless Sallie has completely sunk my career."

Her disappointment hovered over the ensuing silence. He got up and poured himself a shot of vodka and drank it down. "She said I changed her name," Dave said, still facing the bar. "It's true. Do you know what she was calling herself when I discovered her? Sue Storm. After some comic book character. How's that for being who she really is?"

He turned around and saw that Judy was no longer on the couch. He heard her in the kitchen, reciting his address. She was hanging up the wall phone as he walked in.

"Don't go," he said. "I'm really sorry."

She braced herself against the kitchen island, holding on with both hands. "I like you, Dave, but you've got some serious unfinished business here. Six months or a year from now, if you get past it, give me a call, maybe we can try again. But I'm not going to fight over you with somebody who's not even here."

She pushed past him, headed for the front door. "Where are you going?" he asked.

"There's a cab on the way. He should be here in ten minutes."

"I can take you—"

"I don't think that's a good idea," she said, and let herself out.

Dave made it to the bar and poured himself another shot. He didn't remember drinking it, or anything else until he woke up at four AM, sprawled on the couch with a caustic taste in his throat and his head thudding.

"'In control?'" he said to the empty house. "When were *you* ever not in control?"

CABS CRUISED THROUGH SoHo now, at least during daylight hours and in the four square blocks that the galleries had civilized, from West Broadway east to Greene, and from Houston south to Prince. In her first two months, when she was still struggling not to pronounce the street name like the name of the Texas city, Madelyn frequently had to walk across Houston to the NYU campus to even see a cab, and most evenings she kept walking until she got to her ritzy and secure studio apartment on University Place, north of Washington Square.

The changes that she'd witnessed in the last year had mostly been for the good, though she missed the smell of arroz con pollo that used to leak through the wall that Kindred Gallery East had shared with a now-defunct Puerto Rican restaurant. The last of the sweatshops and textile merchants were clearing out; the city had finally granted a historic designation to the local cast-iron buildings with the arched, gray-painted facades that gave the neighborhood its character.

It was 6:19 on a Saturday evening in late September, she had just locked the doors of the gallery, and the first drops of rain had started to fall out of a gray sky. At that moment a cab stopped in front of her and she chose not to argue with fate, laying hold of the door handle before the previous fare, a guy in a white corduroy car coat, could close it.

The rain was pummeling the cab by the time it pulled up across the street from her building; she was soaked before she got to the front door. Water cascaded off the overhang all around her in a liquid curtain. She unlocked the heavy glass door and made sure the lock clicked solidly behind her. She tracked water across the black marble lobby, rode the brushed chrome elevator to the 11th floor, let herself into her apartment, and shed her wet clothes by the door.

As always, a hidden tension relaxed once she was in her space, the sanctuary that enabled her to endure the lonely and intimidating megalopolis. The single room was too small to permit any disorder, so everything was precisely placed, from the thrift-store single bed and sofa to the rugs and potted plants to the posters on the walls by her beloved Pre-Raphaelites: Byrne-Jones's *King Cophetua*, Rossetti's *Beatrix*, Waterhouse's *Mermaid*.

She took a quick shower and dressed in black jeans, black turtleneck, and African print jacket. Alex called as she was putting on her mascara. Her destination that night was an opening at Paula Cooper's newly relocated gallery on Wooster, and Alex was eager to go. He'd only been in the city three weeks and was still

finding his way around. He'd had a rupture with his father and
was trying to get by on financial aid and student loans from NYU
film school, plus a part-time photo-processing job at a Duane
Reed pharmacy. He'd rented a tenement apartment a few crucial
blocks east of SoHo on the Lower East Side, a tough Jewish and
Puerto Rican immigrant neighborhood with the Spanglish nickname Loisaida. Madelyn worried about him; for his part, Alex
seemed liberated. "I'm a poor Mexican kid in the barrio, living
in a crappy apartment and wearing ropa usada. Why would anybody want to fuck with me?"

They'd gone out every two or three days since he'd arrived, and
Madelyn remained unsure of his intentions. Thus far everything
had been comfortably platonic, and he'd insisted on separate
checks and paying for his own movie tickets. Madelyn was unsure
how she would react if he came on to her. He'd gotten more physically attractive as he'd grown up and filled out, but the flashes of
cynicism she'd seen in him over the years had left her wary. Their
tangled relationships to Cole and Denise also gave the idea a whiff
of the incestuous.

For the moment she was happy to have the company, not to
mention the ferocious critical sensibility he brought to watching
films. Over a glass of wine afterward he would point out the myriad
ways that the cinemaphotography, the music, the verbal clichés,
the very essence of the typical Hollywood movie was designed to
deaden the mind and dictate the reactions of the emotions. She'd
asked him why he kept watching them, and he said, "You learn
more from what you hate than from what you love."

As always, Alex wanted to eat at FOOD, Gordon Matta-Clark's
conceptual art restaurant, and Madelyn demurred. The dinner
menu was unpredictable, with a risk of something presentation-
ally brilliant but inedible, and ever since the *New York* magazine
review, crowds had been a problem. She was tired of Fanelli's, the
only other restaurant in the neighborhood, and she convinced
him to go to Little Italy, where they could be sure of a good,
cheap meal.

They got to the Cooper gallery well after nine. Despite Madelyn's
having been on the scene for over a year, she couldn't help the

charge she got the minute she passed through the door, knowing she was at the absolute forefront of visual arts for the entire planet. The inside was cavernous, managing to look battered and sleek at the same time, from the exposed joists overhead to the original distressed wooden floor that had been refinished and buffed to a high gloss, to the islands of light where massive, mysterious objects disrupted the flow of a jittery and hyper-verbal crowd.

Paula herself was hovering near the door and hurried over to press her cheek to Madelyn's and say, "Madelyn, I'm so glad you could come. You look fantastic."

"I wouldn't have missed it," Madelyn said, not letting herself reject the compliment—audibly, anyway. Paula was 35, tall and stunning in the classic New York tradition, full lips and enormous dark eyes, long dark hair held loosely in a silver barrette. She had a wide-collared white shirt, a black blazer, and a cigarette in her left hand. Madelyn knew the welcome was sincere. Paula, like most of the artists and gallery owners in SoHo, seemed immune to envy or competition, as if they were all part of a crusade against the business-as-usual of art. Half of the artists were making works that couldn't be sold, either because they were too gigantic or too ephemeral, like Sol LeWitt's wall drawings, executed on the actual walls of the gallery and then painted over when the show closed. Madelyn had to admire the suicidal purity of the ideology.

"This is an old friend, Alex Montoya," Madelyn said. "He's in film school at NYU."

Paula took his hand, sized him up quickly, and said, "If you do something interesting, I want to see it."

"Absolutely," Alex said.

They moved into the smoke-filled exhibit space. As many as a hundred people ebbed and flowed through the room, dealers and collectors and critics in coats and ties or black dresses, artists and hangers-on in jeans and T-shirts and sweat shirts. The exhibit was Donald Judd's latest collection of rectangular boxes, or "specific objects" as he preferred to call them. His "vertical progressions" consisted of identical cuboids, made of steel and plexiglass, mounted one above the other directly on the gallery wall. The main floor held a scattering of more massive pieces, including a large ply-wood cube, open on one side, with a panel tilted diagonally inside it from the top almost to the floor.

"That's shaped exactly like the inside of a bass speaker cabinet," Alex said quietly as they stood in front of it.

"Is that a good thing or a bad thing?" Madelyn asked. She saw that Judd himself—barrel-chested, light-brown hair pushed back from his high forehead, full beard failing to hide his easy smile—was out of earshot. The last thing she needed was for him to overhear her half-baked thoughts about his work.

"I don't know yet. It's certainly nicely made."

"He doesn't build them himself. He has them professionally fabricated."

Alex raised an eyebrow.

"People were scandalized when he first did it," she said. "Now-adays it's pretty common. I don't know. I have mixed feelings. The point, as I understand it, is to make something that doesn't *mean* anything, that isn't trying to tell a story, that is just itself, occupying space and creating space."

Alex nodded and she watched him drink it in, saw him look at it differently, and she had to admit it gave her a thrill.

"Interesting," he said. "I can see that now."

"Is this in the same category as Bernini's *David*? That I can't answer."

She suddenly noticed a woman staring at them. When Madelyn stared back, the woman didn't look away. She was severely thin and oddly dressed: horizontally striped knee socks in red and green, a brown tweed skirt, a long-sleeved T-shirt with thin, dark blue horizontal stripes on white, a black bandana, and a red plaid tam o'shanter. Dark circles under her eyes, combined with too much rouge and lipstick, made her clownlike. Her long, reddish brown hair fell to the middle of her spine and her cigarette was screwed into an antique red Bakelite holder.

"Hello," Madelyn said, in an attempt to defuse the intensity of her look.

"Hi," she said. "I was eavesdropping. You've read 'Specific Objects'?"

That was the title of Judd's 1966 manifesto. "I tried," Madelyn said. "I found it pretty tough going. As best I could tell, he wrote off the entire history of western art, which I'm pretty attached to."

The woman shook her head impatiently. "You missed the point. All he's saying is, after Van Gogh has painted *Wheatfield with Crows* or whatever, it's brilliant, it's wonderful, and now it's been done. We can't keep painting *Wheatfield with Crows* over and over. Let Henry Moore keep on making Henry Moore sculptures, but don't ask somebody of our generation to make Henry Moore sculptures. That's all."

Madelyn, who had been raised with Southern manners, had difficulty not finding this woman rude. Alex, on the other hand, was intrigued. He offered his hand and said, "Alex Montoya."

She parked the cigarette in the corner of her mouth, squinted against the smoke, and gave his hand a single, abrupt shake. "Hi."

Alex turned on his most charming smile. "Your turn."

She smiled back at Alex. It was quite dazzling, though Madelyn suspected sarcasm. "I was never one for rules."

"And I," Madelyn said, "have spent my life in thrall to them, I'm afraid. I'm Madelyn Brooks."

"From Kindred Gallery East?" The woman held out her hand. "I'm very glad to meet you. I'm Callie Janus."

Madelyn pressed Callie's hand gently. "I've heard of you." She was one of the many up-and-coming neighborhood artists who were said to be on the verge of being ready for a show, though Madelyn hadn't yet seen her work.

"I'm flattered," Callie said. "That's a beautiful space you've got, tastefully curated."

"Ben makes the final decisions," Madelyn said, "but thank you." Madelyn knew Callie was working her, yet at the same time the compliments had authority and conviction.

"What kind of stuff do you do?" Alex asked. Madelyn felt his impatience; Callie had exiled him to conversational Siberia.

"I don't like to be pinned down," Callie said. "As you may have already guessed. I suppose I'm trying to find some kind of midpoint between painting and poetry." She paused, then, deadpan, said, "And pretentiousness, needless to say. The three Ps."

Even her self-deprecating joke seemed directed inward, as if she didn't expect anyone else to get it.

"What do you think of this?" Alex gestured at the massive plywood box.

"I think Don is smart. Really, really smart. He's created his own niche and fully occupied it."

Alex said, "If I saw this sitting on the sidewalk outside a factory, I don't know if I'd look at it twice."

"Duchamp's urinal. Or more likely Elsa von Freytag-Loringhoven's urinal, but that's another argument." She dropped her cigarette butt on the floor and crushed it with one pink Ked. Madelyn cringed on behalf of the wood. "Do you often see something on the street and think it's art?"

"I'm a filmmaker," he said, in the way he might have said, "Of course."

"If you saw this outside a factory," Callie said, "you would assume utility from the context. Here it's obvious that it has no purpose. It's not pretending to *be* anything or *represent* anything. It's pure. It's truthful. It has integrity. What's funny?"

"I was just thinking. We were trying so hard to find that integrity in sixty-five, sixty-six. Folk songs, blues, jazz."

"You can't borrow somebody else's integrity."

"Wow," Alex said. "That's profound."

Madelyn edged away. Alex was no longer the cocky opportunist she remembered from the Castle in Austin; he'd matured into someone more open and genuine. Even so, Madelyn was uncomfortable seeing him smitten and struggling for Callie's serious attention. She opted to give them their privacy.

She joined the crowd around Judd, who was talking about how much he loved being in Texas. He'd relocated the year before to Marfa, the flat wasteland where they'd filmed *Giant*. Judd saw her and winked. "Madelyn can tell you. She's from Texas." He put on a drawl. "Am I right, hon?"

She had been introduced to him at a loft party a few days ago; she was flattered that he remembered her. After a moment of being tongue tied, she said, "You better believe it, sugar."

He laughed. "You know Marfa?"

"Been through it on my way to Big Bend. It's, uh, spacious."

That provoked general laughter, Judd laughing hardest of all. Then somebody else hijacked the conversation, wanting to know more about how he wrote up his specifications. A couple of minutes later, Alex showed up at her side, alone.

Madelyn led him away from the main attraction. "She got away?"

"I failed to set the hook."

"Probably for the best," Madelyn said. "She looks like a lot of fight for not much fish."

"I thought she was incredible. Smart, educated, gorgeous, totally her own person. What's her art like?"

"I have no idea. And I'm not going to offer her a show just so you can get her into bed."

"I wouldn't dream of asking you to do that." He gave it a long second. "You could take a look, though, and if the work is good..."

"I'll think about it."

Alex checked his watch. "Is there anything else to see besides these boxes?"

"There's the people. If you're bored, you don't have to hang around."

"I was hoping I could convince you to go with me. I've been invited to a disco."

"I've heard the word," Madelyn said. "It's a dance club where they play records, right?"

"This place is more than that. It's called The Gallery, up in Chelsea, invitation only. Supposedly they have this incredible sound system, huge crowds, the DJ is remixing the music as it plays. People go into altered states from the dancing."

"Sounds interesting, but why do you need me?"

Alex looked embarrassed. "It's, uh, it's a big 'gay' scene. I don't want to get hit on all night long."

"So you want me to be your beard?"

"My what?"

Now Madelyn was checking her own watch. "Never mind. I have to schmooze for another hour or so. If you can wait that long, I'll give it a try."

*

THE CROWD HAD spilled out onto West 22nd Street, and as the cab pulled to the curb, Alex began to have second thoughts. People were clustered in threes and fours, mostly male, mostly black and/or Chicano, most of them somewhere between fit and scrawny, wearing sleeveless T-shirts or vests with no shirts, or silk shirts unbuttoned to the waist, showing provocative quantities of hairless black and brown and tan skin, sleek and shiny with sweat. They wore giant Afros and fedoras and yachting caps and cowboy hats, outsize sunglasses, blonde wigs, feather boas, harem pants, basketball shorts, Cuban heels and curly-toed shoes out of the Arabian Nights. They drank wine and sniffed cocaine off of hand mirrors and draped themselves over each other like discarded clothes on furniture.

"Holy fucking shit," Alex said.

"That'll be two sixty-five," the cabbie said. Madelyn paid him while Alex tried to decide whether he wanted to go in. A tall black man with a shaved head, dressed in leopard print from shirt collar to shoes, opened the cab door and said, "Welcome to the Gallery. First time?"

Alex nodded.

"Invitation?"

Alex showed him the business card that the guy from his editing class had given him, and the man made a sweeping motion with his hands as the cabbie said, "In or out, pal, I don't got all fuckin' night."

They got out. Alex immediately tucked Madelyn's arm inside his own as the cab sped away. "Up the stairs," the Leopard Man said unnecessarily. You could hear the music clearly on the street, especially the bass, as if the amperage had turned the entire building into a loudspeaker. At the top of the stairs, Alex showed his card again and Madelyn volunteered to pay the steep seven-dollar cover charge. They passed through a steel fire door into the club.

Alex found himself in a converted industrial loft like the ones in SoHo, the exact dimensions hard to pin down because of the mirrors on the walls, the colored lights and strobes, and the sheer number of human beings, all of them pulsing to the music. A cage full of brightly colored balloons disguised the exposed girders on the high ceiling. The outfits they'd seen on the street had only been a preview. Alex saw Marilyn Monroe, a soldier in scraps of camouflage and a green beret, Elvis in gold lame, and an Arab sheik. One guy wore nothing but a skimpy loincloth and another wore a bustier and bloomers.

They pushed through the writhing bodies until Alex found a wall he could put his back to. The place smelled like the locker room at St. Mark's, mixed with cigarette smoke and cheap cologne. The sound system was amazing—as loud as it was, Alex heard no distortion at all. He could pick out every individual instrument and feel the bass rise up through his feet. The music itself sounded like a Gamble-Huff production out of Philadelphia, with gospel-style female singers, throbbing rhythm, and aggressive strings and horns. As the long coda began to fade, the DJ brought up "Money" by Pink Floyd, its looped cash-register sound effects perfectly synchronized to the hi-hat in the previous song.

He could not have pictured a place like this five years ago. Once you started knocking down walls, you never knew who was going to come in.

Alex didn't notice that he was moving to the music until he saw Madelyn smile at him. "Feeling better now?" she shouted in his ear.

He nodded. The dancers around him ranged from people swaying in place to a few obvious modern dance professionals, spinning and making dramatic gestures with their hands. Many of them, Alex suddenly realized, were tripping. He hadn't done acid himself in years, though the thought cheered him up.

From Pink Floyd the DJ took them to "Green Onions" by Booker T. and the MGs, a song The Chevelles used to play before their breaks, as did The Other Side in Austin. Suddenly Alex's emotions all bubbled up at once—nostalgia, loneliness, desire for that artist, Callie, that he'd just met, fear of the future, regrets over his break with his father, and yet above them all a wild exhilaration at being in New York, on his own, in a crazed and somehow welcoming environment.

He grabbed Madelyn's hand. "Let's dance," he said.

*

THAT PAST JUNE, Alex had ended up with a BS in film from UT, an acceptance in hand from NYU, and a half-dozen black and white prints of a 20-minute film called "Nimbus" that had been his final project for his degree. The film used two non-actor friends who were lovers, speaking improvised dialog and backlit by various natural light sources including, at the end, the setting sun.

He felt a sense of urgency he couldn't clearly articulate. Nixon, after senselessly prolonging the war for four years, had finally kept his campaign promises and pulled out of Vietnam at the start of his second term. Instead of the dawn of a new era, it felt like the end of everything. Alex's economics classes had taught him that you didn't get runaway inflation, high unemployment, and stagnant economic growth all at the same time, yet that was exactly what was happening, and people were freaking out. Meanwhile, Nixon had been caught burglarizing the Democratic National Convention headquarters, and like some pathetic sitcom President, he'd kept piling on the lies and evasions until it looked like he meant to take the entire ship of state down with him. Integration was back in court because the US had managed to get its neighborhoods so segregated that the only way to get the races together was to bus kids from one end of town to another. People flocked to cults like the Hare Krishnas and the Moonies or turned into Jesus freaks. A research institute had published a book called *The Limits to Growth* that said unless we stopped overpopulating, civilization would collapse by the middle of the next century.

The time had come, he knew, for him to go out on his own and try to do the thing he wanted to do, and to take the responsibility, financial and otherwise, for whether he succeeded or not.

He had screened "Nimbus" for his parents, and afterward told them he was moving to New York. His father hadn't understood either one, as Alex had known he wouldn't. But Alex had hardened his heart.

It was time to grow up.

1973

★

BY TWO AM, Madelyn had passed through exhaustion into an ecstatic high unlike anything she'd ever experienced. She was energized, clear-headed, completely happy, and full of love for everyone around her. The mood didn't feel thrust upon her, like with booze or dope, instead felt more like returning to some primitive, Rousseauian natural state that she'd lost touch with because of too much work and the mundane depredations of the material world. She couldn't think of a reason not to feel this way all the time.

Alex was powered by an altogether different fuel. Shortly after midnight they'd run into Jamie, the film school friend from whom Alex had scored his invitation, dressed in a motorcycle jacket, cap, and boots, a pair of white cotton briefs, and nothing else. He'd offered them coke, which Alex was up for and Madelyn was not; she didn't care for the narcissistic and talkative person it turned her into. Alex had brought her along anyway, no doubt due to Jamie's refusal to believe that Alex was straight. They'd squeezed onto the fire escape with far too many like-minded others, and Madelyn closed her eyes and focused on the sensations on her skin, alternating between the chill of the night and the heat from the bodies around her.

Once they were back inside, Alex had been frenzied for a time, at one point breaking into jumping jacks. Madelyn had ignored him when he threatened to spoil her mood, turning away and letting the music carry her.

At three AM she leaned into Alex in mid-song and said, "I think I've had it."

They only had to wait ten minutes for their turn at a cab. The party continued around them on the sidewalk, Alex with a frozen grin on his face, Madelyn relaxed and going with the flow, accepting a taste of warm champagne from a drunken threesome, ignoring the alcove of the building next door, where a man was on his knees, his head moving rapidly forward and back, hands from an unseen partner in his hair.

The cab dropped Alex off first, and as soon as he got out he said, "You're going to check her out, right?"

543

Madelyn blinked, her mind elsewhere. She couldn't remember when she'd been so exhausted.

"Callie," Alex said. "Callie Janus."

"Yeah, sure, okay."

"You won't forget."

"No," Madelyn said. "I won't forget."

ON TUESDAY AFTERNOON, one of the collectors visiting the gallery mentioned the Donald Judd show and Madelyn realized that she had, in fact, forgotten Callie Janus. She checked her file cabinet and sure enough, she had a set of slides, tucked professionally into the pockets of a three-hole-punched plastic holder, along with a business card that appeared to have been produced with a child's toy printing press and a set of rubber stamps and cut with dull scissors from the inside of a cereal box. Madelyn wasn't sure if she was charmed or embarrassed by it.

As to the art, it would stand or fall based on the back story that went with it. It involved paint on wooden slats, collage, and hand lettering and sketching on top. Details were hard to make out without a projector.

On impulse, she dialed the number on the card. A mumbling voice at the first number directed her to a second one, where eventually someone found Callie and got her on the line. Madelyn, suddenly wishing she hadn't come this far, arranged to visit her loft after work.

The loft was two blocks away and four flights up. The temperature outside was 60 degrees; inside the loft it felt distinctly colder. Drop cloths and hammers and sketchbooks were piled on the non-functional radiators. Many of the lofts didn't have running water, let alone toilets or showers, keeping the rents affordable for tenants who were still struggling for their first break. It was not a mode of existence that Madelyn could imagine for herself, though the conditions that Alex was living in were not much better.

The space was thirty feet wide and a hundred feet long, shared by five artists, all of them male except Callie. One was asleep on a mattress under a canvas splotched with brown acrylic; one sat on the floor cutting up magazines; one was cooking something on a hotplate; one sat cross-legged on the ravaged wooden floor, watching Callie sketch on a newsprint pad.

Three work lights hung from the ceiling, only partially relieving the gloom as night fell. They'd improvised a few fixtures to illuminate posters, paintings, and bookshelves made of boards and bricks. What furniture they had was arbitrary: a gray metal office desk; red and orange plastic chairs that looked like they'd been liberated from a laundromat; a wooden hat rack layered with clothes.

No one, including Callie, reacted to Madelyn's arrival. Madelyn resisted the temptation to walk out, and instead looked at the art on the walls, perversely hoping to find something extraordinary by somebody other than Callie, whom she could elevate to stardom while Callie looked on in bitter disappointment. Sadly, most of the work was second-hand: a white T-shirt pasted to a canvas with a thick coat of white paint, à la Robert Ryman, or an assembly of incandescent light bulbs imitating Dan Flavin's fluorescents.

She stopped at the first of Callie's paintings. The surface was constructed from a grocery store fruit crate, the thin bottom and side boards removed and then nailed side by side to the thicker end pieces. The partially visible label advertised Washington "Delicious" Apples. Callie had glued a sheet of drawing paper to the slats on which she had laboriously printed, using her rubber stamps, a variation on a word ladder, a game that Charles Dobson had invented:

```
         LEAF  LEAF
      LEAF  LEAF  LEAF
   LEAF  LEAF  LEAF  LEAF
   LEAF  LEAF  LEAF  LEAF
      LEAF  LEAF  LEAF
         LEAF  LEAF
            LEAN
            BEAN
            BEEN
            SEEN
            SEED
```

She'd painted over the words with a light pink wash and then scribbled a few childlike drawings in graphite on top: three birds perched in the tree and a single apple. On looking more closely, Madelyn saw that the drawings had real authority and a strong gestural quality that betrayed skilled draftsmanship.

Madelyn caught a strong whiff of Chanel No. 5 mixed with cigarettes and saw that Callie was now standing next to her. The Chanel seemed weirdly out of place in a SoHo loft.

"Pink?" Madelyn said.

"It was the least expected color I could think of. So you would have to decontextualize it."

"There's a faux naiveté here that's undercut by the craftsmanship," Madelyn said. Callie flinched, so Madelyn hastily added, "I mean that as a compliment. It's what I like best about it. You've been to art school, clearly."

"CalArts," she said, as if admitting to something embarrassing. "I dropped out after my sophomore year."

Artists and their tissue-thin egos, Madelyn thought. "Are you from LA?"

"Chillicothe, Ohio." Then, after a pause, "I was a cuckoo."

"Beg pardon?"

"My egg was laid in the wrong nest. I was too weird for anybody in that town. I couldn't wait to get the fuck out of there."

Madelyn felt the sting of compassion. The odd clothes, the insular humor, the contentious erudition, all made oddness into a defensive weapon. There but for fortune might Madelyn herself have gone. The survival tactics of childhood were so hard to shed, even when long outgrown. "That's where the Indian mounds are, right?"

"I used to freak the other kids out by pretending to be possessed by the spirit of a Hopewell shaman." She pointed to another fruit crate painting. The overlaid paper consisted of an incomplete game of Hangman, S H _ M _ N. Underneath were the attempted letters O,U,T,C. The gallows, body, and two legs were drawn above; in place of the head she had glued an Indian-head nickel. The wash was a thin olive-green.

"After what you said on Saturday, I'm a bit surprised that your paintings tell stories."

"I was talking about Don's work. You don't want to put me in the same box with him."

Madelyn studied her face, in vain, to see if the pun was intentional.

"I think of myself as a poet first," Callie went on. "Poetry with no story is Dada. Which is great, but it's been done."

Callie had three other paintings in the series, and Madelyn had to move one of the hanging work lights closer to see them all properly. Each had something going for it, and together they had a cohesion that would play well in a gallery. She hadn't entirely warmed to Callie as a person, though she was confident that Callie could lay down a convincing enough patter to impress her clients. Was the work actually any good? Or would shrill cries ring out at the opening, revealing both artist and dealer as rank imposters?

"I think the work is very interesting—" Madelyn began.

"'Interesting'?" Callie said, with a bitter edge.

"—and I can't give you a yes or no on the spot. But I'll think about it, and talk to my boss, and I'll get back to you one way or another by the end of the week."

"You'll call me either way?" Callie said. "You promise? Because that's what kills me, the waiting and never knowing." She lit a cigarette; her hands were trembling. "With all the theory and posturing and intellectualizing that happens around here, when it comes down to it, I am pouring my heart into this. This is what I live for. I can handle it if you don't like it, as long as you take me seriously. You know? Whether it's great or it's worthless, it matters. It matters to me."

Madelyn nearly let her guard down and admitted her own inexperience and self-doubt; her natural reticence saved her. "I promise," Madelyn said, "to have a decision for you by noon Friday."

That seemed to cheer Callie up and she shook Madelyn's hand and walked her to the stairs. As Madelyn started down, Callie called after her. "That cute guy who was with you Saturday, is he your boyfriend?"

"A friend of my husband's." What she lost in strict accuracy she gained in concision.

Callie smiled. "Okay."

Madelyn continued down the stairs, thinking, Uh-oh.

SHE CALLED KINDRED in San Francisco as soon as she got home. He had a copy of Callie's slides and glanced at them quickly. "You say it presents well in person," he said, "so I say let's try it. We can put her with a couple of slightly more established neighborhood artists and get some press and some goodwill, at the very least, for supporting the locals. And if she hits, we make out like bandits."

"And if she tanks?"

"You need to be more positive. Critics can smell fear before they get in the door."

"I am terrified."

"Have a glass of wine. This is a milestone—your first discovery."

She was not overly tempted to call Alex. He had no phone in his apartment, and negotiating in Spanish with whoever answered the hall phone was more than she was up to. She also decided to hold off on informing Callie, so that she could sleep on her decision. Callie herself might not sleep, but Madelyn was prepared to live with that.

She called the loft the next day at noon and Callie answered. If Madelyn had expected her to scream with excitement like a radio contest winner, she would have been disappointed. All Callie said was, "Thank you. You won't regret it."

Madelyn explained that there would be two other artists, yet to be determined, that the gallery took a standard 50 percent commission, that they would have exclusive rights to sell the pictures for a year from the date of the opening, and the rest of the fine print. Callie was unfazed and agreed to come by the gallery on Friday to sign the contracts.

Feeling equal parts pleased with herself and panic-stricken, she called Alex and invited him to a late lunch.

ALEX COULD NOT REMEMBER the last time he'd suffered through such an agonizing cocktail of obsession, helplessness, and desire.

He sat in Madelyn's office on Friday afternoon and waited to "accidentally" run into Callie, who was already later than Alex had been early. Alex was talking about his next-door neighbor, Maelo, who was in the Young Lords.

Madelyn said, "Aren't they like the Puerto Rican Black Panthers or something?"

"Kind of. Less gun waving and more community action. They changed their name to 'The Puerto Rican Revolutionary Workers Organization,' which I think was kind of a dumb move. Everybody, including Maelo, still calls them the Young Lords."

"They wear berets, right?"

"Yeah, purple ones. That's the only uniform. If there's an action and the cops come, they take off their berets and blend in with the crowd."

"What kind of action?"

"The one they're best known for was in sixty-nine. They got hold of a bunch of brooms, swept all the garbage into big piles in the street, and set fire to it. They forced the city to start picking up garbage in the Latin neighborhoods."

"They didn't have garbage pickup?"

"Life in Fun City," Alex said. "Anyway, Maelo is after me to make a film about them, and I'm thinking about it."

Callie stuck her head in the door. "The girl said I should just come on back." She glanced at Alex. "Hey."

"Hi," Alex said. He stood up. "I guess I should be going."

"Aw," Callie said. "Do you have to?"

Thank you, Jesus, Alex thought. "Well... not really, I guess." Callie smiled at him and at that moment he only wanted to please her. "I'll, uh, hang around out front for a while."

Twenty minutes later, when Callie came out of Madelyn's office, Alex was staring at a canvas on the gallery wall. It had been laboriously hand-painted from a halftone photo as different-size black dots on a canvas that was 12 feet on a side. From a normal viewing distance you only saw the dots themselves, and you had to stand on the far side of the studio to resolve the image into that of a dark-skinned girl in a dirty dress, sitting on a sidewalk and crying. Alex had spent the last few minutes trying to find the exact point at which the random became meaningful.

"I overheard you guys," Callie said. "Were you talking about the Young Lords? They are just the coolest."

And they were off, both of them talking fast, sometimes on top of each other, as if the contents of their brains had been under pressure and were spraying out uncontrollably. At some point they moved from the gallery to the street and by a mysterious, unspoken consensus walked east through Little Italy to Loisaida and into a working class Puerto Rican restaurant. Callie ordered pastelón, a casserole of ground pork, eggs, plantains, and green beans, while Alex went for the less adventurous chicharrones de pollo, fried chicken strips. They both drank one Cerveza India after another.

Callie was the single most opinionated person Alex had ever talked to. She loved Van Gogh and hated John Singer Sargent, loved Otis Redding and John Coltrane and hated Motown and Steely Dan, loved *Breathless* and hated *The Godfather*. Just when Alex thought he was beginning to get a grip on her taste, she would passionately defend Jacqueline Susann or Norman Rockwell and attack Stockhausen or Albee. Her disdain for what she deemed Alex's lapses in taste seemed absolute, yet before the pain completely registered, she had moved on.

The personal stuff came out only in passing. Alex touched on his rich father and private school background and told her he'd broken free and was living on a shoestring. She skimmed over an impoverished childhood, scholarships, CalArts.

At 11 PM they had ended up standing in front of Alex's tenement. "This is where I live," he said. "Want to come up and see my movie?"

They smoked a joint first and then sat on the floor, leaning against the bed, while Alex projected it onto one dingy wall. When it was over, and Alex had turned off the lamp, and they sat listening to the quiet whirr of the fan, the silence was both profound and natural. Alex felt he'd watched the film through her eyes and seen that it was good. Finally he switched off the projector fan and she said, "Wow."

She made love with a ferocity he had never experienced, scratching, biting, making guttural noises, at one point flipping him onto his back so that she could straddle him. He was crazy for her body, for the hard edges of her ribs, her shoulder blades, her hip bones straining against her pale skin. After he came she had him bring her to a climax with his fingers, then she took him in her mouth until he was ready to go again. When they were finally both exhausted, a dark mood rolled over her, and she turned away from him.

"What's wrong?" he asked.

"Don't mind me," she said. "I'm just loony tunes. Go to sleep."

When he woke up a few hours later in the gray dawn, she had left nothing behind except a few cigarette butts stubbed out in a saucer and the smell of sex and Chanel No. 5 in his sheets.

LATE SATURDAY MORNING Madelyn got a call from Alex. After a wild night of passion, Callie had neglected to leave her phone number.

"Alex, I can't give out personal information about my artists, it's a breach of confidence. I could lose my job."

"After last night, believe me, we don't have any secrets from each other."

"Apparently there's *one*."

"Why are you so dead set against her?"

"I'm not. I do think this is precipitous." Then, unable to stop herself, she said, "At the very least, I think she's manipulative."

"Why do you say that?"

"For one thing, because she didn't give you her phone number."

Alex's panic seeped through the phone. "Look, will you call her and ask if it's okay? If she gives you permission, you can do it, right?"

"You're putting me in a really lousy position, here."

"I'm desperate."

Madelyn sighed. "All right, I'll ask her to call you."

"Thank you. You're wrong about her, you'll see."

Knowing it was a bad idea, she called the loft. When she asked for Callie, a male voice said, "You want me to wake her up?"

Madelyn checked her watch. Eleven-fifteen. "No, that's okay. I'll try later."

"Hang on, I think she just woke up."

Half a minute later Callie said, "'Lo?"

"It's Madelyn. This is really awkward…"

"That's cool. Awkward is the story of my life."

"Alex called me. He's concerned that he doesn't have a way to get hold of you."

"Did you give him my number?"

"No, I consider that confidential."

"Good."

Madelyn couldn't get a handle on Callie's mood. She was cheerful enough, with no audible hostility toward Alex, and yet she had also shut down the conversation. "Well, okay then. I won't bother you any further."

"It's no bother at all. I'm really looking forward to working with you."

Madelyn couldn't bring herself to reciprocate; she said, "I'll talk to you soon," and hung up.

Alex was predictably incredulous. After she went over the entire conversation, word for word, he said, "What am I going to do?" He sounded very young.

"She knows where to find you. The best thing you can do in a situation like this is to play it cool."

"Cool is not what I'm feeling."

"Well, these artist types all know each other. You could walk around SoHo and ask everybody you see in ratty clothes if they know where to find her."

She had meant it as a cruel joke, but Alex said, "That's a good idea."

"Alex—"

"Do you not remember what it feels like to be in love?"

If it had been anyone else she would have hung up. "I consider that a highly insulting question."

"Sorry. I'm half out of my mind."

"Which is exactly the condition she wants you in. The only way to win this game is not to play."

"Not an option," Alex said.

After she hung up, Madelyn asked herself if Alex could be right. She hadn't defined herself in terms of a relationship since the early days with Cole. Was she jealous because Alex had not fallen madly and desperately in love with her? That in fact no one had, or even come close to it, in years? She didn't think that was the issue. That kind of love seemed a hysterical condition, kin to the "vapors" of the Victorian era, exacerbated by too much introspection.

Some up-and-coming artist was having a party that night at his loft. Callie would probably be there, and Madelyn could have brought Alex, except that she was annoyed with both of them and regretting that she had let them violate the boundaries she had so carefully maintained around her work. Instead she decided to barricade herself in her apartment with leftovers and public access channels C and D of New York City cable TV.

AROUND EIGHT, Alex got a bowl of soup at FOOD, all he could afford, and tuned in to the surrounding conversations. The group two tables over, clearly identifiable as artists by their paint-spattered jeans and inappropriate hats, were on their way to a party at the loft of somebody named Julian. Everybody, it was said, would be there. When they got up, Alex did too.

"Did I hear you say you were going to Julian's party?" he asked a rather severe woman in cat-eye glasses and a leopard print dress. She smiled and nodded. "I'm Alex. I'm headed that way myself. Mind if I tag along?"

"Not at all," the woman said, and offered her hand. "I'm Becky."

She introduced him to a few of the others as they walked down Wooster to Spring Street, then east to Mercer. Alex let it come out that he was working in film, which piqued their interest. Everyone argued about Art, but they all loved movies.

Nobody vetted the guests at the loft. After a few minutes Alex broke off from Becky and her friends and roamed the perimeter, stopping only to pour a Dixie cup full of Gallo Hearty Burgundy from a jug and eat a handful of off-brand pretzels. He was in a lousy mood. Maybe it was Callie not being there. The paintings on the walls, presumably Julian's, were crude knockoffs of late-period Picasso. The scraps of conversation he overheard were frustratingly pedestrian, the kind of thing he could hear anywhere:

"George Lazenby in a kilt was bad enough, but Roger Moore? I don't think the world is ready for a gay James Bond."

"Sure Lindsay supports the arts, but he's wrecked the city."

"My accountant says if I don't turn a profit this year the IRS will reclassify me as a hobbyist."

"Did she really? And went back the next night for more?"

"If the tapes weren't incriminating, Nixon would have already turned them over."

"The Mets are going to the series. They got hot bats and momentum."

At 10:30, as he was ready to call it quits, a disturbance broke out at the elevator. He turned and saw Callie screaming with delight as she hugged a black guy in an ancient raccoon coat, attracting the attention of the entire room. Surrounded by women in jeans, turtlenecks, T-shirts, and cast-off men's shirts, she radiated color and light. She wore a tight red 1960s minidress, striped knee-high socks, and a brown leather bomber jacket that was too big for her. Her hair was halfway pinned up and already in sensual disarray. Her eyes were lined in black, her lipstick the same red as her dress.

Alex was dizzy and heartsick. She belonged in this world and he was an interloper. Madelyn had been right, he should have played it cool. He had absolutely nothing to say to her under these conditions. While she was distracted, he crossed the room to the stairs, keeping his back to her, and slowly made his way down. He felt like he was fighting the gravitational pull of the sun. After the first flight it stopped feeling impossible and became only brutally painful. Then he heard her voice say, "Alex? Alex, is that you?"

Though he instructed himself to keep walking, his legs stopped moving and his head turned around and up and he locked eyes with her. She'd been smiling until she saw his face, which he imagined to be a cartoon of pathos and misery. They stared at each other for a timeless moment that stretched and finally snapped. Alex resumed his descent, moving quickly now, and emerged into night air chilly enough that he could see his breath. He struck out for his apartment, his feet slapping against the empty sidewalk. At the end of the block he stopped, again fighting his better judgment, and looked back. His disappointment and self-loathing nearly overwhelmed him when he saw that she hadn't followed.

He called himself names all the way to his tenement, "idiot" and "pendejo" and "loser" among many others, only to get there and realize that the very idea of going up to his room was not bearable. So he walked back to Mercer Street, promising himself he would not go upstairs, merely absorb a little heat from her proximity, and then he would be able to go home again.

When he got to the building and saw Callie leaning against the mailboxes, hazed by cigarette smoke, one sneakered foot artfully positioned against the wall, he experienced a moment of suspended animation, no breath, no pulse, before his heartbeat went into double time. As he approached, she pushed herself off the wall, flicked the cigarette away, and said, "Let's walk."

They headed north, not touching, both of them with hands stuck deep into their coat pockets. "This is not going to work out," Callie said. "I'm the one who makes with the drama and the self-pity and starts the fights. If we both do it, neither one of us is going to get a moment's peace."

All that Alex heard was "we" and "us." He had bounced hard and now was sailing high. Opening his mouth was an unnecessary risk.

A block later, Callie zigzagged west, the opposite direction from Alex's apartment, and said, "I can't handle expectations. There's this part of me that says, 'What gives you the right?' It's been like that since I was a kid. My parents were smart, pulled reverse psychology on me so I would get good grades." She glanced at him. "In case that gives you ideas, I'm wise to that shit now."

"Okay," Alex said happily.

"That's one of the things I love about the art scene here, the way it fucks with its audience. You want art you can commodify and hang in your living room? We'll make canvases 20 feet tall or paint it on the side of a subway car."

"And if I think you should give me your phone number because we had incredibly great sex," Alex said, "that's just tough shit for me. I get it. But it *was* incredibly great sex. Admit it."

She shrugged. "If you like sex."

"What?" He stared at her in astonishment until she cracked a smile.

He grabbed her by the neck and pulled her into a kiss. She let out the most enticing sound, a whimper crossed with a sigh, and kissed him back, holding the sides of his face with her hands. He was crazy with desire. "Let's go to my apartment," he whispered.

She took a double handful of his hair and pulled on it, turning it into a caress at the point of pain. "Nice try," she said. She started walking again. "I haven't eaten all day. Have you got any money?"

"Stone broke."

"Follow me." She walked quickly across Houston, around NYU, and into the Village. The streets were suddenly full of tourists and couples on dates. As they turned onto Bleecker Street, she pushed him against a wall and said, "Stay in the shadows."

Pubs lined the north side of the street, including the Bitter End, a legend in the days of folk, so long ago now. With her bomber jacket hanging open, smiling shyly, she walked up to the first man she came to. Alex only heard fragments of her side of the conversation: "lost my wallet," "trying to get home," "anything you can spare." The man's expression slipped from pleasure to annoyance as he shook his head, then to wistful as he turned to watch her walk away. The next man gave her some coins, the next two shouldered by her, then an older man with a white beard approached her and gave her a folded bill. She squealed and threw her arms around him and kissed his cheek, and he stumbled away with a dazed smile.

She ran back to Alex and showed him a five-dollar bill. "You take it," she said. "I hate money." They bought two slices of pizza each and ate it on the street. Now that he was broke enough to miss meals, Alex was hungry all the time. Callie's easy success at panhandling had turned her mood around and she became talkative and rambunctiously affectionate. She insisted that they spend every penny that she'd "prostituted" herself for, and they got two cans of Budweiser and a can of Planter's Cocktail Peanuts, leaving the change on the counter. They walked up Macdougal to the park as Callie wound the key around the peanut can and then threw the key and the lid in the street. Alex told her about seeing Dylan in '65 and The Chevelles and how so much of the music they played started there in Union Square.

"I remember folkies from high school," Callie said. She filled her mouth with peanuts and handed Alex the can. "Black turtlenecks," she said with her mouth full, "glasses, so fucking earnest. None of them had a prayer of getting in my panties."

"Once they plugged in and got a drummer I bet you changed your mind."

She laughed and grabbed his arm with both hands. "Maybe. But I don't want to talk about the past. I hate it. It just gets bigger as the future gets smaller."

They found a bench to themselves facing the fountain, with the arch in the background, and drank the beer and ate the greasy peanuts. "You talk about this guy Cole a lot," she said. "Did you guys make it together?"

"Are you kidding?"

"Nothing wrong with it. I make it with chicks sometimes."

"No," he said. "It's not like that."

"If you say so."

Kids with guitars still wandered the darkness, ten years too late. Callie laughed at them and said, "They never give up, do they?"

"What's Callie short for?" Alex asked impulsively. "Calpurnia? Caledonia? Calliope?"

"Calamity," she said.

Alex laughed. "No, really."

She looked at him. "Really."

"Calamity... Janus?" He felt like he'd been mugged. "So that's not even your real name. It's another joke."

"What is reality?" she said.

"Jesus Christ. It's like trying to grab hold of a wet bar of soap."

"Soap is clean. I'm dirty." She leaned in to kiss him, sucked his lower lip into her mouth, and bit it sharply.

"Ow!" Alex pulled away. "What am I supposed to call you? I'm not going to call you Calamity."

"You know Bob Dylan's name isn't Bob Dylan, and you still call him that."

"You're not going to tell me your real name, are you? The one on your birth certificate?"

"You should make up your own name for me." She paused. "Just don't *expect* me to answer to it."

At three in the morning—after walking up 5th Avenue to Midtown and back, with Callie critiquing the fashions in the shop windows, telling elephant jokes, reciting Sylvia Plath poems, and taking a number of liberties with Alex's person—they ended up at the top of the stairs outside her loft, kissing passionately. Alex was reduced to Paleolithic lust. "Let me come in with you."

"No. Too many people."

"I don't care."

"I do."

He kissed her again, lifting her skirt and slipping his fingers inside her panties. He pushed her gently against the wall and found his way quickly to the heat and wetness between her legs. Her hands were in his hair and her mouth was on his neck. Gradually her breath came faster and faster, and then she was moaning and biting, and then at the end she wrapped both legs around him and let out a stifled cry.

He held her there as she slowly relaxed and her legs fell like dead weight. She gently pushed him away and straightened her dress, smiling dreamily, and kissed him on the nose.

"I want to see you tomorrow," he said.

She'd turned away to unlock the door. She looked over her shoulder and said, "Two five five five oh nine oh." While he repeated the numbers to himself, knowing he would get no second chance, she got on the other side of the door and the locks thudded into place.

ALEX HAD TO BE at work Sunday morning at 9. Running on less than four hours of sleep and distracted besides, he ended up exposing some poor bastard's roll of color film. Moshe, one of his co-workers, said, "Mark it as 'Defective Canister.' Fuck it, it happens." He couldn't get past it, however, so overwhelmed by sadness and anxiety and guilt that he barely kept himself from quitting on the spot.

At noon he called the number Callie had given him. A man answered and told him Callie was out. He didn't know where she was or when she'd be back. He dutifully wrote down Alex's work and home numbers.

Alex called again when he got to his apartment and she was still out. He collapsed and slept until eight, then cooked one of the dozen Swanson Chicken Pot Pies from his freezer, 30 cents each at the corner bodega, and tried to study. His thoughts ricocheted between the golden strip of exposed film and the memory of Callie's pubic bone against his hand from early that morning.

He refused to make another call to the loft. "Fuck you," he whispered, so as not to drown out the phone if it should ring downstairs. "Fuck you if you don't want me."

He compulsively replayed their conversations from the night before, out of the context of her body heat. "If you like sex... what gives you the right?... this is not going to work out... neither one of us is going to get a moment's peace." She'd tried to warn him and he'd refused to listen.

All day Monday he tortured himself with visions of her with other men. He was too stubborn to call again. As he waited for sleep Monday night, he tried telling himself that it was over and that he was better off that way.

Tuesday she was waiting outside his building when he got home from Duane Reed at 4:30 in the afternoon. She was in her oversize bomber jacket, hugging herself against the chill, her skinny legs protruding like popsicle sticks. They stood three feet apart, Alex warily studying her face, Callie looking at her shoes. He'd never seen her so subdued. When she finally looked up, her eyes were damp. "Alex," she said, "can you ever forgive me?"

He discovered, with some satisfaction, that he wasn't over being angry. "For what?"

"For running away."

"Come on upstairs." He looked back twice on the stairs to make sure she was following, and had to wait for her once he had the apartment door open. "You're cold," he said as he locked the deadbolt. "I can make some tomato soup."

When he turned, she was standing by the bed. She had let the jacket fall halfway to the floor, hanging from her arms as she held them out from her body. She had nothing on under it but an over-size pair of boxer shorts and a white sleeveless undershirt. She looked young and vulnerable.

"I'm scared," she said. The apartment was cold and as she raised her eyes to him she was trembling.

"Of me?" Alex asked incredulously.

"I've been with lots of guys, and I've always called the shots because I didn't care that much. But you..."

He had taken a step toward her without realizing it. She let the jacket fall and reached out to him and he was lost.

She was a different person in bed, passive, melting, enveloping, responding to everything he did, initiating nothing, except, near the end, when she put her hand down between them and touched herself as he moved inside her, bringing herself to a climax that triggered his own.

"I hate this," Callie said eventually, her arms still tight around him. "I hate you for making me feel like this."

"Like what?" Alex's contentment was undercut only by his anxiety about what Callie might do next.

"Don't make me say it."

"Since I met you, you've consistently shown me that I have no idea what you're feeling from one moment to the next."

"For feeling like I need somebody else. I don't need anybody else."

Alex felt as euphoric as if a hit of acid was coming on. "Don't be afraid. This is all new to me too. I'm in love with you, and I've never been in love before. Not ever." The words surprised and frightened him when they came tumbling out of his mouth, but he saw that they were true.

"Taking it as it comes is not my style," Callie said. "If I'm going to fall, I'm going to kick and scream and gouge fingernail marks in the walls all the way down. You don't want to be in love with me. I'm crazy. I'll make you miserable."

"If this is miserable, I'll take all of it I can get."

She sat up, pulled some tissues from the box next to the bed, and scrubbed at the wet spot between her legs. "And I," she said, "would take some of that soup if it's still on offer."

LATER SHE TOLD HIM that she'd run into Paula Cooper at a party. "I mentioned that you were making a film about the Young Lords and how good you were. She was really interested."

MAELO WAS HANGING OUT in the hall on Friday morning as Alex was leaving for his 9:00 acting class. "Listen," Alex said, fighting an odd reluctance, "are you still interested in doing a movie? About, you know, the Young Lords?"

Maelo was six feet tall and maybe weighed 150 pounds, much of it in his enormous Afro. His skin was dark brown, his nose wide, his eyes perpetually bloodshot from smoking dope. "Yeah, man, are you up for it?"

"I'm thinking seriously about it."

"Righteous, man. Whenever you're ready we'll go uptown, talk to some of the brothers and sisters."

What he wanted to say was that he would let Maelo know. What he said instead was, "Is there a good time this weekend?"

ON SUNDAY AFTERNOON they took the 6 train up to Spanish Harlem. Alex had an Arriflex BL 16 mm camera, a heavy wooden tripod, a Nagra IV audio tape recorder, sync cable, boom mike, and a half-dozen canisters of black-and-white film stock, each good for a bit over 11 minutes. Altogether it added up to thirty or forty thousand dollars of NYU's equipment that he and Maelo were about to take into the highest crime neighborhood of the most dangerous city in North America to make a film he wasn't sure he was ready to make. He couldn't stop sweating.

Maelo had recruited a couple of members from the Loisaida branch office for "security" and also, apparently, so he wouldn't have to carry any of the gear. Miguel was barely over five feet tall and still somewhere in his late teens, with a crew cut and religious-themed tattoos and a homicidal look about him. Felix was not much older, five-ten and soft looking, with round glasses. All three wore their purple berets.

They got off at 110th Street and hiked from Lexington east across Park to Madison, past windowless shells of buildings stained by fire, past red-brick public housing like prison compounds, past people sleeping in doorways in the middle of the afternoon, past kids barely old enough to walk who were wandering alone and barefoot on the sidewalks and pissing into the gutters. Garbage had piled up in the alleys and the air carried the sour stench of it. Traffic was sparse, the cars mostly junkers from the fifties and early sixties. Alex didn't see any cabs.

They turned north on Madison, crossed 111th, and then Maelo pointed out a white brick building ahead. "That's the office there." A guy in jeans, a blue work shirt, and purple beret lounged against the door with an M-1 carbine in port arms position.

"Holy shit," Alex said. "The cops let him stand there with a rifle right on the street?"

«Mejor hablar español aquí,» Miguel said.

«Sorry,» Alex said in Spanish. Maelo had advised him to play up his Mexican side.

«Cops don't come here,» Maelo said.

«If they do come,» Miguel said, «they come with respect. And fear.»

Alex himself was terrified. To put off his confrontation with the Central Committee, he suggested they take a few exterior shots from across the street. «Chévere,» Maelo said. «I'll tell him what we're doing.» Maelo approached the door guard with his right fist shoulder-high. They ran down some kind of complicated handshake that involved five or six different moves. After an inaudible conversation, Maelo looked at Alex and gave him the okay sign. While Alex mounted the camera on the tripod, Maelo crossed the street to join him, unfazed by oncoming cars. Maybe, Alex thought, the beret really did buy him something in the barrio. Alex loaded a film canister and Maelo made a frame with his hands and pretended to pan up and down the street, a gesture he must have seen on TV.

Alex felt like more of an imposter than Maelo. You had to be crazy to shoot a bunch of footage and hope to make sense of it later. Nevertheless, he plugged in the Nagra and said, «When I get rolling, you tell me how you got started in the Young Lords. Spanish or English, it doesn't matter.»

He showed Felix how to hold the boom mike, then he focused on the guard. He liked the blur of passing cars in the foreground. He switched the camera on and nodded to Maelo.

"Hello, ladies and gentlemen," Maelo said in English. "My name is Ismael Cienfuegos, but everybody calls me Maelo, the nickname of Ismael Rivera, who is a hero of mine, who sang with Rafael Cortijo y su conjunto in Puerto Rico, where I was born."

Alex stopped the camera and said, «Bueno, Maelo, you don't have to talk like you're onstage at a theater or something. Be casual, like we were sitting around smoking some yerba and rapping, you know?» Alex had to pay for his own film stock, thirty dollars a roll.

«Sorry,» Maelo said. «Let me try again.»

«Just keep it short and simple, okay? Like maybe it was the rats and garbage...»

«Truth is, my parents had a pretty okay building, we didn't have any rats.»

The silence stretched uncomfortably. «So,» Alex said at last, «what made you want to join?»

«It was because I'm such a culero, man. Can I say culero? My father is so burgués, so *bourgeois*, you know? I wanted to piss him off, so I joined up, thinking it was a street gang.»

«Bueno, tell me about that, but—»

«I know, like we're smoking maría.»

Alex got his focus, started the camera, nodded to Maelo.

"Hey, primo," Maelo said in a pinched voice. He pantomimed smoking a joint and hissed in his breath. "Some righteous shit, man."

Alex switched off the camera again. A crowd had gathered, teenaged kids of both sexes, a few older men who looked like they lived on the streets. A half-circle had formed on the sidewalk and they'd started to bump and jostle.

«We can do the interview later,» Alex said. He tried to remember how he'd made "Nimbus." The difference was that he'd had a clear vision of "Nimbus" in his head before he started filming, and he hadn't had to shoot it on the streets of Spanish Fucking Harlem. «I'll just get some establishing shots.» He told Felix to hold the boom mike out toward the street, and even so the crowd noise was distractingly loud.

«¡Oye!» Miguel waved his arms, then whistled sharply. «Everybody shut the fuck up and give the man some room, right?»

Alex zoomed in on the building entrance, panned up the three stories above it, then up and down the block. He thought that not too much of his trembling translated to the camera.

They crossed the street and Alex set up in front of the entrance, a storefront where the windows had been completely papered over with handbills. He asked the guard to say his name and that they were in front of Puerto Rican Revolutionary Workers Organization headquarters. He needed four takes to get it loud enough for the Nagra to pick up, and then he was awkward and embarrassed. This, Alex thought, is why people use actors.

Inside, one solemn face after another stared down at him from the walls, not just the obvious Fidel and Che, but hardcore shit like Lenin and Stalin, Ho Chi Minh and Mao, with quotes like, "Thousands upon thousands of martyrs have heroically laid down their lives for the people; let us hold their banner high and march ahead along the path crimson with their blood!" The light was too feeble for Alex to even think about shooting.

«This room here was where we used to have daycare,» Maelo said. At one point it might have been a kitchen. At the moment it was stacked with cardboard boxes bearing logos for Pepsi and Sugar Frosted Flakes and Pampers.

«What happened?»

«Long story,» Maelo said. «Priorities changed.» They moved down the hall. «This is the library and classroom.» A couple of metal shelves held a few hundred beat-up paperbacks. Alex recognized the same Penguin edition of *Capital Volume 1* that he'd tried to read in Austin. Sagging boxes and overflowing file cabinets lined the other walls. The two chairs in the room were both broken, and back issues of the movement newspaper, *Palante*, were scattered everywhere. The air smelled of moldy paper. «This is where we have the political education classes. After you take the classes you'll be on probation for a while, and then eventually you can join up for real.»

Across the hall was a room with a beat-up desk and a mail sorter. A handwritten sign on the wall, faded to illegibility except for the title, said, "Office Rules." The woman behind the desk had reddish-black skin and a short, uneven Afro. "Who's this?" she asked in English.

«Mi primo Alejandro,» Maelo answered in Spanish. «He's going to make a film about us.»

«There's already a film. Does Gloria know about this?»

«We're going to talk to Gloria.»

«¿De veras? When? Does *anybody* on the Central Committee know about this?»

«Don't break my balls, Lidia.»

«Your balls and your prick are fucking counterrevolutionary and I'm tired of hearing so much noise about something so tiny.»

«Come on,» Maelo said. «Obviously Lidia is having la regla.»

«Chingate, Maelo.»

In the hall, Alex heard Lidia dial her old-fashioned rotary phone. Flipping the light switches did nothing. "Yeah, hi, Gloria," Lidia said. "Maelo's here and he's got some guy with him with a camera and shit... Yeah, I thought you might want to come down and see what the fuck is going on... Okay, see you in a few minutes."

«Maybe we should go,» Maelo said. «I'll meet with Gloria later, get this shit straightened out, we'll do it another time.»

Alex strongly doubted there would be another time. They gathered up the gear, Alex made sure they had it all, then they headed south on Madison.

«Oye, what about my interview?» Maelo said. «The park's a couple of blocks away, we can do it there.»

Alex didn't see any way out of throwing good money after bad.

Clouds had massed up and the wind tugged at their sleeves. Maybe they would get rained out.

They all sat in the grass with the rippling water of the Harlem Meer in the background and Maelo used up the rest of the roll as he meandered through his story. When Alex tried to pack up, Maelo said, «You've got more rolls. You need to give the other brothers their time.»

Alex dutifully changed the canister and Felix, wide-eyed and hurrying, said, "My brother was in the Lords, so I joined too."

"That's it?" Maelo said, following him into English.

"That's it."

Alex stopped the camera and got Miguel set up, thinking, not much longer. But once he got Miguel's face in focus, he thought he saw something there, a calm authority. The clouds were really moving overhead and the light was dramatic.

"You ready?" Miguel said.

"Go."

"I have to back up some, is that okay?"

"It's fine."

"See, I used to jitterbug. You know what that means?"

"Like dancing?"

Miguel laughed. "Maybe where you come from. To us, jitterbug means run with the gangs, to fight, right? To rumble, to bop. I was a Dragon, because Loisaida was Dragon turf, the Lower East Side, you know? Sometimes we would go up to El Barrio to help our Dragon brothers kick the asses of the Red Wings, which was this Italian gang from like Jefferson Park. And sad to say we would also bop with the Viceroys, who were our Boricua brothers, but we had no consciousness at that time, we were illiterate motherfuckers who didn't know no better."

"How old were you?"

"I got initiated at 14 years old, young on top of being stupid." He turned thoughtful and his initial momentum was fading.

"When you would fight," Alex prompted him, "it was, what, with fists? Switchblades? Broken bottles?"

"Everything. Bike chains, shivs, zip guns. People got bad hurt, people died. I had this zip gun, right, a real piece of shit I made in shop class when the teacher wasn't looking. Held one .22 LR cartridge, then you had to practically take it apart to reload."

"Did you ever use it?"

"Shit, yeah. That's how I ended up in the Young Lords." He got thoughtful again, and this time Alex waited him out. "I had a beef with this cat Enrique Ramirez who was in the Viceroys. He was 17, had this greasy DA haircut, this pathetic fucking skimpy-ass mustache, and he was always after my sister Lupita, who wouldn't have nothing to do with a douchebag like him, so he put it on the street what a slut she was, and making up details and shit. So me and some of the compañeros go up to El Barrio and we jump him and some of his friends. My guys take care of the friends so it's just me against him, and I put him on his ass because I was a mean little motherfucker in those days, and I put the zip gun right in his eye and tell him to shut the fuck up about Lupita thenceforth, right? Only he's got more balls than brains and he starts telling me about the noises she made when he fucked her and how she was begging for more and I lost it and shot him in the eye.

"The eye popped like a raw egg and all this goo ran out of it, and the bullet went right into his brain and killed that motherfucker stone dead. And I was so happy about it, I wanted to kill him five or six more times, but the compañeros pulled me off and we ran like hell."

"You killed him?" Alex said.

"Are you listening, or what? Fuck yes I killed the scumbag. Now, the gangs, we settled our own scores, right? The cops came around and asked a lot of questions and nobody told them nothing. It didn't matter, I knew I was a dead man. Enrique had a brother Vicente who was 15 and a hardass, not as hard as me, maybe, but he would bring help. My options were basically leave the country or get ready to die. But that life, the jitterbug life, it makes you crazy. You're all into honor and loyalty and shit, and you don't care if you live or die. I mean, nobody gets into a gang in the first place if they got anything to live for, right?"

Alex nodded, waited on Miguel again. Maelo and Felix seemed hypnotized and didn't try to interrupt.

"This was in April that I killed Enrique, so I stopped going to school, and if I went out of the house to buy a Yoo-hoo I had three or four compas with me, packing heat. Then I fucked up. This was in June, the middle of June, I went to church on Sunday with my moms, because church was off limits, right, only as we were coming out this chica I knew from school, Diana, she was fully developed at 14, you know what I mean? And beautiful. She says, 'Mikey, where you been? I been worried about you,' and all like that. And like an idiota I let my moms go on ahead so I can talk to Diana, and of course she was a decoy and the Viceroys jumped my ass. I fought but there were five of them and they handcuffed me and tied up my legs and the last thing I saw before they put the blindfold on me was Vicente, so I knew I was well and truly fucked.

"They threw me in the back of a car and they took me uptown and dragged me up a bunch of stairs and into an apartment, and I'm still fighting, because it's machismo, right, you do not go gentle into that goodnight. And they are like punching me a little to keep me under control, nothing like they could have been doing, and then they tie me to a chair and take the blindfold off and I'm facing a couch where this middle-aged lady is sitting, wearing a black dress and a hat and a veil, like she just got back from church, which she had. The only light in the room is this table lamp next to her, it's sitting on this doily and it's got a fringed lampshade. I'm noticing all this shit because I figure it's the last shit I will ever see. The Viceroys, they're all standing behind me and I still haven't seen any of them except Vicente. 'Do you know who I am?' this lady says. They've tied a rag in my mouth so I can't talk, so I shake my head and she says, 'I'm Enrique's mother. That was my son you killed.' Then she snaps her fingers and Vicente goes over to her, and she says, 'This is Vicente, Enrique's brother,' like I don't already know that. And Vicente is fucking crying, man, I can't believe it.

"She says, 'Vicente was the one who had to tell me that Enrique was dead. He had to listen to my screams. And he told me they knew who did it, and they were going to kill you to make it right. For a few days I tried to take comfort from that. But even to a foolish old woman like me it was obvious that the next thing that would happen is that your friends would have to kill Vicente, and back and forth and back and forth. So I started to think about what it would take to *truly* make it right, as close to right as anything could. And the only thing I could think of was that you would have to give me your life. Not your death. Your *life*.'"

Miguel was fully into it now, and all Alex had to do was keep nodding.

"My first thought is, holy shit. They're not going to kill me? What a bunch of fucking pussies. But then she starts to run it down, all the shit she expects me to do. First, I have to quit the Dragons. Second, I have to go back to school and make up the tests I missed and stay there and graduate high school. Third, I have to report to her and Vicente once a month, like probation, right, and explain to them what I'm doing to 'make something of myself.' Because Enrique will never get the chance to be a doctor or a priest or a senator, so now I have to. It's a good thing there was a gag in my mouth or I would not have been able to keep from saying that the only thing Enrique was going to be was a fucking welfare-cheating junkie pimp, if he lived that long.

"And then Vicente says, 'I hope you say no. I hope you go back to the Dragons and drop out of school and keep going the way you're going, because then I will kill you with my mother's blessing.' And I remember thinking this might be a good campaign for Mayor Lindsay, 'Stay in school or I will personally kill your ass.' Because once I had glimpsed the idea that I might actually live through this shit, suddenly it was much harder to not care whether I lived or died."

Alex, nodding, checked the film gauge. Still half a reel.

"They put the blindfold back on me and untied me from the chair and drove me back to Loisaida. They took the handcuffs off and untied my legs, and when they dumped me on the street in front of my apartment I still had the blindfold on and by the time I got it off and got on my feet the car was gone.

"I didn't sleep for a couple three nights, and when some of the guys came around and wanted me to bop I told them not this time. After this happened a few times some of the Dragons said

I'd turned pussy, but after I whipped their asses they decided then again maybe not. I told myself I was just trying to give myself time to decide, but when the middle of July rolled around, there's a note under my door with a date and time and directions to Vicente's apartment, and I went."

"Were you afraid?" Alex asked.

"Fuck yes I was afraid. I don't know who in El Barrio knows my deal with Vicente and who doesn't. I see Viceroys on the sidewalk, I cross the fucking street. And they're all watching me, right? Like one false move, I'm hamburger.

"Vicente answers the door, and when he sees it's me he walks away without saying nothing, because he clearly does not dig this any more than I do. His mother has made dinner, mofongo relleno de camarones, sorullitos de maiz, yuca con cebollas, holy Mary mother of God. My moms, I love her always, can't cook for shit and the smell coming out of that kitchen, well, that was pretty much the end of my resistance.

"I go back to PS 188 and I take some makeup tests and shit, and in September I start eighth grade. Meanwhile Vicente, his mother has made him quit the Viceroys, which as you can imagine brought a world of shit down on him from his former compañeros, calling him mama's boy and all like that. Me and Vicente were going through the same thing, because for both of us the gang was our family, our friends, our sports, our chess club, everything. So that was like this unspoken bond we had that was starting to get stronger, in spite of everything.

"One day I was there having dinner—carne guisada, habichuelas guisadas, ay cabrón—and after, Vicente says, 'I want you to come meet somebody.'

"I look at his mother, because this is not part of the deal, and she says, 'Vicente has told me about this. I want you to do it.'

"We walk over to the Young Lords Party headquarters, same place we were at this afternoon, and on the way Vicente tells me about this guy Georgie, he used to bop with the Viceroys, he's been in the Youth House, the Children's Village, the Tombs, Riker's Island, he's one serious motherfucker. Vicente knew him from back then, and a couple of months ago he ran into him on the street and Georgie told him about the Lords. Now, I heard of the Lords, and I thought they were just another gang, right, so I'm thinking chévere, I'm down with this.

"Georgie turns out to be this little guy, like me, with a thick mustache and these big-ass sideburns, and he's got this purple beret with all the pins on it, and there's this way about him. No macho bullshit, not trying to prove nothing, talks so quiet you have to listen up hard to hear. He wants to know what I did with the Dragons and it feels weird in a way I never felt before when I tell him I killed Vicente's brother, telling him right there in front of Vicente."

"Weird like how?" Alex asked.

"It's hard to explain. It's like I'm trying to find other words to make it sound like it just *happened* instead of being something I *did*. You know? To make it something I can look away from and not this humongous big deal, which it has suddenly turned into.

"Then I tell him how Vicente's mother made us both stop jitter-bugging, and I say, 'Which is why I don't understand what we're doing here.'

"And Georgie smiles this big beautiful smile and says, 'This is not a gang, chico. This is the Revolution.'

"He gives me this book and tells me to read something called 'El socialismo y el hombre en Cuba' by Che Guevara, and I'm thinking, yeah, right. It's like pages and pages, I'm really going to read that. But walking to the bus stop after, Vicente says, 'This is now part of the deal. Next month, when you come for dinner, you need to have read that and be asking me questions.'

"And I say, 'Really, Vicente? You would really kill me if I don't read this shit?'

"And Vicente says, he says, 'You are standing at the crossroads. You read Che, and you open your brain to what he has to say, and you will be on the road to being a real man, and maybe you and me will be brothers in the struggle. But if you close your mind and don't read it, you will be just another spic on the corner, a waste of the good food my mother gives you, a waste of the air you breathe, and no, I won't give a fuck if you live or die, and nobody else will either.'

"I start reading it that night and I'm thinking, if it's either read this shit or die, I have a very tough decision to make. You understand, up to this point, I never read a whole book in my life. I did the least amount of homework I could get away with. I printed my words like a third grader. But I got my moms to help me with the Spanish and I wrote down some questions. What happened at Playa Girón? What the fuck is 'dialectical unity'?

"Then something happened. I figured out that the reason Georgie and Vicente wanted me to read this is that the 'new man' that Che is talking about, that could be me. Whoa! That completely fucked with my head. Suddenly all this shit that was abstract and boring, now it's personal. It's not some faceless masses that are getting fucked by capitalism, it's me. And my moms, and all the guys in the Dragons and the Viceroys, and even those assholes in the pinche Red Wings. Everybody in New York City that's ever been called nigger or spic or wop. It was like being asleep for fourteen years and you suddenly wake up, and man, you are ready to go.

"There was plenty to do. Free breakfast programs. Clothing give-aways. Testing for lead paint poisoning and TB. Garbage cleanup. And reading. Marx, Mao, Lenin. And not just political shit. Pablo Neruda. Julia de Burgos. Dylan Thomas.

"Me and Vicente got initiated at the same time. I was proud of that, and him too. The first action we did together was Lincoln Hospital, July 1970, a year from my first dinner at Vicente's house."

"Lincoln Hospital?"

"Lincoln was such a shithole, man, it had been condemned for twenty years and they were still using it. People died in the halls waiting for somebody to see them, and they died of septicemia if somebody did see them. We occupied it with guns, to show we were serious. Because we were not a gang, right, we were an army. Like the Panthers or the Weathermen. And we won, because they are building our new hospital now. Like we won all our actions, because we had the community behind us, because we listened to what they wanted."

The film was going to run out. "Hold that thought," Alex said, and changed cartridges. He repositioned the camera to one side, had Felix adjust the boom mike, got his focus and started again.

"Whenever you're ready," he said to Miguel, "turn and look at the camera and pick up where you left off. You were talking about being part of the community."

Miguel was quiet for a few seconds, then you could see his mood change, turn somber. "It was great for another year, then it all went to shit, like it did for the Panthers and the Weathermen and every other revolutionary organization in the United States."

The first drops of rain started to fall. Alex peeled off his jacket and held it above the camera so the rain wouldn't streak the lens. "Somehow we ended up committed to Puerto Rican independence, and all the community work stopped and the Central Committee went to the island, and that was a total failure, and when they came back we were all factionalized. That was when they changed the name, and Gloria was now top dog, and she exiled Yoruba, man, she exiled Fi, and most of the old guard walked out, including Vicente. When Vicente quit, man, that broke my fucking heart."

"Why did everything change?"

"You know what COINTELPRO is, right?" Alex shook his head. "It's the fucking feebs, man, the FBI, infiltrating revolutionary organizations, pushing the leadership to do stupid things, inciting them to violence, driving them to extremes. They got to the Panthers, to the SDS, the Weathermen, everybody, and they got to us.

"That's part of the story. And part of it is the kind of people who get involved in a movement like this in the first place. You got idealists with their heads in outer space, and you got narcissists that always got to be looked at. And you got people like me, ordinary people of good will, that need somebody to lead us.

"I keep on because... I don't know. I'm not so sure anymore. Hoping for a miracle? There's no miracles in El Barrio or Loisaida. Just a lot of poor people who had some hope for a while and now they don't anymore."

Miguel looked away. Alex kept the camera running until Miguel, still staring off into the trees, made a throat-cutting gesture with the flat of his hand. "Se acabó. That's it."

Alex had a vision of how he could shape it, take out the questions so it was just Miguel talking. He shot another half-roll to use as cutaways—birds flying over the Meer, Miguel looking thoughtfully into the distance, a close-up of his interlaced fingers holding his knees, raindrops clinging to a blade of grass.

WHEN THE WORK PRINT came back, Alex put the picture roll and the sprocketed soundtrack tape on rewinds on an editing table. He cut off Felix's feeble speech and saved it on separate mag and picture rolls. He cut out his own questions and a few of Miguel's sentences here and there and spliced in the B-roll footage to cover the cuts, editing the mag tape to keep the picture and sound in synch as he went. He watched it a couple of times on the little Moviscop viewer on the table and gave himself chills.

He kept thinking about Miguel with his beret and rifle marching into Lincoln Hospital, surrounded by his compañeros, all of them carrying guns "to show they were serious." Alex wondered if he'd ever been that serious. What if it had come to that at UT? Would he have been able to harness his rage to a gun? Harness his principles to one?

Callie was supposed to come to his apartment at seven PM and didn't arrive until 8:45. She smelled of linseed oil, not unpleasantly, and her unwashed hair was pinned up in a wad on top of her head. Under her bomber jacket she wore paint-streaked jeans and a flannel shirt and a testy attitude. "Sorry," she said. "I was working."

Alex hadn't seen her for two days and wasn't sure whether he was more eager to show her the piece of film or get her into bed. What he ended up doing was making the grilled cheese sandwiches she asked for while she talked about Spiro Agnew, who'd been busted for taking over a hundred thousand dollars in bribes when he was governor of Maryland. Like with Capone, it was failure to pay taxes on his illegal income that did him in.

"The fucker pleads nolo contendere," Callie said venomously, "pays a lousy ten grand, and gets three years unsupervised probation. Oh, and he has to give up being vice president of the United States."

Alex was glad to see the mean-spirited bastard go down, though he wouldn't be truly satisfied until Nixon himself was doing hard time on a chain gang. "Well," he said, "at least he put the vice back in the vice presidency."

Callie stared at him as if he was a babbling lunatic. "This is serious."

"Sorry," Alex said.

"What's got into you tonight?"

Alex wondered if the question had been pointed in the right direction. "I really want you to see this footage."

By the time he got her up to the ninth floor of the East Building, home of The Institute of Film and Television, it was after ten. The editing room was a big open space carved into separate work areas—editing tables with hand cranks, Moviolas, and one new Steenbeck flatbed editor, a veritable Maserati next to the Moviola's Model T. His Fundamentals of Filmmaking teacher, Mr. Scorsese, was on the Steenbeck, hunched over, his long, dark hair hanging everywhere, whizzing film and a couple of mag tapes back and forth with nervous energy.

Which left the Moviolas, four-foot-high, green-gray, cast-iron praying mantises with viewers for heads and backward and forward pedals for front feet. Alex pulled up a stool and threaded in the film and the mag track. "Grab a stool and look over my shoulder," Alex said.

"I want to run it," Callie said.

"No way. This thing is a bitch with sixteen millimeter, and it'll chew up a work print in the blink of an eye."

He read annoyance in her silence, in her hesitation at the edge of his vision. "Look," he said, "if you don't want to see this, we can do it another night."

"I didn't say that." She moved behind him, standing, not touching him.

"Can you see okay?" he asked.

"Yeah."

He let out the clutch and Miguel looked at them and said, "See, I used to jitterbug."

Callie watched in silence. Alex got carried away with the

performance all over again and was close to tears at the end. He got himself under control and rewound both the film and the tape. "Well?" he said at last. "What'd you think?"

He shifted around on the stool. Callie looked preoccupied. "The kid's a natural," she said. "People will eat that up, that whole quitting the gang and finding his social conscience bit."

"But not you."

"Well, you know. It's a bit predigested, isn't it? All kind of neat. Like an After School Special."

"A what?"

"You know, those TV movies for kids. Troubled teen triumphs over adversity thanks to hip and caring adult."

Alex took off the split reels and put both rolls back in their cans. Mr. Scorsese looked up from the Steenbeck and said, "Alex, how you doing? You got something?"

"I don't know yet," Alex said.

"Yeah, sometimes that's the best kind."

Alex and Callie rode down the elevator in silence together. He'd tiptoed around her moods before, or managed to distract her, but tonight he felt like one of those GIs he'd read about in Vietnam, who'd stepped on a landmine and heard the click, knowing it would explode as soon as he took his weight off. "Maybe I should walk you home," he said.

"Why, because I didn't go apeshit over your movie?"

"You don't seem that into being with me tonight."

"I wish you wouldn't tell me what I'm feeling."

Alex stopped. "Look, I don't want to fight."

"Fine, then don't start one."

Alex had always thought of himself as a reasonably mellow individual. Callie had the ability to turn him into a mass of seething chemicals inside a hot, thin skin. He shoved his hands in his pockets, the film reels pinned under one arm, and strode off toward his apartment, not looking to see if Callie was following.

She caught up to him at the front door of his building. "You know," she said, "if you're going to be an artist, you have to learn to accept that people are going to have their own opinions about your work."

As badly as he'd missed her the last two days, that was how much he now wished she would go away. The highs and lows of the day had left him exhausted. Back in the apartment, he said, "I'm going to bed."

Callie was rummaging around in his fridge. "Suit yourself. I'm going to stay up and read for a while."

The hissing of the radiator covered most of the noise of her shifting around on the creaky couch and flicking the pages of her book. Eventually he went all the way under. At three AM he woke to Callie crawling into bed next to him. He kept his back to her and felt her flannel shirt against his skin as she draped an arm over his chest. Lust dueled briefly with resentment and lost, and Alex went back to sleep.

HE WOKE LATE the next morning, alone, to pounding at the door. "Phone, Alex," the landlady said.

He put on some random clothes and went downstairs. His mother was on the phone with bad news from Guanajuato. His grandmother had been sick and it had turned to pneumonia. His grandfather had been keeping vigil by her bedside and had a fatal stroke. His grandmother was not expected to last the week.

They were both in their early 70s and old before their time, having only had any luxury in their lives for the last dozen years. Alex had always found his grandfather remote, stern, and formal, and his grandmother had devoted her life to pleasing her husband. He had trouble feeling more than a superficial sadness, and most of that was for his own vague and happy memories of their houses in Monterrey and Guanajuato.

His parents would fly down the next day. "I know it would be hard for you to get away," his mother said, "but if you want to come…"

"I want to," Alex said. "Between school and work…"

"I understand," his mother said.

As he climbed the stairs he was torn between relief and guilt, relief that his mother had made it so easy for him, guilt because it wasn't school or work keeping him in New York. It was Callie.

★

HURRYING HOME from class on Monday afternoon, with an hour to grab a bite before work, Alex saw Maelo leaning against the front of their building, smoking.

«¿Qué pasó, Maelo? Where's your beret?»

"Gloria kicked us out," Maelo said in English. He was smiling. "All three of us."

"You're kidding."

"No, man, straight up."

"Oh, shit, man, was it because of the movie?"

"That was her excuse. Really, she's been about to do it for the last year. To her we're reactionary. Anybody is who's to the right of Mao. It's a sinking ship, and Gloria's going to take it to the bottom of the sea, all by herself."

Alex was suddenly furious. At Gloria, at the lack of justice in the world, at the trouble his own half-assed ambitions had caused. "That sucks."

"Hey, it sucks for you too. You won't be able to make your movie now. Gloria said if you came around again she would break your camera. I'm leaving out some words between 'your' and 'camera.'"

Alex noted that he didn't like being threatened. Not by cops in Austin, not by Maoist revolutionaries, not by Callie. "What about Miguel? He must be really disappointed."

"No, man, not at all. His heart wasn't in it anymore either."

Alex seemed to be the only one who cared. He'd become invested second-hand, his own unfinished business with the Revolution come back to haunt him. "What are you guys going to do?"

Maelo shrugged. "What everybody else does, I guess. Look out for number one."

APPARENTLY ALEX HAD not yet had enough bad news. Three days later, at ten PM, eating a chicken pie and obsessing over Callie, he got called to the phone again.

"Alex?" said a vaguely familiar voice. "Alex, is it you?"

"Frederica?"

"Yes, honey, it's me. Your mama gave me your number, but I can't stay on the line, I'm at a pay phone with some change." Her voice sounded weak.

Frederica had "retired" in 1970. His father had made some kind of financial arrangement with her and Alex hadn't asked about the details.

"Are you okay?" Alex asked.

"I'm not doing so good. I got the rheumatoid arthritis in both my hands and I can't work. The little money your daddy gives me every month is not enough. I'm 65 now, but nobody ever paid Social Security to my account, so they tell me there's no benefits to take out." She sighed. "I don't want to unload all my troubles on you, honey, this isn't any of it your fault. I just need help, is all, and I know you've still got love for me in your heart."

Guilt and helplessness swallowed Alex whole. He'd lavished his empathy on French students with cobblestones, while knowing that Frederica was spending two hours on the bus every day to work for two dollars an hour, barely more than minimum wage. Now, when she needed him, he had nothing to give her.

He tried to explain his financial situation, and in the middle of it the phone started beeping and she was gone. He didn't have a number to call her back and his parents were in Mexico.

Duane Reed pharmacies, Callie, film school, the Lower East Side, what the hell did he think he was doing? Who was he trying to kid? He didn't belong here any more than he did behind a bass guitar at a frat house.

EARLY IN THE AFTERNOON on the Sunday before Christmas, Madelyn stood among the flags in Rockefeller Center and let thick, wet flakes of snow fall on her as she watched the skaters glide across the rink below. The idea was to raise her spirits by glutting herself on the New York Christmas experience. She'd already spent an hour attempting to admire the overdressed windows on 5th Avenue and she was headed uptown to see Central Park covered in white. The beauty and the melancholy were seamlessly intertwined.

"Young SoHo Originals" had opened on Friday, December 6. The other two artists, Kindred's picks, sold enough to keep the show from being a complete disaster; Callie Janus had so far failed to sell a single painting. The reviews hadn't helped. Hilton Kramer, the *Times*' new, extremely conservative art critic, had insinuated that she'd gotten into the show purely on the basis of her gender. In the *Voice*, John Perreault wrote, "In an era where art is attempting to redefine itself in terms of space rather than story, Janus's rather awkward paintings are all about 'words, words, words,' as Hamlet said. She is swimming upstream, but she has failed to spawn."

Kindred had laughed off Callie's failure, saying, "You can't predict a painter's success any more than you can predict a hit record. There are too many variables. You have to follow your heart and hope for the best." Madelyn, however, saw it as her own failure, the fault of clouded judgement and inexperience and her predilection for academia.

Callie herself had put up a brave front, dismissing Kramer as a "fascist asshole" and accusing Perreault of being jealous, though of what she didn't say. Now she was in Dallas, where Alex, to Madelyn's astonishment, had flown her. Alex had assured her that it was not what it sounded like. "It's just a place for her to spend Christmas. She doesn't really get along with her own family."

Madelyn had refrained from asking who, exactly, she *did* get along with; the answer seemed to be Alex. Sometimes.

Despite her best efforts at Christmas cheer, Madelyn wanted nothing more than to be in Dallas herself. Kindred had offered to let her go, with poor enough grace that Madelyn had known better than to take him up on it. Her parents had originally planned to fly up, and then Julia had totaled her car; she was not seriously injured, but they'd needed the money to help her get a new one.

She'd been back to the disco a couple of times on her own—Callie didn't dance, and thus neither, now, did Alex—and it had provided some small release. When she wasn't on the dance floor, however, it seemed impossibly hard to justify the hours away from her textbooks, the lost hours of sleep.

Beyond the loneliness, beyond the guilt over Callie's show, beyond the chill of the big city, she was exhausted. She had turned in her last paper the day before, completing her fifth year of full-time school and nearly full-time work at the gallery. In the spring she would receive her master's; she would then face four more years, minimum, to get her PhD. In a field that was not her own. Followed by five years to work off her commitment to Kindred, by which time she would be well into her thirties. No, not well at all. Badly into her thirties.

She was in danger of crying. She declared the experiment in Christmas cheer a failure—another failure—and walked to 5th Avenue to catch a cab.

As the cab pulled up in front of her building, she noted with a mix of empathy and discomfort that a homeless person was standing in the snow near the entrance. Long hair protruded from a black watch cap, and most of his face was hidden by a light-brown beard. He had a cheap guitar case and a knapsack, both dusted with snow, and an Army surplus jacket that was inadequate for the weather.

She paid the driver, took out her key before getting out of the cab, and walked quickly toward the door. Then something made her stop and look again. Boots. He was wearing cowboy boots.

The man was moving toward her, looking into her eyes, and she felt the key slip out of her limp hand and heard it clatter on the marble step.

"Dear God," she said. "Cole?"

COLE LEFT WOODSTOCK with the clothes on his back, a toothbrush, and 47 dollars in his wallet. He and Laramie hitchhiked to Wytheville in three endless, hot August days, dozing fitfully in back seats and the beds of pickups, eating from vending machines in truck stops, stoned on lust and lack of sleep and their own recklessness.

They arrived in red-brick, two-story downtown Wytheville late Thursday morning, in time to see a heavyset man in a beard, long hair, and overalls put a bag of seed into the back of a 1940s-era pickup truck that was held together by several coats of fading lavender house paint.

"Hey!" Laramie called from half a block away. "You know Sugarfoot?"

The man turned, squinted, and looked them up and down. Then he nodded and beckoned them over with a slow crook of the wrist.

The three of them crowded into the cab, the broken springs of the seat groaning with their weight. In his exhaustion, Cole registered only fleeting images as they drove—clapboard mansions on the edge of town, a winding uphill road, deep green forests of oak, maple, and pine, a wooden bridge over a swollen river, a rusted metal gate, a dirt road through fields gone to weeds and saplings.

The truck pulled up at a two-story Victorian with a sagging porch, a couple of cracked windows, and most of its paint peeled away. A sign over the door read EDEN FARM. Sugarfoot sat barefoot on the front steps, still shirtless, still in his leather cowboy hat, and when he saw Cole and Laramie step out of the truck he did a little dance in the dirt, waving his hat around and laughing. "I can't believe it!" he said. "You made it!"

The house smelled musty and the edges of the linoleum in the kitchen had curled. Mice in the walls and loose nails in the floorboards. A propane gas tank for cooking, kerosene lanterns, running water from an Artesian well. No phones, no electrical wiring. A battery-operated CB radio for emergencies, toilets that flushed into a septic tank. The usual posters on the walls: "You have not converted a man because you have silenced him," "War is not healthy for children and other living things," Hendrix in his vintage military jacket.

The tepee was pitched a hundred yards from the back porch, and most of the people slept there. Sugarfoot said that Cole and Laramie could stay in one of the bedrooms for a couple of days while they got their wind back. Three women were in the kitchen cooking and a few guys sat in the living room, one of them noodling on a harmonica. Cole said hello but didn't retain any of their names.

Sugarfoot showed them their room and found Cole a pair of overalls and some clean socks and left them alone. They bathed and ate and spent the rest of the afternoon and night making love and sleeping, Cole fighting hard to stay in the moment and not think about what he'd done or what was going to happen next. As in the Vince Guaraldi instrumental that Cole had heard a hundred times going into the news at the top of the hour, he had cast his fate to the wind. And having had that thought, the tune played in his head all night long.

In the morning, Sugarfoot called a meeting.

"As many of you already know, it's August." They were sprawled in the field between the porch and the tepee. The sun was already blazing, and half a dozen dogs raced around and through them, barking and nipping at each other. Cole counted 21 men and thirteen women, including himself. Most were Cole's age, a handful in their late 20s or early 30s, all the way up to one guy who looked to be in his 50s. Not enough people for the work ahead of them, and Cole suspected the gender imbalance would create its own share of tension.

In the silence, Cole heard the electric hum of cicadas in the distant trees. Shaking his head, Sugarfoot said, "That was a joke. I expect even Donnie and Carl to know what *month* it is."

Next to the harmonica player was another kid who looked like a serious doper, who laughed and shouted, "It's Octember, right?"

"The thing is," Sugarfoot said, "it's too late now to plant much of anything. We have to somehow get through a long, cold winter before we can turn this place into a working farm. Now, I've got a plan, and some of y'all are probably not going to like it. That's okay, we can discuss it, but I want you to be cool and hear me out before anyone starts pissing and moaning.

"And there's one more thing I want to say up front. I want us to make decisions as a group as much as possible, and I want everybody to know that they can speak freely and raise all the objections they need to. But at the end of the day, somebody has to be in charge, and that somebody is me. I've thought long and hard about all this, and what it comes down to is, I'm providing the land and the vision, and I reserve the right to a final say. I hope it doesn't come to that, but if it does, don't say I didn't warn you."

The guy who drove them in from Wytheville held up his hand. Sugarfoot said, "Chuck, if you'll bear with me, I want to get through the rest of this, then we can have questions. Is that okay?" Chuck nodded and put his hand down.

"There are only two major rules for living here. They're kind of like mathematical postulates. They're the things we grant as assumptions that all the theorems, all the day-to-day rules, are derived from. I've talked to most of y'all one on one and I think you're all down with them, but I want to make sure they're clear to everybody.

"The first postulate is, 'From each according to his ability, to each according to his need.' Which means there's no private property here. Everything is held in common, and everybody is responsible for taking care of it. It means the Golden Rule, putting the good of the community ahead of personal desires, all of that.

"The second postulate is no violence. That doesn't just mean no fighting and no non-consensual sex. It means we don't do violence to animals either, so from now on we're all vegetarians." Cole flashed back to Sunny's exotic meals at the Castle and had a pang of homesickness. "It's healthier," Sugarfoot went on, "it's more economical to eat lower on the food chain, and it changes you as a person in really good ways. No violence also means no poisons, which includes insecticides, chemical fertilizers, cigarettes, and any booze stronger than beer or wine, or beer or wine to excess."

He waited a few seconds, looking around to make sure nobody was freaking out, and then went on. "Now, we're going to need a lot of things to get through the winter, and the number-one thing is money. We've got no crops to sell, and unless somebody's keeping a secret, there are no trust funds among us. So what I'm proposing is that those of us who can get jobs in town do so, at least from now until spring, and we pool our earnings. Are there any carpenters here?"

Cole raised his hand, as did the old guy and two others.

"Plumbers?"

One young guy raised his hand. "Apprentice for a year."

"Good enough," Sugarfoot said. "Electricians?"

The old guy put his hand up again and Sugarfoot nodded. "We're going to need as much work from y'all as possible. You'll have the easiest time getting day jobs, and on top of that we're going to need to build a bunkhouse, and chicken coops, and do some repairs on the Big House. If you're willing to pitch in, you'll be first among equals. You'll sleep in the Big House and you'll be first in line for chow. If everybody follows Rule Number One, there'll be enough for everybody.

"One last thing. Those of you going job hunting." He seemed seriously uncomfortable for the first time. "The reality is we are in the South. If we go into town in long hair and bell bottoms and love beads, people are going to be hostile. I'm not defending that attitude, I'm just pointing out that it's there. If any of y'all are willing to cut your hair and shave and wear straight clothes and basically take your freak flags down for the duration, it could make a big difference to the economic prosperity of our enterprise. This is not a mandate, this is just something I'm asking y'all to consider."

He took his hat off and scratched his long, thinning hair. "I guess that's it for now. Questions?"

The questions and comments went on for over an hour. Most people came down on the side of optimism, believing that love and hope would get them through. Some were hushed and incredulous, as if they'd closed on their dream house only to find cracks in the foundation. A few potential dissidents worried that Sugarfoot had set himself up as some kind of Maharishi, living off of other people's work, screwing all the women, dispensing wisdom from on high. Sugarfoot assured them he would be getting a haircut and a job and sleeping in the tepee like everybody else.

The old guy, whose name was Phil, wanted to know how they were going to do massive building projects without power tools, and Sugarfoot said that they had a gas-powered generator in the barn.

One of the women wanted to know about birth control pills, and another asked who was going to do the laundry, and how. Sugarfoot dutifully wrote down the questions in a spiral notebook and said he'd get back to them.

Somebody asked about dope and Sugarfoot said he'd set aside a growing field a couple of miles away that was accessible only by foot. "Like I said, this is the South. We have to be aware that some of the locals are going to want us out of here, and if we're not extremely cool with the dope, we're giving them a weapon to use against us."

After the meeting, Cole and Laramie took a walk toward the tree line. "I can get a waitress job," she said. "I've done it every summer since eleventh grade. Show some cleavage, get good tips. But if that's all this is, waitressing and hiding our dope and a crappy place to live and boring food, I'd be better off back in Chicago."

"It's just for the winter. Besides, you'll be bunking with me in the Big House. Rank has its privileges."

"You can make more money playing guitar on weekends than from working all week in construction."

Cole was not at all sure that was true. He pretended to write it down in an invisible notebook. "I'll get back to you on that."

"Is this all a joke to you?"

Cole shrugged. "I don't know what my expectations were, if any. I don't want to be that guy on stage at Woodstock anymore, knowing I'm fucking up, knowing I'm not reaching anybody. I don't want to have to think a lot or be responsible for anybody else. Being a carpenter in rural Virginia is fine right now."

"Is this how we change the world?" Laramie asked.

"I guess it's where we start. Ask me again in a year."

Cole's one-on-one with Sugarfoot came the next evening. They sat on the front porch in a couple of peeling Adirondack chairs as the sun went down on the other side of the house.

"How did you come to own all this land?" Cole asked.

"My parents own it. What I have is a notarized document leasing it to me for ten years for the sum of one dollar. My great-grandfather owned this place, and they have their own spread about five miles up the road. Nobody else wanted it, and if I hadn't taken it over, it was going to rot away. We'd pretty much stopped talking to each other until I came up with this idea. Now I'm at least in proximity, and farming again, and I guess they saw it as their last, best hope for reconciliation. That after I fail at this, I'll want to keep farming and come back home."

★

COLE WAS NOT SURPRISED when some of Sugarfoot's principles crashed and burned against the brick wall of human nature. Electric guitars and a drum set appeared in the barn, and the generator ended up powering jam sessions, record players, and an old console black-and-white TV. People were allowed to hang on to their clothes and a few personal possessions like watches, jewelry, posters, keepsakes. The kitchen was occasionally commandeered to cook up LSD or psilocybin tea.

Even so, they lost half their people over the winter. Some of them simply disappeared overnight with no goodbyes. Others left over ideology. A guy in his 30s named Mike, hard-working and previously quiet, stood up in a meeting and announced that social-ism wasn't doing it for him anymore. He and Jean, his girlfriend, had been living in a curtained-off corner of a 16 × 32 Army surplus tent, and they wanted to keep half of what they earned so they could buy a used trailer and have their own space. Everybody should keep half of what they earned, he said, to give them some incentive. Everybody needed a little luxury now and then. He pointed out that people were pocketing money anyway, and the only way to stop it was to legalize it.

Cole knew this to be true. Phil, the old guy, had ended up work-ing with Cole on several construction gigs. He had hamburgers and Cokes for lunch, negotiated kickbacks with the foreman, and put part of his pay in his shoe every Friday. He didn't try to hide it from Cole, and thought Cole naïve for not doing it himself.

Sugarfoot offered a compromise. He would set some money aside in an entertainment fund, and everyone could vote on how to use it. Mike and Jean were not satisfied, and as they left with their meager belongings, another couple joined them. A week later, a hardline hippie chick who called herself Sirocco complained that it was hypocritical to claim to be vegetarian and still wear leather. She found Cole's boots offensive and objected to the leather tool belts that the commune had funded for the construction workers, including Cole. Sugarfoot explained that he made a distinction between leather, which you could salvage from a cow or goat that died of natural causes, and meat, which necessitated killing.

"It's about drawing lines," he said. "We'll be giving our chickens vegetarian feed, but I will tell you from experience that there is no way to keep a hen from eating a bug or a frog that gets in that coop. If you say no leather, do you also say no to manure? That compost pile in the shed is not going to be enough, and we for sure don't want chemical fertilizers. The point is, unless you compromise somewhere, you end up with nothing."

The debate went on long after it ceased to be interesting, until Sugarfoot called for a vote. The pro-leather contingent handily won, perhaps in backlash against Sirocco's personality. She fled the room in tears and was gone two days later.

Laramie left in January. She had trimmed off the last of her blonde hair the week before, marking the end of her transformation, and it turned out that Cole and Sugarfoot were part of what she was leaving behind. Cole borrowed the pickup to drive her into Wytheville. Sugarfoot had taken it on a run to some neighboring stables that morning and the bed still smelled of horse manure. They both cried at the bus station, though afterward Cole felt mostly relief. She had never, Cole thought, made an effort to know him. Her years of being constantly uprooted had taught her to form quick attachments with shallow roots, and to move on when her interest waned. Cole sympathized, though his similar upbringing had led him to get as deep as possible as quickly as possible. Their lovemaking, while physically pleasurable, had never given him the emotional satisfaction he'd felt with Madelyn. That lack had made him withdraw, and she'd done the same.

Madelyn was never far from his mind. He'd given up, under the weight of his guilt, all the letters he'd started. Though the Silvertone acoustic was now commune property, Cole took it up to his room on weekends for an hour or two to keep up his calluses. His attempts to write a song for Madelyn turned out no better than his letters.

In February the remaining nine men and six women met in the living room of the Big House to vote on whether to go on. Six inches of snow lay on the ground outside. The inside temperature varied from blazing hot next to the wood stove to bitter cold near the exterior walls. They had a lantern lit though it was midday. Between the chill in the two indoor bathrooms and the limited hot water supply, people tended to bathe no more than once or twice a week, Cole included, as was all too obvious from the aroma in the room.

Sugarfoot's confidence was unshaken. "We can't quit now. We are more than nine-tenths there. The bunkhouse is mostly done. The chicken coop is ready for chickens. In a month we can plant spinach and lettuce and collards. By summer, once the word gets out, people will be flocking here.

"We've weeded out the ones who don't share our vision. We'll make sure that the new recruits are on the same wavelength as us. Those of us in this room are the seeds that are going to sprout into a whole new civilization."

In the face of his enthusiasm, no one else had much to say. The vote was 14–0 to carry on, with much tearful hugging afterward. Cole was the only abstention, and Sugarfoot cornered him in the hall. "I would have been happier if it had been unanimous."

"I'm here," Cole said. "Actions speak louder than words."

"Sometimes you need the words to make the actions happen. For morale, for inspiration. Like wedding vows. To help you make it through the tough times."

Cole didn't mention that his wedding vows had not gotten him through the tough times.

"You're the best man I've got," Sugarfoot said. "You've got the skills, you work hard, you never complain. But you make me nervous because I'm not entirely sure why you're here."

Cole knew better than to say he wasn't sure either. "I'm not going anywhere."

"I hope not," Sugarfoot said. "We'd be in a bad way without you."

"Thanks," Cole said. Maybe that was reason enough. To be tired at the end of the day, to feel like you were making a difference, to be appreciated.

COLE MISSED his records and his stereo. Though he'd been tempted on multiple occasions to sit in with the ever-changing personnel in the barn, he couldn't shake a snobbish conviction that he was too good for them. Few of the farm's many books appealed to him—multiple copies of *Stranger in a Strange Land* and *Lord of the Rings*, beat poets, Vonnegut, Brautigan, Harold Robbins, the *Bhagavad Gita*, *The Whole Earth Catalog*, a dozen books on astrology. Despite weekly trips to the Wytheville Library, where he checked out thick volumes of nineteenth-century literature—Dickens, Eliot, Hugo, Gaskell, Stendhal, Tolstoy—he had a recurring dream of walking into Safeway and finding a new Matt Helm and a new Joe Gall in the same rack. In the dream he could smell the ink on the pages. He missed drinking, the feeling of being seriously drunk. He missed going to the movies.

At the same time, he had become attuned to natural cycles in a way he never had before, energized at the full moon, waking at sunrise, and when the first buds opened on the trees, he felt himself about to burst like a dogwood blossom.

As Sugarfoot predicted, things improved as soon as February turned to March. Sugarfoot had already plowed up a couple of acres with the commune's 1948 Ford 8N, a Model T motor on a tractor frame affectionately known as Old Paint, turning under the grass and weeds. All the workers left their straight jobs and began to cover the broken ground with composted horse manure and kitchen scraps, with a sprinkling of lime dust as recommended by the soil analysis that Sugarfoot had gotten from the Ag school in Blacksburg. Sugarfoot came through with the tractor again, turning the compost under, then he broke up the dirt clods with a disk harrow, and finally he hilled up the rows.

Meanwhile, kids were showing up at the front gate. Sugarfoot took them into his office, the former sitting room of the Big House, and delivered an agreed-upon lecture. Visitors were welcome to stay in the bunkhouse for two days and look around. On the third day they had to go to work or move on. After two weeks, if they wanted to stay, they had to be voted in by a majority of the existing members, at which point their excess personal goods became the property of Eden Farm.

Some of the new arrivals included people who'd left during the winter. They were now subject to being voted in, like anybody else, and if they left again, it was for good.

One of the returnees was Sirocco. A few days into her probationary period, Cole wound up planting spinach beside her. They worked parallel north-south rows, 30 inches apart, using bamboo planting sticks to open a hole and drop a seed. When the seed was in, they pushed dirt in the hole with one foot and made the next hole two inches on.

She showed no lingering hostility from the leather incident, hadn't so much as cast a withering look at his boots. After a few polite words, they'd worked in silence for a while. The morning was cool and damp enough to turn their breath to steam, and Cole's fingers had been stiff at first inside his leather work gloves. He'd never used a planting stick and Sirocco advised him on the proper twist of the wrist. Cole thanked her and then said, "Why'd you come back? If you don't mind my asking."

She was tall, only an inch or two shorter than Cole. Her weight was nicely distributed, curving in and out in a way that reminded Cole he hadn't been with a woman since Laramie left. She wore wire-framed oblong glasses. Her ankle-length skirts and long-sleeved blouses were cream-colored unbleached muslin. Most days she covered her shoulder-length blonde hair with a blue bandanna.

She sighed. "Sugarfoot's wrong about a lot of things. But out there in the straight world, they're wrong about *everything*."

They exchanged some personal history. She was from upstate New York, so Cole asked her if she'd been at Woodstock.

"I was helping a friend deliver her baby, so I missed it. I heard you were there, though."

"Yeah." He opted not to elaborate. "That's where I met Sugarfoot."

"And Laramie?"

"Yeah."

"I liked her. She was smart. And really pretty."

"I got the idea you didn't like much of anybody."

"Well, you were wrong."

Cole let out short, involuntary laugh.

"What?" she said.

"You seem more concerned with right and wrong than a lot of people I've met."

"Now that's the most diplomatic way I've ever heard that put. You don't have to tiptoe around me, by the way. You can call me an opinionated bitch and I won't disagree with you. I will tell you one thing, though. I'm smart, and I spend a lot of time thinking before I make up my mind, which is why I don't like to back down. And I know a lot about farming, and midwifery, and herbal cures. I know a fair amount about machinery. People say I intimidate them, and I have to stop myself from saying, 'If you can't keep up, get out of the way.' Now what?"

Cole had laughed again. "Nothing," he said. "I like you, that's all. It's a nice surprise."

Cole had built some picnic tables and a ramada next to the kitchen. They sat there and talked some more over lunch. Pinto beans, corn tortillas, spinach salad, cold well water. Cole didn't want to talk about his former career, because of not wanting to put on airs and also because of some residual pain. In fact Sirocco was more interested in what his parents were like, how much Arabic he remembered, whether he believed in God.

She'd taken acid a couple of times and didn't care for it any more than she did for alcohol, marijuana, or cocaine. She liked her thought processes straight up. If she wanted to get high, she said, there was always folk dancing. She didn't care much for fiction and she thought TV was the new opiate of the masses.

They worked through the afternoon, until the sunset leached the heat out of the air so quickly that it made Cole shiver. He was dusty and tired and sore and looking forward to dinner. "It's too dark to work anymore," he said. "I think we're done."

"Yep. I could use a shower." She looked at Cole. He could see the whiteness of her face in the last of the daylight, but not read her expression. "Join me?"

The implications brought Cole to life. "Sure."

"If we go now, everybody else will be lining up for dinner. Why don't we get some clean clothes and I'll meet you there?"

Over the winter Cole had helped build the shower building, nicknamed the Turkish Baths, or "the Turkish" for short. It featured a big open area for those who didn't mind showering together, which turned out to be most of the men and none of the women, with some cubicles for privacy. When Cole got there, Sirocco was sitting on the waiting bench outside. "We're almost out of towels again," she said. "I grabbed us a couple."

The commune had bought eight identical washers from a bankrupt laundromat, both in expectation of more arrivals and to cannibalize for parts. They were in the barn with the generator. People were expected to take care of their own clothes, but the towels were a rotating task that frequently fell through the cracks. Which meant that people tended to steal them to be sure of having one, prompting lectures from Sugarfoot at the Sunday meetings.

"Thanks," Cole said, and followed her down the hall to a private shower, his heart beating in his eardrums. Each shower had a small anteroom with clothes hooks and wooden racks on the floors. "Our lucky day," Sirocco said. "There's soap *and* shampoo."

Quarters were tight. As they undressed, they constantly brushed up against each other, and by the time they were both naked, Cole's desire was evident. He waited for Sirocco to make the first move. She looked him up and down with a smile, then took her glasses off and dug a blue plastic case the size of her palm out of her stack of clean clothes. Cole, who had never seen a diaphragm before, quickly figured it out. She smeared the cup with clear jelly from a glass jar, then stuck it between her legs, shifting her weight from side to side until she got it settled into place. Then she turned her back to him and started the shower.

The rule was to only run water at the beginning and end, turning off the tap to lather up. The place was heavily insulated, with three separate water heaters, so the steam kept the air comfortably warm except for early winter mornings. Sirocco got herself thoroughly wet, including her hair, then made room for Cole. She shampooed while Cole turned off the water and lathered up, and then she turned away and said, "Do my back?"

Cole obliged. He got her back slippery clean, then put down the soap and began to work her trapezius muscles, which were as hard as two bags of cement. She groaned and leaned forward, putting both hands flat on the wall. He worked his way down her back, then rubbed her big, beautiful buttocks. "Mmmm. Don't stop," she said. He reached between her legs and she stepped apart to accommodate him. He was trembling. He bent his knees and moved in over her as she guided his right hand to her clitoris. He tried a few different movements until her breath pushed her spine harder and harder against his chest. In the moment before she came she stopped breathing entirely, and then she let it out in an explosive sigh and he felt her contractions in his hand. He couldn't wait any longer, and he slid inside her from behind. It had been so long, and it was the best feeling he knew, to be inside a woman. She pressed back against him, finding his rhythm and moving with it. His eyes rolled back in his head. His hands moved up her hips and waist and then slipped around to cup her breasts, her skin rubbery with soap suds, her nipples hard knots against his palms, and all too soon the pleasure was unbearable and he came so hard he thought he might never stop. When it was over he went to his knees and she turned and they both slid to the floor, Sirocco ending up half on top of him, both of them laughing.

Eventually they got rinsed off, and Cole was staring at her lips, heavy and curvaceous like the rest of her, and realized he'd never had sex without kissing before. He leaned in to rectify that and Sirocco put a finger on his mouth as if to shush him. "No attachments," she said. Her eyes were a cool gray. "No expectations. Right?"

"Okay," Cole said.

She pushed him away gently and threw him a towel. "Get dressed. I'm starving."

They sat together at the oversized dining room table at the Big House. The first round of diners had mostly departed. Phil, the old guy, was on Sirocco's right and she immediately started up a conversation with him. Cole, who had an empty chair on his left, ran down the possibilities. She could be deliberately trying to make him jealous, which didn't seem her style. She could be indifferent to Cole's feelings. Most likely she wanted to reinforce her point that Cole had no claim on her. Sirocco, so relentlessly doctrinaire, would have been appalled by Phil's meat-eating, cash-embezzling, caffeine-drinking ways. Cole knew that any attempt on his part to narc him out would backfire. Instead he ate his tiresome beans, greens, and cornbread in silence, excused himself when he was done, put his dishes in the soaking pan, and went up to bed.

He waited a long time for sleep. In the living room downstairs they were passing the guitar around and singing Weavers songs like "Michael Row the Boat Ashore" and Carter Family songs like "Wabash Cannonball." Somebody played a plastic Tonette out of key and Donnie grated away on his harmonica. Cole told himself that if he'd met Sirocco outside of the commune he wouldn't have given her a second look. Her own self-regard was contagious. But it was more than that. She was smart and capable, comfortable with her own body, unashamed to take what she wanted.

For two days he only saw her at a distance, then on the second night he woke to a tapping. Before he could answer, the door opened and Sirocco stuck her head in. "Mind if I join you?"

"No," he said, his throat suddenly tight. "Not at all."

She undressed in the moonlight, taking her time. Without quite falling into the artifice of a striptease, she paused at critical moments to make sure she had his attention. When she was done, she set her glasses and diaphragm and jelly on the nightstand. "What would you have done," Cole said, "if I hadn't been alone?"

"Asked if you minded sharing."

She got in between the sheets and Cole smelled mint and patchouli on her skin. This time when he tried to kiss her she put both arms around his neck and pulled him in. Her mouth was everything he'd imagined it might be.

"Um, do you need to put the diaphragm in?" he asked.

"In a while. The spermicide is organic, lemon and aloe vera, but it probably doesn't taste very good." He raised his eyebrows. "I want you to do what you did in the shower," she said, "you know, at the start? Only I want you to use your mouth. Don't worry, I'll show you. And all the women you make love to after me will be ever so grateful."

Much later, she kissed his forehead, making him aware that he'd drifted off as they lay on their sides together. She disentangled herself and reached for her clothes. "Why don't you stay?" Cole said. "It's cold out there."

She finished dressing and came back to sit on the edge of the bed. She ran her fingers through Cole's hair. "There's a part of me that would like that. Part of me wants to leave out the diaphragm and let you knock me up and help me raise a bunch of squalling kids who'll grow up to be perfect anarcho-syndicalists and smash the state."

Cole knew that his brain was awash in sexual chemicals, still, he'd heard plenty of worse ideas. He was sure he could do a better job than his father had. "Why don't you?"

"Because we're just kids. Because I'm not ready to do just one thing or be just one thing for the rest of my life. It was sweet tonight. There can be more nights like this if we both want. We don't have to own each other."

"Yeah, yeah, I know. Property is theft."

"It really is, you know." She kissed him tenderly. "Good night, Cole. Sweet dreams."

In April, Cole ate his first truly fresh eggs, out of tan and brown and green colored shells, the yolks fat and dark orange, tasting nothing like the ones his mother used to overcook. Later that month he thinned the spinach that he and Sirocco had planted, putting most of the culled plants into a bag for dinner that night, eating the rest straight out of the ground, the leaves impossibly tender and subtly nut-flavored, a whole different vegetable from anything he'd eaten before.

They planted potatoes early in the month, a back-breaking job that involved setting pieces of seed potato, eye side up, in a deep, manure-filled trench. Once the potatoes were in the ground, the construction crew put up chicken wire around all the planted fields to keep out the rabbits and the deer.

The outside world made its occasional intrusions. On May 1, Nixon expanded the war into Cambodia. College campuses around the country erupted and the National Guard killed four kids in Ohio. Cole thought of Alex and wondered if he'd gotten drawn in, if he was safe. Walter and Leon, the commune's radical fringe, wanted to have an "action" of some unspecified nature. Cole left the meeting early and heard later that it had dissolved into factionalism and pointless alternatives. Sugarfoot had finally shut it down, saying, "We are not part of the war, or the war against the war. We are the alternative to war."

In the meantime they had work to do. Early May was the season to plant corn. Sugarfoot taught Cole how to run the disk cultivator to keep the rows neat and weeded, and Cole taught Sugarfoot basic engine maintenance. Late in the month they harvested the spinach and replaced it with tomatoes, eggplant, hot peppers, okra. As soon as they finished one job, two more were overdue.

As compensation, they threw a party after every planting, and while most everyone put in long days, Frisbees, water balloons, and nude sunbathing helped break up the monotony.

By mid-summer the population had tripled to 45 and the entire chemistry had changed. They had their first black guy, a skinny kid from New Orleans who called himself Big Easy. They had their first Chicano, a Honduran named Jaime, which meant that Cole got to dust off his Spanish. They had a Vietnam vet who claimed to be against the war, yet constantly butted heads with Walter and Leon. Married or otherwise committed couples, plus a couple of single mothers, had brought in a total of seven kids who ranged in age from newborn to 5 years. The ones old enough to walk ran wild with the dogs. Various women were coming up pregnant, and Sirocco had lined up volunteers to learn midwifery. For the moment the couples were staying in partitioned 16×32 Army tents, acceptable in the hot and humid summer, hopelessly inadequate for the winter to come.

In August, with the population at 52 and climbing, Sugarfoot asked Cole to take a walk with him after supper. The sun was low and the temperature was in the low 80s, cooler than it had been in a few weeks.

"Today is the first anniversary of Eden Farm," Sugarfoot said. "We should have had some kind of celebration, but I couldn't see my way to it. It's not like there's a shortage of parties here any-way." They'd been walking for ten minutes and still hadn't come to the end of the cultivated fields. Cole hadn't taken the time to look around for weeks, and the sight of all those neat rows of crops filled him with pride and weariness.

"I've got some decisions to make," Sugarfoot said, "and none of them are going to be easy."

"First one's got to be accommodations for the winter," Cole said. He'd gotten unused to the sound of his voice, which came out low and Texan.

"Yeah. We can throw up some tarpaper shacks, or we can build some sturdy housing with concrete slabs and wood stoves and running water, and we'll be in danger of going broke by spring."

"That bad?"

"People are showing up with empty pockets. The harvest's been good, but we can't turn that into cash."

"What about the roadside stand?" Cole asked. In May, he and Phil had knocked together a tin-roofed shelter with no walls and long tables where the commune land intersected the county road. One of the women had painted signs promising "Fresh, Organic Produce." They'd sold three hundred dollars' worth of vegetables on their opening Saturday, and the next day Wythe County Sheriff P.J. Mackie had shut them down. "Are they still jacking you around over the permit?"

"Now they're saying the city council has to take it up at the September meeting. Meaning no chance of income this year."

"They're looking for la mordida," Cole said. "Grease for the palms."

"I dropped some hints. I think it's more a case of fucking over the hippie freaks."

Cole remembered the schooling Alex had given him. "Offer them ten percent if you can reopen the stand this weekend. Tell them it's for the civic improvement fund or whatever worthy cause they think is appropriate. Be sure to tell them that you're making this donation because you care about our neighbors and want to be a contributing part of the community. If they don't go for it, raise it to fifteen, or even twenty. If that doesn't get it, start to walk out and they'll come around."

"Where did you learn that?"

"Living in Mexico. Mexico is like the future, after the collapse of civilization."

"Assuming that works, what about the housing?"

"Do it right," Cole said. "If we start thinking short term, we're sunk. What are you smiling at?"

"You said 'we'." They walked on, past the end of the fields, up a low hill covered with live oaks and a few Winesap apple trees they'd planted in June, six feet tall and severely pruned, still a few years from making fruit.

"There's this other thing," Sugarfoot said, looking at his feet. "It's, uh, more personal. I mean, I guess it's, like, totally personal."

"Spit it out, man."

"I've been… I mean, kind of for the sake of keeping everything… I haven't…" He heaved a huge sigh. "I've been celibate since we got here."

"For god's sake, nobody expects that of you. The opposite, in fact."

"It's not that simple." Sugarfoot's discomfort was so extreme that it was contagious, making Cole awkward and anxious himself.

"Why not?"

Sugarfoot stopped, ground the toe of one boot into the dirt. "Because I'm gay." When Cole stared, he said, "Queer. Homo."

"Really?" Cole said. He was lost for an intelligent response.

"You hadn't suspected?"

"Not at all. Who else knows?"

"There's a couple of the new guys who I think suspect. Because they're, you know, interested. I think."

"So what's the problem?"

"Don't be naïve. Are people going to sit still for me making decisions if they're thinking 'faggot' in the back of their minds?"

"You've got to live your own life," Cole said. "If anybody's uncomfortable with it, I can't believe they'd say anything, it would be too incredibly unhip. It would be like saying something racist to Big Easy."

"Big Easy is one of the ones I was talking about."

"The ones who are interested?"

"Yeah."

Cole, hating himself for his own lack of hipness, felt like the ground had shifted under him. "I guess I really am naïve."

"It's kind of charming, actually." Sugarfoot paused, then turned and started back in the direction of the Big House. "Sirocco was saying that the other day."

Now Cole was embarrassed. "You guys were talking about me?"

"Only good things. We were talking about who should take over if anything happened to me. I should have an heir apparent."

"Oh no," Cole said. "Not me. No way. The only person other than you who can possibly run this place is Sirocco."

"A chick? Never happen."

"Then what are we doing here? Seriously. If we can't have a smart, capable woman in a position of authority, if you have to hide your sexuality, if we have to keep working day jobs, what's the fucking point?"

"We are fighting one battle at a time, is what we're doing. And that battle is against capitalism. That's going to take everything we've got. That's like the root of all evil, that's the addiction we've got to kick. If we can get past that, everything else will fall into place. My grandmother was Russian, and she used to say, 'The man who chases two rabbits catches neither.'"

They were back to the plowed fields. "You won't tell anybody, will you?" Sugarfoot said. "About my... secret?"

"Does Sirocco know?"

More embarrassment. "Yeah. She, uh, kind of propositioned me a while ago, and when I turned her down, she guessed why."

Cole knew Sirocco's terms. Still, this was the first time he'd had to face up to them. "She's got a lot of self-confidence."

"She said y'all have an understanding."

"I understand the way she needs things to be," Cole said.

"Sorry, man."

"It's never simple, right? Not for anybody."

Sirocco came to him that night. He'd had it in his mind to put her off, maybe to politely send her away. He needed to grant himself some power, if only the power to deny himself what he wanted. Then he woke to the pressure of her breasts on the soft skin of his stomach, her hot breath and tongue on his nipple, and the transition from sleep to desire was instantaneous and undeniable.

As they lay together afterward she said, "Did Sugarfoot talk to you?"

"About me being his second? It should be you, and you know it."

"In an ideal world, maybe. If you had the title, we could still work together."

"You calling the shots, me as the mouthpiece?"

"No, as partners. Is something bugging you?"

"Sugarfoot said you came on to him."

She sat up in bed facing him, no longer touching him. "That was always the deal. From the start. I don't want to rub your nose in it, but I'm not going to lie to protect your feelings."

"Jealousy is a pretty normal human response in the circumstances."

"Is it? I'd like to think we can be better than that."

"I'm not sure that 'no attachments' is actually better."

"'No attachments' doesn't mean I don't care."

"If you really cared, why would you want to be with anybody else?"

"Then where do you draw the line? Would I be allowed to kiss anybody else? Hug anybody else? Talk to anybody else? Let anybody else see my uncovered hair, like the Moslems? It's a matter of principle."

"And to me it's a matter of emotion."

"Is this an ultimatum?" Her eyes glistened. "You'd rather give up what we've got than compromise?"

"Why am I always the one who has to compromise? No, don't tell me, I already know. Because you're right and I'm wrong."

He saw the hurt on her face and knew he'd gone too far. She was openly crying as she pulled on her clothes and gathered up her glasses and diaphragm case.

"Sirocco..." She turned her back as he reached for her. She left his door open and ran down the stairs.

IN EARLY SEPTEMBER the tassels of the corn turned brown. They spent two long days harvesting it, then replacing it with soy beans that would end up in the "soy dairy" that Sugarfoot had promised. The corn was the last to mature of the "three sisters" that they'd planted in succession, starting in late spring—corn first, then pole beans to climb the corn stalks and put nitrogen back in the soil, then finally squash, to hold in moisture with its broad leaves. They sold half the crop at the reopened roadside stand, and boiled most of the rest and cut the kernels off for freezing. After the third night in a row of corn on the cob and collards for dinner, threats of mutiny consigned the rest of the harvest to seed.

With the fall, Cole and Phil and a few new recruits were sent back to their construction jobs during the week, and spent the weekends building new family housing units and latrines.

Cole knew by the occasional sudden silences when he sat down to a meal that rumors were going around. He assumed at least some of them concerned Sugarfoot, since people considered Cole to be in Sugarfoot's confidence. Some of the gossip was about Cole himself, he knew from the way a few of the unattached women had been looking at him since his split with Sirocco.

Dating didn't fit well with the realities of Eden Farm. Dinners were strictly communal, no movies, no concerts. When the weather permitted, couples could walk in the woods. On the other hand, it was a post-sexual-revolution crowd, and preliminaries weren't as necessary as they used to be. None of Cole's experiments got very far. One woman wanted to have babies as soon as possible, another failed to engage Cole's intellect, another told him cheerfully the next day that she wasn't "feeling any chemicals" with him.

Sugarfoot and Big Easy kept their relationship discreet, though Cole had a pretty good idea of when it had been consummated by the smiles on both their faces the next morning, Big Easy a bit smug, Sugarfoot relieved. Cole heard only a single explicit reference to it, and that came when he and Phil were hanging sheet-rock together. "I hear Sugarfoot's buttfucking the nigger boy," he said. "I wouldn't have thought he swung that way, but what do I know?" Cole at this point had not been talking to Phil for several months, and Phil had yet to notice. Shortly after that a few people left, though it was impossible to know whether it was related to Sugarfoot's sexual preferences or simply the beginning of the winter exodus.

Cole himself held out until December, at which point he cornered Sirocco in the barn and told her he wanted her back in his bed, under whatever terms she needed. She had looked away, tears coming up in her eyes, and said, "Good. I missed you." Then she got herself under control, smiled, and said, "I'll see you tonight." Without ever conceding anything, she began to show up more and more often until she was there nearly every night, usually falling asleep and staying until morning.

The fall had been difficult in other ways. In the space of a single month, between September 3 and October 4, three of his fellow Woodstock musicians had died from overdoses, first Blind Owl Wilson from Canned Heat, then Hendrix, then Joplin. The night after he heard about Joplin, he lay awake thinking about the lounge at the Holiday Inn in Liberty, her flirting with him, her kissing him on the lips. The loss seemed greater than three musicians. It seemed like a cosmic shift, as if the Aquarian Age had been cancelled due to unforeseen circumstances.

Meanwhile the war ground on and on, killing 6000 US soldiers in 1970 and uncounted Vietnamese, Cambodians, and Laotians. Peace talks continued in Paris and got nowhere. In November Nixon proposed a cease fire, in terms the North couldn't accept. And on and on it went.

At Eden Farm, at the low ebb in February of '71, they still had 67 people, 18 of them kids. Five of those had been conceived and born on the farm and were known as "creoles" in the farm's private slang. Ten more women were in various stages of pregnancy, and Sirocco's midwife team now made themselves useful throughout Wythe County, doing wonders for public relations.

Cole gradually relaxed into the rhythms of the farm. Short hair and clean shaves and for-hire carpentry in the winter, long hair and beard and agriculture in the spring and summer. Eating food that tasted better and made his body feel better than anything he'd ever eaten. Living in a community that had the closeness of a rock band multiplied ten times over, that did yoga together, that shared politics and musical taste, that hugged each other frequently.

Having regular sex with a woman who turned him on physically and mentally, despite his occasional jealousy and her occasional barbs about his boots.

It all peaked in the summer of 1972. The commune was 150 strong, kids underfoot everywhere. People lived in anything they could scavenge, barter for, or convince Sugarfoot to assign the construction crew to build. The roadside stand made as much as the day jobbers had brought in over the winter. Sheriff Mackie, who Sugarfoot now called "P.J." behind his back, came around personally every Monday. He was tall and sunburned and pushing 60, with a pearl gray Stetson that had a sweat stain above the hatband. After he collected his 20 percent, he stayed for a home-cooked lunch where he said, more than once, "Y'all folks ain't near as bad as some try to make out."

"Yankees," Cole liked to tell him. "Spreading lies."

Mackie had in fact warmed to the point that when a couple of deer hunters stumbled onto the pot fields that November and called the law, he went straight to Sugarfoot. This was the Friday after Thanksgiving, and he had the courtesy to run his lights and siren when he drove up so that he wouldn't surprise anyone smoking a joint. Sugarfoot sent for Cole and Sirocco, and the four of them sat at the round laminated table in Sugarfoot's office. Sugarfoot told Mackie how shocked they were that someone would use their land to grow illegal drugs. "Since this has been brought to my attention," Mackie said, "we have no choice but to burn the fields. Any plants we find there, oh, say, next Monday, will have to be destroyed." Everybody at the table managed a properly somber demeanor, and as soon as Mackie's car disappeared in the distance, every available hand was diverted to an emergency harvest. Even so, enough was left on Monday that the burning was very well attended, and the ravenous deputies were all invited to lunch at the farm.

In the outside world, 11 Olympic athletes were murdered by Palestinian gunmen in September. In November, peacenik George McGovern was trounced by Nixon, despite evidence that Nixon had been involved in spying and dirty tricks. Rain gave way to snow, and then more snow.

Cole, for the first time, found himself restless. He brought the communal Silvertone up to his room and played it every night. The heat between him and Sirocco had cooled, and more nights than not she fell asleep to his guitar without their making love.

The spring of '73 got off to an ominous start. In late March, a host of timber rattlesnakes took to sunning themselves in the dark soil of the fallow fields. Sugarfoot refused to kill them, which outraged the parents with small children, a number of whom pointed out that the snakes themselves were violating the prohibition against violence. "Only if they have no other option," Sugarfoot said. "If you leave them alone they'll go away." The ensuing arguments were loud and long, and ended with the creation of a Snake Relocation Team. They scored bag sticks from the hardware store and collected nine adult snakes between three and five feet long. They dumped them in a screen wire enclosure, which a herpetologist from the State of Virginia came to collect.

The rancor from that confrontation had barely subsided when a reporter from WDBJ in Roanoke showed up, wanting to bring out a full news crew to do a story. At the inevitable company meeting to discuss it, Sirocco was adamantly opposed. Sugarfoot argued that not only could it boost sales at the produce stand, it could help send a positive message and further the Revolution. He carried the vote by a substantial margin, though Cole voted with Sirocco. Despite severe rationing, most of the farm continued to be seduced by the fake glamor of TV. The crew spent a full day doing interviews and shooting people at work while Cole, Sirocco, and a handful of other dissenters stayed upstairs in the Big House and played Monopoly. On the day of the broadcast, most of the commune gathered to watch it in the barn, again excepting Cole and Sirocco. Sugarfoot came to the Big House afterward to admit that it had been a travesty. "Outhouse jokes, implications that everybody was having sex with everybody else, screen time for *both* Donnie and Carl so we'd look like a bunch of stoned-out idiots. The interviews were invariably with the dirtiest, hairiest people they could find. Then when they put P.J. on at the end, saying how we weren't 'near as bad as some tried to make out,' it made him look like an idiot too. I wouldn't be surprised if it cost him the next election." Sirocco had the grace not to say anything. Sugarfoot apologized to her anyway, and to Cole, and left in a black mood.

By May they averaged two or three people at the front gate every day, due to word of mouth alone. In '70 and '71 the few applicants had been idealists, earnest back-to-nature types in overalls and beards and second-hand granny dresses, wanting to be part of something bigger than themselves. In '72 came the followers, in headbands and leather vests and peace symbols, the hippie as fashion statement, looking for dope and free love like they'd seen in the *Woodstock* movie. By '73 it was the dregs, the speed freaks, the mental patients, the scammers, everyone who was no longer welcome in the straight world, looking for whatever they could get away with.

Sugarfoot had appointed an ironically-named "Welcoming Committee" who tried to talk the visitors into leaving. Those who insisted could stay for two days. If they failed to show serious promise, they were gently escorted to the highway.

That was how "just Keith" made it inside the gates in mid-June, against the Committee's instincts. Cole happened to see him as they took him on his introductory tour. Pale skin, stringy unwashed black hair, Fu Manchu mustache, black T-shirt too small for his scrawny frame, black jeans, motorcycle boots, silver concho belt, leather bag slung over one shoulder. Eyes small and bloodshot. Cole's first impression was that he was a dangerous psychopath.

Early the next morning, Sugarfoot brought Cole and Sirocco to his office and told them that "just Keith" had made aggressive advances to a number of women during the night, two of whom came to Sugarfoot to complain. Also during the night, a number of personal items had gone missing—jewelry, a baggie of now very scarce pot, a pair of women's panties. "I've got a bad feeling about this guy," Sugarfoot said.

"Two words," Cole said. "Charlie. Manson."

"I radioed the Sheriff's office and P.J. wouldn't take my call." Mackie had indeed blamed the commune for the way he'd been portrayed in the TV show. "The deputy said they don't do evictions for private citizens and we'd have to work it out ourselves."

Sirocco said, "The Welcoming Committee plus the three of us makes eight. We surround him and escort him out."

"We need to search him," Sugarfoot said. "If he stole that stuff, I want it back."

"If there's no private property…" Sirocco said. Sugarfoot gave her a look that said he was not in the mood.

"Worst case," Cole said, "we have to sit on him while we search." He was terrified. He hated confrontations even when they weren't hostile.

"Do we know where he is?" Sirocco asked.

"Sleeping it off in the bachelor's bunkhouse. Apparently he's got a girl with him. That 14-year-old kid who came in with her parents last month. The one with all the hostility."

"Tessa," Sirocco said.

"That's the one."

"Jesus," said Cole.

They found four out of five of the Committee, three women, one man. Maybe, Cole thought, the women would make him feel less threatened.

Yeah, right.

The bunkhouse was nearly empty. It was eight AM, the farming day well underway. "Just Keith" was asleep on his back in the highest bunk of a tier of three, his mattress at Cole's eye level. His right forearm lay across his eyes and he was using his bag as a pillow. Tessa lay half on top of him, long brown hair spread over his chest.

The bunks were open on both sides. Two of the Committee women walked around to Tessa's side and one of them touched her on the shoulder. She came up on one elbow and, ignoring the shushing gestures that everyone was making, said, "What's going on?"

Keith stirred and Sugarfoot make a grab for his bag. At that Keith came instantly awake, one hand on the bag and the other grabbing Sugarfoot's wrist, hard. "The fuck you doing?"

"We're here to ask you to leave," Sirocco said. "We need to check your belongings before you go."

"Let go," Sugarfoot said. "You're hurting me."

"Tough shit," Keith said to Sugarfoot, and to Sirocco he said, "Fuck you. I like it here."

Tessa, wearing only a stained white T-shirt, chose that moment to slide out of the far side of the bunk. Keith lunged for her, which meant he had to let go of Sugarfoot, who snatched back both his wrist and the shoulder bag. Sugarfoot tossed the bag to one of the Committee women, who looked inside and said, "The missing bracelet… the missing watch… the missing panties… the missing dope… some bags of white powder… a good deal of cash… a bunch of rings of keys, god knows to what…"

"What?" Keith said. "You calling me a thief, now?"

"Oh, what the hell," Sugarfoot said. He was trembling with nervous anger. "You're a thief. You're also a statutory rapist, and God knows what else. Get dressed."

Keith considered his options for a second or two, then threw off the sheet. He was naked, and the gust of air from the sheet brought Cole the smells of sex and poor hygiene. They all backed away to let him climb down from the bunk. He got into his jeans and T-shirt and sat down to put on a pair of rank socks and then his boots. He patted his pockets as if he were missing something, and turned half away. When he spun back around, he had a switchblade in his hand, the kind Cole had seen in flea markets across Mexico.

"Give me my bag," Keith said.

The woman holding the bag looked at Sugarfoot. "Give it to him," Sugarfoot said.

"Wait," Sirocco said, and took a step toward Keith. "Give me the—"

Cole yelled, "No!" at the same time that Keith lunged at her.

Cole didn't quite follow what happened next. Somehow Sirocco was standing inside Keith's reach, and she had both hands on his knife arm. The knife clattered to the floor and a second later Keith was on his knees, facing the opposite way, head bowed, and Sirocco was holding his right hand in hers, Keith's arm stiff and bent at an unnatural angle as he made noises like "Ah, ah, ah, ah."

"Do we have any rope?" Sirocco asked calmly.

"I don't think so," Sugarfoot said.

"Twine," the Committee woman with the shoulder bag said. "We've got the twine we use to tie up the plants with."

"That'll work," Sirocco said. "Would you get some for me, please?"

Sugarfoot sat on a nearby bunk, folded his arms over his knees, and rested his forehead on them. The others stood around awkwardly, Keith still making rhythmic noises, until the twine arrived. Sirocco supervised as the woman with the twine tied Keith hand and foot.

"Now what?" Cole said. He wasn't sure if he was frightened because of the way Sirocco had endangered herself, angry because she'd never told him she knew martial arts, or full of homicidal hatred for Keith. All of the above, he guessed.

"Take everything we know for sure is ours out of his bag," Sirocco said. "Leave the other drugs and the money. Drop him off at the Sheriff's."

"I'll be back," Keith said. "I'll come back and kill every one of you fuckers in your sleep."

"Sugarfoot?" one of the Committee women said.

"I don't know," Sugarfoot said. "This is all… this shouldn't be…"

Sirocco knelt beside Sugarfoot and stroked his hair. "Deep breaths. Lots of deep breaths."

"You fuckers," Keith said. "You're all dead."

Sirocco turned to Keith and said quietly, "Unless you want us to gag you, you need to be quiet. If you make me mad enough, I might use one of your own socks to do it."

Keith shut up.

"Sugarfoot," Sirocco said. "We need to do something."

"Go ahead," he said. "Do what you want."

A crowd had gathered outside the bunkhouse. Sirocco took the farm property from Keith's bag, picked up the switchblade with a bandana and dropped it in, and slung the bag over her shoulder. She took Keith's shoulders and nodded to the male Committee member to take his feet. Keith began to buck furiously. Sirocco set him down and put a finger under his jaw. "Hold still. Do you understand me?" He went limp and Cole followed as they carried him out to the lavender pickup and placed him in the bed. "Cole and I'll ride with him," Sirocco said.

Cole climbed in and slammed the tailgate. He sat as far as he could get from Keith, and Sirocco sat next to Cole.

"You might have asked," Cole said.

"What?"

"Before you volunteered me."

"Sorry. I'm a little flipped out."

"Man, you sure don't show it. What was that you did to him?"

"Aikijujutsu. Daito-ryu version."

"You're like a black belt or something?"

"Yeah, first dan only. I was lucky, I had a teacher who studied with Tokimune Takeda himself."

Cole shook his head. "I don't know jack shit about any of that. How come you never told me?"

"Because I don't like it. I want to live in a world where I never have to use it."

Cole shut his eyes. "I want to live in that world too. If you find it, let me know."

At the Sheriff's office, P. J. himself came out to look at Keith. "What the hell am I supposed to do with this?"

"Fix up your reputation," Sirocco said. "He's got what looks like drugs in his bag." She handed it over. "You'll also find an illegal switchblade in there, covered with his fingerprints. He attacked us with it, which is assault, and threatened to come back and kill us, which is also assault. Let the voters know you won't put up with hippies who can't follow the law."

"Clever, ain't you?" P. J. had always had a certain gleam in his eye when he talked to Sirocco. "Bobby, put this trash in a cell and I'll talk to him later."

"Want me to cut this string off him?" Bobby said.

"It's just string," P. J. said. "Can't be hurting him too much."

Keith, who'd been quiet to that point, spat at P. J. "Son," P. J. said, "you shouldn't ought to have done that."

"You need to take statements from us?" Sirocco asked.

"Y'all run along," P. J. said. "I know where to find you."

By the time they got back to the farm, everyone had heard some version of the story, which had swollen into an epic melodrama with buckets of blood, hostages, broken bones, and concussions. Cole tried to return to work, pulling weeds by hand from between the intermingled corn, beans, and squash. People kept interrupting. Two fields over, Sirocco was dealing with the same hassles. At one point a small crowd gathered around her, voices getting strident. Cole went to investigate.

"… never justified," one of the women was saying, an edge of hysteria in her voice. She called herself Zinnia, Cole remembered. Long auburn hair, no sense of humor. "Passive resistance is the only way to respond to—"

"Where's Sugarfoot?" one of the men interrupted. "We need to have a meeting about this."

"He's locked in the office," another woman said. "He won't come out."

"The rules have to apply to everybody," Zinnia said, "all the time. No exceptions."

"Could we all go back to work?" Cole said. "We can discuss this at the next meeting."

"He said he was going to come back and kill us all!" Zinnia said. "We have to decide how we're going to—"

"Did we ask your opinion?" the man said to Cole, interrupting again.

"He's not coming back," Cole said. "He's in jail."

"Since when are we going to the pigs to solve our problems?" another man asked.

Cole felt his own temper rising. Sirocco put a hand on his arm. "Let's go," she said.

As they walked away, Zinnia shouted after them, "This isn't over!"

Sirocco said, "Most of the people who came to talk to me wanted me to teach them self-defense. The others wanted me to leave."

"Sugarfoot has to take control of this mess. I'll go talk to him."

"Good luck."

Cole tried the office door. It was indeed locked, for the first time ever. "It's Cole," he said. "Open up."

The silence dragged on. Cole knocked again, beginning to worry.

"C'mon Sugarfoot, let me in." This time a chair squeaked and then, finally, the lock clacked and the door opened.

The yellow paper shade was drawn on the window and the office was dim. Cole took his usual seat at the table. Sugarfoot locked the door again and slumped in a chair across from him.

"I keep going over it in my mind," Sugarfoot said. "What Sirocco did was wrong. But I can't think of any response that wouldn't have been worse."

"She used the minimum force necessary to protect herself from serious injury or death. She didn't do him any lasting harm. She recovered our property and neutralized the threat."

"What if we had just let him walk away? Maybe he would have left."

"Get real. He wasn't interested in leaving, and even if he did, he would have become somebody else's problem."

"Do you think he'll come back?"

"No," Cole said, not entirely sure he believed it. "Once he's out of jail he'll want to get as far from Sirocco as he can get."

"It's too hard," Sugarfoot said. "I can't deal with it anymore."

"Somebody has to," Cole said. "I don't have the skill. Sirocco's in the middle of it, so she's not a choice. That leaves you. Unless you maybe want Donnie and Carl to run things."

"I'm not sure they could do any worse."

"If you want to feel sorry for yourself, that's fine, as long as you do it on your own time. Right now you need to call a meeting, stand up for Sirocco, and get us past this." He got up and unlocked the door. "Now would be good."

Sirocco wasn't in his bedroom. From his window he saw clumps of people talking and gesturing instead of working. Finally Sugarfoot came out and they all sat down in the shadow of the tepee.

Cole watched from where he stood. Sugarfoot was brief and to the point. He explained what had happened in the bunkhouse, and called on the Committee members to back him up. Zinnia brought up passive resistance and Sugarfoot said the circumstances did not allow it. Somebody complained about using the Sheriff to deal with their internal problems and Sugarfoot reminded them that on four separate occasions they had taken people to the Wythe County Community Hospital for medical care, which was no different. They paid taxes and received police and fire protection in return. As to the possibility of future violence, from Keith or anyone else, he planned to ask Sirocco to teach martial arts to anyone who was interested. The discussion quickly got repetitive and Sugarfoot called an end to it.

Gradually people drifted back to work. Cole lay down for a while and went back to his weeding at 1:30. No one spoke to him. Sirocco had disappeared.

He was ignored again at dinner. He overheard hushed voices and grumbling, and he saw, with fresh eyes, what long odds Sugarfoot had taken on with Eden Farm, how easily one noxious personality could poison an entire community, how quickly years of good will and hard work could be undone.

At four in the morning he woke to a pale fluttering in the moonlight. Sirocco sat on the edge of the bed. She was luminous and he wondered if he was dreaming.

"I'm leaving," Sirocco said. "I'm going to Tennessee, give the Farm a try." It was the largest commune in the world, with a population of over 1500. "This place is finished."

She had not invited him to join her. Though he'd seen this moment coming, the rejection stung and he retreated into himself.

"When?"

"Now. By the time the sun comes up I'll be on the highway with my thumb out."

He searched for a way to change her mind. His brain, numb with sleep, came up empty.

She ran a hand through his hair. "You know what I always liked about you?"

"No. I always wondered."

"You never tried to impress me."

"Would it have worked?"

"No." She, who cried so easily, was dry-eyed now. "You should go back to playing music," she said. "You have a gift."

"Maybe. I have to not want it so much."

She touched his lips with the tips of her fingers. "Go to sleep."

He grabbed her hand and kissed her palm. He already missed the idea of her. "Please don't go," he said.

"Maybe our paths will cross again. If that's our karma."

"I don't even know your real name."

"Shhhh," she said. He saw then that she had already left and he was trying to reason with a shadow, a footprint, the scent of mint and patchouli left on a pillow. She stood up and turned away and she was gone.

IN THE END, neither "just Keith" nor Sheriff Mackie nor rattlesnakes nor WDBJ-TV landed the blow that killed Eden Farm. That honor fell to a baby chicken.

Afterward, they figured out that one of the kids had been playing with the chickens and then forgotten to wash his hands. He ran to see his mother, who was working in the kitchen, and within a few days half the population was sick with salmonella. The farm was quarantined, and though their produce was pronounced safe by the Virginia Department of Health, no one stopped at the roadside stand. Two toddlers died, one of whose grandparents filed suit against Eden Farms and Sugarfoot in specific for criminal negligence. As soon as they were well enough to travel, people fled, sometimes ten or twenty in a day. By mid-September it was down to Cole, Sugarfoot, and 11 others.

Sugarfoot called one final meeting to announce that he was closing the place down. Everyone had two weeks to find another place to live. They were welcome to whatever they could carry away.

No one had any questions. Cole and Sugarfoot adjourned to the front porch of the Big House and drank beer. "What about the debts?" Cole asked. He knew they'd been dodging the propane company for months, and had outstanding bills for groceries and hardware and diesel for the tractor. Not to mention unpaid property taxes.

"My father's lawyer is drawing up the papers for me to file for bankruptcy. And he's going to make the lawsuit go away."

"How pissed is your father?"

"Not at all," Sugarfoot said. "He was so pleased to see me fail and prove him right that it moved him to new heights of generosity. Not that he would ever put it in those terms."

"Where will you go?"

"Chicago. I've been talking to my thesis advisor. He wants me to dump my old idea and write about agronomy in the context of the commune instead. He's going to give me my TA gig again, and says I can get an assistant professorship as soon as I finish the thesis. Which I've already got outlined. I mean, I can see the whole thing in my head."

"You sound better than you have in a couple of years."

"It's a load off. Jesus, what a load off." They sat and drank for a while and then Sugarfoot asked gently, "What about you?"

"I have no idea," Cole said.

COLE WAS THE LAST, other than Sugarfoot, to leave. Sugarfoot insisted that he take his tool belt and tools, the Silvertone guitar, and what was left of the petty cash, which came to $73.09.

He got a room in a boarding house on the western edge of Wytheville and signed on with the same construction company where he'd worked the last four winters. This time he trimmed his beard instead of shaving and left his hair in a ponytail. The foreman didn't seem to care. When Cole told him the commune had folded, he said, "I heard about that salmonella. Tough break." Cole agreed that it was.

He ate supper every night at a diner a few blocks from the boarding house, and after a week he had the waitresses trained in the general principles of vegetarianism. The vegetable soup didn't count if it was made from chicken stock, nor did the green beans that had been boiled in ham hocks. He was patient and smiled a lot and left good tips and over time more and more things turned up that he could eat.

Most evenings he would watch the boarding house TV for an hour or two with the landlady's cat in his lap. He had emerged into a different world. The war was over and Congress was talking about impeaching Nixon over Watergate. The men on TV had hair over their collars and the women were blatantly sexual. A show about doctors in Korea was an obvious allegory for Vietnam. In another show, a half-Chinese guy in the Old West spouted Taoist sayings and reluctantly kicked people's asses with martial arts. Cole's generation had become a desirable demographic. He thought of Sirocco and how much she would hate the pandering.

On weekends he read novels from the library, played guitar, and caught up on the sleep that he seemed unable to get enough of. In good weather he would walk for three or four hours at a time. One Sunday in late October he hitchhiked out to the deserted roadside stand and turned up the long dirt road to Eden Farm. The day was cloudy, dry, and cool enough for the new, dark-gray windbreaker he'd bought two weeks before. The chained and padlocked gate was easy enough to climb over. The front door of the Big House was unlocked, and the furniture was gone, upstairs and down, except for the table in the office. Somebody had sawn it in half, with the apparent intention of carrying it out.

He went out the back door and it took him a second to realize that the thing he was missing was the tepee. He wondered where it had ended up. Most of the other structures he'd built were gone, down to the concrete slabs, in the cases where they'd bothered to pour one. Piles of lumber lay here and there, cleaned of nails and ready to be carted off.

The fields were dry and yellow, the last crop of soybeans rotting on the vine. Cole walked as far as the orchard and picked a few apples that the birds and bugs hadn't gotten at too badly. On the back stoop of the house, he ate one of the apples and wondered where those four years had gone. He had nothing to show for them. He remembered how cold the house had been in the depths of winter, how hard it had been to get up at 5:30 and throw his work clothes on his shivering body, to eat beans and eggs and tortillas and get in one of the farm's barely-running school buses for the half-hour drive into town and the long, cold day on the job site. He remembered the hot, airless nights in the summer when the only thing he wanted in the world was a box fan in his window, when, after dozing off repeatedly in the fields all day, he found himself unable to sleep in the relentless heat. He remembered the endless Sunday morning meetings and a woman named Pat who, every time things wound down, always had one more niggling question.

Then he thought about putting his tools in the barn at the end of a day's work, relief in sight for his fatigue and hunger, and feeling another man's hand on his shoulder in wordless communion. He remembered an afternoon riding home from Wytheville on the bus when somebody had started singing the lick from "Sunshine of Your Love," and somebody else began drumming on the back of the seat, and then everybody on the bus fell in, Cole and another guy singing the lead guitar solo in harmony, the whole thing boisterous and largely out of tune and altogether intoxicating. Or one of the kids he'd watched grow from infant to toddler to miniature human coming to him and asking him to read *The House at Pooh Corner*. Sitting in a field before dawn on the summer solstice with fifty other people, panting the Kundalini Breath of Fire, feeling like they were pulling the sun up over the horizon with the power of their lungs. The incendiary conversations that would spring up out of nowhere about Kierkegaard or blacksmithing or UFOs or acupuncture or chess or numerology or the Dhammapada, as sharp minds made agile by psychedelics fearlessly attacked the eternal questions of the universe.

If happiness, as Sirocco had once postulated, was the ability to appreciate the things in front of you—the clean taste of winter wind, the texture of a wooden spoon, the whisper of your own body turning under cotton sheets—without being overly impinged upon by regrets or anxieties, without being twisted up by anger or needy romantic love, then Cole had been happy, for the first time in his life, for four long years.

Before, loneliness had meant being without a woman. This was an altogether different and insoluble hurt.

ON THANKSGIVING the diner closed early and Cole let a waitress named Sandy take him back to her trailer. She was 28 to Cole's 23, black-haired, wide in the hips and narrow in the shoulders. She smoked Camel filters and the trailer smelled of old smoke and perfume. She'd been married young and divorced young, had wanted to go to veterinary school and never had the money. She fed a collection of stray cats that she'd named Tammy, Loretta, Dolly, George, and Hank. Cole stayed there for two days as they tried to chase each other's sadness away, grateful for the warmth of each other's bodies, unable to connect any other way.

A week before Christmas, five days before his 24th birthday, Cole finally broke down and called the Montoya house in Dallas. He stood at the pay phone in the diner with a stack of change, feeling Sandy's reproachful gaze on him as he dialed.

Alex's mother answered and he said, "It's Cole."

"Cole? My God, is it really you?"

"Yeah," he said, feeling something in his chest relax. "It's really me." He gave her a thirty second summary, mentioning the pay phone. She called him back, put Montoya on the extension, and went to wake Alex up. Susan got on too and told him she'd been worried about him and wished him a happy birthday and merry Christmas. Cole sat on the edge of a banquette next to the phone and talked to Alex for half an hour, trying to absorb all the changes—Alex as radical, Alex as filmmaker, Alex in New York, Alex in love. And Madelyn was in New York too.

"Does she hate me?" Cole asked.

"Madelyn? No, she doesn't hate you. She has the right. Pulling that disappearing act, that was cold. You cost her a lot of pain that she didn't deserve."

"I need to see her."

"I don't think that's a good idea. I can call her and see if she's willing to talk—"

"No," Cole said. "I have to surprise her, face to face. It'd be too easy for her to blow me off on the phone."

Cole was determined and he knew Alex's weaknesses. Five minutes later he was writing Madelyn's address on the back of a napkin.

Before he could hang up, Alex said, "Hang on a sec, Mom wants to talk to you again."

Cole knew what was coming and it left him with a sick, fluttery feeling in his stomach.

"Cole," she said, "I'm going to call your mother and tell her I heard from you. I'm not asking you, I'm telling you. They've both been worried sick for more than four years now."

"Yeah," he said, "okay." Then, grudgingly, "Thanks."

"Your father's changed. Two years ago the company tried to move him to Houston and he refused. He told them he'd moved enough and they could fire him if they wanted. They gave in. But the real reason? The real reason was your mother didn't want to give up the last connection she had with you, which was the house you used to live in. She still keeps your room the way it was when you left."

Cole didn't have it in him to give her the reaction she wanted. "Is she all right?"

"All things considered. I call her every couple of months to check up. She kind of shut down when you disappeared. I'm hoping this will give her a jump start." She paused. "Is there... anything you want me to say to them?"

"I don't think so," Cole said.

By six the next morning he had closed out his bank account, settled up with his landlady, returned his books to the library, packed a knapsack, put the Silvertone in its cardboard case, and hit the road.

As soon as Madelyn understood that it was in fact Cole, back in her life, her first reaction was disappointment. Her second was guilt; did she really want him to have been a John Doe cremation somewhere? The third was anger: He'd been alive all this time and hadn't had the human decency to let her know? The fourth was fear; what if he were mentally ill? The fifth was horror. This ragged, pathetic, homeless person had been lurking inside Cole the entire time they'd been together, waiting to emerge.

She tried to keep the reluctance out of her voice as she said, "Come on upstairs. You must be freezing."

"Thank you," he said, watching her with needy, anxious eyes.

They rode up the elevator together. He didn't have the sharp, vinegary odor of the hardcore homeless, though he was clearly not fresh out of the shower either. She wasn't ready to ask the big questions yet, so she said, "Does anybody else know where you are?"

"I talked to Alex last week." As she digested the implications, he said, "I made him promise not to call you."

She saw that impulse control was going to be required; better to seem cold and distant than to lash out with sarcasm. She unlocked her apartment door and said, "Take the boots off, please, so you don't track snow in." She put her own boots on the newspaper by the door and left Cole to struggle with his. "Want some coffee or tea?"

"Herbal tea, if you have it." He got the boots off, hung his Army surplus parka on the back of the door, and perched tentatively on the edge of the couch. He wore a gray zip jacket over a flannel shirt; his hands were in his armpits, and he stared at the rug under his feet. He was both Cole and Not Cole at the same time.

She put the kettle on and found pâté, a block of cheddar, and half a salami in the fridge. She put a baguette in the oven and it was warm by the time the kettle shrilled. When she set the tray on the coffee table, Cole hadn't changed his submissive posture. She sat in the overstuffed chair with her feet under her. "Herbal tea?" she said, trying to keep it light. "Since when do you drink herbal tea?"

"I spent the last four years on a commune," he said.

She shook her head. "What? How—"

He told her about Woodstock, backing up and starting over a few times to get an adequate level of detail, interrupting himself frequently to eat cheese and bread. Madelyn nibbled on the pâté and sausage, which she noticed Cole hadn't touched. She saw that he was more muscular now, tanned and fit. She tried to tune out his physicality, her memories of their bodies together. As antidote she reminded herself of the cruelty of his disappearance, the loneliness of their marriage.

Cole was clearly uncomfortable with the clichés of betrayal: I met someone, my defenses were down, it was "mostly" physical, whatever that meant. None of it was a surprise, except for the power it had to hurt her. Still. Again.

The sex part she at least understood. Cole's motivation for

joining the commune, for staying on after his new girlfriend went home, above all for not contacting anyone to let them know he was alive, remained slippery. The gist seemed to be that, between the breakup of their marriage and the failure of the band, he was too hurt to go on.

Some of us, Madelyn thought, were hurt and went on anyway.

He asked about the gallery and her family. He told her repeatedly how good she looked and she did not reciprocate. When he awkwardly asked if she were seeing anyone, she told him, politely and firmly, that he had hurt her really, really badly and it would take some time before she was willing to talk to him about her personal life. He was suitably chastised and, she thought, a bit disappointed.

"I'm sorry," he said. "I'm sorry I hurt you."

She said, "It's over and done." She was about to add something trite about forgiveness and Christmas, and that triggered a memory. "Oh dear God," she said. "It's your birthday."

He smiled ruefully. "Yeah."

She asked herself how she would behave if she were truly over him, with no bitterness or residual desire, if they had managed to salvage a friendship with nothing but good intentions for one another. "All right, then," she said. "We're going to go out and celebrate."

She determined that he was in fact now vegetarian and that he was fine with Italian. He asked if he could shower and borrow some scissors to trim his beard. While he was doing that she called Amici 11 and got an early reservation.

Except for Cole's refusal to consider clams vegetables, ruling out the Linguine Con Vongole, dinner was a big success, complete with checkered tablecloth, Louis Prima on the sound system, and signed celebrity photos on the wall. They split a bottle of wine, with Madelyn carefully limiting herself to a single glass. By means of somewhat greater efforts on both their parts, they managed to tell each other funny stories all the way through dinner, then walked back to her apartment in the cold to work off the starch overdose, low clouds making the city for once almost human in its proportions.

Back in the apartment, Madelyn was all raw nerves. She went to make more chamomile tea. Cole came up behind her and held her by her upper arms. She bowed her head. "Cole, no," she said. She could hardly hear herself over the beating of her heart, the rushing water in the sink. "I'm not going back to what we were. I'm not. It's been a long struggle, and, and I'm not going back, that's all." Words, ever her most trusted tools, had failed her.

Cole took his hands away. "Okay," he said sadly.

She turned off the faucet and faced him. "You can sleep on the couch tonight. I've got Alex's spare key, and he'll be in Dallas for another two weeks, so you can stay there until you figure out your next move."

"Okay," he said, and smiled. The beard emphasized the softness of his eyes. "Thank you. It was the best birthday dinner I can remember."

COLE WOKE EARLY, the shortness of Madelyn's couch quickly reminding him where he was. He looked across the room to where she slept in the position he knew so well, on her side, arms crossed, hands on opposite shoulders. He felt an upwelling of love. Her forgiveness was more than he had any right to expect, and he was content for the moment to have won that much.

He performed a quick mental audit. Last night Madelyn had told him that she had taken her rightful half of the money from their joint account and left him the rest. Combined with the cashier's check he'd bought in Wytheville in the amount of $812.79, he would have a few months with no financial pressure. He wouldn't have to buy new equipment—she had also shipped his guitars, his amp, his stereo, and three boxes of clothes and records for Alex to store in the basement of the Castle. Her generosity had left him mute.

In addition, he had a hundred dollars in small bills, distributed between his wallet, various pockets, and his boots. He had not bought a record or a book in four years. It was Christmas Eve and he meant to go shopping.

After a hurried but friendly breakfast with Madelyn, he

stopped by Alex's apartment to drop off his guitar and knapsack. From there he walked to the West Village and spent four hours in record stores. He knew he would have to hit the road soon, and promised himself he wouldn't buy more than five albums, and in the end he only went over by two. He started with the first Santana album, only needing a few seconds to verify that it was the same songs and the same sound he'd heard at Woodstock. Boz Scaggs had split from Steve Miller, and though the clerk pushed his Atlantic debut, Cole fell immediately in love with his second, *Moments*. Boz had put a jazz pianist together with a country guitar player and a horn section that could have come off a Stax session in Memphis, and, as with Santana, Cole knew where all the pieces had come from, but the way they fit together was brand-new and sounded like the future. Led Zeppelin had put out four more records since the one Cole had bought in January of '69, and Cole went with the clerk's recommendation of *Houses of the Holy*. He was partly swayed by the beautifully weird album cover, but mostly by the music, which had matured into something that was textured and nuanced one minute and a sledgehammer the next, as contemptuous of 4/4 time as it was of Western modality. At a used shop he found a pristine copy of a solo album called *Ennismore* by Colin Blunstone, produced by fellow former Zombies Rod Argent and Chris White. Like so much of the music he was hearing, it was based on acoustic guitar, in this case sold by Blunstone's breathy, emotional vocals. At Village Oldies they played something Cole had never heard before, a Jamaican band called The Wailers doing a rough, hypnotic music with an irresistible backbeat on an album called *Catch a Fire* that was primal and new at the same time. The owner looked through the other records in his bag and sold him on a new singer named Jimmie Spheeris and an album called *Isle of View*, a jazzy, soulful kind of folk-rock. At the last record store he hit, as he was trying to decide between Dave Mason's *Alone Together* and Stevie Wonder's *Innervisions*, the clerk convinced him instead to go for *The Wild, the Innocent, and the E Street Shuffle* by a John Hammond discovery named Bruce Springsteen, some kind of crazed Dylan fan who warbled and howled and played gorgeous lead guitar over everything from accordions to tubas to more acoustic guitar and jazz piano.

Eden Farm had owned an AM/FM transistor radio like the one Cole had in high school. After a few months, Cole had stopped listening, believing that it only made him want things he couldn't have. Now, with an overdose of new music burning through his synapses, he felt the way he had so many times when dumped into a new school—left out, unwanted, hopelessly behind. He was afraid to measure himself against what he'd heard on these new records, both musicianship and the sheer inventiveness. At the same time, he knew he would have to try.

His frenzy of capitalist consumption left him with nagging guilt and a bit of nausea, as if he'd binged on Snickers bars. Hoping it was just hunger, he grabbed a slice of pizza and walked up to Macy's on 34th Street, then down to the Strand bookstore, where he found two new Matt Helm novels and a pair of Joe Galls.

He hurried to Alex's apartment to listen to his records, only to discover that Alex no longer had a stereo, or records, or much of anything except cans of tomato soup, a musty unmade bed, and piles of textbooks.

He called Madelyn's work number from the downstairs phone. "Sorry, I forgot to warn you," she said. "He left his stereo in Texas and sold off most of his records because he thought they'd get stolen."

"Oh." Cole could hear the disappointment in his own voice.

Madelyn sighed. "You can listen at my place. Come by the gallery and get my key. And I know it's Christmas Eve, but you really need to stay at Alex's place tonight. Okay?"

"Sure," Cole said. "This means... this means a lot. Thank you."

WHEN MADELYN RANG the bell for her apartment, Cole didn't answer at first, and she had a moment of panic; she had hated to let go of her key, even knowing that Cole's particular irresponsibility was not of the material sort. At last he buzzed her in. When she got to the apartment, he had left the door ajar for her and he was sitting cross-legged in front of the turntable with his acoustic guitar, playing and singing along with an up-tempo song in a minor key about running from the sun and catching the rain. Cole's voice blended with the singer's, and yet Madelyn would have known it anywhere; she had to stand in the doorway for a moment and hold tightly to the frame to get her feelings under control.

The click of the closing door made Cole turn. His eyes shone as he said, "Isn't it beautiful?"

"Yes," she said. "Yes, it is." She hung up her coat. Her better judgment told her to send him away, now. Common courtesy, and a long loneliness, only now making itself apparent, instead sat her on the floor near him and said, "Show me what you bought."

He was patient when he explained who the various singers were, admitting that half of them he'd never heard of until a few hours ago. He was surprised that she'd heard of Springsteen and pleased that she remembered the Zombies, but it was Boz Scaggs that he wanted to play for her, a record that from the first line threatened to hit too close to home: "We were always sweethearts, different in our ways."

"Do you want some wine?" Madelyn said, getting to her feet to shake off the warm, intimate glow that had seeped out of the speakers and suffused the room.

"I should probably go," Cole said. "I promised I wouldn't hang around."

The idea of spending Christmas Eve alone suddenly seemed depressing and a little ridiculous. "It's okay," Madelyn said. "Stay for dinner. We can get Chinese takeout around the corner."

They drank a glass of wine each, and when the record was over they brought home the food and Madelyn set out plates and bowls on the table. They listened to another of Cole's new records while they ate and drank more wine. Madelyn realized she was feeling it more than she should. At the same time she felt in control and comfortable and happier than she'd been in a while; she wasn't ready for it to end.

The wine made her open up. She'd been talking about Alex's obsession with Callie Janus and how that had led to the unfortunate show at the gallery, and Cole said, "Still, you're making it work.

You set yourself this incredibly ambitious goal and by this summer you'll have your master's. That's really amazing. Whereas I got to where I was going and it all fell apart."

She ignored the invitation to feel sorry for him and said, "It's not what I wanted. It's what Ben wanted for me. It's not even a compromise; it's a completely different life. Between work and classes I don't have time to see any plays or read any novels. I want to teach English and study literature, not listen to a lot of intellectually rigorous defenses for emotionally bankrupt art."

She poked at her lo mein with cheap wooden chopsticks. Her own words shocked her; she hadn't realized how much she'd been hiding from herself.

She had also surprised Cole. "I didn't know," he said.

"Sorry," Madelyn said. "I guess that's been building for a while."

"There's nothing you can do?"

"Not without breaking my promise to Ben. And anyway, it's not so bad most of the time. It's just…"

"Yeah," Cole said. "'Tis the season of disappointment."

"I so wanted to be in Dallas for Christmas. I mean, I know people are starving in Biafra and Bangladesh, and sometimes it feels really selfish, but… do I have to give up everything that makes me happy? Am I not allowed to have any fun at all?" She couldn't meet Cole's eyes, which she knew would be warm and sympathetic. "Is it worth making all these sacrifices to not even get what I really want?"

Cole reached across the table and took both her hands. She squeezed back, then, feeling the heat rise in her cheeks, she pulled away and forced herself to take another bite of fried rice. "The record's over," she said.

After dinner they sat on the floor by the stereo and Cole handed her a small, gift-wrapped box. "Oh no," she said.

"It's nothing, really."

"I didn't get you anything."

"It doesn't matter. Go ahead, open it."

Inside a forest green Macy's box, nestled in cotton, was a pair of 14K gold earrings shaped like sea shells. "Oh no," she said again.

"You don't like them."

"They're beautiful. It's too much…"

"They're not quite the right shape, but I wanted to make up to you for the clams you didn't get last night because of me."

She stood up, wobbling a bit, and tried them on in front of the mirror by the door. They were very much her style, delicate, elegant. While she was admiring them, Cole's face appeared in the mirror behind her. "How do they look?" she said.

His eyes were shining again. "Beautiful," he whispered.

This time when he put his hands on her shoulders she didn't say no.

SHE WOKE UP DISORIENTED, her buttocks glued to the sheets with dried semen, sour wine on her breath, Cole snoring gently next to her in the too-small bed. With growing horror she remembered details: her clothes falling to the floor seemingly without human agency and her making no attempt to stop them; the softness of his beard surrounding his familiar kisses; his mouth between her legs, making her crazy with pleasure; him inside her, whispering that he loved her; her hands in his hair, digging into his back, feeling how the manual labor had transformed his body, his biceps hard and smooth as marble; her own voice saying yes again and again.

She crawled out of bed and huddled, freezing, on the toilet. She felt as if she'd finally gotten out of prison, only to somehow end up in a 7-Eleven with a gun in her hand. Or like she'd suddenly found herself at the track with a handful of losing tickets that had cost her life savings. The last year of her marriage unspooled in her head: the cold, echoing apartment when he was on the road; the times he was home and she saw nothing of him but an unconscious body and dirty dishes in the sink; the jealousy he awoke in her, the poisonous silences, those first months after Woodstock when she lay awake imagining him injured somewhere, lost, broken, helpless, because of her rejection.

On top of everything else, she hadn't been on the Pill in over a year.

She sat on the edge of the tub and washed herself repeatedly, thinking, I should have left him in the snow. She hated herself more than him because he was what he always had been and she should have known better.

She took a hot shower and wrapped herself in towels and moved around the apartment in the dark, putting on clean underwear and jeans and a sweater and thick wool socks and finally curling up on the couch in a blanket. She believed in God, even if she couldn't quite picture him in her mind, and rarely made time for church; she could feel his presence out there, floating above the world, and she begged him to just let her get past this awful moment, and she wouldn't ask anything ever again.

IT HAD SNOWED overnight and Cole could see it in the muted, colorless sunlight and hear it in the hush from the streets. He had a few blissful moments before he realized that he was alone in the bed and that Madelyn was huddled on the couch with her back to him.

He got dressed as quietly as he could. Madelyn must have heard him because he saw her pull even further into herself and tug at the blanket. He knelt on the floor next to her and put a hand on her shoulder. He felt the tension through the layers of fabric and it went up his arm and into his stomach.

"Madelyn? What's wrong?"

"Just go away, Cole. Please. Just go away."

"What did I do?"

She turned over, holding the blanket to her neck. "I told you I didn't want to go back. Remember?"

"This isn't back," he said. "This is forward. We're different now, older..." He couldn't continue when confronted with the bleakness in her swollen, bloodshot eyes.

"It's over, Cole. It was over before you went to Woodstock."

"It wasn't over last night. I know what you were feeling last night."

"Desperate. I was lonely and desperate and stupid."

That one, Cole thought, was going to sting later. "I know I

hurt you. I know it's scary to give me another chance. But who knows you better than me? Don't run away from us, from what we can be."

Carefully emphasizing each word in turn, she said, "I don't want you here."

"If you send me away now..."

"What?" she said. "I'll never see you again? That's what I'm asking you for."

It was like he'd switched off his Twin Reverb at the end of a gig. A red light went out inside him and a steady background hum that he hadn't been aware of faded to silence. He gathered up his records and put his guitar in its cardboard case and put his boots on, and his layers of jackets. With one hand on the door knob he looked back and saw that Madelyn had turned away and pulled the blanket over her head.

He spent a few of his remaining dollars on a bus ticket to Newark, where he could pick up I-95. Christmas Day. Maybe somebody would be moved by the spirit of the season.

He had the bus nearly to himself, so he snuck the guitar out of the case and played it so quietly that his fingers barely touched the strings, making just enough sound to quiet the voices in his head. They'd been on him since he closed Madelyn's apartment door, full of self-pity and I-told-you-so, lousy Christmases past and empty futures.

The driver let him off near the I-95 on-ramp, where he stood in the half-melted slush for an hour and a half before a pale-yellow Cadillac wobbled onto the shoulder and the front passenger window powered down. Cole ran over and saw a man inside in a tie and a cashmere overcoat, fifties, dark thinning hair.

"Where you headed?" the man asked.

Without thinking, surprising himself, Cole said, "Tupelo. Tupelo, Mississippi."

1974

JOE WAS WATCHING Darrel Royal's Longhorns get their asses handed to them by Nebraska in the third quarter of the Cotton Bowl. He didn't sit around all day brooding about UT, but on the other hand, he didn't mind seeing them cut down to size either. That was when the doorbell rang.

"Who on earth can *that* be?" his mama said and went to answer, kindly pretending not to notice the way Joe jumped at the sound of the bell. His daddy gave one of his sidelong looks from his Barcalounger so Joe would know that he in fact did notice, and then turned the volume up with the remote that never left his hand so that the Pontiac Firebird commercial would drown out whatever was happening at the front door.

Joe got up and stood in the shadows behind the door, wondering what it would feel like if it was Denise. She still wrote every six months or so, and he still sent her letters back unopened, though lately he had to work himself up to it and his curiosity was starting to itch him some.

The TV was loud all right, and Joe couldn't hear the words of whoever it was on the porch, only the tenor of the voice, which was male and familiar, and he didn't know who it was until his mama said, "That's right, they just call you Cole, don't they?" and Joe understood that he would have to make a decision. "I'm sorry," his mama said, "but Joe doesn't want to see anyone he used to know," which was the line he'd instructed her to say if anybody from his past showed up, but he hadn't thought it would be Cole, and suddenly he thought, what the hell.

"It's okay," Joe said. "Let him in."

His mama hesitated, the way a dog will when you tell it to get up on the couch that's always been forbidden. Joe took himself a deep breath and stepped into the light from the door and said, "Hello, Cole."

He wasn't sure he would have recognized Cole without the warning. All tanned and beefed-up, hair to his shoulders, neatly

trimmed beard, somewhat the worse for lack of sleep and looking
older around the eyes, wearing an Army parka and GI surplus
knapsack, which Joe hated to see for a couple of reasons. Big smile,
though, when he reached out to hug him, saying, "Tupelo! It's so
good to see you."

Joe let himself be hugged, slapped Cole on the back a couple of
times, and said, "Good to see you too, man."

Joe took him into the kitchen where Cole piled his guitar and
pack and jacket in the corner while his mama hovered over him,
trying to get him to eat some leftover Christmas turkey, while he
tried to explain to her that he was a vegetarian, which was not a
word in his mama's vocabulary. Pretty funny, really, and Joe let
the two of them work it out, which ended up with Cole accepting
a cup of coffee and a slice of chess pie.

"Delicious," Cole said, after his first bite. "Why do they call it
chess pie?"

"Nobody knows," Joe said. "Thank you, Mama, me and Cole'll
be all right now."

She dried her hands on a dishtowel and smiled nervously. "Y'all
holler if you need anything."

When she was gone, Cole said, "Shouldn't I meet your father?"

"Later."

"So how the hell are you? Are you all right? Nobody's heard
anything from you since the spring of 1969."

"I'm fine," Joe said, "but you ain't exactly one to talk. Denise
called my mama that fall looking for *you*."

"Yeah. I kind of fell off the planet for a while there. But nobody
was shooting at me. What was it like over there?"

Stupidest question in the world, and folks could not keep themselves from asking it. Like you could describe it in 25 words or
less. "I don't talk about it." He tried to keep his voice even, though
he heard the cold edge in it.

"At least tell me that you're okay physically, that you don't have
a wooden leg under those jeans or anything."

"I got a little shrapnel in my ass when a guy behind me stepped
on a mine, that's all." That had been falling back from Happy
Valley, southwest of Da Nang, October 1970. The monsoons had

started and the gray, pounding rains had left them all on the careless side, and for weeks afterwards, long after he'd gotten out of the field hospital, there had been this tiny scared voice in his head saying, "That could have been me," over and over. He remembered, like it had just happened, hitting the ground and hearing the pieces of PFC Emmett Washington slap into the mud around him, raw meat falling with the rain.

Joe carefully visualized the image as an 8 × 10 glossy and folded it in half, plain white on the other side, folded it again and put it into a wall safe, closed the door and spun the dials, and covered it up with a painting of trees hung with Spanish Moss that was hinged into the wall.

"That's been healed up now for a good long while," Joe said. "I got the GI Bill when I come out, and I went to Ole Miss over to Oxford and finished my BA last year. Now I'm going for my Juvenile Delinquent degree." Cole looked confused, so Joe said, "JD? Juris Doctor? That's law school to you, hippie."

Cole shook his head. "Crazy, man. Listen, can we, like, go drive around for a while or something? I feel like we can't really talk here."

"Drive around?" Joe said. "Drive around? Where you been? The North Pole? There's a gas crisis, son. People don't just 'drive around' these days."

"Okay, how about walk around?"

Joe was starting to wish he hadn't let Cole in. That was the way of impulse decisions, you ended up regretting them like as not. He could have been watching football and digesting turkey and maybe dozing off in front of the TV, and now instead he was getting a mental slide show from not one but two sets of memories, the Nam, which was always there, and Denise, who he had pretty much managed to not think about for a while, plus he was going to have to parade around in the cold besides.

Joe put on his old brown hunting jacket and some boots and they went outside. Out here on the north end of town it was all big ranch-style houses on big ragged lots, two-lane asphalt roads, no sidewalks. Lawns all brown, tall hardwood trees all bare. It was maybe 50 degrees with low-hanging clouds and a pestering breeze.

"One thing I never understood," Joe said, "is why is it y'all wear Army clothes? You're supposed to be against war and for individuality and doing your own thing, and then y'all wear our uniforms. Is it some kind of mockery or something?"

Cole smiled. "I guess the main reason 'we-all' do it is because it's cheap."

Even with the long hair and all, Cole still had that charm thing going on, and it was hard for Joe to keep fighting it. "Where'd you disappear to, anyways?"

To a commune in Virginia, turned out to be the answer. From how Cole described it, it was like being in the Corps in some ways. There was the lousy hours, the being out in the weather all the damn time, the same boring chow every day. There was the comradeship. There was the selflessness.

Just now Cole had been in New York City, trying to get back together with Madelyn, and she'd let him do it one night and the next day thrown him out, which Cole was pretty busted up about. Joe asked him what was next.

"Back to Austin, I guess. Maybe start another band. What about you? You're going to be a lawyer like your old man?"

"Nah. Politics."

"Are you serious?"

"Why not? Nixon made me ashamed to be American. We got to show the world that we're not all like that. Hell, maybe I can stop us from getting into the next war."

Joe stopped where Lakeshire met Van Street and pointed east by southeast. "Yonder about three miles is the house where Elvis was born. That's more of an outing than I'm up for today, and it ain't nothing but a shotgun shack with too many coats of white paint. There's a pocket-size lake due south, and west and south of here half a mile is the Bel Air golf course, nine holes, par thirty-six, pretty nice."

"Golf?" Cole said. He sounded like Joe had confessed to having sex with a goat.

"I'm learning." He pantomimed a tee shot. "Future of this country gets decided on golf courses."

"Is there a future?" Cole said. "I've been off the commune since

September and from everything I've seen and heard it's like we hit some kind of wall. Nixon's like some first-grader who can't stop lying, even though the lies get crazier and crazier. And somehow he's still President. There's this gas crisis thing. All the communes are falling apart. School busing is killing integration, whatever Nixon didn't already kill. The freaks are doing coke and heroin instead of LSD. All our heroes are dead or junkies or sellouts. How did everything go so completely to hell in four years?"

"Y'all couldn't follow through," Joe said, taking another golf swing to demonstrate. "Being against the war was the only thing all y'all could agree on, so once that was over, y'all went your separate ways."

"You said you were against the war too. You smoke dope. Your hair is over your ears. What's with all the us-versus-them attitude?"

"Because there ain't no 'us' that I belong to anymore. I got nothing but respect for the men I fought with, but I ain't no gung-ho Semper-Fi lifer. I was and am against the war, but being over there, hearing about y'all burning flags and cheering on the VC, well, I didn't like it. It felt disloyal. I feel older than you now, years older, but still not as old as my parents. I'm a chronologically displaced person, is what I am."

"Maybe there's a camp where they could put people like you."

"There's nobody like me." He'd said it as a joke, but it came out serious. Cole didn't have a comeback for that, which maybe was what Joe had been shooting for.

"Let's go to the house," Joe said, "grab a beer or two. You'll stay the night, won't you?"

"If it's no bother."

"It's an empty nest, plenty of guest rooms. We'll open up some canned green beans for you for dinner."

PEOPLE HAD A WAY, Cole had noticed, of telling the truth about themselves. When Joe had first talked about being older than him, Cole had thought he was being dramatic. As the evening wore on, it felt increasingly true. The jokes he made were more calculated than impulsive. He only listened with half an ear. Late that night, when he'd gotten a few beers into him and his parents had gone to bed, and he told a story about a five-day R&R in Bangkok where he'd rented a bar girl for the duration—the closest he came to talking about the war—even then he was watchful. Susan's ex, Jesse, had been the same way. The friendship that he and Joe had once had was gone. In its place they had shared history and a certain residual goodwill.

In the morning, Joe insisted on driving him to US 75, even if it did burn up a little gasoline. Cole convinced him to detour past Elvis' birthplace, and it was as uninspiring as Joe had promised. At the highway, as Cole unloaded his stuff, Joe handed him a folded sheet of paper.

"What's this?" Cole asked.

Joe looked embarrassed. "Not sure yet. Maybe you can tell me." Cole started to unfold it and Joe waved his hand. "Not now. Read it tonight or something."

Cole was lucky and caught a vw bus in less than an hour, driven by a longhaired couple on their way to Marin County, as if the last seven years had never happened. Cole read Joe's poem in the back seat. Or maybe it was song lyrics, because Cole could hear a melody. The title was "Could Have Been Me" and the verses were there-but-for-fortune snapshots of various destitute and broken people that the narrator had avoided becoming. Then the chorus turned it around and talked about how he could have been the man of his true love's dreams. "Of all the men I could have been/ Why couldn't I be yours?"

Interesting, he thought.

COLE MADE IT to Dallas at dusk the next day, having splurged the night before on a room at a Motel 6 on the edge of Little Rock rather than freeze to death. The Montoyas were just back from Guanajuato, Alex with Callie, Susan with her new fiancé, a soccer-playing lawyer she'd met while in law school at UT. Jimmy, who was now a UT freshman and staying in Alex's old room at the Castle, had a willowy blonde girlfriend of his own named Amanda. All the cuddling as they sat around the den made Cole feel even more miserable over Madelyn, which in turn led him to more and more Bohemia.

Though he wanted to like Callie for Alex's sake, he found her needy and quarrelsome. Maybe he was jealous. She focused on Alex as if the rest of them were only phantoms. She kept touching him in intimate ways, nipping his ear lobe, resting her hand low on his stomach. When she disagreed with him, she did it at full intensity. She kissed him lingeringly before she went off to bed.

By 11 he and Alex and Alex's father, the last men standing, reconvened in the dining room for more pumpkin pie and whipped cream. And more Bohemia. Cole was not the only one feeling its effects.

"Can I ask a question?" Montoya said to Cole.

"You can ask me anything you want, any time."

"Are you a Communist now?"

"Papa, for god's sake," Alex said.

"It's okay," Cole said.

"Alex marching against the government," Montoya said, "coming home from New York full of Black Panthers and power to the people, you on a commune for four years, it seems like a fair question."

"People in Wytheville were always asking us the same thing. If you're talking about all-out Soviet-style collectivism, no, it wasn't like that. For one thing, we only had one very old tractor. Stalin would have been mortified. On the other hand, one of our basic principles was, 'from each according to his ability, to each according to his need,' which is from Marx."

"Actually," Alex said, "Marx got it from Louis Blanc, who was a French socialist. 'De chacun selon ses facultés, à chacun selon ses besoins.'"

"If you say so." Cole understood that it had been his own choice to bail out of college. He'd sold his education down the river for fame and fortune, and the check had bounced. Ever since, though, when the conversation turned intellectual, whether it was Sugarfoot going on about Thoreau and Emerson, or Madelyn with her French post-structuralists, whatever the hell that meant, it got his back up, made him feel like a bumpkin.

"What about 'a fair day's pay for a fair day's work'?" Montoya said. "That was Franklin Roosevelt. I don't see anything wrong with that."

"The problem," Alex said, "is that it leaves it up to the bosses to decide what's fair. Blanc's idea is that you should decide for yourself."

"And if you're greedy?" Montoya said.

"The hope is," Alex said, "if there's enough to go around, greed will eventually disappear."

"But there isn't enough," Montoya said. "There's not enough oil, not enough of anything. Like in that *Limits to Growth* book. And your farm, it went under."

"We had some bad luck," Cole said. "We were on our own, we didn't have anybody to help us through the crisis."

"If it had been a lot of individual farms," Montoya said, "instead of one big one, would all of you have gone under?"

"Because of the salmonella? No. But I don't know that individual farms would ever have gotten off the ground in the first place."

"Well, I wasn't there," Montoya said. "But I'm willing to bet that some of them would have. The ones where the people worked the hardest. If that's true, it means that combining everything into one big farm made you weaker, not stronger."

"Strong like who?" Alex said. Up to that point it had been a theoretical discussion, and now something had clearly wound Alex up. "Strong like Hitler? Strong like Nixon's National Guard? Survival of the strong, and death to the weak and unlucky? Where's the compassion in that? Where's the humanity? If the price of having a few individual farms survive is having a lot of individual farms fail, maybe that's too high a price. Maybe it's better that we all go down together than that a few of us make it by standing on the dead bodies of everyone else."

Cole was shocked into silence, more by the force of Alex's emotion than by what he'd said. Montoya seemed just as shocked, but then he reached out and took Alex's hand and said, "You make me very proud, son."

Cole's eyes stung and he had to look away.

"I learned it from you, Papa," Alex said. He was still full of bloodshed and defiance. "You taught me, 'ponte en la piel del otro.'"

"Did I say that?"

"Only about a million times. And maybe there would be enough, if we didn't all want so much." Alex's face had gone wistful, as if he no longer believed the words even as he said them.

"'The Skin of the Other,'" Cole said. "That'd be a good title for a film."

"Yeah, well," Alex said. "Somebody else is going to have to make it."

Montoya had also picked up on the weird tone of resignation in Alex's voice. "What do you mean?"

Alex took a deep breath. "I'm quitting film school. Callie and I are moving to Dallas. I'm going to go to work for you, if you'll have me, and she and I are going to get married this summer."

Alex had just handed his father the gift he had always wanted. Montoya sat as if the slightest movement would turn it into fairy dust. Cole, for his part, didn't like the resignation in Alex's voice.

Then Montoya couldn't stand it anymore. He got to his feet and held out his arms. Alex stood up and let himself be pulled into the embrace. Montoya kissed him on the cheek and seemed in danger of crushing him. "If I'll have you? Are you crazy? This is the happiest day of my life. I feel like waking up your mother to tell her the good news."

"Don't, Papa, please. There's time enough tomorrow. Right now it's late and we're all tired."

"I couldn't possibly go to sleep now," Montoya said. "I may be up all night."

"Not me," Alex said, and stepped away.

Cole hugged Alex too. "Felicitaciones," he whispered. "You just completely blew my mind."

"Yeah," Alex said with a tired smile. "We'll talk." He went upstairs.

"Another beer?" Montoya said. Cole nodded and brought two in from the garage. "Did you know about this?" Montoya asked. He was as excited as a kid in a room full of puppies.

"Complete surprise," Cole said. "I wish I could take credit, but I had nothing to do with it."

"I can find you a job too, if you wanted. Maybe something creative, in the advertising department. You could live here until you got on your feet. Then I'd have both my oldest sons together with me. That would make me even happier than I already am."

"Maybe another time," Cole said, moved yet again by Montoya's unencumbered love. "I thought I might go back to Austin, try and put another band together."

"You need a place to stay? Your old room is available. Same deal as before, free rent if you do the handyman work."

Cole took both of Montoya's hands. "I would like that very much." Madelyn would haunt that room, he knew, but in his present mood he wasn't sure that was a bad thing. He remembered how he'd felt when he first saw the house, how he thought it would give him a firm rock to stand on. "If only my father had been more like you."

Montoya shook his head. "What Alex was saying about getting in the skin of the other guy, I hope someday you can manage to do that with your father. We all of us do the best we can. You may not believe that now, but it's the truth."

Cole felt too much tenderness and gratitude to argue. "You want to look at some cards?"

"You must be exhausted."

"I'm good for a while longer."

Montoya sat back in his chair and smiled. "Deal 'em up."

COLE TOOK JIMMY and Amanda up on their offer of a ride to Austin. It was Sunday morning, January 6, and the spring semester started on Monday. They rode down in Jimmy's new 1974 BMW model 2002.

Jimmy had come into his own in the years since Cole had last seen him. Handsome as a movie star, long, dark blonde hair and a high forehead, dressed in a uniform of rayon Hawaiian shirts, jeans, red high-top All-Stars, and St. Mark's blazer, even in the cold of January. He had the self-confidence of somebody twice his age, and yet seemed flattered that Cole wanted to hang out with him. He was in Plan II, as was Amanda, Jimmy thinking about photojournalism, Amanda about sociology. She had a way of combing her hair back with her long fingers and long, long red fingernails that Cole found suggestive and extremely distracting.

Jimmy had an 8-track player, and as soon as he started the car, the fiddle-based hippie swing of Willie Nelson's "Stay All Night" came blasting out of the speakers in the rear deck.

"You heard any of this?" Jimmy asked as he backed out. "Any of this outlaw country stuff?"

"I guess I heard a little," Cole said, leaning forward. "Waylon Jennings, Kristofferson, those guys?"

"Forget them. Austin is where it's happening. The Armadillo, Broken Spoke, Soap Creek, Threadgill's. It's the Texas guys that are driving this. Willie, Jerry Jeff Walker, Michael Murphey, Townes Van Zandt. You should come out with me some night, check it out."

If Amanda, who was kneeling sideways in the passenger seat, had a reaction to Jimmy's "me" instead of "us," Cole didn't see it.

"Do you play?" Cole asked.

"Nah, Alex got all the musical talent. I'm not a creator, I'm a consumer. I mean, somebody's got to buy your records, right?"

"Not so far," Cole said. He hadn't meant it to come out quite so harshly.

As a consumer, Jimmy had a different threshold of saturation than Cole. He was happy to let the tapes cycle through repeatedly, whereas once was enough for Cole, especially with Nelson's nasal whine. He had to keep reminding Jimmy to switch them out.

Of the albums Jimmy played on the three-hour drive, Cole was most impressed with Murphey's, especially a song called "Backslider's Wine," full of powerlessness and regret that got inside Cole's defenses. It made him think of Tyler and the Wagon Wheel and Corrina and poor, dead Jerry who'd always wanted him to have a hat.

The landscape was as flat and barren as ever, with some of the landmarks gone. I-35 went straight through Waco now, and the few formerly empty miles between Round Rock and the outer fringes of Austin had been taken over by shopping centers and housing developments, power lines and fast food restaurants. They were building express lanes on an upper deck to ease the congestion downtown.

Cole was surprised by how much Austin felt like home, despite his only having lived there for nine months. As they drove up the steep incline of 15th Street, the memories flooded in. Walking in Pease Park with Madelyn, playing the Deke house with The Other Side. Discovering the Castle on that first trip with Alex and his father, making love to Madelyn for the first time, the aroma of Sunny's Dal Biryani in the kitchen. Madelyn, Tupelo Joe, Denise, Madelyn, Madelyn, Madelyn.

Jimmy pulled into the driveway of the Castle and cut Jerry Jeff off in the middle of a drunken and decidedly inferior version of "Backslider's Wine." "All ashore," Jimmy said, "that's going ashore."

Cole hesitated at the steps, the Silvertone in one hand, the knapsack in the other. Jimmy, at the front door, picked up on his feelings. "You've got your keys, right?" Cole nodded. "Your bed's made up with clean sheets. You should be set. If you need anything, holler." He glanced inside the house and from the angle of his gaze Cole guessed he was watching Amanda climb the stairs. "Well. You might want to give us a while before hollering." He smiled as he turned away, leaving the door ajar.

Walking through that door, Cole knew, would subject him to the ambush of memory, to countless reminders of failure, to the claustrophobia of having nowhere else to go, to the lonely comfort of self-pity.

Take your comfort, he thought, where you find it.

He crossed the threshold and climbed the stairs. In his room he unpacked his meager wardrobe, freshly washed at the Montoyas', and put his new albums and paperbacks on the shelves. It was 2:17 in the afternoon. His hunger and thirst could wait.

He took the Silvertone down to the basement and stowed it on a top shelf. As promised, La Pelirroja was there in its hard-shell case, along with the rest of what Madelyn had sent. He knew she was not the vengeful sort, still he was relieved when he took

La Pelirroja out and saw that it was intact. He put on the new set of Darco strings that were in the case and tuned it up, sitting on the gray metal folding chair there in the basement. The rich, pure sound of La Pelirroja, after four years of the Silvertone, was a revelation. Without conscious intent, his fingers found a G7 and he sang:

Golden light comes streaming in
On golden hair and molten skin

In for a penny, he thought, in for a pounding. Why settle for a little pain when you can have a lot? Though he had to fumble for some of the words, they came to him in the end, and then he played "Cielito lindo," making a liar of himself when he sang, "Canta y no llores."

BY FIVE COLE had unpacked everything. Meager as they were, it felt like drunken excess to have so many possessions again. He changed the strings on the Strat and verified that his amp still worked, then he hooked up his suitcase stereo and played the Wailers. By that time Jimmy and Amanda had emerged. Jimmy took him around to meet his new roommates. Chip, in Joe's old room, short, dark, and athletic. John, downstairs, a senior pre-med student who already looked short of sleep.

Jimmy insisted on taking Cole to dinner, and Cole, in keeping with his mood, suggested Matt's El Rancho. As they drove through downtown, Cole saw young people everywhere, panhandling on the corners, driving around in vw microbuses, lined up outside the crumbling Paramount Theater. Austin, Jimmy explained, had become the Land that Time Forgot, where hippies still roamed wild in their natural habitat, subsisting on cannabis and Boone's Farm Strawberry Hill wine.

Their waiter, who was not much older than Cole, kept looking at him strangely during dinner, and when he brought the check he said, "Did you use to be in the Austin Blues Group? Played at the Vulcan?"

"That's me." He offered his hand. "The name's Cole."

The waiter, whose name was Roger, invited him to a Sunday jam session, "old blues, rock, country, whatever comes around on the guitar, you know?" He tore the stub off the check and wrote his name and phone number.

Amanda, at least, was impressed. "Does that happen a lot?"

"Less than you might think."

"I'd say it was a good omen," Amanda said. "You haven't been back twenty-four hours and already you're getting offers."

"Well," Cole said. "There are offers and there are offers." He imagined the dingy garage, the smell of old beer cans, the tedious I-IV-V blues progressions.

At the Hancock HEB on the way home, Cole bought some basic supplies and a case of Old Milwaukee. He made nice with Amanda and Jimmy while he put the groceries away, then he took two bottles upstairs to begin his project of serious drinking and becoming reacquainted with his record collection.

OF COURSE SHE was pregnant.

Sometime in the early morning hours, after moving to the couch, Madelyn felt an odd little pinch in her uterus and knew beyond a doubt that something had taken hold inside her and started to grow. She knew it had the potential to be the end of her world, of her safe, if exhausting, routine of school and gallery and fortress apartment.

She took a moment for recriminations. How could she have been so stupid, with Cole of all people? What in God's name was she going to say to Kindred? And so on. Eventually she willed herself into a fitful sleep, waking long enough to send Cole out into the snowy Christmas morning, as if it were all his fault and none of her own, then pulling up the blanket and diving again into her inner darkness.

When she finally abandoned all hope of more sleep, she made a pot of coffee and changed the sheets on the bed. She washed the dishes and sponged off the counters and the table. She put the earrings in the green Macy's box and tucked them into the back of her sock drawer. She was the daylight Madelyn now, strong and capable, and she reminded herself that abortion had been legal in New York State since 1970, never mind last year's *Roe v. Wade*, and it was simply not a big deal anymore. If, in fact, she was pregnant—and she had no rational reason to think so, only a weird feeling after a sleepless night—she could end it before anybody else found out. When her inner voices tried to argue with her, she drowned them out with the vacuum cleaner.

In mid-January, when her period was a week late, she told herself she'd been late before. By the time she was two weeks late, her legs were so tense that she felt lopsided when she walked; her neck was rigid with pain and her eyes bloodshot from lost sleep; she was on the verge of exploding with rage or collapsing in tears whenever anyone spoke to her.

Over lunch on the Wednesday of week three, Paula Cooper said, "Forgive me if I'm out of line, but is everything all right?"

Madelyn felt the blood rush to her face. "Is it that obvious?"

"Well, you might at least apologize to that poor napkin."

Madelyn saw that she had twisted it into a rock-hard spiral of fabric. "It's nothing," she said, and bluffed her way through the rest of the meal.

Back at the gallery, she looked herself over in the bathroom mirror. "You're a wreck," she told her reflection, who responded by holding up her middle finger. "This is what it's come down to," she said. "You're the only one I can talk to." Paula and her other New York friends were little more than acquaintances. She couldn't tell her mother, who would not be willing to even consider abortion. She and Hope had hardly been in contact since high school. The last time she'd tried Irene's number it had been disconnected. Alex had never come back from Christmas break, and he was out of the question anyway, as was Denise; she couldn't put either of them in the position of having to lie to Cole.

Cole, above all, was never ever to know.

Anyway, there was nothing to discuss. It had to be done, like filing her taxes or fixing a flat tire. The sooner she got it over with, the better.

She locked herself in her office, leaving Elaine to watch the front. She looked up the Sanger Center on Bleecker, whose name she knew because she passed it several times a week. She made an appointment for the next day, and the woman on the phone told her not to drink anything before bed and to take a urine sample in a clean glass bottle first thing in the morning.

After she hung up, she waited for calm to descend. She'd made the decision, and she was a day, two at most, from returning to her quotidian existence. Instead she felt worse than ever. Her stomach churned and she kept having to swallow.

If she slept at all that night, she didn't register it. She peed into an empty jam jar and showered and dressed, wandering dazedly around the apartment, her stomach too tense for food. At 9:30 she headed out with the jam jar in a paper sack.

The weather was hallucinatory, the sky completely overcast, tiny snow flurries invisible except in her peripheral vision, pricking her face with needles of cold, vanishing before they hit the sidewalk. She somehow got turned around and ended up in front of her own apartment building, not even recognizing it at first, and had to rush to make her appointment.

The Caucasian-flesh-colored bricks of the Sanger Center were not, Madelyn thought, well considered; once inside, however, the carpeted floors and dark green furniture projected a mood of calm elegance. The receptionist sent her to the lab, where a middle-aged woman in a navy cardigan and long skirt took her sample and said they should have the result by one.

"The sample is for you, not for me," Madelyn said. "She's a girl, by the way."

"You're here for counseling?"

"I'm here to get rid of it," Madelyn said, her harshness shocking them both into temporary silence.

"Come back at one," the woman eventually said. "I've done this long enough that I don't doubt you, but the doctors will want something more objective."

Madelyn turned to go. A poster from a medical company, hanging next to the door, showed a series of curved-bottom triangles of spattered gray. "Sonograms?" Madelyn asked.

The woman nodded. "They do them routinely in England now. How many weeks are you?"

"I'm in my fifth."

The woman pointed to the first picture. "That's all it is at this point," she said.

"All *she* is," Madelyn corrected her.

She gave the smallest possible shrug. "That black circle is the gestational sac, and the little ring inside it is the yolk sac."

The next picture, at nine weeks, showed a pale, cloudy creature, curled on itself like a caterpillar. Two black eyeholes were visible, and rudimentary arms and legs.

The third picture, week 12, showed fingers and toes. That was as far as Madelyn got because everything had gone blurry. She did *not* want this woman to see her cry, so she said, "Thank you," in the steadiest voice she could summon, and said, "I'll be back at one."

On the street, the wind had picked up. As her tears overflowed, they turned bitter cold on Madelyn's face. If it weren't for the salt, she thought, they would freeze. Her head thrummed and her stomach burned. It occurred to her that she needed to eat, though she couldn't imagine getting anything past the blockage in her throat.

She ducked into a deli anyway and stood in front of a glass case full of cheeses. "What'll it be, lady?" said the bulging-armed man behind it.

"Half a pound of the sharpest cheddar you've got," she said, and her mouth suddenly watered so violently that she had to swallow and swallow again. "Thick slices."

He wrapped the slices in paper. "What else?"

"Mustard," she said. "Hot mustard."

The man showed her a jar and she nodded mutely. She gave him money and told him to keep the change and found a table in the back of the room. Her hands trembled as she tore open the paper, fought the lid off the jar, and took a huge bite of cheese and mustard.

She had never eaten cheese and mustard before. The demands, she knew, were not hers. And as a reward for her compliance, a warm, gold-colored glow spread from her navel to the ends of her fingers and toes, up her face and forehead into her scalp. Her headache was gone, her throat clear, her stomach relaxed.

All this from one bite? she asked herself disingenuously, knowing it was not the cheese. It was because, bypassing her conscious judgment, she had realized that she was not going back for her one o'clock appointment.

Now, she thought, for the hard part.

SHE CALLED KINDRED that afternoon and asked when he was going to be in New York again. She told him she had something she needed to discuss with him in person.

"That sounds ominous. Can I at least have a clue?"

"I'll explain when I see you."

"I'll be there tomorrow," he said.

He came straight to the gallery from the airport, carrying a black leather overnight bag like the pilots used. He shrugged out of his black cashmere overcoat the minute he was in the front door, revealing a dark, conservatively cut suit, deep blue shirt, and red tie. He barely nodded to Elaine, gave Madelyn a long, searching look, and strode briskly back to the office.

Elaine, already somber in her straight dark hair, black horn rims, and black turtleneck, looked apprehensively at Madelyn. "Something I should know about?"

"Nothing to do with you," Madelyn said. "Don't worry." Though her own worry had left her slightly nauseated, it was vastly preferable to the numb panic she'd been living with for the preceding two weeks. And she still felt the glow from the deli.

She followed Kindred into the office. The words she'd rehearsed now felt too belabored, so she closed the door and with her hand still on the knob said, "I'm pregnant."

Kindred had always been unflappable, and she saw that she'd been wrong to count on that. All the warmth left his face. "I take it you're sure?"

"Oh, yes."

"Are you getting an abortion?"

"No."

"For God's sake, why not? Do you seriously think you can go to school, manage the gallery, and raise a kid all at the same time?"

"No, of course not. I haven't worked out the details yet. I expect I'll go back to Texas when the time comes and stay with my parents."

"How did... I mean, I didn't think you were even..."

"I wasn't. There was a... chance encounter with my ex-husband."

"The one who disappeared?"

She nodded.

Kindred tugged at the cuff that projected a quarter-inch past his coat sleeve. "When I told people that I was grooming a girl who was still an undergraduate to be my partner, they told me I was crazy. Women are not cut out for business, they said. You can't depend on somebody who's going to make critical decisions based on her hormones. You don't know this woman, I said. She's smart, she's sensible, she's got her priorities straight."

What stung the worst was to be dismissed as a cliché. "I did think I knew my priorities," she said. "Things happen that are watersheds, where you're not the same person afterward, and unless somebody has had that experience himself, it's hard to understand how powerful that can be."

"In other words, until I get pregnant, I'm in no position to judge you?"

"I know I've disappointed you—"

"You have no idea how much you've disappointed me. In fact, unless you've had that experience yourself, it's probably very hard to understand just how powerful my disappointment is."

She couldn't recall his ever lapsing into sarcasm before. "I'm truly sorry to have hurt you. My hope was that we could talk through this and find the best way—"

"I don't think there's anything to discuss. Why don't you give me your keys to the gallery and go on home?"

"Just like that?"

"I don't give my trust easily. When it's gone, it's gone."

"You're firing me for telling you I'm pregnant?"

"We had a contract. You admitted that you can no longer fulfill the terms of that contract. As far as I'm concerned, we're through."

In the last five years she had spent thousands of hours with this man, met impossible deadlines with him, listened to his dreams and petty annoyances, gotten giggling drunk with him, fought off the occasional moments of sexual attraction, anger, and frustration. Through it all she had seen him as deeply honest, even compassionate in his own cautious way. To now see him as a heartless stranger was devastating.

She rummaged in her purse, found her keyring, and broke a fingernail detaching the gallery keys. Putting off the moment she would have to let them go, she said, "I have personal stuff here. Books, coffee cups…"

"Come back tomorrow. You can pack it up then."

She dropped the keys on the desk, gathered her coat and scarf and boots, and walked past him to the door, thinking he would say something, an apology, a conciliatory word of praise. Instead there was only Elaine's voice calling her name as she walked out the front door, pulling on her winter things, into the biting cold of the street.

And yet, in the starkest contrast to the shame and betrayal she believed she was feeling, every step that distanced her from the gallery came more easily than the one before. She hadn't let herself register the weight of Kindred's expectations until they were gone. She had been pushing, every day, against the knowledge that she was on the wrong road, that art was not literature, was not an orange hardcover with all the world inside it, was not the thing that she wanted for herself. The knowledge that she had let herself be owned again.

And then she stopped abruptly in the middle of the icy sidewalk. Had she *let* this happen? Had her Machiavellian subconscious connived for her to sleep with Cole, to get pregnant, because it was the only way out of the trap she was caught in?

The thought was too monstrous to contemplate.

In grade school she'd suffered from Bad Thoughts: the wish that her sister would fall and skin her knees; the memory of the India Ink she'd spilled on the carpet; the doubt that God existed at all. She'd taught herself to banish them by extending her arms at her sides, as if they were wings and she were about to fly away. She lifted them now, oblivious to the downward-gazing New Yorkers around her, and imagined herself rising into the air, up over SoHo, up past the Chrysler Building and the Empire State, to the Long Island Sound and out over the wine-dark sea.

COLE SLEPT UNTIL late morning, and in the afternoons he caught the UT shuttle bus and rode around town, getting off sometimes and walking from one stop to the next, watching people, getting his bearings. He bought himself some sheets and towels and got his boots resoled. Shepler's Western Wear turned out to be the only place he could find straight-leg jeans, in the form of button-fly Levi's that took him a while to master. The weather was mild compared to Wytheville, highs mostly in the 50s and 60s, sometimes with a bonus of blue skies.

In one of his boxes he found the reel-to-reel tape he'd recorded during his acid trip at the motel in San Francisco. His green Japanese recorder was long gone, so he took it to a recording service and had it dubbed onto a cassette. He had no idea what to expect. It had been so long ago, before the Austin Blues Group, before he met Madelyn. The music turned out to be pleasant enough, melodic and played with feeling, but drowned in so much reverb as to be comical.

He bought more new records, and at night he listened to them, and to his old ones, and played along on La Pelirroja and made a mental list of what hurt the most.

On a Friday in the middle of February, Amanda was obligated to a mixer at school and Jimmy insisted that Cole go with him to the Broken Spoke. A local western swing outfit called Asleep at the Wheel was playing, which Jimmy seemed to think was a plus. The club was a straight shot south on Lamar, over the river and past Zilker Park. The sprawling, one-story, red frame building sat in a huge gravel parking lot full of pick-up trucks and beat-up sedans from the early sixties.

A sign on the front door read, "Through this door pass the best country music dancers in the world." Inside it was mostly dance floor. Bar on the left, stage at the back, tables along the sides separated from the dancers by a plank barrier. Another sign drove the message home: "No standing on the dance floor."

Jimmy led the way to an empty table. A couple of hundred people milled around, barely making a dent in the room. The band was tuning up and Cole, who hadn't been on a stage since Woodstock, suddenly missed it with a ferocity that made his chest go hollow and his hands clench in his pockets. The front man was some kind of giant, a head taller than anyone else in the band, with a flaming red beard, long hair, a ten-gallon hat, a three-piece suit, and a blonde Telecaster. Pedal steel stage left, piano stage right, drums and standup bass in back, fiddle and guitar and mandolin in between. Up front, next to the giant, stood a stunning brunette with an acoustic guitar, who gave Cole a pang of another sort.

"You want a beer?" Jimmy said. "I don't know if they have anything but Lone Star."

"Lone Star'll drink if it's cold enough. Thanks."

"Hey, everybody," the giant said. "Welcome to the Broken Spoke. Let's get the party started with a little number called 'Well, Oh, Well.'" He vamped briefly behind a piano intro, then the brunette moved up to the mike and started belting the lyrics. The rest of the band fell into a shuffle, and before she made it to the chorus the couples had started two-stepping counter-clockwise around the floor, the same dance Cole had done with Corrina in Tyler. As he watched, the rhythms came back to him, and the timing on the turns. Jimmy arrived with two longnecks and Cole drank half of his with the first pull.

The band didn't let being tight interfere with an easy, swinging groove. The giant had a relaxed baritone when he sang and a slick patter between numbers. They did Hank Williams and Bob Wills, and then they lit into Fletcher Henderson's "Shoeshine Boy," which Cole remembered from his father's records. He polished off the rest of his beer. "Fish," he said out loud, "or cut bait."

Jimmy looked at him curiously as he stood up. Cole nodded, stiff with nerves, and made his way around the barrier to the dance floor. An older woman with flagrantly dyed blonde hair stood on the sidelines. Cole had seen her dancing, good but not great, likely to be forgiving. He leaned toward her ear and said, "I haven't done this in ten years. Would you—"

"Oh hell yes," she said, and they were off. It took him a couple of seconds to find his place in the music, during which he nearly got run into a couple of times, and he started to panic. But everybody was smiling and he took a breath and started off and it didn't go too badly. At the end the woman introduced herself and said, "Not bad for ten years," which made him think of Corrina again. He smiled and thanked her and grabbed another partner.

By the time he made it back to the table, two dances later, Jimmy had acquired two women and another round of beer. Cole was hyped-up and pleased with himself and he needed a second or two to realize what was wrong with this picture. The woman sitting very close to Jimmy had red hair and electric green eyes and looked like she was about to burst out of her clothes. The other woman was on Cole's side of the table with her back to him, and he saw long dark hair, a battered straw cowboy hat, tight jeans.

"Where'd you learn to do that?" Jimmy said, with genuine admiration. "You surprised the hell out of me."

Cole flicked a glance at the redhead. "I guess that's two of us surprised."

"Cole, this is Sharon," Jimmy said, and the redhead nodded. "That's Charlene."

Charlene turned sideways in her chair. She looked to be a couple of years older than Cole, with a prominent nose and lots of eye makeup. "How do," she said. "Like to dance? Unless you're tired."

"I don't get tired," Cole said.

She stood up. "I like the sound of that."

On the floor she admitted she didn't really know what she was doing. She laughed when she said it, and Cole didn't mind anyway. In her cowboy boots she was eye to eye with Cole and she didn't look away except when she was turning. Cole figured out quickly to mouth the count to her as she came around. When the song finished, the girl singer in the band stepped up to sing a slow one and Cole said, "You want to try another?"

Charlene kept a discrete distance at first. By halfway through the song she had nestled her head on his shoulder and he felt the weight and warmth of her breasts against his chest. His right leg was between both of hers, and their thighs touched and separated and touched again as they turned in a slow circle. She had on a musky, dark-smelling perfume that stopped Cole's brain in its tracks. She had stopped laughing. When they finally let go of each other she fanned herself and said, "Whooeee. I think we better cool down a bit."

The more she drank, the more giggly she got, which didn't bother Cole. She worked at a nail salon called Your Nailed, a patch of grammatical quicksand that Cole opted not to poke at. Sharon was a secretary at an architect's office, "hired for my boobs, but I needed the bread." Charlene had been doing Sharon's nails for a year or so.

Around 11 Jimmy said, "Shall we?" and they all stood up. Apparently everything had been decided by means that Cole was not privy to. Charlene dug in her purse and held out her car keys. "Are you okay to drive?" she asked Cole. "I might be a little drunkie." She giggled.

Charlene's car turned out to be a dark red '66 Mustang with a 289 V8. Cole was halfway tempted to pop the hood and see if she had the four-barrel carb, but knew this was not the time. He got Charlene poured into the passenger bucket seat about the time that Jimmy pulled up in his BMW. When Cole cranked the engine, KOKE-FM blasted out of the dashboard speakers, playing Jerry Jeff's version of "London Homesick Blues," better known as "I Want to Go Home with the Armadillo." Cole turned it down and followed Jimmy up Lamar, noting that the Mustang needed a tune-up and the Cruise-O-Matic transmission was sluggish.

"If your hair was lighter and there was less of it and you didn't have a beard, you'd look just like Steve McQueen in *Bullitt*," Charlene said.

Cole didn't have a ready response, so he said, "How long have you known Jimmy?"

"I just met him tonight. Sharon met him last fall. He calls her up sometimes, tells her to meet him somewhere."

Cole glanced over at her. She was slumped in the seat, hat pulled low over her face. Cole checked the road, looked again, and she had the hat pushed up with one finger and one eye open. "She knows he's got a regular girlfriend."

"She's okay with that?"

"He's got money, he's great looking, he treats her sweet... hell no, she's not okay with it. She takes what she can get in this world, like the rest of us."

"You guys drove together?"

"Yeah, she called me up and told me Jimmy was bringing a friend. I said, 'I'll drive, but you tell Jimmy I am not going home with some stranger.'" She giggled. "'Unless I like him.'"

Cole worried that she might pass out as soon as she got into bed, but she continued to be drowsily amused throughout. She did fall asleep quickly afterward, leaving Cole with a mild case of post-coital remorse. He'd never shared that bed with anyone but Madelyn, though that thought didn't occur to him until Charlene was lightly snoring with her back to him. Nor did his regrets keep him from responding when she came back from the bathroom before dawn, feeling playful, or again when they woke up for good late on Sunday morning and sex proved easier than conversation.

"In case I never see you again," Charlene whispered.

"You'll see me," Cole said, from a mix of guilt and lust.

Eventually, dressed in the previous night's smoke-saturated clothes, they made their way downstairs. Cole felt drained and raw, but he had thought to get Charlene's business card, with her home number scrawled on the back. "I live with my mama," she said, "so watch what you say on the phone."

Sharon was already at one end of the dining room table, drinking coffee and looking at her watch. Chip, the middle roommate, sat at the other end, eating Trix and reading the sports section of the *Statesman*. He looked up long enough to give Charlene a slow, head-to-foot checkout. Jimmy was nowhere to be seen.

"We got to boogie," Sharon said.

Cole walked them out to the Mustang and gave Charlene her keys and a kiss. She tapped him on the chest with one long, shining fingernail and said, "Thanks for the ride." The first drops of a bitter cold rain fell as Cole sprinted up the walk.

Cole's bed smelled of smoke and beer and sweat as much as it did of sex and Charlene's musky perfume. He thumbtacked her card to the bulletin board above his desk and showered and put his sheets and clothes in the wash. In his robe and wet hair he cooked up a mess of factory farm eggs and instant grits and Mrs. Baird's whole wheat toast and drank some frozen orange juice. It was one in the afternoon and Chip had a basketball game blaring in the living room, squealing sneakers and referee whistles and crowd noise. Cole moved his clothes over to the dryer and picked up the Strat and tried a country shuffle on for size. It didn't fit.

Between Charlene and the tasteless eggs and living in the Castle again, Cole was in a mood, and the name of the mood was Settling for What You Can Get, which was not a happy one. It did, however, remind him of Tupelo Joe's lyrics, which were also about not getting what you wanted, and it sent him up two flights of stairs to his bedroom, where he got dressed and sat down with La Pelirroja and Joe's piece of paper and took 45 minutes to turn it into a fully fleshed-out song. Though he'd tinkered with the words a bit and added a bridge, it was recognizably Joe's work. And it added up to something worth singing, Cole thought.

After the basketball game, Cole called Joe from the downstairs phone and played it for him, remembering high school and sitting in the hall closet to play "Laura Lee" for Alex.

"Sounds country," was Joe's reaction.

"I was two-stepping last night," Cole said. "Is that a bad thing?"

"I don't know. I guess I hadn't really pictured it that way."

"How did you picture it?"

"I don't know. Like Creedence, maybe."

"Well, that's my best shot. I won't play it if you don't like it."

"I didn't say I didn't like it."

"You didn't say you did."

"Are you going to put it on an album or something?"

"Not any time soon. I might sing it in public."

"Don't say my name if you do. You can say you wrote it with a friend, but don't say who."

"If you're embarrassed by it..."

"I'm not embarrassed. It's just, if I do more of this, I want it to be separate. You know. From the other thing."

"From your political career."

"Yeah."

"Is there more?"

"There might be."

"Well, frankly, after the excitement and flood of gratitude that this one provoked, I'm not sure I'd feel like working on any more."

"Give me a break. It's kind of a shock to have something all of a sudden grow legs and start walking around on its own, you know? Play it again."

As he sang, Cole pictured himself as John Fogerty in flannel shirt and Beatle haircut, and at the end Joe said, "That's pretty good. Did I really write that?"

"Most of it," Cole said, still feeling snippy.

"Thank you," Joe said at last. "Thank you for making it into a song. I wish I had it on a record so I could hear it again."

"Maybe someday you'll get your wish," Cole said.

After he hung up he checked the refrigerator. The last of his beer was gone, as usual, and nobody had replaced it. The tragedy of the commons, Sugarfoot had called it. The refrigerator belonged to everyone, so no one had stewardship. The nearest 7-Eleven was a long walk away in the pouring rain.

Cole took La Pelirroja upstairs and played a few random chords. One of them sounded like "Time Is on My Side," and he started to play it, then he thought, this is bullshit. Time is not remotely on my side. Time is just a greedy kid who takes and takes and takes and never gives back in return.

He stopped and said the line again in his mind, and this time he heard a guitar behind it. He didn't have another piece of paper, so he turned Tupelo Joe's song over and started writing on the back. "The road ahead holds nothing," he wrote, "but more bridges to be burned."

And away we go, he thought.

ON HIS FATHER'S instructions, Alex dressed nicely but not formally—pressed, pleated khaki pants, black tasseled loafers, a blue checked button-down dress shirt with no tie, his St. Mark's blazer. His father wore slacks and a white shirt and a brown cardigan.

Callie was in the den watching *All in the Family*, and she wolf-whistled when Alex came in to kiss her goodbye. "Take 'em to the cleaners," she whispered.

"Not tonight," Alex said.

His father drove the Cadillac. The night was cold and damp and the late February wind whipped the bare trees around. "Nervous?" his father asked.

"Not too much. You said you're staking me."

"And I expect you to lose a couple of hundred. That would be about right. They'll look forward to having you back, but they'll see you know how to conduct yourself."

"And if I win?" Alex said.

His father smiled. "I'm not too worried about that."

Alex had been on the job a month and a half. He had one of six desks in the Accounting bullpen and he spent his days reconciling job tickets from the delivery trucks with orders and inventory from the warehouse. For the sake of his sanity, he'd started taking notes, tracking patterns, defining categories, looking for a way to automate his job out of existence.

For all his boredom, the memory of the Loisaida tenement was still pungent. He could put up with a lot for the sake of a clean and spacious house, abundant food, the warmth of his father's happiness as they rode downtown together, the ability to send money to Frederica every month, the contentment of sharing a bed with Callie every night.

The week before the wedding, they would close on a place of their own near Northpark. It was ten years old, on a cul-de-sac, with four bedrooms and a two-car garage. Alex would never have imagined buying a house like that for himself, but Callie had led the search, with Alex's mother patiently taking her around in the afternoons. Alex's father had offered the down payment as their wedding present, and with the generous salary Alex was making, the payments were affordable—at least in theory. He was still getting used to the woman of easy privilege that had emerged from Callie's hard bohemian chrysalis.

The first cracks had appeared in New York in November. They'd been in bed, talking about their childhoods, and she had finally agreed to tell him her real name. "You have to swear on everything that's sacred to you that you will never tell anyone, ever."

"I swear."

"If you ever use this against me when we're having a fight, we are over. This is the hydrogen bomb, the ultimate doomsday weapon. Is that completely understood?"

"I understand."

"My parents named me Gladys."

"That's not so bad. A little old fashioned—"

"Gladys Glück. With an umlaut." She poked him in the chest with two fingers. "Of course the kids pronounced it to rhyme with 'duck.' In fact, one of the many, many names they called me was Donald Duck. What kind of parents would name a child Gladys Glück?"

"Maybe it was like 'A Boy Named Sue,' maybe your whole artistic career is due to your childhood struggle."

"Some career. When I get married, I'm taking my husband's name so fast his head will spin. And I'm giving my kids names that nobody will make fun of."

"I didn't figure you for a marriage and kids."

"You figured wrong. I want a big house, too, in the burbs, with a big car that when you roll up the electric windows you can't hear anything at all. I want to go to Junior League meetings in tie-dyed coveralls and be so rich that no one will dare complain. I want two kids, a boy and a girl, and I want them to grow up knowing who Schoenberg is, and Kerouac, and Lenny Bruce. Smart, confident kids who'll turn the world upside down by its ankles and shake everything they want out of its pockets." She turned onto her side and faced him. "Am I scaring you yet?"

"I'm not afraid of you," Alex lied.

"Prove it."

He reached for her waist and she slapped his hand. "Not that way."

"What, you want me to propose?"

She rolled away onto her back again. "No, not now. Too late. You missed your shot."

"So if I proposed now, you'd turn me down."

"That's right."

"Marry me, Callie."

"Okay."

"Are you serious?"

"Are you?"

Alex wasn't sure when exactly he'd lost control of the conversation. "Yeah," he said. "I'm serious. Let's get married."

"I don't know. Maybe. I'll think about it." She kissed him on the forehead and turned her back to him. "It's late, let's go to sleep."

Holy shit, he thought. He'd nearly committed himself to something life-shattering without thinking twice.

He didn't know whether he was relieved or disappointed.

It turned into a running joke. One or the other of them would start a sentence with, "When we get married..." Then Alex bought a handful of toy diamond rings at FAO Schwartz and would periodically sneak one into her dessert. It might never have progressed beyond that had they not found, at a thrift store, a 1920s deco wedding dress, embroidered with white-on-white dragonflies. Alex went into the dressing room with her, and when she saw how perfectly it fit, she said, "Fuck. Now we have to do it for real."

ALEX'S FATHER had briefed him on the other players during the drive. Bob, in his forties, was a Korean War veteran, tanned and handsome, and was high up at Pepsico. Wade, in his fifties, was in oil. He had a thick East Texas accent, a starched white shirt, a sun-crinkled face, and a stained straw cowboy hat that he claimed was the source of his luck. Donny, also in his fifties, was heir to a major regional department store, heavy-set, with a gold medallion conspicuously nesting in the chest hair exposed by his floral-print double-knit shirt. He also owned the far-north Dallas house where they were playing. The last to arrive was Julie Greene, the gentle, balding banker who had put up the money for "Laura Lee," wearing a forest green polo shirt and plaid sport coat.

When Alex shook his hand, Julie said, "I'm so sorry the way things turned out with your record."

"I should apologize to *you*," Alex said. "It was your money."

"You can start making up for that tonight," Julie said, with a wink.

They moved into the game room. Alex was not sure he'd ever been in a house where the games had their own room. The table was eight feet in diameter, dark cherry, with a green felt surface. Each place had a side table for drinks, ashtray, and snacks. On the table itself sat six stacks of chips, each worth $500.

Alex's mouth had gone dry. He admitted to himself that he was intimidated. The net worth of the four non-Montoyas was somewhere north of a billion dollars and the air of self-confidence and privilege around them was palpable. These men had no interest in impressing anyone. They took what they wanted and had their people come around afterward to clean up the mess.

An elderly black man in a white jacket took their drink orders, and when Donny introduced Alex to him, the man, whose name was Jedediah, stood far enough away that Alex understood he was not to offer his hand. Bob ordered Glenlivet, Wade a Coors, Donny Wild Turkey, and Julie a brandy. Alex's father asked for a Bohemia. When Alex said, "Just a Coke, please," he felt like a kid in sockfoot pajamas sitting at the grownup table for the first time.

"Don't get too wild, there, Alex," Wade cackled.

Without thinking, Alex told the truth. "I figure I need to keep my wits with you sharpies around."

For a fraction of a second Alex thought he might have crossed an invisible line, but then Wade cackled again and said, "You got that just about right," and there was laughter all around.

Donny produced two sealed boxes of Bicycles and passed the blue deck across the table to Alex. Alex tore off the cellophane, broke the seal, and fanned the cards face up on the table, making sure all four suits ran continuously from ace to deuce. He plucked out the jokers and the ad and the spare, put them back in the box, and put the box on his side table. He swept the cards back together and used a dealer's shuffle that he'd been practicing for the last two weeks that kept the cards flat on the table. Julie turned to Alex's father and said, "I don't know, this kid is looking pretty sharp himself."

Alex caught the high card for the first deal. He offered the blue deck to Wade for the cut and Wade did it by the book, cutting toward Alex and letting Alex finish it. Everybody threw in a dollar ante. The chips, Alex saw, were made of dyed and embossed leather, well worn. He said, "How about we ease into it with a little seven stud?" He made himself deal more slowly than usual rather than risk a misdeal. He called out the up cards as he went around the table, and when he gave Wade a king he couldn't resist saying, "A cowboy for the cowboy," and got a laugh for it.

Wade, who was high, said, "Pair of cowboys bets a dollar."

"Nothing like starting your bluff early," Julie said.

Alex folded quietly after the second up card. Wade turned out to have the second king, which, with a pair of deuces, took the pot.

He folded the next three hands. Other than his own awareness of the stakes, it was like any other friendly poker game, with lots of shit given and taken. Wade bragged on his cards and Julie kvetched. Donny was restless, drumming his fingers, sipping his drink, and Alex's father did his snake-in-the-grass routine. Bob played conservatively and bailed when the betting got serious.

The fifth hand was five stud and Alex had tens wired. He waited until the next card, a deuce, to bet as if he'd just paired. When the third ten arrived, he bet it like two pair and kept Wade and Julie in to the end with lesser hands. It was a decent pot, and Donny said, "Well played." That got Alex a smile from his father.

They took a break after an hour and a half for calls of nature, fresh drinks, a chance to stretch. Alex was up a couple of hundred, Wade and Julie each down a hundred. Conversation touched on the new polo and hunt club in Plano, the Cowboys losing the conference championship to the Vikings, the ongoing bear market that had turned into a recession, the lousy performance of GE compared to Boeing, the soaring inflation.

"You're making me suicidal," Julie said. "Can we please go back to the table where I can lose my money honestly?"

When they sat down again, you could feel the focus sharpen. The chatter dropped off and nobody drank. A few hands in, as Bob dealt Spit in the Ocean, he said, "How about that Ronnie Reagan? You think he's going to run?"

"Hell yes, he's going to run," Donny said. "He's working the TV networks like a pro."

Wade said, "I like the cut of that man's jib."

Bob said, "He'd get the economy straightened out, that's for sure."

Alex, who'd chased the last two hands and lost them both, tried not to visibly bristle. His father, who didn't care for Reagan either, said, "Now, gentlemen, we're not supposed to talk politics at the table."

"Hell," Wade said, "we all businessmen here. Reagan's the only candidate out there who understands business. If Nixon had two brain cells to rub together he would have picked Reagan for Vice President. Now when they impeach him we'll be stuck with that moron Ford."

Alex bit his tongue. How did Reagan become a business expert? By hosting *GE Theater*?

Things continued downhill from there. When he had a good hand, the others seemed to instantly know it and fold, leaving him with minimal pots. His promising hands died on the vine. By 11:30, with half an hour left to play, he'd lost his $200 lead and another hundred besides.

Julie was dealing seven stud high/low. Alex had one queen down and one up in the first three cards and he knew this was going to be his hand. He opened with a five-dollar bet and said, "It's late and I've got some money to win. Cowards out."

His father and Bob both took his invitation and folded. After two more rounds, when Alex got his second queen up, Julie dropped as well, folding the fourth queen with his up cards. The battle lines were drawn. Donny was working a straight flush, showing the 4, 7, and 8 of clubs. Alex knew he wouldn't get it, because Alex himself had the 6 of clubs in the hole and the 9 and deuce had both come up in other hands. That meant Donny would have to settle for a straight or flush at best, and if Alex got a second pair to make a full house, he would beat either one—only four of a kind or a straight flush could top him. Meanwhile Wade was clearly going low, with a 2, 5, and 3 of various suits.

"Round again," Julie said. He dealt the 5 of clubs to Donny and you could hear everyone suck in their breath. Wade got a 7 and this time people were muttering under their breath. The murmurs got louder when Alex got a second 10, giving him two pair showing.

"Queens and tens are tall," Julie said. "Bet 'em."

It was time to let Donny take the lead. Alex stifled his elation and said, "Check to the straight flush."

The maximum bet and maximum raise were $30. Donny looked Alex in the eye, as if trying to decide how high he could go without Alex folding. "Ten dollars."

Wade, who figured on having the low to himself, said, "Up thirty."

Alex threw in $40 and Donny, of course, raised another 30. Wade took it to the three-raise limit with another 30. Alex had never paid a hundred dollars to see a card before in his life. This would be the biggest pot he'd ever won. He called and Julie said, "Down and dirty."

Alex and Donny glanced at their final cards. Wade didn't bother. Alex's was the jack of hearts, meaningless. "Queens and tens," Julie said.

Alex went the limit, as did the others, putting another $120 into the swollen pot.

"Declare time," Julie said. "Zero for low, one for high, two for both ways."

They each took two chips under the table and came up with a clenched fist. Alex was so tense he was afraid of crushing the antique leather. Julie counted to three and they opened their hands. No surprises. Wade went low, Donny and Alex high.

With no hesitation they went around again, $30 bet and three $30 raises. By this time there was so much money on the table, over a thousand dollars, that Alex tossed out another 120 with a kind of drunken nonchalance. You could work a month at Duane Reed for less than what he'd just spent on a single round of betting. Don't think about that, he told himself. Think how far ahead your half will put you.

"I believe you're called," Donny said. "Have you got the boat?"

Alex turned up the third queen. "And," he said, "you don't have the straight flush." He flipped the 6 of clubs.

Julie whistled and Bob laughed out loud. Wade said, "I'll be goddamned!" and leaned over to slap Alex on the back.

It was Donny's signal to fold his up cards so Wade and Alex could divide the chips. Instead he smiled and said, "You're right. I don't have the straight flush."

He turned over the first of his three hole cards. It was a second 8. Alex felt the floor tilt.

Donny turned over another 8, and Alex thought, maybe he's fucking with me. He can't possibly have the fourth 8.

He did.

"I'll be goddamned," Wade said again.

"I've been playing cards fifty years," Julie said, "and I've never seen a hand like this."

Somebody said, "Incredible," and another voice said, "Unbelievable." Alex's vision was too blurred to tell who. He sat back in his chair and listened to the air go in and out of his mouth as Wade and Donny began to divide up the money.

"Take five blues," Wade said. "Again."

On autopilot, Alex turned his cards face down and gathered them up and piled them somewhere near Julie. All he wanted was to get up and walk away from the table, and it was the last thing he was permitted to do. His job now was to sit through another twenty humiliating minutes and pretend to act normally.

The fact that the money he lost was his father's only made it worse.

The deck passed to Donny. "That was fun," he said. "Let's play that again."

ALEX MADE HIS few remaining dollars last until midnight. He had enough to ante and stay in for a card or two, then fold once the raises began. At one point his father caught his eye and mimed pushing a stack of chips toward him, and Alex shook his head.

The worst was after they cashed out. Donny shook hands and said, "I'll be telling the story of that hand tonight at every poker game I'm in for the rest of my life."

"Not if I'm there," Alex said, faking a smile. "Please!"

Julie put an arm around his shoulders and said, "You played like a pro. You're welcome at our table any time."

"As much as I lost, I should think so," Alex said, and everybody laughed.

In the car, his father gave him a few minutes of silence and then said, "You made me proud tonight."

"For what, taking a sucker's bet?"

"I would have played that hand the same way. So would every man at the table. He didn't even catch the fourth 8 until the last card."

"He knew I had the boat. He knew I was not going to back down. If he didn't have me beat, he would never have called on the last raise."

"By which time the betting was over. You're second guessing yourself. All that matters in the long run is that you played well and you were a good sport."

"An important character trait in a loser."

His father rebuked him with silence, and Alex felt guilty for his poisonous mood. Which didn't change the fact that he'd been humiliated, put in his place as surely as he had been by the 7-Up plant manager in Austin.

When they got home, he kissed his father on the cheek and took a deck of cards up to his room, where Callie was reading French *Vogue*. She saw his face and said, "Uh oh."

She was not a poker player, so he had to explain everything as he recreated the hand on the bedspread. He felt better for walking through it, like a football player watching the game films from a blowout loss. Her eyes were mostly on him, but she got the gist. "The odds against this must be phenomenal. Your hand just so, his hand, the other people's up cards."

"At least a million to one."

She nodded. "It figures."

"It does?"

"The rich always win."

She could make him smile as easily as she made him crazy. He said, "You won't be able to say that in the third person much longer."

"The world will always be in the third person to me."

Alex wasn't sure what she meant, but it sounded like poetry. He gathered up the cards and let it go.

"ONE LEG AT A TIME," Madelyn said. It was a Wednesday, the first of May; the sun was out, so the mall was deserted.

"Hi, dear, I'm sorry to call you at work, but…"

"What is it, Mother?"

"I'm afraid it's Cole. He called here. Somebody he knew saw you at the store—"

"Oh dear God."

"I told him I didn't know where you were, which wasn't entirely a lie, I mean, you might have been at lunch—"

"When did he call?"

"Just now. I think he may try to call you there at the store. I didn't tell him anything, he already knew. He left a number, Austin area code." She rattled off the digits to the downstairs phone in the Castle. The past suddenly felt like a dry-cleaner's plastic bag, suffocating her.

At that moment the second line buzzed. Beth, at the register on the far side of the store, picked up. Madelyn glanced at her and she mouthed, "For you."

"That's him now," Madelyn said. "Thanks for the warning. I'll talk to you later."

"What are you going to say?" her mother asked.

"I have no idea," Madelyn said.

She pushed the button for line 2. "This is Madelyn."

The silence at the other end went on so long that she was about to hang up. "Sunny saw you," Cole finally said. "He was home on semester break from Duke Medical School. He said you were pregnant. He guessed four months."

She had glimpsed someone who looked like Sunny the day before. She'd hidden in the back and hoped he hadn't seen her.

"Well?" Cole said. "Is it true?"

"I don't want to have this conversation."

"Is it mine? If it's my child I have a right to know."

His moral superiority undid her patience. "You didn't care

enough at the time to ask if precautions were necessary. You just took what you wanted. What is it you're offering, here? Did you want to help pay my expenses?"

A long, embarrassed silence ensued. "This is not a good time for me financially. I'm trying to put a new band together…"

"You didn't have a problem working construction in Virginia."

"So you're determined to go through with it?"

"Yes. I'm determined to go through with 'it.'"

"And my feelings don't matter at all?"

"Get a real job, start sending me money, and maybe—*maybe*—we can talk. Otherwise I don't want to hear from you."

"Madelyn, that's not fair—"

"I lost my job and my academic career because of you, and now I'm working in a jeans store for minimum wage. You want to talk fair?" She was going to lose another job if she didn't keep her voice down. "Fuck off, Cole," she said quietly and hung up.

Seconds later the phone rang again. Madelyn shook her head and held an open palm toward Beth. Beth nodded and Madelyn went in the back and washed her face. Her hands shook. She'd never told anyone to fuck off before. She rather liked it. What a relief it had been to blame everything on Cole. In reality, the amount of blame she awarded to herself varied between 40 and 90 percent, depending on how many times her bladder had woken her during the night and the extent of the swelling in her ankles, exacerbated by working retail, the only job she'd been able to find, and then she'd been lucky that the owner was a woman with two young kids of her own.

She wondered, briefly, if Cole would show up in person to harass her. Let him, she thought. She'd befriended several of the Valley View Mall security people, and she imagined them dragging Cole away, a cop on each arm, his legs kicking in futile rage, and the thought was deeply satisfying.

She dried her face and went out to relieve Beth at the register.

THE WEDDING WAS BOOKED at Christ the King, just south of Preston Center and the Studio Club, for Friday afternoon, May 31.

Alex hated the obscene wealth of the diocese, the pretentious stone arches and massive vaulted ceiling of the cathedral itself, the outrageous expenses that kept piling on, the overbearing weight of tradition and social status that constrained every decision. Between his father on one side and Callie on the other, he was helpless to stop the juggernaut. In the end he went where he was told to go and did what he was told to do.

Cole drove up from Austin with Jimmy and Amanda on Wednesday afternoon. Alex had barely had time to say hello. Thursday would be the rehearsal and the rehearsal dinner, followed by the bachelor party. Cole, as best man, was responsible for the party and suggested that the traditional stripper popping out of a cake was not very enlightened and that they should invite the women and have live music. He'd talked Alex into renting the new Studio Club location, down the street from where The Chevelles had played, and had hired a band called The Stone Brothers, which had evolved out of the Novas.

The rehearsal started with Alex being introduced to Callie's parents, the Glücks. The father had a big belly and short legs and a cheap brown plaid suit, and Alex had to fight not to think of Donald Duck. Hysteria was within easy reach. The mother was short and heavy too, with artificially bright copper-colored hair done up in tight curls that hurt Alex's eyes. Neither Glück bore any resemblance to Callie, as if she had changed her own genetic makeup through sheer force of will.

They walked from cue to cue, skipping most of the lines, including the vows that Callie had written for them, incorporating snippets from Blake's *Songs of Experience*, Ionesco's *The Chairs*, and Gregory Corso's "Marriage." At the point where Cole was supposed to produce the rings, he instead offered them two ring-pull tabs. It all seemed like a put-on, a tech rehearsal for a high-school play, nothing he could possibly take seriously.

The rehearsal dinner, at Lucas B&B in Oak Lawn, was even more awkward and artificial. Callie, seated next to her parents, didn't bother to hide her contempt for them, leaving Alex to wonder why she'd insisted on flying them in. Maybe, he thought, she meant to show them how well she'd made out in spite of them.

1974

Not helping the mood was the fact that Callie's sister had canceled at the last minute, offering no excuse, and leaving only two bridesmaids, Alex's sister Susan and Jimmy's girlfriend Amanda, desperate choices they'd fallen back on when the only friend Callie could name was Madelyn. Cole, Susan, Amanda, and both of Alex's parents tried repeatedly to lighten the mood and get the conversation moving, but it sprang one leak after another and sank again and again. Alex cut his steak into increasingly smaller bites and pushed it around his plate without eating anything.

At eight they moved on to the Studio Club. The Stone Brothers, per instructions, kept it quiet for the first set of Beatles, Byrds, and Gerry and the Pacemakers. The crowd, mostly standing in the middle of the dance floor and trying to be heard over the music, included people from his father's office, a few friends from St. Mark's, some out-of-town relatives on his mother's side, Uncle Jesús from Guanajuato, and a lot of young women he'd never seen before. The hard liquor was flowing and Alex understood what it was there for. He skipped the Bohemia and went straight to the screwdrivers.

Cole appeared and put his arm around his shoulders. "Good band, huh?"

"I can barely hear them," Alex said.

"Wait till the old folks clear out."

"Where did all these women come from?"

"The band, mostly. And some friends of friends. I had them put the word out to all the good looking, available women they knew that there was going to be free booze, music, and lots of single rich guys."

"You dog."

"Are you all right? I mean, is this just nerves, or something worse?"

Alex drained his glass and felt the alcohol go from his empty stomach to his crowded head. "You don't like Callie, do you?"

"Nothing against her. She doesn't seem to care much for me."

"You think I'm making a mistake?"

"You're in love. That makes me happy. I've been waiting for it to happen as long as I've known you."

Alex supposed it was the best answer he was going to get.

By nine, most everyone over thirty had left. The band took a break and Cole escorted him out to the street for "air."

"What's this about?"

"Nothing, really. Getting your surprise set up."

"I thought we decided not to do the girl and the cake."

"Did we? I guess I forgot." Cole looked at his watch. "We can go in now."

A new drummer and guitar player were on stage. The drummer was stomping his bass drum and adjusting the snare height or Alex might not have noticed. They looked oddly familiar. Before he could make the connection, Cole said, "I brought your bass. It's onstage, in tune. Let's go. The Chevelles are back."

Holy shit, it was Mike Moss and Gary Travis. Mike was wearing khakis and a striped dress shirt, his hair already starting to recede. Gary had a short black beard, shaggy hair, worn jeans and T-shirt. "Where the hell did you find them?"

"It wasn't easy," Cole said. "Mike is married and living in San Antonio. Gary was on a farm in Granbury. Mike hasn't played in two years. We're going to sound like shit, but I don't care."

Alex's buzz had left him reckless and ready to go. He got up and slapped hands with Gary and Mike and then strapped on his old Gibson EB-0 bass. He looked for Callie and couldn't find her in the crowd.

"It's your party," Cole said. "What do you want to do first?"

"I don't know." He barely remembered their set lists. "How about 'Laura Lee'?"

Cole was right, it was terrible. Nobody in the band cared, and the audience certainly didn't. They danced and yelled and shouted requests, and if it was something the band used to do, they tried to play it.

During "You Really Got Me," he finally located Callie, standing at the back of the room with folded arms. He grinned at her and winked. She looked away and walked to the bar.

He told himself not to let it get to him. Her mood would surely pass, and Cole had worked so hard to set this up. Who knew if he would ever play with a band again? Thinking that, he called for "Last Time," hoping she'd get the message.

1974

They did two more songs after that, then Cole called Jesús up and handed over his Strat, and they sang "Cielito lindo," and Jesús played a solo that brought tears to Alex's eyes. When it was over he did all the right things, hugging and thanking everyone before he went to look for Callie.

He finally found her outside, smoking. "What's wrong," he asked.

"Nothing."

"Yeah, right."

"Look, it's fine. It's a very macho thing, you guys up there preening and stroking your phallic symbols. This is your party. I don't have to dig everything you do."

"Sorry. I thought it might turn you on."

"Oh, I'm sure there are plenty of girls in there who are hot and wet over you."

"It has been known to happen," Alex said.

"Oh, that's nice. Remind me of all the floozies you've fucked on the night before our wedding."

"Maybe it's not too late to call it off," he said, and walked away, rage making his teeth rattle. He ordered another screwdriver. The Stone Brothers had started again, and cranked the volume, as promised. A girl standing near the stage, tall, dark haired, wearing a tight, red knit top, looked at Alex. She smiled shyly and looked down. Goddamn, Alex thought. There was a time he could never have passed that up. He drank off half the screwdriver and made his way to the table where Cole and Gary and Mike were waxing nostalgic.

He didn't remember how he got home. In keeping with tradition, he and Callie had already made plans to sleep apart. Cole wanted to surrender his bedroom, but Alex insisted on taking the living room couch.

He gave up on his restless sleep at 11 the next morning. His head felt like a balloon in a vice. His stomach, which hadn't had anything in it other than vodka and orange juice for 24 hours, was okay as long as he didn't think about eating.

Nobody suggested that the wedding might be canceled. Callie was long gone, taken by her bridesmaids for brunch and hair and nail appointments. Alex wouldn't see her until her father waddled down the aisle to give her away. The momentum seemed unstoppable. The flowers were ready to wilt, the reservations past changing, the multitudes of guests all assembled.

And so, running on two pieces of buttered toast and two cups of coffee, Alex found himself at 5:20 in the afternoon standing in front of the altar at Christ the King, a 30-foot-high medieval icon of Jesus staring down at him with two fingers raised in benediction, wearing a rented charcoal morning coat, striped trousers, and tan vest, watching Callie walk toward him, looking more beautiful than he'd ever seen her. She'd opted for no veil and her dark eyes burned into his for the entire length of the church. What he saw there, more and more clearly the closer she came, was hunger, passion, need, and it was all for him. She moved like a big cat, slow, sensuous paces, as if at any moment she might break into a run and take him to the ground.

His doubts boiled away in the heat of his desire.

They'd booked the reception into the Royal Coach Inn on Northwest Highway, a labyrinth of half-timbered buildings that included a tower, formal gardens, and multiple swimming pools. A DJ had set up at one end of the enormous function room, and the buffet line and tables were at the other. During the planning stages they had argued long and bitterly over their first dance, finally compromising on "When a Man Loves a Woman" by Percy Sledge.

Now, as they swayed together, barely moving, as he felt the heat of her body and smelled the sweet skin of her neck, he surrendered the last of his pride and said, "I love you."

"I love you too," she said. Her arms tightened around him and her fingernails dug into his neck. "I want to always feel just like this." Her breathing stuttered as she started to cry.

"Okay."

"Always?" she said. "Do you promise?"

"I promise," he said, and lifted her and spun her around and around.

*

ALL THROUGH the wedding weekend, Cole had the conviction that if he turned around, Madelyn would be there. The worst was the reception, watching Alex and Callie together. For all her many faults, the passion that she and Alex shared was undeniable. Cole was sick with jealousy, not for the woman, but for the feeling.

More than once he'd considered borrowing Jimmy's car and confronting Madelyn. He'd looked up the store, which was in the new mall at Preston Road and the LBJ Freeway in far north Dallas. If she wasn't there, she'd be at her parents' house. His fantasies invariably seized up at the first sight of her, swollen with his child, no warmth for him in her eyes. Smarter than he was, more determined, more in control of her emotions. What chance did he have?

Alex and Callie spent the night at the Royal Coach Inn, doubtless setting the sheets on fire, and took a limo early Sunday afternoon for the brand-new DFW airport, bound for New York and then Paris. Cole ate wedding leftovers at the Montoyas' and caught a ride back to Austin with Jimmy and Amanda.

THE FIRST TIME Cole saw Valentina was when Bugs Henderson called her onto the stage of the Armadillo World Headquarters during his encore. It was August and broiling hot inside the old National Guard Armory. Cole was driving the bright blue 1969 Chevy Nova with the 307 V8 and Muncie four-speed that he'd bought the week after Alex's wedding. He was bored and restless and on his own on a Thursday night. Bugs had been playing a lot of Texas-style blues, with a few departures like "Public Execution," the hit single by Mouse and the Traps that he'd played lead on back in 1965. The sustained guitar notes and the cymbal crashes echoed brutally off the brick walls and the shallow inverted V of the metal ceiling. Bugs was a grizzled veteran at 30, and the crowd, sitting on stained carpet pieces on the concrete floor, was small.

Valentina woke them up. She was five-ten in her bare feet, with glittering straight black hair down her back. Her cutoff jeans and cutoff T-shirt exposed a lot of lanky, dark brown body. She plugged a bright blue electric violin into the cable that a roadie offered her, and then licked her soft, oversized lips. She and Bugs conferred briefly and then tore into the Bobby "Blue" Bland classic, "Further On up the Road."

Cole was not usually one for fiddle players, but Valentina played in the mariachi style, rich and sonorous, and when she stepped up to the mike she wrapped instinctive harmonies around Bugs' sandpaper voice that conjured vistas of beauty and loss. Cole couldn't stop imagining the possibilities. From there they went to "Stormy Monday Blues," and Valentina played a solo that reminded him why they talked about Jimmy Page's "violin tone."

The re-energized audience crowded in front of the stage, yelling until Bugs and Valentina came back one more time. They closed with "Cielito lindo," as if they'd heard Cole's silent request, and when they were done the house lights went up.

Cole headed for the dressing room, and passed Jim Franklin in the hall. He was balding and shaggy-bearded, dressed in loose jeans and an Armadillo T-shirt of his own design. Cole had known him at the Vulcan, where he was part-owner and primary poster artist, and now he was in the same position with the 'Dillo.

"Hi, Cole," he said. "How's it going?"

"I have to meet her."

"Let me guess. That would be Valentina, right?"

"Where the hell did she come from?"

"She showed up from El Paso a month ago. She's been playing around, looking for a steady gig."

"She's amazing."

"You haven't seen anything yet. She plays the harp, you know, that little Mexican harp? And guitar and mandolin. And sings. Well, I guess you heard her sing."

"Introduce me, will you?"

Franklin walked him to the dressing room, where Bugs was in the process of rolling a plastic garbage can full of ice and Lone Star out into the corridor. Twenty or so people had crowded into a space that might comfortably hold half that, in cooler weather. Most of them orbited Valentina. Franklin eventually caught her eye and beckoned her over.

"It's ten million degrees in there," she said when she'd pushed her way out. She mopped the sweat off her face with both hands.

"I want you to meet Cole," Franklin said. "He's an old friend from the Vulcan days, and one of the better guitar players in town."

"Hi," she said. The wattage of her gaze didn't go up or down when she looked at him.

"You've made a conquest," Cole said.

"Not a battle I was fighting, I assure you," she said. Before he could recover, she said, "Who do you play with?"

"I'm, uh, considering my options at the moment."

"Ah, unemployed. I can dig it."

Cole felt the moment slipping away from him. "I think we should start a band together."

"Well, you've got a lot of balls, I'll give you that. Why would I want to be in a band with you?"

"If we can borrow a guitar from somebody, I'll show you."

She looked at Franklin. "You're sure he knows what he's doing?"

Franklin nodded, and with obvious reluctance she fetched a guitar case from the dressing room. Cole grabbed a folding chair and she handed him a nice spruce-top Guild D-series acoustic and said, "Please don't fuck it up."

Cole checked the tuning and made a minute adjustment to the D string, mostly for show. He played the insistent flamenco strum to "Malagueña" and started the first verse, "Que bonitos ojos tienes." It was a song of seduction, the singer enchanted by the woman's beauty and yearning to kiss her lips. He'd done well with it before. As he started the second verse he looked up at her, inviting her to join in, but she stood with her arms folded across her chest. He had the bystanders on his side, though, he could feel it, especially when he broke into falsetto on the chorus like Trio Los Panchos, and followed it up with a languorous lead with lots of finger tremolo. The last verse was the killer, "Si por pobre me desprecias," if because I'm poor you disdain me, I don't offer you riches, I offer you my heart. He wrapped up with a big flamenco finish and everybody applauded.

Except Valentina. "All due respect," she said, "if I wanted to play 'Malagueña' I could have stayed in Mexico."

"What *do* you want to play?"

"I'm not sure I've heard it yet."

Okay, Cole thought, one more roll of the dice and I'm out of here. He started into "Time and Tide," the song he'd written on the back of Tupelo Joe's lyrics. He played it straight, Tim Hardin style, laying the words out there for her to take or leave, and this time he connected.

"You wrote that?" she said.

Cole nodded.

"You got more like it?"

Cole nodded again.

She took a business card and a Bic pen out of her guitar case and scrawled a phone number on it. "Call me. Tomorrow afternoon is good."

"Okay," he said, and traded the guitar for the card.

A male voice in the crowd said, "Sure would admire a look at that there piece of paper."

Valentina smiled in his direction. "You're wasting your time, brother. I play for the other team." She put the guitar in its case and walked away to wolf whistles and applause.

"Nice audition," Franklin said.

"Did she mean…"

Bugs Henderson's drummer popped a beer near Cole's ear. "Yep," he said. "She's a carpet muncher. Hell of a waste, ain't it?"

COLE DOUBLE-CHECKED the address and verified that the run-down two-bedroom bungalow in South Austin was Valentina's. Peeling wood siding, set well back from the street in an acre of weeds and sycamores. A woman with brown hair like a haystack, wearing an oversize T-shirt and the remains of the previous night's eyeliner, unlatched the screen door for him. "Mind the cats," she said, and wandered away. Valentina sat in the living room on a thrift-store couch covered with a Mexican rug, reading the *Statesman* and drinking iced tea. All the windows were open and a couple of oscillating fans tried to push the air around. Valentina wore blue jeans and a black T-shirt with the sleeves rolled up and didn't seem fazed by the heat. She apologized for not having a sidewalk and insisted on helping him carry in his amp, after which she brought him a glass of tea with a slice of lime in it. A cool politeness had replaced her belligerence, leaving her the same distance away. Finally she sat on the couch and Cole sat on top of his amp and they got their guitars in tune.

"So what's your idea for a band?" she asked.

"I can't put it in words too well. If you take Big Bill Broonzy and Tim Hardin and The Beatles and Trio Los Panchos and Judy Collins and Don Covay and Led Zeppelin and Don Gibson, and you take that place where they all overlap, that's where it's at."

"Acoustic folk music, is where that is."

"But folk music that kicks ass, and knows how to drive a tractor, and speaks Spanish, and has missed some meals. And that you can dance to."

"Bass and drums?"

"Definitely."

"Pedal steel?"

"No. Not unless you play one."

"I can. But I can't afford one. All originals?"

"Maybe half and half. Do you write?"

"Some."

"Can I hear one?" Cole said.

She played something called "Take Me with You" that sounded like the Sir Douglas Quintet, with some New Orleans and some rockabilly thrown in. Driving rhythm, great hooks on the chorus, a bridge that suspended everything, including a D9, while it swirled around for eight bars before the beat came back strong.

Cole was too knocked out to play along. "Have you recorded that?"

"Not yet," she said.

"That's a top ten record. Jesus Christ."

This time when she smiled it was for real. "Your turn."

They traded originals for close to an hour, then threw a few obscure cover tunes at each other. He guessed a couple of hers and she knew all of his. "My old man owns a record store in El Paso," she finally admitted. "I don't stump easy."

The girl with the haystack hair stuck her head in. "I'm going to HEB. You need anything?"

"I'm good," Valentina said. "Thanks."

When the front door closed behind her, Cole said, "Is she your..."

"She's my roommate," Valentina said. "If we're going to work together, and that's still a big if, you're going to have to learn to mind your own business where my sexuality is concerned. I'm not some exotic subject for your anthropological study. And if you're nursing some Pussy Galore fantasy of me saying, 'I guess I never met a real man before,' you need to wake the fuck up."

Cole was hot with embarrassment. "Sorry," he said. "I really want to play with you." In a fit of self-consciousness he added, "Music, I mean. In a band."

She nodded. "I know a drummer, Linda Henried. Her band may be about to break up. She's good. Maybe she can bring her bass player along for a trial run, see what happens."

"Sounds great."

"Aren't you going to ask if she, you know, likes girls too?"

"No," Cole said.

"That's good. Now if you can keep from thinking it, you'll be getting somewhere."

"Are you this tough on all the guys?"

"I've mostly been in all-girl bands, to tell you the truth. Guys can be a fucking pain in the ass. But I think there might be hope for you."

"I'm glad to hear it," Cole said, not sure if he was being sarcastic. "Can we talk about a song list?"

LINDA WAS IN FACT a terrific drummer in the Keith Moon/John Bonham mold. She stood five six, big in the chest and thighs, with muscular arms and straight brown hair cut in short bangs. She locked down a tempo as tightly as anyone Cole had ever heard, with plenty of dynamics and syncopation and an overall sense that not even an atom bomb could derail her.

The bass player, Jonathan somethingorother, wore tie-dyed

T-shirts and had a fringe beard with no mustache. He lacked sparkle and Cole didn't think he'd make the final lineup.

The biggest problem was reconciling Linda's big drum sound with the songs where Cole wanted to play acoustic and Valentina was also on acoustic or harp. When Linda admitted that she was taking conga lessons, the last pieces fell into place.

Cole argued against the Crosby, Stills and Nash "wooden" versus electric dichotomy, and wanted to mix it all up, all the time. He also pushed for more songs in Spanish. Linda spoke a little Spanish and sang backup, so her vote carried the day. Behind songs like "Perfidia" and "Cielito lindo," the harp let loose cascades of trilling notes and thick powerful chords that sounded like dry dust and ancient civilizations and dancing women flicking long white embroidered skirts. The rock songs, meanwhile, shook the walls, thanks to Linda's power drumming and Valentina's violin.

The first practice, rough as it was, eliminated any doubts about going forward. They set up a four-day-a-week rehearsal schedule, and afterward, when Jonathan and Linda had left, Cole and Valentina would sit at her kitchen table and work on the set list and arrangements. Gradually they told each other their stories.

She'd been born in Veracruz, and learned violin in the school orchestra. She'd picked up the harp in Parque Zamora, where her father got his start selling records out of cardboard boxes on Sunday afternoon under the palm trees. He loved every kind of music, but his absolute favorite was danzón, the stately, clarinet-driven melodies that brought dancers in their white suits and hats to La Plaza de Armas on Friday and Saturday nights. Second came son jarocho, with its high-strung requinto guitars and harp, and its relentless, churning rhythms. He bought records wherever he could find them cheap, cleaned them, played them until he got tired of them, and then sold them for a profit. When Valentina was born, the first of six children, her mother was supporting the family as a waitress. Within five years her father had a mail-order business and was selling to collectors in the US. He'd saved enough to move the family to El Paso, where one of his best customers had a record store. Her father had started as a clerk and ended up owning the place, and Valentina had worked weekends to pay for music lessons and instruments of her own.

She dug out a scratchy old record by Lino Chavez, the godfather of son jarocho, and Cole loved it immediately, at the same time that he found it maddeningly familiar.

"That's because of Ritchie Valens," Valentina said. "'La Bamba' is an old son jarocho."

"We have to do it."

She showed him a pained expression. Her own cover choices tended toward Zeppelin's "Black Dog" or Blue Cheer's "Just a Little Bit" or Black Sabbath's "Paranoid." "How are you going to explain this to a promoter?" she said. "What are you going to put on a poster that tells people who we are?"

"We need the right band name," Cole said. "Then, after people hear us, we become our own genre."

Valentina sighed heavily. "I suppose you want something in Spanish."

«Claro que sí.»

She thought for a minute. "How about Los Lobos?"

"Wolves are too violent."

"Los Pájaros? Like a joke on The Byrds?"

"Gringos can't pronounce it. They'd say puh-*jar*-ohs." They both looked at the scarred tabletop for a while, then Cole said, "Los Cuervos. Easy to pronounce, people know it from the tequila."

"Maybe."

"Plus, it sounds like curvas, which could be a reference to your curves, as in, tantas curvas y yo sin frenos."

"Watch it, Cole."

"Not speaking for myself, of course."

"Right." Her mouth spasmed briefly. "Meanwhile, we've got another problem. Jonathan is not making it."

"No."

"I was thinking. What would really fit with these lunatic ideas of yours would be a standup bass player, somebody with some jazz chops."

Cole immediately heard Eldee Young in his head, the long, groaning, descending riff in the Ramsey Lewis instrumental of

"The In Crowd." "Oh, hell yeah. That's a great idea. Where do we find one?"

"I guess we go looking."

And so they did. Joe's 6th Street Deli, Cactus Café, the Victory Grill in East Austin, wherever there was a jazz jam session. It was frustrating, but mostly fun. Cole still felt like she didn't respect him, and it stung when she directed her sarcasm at him. On the other hand, it did keep him from kidding himself that they were out on a date. Meanwhile, they put up ads at all the music stores and Valentina called the director of the UT Jazz Orchestra.

The first outcome was that Jonathan showed up for practice on a Wednesday afternoon without his equipment and on a slow boil. "I saw an ad at Straight Music looking for a bass player and it had your phone number on it."

Valentina said, "What, were you looking for another gig?"

"None of your business what I was looking for. If you're going to fire me, you could have had the guts to tell me to my face."

"Sorry," Valentina said. "We were hedging our bets. We didn't want to fire you until we were sure we had somebody better."

Her frankness knocked Jonathan off his high ground. His face got red and he said, "Well, well, well, I hope you... I hope you don't find *anybody*." He banged the screen door on his way out.

Their first audition was that weekend. Receding sandy hair, tattoos on his forearms, mid-thirties. In the course of an hour he mentioned Charles Bukowski twice, referring to him as "Hank," and alluded to a stint in the Navy. Cole, recognizing something in his demeanor, offered him a beer. From the gratitude in his eyes and the haste, in spite of himself, with which he drank it, Cole suspected trouble. Despite a solid rockabilly technique, the feel of the Mexican tunes eluded him. "I can pick it up," he said. "I just need to hear it some more."

Cole and Valentina nodded, and after he left they looked at each other and said, "No."

Number two had hair to the middle of his back and a full beard. It quickly came out that he had a few years' experience on electric bass and only a few months on acoustic. "I'm picking it up pretty fast," he said. "I know I've got a ways to go."

Number three was a UT student named Aaron with great technique and not a lot of soul. He was not up for road trips and would have to miss a week here and there because of concerts and exams. Valentina explained that it was a problem, and he shrugged and said, "Oh well." As he was hoisting his bass to carry it back to the car, and as Cole was remembering the agonizing months in San Francisco before Gordo, Aaron said, "You know... there's a guy that graduated two years ago that was pretty hot shit. I think he might be what you're looking for."

By the time Luke Buckler called two weeks later, they had to be reminded who Aaron was. Linda was on the verge of quitting, her refrain of "Sucks without a bass" getting louder every practice, and their momentum had stalled.

Luke was from Lubbock, where he'd grown up loving Buddy Holly, and especially Buddy's upright bass player, Joe Mauldin. His bass looked like it had lost a couple of bar fights, and had a Shure ball mike duct-taped under the tailpiece. He showed up for his audition wearing a short-sleeved dress shirt and red-brown double-knit slacks and K-Mart shoes with buckles, and he had a flat-top haircut that hadn't been in style since The Day the Music Died. He used the word "gosh" in conversation, especially when talking to Valentina, with whom he had clearly fallen in love at first sight.

On the country and rockabilly songs, he was great from the start, snapping the strings, slapping the fingerboard between notes, spinning the bass on its endpin. He was good on the blues, and though he got buried on the loud rock, his time was in the pocket. Only on "Cielito lindo" and one of Cole's songs with a reggae backbeat did he fail to swing.

"I hate to do this," Valentina told him, "but can you wait outside for a few minutes while we talk this over?"

"That Mexican stuff—no offense—kind of threw me," he said, looking only at Valentina. He wasn't pleading, quite. "But I can get it. And I need to listen to that Zeppelin song some more..."

"Don't worry," she said, and gave him a smile to build a dream on. "We threw a lot of different stuff at you."

Once he was outside, Cole said, "I think he's worth a shot."

"Fuck yes," Valentina said. "He's obviously got the shit. I just wanted him to think we had the upper hand. Linda?"

Linda, who was not a talker, stuck up one thumb.

"Where did he get that haircut, though?" Cole said. "I bet he has to go to Lubbock for it."

"I thought he was kind of cute," Valentina said. When Cole stared at her in disbelief, she said, "Just fucking with you, Cole."

"He's in love with you," Cole said.

Valentina shrugged. "It happens."

MADELYN WOKE UP at 2:07 AM. The date was September 27, 9/27, and nine equaled two plus seven. It was the 243rd day of her pregnancy, counting from conception—the doctors insisted on counting from the first day of her last period, which had nothing to do with anything—another two and another seven, if you added the three and four. The numbers were ridiculously auspicious. Evidently Ava agreed, because she had let Madelyn know she was ready.

Madelyn had been thinking of her as Ava starting four months in, as if the idea had come from the child and not from her own imagination. She liked the fact that it was a palindrome, that it evoked Eve and the Garden, that it went from A quite nearly to Z and back again in three letters, that it reminded her of Ava Gardner, smart and beautiful and unapologetic about her sexuality.

She had to sit on a white plastic lawn chair in the shower. After drying off, she put on eyeliner and mascara and got dressed. She packed her suitcase for the hospital, then compared the contents to the list she'd written weeks ago. She was pleased to see that she'd remembered everything. After one last check in the mirror, she went to wake up her father.

If she'd thought she had a prayer of succeeding, she would have asked to drive. Her father was so nervous that she had to warn him repeatedly about speeding and red lights. Her mother sat in the back seat and smiled and shook her head. Fortunately the streets of North Dallas at 3:00 on a Friday morning were empty of danger.

By the time they got to Presbyterian Hospital, the contractions were coming every three minutes and lasting more than a minute each. She felt the hormones kick in. The naturopath she'd been seeing had told her that her body's own painkillers would be released with each contraction and that the painkillers in turn would enhance the next round of contractions. She was giddy, and the contrast between the stories she'd heard about unendurable pain and what she was actually feeling only increased her sense of her own good luck. The good luck to get knocked up by her perpetual adolescent of an ex-husband? The thought made her giggle because it was so self-evidently true.

She was barely on the gurney when her water broke. The contractions slowed, then started to come in double waves. The OB nurse wheeled her into an exam room and took her vitals and asked her to describe how she was feeling. Madelyn giggled again and the nurse turned to her father. "Is she on something?"

Her father blinked in confusion. "On something?"

Her mother said, "She's fine. I was the same way when I had her."

The nurse, skeptical, looked under Madelyn's gown. She had a furtive quality that Madelyn found hilarious. "Can you stop laughing, please?" the nurse said. "You're crowning. We need to get you to Delivery."

Ava took her time, waiting another hour to fully emerge. As the doctor held her up to evaluate her Apgar score, Ava was already losing the reddish-purple color she'd worn in the birth canal and turning to gold. She was perfect. The doctor confirmed it, telling the nurses, "Take a look. You don't see too many perfect tens."

At that moment Madelyn realized that the bare-bones existence she had imagined for the two of them was not going to suffice. To be worthy of this child, she herself would have to be more and better. She would have to remake herself in the image of her own excellence.

The nurses crowded in to see, which prompted Ava to let go a long stream of golden urine that soaked the doctor's gown. Madelyn laughed and Ava laughed. Madelyn reached out and took Ava to her breast.

1974

*

THE WEDNESDAY BEFORE THANKSGIVING, Ava dozed between Madelyn's breasts while Madelyn read *Pride and Prejudice* aloud. Ava liked British writers best, and Henry James the best of the Americans. Something in the formal cadence of the language soothed her.

Mail fluttered through the front door slot, and Ava allowed her to slowly get up and collect it. The only envelope addressed to her had familiar handwriting that she couldn't quite place. The note inside had no salutation:

"Look, this is ridiculous. You and I have always had our own friendship that has nothing to do with Cole, especially when we were in New York together. Now we're both in Dallas and you must have had your baby, and I'm dying of curiosity and I miss you. If you will just call me, none of it will get back to Cole unless you specifically request otherwise."

It was signed "Love, Alex," and had his phone number below the signature. She felt so grateful that she started to cry. Lately she cried because of the particular blue of the sky or the background music in TV commercials, so she had a Kleenex handy. She blew her nose and dialed Alex's number.

1977

COLE NEARLY BACKED OUT more times than he could count. Even as he stood outside the offices of Bill Graham Presents, in a run-down South of Market neighborhood full of warehouses and old Victorians that had been chopped up into apartments, he wanted to turn around and get on a plane back to Austin.

Instead he opened the door and stepped inside. A woman in her 20s was at the front desk, dark brown hair, big smile. "Can I help you?"

"Is Bill in?"

"Do you have an appointment?"

"No," Cole said. "I don't imagine this will take that long. He'll scream his head off and maybe throw me out a window, and that'll be that. Probably five minutes, tops."

"Uh oh," she said. "What did you do?"

"You don't want to know," Cole said.

She picked up the phone. "What's your name, so I can notify next of kin?"

"Cole. Jeff Cole. Formerly of The Quirq. There's a good chance he won't even see me."

"I'm Regina," she said, and squeezed his hand briefly. "There's a Jeff Cole here for you," she said into the phone.

Cole heard Graham's response both through the earpiece of the phone and from the depths of the office. "Jeff COLE? Jeff Cole from the fucking QUIRQ?" Regina held the phone away from her ear and winced.

"It's only been eight years," Cole said. "I don't know why I thought he might have cooled down."

Before Regina could respond, Cole heard a door crash open and Graham yell, "Where is he?"

"My advice?" Regina said. "Run for your life."

Graham emerged from a hallway. He looked the same as ever, hair still dark, body stocky and fit, wearing loose jeans and a Rolling Stones T-shirt. Cole remembered how he'd always felt a smile lurking behind Graham's rages, as if it was all a put-on. He didn't see that smile now.

Cole looked down, clasped his hands behind his back, and left himself completely open to a physical attack. Graham stood with the toes of his shoes against the toes of Cole's shoes, went up on tiptoe and leaned forward. "YOU HAVE THE UNMITIGATED FUCKING GALL TO COME INTO MY OFFICE? INTO MY OFFICE? YOU FUCK! YOU UNGODLY PIECE OF FUCKING SHIT! DO YOU HAVE ANY IDEA WHAT YOU DID? YOU MADE ME GIVE MONEY BACK TO PROMOTERS! THOUSANDS OF FUCKING DOLLARS, YOU COST ME! DO YOU HAVE ANY IDEA HOW MUCH I HATE TO GIVE MONEY BACK TO PROMOTERS?"

Cole started to say, "I'm sorry," and Graham upped the volume to cut him off. "DO NOT DARE OPEN YOUR FUCKING MOUTH! THERE IS NO APOLOGY FOR WHAT YOU DID!"

The tirade went on and on. It felt like hours, but surely was no longer than five agonizing minutes. When Graham was finally done, without ever having stopped for breath, he said, "NOW GET THE FUCK OUT OF MY OFFICE AND DO NOT EVER SHOW YOUR FACE TO ME AGAIN!"

Cole turned slowly and walked outside. His ears rang and his face was damp from Graham's spittle. He dried his face on his T-shirt and decided that it had gone about as well as he'd expected.

The warm February afternoon blazed with sunshine. Cole had rented a Chevy Vega hatchback at the airport, and he drove it up 11th Street to Market, where the Fillmore West had been. The building was deserted. In keeping with the penitential theme of the day, he crossed over to Oak Street and drove to the apartment he'd shared with Madelyn and Lenny, two of the people he'd loved most in his life, both of whom wanted nothing more to do with him. The paint was peeling off the old wooden siding, and the surrounding neighborhood had continued the downhill course it had been on in 1969—cardboard for window panes, unrepaired damage from fire and decay, broken glass and dog shit on the sidewalk.

Cole parked and sat on the front steps and remembered the last time he'd walked down them, on his way to Woodstock, dreaming of glory. Now he was poised to try again. Los Cuervos was one of the top bands in Austin, headlining at the Armadillo and Liberty Lunch. Two albums out on local Fable Records and a new one on Warners scheduled for July release. They were supporting themselves and then some, playing festival gigs in Houston and San Antonio. They were ready for the next step. Valentina was star material and Cole recognized that they had to make the transition to a national act or he would lose her.

He'd bought his own plane ticket to test the waters with Graham. If Cole could miraculously get back in his graces, it was a shortcut to the top. If he failed, it would only cost him his pride, a couple of hundred dollars, and some painful memories. Nothing he hadn't paid before.

He got back in the Vega and zigzagged south and west to Haight Street. Before the sunshine had faded, the neighborhood had gone dark. Most of the stores were closed and junkies nodded off in shuttered doorways. Cole ducked into a Chinese restaurant for mediocre noodles and a couple of bottles of Tsingtao.

The *Berkeley Barb* was still publishing and Cole flipped through it as he ate. He no longer recognized the music scene. Most of the space went to national touring acts at the Cow Palace and the Great American Music Hall, and the rest was bands he'd never heard of at venues he didn't know. The only thing scheduled for the Winterland was a Kinks show two weeks away on the 19th. The economy was gone that had once supported three nights in a row of the Grateful Dead or Quicksilver at the Fillmore. Bands wanted more money, and the kids that had showed up to hear live music every night had moved away or gotten day jobs.

He decided not to take musical potluck. He was exhausted from nervous tension and the long flight, so he had another Tsingtao for the road and drove to his motel.

At 11 the next morning he was back in Graham's office. This time when Graham emerged he wasn't shouting. "You've got some fucking balls, I'll give you that. Did I not tell you to never come here again?"

"Yes, sir. But I flew out here to apologize and I never got a chance yesterday."

"One of my trade secrets. Never let the other guy get a word in."

Cole took a breath. "I fucked up and I'm sorry. I know the reasons don't matter, but my marriage was breaking up, and the band sucked at Woodstock, and Lenny quit, and I had a kind of a breakdown. You went out on a limb for us and got us a lot of breaks, and I was irresponsible and cost you money."

"Is that it?" Graham had already started to turn away.

"I want to pay you back."

"Really? How do you pay somebody back when you've betrayed their faith in you?"

"I have a new band—"

"Oh no," Graham said, the volume starting to rise. "No fucking way. I can't believe you make this cornball apology and immediately turn around and try to sell me something."

The important thing was not to sound desperate, to keep his voice calm. "If you booked us, you could keep my share of the money until you felt like you were satisfied. I don't want the rest of the band to suffer for my mistake. It's a great band. We do a lot of Latin material that you would love."

"Out," Graham said. "Get the fuck out of here." He was louder, but he wasn't yelling.

When Cole returned later that afternoon, Regina stared at him. "You must not value your life."

"I wanted to drop this off," Cole said. He gave her a rough mix of the Warner's album, *Something to Crow About*, on cassette, a pub shot of the band with Valentina looking particularly sexy, and contact info for their management and booking. "Give me at least a ten-minute head start before you pass those along."

"You'd really play for no money?"

"What can I say? I know it's supposed to be every man for himself these days, but…" He couldn't think of a way to say what he wanted that didn't sound pompous or self-righteous, so he shrugged and smiled instead.

Regina smiled back. "I'll do what I can for you."

★

ALEX COULDN'T STOP trembling, maybe from fear, maybe from anger, maybe both. He'd been standing outside his father's office for over three minutes and was still not under control. He gave up and went in.

His father was on the phone. He motioned Alex to sit down, which Alex was too wound up to do. Alex leaned against a wall out of his father's line of vision and continued to vibrate.

The phone call went on and on. The fact that his father sounded so relaxed and was making jokes only stoked Alex's outrage. When he finally hung up, his father spun around in his chair and looked at Alex with concern. "Are you feeling okay? You don't look well."

Alex laid the manila file folder on his father's desk. His father looked a question at Alex and opened the folder. He paged through the documents inside and smiled. "I remember this. This was a real piece of luck."

"Luck? That's the best luck I've ever seen. You bought that land for seventy-five hundred an acre. It's worth, what, half a million an acre now? The southern boundary picks up exactly where the northern boundary of DFW airport leaves off. I mean, exactly."

"Making it a great location for a hotel," his father said. "Which is why I put one there."

"The only thing is," Alex said, the tremor now in his voice as well, "you bought this land in February of 1964. Which was before the site for the airport was chosen."

"Officially," his father said. "A smart man could see where things were headed."

"It takes more than brains to see an exact latitude and longitude. It takes inside information."

"It takes more than that. It takes some pull with the guys who draw the final lines."

Now Alex did sit down. "I can't believe you're bragging about it. This is *illegal*. You could go to *jail* for this."

His father looked troubled, for the wrong reasons. He shook his head and said, "Alex, I love you, my son, but you are a long way yet from understanding business. This is the way the game is played. Nobody got hurt. There's nobody to complain."

"What about the farmer who sold you the land? You cheated him out of millions of dollars."

Alex saw that he'd crossed a line. His father's smile dropped away and one eye narrowed. "Don't use emotional language to muddy up the truth. The man who sold me that land knew I was speculating. He could have kept it for himself, but he got greedy and wanted to take the short-term profit."

"He didn't know what you knew."

"He knew I knew something. Because he, *unlike you*, understood business."

Alex had forgotten the potency of his father's disapproval. It had been many years. Still he said, "This was wrong, Papa."

His father closed the file and held it out. "Put this back where you found it. And go back to work."

Alex sat at his desk for an hour, his guts churning, then drove home. Magdalena, the Honduran nanny, was about to put Gwyn down for her afternoon nap. Alex gave her the rest of the day off and picked up the battered copy of *Mr. Brown Can Moo*, Gwyn's current favorite. Gwyn was two now, and talking most of the time she was awake, though much of what she said was in some private language and the rest was evenly split between English and Spanish. Callie thought it was wonderfully creative and encouraged her, one of the many, many things that she and Alex disagreed on.

Callie herself was in Marfa that week, at the Donald Judd ranch. She'd been making trips there for a year, and Alex suspected she was having an affair—not with Judd himself, who was married and seemed a decent sort, but with one of the many hangers-on who had answered the gravitational pull of Judd's project. Some days it made Alex frantic with jealousy. Today it was just one more straw.

He was able to read *Mr. Brown* without engaging his conscious brain, leaving it free to torment him. More than anything, he wanted to quit, to run away to New York or Austin or Mexico. Bad enough that he hated the job, hated the fact that he was slowly turning into his father, hated the house and the nanny and the polyester slacks and shirt and necktie that he wore every day, hated his routine of poker every Friday, dinner every Saturday at his parents' house, tennis every Sunday with Stanley Marcus of Neiman Marcus. Now the job had driven a wedge between him and his father, as if to prove that there was nothing it couldn't contaminate.

Yet he couldn't quit because there was no other way to make the money to pay for the house that was a condition of his unhappy marriage. And he couldn't leave the marriage because of Gwyn.

When Callie had turned up pregnant, Alex wasn't sure either of them had what it took to be a parent. Callie surprised him when she quit smoking the day her test came back positive, and then again when she started taking Lamaze classes. From the start she had loved the baby cheerfully and unconditionally.

Alex too. Which meant he could neither give Gwyn up, nor ask Callie to. The trap was perfect, inescapable. He had a vision of himself running down an infinite hallway, doors on both sides slamming shut as soon as he approached. If he didn't come up with something soon he'd be howling in the streets.

Gwyn's arms relaxed at her sides and her fingers began to twitch. Alex slipped out of her bedroom and put on the first side of *Live Dead*, keeping the volume low enough to hear Gwyn if she called.

He sat at the kitchen table and thought of his anti-capitalist rhetoric in college, of his father's land fraud that had helped pay for it. He fantasized about the many young and available women in the office that he knew better than to approach. He wished he were stoned or drunk or tripping, knowing that even that small release was unavailable without somebody to look after Gwyn.

He could ask Madelyn. She showed up once or twice a month, usually on very short notice, to take advantage of whatever baby-sitting arrangements were in place for Gwyn. She was always wary, as if he might have Cole hidden in a closet somewhere. He wasn't sure their current relationship allowed him to ask for quid pro quo.

He had nobody to call and unload on. Susan had too many problems of her own, as she watched her loveless second marriage come apart. Cole would make excuses for his father and ever-so-nicely imply that Alex was to blame for marrying Callie in the first place.

Which left him circling the idea that had been lurking in his head for six months, ever since the last family trip to Guanajuato. He and Callie had been sitting on a bench in the Jardín de la Unión when he thought he saw a familiar face. «¿Álvaro?» he said.

The man turned. «¿Alejo? ¿Eres tú?»

Mexico had been through a financial crisis at the end of August where the formerly fixed exchange rate had been cut by nearly 50 percent. Overnight people lost half their savings, half their paychecks, half the value of their houses and cars. Wage and price controls had artificially slowed the resulting inflation and the economy had collapsed into recession. In the midst of these hard times, Álvaro looked prosperous in bell-bottom jeans with chrome studs, a double-knit shirt with a loud floral pattern, and a brand new black cowboy hat. He was obviously also eating well. Alex stood up and Álvaro grabbed him in an abrazo, squeezing hard. When he finally let go, Alex introduced Callie.

In formal Spanish, Álvaro said, «Clearly you are an amazing woman, to have captured the restless heart of mi primo Alejo.»

«No hablo,» Callie said with a forced smile.

«Qué lástima,» Álvaro said, and winked at Alex. «Perhaps you can translate for her later, in private.»

Alex gestured at his clothes. «Did you give up el mariachi for norteña?»

«No more music for me, primo. I've become a man of business.»

«What kind of business?»

Álvaro looked both ways. «The yerba business. We should talk, but not here. You free for lunch tomorrow?» He glanced at Callie. «Just you?»

The next day at one in the afternoon they met at the Hotel Posada Santa Fe on the plaza. Álvaro wore an expensive suit and an open-collared white shirt. In daylight he looked a good five years older than his chronological age, as if his internal clock was running fast. His mustache was still thin, and his eyes still tended to go off in different directions. He'd been a spooky-looking kid, and now, with physical heft and self-confidence, he exuded danger. Sitting across the table from him made Alex feel nervous and flattered at the same time.

Minding his manners, Alex kept the conversation to mutual friends, family, fútbol, and other neutral topics until they were well into the meal. «Bueno,» Alex finally said, «how's business?»

«Business, mi primo, is very, very good.»

«Is it safe to talk here?»

Álvaro smiled. «As long as we don't shout.»

«I read in the papers about Operation Condor, and it sounded like they poisoned all the yerba in Mexico with this paraquat mierda.»

«They did poison a lot of yerba... in Sinaloa. But you guys in the US, you have such an appetite, and we don't want you to do without. Sinaloa dries up, Guadalajara steps forward. And Veracruz, and Columbia... Paraquat was great for our business.»

«I would like to buy a little from you before I go back.»

«You can buy a little... or buy a lot.»

Fear narrowed Alex's vision to the plate of carne asada in front of him. «What are you saying?»

«I thought about you last night. Because of your father, you're in a perfect position to help us out. And make yourself a lot of money. Your father has refrigerated trucks that run from Monterrey to Laredo and then all the way up the highway to Dallas. Everybody knows those trucks. Nobody would ever search one of them. Add a few kilos of yerba to each one...»

Alex shook his head. «No, never, I would never risk my father's reputation by doing something like that.»

Álvaro put a big hand on Alex's forearm and looked genuinely repentant. «I apologize. I should never have suggested such a thing. Your father is a good man and you are completely right.» He squeezed Alex's arm, and then smiled. «You, however...»

«I'm not the man my father is, that much is certain.»

«You could, without involving your father in any way, drive a fancy rented car across the border at Laredo, and return with a couple of well-hidden kilos.» He held up one hand. «Don't say anything now. Give it some time.» He pushed a business card across the table. «That number is good twenty-four hours a day. Leave a phone number with whoever answers and I'll call you.»

As Alex walked home, the streets were full of students and young Mexican tourists, their lives still rich with possibilities, their hands flying in all directions as they laughed. He knew that the rivalries between the Mexican drug gangs were getting more and more violent. Álvaro's assurances of how easy it would be to cross the border with a few kilos of dope were pure fantasy. Still he couldn't stop thinking about it, not on the long walk home, and not in the six months since.

He was still not prepared to use his father's trucks, even after what he'd learned, even though it would serve his father right, and take away some of the bitterness of the memory of sitting there with Álvaro and praising his father's nobility. He was, however, more prepared than ever to consider the other possibility, the possibility that scared the living shit out of him, the possibility that sent a jolt of electricity through his life, that might just make it bearable.

FRIDAY EVENING, when Cole and the rest of the band pulled up in a limo for sound check, hundreds of kids were already in line at the front gates of Oakland Coliseum. No reserved seats, which would mean a stampede when the gates opened at nine the next morning. Los Cuervos were supposed to start at 11:00, followed by Rick Derringer's band, followed by Zeppelin at 1:00. Cole saw kids no older than 13 or 14, dozens of them, on their own, guys with hair past their shoulders, girls in lots of makeup and skimpy clothes, smoking cigarettes and dope, drinking anything that came their way. He wondered if their parents knew where they were.

Three Zeppelin security guards opened the limo doors. Cole was the last one out. The guards were enormous, all dressed in black tour T-shirts with the falling angel logo from Zeppelin's record company, all in sunglasses against the last of the July sunlight. Their silent menace took away Cole's normal affability and muted the excitement he'd been feeling for days. He'd heard stories about the brute force that manager Peter Grant used to protect his clients. This was something else again, poisonously bad vibes, like something out of a gangster movie. He glanced at Valentina, who'd been smiling less than a minute ago. Her face was unreadable.

The guards led them through a series of concrete tunnels and overpasses to stage left, where Linda's drum cases and their amps sat in orderly piles. One of the thugs said, "Get your gear ready, then sit." He pointed to a row of folding chairs. A few yards away, a couple of Derringer roadies were unpacking Vinny Appice's drums and mounting amplifier heads on speaker cabinets.

Cole had a good view of the oversized stage, complete with fake standing stones and a giant cloth hanging in the back painted in red and orange rays. A big redheaded man, long-haired and bearded, was tuning Jimmy Page's sunburst Les Paul to the piano. Lined up in the near corner of the stage were Page's purple Telecaster, his famous double-necked SG, another sunburst Les Paul, two full sized acoustics, and a mandolin. The man approached one of the vocal mikes and said, "Ready for me, mate?"

"Give it a go," said the voice from the monitor speakers.

The man plugged into a Marshall stack and played the signature riff to "Whole Lotta Love," which echoed massively off the walls of the empty stadium. Cole, despite the negative energy all around him, felt his spirits lift at the reminder of where he was and what he would be doing tomorrow. The man then stepped on an orange effects pedal and played the phase-shifted intro to "Achilles Last Stand," followed by the opening rapid-fire chords. When he paused, the monitors said, "That's lovely. Give us a bit of the Tele, then."

The man changed guitars and played a minute or so of legato single notes, timed to the natural reverb of the space. Cole found himself holding his breath. The melody was passionate and vastly sad, more like something from Jeff Beck's *Blow by Blow* than one of Page's tortured metal solos.

"Right," the monitor said. "Let's keep it moving, yeah?"

Another from the endless supply of big men came out and made a few adjustments to Bonham's custom Ludwig set. He had only a single bass, single riding tom, and a couple of floor toms, though the drums themselves were huge and looked to be made of gold-plated steel. Plus two tympani and a monstrous gong. A ridiculous amount of equipment to cart all over the world for a few seconds of effect. While the sound man got levels on each of the dozen drum mikes, the red-haired man played the rest of Page's guitars and then ran through Jones's gear—electric bass, standup bass, and a triple-necked acoustic with mandolin, 12-string, and 6-string on the same body.

By that time Linda had her drums assembled and they settled onto the hard metal chairs. Cole would rather have stood at the edge of the stage, but a glance at the head gangster convinced him not to bother asking. The Zeppelin crew finished their sound check and the red-haired man walked past Cole. "That piece you played on the Telecaster," Cole said. "That was amazing."

The man stopped, and for a second Cole was afraid he'd broken some rule of silence. Then the man grinned. "Twats in the booth didn't think as highly of it as you did, unfortunately." He offered his hand. "My name's Ginger. On account of the hair."

"Like Ginger Baker," Linda said.

"Yeah. Right bastard that he is."

"I'm Cole," Cole said. "This is Linda."

Ginger crouched in front of them. "Our tour manager's name is Cole, but everybody calls him Ricardo. You lot don't look like Derringer, so I take it you're Los Cuervos?"

Cole introduced the others as Appice's elaborate drum set was loaded on in front of Bonham's platform.

"I don't envy you playing tomorrow," Ginger said. "Zeppelin's crowds eat opening bands for breakfast. My advice is, keep it loud, keep it coming, and don't overstay."

"Thanks," Cole said. Ginger patted his shoulder with an over-sized hand and walked away.

"Guess we better rethink the set list," Valentina said.

The Derringer roadies were quick. The guitar tech played less than a verse of "Rock and Roll Hoochie Koo" before being dismissed by the sound crew. The drum tech got only a handful of microphones and a minute and a half.

Then Cole was rolling his Twin Reverb onto the stage and trying to find a place for it in front of the other gear. He plugged in the Strat and played a few notes of Zeppelin's "Black Dog," a song they would definitely *not* be playing. The echo hypnotized him. He almost regretted that a hundred thousand bodies were going to be there to kill it on Saturday and Sunday.

The sound crew finished with them in moments—nobody cared how the opening band sounded—but Cole couldn't resist playing another minute of solo guitar just to listen to it come back to him out of the twilight.

"Yeah, thanks, Clapton," the sound man said, "but we haven't got all fucking night."

Cole put the Strat away and looked up to see Ginger loitering by one of the fake standing stones. "You've got a nice touch," Ginger said. "Fancy a pint? Or whatever odd configuration of piss-water lager you poor bastards have on offer over here?"

Ginger rode to the Hilton in their limo, doing his best to charm Valentina and Linda, with limited success. Cole wasn't sure they understood what he was saying. Cole himself had read so many English spy novels that he was able to get at least the gist of the slang.

The rest of the band left Ginger and Cole to stake out a table in the bar. Word had leaked that Zeppelin was staying there and teenagers thronged the lawn and sidewalks outside. Periodically one or two rushed the lobby and got ejected by hotel security. "They don't even look like they're having fun," Cole said.

"Nah. More like they're offering themselves up as sacrificial victims to their gods. And in the case of the little girls that get taken upstairs, sacrifice is the word. You been at this long?"

"Ten years or so. I played at Woodstock."

"Ah. About ten years for me too. That was a whole different scene then, you know? Took acid for cosmic insight, didn't we, and now these kids take it just to get fucked up. The music meant something then."

Cole shrugged. He'd witnessed the mystification of Woodstock over the years, as kids who'd been nothing but wet and miserable now claimed to have had life-changing experiences. "I don't know. Seems like most rock and roll has always been about, 'let's get high, let's get laid.'"

"At least there was an, 'I love you, baby,' before the 'let's fuck.' Not just, 'gonna give you every inch of my love.' You know what I mean? There's a big empty place in this music where the heart should be."

"Still, you have to give them credit. It's beautiful stuff. 'Achilles Last Stand,' like you were playing tonight, 'Kashmir,' nobody else makes music like that."

Ginger shook his head. "People make music like that, just not as well. I mean, Black Sabbath, for Christ's sake. I don't know, maybe it's knowing them personally puts me off the music."

"I've heard some of the stories. Mudsharks, whips and hand-cuffs…"

"It's not just the sexual stuff, though I'll say it again, god help those poor little girls. You know Jimmy is into all this Aleister Crowley bollocks. 'Do what thou wilt shall be the whole of the law.' That's just an excuse to indulge his slightest whim without regard to the consequences for anyone else. I mean, look at the lives they lead on tour. They can't leave their bloody rooms except to go to some stadium and be worshipped, or to get on their private aeroplane to fly to the next city they'll never see except through a limousine window. Totally divorced from reality. Bonham, who is more sensitive than you might think, goes barking mad after every show, Jonesy withdraws from everybody, G—that's Peter, Peter Grant—snorts mountains of coke, Jimmy shoots up. Robert is the only one close to normal, and he's not all that close."

"You're a terrific guitar player. Why don't you quit and play in your own band?"

"Look at me. I'm not some waif-like pretty boy like Jimmy, I'm a great ugly bastard that gives girls nightmares." He held out his massive hands. "These are all right for power chords and slow stuff, but… have you heard this kid Eddie Van Halen? That's what they want now, speed. At least working for G, he values me being big and ugly, more muscle when it comes time to put the boot in."

"Do you really do that? You don't seem like the type."

Ginger drank off the last of his current beer. "Yeah," he said, "it gets rough sometimes. I don't like to hurt anybody, but some of these kids, they're so crazed, they could hurt the band or hurt themselves and you've got to restrain them. I mean, that's the thing about G. He lives and breathes this band, it's all he does. He takes care of his own, and fuck everybody else."

The beers kept coming and Ginger put them away twice as fast as Cole. He talked about working for Cream and pulling his namesake off of Jack Bruce on multiple occasions, not to mention cleaning Baker's vomit off his drums and the surrounding stage. "It was the heroin made him puke. Fortunately Jimmy's got a stronger stomach."

"Jimmy's on smack?"

"Fucking right he is, have you not seen him staggering about the stage?"

"No, I've never seen him before."

"Henry is their little code name for it. Charlie for cocaine. He mixes them up in some exact combination that lets him function, barely. Though it's got so bad a couple of times lately he'll forget how the songs go and Robert has to sing them for him right there on stage. I don't know how they can keep on going, with everything getting madder and madder, the band stir-crazy in their rooms, G hiring these gangsters like John Bindon who then assault journos and punters and staff, millions of dollars in cash flying about, where does it all end? Where's the joy in it? Is this the music that was supposed to set us free?"

At 11:00 Ginger announced, "Bollocks. I'm knackered, and pissed as a newt. And we've got an early call tomorrow."

"Yeah." As Cole stood up, he felt a drunken rush of affection. "It's been good talking to you. I really enjoyed it."

"Yeah, me too, mate. You're all right." Then a troubled look crossed his face. "You're not... nah, of course you're not."

"What?" Cole said.

"You don't... I mean, you're not..."

Looking into his eyes, Cole saw pain, doubt, fear, and something else. "You mean... am I gay?"

"I knew it was a stupid question. Should have kept my gob shut."

"No, it's all right. I'm just... I'm sorry, man."

Ginger waved a large, drunken hand. "Forget I said anything, yeah? I mean, if G or the other fellas found out, it'd be my job. Probably beat me half to death first."

Cole, torn between sympathy and his own discomfort, held on to the back of his chair with both hands. "Yeah, not a very open-minded bunch, I imagine. It must be hard."

"It's fucking lonely, I'll tell you that. And being around Robert all the time, he's always running around with his shirt off and his tackle bulging out of his jeans and me trying not to look..." In a split second, his defenses snapped back into place and he sat up straight and shook his head like a dog coming out of the water. He fixed Cole with an intense stare. "Seriously, though. You'll keep schtum, won't you?"

"I promise," Cole said. "Get some sleep, Ginger. I'll see you in the morning."

Cole had to show his purple backstage pass three times to get to the sixth floor—once to a hotel bouncer and twice to Zeppelin's own security. Bill Graham had booked them into a suite, two bedrooms with two beds each. When he let himself in, Linda was on the couch watching TV. Moaning noises came from one of the bedrooms.

"Val scored, I take it," Cole said.

Linda looked up, held his eyes a second too long, and then looked away and nodded. "Luke's already sacked out."

Cole showered and brushed his teeth, careful to wear a robe when he passed through the living room. He felt Linda watching him. He got into bed in the dark and tried to tune out Luke's soft snoring. His thoughts turned, inevitably, to sex.

He and Charlene had been an on-and-off thing for a year or more, both of them fooling around on the side, both up for a bit of fun when they ran into each other at the 'Dillo or the Broken Spoke. Then a drunk had run a red light and T-boned Charlene's Mustang. She'd broken 17 bones and been in physical therapy for seven months. They'd done their best to put her face back to what it had looked like before the accident. Cole was okay with that, thought it gave her character. She'd also gained a lot of weight in the hospital, which was not in itself a deal breaker. The problem was that she was in constant pain, and the doctors insisted it wasn't real. They had stopped prescribing Percodan and so she'd moved out of her mother's house and started using heroin. The last time he'd spent the night with her, mostly out of pity, he'd caught her emptying his wallet in the middle of the night and he'd told her to call him if she ever got straight.

Once Los Cuervos were making good money he'd left the Castle for a new two-bedroom apartment across the river in South Austin. He'd brought home his share of women from the shows, none of whom had stuck, and he had to admit it was not the ideal way to start a serious relationship.

He'd never intended for the business with Linda to happen. The band had played an ill-advised and worse-attended show in Waco, and somehow he and Linda had ended up in his motel room with a couple of six packs and nature had taken its course. Cole had felt guilty and disgusted with himself afterward, but Linda, it turned out, had been nursing some feelings for Cole for quite a while. In fact, she had quite a lot of feelings, which she tended to hide under several layers of sullenness and aggression. And Cole, having been there once, found himself on a couple of other occasions of drunkenness and desperation unable to resist the easy opportunity, until Valentina had taken him aside.

"This bullshit with my drummer is going to stop, right now."

"*Your* drummer?"

"She's a human being, Cole, and you are going to treat her that way. You will show her kindness and respect and nothing else. You will not have anything even vaguely resembling sex with her again as long as you are in this band, or you will no longer be in this band. I'm going to give her this same talk, so as of now you two are no longer an item, not even the half-assed, at your pleasure item that you were."

Valentina had never used that preemptory tone with him before, and Cole saw that he had just ceded control of the band. He was smart enough to walk away in silence, turning his fury inward as he always did, driving back to his empty apartment to drink himself into a long, self-pitying sulk. The one time he'd tried to apologize to Linda, she'd said, "Yeah? What exactly is it you're sorry for?"

In the end, the band didn't suffer for it. Linda hit the drums as hard, if not harder, than before, and Cole stood back and let Valentina call the shots.

IN THE LIMO at ten AM, Valentina handed out a revised set list.

"You pulled all the songs I sing lead on," Cole said.

"We share the vocals on nearly everything, and you've got the lead on 'Time and Tide.' I can't help it if you sing a lot of candy-ass Mexican songs. Today is not the day for that shit."

"We should at least end with 'Cielito lindo.' Everybody knows it, we'll get them singing along. Up the tempo, do it electric."

"With no rehearsal?"

"We change stuff around all the time."

Valentina looked at Linda, who said, "I don't care." Luke shrugged.

"Oh, all right," Valentina said. "If it sucks, we're not doing it tomorrow."

At 11:05, a massive thug with a walkie-talkie gave Bill Graham the go-ahead to introduce the band. The boos started when it became clear he wasn't introducing Zeppelin. As soon as the words "Los Cuervos" left his mouth, they hit the stage running. Valentina shouted "Good morning!" into her mike as Linda counted off "Good Morning Blues," the old Leadbelly song that they'd given a Zeppelin-style makeover with churning guitar riffs and Linda hammering the toms. The sound man gave them plenty of PA volume and it should have knocked the audience back in their seats. Instead they waved their middle fingers and shouted for Zeppelin.

Valentina acted like the widely scattered applause at the end of the song was a massive ovation and shouted a "Thank you!" that sounded like she was having the time of her life. As the rest of the band started into "Just a Little Bit," she announced it as "a song by one of the greatest Bay Area bands ever, Blue Cheer," a name that meant nothing to these demented children. Still, when

Linda slammed into the drum break at the end, gradually picking up speed until her hands and hair were flying and her drums completely filled the stadium, the Bonham freaks recognized one of their own and the whistles and cheers began.

They kept their tenuous hold on the audience until the last couple of songs, at which point Cole saw that Valentina was right and he was wrong, and he walked up to her in the middle of "Give It Up," one of her raucous originals, and said into her ear, "Fuck 'Cielito lindo,' do 'Take Me with You' instead." She nodded and he passed the word to the others. They pulled it off, and got decent applause, which died too quickly to justify an encore. Deep Purple's *Machine Head* blasted out over the PA and Zeppelin's road crew shoved the band's equipment offstage.

Ginger was pushing Cole's Twin Reverb and he raised his thumb. "Well done. You actually got those bloodthirsty bastards on your side."

"Thanks to your advice," Cole said.

"All in a day's work. You staying for the main event?"

"I wouldn't miss it."

"Come round the caravans after, I'll see if I can get Jimmy to say hi. No promises, but I'll give it a go."

Bleachers had been set up behind the stage for guests. Cole located a couple of cans of beer and sat with his bandmates to watch Derringer. Their stage show was self-conscious and theatrical, bare chests and perms and lots of running around the stage. The crowd went for it, especially the hit, "Rock and Roll Hoochie Koo." Derringer was a great singer and a fine guitarist, but Cole had liked him better when he led the McCoys. Linda was guilelessly into the show, Luke was bored, and Valentina was shaking her head. "Even with the dumbed-down set we did, we were better than this."

"I know," Cole said. "But there's ninety thousand people out there who disagree."

"That kind of hurts my feelings."

"Yeah," Cole said. "Mine too."

Derringer kept it under an hour, with encore, and then the long wait began. Side Two of *Machine Head* played, then *Disraeli Gears*.

The backstage area was dead and eventually Bill Graham got up and began telling lies about equipment problems. Cole wandered out into the crowd, unable to keep from making comparisons to Woodstock. This crowd was one-sixth the size, and pent up in a concrete facility in the middle of an urban sprawl. They were younger but less innocent—barely pubescent girls danced with calculated eroticism and shirtless boys shoved each other, long hair flying. The heat and the drugs had caught up with the kids who'd been lined up all night. Cole watched uniformed workers being booed as they carried two of them off on stretchers.

Where do we go from here? he wondered. What is this scene going to look like in another ten years?

An hour or so later he was hanging out with Ginger by the backstage gates when a limo pulled up. A disoriented Jimmy Page, in sunglasses and black silk pajamas with dragons on them, got out and started in the wrong direction. One of the bouncers gently caught him and turned him around as the other three climbed out. They were maybe twenty feet away and Cole was starstruck.

"Better clear off, mate," Ginger said. "They don't like to be distracted before they go on stage."

"All right," Cole said. "I'll see you later."

Despite the bad omens, Cole's excitement kept bubbling up. The biggest band in the world, a band he'd loved since their first album, when nobody else had heard of them, and he would be practically on stage with them. The vibe in the stadium had already changed as the crowd sensed their presence. People were screaming "Led Zeppelin!" and "rock and roll!" and, already, inevitably, "Stairway to Heaven!" as if the band might somehow forget to play it.

The tension kept mounting, the audience feeding on its own hysteria. Scuffles broke out below stage right, where a huge US flag flapped listlessly. Finally Bill Graham came out and thanked everyone for their patience, drowned out by the yelling of the crowd, in turn drowned out by the opening staccato chords of "The Song Remains the Same," played crazy fast, the start-stop rhythm at such high volume that it threatened to disrupt Cole's autonomic nervous system, the drums and bass locked in mechanical precision with the guitar, Page looking unsteady yet managing to play the top, 12-string neck of his double-neck SG in perfect time. Cole glanced at Linda, whose gaze was riveted on Bonham. Her jaw had gone slack.

When it finished, Plant, wearing a baby-blue "Nurses do it better" T-shirt, said, "Good afternoon! So this is what they call daylight!"

"I'll never be that good," Linda said.

"You were fantastic today," Cole said. "You saved our ass."

"I wasn't like that," she said, pointing at Bonham.

"Well, maybe you won't wreck hotels and punch women in the face like he does."

Linda shook her head in disgust. "Don't try to cheer me up, Cole. It just shows how little you understand."

Cole was stung into silence, which the band promptly filled with "Sick Again," a song about underage groupies in LA, and then on through a set of meticulous, virtuosic, pile-driving rock songs, the rhythm section impeccable, Plant in shrieking good voice, and only Page unable to fully deliver the goods, his long solos slightly off, never catching fire. Still Cole wished he could see his fingers for more than the occasional glimpse when he turned his back on the stadium. The only serious lapse came during "Ten Years Gone," when Page lost his way and had to bail out on the lead and hand the song off to Plant.

After that they all sat on stools at the front of the stage, Page with acoustic guitar, Jones with his triple-neck, Bonham with a tambourine. The crowd, so completely in their thrall moments before, was not in a mellow mood. The boos—only a few at first—started as soon as the stools came out. When they yelled for "Stairway" again, Plant cupped his ear as if he couldn't understand them. Cole was shocked. The band was narcissistic, but how much worse was the audience, screaming for instant gratification?

They started with "Battle of Evermore," with Jones singing Sandy Denny's part. By the time the acoustic set had passed the half-hour mark and Page was noodling by himself in the middle of "Bron-Y-Aur Stomp," the crowd was actively heckling. Plant made intermittent and ineffective shushing gestures until finally Bonham came in on bass drum and tambourine and they tied it off. They got off their stools and Plant said, "You want to rock?" The audience exploded. "We're going to rock your arse off."

Which they proceeded to do, building to "Stairway" as a climax, then leaving the stage while the audience whipped themselves into a frenzy again, before they came back for "Whole Lotta Love" and "Rock and Roll," then did "Black Dog" as a second encore.

When it was finally over, Cole was wiped out. Valentina buzzed with energy and Linda was despondent. Luke had left after the acoustic set.

"I really need to get laid," Valentina said, stretching provocatively. "See you guys at the hotel."

"I'm going to go drink," Linda said. "You coming?"

"Later," Cole said.

He tried to make his way toward the trailers they used for dressing rooms, and Zeppelin security blocked his way. He showed his performer's pass and said, "I'm supposed to meet Ginger."

"Nobody goes back there until the band clears the arena."

"Could you please ask Ginger?"

"I don't ask Ginger nothing, mate. Now could you please fuck off before you get hurt?"

He got another beer, drank it in three long swallows, then used the staff restroom. When he checked back, the thugs were gone. Which probably meant the band was gone as well. He made his way to the cluster of trailers parked under the lip of the stadium, inside the security fence. Three were set up for dressing rooms, though as far as Cole knew, nobody had used them. One of them was painted with the Bill Graham Presents logo, and Cole saw Jim Matzorkis, one of Graham's security guys, climbing the steps with a clutch of wooden signs under his arm.

"Hey, Jim," Cole said.

"Hi, Cole. Good show this morning."

"Audience didn't seem to think so."

"Hey, what do they know, right?"

Cole waved and walked on, then thought to ask if Matzorkis

had seen Ginger. At that moment four men and a boy walked up to the trailer and Cole instinctively stepped into the shadow of a concrete column. In the lead was Zeppelin drummer John Bonham, massive, bearded, a look of barely concealed rage on his face. He was followed by Peter Grant, 300 pounds, six foot three, scraggly beard and stringy hair. Beside him was a long-haired kid, maybe 10 years old. Then came the road manager, the one Ginger called Ricardo. He was the smallest of the four, not by much, with big dark sideburns and mustache. Bringing up the rear was a blond hulk, clean shaven and handsome except for the air of thoughtless, arrogant menace that came off him. Cole held himself absolutely still.

"Him!" the boy said. "That's the one." Cole realized they were talking about Matzorkis. This is bad, Cole thought.

"You," Bonham said. "Come out here."

Matzorkis appeared at the top of the steps.

Bonham pointed at the boy. "You know who this is?"

"No. He was stealing the signs from the dressing rooms a few minutes ago. I never saw him before that."

"That's Peter Grant's son, you fucking cunt."

"Did you put your hands on my kid?" Grant asked.

"I took the signs away from him, that's all." Matzorkis was a big guy, but he was badly outnumbered and Cole heard an edge of nervousness in his voice.

"Did you hit him?" Grant said.

"Absolutely not. I just told him he couldn't have the signs."

"He says you hit him," Grant said. "Are you calling my son a liar?"

"This is a misunderstanding," Matzorkis said.

"You don't hit Peter Grant's kid, you cunt," Bonham said, and he lunged up the steps and kicked Matzorkis in the crotch. Matzorkis flew backward into the trailer and the others went up after him.

Cole ran. He saw a couple of Graham's security people and shouted, "Get to the storage trailer, they're killing Jim. Call the cops, call somebody." He ran on to the office trailer at the end of the row.

Graham was on the phone. Cole said, "Bill, you have to come, they're killing Jim Matzorkis."

Graham said, "I'll call you back," and jumped out of his chair. "Who is?"

"Bonham, Peter Grant, some other guys."

"What happened?"

"I don't know, something to do with Grant's kid."

By the time they got to the storage trailer, Matzorkis was gone. Bonham, Grant, Ricardo, and the blond paced back and forth, in a standoff with a handful of Graham's security people. Cole could smell the testosterone in the air.

"Bill," Grant said, "I'm very unhappy with you. One of your people hit my boy."

"Hold on," Graham said. "I know this man. He would not hit a kid."

"My son is not a liar."

One of the security guys took Graham aside and whispered in his ear. Graham nodded and said, "Why don't we all sit down and talk this out?"

Cole, on the fringes, slumped down on the oil-stained concrete and leaned against one of the trailers. He had managed to go his whole life without ever getting in a serious fight, just a few ineffectual body blows between kids that were over before they started. He had never seen cold-blooded, animal violence first-hand, and it made him sick and scared and angry. Ashamed that it had come to this. The Stones, Zeppelin, The Who, destroying everything in their paths, protected by their armies of homicidal maniacs. He understood that Graham had to placate them, that the second show was less than 24 hours away and if the band refused to play, a full-blown riot would result. Still Cole wanted their blood.

The longer Graham talked, the quieter Grant and the others got, until it seemed like it had blown over. Grant said he just wanted to meet with Matzorkis, one-on-one, to "make peace and settle this."

"I have your word?" Graham said. "Your word as a gentleman that that's all you want?"

"Yes."

Graham turned to the guy who'd whispered in his ear and said, "He's at the Winnebago?"

The man nodded. In addition to the trailers inside the gates, Graham had a mobile home in the public parking lot on the south side of the stadium, which was apparently where Matzorkis had holed up.

The entire group walked there together, Grant and Bonham, Ricardo and the blond, Graham and his people, a handful of other Zeppelin security guys. Cole, unable to look away, followed a few steps behind.

The sun was low in the sky and long shadows carved up the asphalt of the deserted parking lot. The Winnebago was parked next to a row of stanchions, thigh-high lengths of metal pipe filled with concrete, meant to keep anyone from driving through the open gate.

At the door of the Winnebago, Graham said, "Let me just talk to him first."

Grant opened both hands, as if to say, "Of course."

Graham went in and closed the door. He was only gone a few seconds. The body language in the Zeppelin camp was neutral. Graham opened the door and motioned Grant in. "After you, Peter."

Grant got on the RV. Graham turned to follow him and in an instant the huge blond man had jumped up behind him. A crash came from deep inside the vehicle and Cole involuntarily sucked in a lungful of air. The blond appeared at the top of the stairs, carrying Graham like a stack of lumber over one shoulder. He set Graham on the tarmac, gave him a gentle shove, and got back on the bus and shut and locked the door.

Cole heard Matzorkis yell for help over the sound of crashing furniture and breaking glass. The entire Winnebago shook with the violence of it. Graham pounded on the locked door, then ran back and forth alongside the trailer shouting, "Jim! Jim! Are you all right?"

One of Graham's people said, "I've got a gun in my car," and took off at a run.

Suddenly Ricardo, a crazed look in his eyes, came running toward the Winnebago with a piece of aluminum pipe. He apparently meant to go after Matzorkis with it, but he couldn't get in the locked door, so he stood guard there, swinging the pipe like a bat.

Matzorkis, miraculously, had broken free, but was now trapped in the trailer by Ricardo. Cole heard him pounding on the door, crying for help. One of Graham's people went for Ricardo, but had to jump back from the path of the metal pipe. "Cocksucker!" he yelled at Ricardo. "Fucking Limey cocksucking son of a bitch!"

Ricardo, clearly out of his mind on coke, lunged for him, and the guy ran out into the parking lot, Ricardo in pursuit.

The door of the bus flew open and Matzorkis stumbled out, Grant and the blond right behind him. Suddenly, too late, Cole realized he was in the line of fire. He turned to run as somebody he never saw hit him in the back, yelling, "Out of my way, ya cunt," and Cole went into the stanchion, the edge of it hitting his collarbone. Agony flooded the left side of his body. He fell on his right side, hitting his head, and curled into a ball, grinding his teeth against the pain.

He heard yelling all around him. He felt like he was inside a giant red membrane, darkness below. He wanted to go into the darkness and the pain wouldn't let him. He lay there on the hot pavement as the pain flashed endlessly up and down his shoulder and left arm.

Finally an American voice said, "Hey, this guy's hurt too."

He heard Graham say, "Cole, what the fuck?"

"Knocked me down," Cole said. "Broke something..."

"Hey!" Graham yelled. "This guy needs to go in the ambulance too!"

"Fuck," Cole said.

"It's okay," Graham said. "There's an ambulance. We'll get you taken care of."

It wasn't that. It was that he was 16 again, Elton half-carrying him off the oil rig, being loaded into the ambulance next to Jerry's dead body.

"Over here!" Graham yelled.

Somebody leaned over him. Did he have red hair and freckles, or was Cole having a flashback?

"Where are you hurt?"

"Collarbone," Cole said. "Left side."

"I'm going to turn you on your back, real slow."

Unfortunately, Cole failed to black out from the pain.

"Yeah, clavicle fracture. You're going to need an X-ray, but it looks like it's not displaced. That's the good news."

"Hurts," Cole gasped.

"That's the bad news. These things hurt like a sonofabitch. We got stuff for that, though."

The power of suggestion, Cole thought. He could practically feel the Demerol rush through him. Then the needle appeared, and went into his right arm, and the bright red of the pain turned pale pink.

Oh god, Cole thought, how I have missed this.

They loaded Cole on a stretcher and put him in the ambulance. Matzorkis was already there, sitting up. His face was swollen and bloody, his eyes puffed shut. "Cole?" he said.

"Yeah. I got in somebody's way. Knocked me into one of those barrier things."

"Oh, man."

"I can't believe you made it out of that trailer alive."

"That big blond guy, they had me on the floor under the table, and he was gouging my eyes out. I mean, he was going to take them out. I had some kind of adrenalin rush, man, like I never had before. What kind of person would do something like that to another human being?"

One of the medics got in back with them. "You guys should try and rest."

"Fuck," Cole said. "How am I going to play guitar tomorrow?"

The medic laughed. "You can forget about playing guitar for a while."

COLE LAY ON his back, the head of the bed cranked high. His left arm was in a sling and the sling was bound to his chest to completely immobilize it. His head was turned so he could see out the window. Darkness had settled on Highland Hospital, and Demerol had made the slow sunset compelling and emotional. Though the last light had been gone from the sky for a long time, he had no urge to do anything other than watch the night sky.

"Cole?"

Bill Graham had come in.

"I just saw Jim," Graham said. "He's going to be okay, eventually. I'm taking him home with me tonight, just to make sure those bastards don't try to come after him again."

"That's good," Cole said.

"What the fuck happened to you?"

"One of them, one of the Brits, shoved me out of his way. I didn't even see who it was."

"They're going to pay. I'm flying twenty-five of my guys to their next stop, which is New Orleans, and there is going to be payback."

"Okay," Cole said. The problem, he thought, lay with a universe in which the events of the day could have occurred at all. More beatings wouldn't solve that. Though he did want to see the four of them, Grant, Bonham, Ricardo, and the blond, slowly tortured to death. Followed by Page, because if there was a god who had watched from on high and allowed it to happen, it was Jimmy Page.

"Their lawyer is forcing me to sign a paper indemnifying the band against any legal action," Graham said. "Because otherwise they might be too upset to play tomorrow."

"You're not going to sign it?"

"My guy says it's economic duress, anything I sign under those circumstances is worthless."

A rising, helpless anger fought the Demerol for control of his emotions. "Speaking of playing tomorrow," Cole said, "I'm not. You may have figured that out."

"They told me you're sidelined for at least two months. I can't believe I gave you another chance and you let me down again."

Cole saw that it was meant to be a joke. "What are you going to do?"

"I was just going to cancel the opening slot, but there's an

English heavy metal act in town, Judas Priest, and they said they can cover for you."

"And nobody gives a shit about the opening act anyway, right?"

"Not at a Led Zeppelin show."

"I appreciate your coming around to cheer me up, Bill."

"Get some rest. We'll talk later."

"Bill? Take care of Jim."

"Don't worry."

A while later Linda and Luke came in. Linda's eye makeup was badly smeared and she looked like she'd been halfway to drunk and then forced to sober up. She had a couple of roses that she must have bought on the street outside the hospital. She stuck them in his plastic water pitcher.

"What happened?" she said, and Cole told her the whole story.

"Bonham?" Linda said. "No way. It can't be."

Cole closed his eyes.

"Bill Graham came to the hotel," Linda said. "He told us about you, said he was putting another band on tomorrow. Val tried to talk him out of it, said we could do the show without you, but he wasn't buying."

Cole opened his eyes. "Where *is* Val?"

"She, uh, she doesn't like hospitals," Linda said.

"She's pissed," Luke said. Luke had once told Cole that he didn't talk much because he had loud music playing in his head all the time. It had explained a lot.

"Luke, shut up," Linda said.

"She thinks you should have come back to the hotel with us and this would never have happened."

"She's going to be more pissed," Cole said, "when she finds out I can't play for two months."

"Fuck," Linda said. "Really?"

The conversation stumbled on for another couple of minutes before Cole told them he needed to rest. Linda failed to conceal her relief. Once they were gone, he rang the nurses' station. "I'm in some pain here," he said. "Can I get another shot?"

★

COLE WAS DISCHARGED Monday afternoon, but not before he had the pleasure of seeing Grant, Bonham, Ricardo, and the blond, who was apparently a gangster and sometime movie actor named John Bindon, on the local noon news as they were marched in handcuffs out of the Hilton and placed under arrest. Released immediately on bond, of course. Nonetheless the best moment Cole had had in a while.

Regina at Graham's office had rescheduled his flight for Tuesday morning and gotten him a room at the Hilton. Eating in the deserted hotel restaurant, he heard a waiter say that Zeppelin had done $10,000 worth of damage to the hotel, the drummer alone having thrown five TV sets and a desk out of the shattered windows, narrowly missing spectators below.

The hospital had sent him home with Percodan and Cole managed to restrain himself from washing them down with alcohol. He got in to Austin late Tuesday night and on Wednesday afternoon Valentina dropped by.

"Did you hear about Plant?" she said by way of greeting. Cole shook his head. "His son died, over in England. He got a phone call in New Orleans from his wife last night. Some kind of viral infection. Bam, just like that. They cancelled the rest of the US tour and they're all flying back to England. People are saying it's karma for what happened in Oakland."

"Karma," Cole said. Words failed him. Nobody deserved to lose their son.

Valentina declined to sit down. "I wanted to tell you face to face that we're going to use a substitute guitar player until you can come back. With the album just out, the Oakland publicity, we need to do what we can to keep some momentum going. Whenever you're ready, you can have your job back and she'll step down."

"She?" Cole said. "You already know who it's going to be?"

"Rest up, get well soon."

"At least Linda brought me flowers," Cole said.

"We'll talk," Valentina said, and then she was gone.

*

THE ALARM WENT OFF at 7:30, Alex's usual Monday wake-up time. He'd scheduled the day in detail, with time allotted for a breakfast that he had no appetite for and a futile five minutes of sitting on the toilet. The idea was not to give yourself a lot of leeway to change your mind, or even to think at all.

Magdalena arrived before 9, as usual, and Alex confirmed that she was still willing to spend the night. Callie was in Marfa again, and Alex had written out a message in English for Magdalena to read to her if she happened to call.

He wore a new suit and an open collared white dress shirt. He drove to Love Field and left his car in long-term parking, then caught a shuttle to Avis, where he picked up a late model Buick Regal, dark gold, with a Landau roof, one step down from a Cadillac. It had an 8-track player, and one of Alex's two briefcases was full of tapes—Dylan, the Dead, the Stones, the Doors, Stevie Wonder, Lou Reed, the Allman Brothers, and of course Led Zeppelin. The other held $5000 in twenties, the fruit of five separate trips to his bank over the space of two months, using the excuse that he was paying cash for work on his house.

I-40 ran uninterrupted to the border now—you just pointed the car south and tried not to think too much. You didn't want to think, for instance, about driving west instead and maybe catching Callie in flagrante. Or stopping in Austin to see Cole, who would be back from San Francisco by now, full of stories of the aforementioned Zeppelin and their major flagrante.

South of Waxahachie he put the hammer down, paying no more attention to the 55 m.p.h. signs than anyone else. Eventually he fell in behind an 18-wheeler that passed him doing 80, assuming the driver had a radar detector and a CB. Sure enough, he slowed all the way to the double-nickels for the notorious speed trap in Selma, north of San Antonio, and Alex stopped for gas when the truck did, buying jerky and doughnuts and candy bars for lunch.

Moving at that kind of speed was an end in itself, celebrated in a thousand highway songs—a remedy for the blues, a surefire way to leave his worries behind. He sang along to the tapes and let the music transport him to San Francisco, to Mexico as a kid, to the Castle, to playing with The Chevelles.

1977

At the Mexican border, I-35 became Carretera Federal 85, the old Pan-American Highway that passed through Monterrey, home of the Cerveceria Cuautémoc, on its way to Mexico City. When Alex was little, before Jimmy was born, the family had driven from Dallas to Monterrey a couple of times a year, at Christmas and at the start of summer vacation, so that his father could maintain his personal contacts at the brewery. The trips meant new comics to read in the car, getting to speak Spanish, which had seemed transgressive at the time, staying in a hotel with pink tile floors and ceiling fans, and eating all kinds of ice cream and sweets on the street.

Alex hit the International Bridge by four in the afternoon. Most of the traffic was headed north, but he still ended up in a long line of cars in the broiling August sun. The guards on the US side waved him through. On the Mexican side, he put a five-dollar bill in his passport and smiled at the soldier in the green uniform.

"What is the purpose of your visit?" the soldier asked in English.

«To see my mother,» Alex answered in Spanish.

«And how long will you be staying?»

«Just tonight.»

The guard neatly extracted the bill. He handed back the passport and saluted. «Enjoy your stay.»

Álvaro's instructions took him past the Mercado Maclovio Herrera, a two-story tourist trap full of piñatas and embroidered dresses, where he and Susan had always made his parents stop. He remembered the rich, warm smell of the cowhide belts and holsters, the gleam of the endless varnished straw cowboy hats, the sweet odor of roasting meat and corn, the rainbow-colored tissue paper that wrapped the caramelized goat's milk candy in its wooden containers the size of a cat food can that you would spoon out with broken pieces of the lid.

A year into deflation, business had still not recovered. Tourists swarmed around the building, taking advantage of the hunger for US dollars. The faces of the locals were pinched and tired, the streets unswept, the windows of neighboring buildings boarded up.

Past the Mercado, Alex zigzagged through deteriorating neighborhoods until he arrived at a different sort of trap, a cantina with

717

bat-wing doors and a scratchy waltz-time corrida wailing out into the street from the jukebox. A burro was tied to a hitching post outside, and an old man with a Polaroid camera stood next to a sign offering photos for a dollar.

Alex found a place to park and locked the car. The loss/damage waiver that had doubled the rental price was looking more and more like a smart investment. He put the briefcase with the tapes in the trunk and carried the other one in his left hand. For the first time he considered the possibility of a double-cross. He and Álvaro hadn't been close since they were kids. Would Alex's life be worth five thousand dollars cash? They wouldn't even have to kill him. If they took the money and car at gunpoint, what could he do?

Standing in a dark suit under the murderous sun was not the place to have second thoughts. He'd come too far, and if he couldn't trust Álvaro, he wasn't sure he cared what happened to him.

Inside the bar Alex found a thousand square feet of peeling green linoleum, a row of unused and splintery wooden booths, and a long, mostly deserted bar. A tourist in Bermuda shorts took photos of the quaint inhabitants with a camera that he would be lucky to get out of the neighborhood with, while his blonde wife and daughter edged toward the door, saying, "C'mon, Phil, we need to get back to the car."

At the bar, Alex said, "I'm looking for Álvaro. He's expecting me."

The bartender never made eye contact. "Upstairs," he said.

As Alex's eyes adjusted, he made out the staircase in the corner farthest from the bat wings and next to the bleating juke box. As he climbed, the blonde woman said, "Phil, *please.*"

The stairs led to a long, dim hallway. Alex felt his shirt wilt and dampen in the heat. The doors on his left were numbered, and on the right was an arch with a bead curtain. Alex pushed through it into a lounge. At a table along one wall, a woman in a tank top and flannel shorts and nothing else bent over a mirror and snorted coke through a short piece of red-and-white-striped plastic straw. In one of the mismatched armchairs, a guy with a long, black pony tail, ragged facial hair, and missing teeth watched with hooded eyes while a woman in hot pants and a tube top stroked his cock through his jeans. On the other side of the room, a heavyset man with a scar from eye to ear, wearing a blue Policía Federal shirt over blue jeans, smiled and talked intently to a woman in a filmy nightgown who was reading *El Libro Sentimental*, a digest-sized romance comic. Three barely teenaged boys in dirty white T-shirts sat on the floor in the corner, sorting pills on a sheet of newspaper and putting them into plastic sandwich bags. Old fashioned paper shades blocked the windows. The room smelled of sour perfume, cigarette and marijuana smoke, sweat, and, faintly, of ether.

Álvaro sat on a couch next to another man, both of them in jeans and T-shirts, both holding acoustic guitars, Álvaro trying to teach the other man to play "Malagueña." When Alex walked in, Álvaro's face lit up. «Fuck you, Ramón, here's a guy who knows how to play the guitar.» He tossed the guitar on the couch and jumped up to crush Alex in an abrazo.

«Órale, Chuy,» Álvaro said to one of the boys. «Take the señor's car to the garage.» To Alex he said, «Give him your keys.»

Alex tried not to show his reluctance. «It's the gold Buick across the street.»

Álvaro laughed. «Don't worry, he's been driving since before he could see over the wheel.»

Alex held out the keys and the kid grabbed them and sprinted downstairs, as if Alex might change his mind. And maybe he would have, if he'd had a minute to think, but he'd come this far on autopilot and now it was too late.

«Ramón,» Álvaro said, «give mi primo Alejo the guitar and watch how it's done.»

Ramón was maybe 20, with bloodshot eyes from yerba and bad teeth from growing up poor and a catlike grace that told Alex he could be dangerous in a fight. He handed over the guitar with deference, and the sight of it unlocked something in Alex's heart. Álvaro projected the same respect, a respect he'd never shown before, and it was not because of who his father was, it was for the courage Alex had shown in coming there, and for the power that the money in the briefcase, Alex's own money, brought with it.

«I haven't played in years,» Alex said, though since Callie had been going to Marfa, he had pulled out his acoustic and fooled with it a few times. "Malagueña" came back as soon as he started to play. It had always been one of Cole's favorites, a natural for getting girls' knees in the air. Alex took the lead vocal and Álvaro fell naturally into the high harmony. The girl who'd been sniffing coke sat back in her chair and tears ran down her cheeks. Ramón, sitting with his head slightly bowed, looked like he might cry too.

After that they played "Guantanamera" and everybody sang along, then Álvaro passed around a fat joint. Alex knew he shouldn't have any, but he was afraid to refuse. Besides, he thought, it might help his jangling nerves.

When it was gone, Álvaro said, «You want to get something to eat?»

«There's, uh, the matter of the briefcase.»

«Ah yes, el maletín. Come with me.»

At the end of the hall was a small office with a fluorescent desk lamp and an adding machine and a three-foot high freestanding safe. Álvaro closed the office door, ran the combination, and opened it up while Alex popped the latches on his briefcase. He'd put a change of shirt, underwear, and socks and a shaving kit on top of the stacks of bills, and now he wondered if they made him look like a rube. He passed the bundles of twenties to Álvaro, who stacked them neatly in the safe.

«You don't want to count it?» Alex asked.

«There's an accountant guy who'll count it on Monday. I trust you. I'm too hungry to spend an hour counting all this shit.»

After his saying that, Alex was too embarrassed to ask for a receipt. It was ridiculous how little he knew about what he was doing, what the standards of behavior were. So far it had been as fast and loose as the parties the teenaged Álvaro used to hold when his parents were out of town.

When all the money was in the safe, Álvaro locked it and said, «Let's eat!»

They climbed into Álvaro's new black GMC, Jimmy, Alex and Ramón and Álvaro in the front, the guy in the pony tail and another of the kids sitting in the covered bed by the tailgate. Álvaro drove with careless speed while Alex watched his own tight-lipped smile in the rear-view mirror. Eventually Álvaro pulled up to the curb in a no-parking zone and left the kid to watch the truck.

The restaurant was large and comparatively expensive, by Nuevo Laredo standards. Álvaro ignored the long line of mostly gringos outside the door. A maître d' in a tux took them to a table on a balcony overlooking a stage where a ten-piece mariachi band, in glittering red and gold trajes de charro, played "Allá en el Rancho Grande." Except for Alex, their group was the worst-dressed in the room. Álvaro was completely unselfconscious. The maître d' treated them with a mixture of affection and respect, and Alex understood that once again Álvaro was making a statement about his status.

At Álvaro's urging Alex had the chile relleno, and it was in fact good enough to make him forget his fear for a few minutes— the huge poblano pepper just hot enough to tingle his tongue, the cheese rich and the salsa tart. The mariachis left the stage, playing "Guadalajara," and wound their way through the tables and up the stairs, ending up, not surprisingly, at Álvaro's table. Money subtly changed hands and Álvaro asked what Alex wanted to hear.

«Do you know 'Quién será'?» Alex asked the lead violinist.

«¿Como no?» He smiled as if no one could have chosen a more perfect song. It was an old Pablo Beltrán cha-cha-cha that Dean Martin had covered as "Sway." The Spanish lyrics were darker, full of longing. Who will be the one who loves me, I want the passion and heat that will make me feel again.

Once the song began, he saw that it was in danger of knocking him on his ass. Because he was in Mexico, and drinking, and in the company of men, however, sorrow was permitted. Everyone cheered when he wiped at his eyes.

It was 10:00 by the time they got back to the room above the bar. Alex had allowed himself two beers with dinner, but he was instantly sober when he saw the boy Chuy, jingling Alex's keys.

«You should stay the night,» Álvaro said. «We can play some poker. Remember when you taught me to play? And we can sing and smoke some yerba. Then one of these ladies can help you to bed.»

When Alex looked in the women's eyes, he saw only a stoic determination to please. «Better to get it over with,» he said. «Then I won't have to spend the night being nervous.»

«As you wish,» Álvaro said. «But I swear to you there is nothing to be afraid of.»

«We'll see,» Alex said. He held out his hand to Chuy and the boy tossed the keys in a high arc. Alex snatched them out of the air and thought, all I have to do is be the man they believe me to be.

In the street, he unlocked the trunk to trade the briefcase that had held the money for the one with his tapes. It was okay to open the trunk at the border, Álvaro had said. Everything was well hidden, and Alex was better off not knowing where it was. So he was somewhat puzzled to see a couple of woven plastic shopping bags. He couldn't make himself look inside.

He slammed the trunk and got in and started the car. His mouth was dry. He'd pocketed a couple of peppermints at the restaurant, and he put one in his mouth and pulled away from the curb. He rolled down the power windows and headed for the bridge.

In line at the river, the air no longer felt cool. He started to sweat. He rolled the windows up and turned the air conditioner on full blast. His hands went cold and the stream of air dried his face while the sweat continued to flow under his arms, soaking his shirt. You're going to give yourself away, he thought.

He lowered the A/C as his turn finally came. He rolled his window down and held out his passport with another five enclosed. The guard was the same one from that afternoon. «How was your mother, señor?»

Alex tried to summon the melancholy that "Quién será" had brought him. «Sadly, she is becoming someone else. Someone who barely knows me.»

The guard nodded. «It happens. The years can be very hard on us.»

«Also hard on those of us who love her.»

The guard expertly palmed the bill without losing eye contact and handed back the passport. «Claro. Go with God, señor.»

«You, too.»

His pangs of guilt at deceiving the man were easily outweighed by the thrill of it. His confidence surged. The performance he'd just given was no different than playing bass, something he already knew how to do.

The guard on the US side was gringo, with aggressively short hair and some kind of quick draw holster that made the handle of his revolver stick out an angle from his leg. "Evening," Alex said, holding out the passport, this time without the bribe. "How you doing?"

"Turn the car off and step outside, please, sir."

His high was instantly gone. This was what you asked for, he thought. You wanted to be scared, and now you've got it. And it had worked. He wanted nothing more in the world than to be able to go into his father's office and sit at a desk and not be afraid. "Sure," he said.

The man read out the address on the passport. "Is that still correct?"

"That's right." Don't ask if there's a problem, he thought. There is no problem.

A drop of sweat rolled down the inside of his left arm and stopped at his watchband.

"Open the trunk, please."

He had to reach into the car for his keys and he willed his hand not to shake. What if he asks what's in the shopping bags? he thought. I should have looked. He walked around to the trunk and unlocked it and stepped aside.

"Are your total purchases fifty dollars or less?"

"Yes."

"Any meat or agricultural products?"

"No, nothing like that."

The man nodded. "You can close the trunk. You looking to drive all the way to Dallas tonight?"

"No way," Alex said. "I'll catch a motel in San Antone. Just wanted to get back in the USA tonight."

"Sounds like a plan. You have a good trip."

Alex put the passport in the breast pocket of his suit coat. "Thanks." He got in the car and drove through as the wooden barricade lifted. He rolled his window up, put the A/C on high again, and waited until he was well into Laredo before whooping and hollering and bouncing in his seat.

What a rush. He was ready for one of Álvaro's women now, maybe all three of them. He wanted to get drunk and stoned and run naked through the streets of North Dallas.

Instead he kept the music low enough that he could hear a siren over it and held his speed to 60. He got home around four and looked in briefly on Gwyn. Magdalena, sleeping on the day bed in Gwyn's room, woke and said, «¿Quién es? ¿Qué hora son?»

«It's me, Alex. It's very late. Go back to sleep.»

The next afternoon Alex drove the Buick to a garage in South Oak Cliff that looked like it hadn't been repainted since the 1930s. Per instructions, he left an empty briefcase on the front seat. He watched a baseball game in the waiting room on an old black-and-white TV where the picture rolled every few seconds. After half an hour a middle-aged Chicano brought him his keys and said, in English, "I think you'll find everything is in order."

He drove a mile or so before he pulled over and looked in the briefcase. It held ten stacks of bills in various denominations, each secured with a rubber band, each adding up to $1000. Five thousand dollars profit for a long day's work.

Holy shit, Alex thought. Holy fucking shit.

SUNDAY AFTERNOON was the apex of Madelyn's week. She parked her battered Pinto wagon under a live oak at the Preston Royal branch library and helped Ava out of her booster seat. The doors had just opened at one. She tucked a stack of books under one arm and led Ava inside with the other hand.

Madelyn was not a believer in biological determinism, yet the way Ava loved books was uncanny. From the first she had been gentle, almost reverent in the way she handled them; now, at age three and a half, she was sounding out the words. When Madelyn had tried reading her the *Odyssey*, Ava had made it clear that she would choose her own books and, preferably, read them for herself.

She waved to Charlie, the librarian who had a crush on her. He was in his thirties, a bit sharp-featured and overeager. She wished she could reciprocate; he was bright and had a high success rate at predicting her taste.

She fed her books into the return slot and left Ava in the children's section. Ava went immediately to the letter O, where she'd left off the week before, and sat cross-legged on the carpet with the first five candidates for her selection process, which often involved smelling the pages as well as reading them.

Madelyn took the current *Times Book Review* to a table where she could keep one eye on Ava. She read the lead review for Toni Morrison's *Song of Solomon*, then dutifully noted the title in a pocket spiral notebook.

She'd cut back to 28-hour weeks at the jeans store after Ava was born, and her life was full of opportunities to read: watching Ava at the playground, waiting in the pediatrician's office, putting herself back to sleep after Ava woke her in the night. Madelyn paid for her own food and helped her mother with the cooking and cleaning; the rest of her pay went into her PhD fund. Four years on, the balance remained depressingly small. Books helped her feel connected to the destiny she refused to forsake, feel that this was a hiatus and nothing more.

Julia, amazingly, was in New York, getting small parts in off-Broadway shows, soaps, and local ads. At early morning low emotional tide, Madelyn wondered how it had come to pass that Julia was in New York and she was not; that was usually her cue to escape into another book.

She finished the *Book Review* with her usual twinge of regret, then browsed the shelves until 3:00 and the end of Ava's remarkable attention span. Madelyn sat down and they showed each other what they'd found, with Ava seeming particularly interested in a horror novel called *The Shining* that everyone was talking about.

At the checkout desk, Charlie said, "How'd you like *The Honourable Schoolboy*?"

The truth was that it was hard for her not to think of Cole when she read it. Cole had thought LeCarré "ponderous," but even so, reading any kind of espionage fiction left her feeling that she had surreptitiously crossed Cole's borders by dead of night.

"Good," she said to Charlie, with whom she did not share such intimacies. "Not as good as the last one. What do you have for me today?"

"Two things," he said.

The first was a travel book called *In Patagonia* whose characters he promised she would love. She took it dubiously and said, "What's number two?"

"Wait here."

He lifted the counter and let himself out, then walked over to a table where a man sat reading a massive volume. Charlie said something in the man's ear, and the man looked up and into Madelyn's eyes.

Her first reaction was purely hormonal. He was ridiculously good-looking: dark, slightly shaggy hair; dark, sparkly eyes; strong nose and full lips. He wore jeans, a pink polo shirt, a sport coat, and tennis shoes. He gave her the sort of easy, confident smile that she was a sucker for and walked over with his hand out. "Paul Kirk," he said. "Thanks to Charlie, I feel like I already know you." The voice was deep, soft, and melodious.

"I'm Madelyn—no, I don't need to say that, do I? Since Charlie has already briefed you?" She was unable to find the verbal facility she'd had only moments before. Briefed? Dear God, where had that come from? She struggled to remember what Charlie had told her about this person. He was a high-school friend, recently moved back to Dallas, she would like him.

Paul had squatted down to look Ava in the eye. "And you're Ava, right? Who's already reading? That's pretty amazing."

Ava responded by hiding behind Madelyn's legs. "Say hello, Ava," Madelyn prompted.

"Hello, Ava," she said. It was one of their oldest jokes and rarely failed to make her laugh. Today was one of the exceptions.

Paul, however, laughed heartily. He straightened up and said, "I hear you read *State of Revolution*."

This was Robert Bolt's new play, which had opened to mixed reviews in the UK. "Yes, Charlie managed to get me a copy of the script, though I don't know how."

"It was through Paul, actually," Charlie said.

Paul shrugged. "I know some people in London. What did you think?"

"Not to be unappreciative, but... it's not quite *A Man for All Seasons*, is it? It was interesting, but it didn't speak to me emotionally."

"I feel exactly the same way. The best hope for sympathy was Trotsky, who Bolt mostly left out of it."

"Some might even say that Trotsky was the best hope for the revolution," Madelyn said, having heard those sentiments from her father throughout her childhood.

"Exactly!" Paul said, genuinely excited. "And Stalin knew it, too."

"Easy, you two," Charlie said. "This *is* a library. Big ideas are only permitted at a whisper."

"I know this is presumptuous," Paul said, "but if memory serves, there's a fountain at the drug store across the street. If the two of you happened to like ice cream and you would let me treat, I believe they allow conversation there."

For the briefest of moments, Madelyn wondered how much of the preceding dialog had been prearranged. She was not sure she cared. "Ice cream," she said, "sounds lovely."

Madelyn had chocolate chip and Paul and Ava went for the Dutch chocolate. He seemed too good to be true; he kept Ava in the conversation, actively listened and responded to what Madelyn said, and showed minimal interest in talking about himself. After an hour she had only a few bare outlines of his story: He'd graduated from Berkeley in 1968, leaving the Bay area for the Peace Corps around the same time that she and Cole arrived in San Francisco. Something mysterious had happened by the time he got back to the States, and by 1973 he was getting an MBA at the University of Chicago. He'd used that to get a job with GE Capital, who had just transferred him to Dallas.

"I don't understand," Madelyn said. "How did you go from Berkeley radical to running dog capitalist?"

"It's not the about-face it looks like," he said. "It's way too complicated for a first date, and I don't want Ava to fall asleep and end up with her face in her ice cream dish. Mostly it's about using my energies to make substantive changes rather than wasting them trying to swim upstream against a flood tide."

"I didn't realize this was a date," Madelyn said.

"Ha! Just as I intended. It's too late to back out now, the deed is done."

Ava was quite convulsed by Paul's adenoidal delivery, and as for Madelyn, she had to admit she was smitten.

He was gentleman enough to not try to kiss her after walking her back to the library, though he did hold their handshake a trifle long. And he did talk her into giving up a page from her spiral notebook and writing her phone number on it. He drove off in an orange Karmann Ghia, halfway between a Beetle and sports car, and she stared after him, unable to look away.

FOR THE FIRST three weeks, Cole didn't move his left arm at all. The only time he took it out of the sling was when he bathed—showers were too risky—and then he let the forearm rest against his chest. When the doctor finally let him do a few simple exercises, like raising and lowering his shoulder, or squeezing a tennis ball, the arm felt like it had no strength at all.

All the one-handed techniques he'd learned when he was 16, from opening cans to driving a car to washing dishes, he had to learn with the opposite hand. Boots and lace-up shoes were out of the question. He wore T-shirts over the sling rather than try to thread his left arm through the sleeve, wore sweat pants with elastic waistbands rather than wrestle with jeans and belts.

He had the occasional phone call with Alex, and he kept his monthly phone date with his mother, though he didn't tell her about the fracture. Otherwise he saw no one he knew. He read and watched TV and listened to records, sleeping as much as 12 restless hours a day. Mostly he thought about Demerol.

Alex, it turned out, had seen Madelyn. And he'd seen Cole's daughter. Once he got Alex to confess that he was sometimes babysitting for her, Cole went silent, battered in succession by anger, betrayal, sadness, and guilt. Finally Cole said, "Tell me about her."

"She's got blonde hair and green eyes. She's smart and healthy and pretty happy."

"*Pretty* happy?"

"Madelyn is wary of me, because of you. And you can see that Ava's picked that up from her."

"Ava? That's her name?"

Alex hesitated. "Yes."

"I want to see her."

"No way. Madelyn's going to be pissed if she finds out I let this much slip."

"Goddammit, Alex, she's my daughter."

"Will you use your fucking brain for once? Right now you've got a situation where somebody who is on your side is getting to see her and maybe put in a good word for you once in a while. If you fuck that up, you'll have nothing at all, not even second-hand reports, and you won't see her until she's eighteen. If then."

He'd been thinking lately that he was doing well enough that he could send Madelyn some money. His collarbone had shelved that, but maybe, once he was back with the band...

"Listen," Alex said, "I know how you feel. But I gave Madelyn my word and I'm not breaking it."

"Yeah," Cole said. "Okay."

After the first Percocet prescription, which Cole had sailed through in three days, the doctor had cut him off. To prove he still had discipline, Cole wouldn't let himself have his first beer until noon. Once he started, though, he drank all day, and switched to Jack Daniel's at night.

Throughout September he wore the sling less and less, and by the end of the month he took it off for good. The problem now was the atrophy of his muscles. The first time he tried to play guitar he could barely form a chord. He wondered if he had it in him to learn to play for the third time.

Apparently he did. What else was there to do? By the second week in October he had his calluses back and was playing most of the day.

Valentina hadn't called to check on him. The band, now known as Valentina and Los Cuervos, showed up regularly on KLBJ in ads for gigs at Aqua Fest, at the Armadillo, at a new club on Sixth Street called Steamboat. Cole couldn't help but note that the background music for the ads featured him on guitar.

It was past time for him to take his job back. He didn't understand why it was so hard for him to pick up the phone. She'd said, "whenever you're ready." Day after day, by the time he'd worked up the courage, he was too drunk to make the call.

His life had devolved to the point of making deals with himself, so in the end he made another. No booze tomorrow until you get it over with.

He woke up at ten. At ten-thirty he dragged himself out of bed and got dressed. He had two bowls of Sugar Frosted Flakes and a big glass of orange juice and a cup of coffee. Then he sat on the couch and stared at the phone, where it sat in easy reach.

He started to sweat.

This is ridiculous, he thought. He picked up the handset and dialed Valentina's number. As it rang, he thought, maybe they're on the road. Maybe—

"Hello?"

"It's Cole. I'm ready."

"That means you can drive?"

"I'm all healed up. I'm a hundred percent."

"Come on over and let's talk."

"Should I bring my guitar?"

"Just talk."

He wondered if he should have a beer first. The arbiter of deals in his head said no, that way lay a second beer and a third and a failure to show.

Valentina answered the door and pointed him toward the living room. Linda was there, avoiding eye contact. Valentina didn't sit down, so neither did Cole.

"I felt like I should say this in person," Valentina said. "There's no point in dragging it out. It was decided that we should keep Gilda on guitar and let you go."

Though he had halfway expected it, Cole felt gut-punched. "Nice use of passive voice," he said. "It's almost like it wasn't your decision at all."

"She stuck up for you at Warners," Linda said. "She said you had the original vision for the band, that we needed your vocals. But Ted said he liked the new direction and we should go with it."

"New direction?"

Valentina looked embarrassed by Linda's testimonial. "We're, uh, transitioning away from the Mexican stuff, going for a heavier sound."

"Like Led Zeppelin."

"That's right. We're dropping the Cuervos crap, it's going to be just 'Valentina.' Ted thinks the time has come for an all-girl band that writes their own stuff and plays their own instruments."

"Ted?"

"Our new producer."

"Where does that leave Luke?"

"He quit when we... when the decision was made to let you go."

"He said," Linda broke in, "he wasn't interested anymore if you weren't going to be in the band."

Cole's eyes stung. "Well." He couldn't think of anything else to say.

"One more thing," Valentina said. "I made Warner's come up with some bread. Like, severance pay. It's only a thousand bucks, but it's something." She held out an envelope.

In truth, he needed the money. The civil suit against Zeppelin was dragging on and on, with lawyers eating up any potential settlement money in endless maneuvering. Cole had medical bills and, now, no job.

Yet he could not bring himself to walk over to Valentina and take the money out of her hand. He saw in her face that she understood. He walked out of the house and got in his car.

He gripped the wheel and nearly went back in the house to ask for the money. You fucking idiot, he thought. What are you going to do now?

The answer to that, at least, was simple. He was going to go home and have a beer, and then another.

★

THE PHONE WAS RINGING as he unlocked his apartment door.

"Cole? Bill Graham."

"Bill. How are you?"

"At the moment I am pissed off. The Zeppelin guys pleaded no contest and walked away with suspended sentences. Fucking Oakland, man. Any other city in the US, what they did to Jim would be felony assault. In Oakland it's a fucking misdemeanor. Like throwing a gum wrapper on the sidewalk."

Cole made a noncommittal noise.

"It sucks, but there's nothing we can do about it," Graham said. "There's still the lawsuit, right?"

"Right."

"Hey, I saw in *Billboard* that Ted Templeman is going to produce you guys. That could be very big for you."

So that, Cole thought, was the Ted they'd been talking about. He'd made a fortune for the Doobie Brothers and would doubtless serve Valentina well. Cole didn't have the heart to tell Graham that he was no longer in the band. "We can only hope," he said.

"All right," Graham said. "You hang in there." And then he was gone.

COLE TURNED OUT to be correct in his guess that Alex's brother Jimmy would know a guy who knew a guy. After the buy, he drove to Charlene's shoddy apartment in South Austin without calling first, unsure what he was likely to find and not caring.

She answered the door after his second knock. She'd lost some weight, and the spark was gone from her eyes. She looked Cole up and down and said, "Yeah? What do *you* want?"

Cole showed her the translucent envelope of white powder he'd just scored. "I was thinking you might show me how to use this. You alone?"

She nodded. "Is that what I think it is?"

"It is."

Charlene was a movie fan, and not above the occasional touch of drama herself. She pulled the door wide open and said, "Enter freely and of your own free will."

*

Madelyn's consciousness had just started to float away, like a balloon from the hand of a careless child. She was vaguely aware of the clean smell of Paul's skin where her head rested on his chest, and then she wasn't, and then his voice pulled her back. "Let's get married," he said.

"Can't," Madelyn said. "Sleeping."

"Did you hear what I said?"

She'd heard, but hadn't processed it. The surprise made her eyes pop open. She got up on one forearm to look at him. The only light came from a lamp with a bandana draped over the shade. "You've known me three months. I think we should wait and discuss this when you're not experiencing post-coital hormone distortions."

"When it's for real, it happens fast. I knew I wanted to marry you the first time I met you."

"Let's stipulate, for the moment, that you really do know me as well as you think you do. I still haven't got you figured out."

"That's because," he said, "you're still trying to pigeon-hole me. Pinko radical or capitalist tool."

"I want to know what turned you from one to the other."

"I'm the same person I was when I occupied Sproul Hall."

"Only with an MBA and working for General Electric."

"Exactly. And, if things work out, for the IMF."

"Would the Paul Kirk of 1965 have taken a job with the IMF?"

"If he knew what I know now. You don't give up, do you?"

"Not as a rule, no. I think something happened to you in Africa, which you're keeping me in the dark about."

"I talk about it."

"C'mon, Paul. Get real."

"If I tell you about my life-changing Peace Corps experience, then will you marry me?"

"I damn sure won't marry you if you don't."

He changed position so he was looking her in the eye. "Nothing happened to me personally. But I saw things... They sent me to Nigeria, okay? In 1968."

"Sorry, those years are a little blurry for me."

"How about Biafra, does that ring a bell?"

Though he wasn't being sarcastic, she heard the bitterness in his tone. "Oh," she said. "Oh, no."

"Biafra tried to secede from Nigeria in 1967, which started a civil war that lasted two and a half years. It was tanks and guns, but it was mostly a war of starvation. At one point ten thousand people a day were dying of hunger. A *day*. Every day. Day after day after day. They killed over two million men, women, and children.

"Biafra was in the southeast, and the Peace Corps sent me to the north. Which, to give the rebels their due, probably should have been a separate country. They were Moslems and they had a Sultan who was the civil and religious leader all in one. The Biafrans were mostly Christian, ethnically Ibo, had a democratic political system. I was teaching secondary school, ten- to sixteen-year-olds, and that part was pretty great. The kids were hungry to learn. Almost entirely boys, of course. But the poverty—I mean, kids with flies crawling in their eyes, dirt-floored houses that people shared with their goats and chickens, if they were lucky enough to have goats and chickens. No running water or toilets, just buckets that got emptied twice a week onto a truck that you could smell a mile away.

"We got refugees all the time. I know you've seen the pictures, these kids with stomachs like basketballs and little pipestem arms. And no matter how many times the government tried to warn them, and I tried to warn them, they would let the kids have whatever they wanted to eat and then the kids would get refeeding syndrome in three or four days because their electrolytes were all screwed up, and they'd go into a coma or cardiac arrhythmia or convulsions and end up dead anyway, just when they thought they'd made it and their worries were over.

"Those refugee kids, they'd tell stories of piles of corpses, and rape, and torture, I mean, kids who should have been playing with dolls or puppies, kids the same age as Ava. If they did manage to survive, those kids are going to have those images in their heads for the rest of their lives.

"But that wasn't what did it to me. What did it was the money. They raised millions all over the world to help those starving kids and the Army and the politicians hijacked virtually every dollar of it. That was what made me see that most of the ways we try to change the world are a complete waste of time and moral energy. I mean, people were signing petitions, for God's sake, saying, 'Please stop starving people to death.' And sending them to somebody who had already said, in public, that he considered starvation to be a legitimate weapon of war.

"That's not even the worst. The worst is that Britain was sending military aid to the Nigerians. Why? Because Biafra includes the Niger Delta, and Shell and British Petroleum didn't want to give up their oil profits. So it's okay to kill two million people to protect your profits. You can still be friends with the US, and not have to answer to any kind of court or authority or have any sanctions put on you or anything."

They were quiet for a while, and then Madelyn said, "What are we supposed to do? How *do* you change the world?"

"With money and power. You say, 'I will loan you the money to fix your country, but only on the condition that you actually use the money to fix your country.' One person can't do it. A bunch of long-haired kids can't do it by sitting around listening to the Grateful Dead. The Army can't do it and Gandhi can't do it."

"And you think the IMF can."

"They're not perfect. But they're the best shot we've got."

"So if they offer you the job, you're going to take it. And move to Washington." Until now, Paul had been vague about his chances at getting the job and about its potential effect on their relationship. Now it was clear that the effect would be seismic.

"Yes. I want this job. And if I move, I want you and Ava with me. Which is why I'm asking you to marry me."

Madelyn could come up with a hundred reasons not to marry him. The only one that scared her was the idea that he might have something cold in him that wanted money and power for its own sake. In three months, she'd seen no hard evidence of it. He seemed like the most compassionate man she had ever known, next to her father. He was patient and gentle with Ava, and patient and gentle in a completely different way with Madelyn in bed. "I love you," she said, not for the first time, but for the first time with a whole heart.

"I love you, too. So will you for God's sake marry me?"

1980

JOE HAD ALWAYS understood that the Mississippi Democratic
Party was not the usual political machine. Only as he began to
worm his way into its rotten core—attending school board and
city council meetings, volunteering at campaign headquarters—
did he appreciate the extent of the difference.

For one thing, the state had two completely different Democratic
Parties, the "regulars," who were white, racist, and reactionary,
and the "loyalists," who were progressive, largely black, and substantially younger. In 1968, the first year that black Mississippians
were, theoretically anyway, allowed to vote, Mississippi sent two
delegations to the national convention in Chicago, and the credentials committee gave the seats to the loyalists.

The regulars were only the latest eruption of the state's deep-
seated white supremacy, a grand tradition that included such
highlights as walking out of the 1948 national convention after
Minneapolis Mayor Hubert Humphrey succeeded in getting a
civil rights plank in the platform, and then forming the Dixiecrat
Party to try to keep Truman off the ballot in the Deep South.
There'd been a pitched battle for convention seating again in
'72 and '76, both of which the loyalists had won, and there was
every reason to expect another fight this year in Madison Square
Garden.

After he passed the bar in 1976, Joe had applied only to law
firms where the senior partners were high in the loyalist ranks. He'd
landed an associate's slot in a partnership headed by a longtime
liberal Democrat and former judge named Winter. Joe had made
no bones about his ambitions, and he'd raised his profile with pro
bono work for poor black families. He didn't sleep more than six
hours a night and worked through the weekends, counting his
attendance every Sunday morning at East Heights Baptist.

He'd met Peggy at East Heights the previous fall. She didn't
have the kind of looks that stopped him in his tracks. What she
had was a neat figure and a face where he could read everything

she felt, and when she was happy, it was a face Joe dearly loved to look at. She'd sat at his table at a church potluck one Wednesday night in October and introduced herself by saying, "That's my corn casserole you just took a double helping of." As they progressed to dinners on their own, she admitted that she'd been "kind of wild" in college, and hadn't found the Lord until late in her senior year. She had a spark in her eye that suggested she might have a bit of wildness in her yet.

Joe found himself telling her things he'd never put in words before. "I guess I always believed in God," he said, "but he was like... Charles De Gaulle. I mean, I knew he was there, somewhere, but I never saw him or talked to him and he didn't have any effect on my life. Then they sent me on my first night patrol."

He took it as a good sign that he was able to talk to her about the war. With anyone else he would have been wound up like a cornered bulldog. "When you first get over there, nobody wants anything to do with you. You're an FNG, where the NG stands for New Guy, and you're a liability because you don't know the ropes and you're likely to get killed and maybe get somebody else killed along with you. So they don't even train you proper, they just throw you out there and if you survive and pull your weight, after a few weeks they might bother to learn your name.

"Which means on my first night patrol, I don't know what I'm doing, I'm scared to death, and all I'm getting is, 'Why'd we get stuck with the FNG?' and 'Keep away from me, man, I don't want to have to wash you out of my fatigues.' I'm trying to do like everybody else, but I can't see them in the dark, and my eyeballs are so tense they hurt, and every sound I hear sounds like a tripwire for a booby trap, or maybe a pit viper in the bushes, or a VC, and there's all these smells—rotting fruit, and dust that doesn't even smell like American dust, it's got this curry powder kind of smell, and there's my own sweat, and this kind of heavy green jungle funk. It was worse than fear, it was feeling more alone than I ever have in my life. I was so freaked that I started to pray without realizing it. I offered God a deal. I said I would do anything he wanted if he would just get me through this night. Right away, that second, I felt this warmth in my gut, like when my dad used to hold my hand sometimes when I was little. I was still terrified, but I could relax with it some, and I could see better and my brain could function, and I got through the night and the next thirteen months.

"God kept up his end of the deal, so here I am keeping up mine. The guys I went to school with in Austin, any kind of religion was the same to them as naked savages dancing around a campfire or burning witches. Unless it was a Buddhist thing, which they had decided was cool. I could never have talked to them about God."

"That's sad," Peggy said, "but it makes me feel special."

Judge Winter had told him the right wife would help his chances, and Peggy was made to order, pleasant-looking without being showy, firm in her religious commitment and malleable in her politics, not well-off but well connected to important Tupelo families, smart without real ambition for herself, capable yet willing to follow Joe's lead. He proposed to her on Valentine's Day, booked East Heights Baptist for a June ceremony, and, when Judge Winter asked if he was ready to try for the State House of Representatives in the November election, Joe said, "Let's do 'er."

They were sitting in a couple of leather armchairs in the Judge's office. Hangin' Judge Winter, they called him, because he was strict, and also because he didn't hold with cronyism. More to the point, he tempered his compassion with realism. "You can sound noble on the TV, or you can get the job done. I prefer to make people's lives better."

He was no fan of Reagan, who told people what they wanted to hear, whether he could deliver or not. "There's no doubt he's changed the political climate. People want it to be 1950 again, when we were on top of the world. Thing is, it's a different world. In 1950 we'd just won a world war. Europe was a pile of rubble and Japan was a stomped-on ant hill. Now the Germans and the Japanese have had them a resurgence, and there's not as much of the pie left for us. People don't care about the facts, though. Either you dance to Reagan's tune or you sit out."

"I got things that are important to me," Joe said. "Social programs. We got to finish up what the Civil Rights Act started. And I want to stop the next war before it gets started."

"All admirable. If you take it in stages. All these things you're talking about belong to Stage Two. Stage One is where you say what you got to say so that you get elected. There's ways to let folks know what you truly believe. But you must never, ever come out and say it."

BEFORE HIS FIRST TIME, Charlene had told Cole that there were only two kinds of heroin users: the ones who were out to kill themselves from the get-go, and the ones who killed themselves by mistake. "If all you want is to die, I'll give you what you need and you can go do it at home right now and get it over with. Leave your door unlocked and I'll have the cops come by tomorrow before you start to stink too bad."

"I don't want to die," Cole said. "I just want some peace."

"Well, this here is the peace that passeth all understanding, as my momma likes to say, though she wasn't talking about smack." Charlene had a set of rules that allowed her to function. "I don't do it but once a week. If you're strong, and you know you got it to look forward to, you can make it through the week. You can keep your job and not have to be out stealing to pay for it. The other thing is, I don't put it in my veins. I either snort it or shoot it IM. You get almost the same high, only it comes on slower, instead of hitting you like a train, and you don't get hooked so bad."

For a few weeks Cole took his little glassine envelope over to Charlene's on Saturday afternoons. Sometimes they would make love before they shot up, and sometimes Cole was so eager for the drug that he couldn't wait. Charlene's tolerance was higher, so she needed twice as much, and eventually Cole got tired of sharing.

Timing was also an issue. Charlene needed her weekly shot on Saturday so she could get over her junk sickness on Sunday and be back to the nail salon on Monday. Whereas Cole was trying to play some solo acoustic gigs and needed to be functional on Saturday night.

He also figured out that once a week was not going to cut it for him. Charlene was obviously more resistant to the drug. He dosed himself on Sundays and Wednesdays, and it was all he could do to hold himself to that.

Within six months he saw that he'd made a terrible mistake. The drug had become the whole of his existence. When he wasn't high, he thought about little else. His sleep was shallow and restless. At one point in late '78 he decided it couldn't be any harder to quit entirely than to go on the way he was. Twenty hours of sickness and craving in exchange for each hour of being high, and the high was not particularly high anymore. Hating himself for nodding out because it was precious junk time that he was not able to consciously appreciate. So he tried to kick, using booze as a substitute. The booze nauseated him and he was unable to sleep at all, just like when he'd gotten out of the hospital when he was 16, and in less than a week he was back on schedule.

Valentina's new lineup had made the Billboard top ten album chart and Templeton had done his magic on the high end, making the acoustic guitars sparkle, the harmony vocals soar, the violin and electric guitar solos scream. The bass and drums had a propulsive bounce and Cole, even in his drug obsession and bitterness, had to admit it was a great pop record. Best of all, it pulled the first Warners album onto the lower reaches of the charts, and the royalty checks meant that Cole didn't have to move back into the Castle. He managed a restaurant gig or concert opener once or twice a week, and, when the managers would pay for it, he'd get Luke to back him on standup bass and harmony vocals.

If there was a path from there to something bigger, Cole couldn't find it.

Though he didn't have the heart to make it to any of Valentina's shows, he did get out a couple of times a week as a spectator, hoping for something that might resuscitate his comatose muse. In the spring and summer he favored Liberty Lunch, a former downtown lumberyard, with a dirt floor and no roof. The Lotions, a great local reggae band, had a regular Tuesday gig there, and Beto and the Fairlanes played Latin jazz on Thursdays. Stevie Vaughan, the little brother of Chessmen guitarist Jimmie Vaughan, was at the Rome Inn near campus, and Antone's on Sixth Street had touring blues acts. The Armadillo had overbooked itself into bankruptcy, yet somehow kept the doors open, and Jim Franklin, if he was around, always let Cole in for free.

Meanwhile, a joint named Raul's, on the Drag across from UT, switched from Tejano to punk and by 1979 had become a national epicenter. The also-rans played the old Vulcan space downtown, rechristened Duke's Royal Coach Inn, where short-life-span bands worked for a share of the door and the audience pogoed and spat on the floor and wore safety pins and ripped T-shirts. Cole liked the energy and sixties garage combo vibe of some of the bands, and he got a weird masochistic charge from being in the same place where the Austin Blues Group had begun its journey to becoming The Quirq. He even auditioned a couple of times, though he understood that he was too old, too hung up on technique, not angry enough.

Definitely not angry enough. Despair was more his style.

Alex had told him about Madelyn getting married and moving to DC. Fortunately the call came on a Sunday as Cole was waiting around for his four PM shot. He didn't ask any questions about the new husband, who was apparently some rich accountant or something, and he pretended to Alex that Madelyn was ancient history. When he got off the phone, he took his shot and put on *Garvey's Ghost*, the dub version of Burning Spear's *Marcus Garvey*, and didn't think about anything at all.

He was amazed that the days could go by so slowly and the years go by so fast, leaving nothing to show for themselves.

In the spring of 1980, Tupelo Joe called him up. "I talked to your dad. He told me he didn't know where you were."

"He was lying," Cole said. "I talk to my mother..." He trailed off because he couldn't remember the last time he'd talked to her.

"Well, that's why I told him to put her on, and she gave me your number. She misses you. You ought to go up to Dallas and see her sometime."

"I hope that's not the reason you called."

The reason, it turned out, was that Joe was getting married in June. He wanted Cole to come, and Cole said he would have to see.

Joe had done exactly what he said he was going to do, gotten his JD and started his political career. Madelyn was headed for George Washington University, in English at last. Alex was making the big bucks working for his dad. In life as in marriage, Cole was the only failure in the bunch.

Cole sidestepped most of Joe's questions, and some awkward silences ensued. Cole understood that he was a junkie now, and that was what junkies did, hurt people's feelings and let them down.

"Maybe this was a bad idea," Joe said.

Cole apologized, blamed Madelyn's remarriage and his lack of a working band, which was a long way from the whole truth. That was another thing junkies did, which was lie. "You called to ask me something. Go ahead."

"Well, it's like this. I was thinking maybe I was ready to try again. With the, ahhhhhhh, the songwriting thing."

Los Cuervos had put "Could Have Been Me" on one of their local LPs and Cole had sent five copies to Joe, followed later by a check for a share of writing royalties that came to $73.25. A tone of vague disappointment hovered over Joe's thank-you notes.

"It's for Peggy," Joe said. "I wrote a couple of poems, songs, whatever you want to call them, for her. I want to hire you to set them to music and put them on tape. Then I want to have them pressed up on a single as a wedding present."

Cole couldn't think of a graceful way out. "Send them to me," he said. "I'll take a look."

By the time he hung up he was in the sort of mood that couldn't bear much scrutiny. It was Thursday, meaning he had the usual flulike symptoms from the previous day's shot and three more days to wait for the next one. According to his inviolable weekly schedule, Thursday was also housecleaning day. He found the idea unbearable. He went back to bed and hugged his knees and waited for the time to pass.

AT THE END of March, Cole's connection told him that the new shipment was unusually pure and that he should watch himself. There had supposedly been some overdoses.

Cole took him at his word and measured out only half his usual dose on the following Sunday. He always shot up in the bathroom because sometimes there was blood. Left hip on Sunday, right on Wednesday. He leaned against the counter, naked from the waist down, and shifted all his weight to his right leg. He pinched a handful of buttock with his left hand and reached around to stick the needle in with his right. A single dark drop of blood broke and ran down the back of his thigh, and he mopped up with a wad of toilet paper dipped in rubbing alcohol.

Fifteen minutes later he felt no more than a mild buzz, maybe no more than a Pavlovian reaction to the needle. Disappointed and desperate, he melted another quarter dose and gave it to himself in the other hip. After another 15 minutes he was raging at the dealer, at the fake heroin, at the universe.

He was due a high. He rummaged through the medicine cabinet and found his last two Percocets and washed them down with a beer.

Finally, after another ten minutes, he felt the high come on and he lay down on the couch. The high kept coming, and suddenly he felt like he was slipping down a long playground slide, with no edges to grab onto. At the end of the slide was darkness.

In a panic, he made himself sit up. He was so dizzy. He couldn't keep his eyes open, couldn't stay upright. He kept thinking about Hendrix, how he must have felt the same way.

He threw himself off the couch onto the floor, banging his shoulder on the coffee table. The phone landed on the floor next to him, the receiver bouncing out of the cradle and the dial tone loud in his ear.

He rubbed his hands on the carpet and the pain helped, briefly. He managed to punch in Charlene's number. He heard her pick up, heard the day-after congestion and irritability in her voice as she said hello, and said it again. She was going to hang up.

"Help," Cole said.

"Cole?"

"Help me."

"Oh, shit. Cole, did you OD, you stupid motherfucker?"

He was drowning. The effort to keep his head above water was more than he had strength for.

"I'm on my way," she said. "Keep moving. Don't stop moving, you stupid piece of shit."

He crawled to the door and unlocked it, and then he started toward the bathroom. The effort made his shoulder muscles burn. Every stab of pain helped him stay conscious another second. Cold tile under his hands. He stuck his head under the shower and got cold water drizzling on it. He had his sternum against the side of the tub and his stomach started to heave, then he was throwing up. He thought it would make things better, but the vomit went up his nose and he was spluttering and spitting, even as he wanted to let the thing that had him by the ankles pull him the rest of the way down.

He cupped some water in his hands and rinsed his mouth, and that was the last of his strength. He collapsed there, arched over the side of the tub, head and shoulders under the shower, legs stretched out behind him, and it was like the summer rain, cool and sweet, and the darkness won.

Suddenly somebody was shaking him, yelling, "Cole! Cole! Wake up, goddamn you!" A hand grabbed him by the collar, and pulled him out dripping onto the bathmat. "On your feet."

Charlene stood over him. "Can't," he said.

She slapped him across the face, hard. A red strobe light in the darkness. She pulled one arm until he was on his knees, gasping, and pulled again until the arm went around her neck and she was dragging him around the apartment. "Walk!" she said. "Use your goddamn feet!"

After a few laps he was able to continue by himself in a flat-footed shuffle. Whenever he stopped to lean his head against the wall, Charlene's voice came from the kitchen, "Keep walking or I call 911." Cole smelled coffee. It smelled good.

Eventually they sat at the kitchen table and drank the coffee. Charlene's T-shirt was wet and Cole had tracked water all over the living room. She made him tell her what he'd taken.

"You stupid shit," she said. "People almost never overdose on pure heroin. It's mixing it with pills and booze that kills people. Don't you know anything?"

Cole started to cry.

"A junkie's tears," Charlene said. "Is there anything cheaper?"

"When did you turn so cold?" Cole said. "I'm scared. I'm fucking petrified. That's the scariest thing that ever happened to me."

"Don't call me cold, you son of a bitch. I'm the one who just saved your worthless, washed-up excuse for a life. I thought twice about it on the way over here, too. Call me cold? After all the times you used me and then wadded me up and threw me aside? I should have called 911 and let them deal with you."

"I'm sorry," Cole said. He couldn't stop the tears, and now he was shaking besides. "I'm really sorry."

"Yeah," Charlene said. "Me too."

MADELYN'S PARENTS took the bus from Dulles to the Metro, whence they had a straight shot on the Silver Line to the Foggy Bottom station at GWU. She'd made a token offer to pick them up at the airport, knowing her father would insist on taking public transportation; it made him feel righteous and democratic.

Naturally Paul was at work when her father called from a pay phone at the station. It was 2:15 on a Friday, and Madelyn had gotten one of the other TAs to teach her class. She grabbed Ava, who was red-faced with excitement, and walked to campus. Her parents were sitting on the bench she had described to them, at the 23rd Street entrance to Washington Circle, and as soon as Ava saw them she pulled her hand free and broke into a run, shouting, "Grandpa, Grandpa!"

"Ava!" Madelyn screamed, and Ava froze, thank God, before running across 23rd Street. Traffic, as always in DC, was ferocious, everyone consumed by a pathological sense of self-importance and urgency. Madelyn's heart had gone supersonic.

"I wasn't going to cross without looking," Ava said, already as distressed, at age five and a half, about being treated like a child as she was at having upset Madelyn. "Honest."

"I know you weren't, darling. But you have to remember your mother's nervous condition."

"Whose name," Ava said somberly, "is Ava."

Grandpa was the only male authority figure that Ava had known since birth, and nothing could dislodge him from the top spot in her heart, to Paul's eternal disappointment. She hadn't seen him since Christmas, and now the cherry blossoms were already in bloom.

He charged at Ava as if to swoop her up, then pretended she was too massive to lift, a lovely bit of cartoonery that convulsed her with joyous laughter.

He hadn't been to DC since he was a teenager in the middle of the Depression, so he was hungry to see everything. Madelyn walked them past the Gelman Library on campus, where she spent most of her life these days, then down Pennsylvania to the White House, where her father said, "I bite my thumb at you, all you servants of Mammon." He then proceeded to carry out his word, to Ava's great delight. He then coached Ava on the fine points of thumb-biting, including flicking the thumbnail against the front teeth, "for equal-time offensiveness to people from India. Don't do this with actual Indian persons present."

Dear God, Madelyn thought, one more way for Ava to get herself into trouble.

Madelyn's mother was awed to be around so much political power; her father was far more interested in the Smithsonian and the Folger and the National Gallery. "Save them for tomorrow," Madelyn said. "We have to get home for dinner."

Paul was late, and more irritable than usual. He'd managed to rebel against his own parents twice: first in his Free Speech anti-establishment phase, and then, as his parents mellowed in the seventies, by "meddling in other countries' affairs," as his father put it. Madelyn's closeness to her parents annoyed him; he wanted to be a fully independent foursome consisting of himself, Madelyn, Ava, and a child of their own that he was pressuring her to conceive.

As they passed around the Indian take-out that Paul had brought home, Ava recounted the thumb-biting incident. Paul chuckled initially, then said to Madelyn's father, "I thought Carter was your guy."

"His pious, aw-shucks manner is just an act," her father said, "to disguise a canny and ambitious politician. Even so, he's vastly better than Reagan."

"If Reagan were to get the nomination," Madelyn said, "surely he couldn't win against a seated president."

"He's close to having the nomination sewed up," Paul said, "and he can and will win the election."

"Carter's vulnerable," her father said.

"Because of the hostages?" Madelyn asked. Fifty-two Americans had been captured by Iranian students in November, and Carter had been helpless to get them released.

"That isn't helping," her father said. "But what's going to kill him is gas prices and the economy."

"That's crazy," Madelyn said. She and Paul had an unspoken agreement to avoid political discussions at the dinner table. She couldn't resist the chance to speak her mind now that she had her father to back her up. "Reagan's economic plan is inherently ridiculous. Balance the budget by lowering taxes on the rich? That's like ending hunger by burning food."

"A lot of trained economists don't think it's ridiculous at all," Paul said mildly. "Common sense told us the earth was flat and that the sun revolved around it. To pick a better example, quantum mechanics is full of things that seem to defy common sense, but are perfectly understandable to a physicist. Like Bell's Theorem."

"Only at the atomic level," her father said, bless his dear heart. "At the macro level, where humans interact with everyday objects, quantum mechanics has to agree with observable reality, or it's useless. Bell knew that as well as anyone. There is no evidence of supply-side economics ever working in the real world. It doesn't even merit the term 'theory.' It's purely hypothesis, and a very silly one."

Paul's face turned red. Madelyn had never seen that happen before. They had crossed into unknown territory. "Milton Friedman doesn't find it 'silly,'" Paul said, "and he's the smartest man I've ever known."

"Present company excepted," Madelyn said, perhaps too quietly to be acknowledged.

Her father, having made his point, retreated gracefully. "Madelyn tells me you studied under Friedman at Chicago. That must have been transformative."

"It was."

"I've read *Capitalism and Freedom*," her father said, "but I appreciate that it's no substitute for knowing the man himself."

Paul was quiet for a long time, and then he said, "What you're saying, about the real world. That's what I struggle with every day. Idealism tells you that people are inherently good and altruistic, and my experience of the real world, which gets reinforced every day, tells me that people are greedy. Friedman acknowledges that greed. His theories predicted stagflation, which Keynesians still can't explain."

"Predicting is one thing," her father said. "Solving is another. But it looks like he's going to get his chance. I wish him luck."

Madelyn's mother, who had an irrational fear of any kind of conflict, jumped in. "That's more than enough politics. Can we talk about something really important, like who shot J.R.?"

"Mother, don't tell me you watch that awful show," Madelyn said.

"If I didn't, I wouldn't be able to have a conversation with any of my friends."

The talk moved on, without Paul, who'd turned inside himself. He waited a few minutes after the table was cleared, then said he had a loan proposal to review.

Madelyn sat on the couch with her father and said, "I apologize for Paul. He's been under a lot of pressure at work…"

He patted her knee. "You don't have to make excuses, dear. I don't want you to think I'm criticizing Paul. He's in the trenches with these issues, and all I do is read books and think about them, which is never going to change the world."

"Remember *Middlemarch*? You've changed the people around you, and we are going to change the world. I know I plan to, one student at a time."

Her father took his glasses off and rubbed the bridge of his nose. "I think there are a lot of people like Paul who were very idealistic and outspoken in their younger days and got frustrated and decided to change things from inside the power structure. Which does not like change. And they end up compromised and disappointed and don't want to admit it, not to themselves, and especially not to people they don't particularly like."

Madelyn started to object, and her father held up his hand. "It's okay, dear, we always did call them straight up, you and I. The thing is, this may turn out to be the most important election in the history of the human race."

"Oh, Daddy, you do love your hyperbole."

"I hope that's all it is. From where I sit, the drama is real. Reagan is the classic optimist and Carter is willing to look at hard truths. Reagan says we need energy independence, so we should burn more coal. 'But Governor Reagan, what about the pollution? What about the rising CO_2 levels? What about the Greenhouse Effect?' And Reagan just waves his hands and says, 'It'll be okay.' Carter says we have to tighten our belts, which demonstrably we have to do. He lowers the speed limit, he puts solar panels on the White House, and people go nuts."

"I don't deny that Reagan is bad," Madelyn said. "But this free market mania is everywhere. It's like a contagious disease, and Carter's caught it too. He deregulated the airlines, and now he's deregulated the banks."

"I know, I know. And Mrs. Thatcher in England, selling public utilities to the highest bidder. People don't want to hear about limits. They don't want to be told they can't have something for nothing. And they have this unshakable faith that the rich have their best interests at heart. Wasn't your generation going to hang the rich?"

"Cooler heads prevailed. Maybe this is just a phase. Who always told me, 'This too shall pass'?"

"I hope so. I dearly hope so."

A bit after midnight, Madelyn climbed the stairs, checked on Ava, and brushed her teeth. She thought, for the hundredth time at least, of the nights she'd gone dancing in New York. She'd even located a club called Pier 9 that promised to be even wilder than the Gallery. Paul had dismissed the idea, unsurprisingly, and she had failed to muster the time and rebelliousness to go on her own. Someday, she thought. Maybe.

Paul was still awake. He had a thick, bound document open on his lap, and he was staring into space. Madelyn undressed with her back to him, acutely self-conscious as she pulled a nightgown over her head.

She got into bed and said, "Do you want to talk?"

"About what?"

She ignored the warning and plunged ahead. "Are you disappointed in your job? Is it not working out the way you wanted it to?"

"Where did you get that idea? From your father?"

"From you. You don't seem happy."

"It's not a day-to-day happy kind of job. It's a long slog, hope for some satisfaction at the end kind of job."

He was not going to let her pull anything out of him. "Don't stay up too late," she said. He nodded and picked up the document.

She lay down, facing away from him, and closed her eyes. I tried, she thought. At least I tried.

ALEX BARELY REMEMBERED the last time he'd seen Cole in the flesh. He'd driven to Austin one weekend to see him with Los Cuervos at the Armadillo in, what, '76? Had it really been four years? There had been phone calls and letters, and for a while Cole had sent the occasional thrift store postcard, pretending to be in Tangiers or Bora Bora. After Cole found out that Alex was seeing Ava, the postcards had stopped. Cole had nursed his unhappiness for six or eight months while Alex continued to write or call every few weeks, offering no apologies, until he wore Cole down. Once Madelyn moved to Washington, Cole had finally stopped asking about her, and now he was coming up to spend Labor Day weekend.

While Alex was counting years, he couldn't believe that six of them had now gone into working for his father. Every time his alarm clock went off, he wondered how he was going to make it to dinnertime. Any minute, the bottom was going to fall out of his life and litter the ground around him with his own lies and deceptions. He wasn't sure if he cared.

Pride of place went to his drug smuggling. Three or four times a year he made a run to Nuevo Laredo and put another five thousand in the antique safe, like Álvaro's, that he maintained in an airconditioned storage unit out near Love Field. He kept a few other items there that he didn't want Callie to know about, like a box of *Penthouse* magazines and a loaded Smith and Wesson snub-nose .38. He didn't care about the money, and he didn't know why he kept a gun that never left the shed, he only knew that the fear they inspired was part of the cocktail of risk that allowed him to tolerate his existence.

Brenda was another part of it. She was a graphic designer who occasionally freelanced for Compu-Tex, the local computer company that Alex had hired to automate the most tedious parts of his job. She was a few years older than Alex and not given to showing off her femininity or hiding her intelligence, both of which were ample. Their attraction had been mutual and immediate. She claimed not to care that he was married, and he let himself believe her. They met for athletic lunch-hour sex once or twice a week, always at her instigation, and whatever guilt he might have felt never pained him deeply or for very long.

Then there was Gwyn. Alex tried to shield her from the pitched battles between him and Callie, but Callie burned hot when she lost control. More than once Gwyn had opened the door of whatever room they were fighting in, sobbing in fear and confusion, and Alex had choked down his own rage to comfort her. You can't hide a collapsing marriage from a kid, and even when they managed a pretense of normalcy, Alex could see the light of her childish joy starting to fade. He would have given up his drug money and his mistress to bring it back. A divorce would only make it worse, and he didn't trust Callie to raise a child without his constant moderating presence. Not to mention what Callie might turn up to use against him in court.

When they were both at home, Alex mostly stayed in his "office," a bedroom at the back of the house that he'd fitted out with a single bed, a desk and armchair, a TV with a cable connection, and a Betamax recorder. The room had developed a lingering smell of marijuana.

At the moment another smell had penetrated the room and Alex went to investigate. Callie was washing dishes, and steam trickled from the cover of the electric skillet. Gwyn sat on the counter in a playsuit powdered with flour and stained with Kitchen Bouquet.

"Is that pot roast?" Alex said.

"Yes."

"You realize Cole is coming for dinner?"

"Yes."

"And Cole is a vegetarian?"

"There's potatoes and carrots in there."

"Cooked with the meat."

"A potato is a potato."

His sister Susan was at TCU in Fort Worth, studying psychology, and Alex had told her everything. Well, everything except the dope stuff. Susan said Callie was passive-aggressive, acting out her hostilities in a way calculated to drive Alex crazy. Knowing the technical terminology didn't help.

"Besides," Callie said, "Gwynnie wanted pot roast."

"Potroastpotroastpotroast!" Gwyn yelled happily.

Alex knew that if he said anything at all he would start screaming, despite Gwyn being there. Callie was expert at this, able to torment him endlessly and leave him no way to retaliate.

The doorbell rang.

"Your friend's here," Callie said. She dried her hands, took off her apron, and swooped Gwyn up under one arm, Gwyn laughing in delight.

Cole stood on the front stoop, a knapsack in one hand, his acoustic guitar case in the other. He looked like hell, hair long and oily, ragged beard, clothes tattered and loose on his wiry body. Without letting him in, Alex set the knapsack and guitar in the living room, then stepped outside and shut and locked the front door. "Hungry?" Alex said.

"I ate some veggies at the Turkey Shop," Cole said. "But I could eat again."

"Let's go."

Alex opened the garage and noted Cole's reaction to his current set of wheels, a candy-apple red Z28 Camaro.

"Holy Christ," Cole said. "What's it got?"

"A three-eighty-three stroker," Alex said. "It's quick."

They got in and Cole caressed the black vinyl dashboard. "So we're just going to skip the 'how long has it been, so great to see you' part?"

As he backed out the driveway, Alex saw Callie at the front door, screaming, "Where are you going? I have a party tonight!"

The neighbors on one side had tried to have them evicted, and the ones on the other side had put their house up for sale. You lived in a ritzy neighborhood like this one so you could play string quartets on your fancy stereo at low volume, not to listen to no-class low-life assholes screaming at each other in their front yard like they were in South Oak Cliff.

Alex left a little rubber on the street to express his feelings about Callie's party and the neighbors' disapproval. "You and me," he said, "we're the kind of friends who can just pick up where we left off."

"I don't remember leaving things quite like this."

Alex drove to the Black-eyed Pea on Cedar Springs, sticking to the surface roads since it was rush hour, and he never got a chance to open up the Camaro like he wanted to, not even for two seconds, and eventually the tremor left his hands and he was able to breathe normally. As he drove, he told Cole everything, Brenda, the drugs, the job, all of it. He looked over a couple of times and Cole's face showed nothing but sympathy and interest. When he was done, Cole said, "I wish I had an answer. All I can say is yeah, man, it really sucks."

"Well, that's something. At least I'm not missing an obvious solution."

"Not that I can see," Cole said. "And now my turn."

Cole, it turned out, had been shooting heroin a couple of times a week since the Led Zeppelin fiasco. He'd had an OD scare in March that had kept him straight for two months, but now he was using again every week or two, "whenever I absolutely can't stand it anymore."

"Wow," Alex said. "What a pair of losers we are."

They lingered over dinner, splitting a pitcher of beer, of which Alex only took a couple of glasses. He got them home by eight, and as soon as he pulled in the driveway, the front door swung open and Callie stomped out, her hair piled high, wearing a Calvin Klein sheath dress he'd bought her at Neiman's and high-heeled cowboy boots. She got into her Fiat Spider and was already backing out as Alex pulled into the garage.

"You know what's weird?" Alex said as he turned off the engine. "We still have sex. It gets a little rough sometimes, and there's no pretense that we're making up or anything. We just fuck each other."

"That's really screwed up," Cole said.

"Tell me about it," Alex said.

They went inside. Gwyn was watching HBO, where guys in baseball uniforms and weird makeup were beating people with bats. Alex hurriedly switched the set off and said, "Time for your bath, sugarplum."

Gwyn looked up at him. He wished he could vacuum those violent images out of those dark, innocent eyes, wished he could teleport Callie to Mars and raise Gwyn on his own, wished he could make everything okay, if not forever, at least for a few years.

Gwyn pointed at Cole. "Who's that?"

Cole squatted next to her. "I am your long-lost Uncle Cole, come all the way from the other side of Texas to see you at last."

"Will you read to me?"

"Eventually, but before that we are going to do something even better. Your daddy and I are going to sing to you... in Spanish! Because long, long ago, before you were born, when dinosaurs roamed the earth, your daddy and I were known as... El! Mariachi! Montoya!" He blew a trumpet fanfare into his fist.

Gwyn gave him the bored look she'd learned from Callie. Cole, who'd obviously thought charming kids was as easy as charming women, wilted. Alex laughed until tears ran down his face.

And yet, when Alex got her bathed and into her pajamas and tucked in, when they brought in a couple of stools and tuned their guitars and turned off everything but her Pokey Little Puppy night light, when they started to sing slowed and quieted versions of the old songs, "Bésame mucho" and "Quién será" and "Perfidia," she was asleep within ten minutes.

They took the guitars into the living room and carried on for another hour. Alex couldn't get over how easy it was, the way their voices blended, the way his fingers knew where all the chords were, the way Cole's guitar parts locked into his. He hadn't felt that close to peace in a very long time.

*

ALL SATURDAY MORNING, Callie made an exaggerated show
that Alex and Cole were invisible and inaudible, and by mid-
afternoon Alex couldn't take it any longer. They put Cole's guitar
in the back seat of the Camaro and drove to White Rock Lake.
The afternoon sun was relentless and the park was mobbed with
bumper-to-bumper stop-and-go traffic. Finally Alex crossed over
to the west side, where there were no picnic areas and fewer trees.
They ended up in a vacant lot a few blocks from the lake, near
an abandoned railroad trestle and piles of broken concrete slabs.

"Scenic," Cole said.

"Humble, but our own." They got out of the car and leaned
against the shady side, facing away from the road, and Alex took
a joint out of his shirt pocket. "This is a sample of my wares,"
he said. "I think you'll find it has a pleasant bouquet and quite
powerful legs."

"Fire it up," Cole said.

Alex had the joint in his hand, half-smoked, his lungs full and
a good buzz in progress, when, loud as an explosion, came the
unmistakable single whoop of a police car siren and an amplified
voice shouting, "Freeze!"

Panic hit Alex's brain like a lightning flash. He couldn't see,
couldn't think. He threw the joint into the dried grass nearby
and clawed the other two joints of out his shirt pocket and flung
them in the same direction. By then the cops were on them, two
of them, in black short-sleeved uniforms, sunglasses, and peaked
caps.

This can't be happening, Alex thought. This is the end of everything.

"Well, well, well, well, well," said one cop. He was taller, with
light brown hair and a mustache. He had his nightstick out and
was tapping it in his palm. "What do we have here?"

"On first inspection," his black-haired partner said, "it looks
like we have us a wetback and some kind of street person."

"Smoking themselves a little weed, it appears."

"It does look like that." The second cop walked over and picked up the lit joint. "Why, look here, I believe this little number is still burning, right here among all this flammable material."

He showed the joint to his partner, who sniffed at it and smiled. "Yes, indeed, I have to agree that this is a bit of a smoking gun, as they say."

The second cop stubbed out the joint on the bottom of his highly polished black shoe and put it in a plastic bag. Then he picked up the other two joints and dropped them in after it. He looked at Alex. "You speak English?"

"Yes," Alex said. "Quite well, actually."

"Which one of you is doing the buying and which is doing the selling? And how much more of this stuff have you got in the car?"

Cole spoke up. "Officer, I think there's been a misunderstanding. This isn't a drug deal. We're old friends, just out enjoying the summer afternoon. We're not hurting anyone. Surely you could..."

"Could what?" the first cop said.

"Give us a break?" Cole said, with an ingratiating smile.

The first cop said, "Both of you turn around and put your hands against the car. You're under arrest for felony possession of marijuana, creating a fire hazard, and suspicion of trafficking in narcotics." He then ran through the Miranda warning in a singsong voice and said, "Do you understand the rights I've just stated to you?"

"Yes," Alex said, his brain still frozen in panic mode.

"Yes," Cole said.

The second cop patted Alex down roughly, took his car keys, then frisked Cole. "Going to need to delouse this one when we get to the station," he said, then he grabbed Alex's right arm and jerked it behind his back, slamming him into the car. Alex felt a handcuff cut into his right wrist, then the cop pulled the left arm back and put the other cuff on. The hot metal of the car roof burned his cheek.

While the first cop handcuffed Cole, the second cop pulled Alex backward onto his feet and pushed him toward the squad car. "Let's go there, Frito Bandito. Your chariot awaits." Alex, to his shame, had become totally submissive. The cop shoved Alex into the back seat and slammed the door. Wire mesh separated the front and back seats and the back doors had no handles on the inside. The engine was running, and the air conditioning made Alex tremble.

Through the window he saw the cops double-teaming Cole, pointing fingers, getting in his face. Alex's brain had started to thaw and his thoughts were desperate. Ten years in prison. Losing Gwyn in an ugly divorce and not being able to see her until she was an adult. His father's humiliation. The life that had been unbearable to Alex yesterday now seemed impossibly sweet.

They made Cole lie in the dirt while they searched the car. They took their time, and Alex heard their laughter over the purring engine and the chatter on the police band radio. When they were done, both doors and the trunk of the Camaro stood open, and Cole's guitar case, the spare tire and the jack, and some old towels were strewn around it in the dirt.

They marched Cole to the squad car and put him in the back seat next to Alex, then the first cop got in the driver's seat and the second cop got in the other side.

"Where to, ladies?" the first cop said, looking in the rear-view mirror. "Just kidding."

Cole said, "Listen, could you maybe not just leave that guitar lying there? It's really valuable."

"Oh yeah?" the second cop said. "My girlfriend plays guitar. What kind is it?"

"It's handmade by this guy in Mexico. He's famous down there."

The two cops looked at each other and the second cop got out and fetched the guitar and put it in the trunk of the squad car.

"Thanks," Cole said, when the second cop got back in.

The second cop grinned and said, "Don't mention it."

Alex was afraid to ask what was going to happen to his car, so he sat in silence while the second cop called in a report of their arrest. He realized that he'd still been hoping the cops might change their minds, and now it was too late and everything was official. They drove through the park land north of the lake and then through a tree-lined commercial district. Alex tried to imagine himself making his one phone call to his father, then his mind darted away to prison horror stories—getting lost in the system and never coming out, rape, beatings, gangs, riots, shivs.

The police station occupied a sprawling, one-story mid-sixties industrial-style building. A metal sign read, "Northeast Patrol." They parked in the rear and the cops immediately split them up again. Alex sat in an interview room alone for forty endless minutes before the cops returned. The second cop was grinning. "Your so-called pal Freddy the Freeloader just sang like a canary. He said it was your dope and you offered to sell him a kilo. He may just waltz out of here while you go on a long Huntsville vacation."

Alex flushed with rage at Cole and then, a moment later, he realized that Cole would never have come up with the nonsense about the kilo. "I think I'll wait until my lawyer's here," he said.

"There's a good chance," the first cop said, "we can make this all go away if you tell us where you got the dope. You might want to think about that. And think fast, because this is definitely a limited time offer."

"That's okay," Alex said. "I'll wait for my lawyer."

When they saw he wasn't going to budge, they took him to the booking desk. A woman in her forties with hair the color of redwood fence paint typed up his paperwork and took his wallet and belt. "What about my friend's guitar?" Alex said. "Can you write down on that paper that they took his guitar?"

"No guitar here," the woman said.

Alex looked at the second cop, who said, "Don't worry about it. I'll take care of it."

"You got change for the phone?" the woman said. She sold Alex a dollar's worth of quarters and, hands shaking, he dialed his parents' number.

His mother answered and Alex said, "It's me. I've been arrested."

"Are you hurt?"

"No."

Her voice was calm. "Tell me what happened."

"The charges are possession of marijuana." The cops were not even pretending not to listen. "We're at the Northeast Station, out by White Rock, but I think they're taking us downtown to the courthouse to be arraigned."

"Okay, m'ijo, I'll call Mac now."

"There won't be anything he can do until they set bail," he said, repeating what the cops had told him. "Which will be at the arraignment, which probably won't happen until tomorrow morning."

"Okay. What else can I do? You want me to call Callie?"

Oh, God, he thought. "Yes, please."

"Does Cole want me to call his parents?"

"No, please don't. There's nothing they can do." He felt 6 years old. Tears ran down his face. "I'm so scared."

"Be brave, sweetie, we'll take care of this. You'll be okay."

"I love you."

"You, too."

He hung up, not wanting to turn around and let the cops see him crying.

"Come on, Frito," the second cop said. "Finger-painting time."

THEY TOOK ALEX to a cell. Cole was already there, along with a large, drunk, black man who lay on the only bunk and snored, and an old, barefoot white man in ragged clothes who smelled like ripe garbage and hit them up for spare change. An hour later they brought in a white guy in Bermuda shorts and a polo shirt and a visor who paced back and forth all afternoon.

At six a woman came around and handed plastic-wrapped ham sandwiches and cans of Coke through the bars. Alex felt a flicker of animal pleasure at the sight of food. Cole, however, looked at his and said, "I'm a vegetarian. Is there any chance I could get a plain cheese sandwich?"

"No," she said.

Cole handed Alex his sandwich and sat in a corner.

Around eight PM, a pair of guards put them in leg irons and herded them into a van. Nobody came running out with a reprieve. The van took them to the courthouse where they were herded from room to room and finally put in a heavily crowded cell filled, from the looks of things, with DWIS. One of them threw up in the middle of the floor shortly after arriving, and in the hour before a custodian came to clean it up, the smell made three others vomit as well.

Wall space for leaning was at a premium, so Alex and Cole curled up on the hard tile floor. Alex withdrew into a mindless state from fear and exhaustion and ended up with maybe a couple of hours' sleep. At seven AM they got sweet rolls and cups of lukewarm coffee and lined up to use the seatless toilet in one corner of the cell.

At eight a bailiff called the first set of names and at 9:15 Alex and Cole got paraded past the judge. The charges were read, Mac McKinney, his father's lawyer, stepped up to settle the bail, and they were processed out. Their belongings had been transferred down with them, so they got their wallets back. There was no sign of the guitar.

Mac, who was six foot four, whose hair generally stuck up in one or two oddball places, whose suits never quite fit, looked unusually rumpled, having spent a few early morning hours passing the word to anyone he could get hold of that he expected Alex and Cole to be treated well. Alex's father claimed the bumpkin look was part of an act designed to get Mac's adversaries to underestimate him. That morning he'd made it clear that he was not to be fucked with.

Mac drove them past the lot where the bust had gone down, on the off chance that Alex's car was still there. Apparently it had been impounded. Before he let them off at Alex's house, he said he'd find out what had happened to the guitar and the car, but not to expect to hear anything until after the holiday on Monday. He asked Cole to stick around for a few days so as not to look like a flight risk, and Cole agreed.

Callie and Gwyn were watching *The Rescuers* on videotape when they walked in. Callie looked at Alex with a neutral expression and said, "Are you all right? All things considered?"

"All things considered," Alex said.

"Good," she said, and turned back to the TV. Alex knew that

worse would follow, once they were alone. At the moment all he could think about was his love for Gwyn. He knelt and scooped her up in a hug. She squirmed so that she could see the TV and said, "Daddy, you *stink*."

"Both of you," Callie said.

Alex kissed Gwyn on the top of the head and let her go.

THOUGH COLE HAD BEEN intellectually prepared for Alex's new life, he'd still been shocked by the four-bedroom house in the exclusive neighborhood, the expensive cars, Callie's designer wardrobe, the weight Alex had gained around the middle. Like a double exposure of the Alex he knew with Alex's father.

He hadn't realized how bad he himself looked until he saw it in Alex's eyes. And yet, none of it mattered once they started telling each other the truth. Maybe it took both their lives being in the toilet to bring them back together. Whatever the reason, Cole was glad for it.

Until the inconceivable happened and two would-be comedians came out of nowhere to destroy their lives.

Cole got through the afternoon and night of the bust by dreaming of heroin. He played out the whole sequence in his mind, from scoring in the parking lot to the sour smell of cooking the dose over a candle flame, the bite of the needle, the slow warmth spreading through his body, so sweet that it made him lick his lips, even as he lay on the hot tile floor of the county jail.

Back at Alex's place, bathed and in his guest bed, Cole found he still couldn't get to sleep. He wanted a shot more than life itself. Without heroin, his skin felt like poorly fitting woolen underwear and he couldn't get away from the voices of fear in his head.

He got dressed and went into the living room. The TV was off and Callie and Gwyn were playing War on the carpeted floor. Cole watched for a while, remembering playing with his mother when he was Gwyn's age, wondering how he was going to tell her what had happened. "Can I have a beer?" he asked.

"If we have any," Callie said.

They had Bohemia. Cole drank one in the kitchen and took a

second one to the living room. "I'm tired," Gwyn announced. It was two in the afternoon. Maybe it was nap time. She looked at Cole. "Can you do Matty-Tutcheys?"

"Mariachis?" Cole said. "I can't. I lost my guitar."

"You can use my daddy's."

"What's this about?" Callie said.

"We sang her to sleep Friday night with some mariachi songs. It worked pretty well."

"Infecting her with the music virus?"

"It's not like she hasn't already been exposed."

Callie abruptly walked out. One good thing about prison, Cole thought, is it will get Alex out of this marriage. He asked Gwyn, "Do you have a favorite song?"

Gwyn sang, in a clear voice, "This old man, he played one, he played knick-knack on my drum…"

"I know that man," Cole said. "But he played knick-knack on my thumb."

"Too easy," Gwyn said. "Everybody plays knick-knack on their thumb."

Callie came back, carrying Alex's guitar by the neck, like a skillet, and held it out to Cole. Cole checked the tuning while Callie sat down and Gwyn crawled into her lap. "Allá en el rancho grande," he sang quietly, "allá donde vivía…" He held the note a ridiculously long time, finally poking himself in the nose to move on to the next line. Gwyn laughed, so he continued to ham it up whenever the chorus came around. He saw she was getting wound up, so he slowed it down with "Perfidia," achingly slow. Infidelity was probably not the best topic, considering Alex's ongoing aventura, but then Callie didn't speak any Spanish as far as Cole knew. Gwyn was yawning by the end, and out cold by the time he played "Siboney."

Cole put the guitar down. Playing made him think about La Pelirroja, which made him feel enraged and helpless. Callie continued to sit with Gwyn in her lap, gently rocking, so Cole asked, "Are you still painting?"

"Something like that," Callie said.

Cole didn't know how to respond. The silence stretched, and

then Callie said, "It's so hard to find anything new. It's all been done. And you can't just make something, you have to have a concept and a manifesto."

She rocked Gwyn for a while and then said, "I knew I was an artist before I was old enough to read. I was always drawing. Sometimes I wish I'd been born a man in the Renaissance. I could have joined the Guild of St. Luke by the time I hit puberty and been signing my canvases by twenty. No identity crises, no agonizing over form, just paint and more paint. Did you always know you were a musician?"

"Alex knew it before I did. My whole career was his idea."

"Too bad he didn't think it through." Cole couldn't help but laugh, and Callie finally cracked a smile. "At least you and I know what we want," she said. "Alex is still in search of his métier."

For the first time Cole understood what Alex saw in her. She brought her passion to everything. He could see how that could get maddening on a daily basis, yet it was also compelling in a way that reminded him of Madelyn. The women Cole had been involved with since might have had any number of qualities, but that kind of white-hot intensity was not one of them.

"I have to tell you," Callie said. "If you guys go to prison, Gwyn and I won't be here when you get back."

COLE AND ALEX had dinner that night with Alex's parents. Cole hadn't seen them since Alex's wedding. The mood was somber and the small talk died without ever taking wing. Susan was in Fort Worth, Jimmy in Austin, and Callie had stayed home with Gwyn.

After dinner Cole and Alex and Montoya played poker at the dining room table, using imaginary money. As well as he knew Montoya, Cole was still amazed that he didn't offer a word of reproach, or ask whose dope it was. The only time he directly addressed the subject was to say, "If worse comes to worst, there's always Mexico. Alex could work out of the Monterrey office, and we could get you a job there too."

"We could never come back to the US," Cole said.

"No," Montoya said. "But you wouldn't be in prison."

On Tuesday, Mac called to say that the prosecutor had sent a complaint to the grand jury, who would respond on Thursday. "There's always the possibility that they might no-bill you, that is, refuse to indict. That possibility is small. They've got evidence, they've got the two officers, there's no pressure on them not to indict. I wouldn't look to anything there."

Wednesday they stayed up drinking at Alex's house. Alex had flushed all his dope on Sunday afternoon.

"Are you thinking about it?" Cole asked. "Mexico?"

"No way Callie would come. So I would never see Gwyn again. I can't do that. You?"

"I don't know. I don't know if I could make a living playing music down there, not the kind of music I want to play. If it meant working a day job for your father... well, that's just another kind of prison sentence, isn't it?"

"Tell me about it."

They drank for a while and then Cole said, "Remember all those flag decals they used to give away, back around sixty-nine, seventy?"

"Yeah, what bullshit that was. I hate flags. A flag is inherently divisive. It says, 'we are us, and fuck you.'"

"I put one on the windshield of the bus we had at the commune. Took a lot of shit for it, too."

"I can see why."

"Yeah, well, there was a part of me that didn't see why the red-necks should get to own patriotism. What with the time I spent overseas—"

"Armpits, was I believe the word you used."

"I remember how good it felt to come home. I used to love this country."

"Used to?"

"It doesn't feel the same anymore. Not after Nixon and now Reagan's campaign, all the backlash against, I don't know, against you and me, is what it feels like. It's like Reagan has disowned us."

"For me it was Kent State. It was never the same after that. I think I could live in France and never look back. Maybe I could talk Callie into that."

"Maybe they'll let me have a guitar in prison. Maybe I'll write the next 'Folsom Prison Blues.'"

"Maybe Iran will start a world war and we'll all die."

Cole saluted him with his beer bottle. "We can only hope."

THE PHONE RANG Thursday at noon. Cole was sitting on the couch, flipping through the channels. Callie and Gwyn were out and Alex had shut himself in his office.

Cole answered on the third ring when Alex didn't pick up. It was Montoya, sounding grim. "Mac called and said for you and Alex to come over here."

"Now?"

"If you can."

"It's bad news, right? Can't you just tell us over the phone?"

"Mac wanted you here."

Cole hung up and had a moment of panic. What if Alex had killed himself? He walked down the long hallway and tried the door. The knob turned in his hand and the door opened. The lights were off and the blinds were closed. Cole needed a few seconds to see Alex lying on the day bed, eyes closed, loud music leaking from the headphones over his ears.

Cole shook him gently by the foot. Alex's eyes slowly opened and he took the headphones off.

"Come on," Cole said. "We're going to your folks' house."

Mac's Sedan de Ville was in the driveway when they arrived. "If we don't go in there," Alex said, "we don't have to hear the news."

"Schrodinger's Indictment. Good plan. We can still turn this thing around and head for Mexico." Even as he said the words, Cole parked next to the de Ville and turned the engine off.

"Let's do it," Alex said.

"Go in, or run for it?"

"Run for it," Alex said, and opened the door.

Mac and Montoya sat at the dinner table. No papers lay on the table, no briefcase, no books or pens. They sat down next to each other, facing Mac. Cole had to remind himself to breathe.

"You lucked out," Mac said. His expression was so grimly at odds with his words that Cole wasn't sure he'd heard right. "Lucked out?" he said.

"You were no-billed."

"No shit?" Alex said. "For real?"

Cole didn't know how tense he'd been until it went away. He slid down in his chair and leaned his head back and closed his eyes. "Thank god," he said. "Thank god."

"And," Mac said to Alex, "you can pick up your car at the auto pound in West Dallas. You got lucky there, too. The burden of proof for forfeiture is significantly lower than for criminal charges. They could have legally gotten away with it."

"Oh man," Alex said. "Thank you."

"What about my guitar?" Cole said.

"No guitar."

"What do you mean, 'no guitar'? That fucking cop stole it. He did it right in front of us, put it in the trunk of the cop car."

"There's no official record of the guitar, so there's nothing we can do about it."

"Have him arrested," Cole said. All of his relief had turned to righteous indignation. "That guitar is one of a kind, irreplaceable. It was a gift from the Montoya family, handmade by Alex's uncle."

"Cole," Mac said, "listen to me. Let it go."

"I'm not going to let it go," Cole said. "I'll get my own lawyer and sue his ass."

Mac stood up. "Let's take a walk."

"Fine," Cole said.

They walked toward the grade school in the suffocating heat. "I had hoped to keep this from you," Mac said. "Since you won't back down, here it is. It was not luck that got you the no-bill."

"What are you saying?"

"The cop who took your guitar is named Ralston. In fact, it was because he took the guitar that I knew I could approach him. A discreet offer was made, which he chose to cut his partner in on. Money changed hands. The evidence bag got misfiled. Their testimony before the grand jury was confused and unconvincing. Am I making myself clear here? The guitar, it turned out, was a non-negotiable item. Compared to hard time in prison, it seemed an easy choice. Even if you don't agree, it's too late now. It's gone too far. Too many people are involved. Do you understand?"

"Does Alex's father know?"

"The specifics? No. But he told me that the two of you—and he was very specific that it had to be both of you—were to be kept out of prison, and I quote, 'at any cost.'"

It was one shock too many. Cole couldn't take it in.

"This is how the world works," Mac said, his voice gentler now. "Where there's enough money, pretty much anything is possible. I know that's not the world you guys had in mind when you were in college. I'm sorry I had to be the one to tell you."

They started back toward the house. "Are you going to tell Alex?" Cole asked.

"No. Are you?"

"I guess not. Not if I can help it. I'm not going to lie, but... I'm not going to volunteer anything either."

"That would be wise," Mac said. "The fewer people that know about this, the safer everyone will be."

THE NEXT NIGHT, Alex took down close to four hundred dollars at the poker game. "Gentlemen," he said, as he raked in his third hundred-dollar-plus pot of the evening, "when you're hot, you're hot."

COLE STARTED BACK to Austin on Saturday morning. Alex had offered to buy him a new guitar from his poker winnings and Cole had refused. "Let it be a lesson to me," he'd said. He felt fifteen years older than Alex.

The no-bill had, if anything, made his craving for heroin stronger. He could already taste the drug on the back of his tongue as he pulled out of Alex's driveway. He couldn't concentrate on the highway and he kept speeding up and slowing down.

He exited in Waxahachie and pulled into a parking lot. He sat there for ten minutes, shaking, then he drove 25 minutes back to

North Dallas, to Alex's father's house. He rang the doorbell and
Alex's mother opened the door. "Cole?" she said. "What's wrong?"
"I need help," Cole said. "Help me. Please."

THE LAST-EVER SHOW of the Armadillo World Headquarters was
scheduled for New Year's Eve, 1980. Commander Cody and the
Lost Planet Airmen would co-headline with Asleep at the Wheel.
It was the end of not just one era, Cole thought, but all eras. John
Lennon had been gunned down on the streets of New York, the
Middle East was at war again, and they were shooting nuns in
El Salvador. The future was Ronald Reagan and high-rise office
buildings, short hair and fraudulent family values. A good night
for the two-step and a bad night to be sober.

Yet sober was what Cole had been for four long months. No
booze, not even beer. No marijuana, no Percodan, and most of all,
no white powders. Montoya had paid for six weeks in Baylor's
rehab unit, and Cole had been determined not to waste his money.
He'd gone through the initial detox, and then made it to all the
group sessions, in spite of the God talk and the devotion to the
12-step doctrine, in spite of the casual dopers who were there for
the attention and the hardcore junkies who were scoring from the
hospital staff. He spent his free time in the hospital gym, which
had the side benefit that it helped him sleep through the endless
lectures and films.

Gradually the periods when he felt close to normal got longer,
from minutes to hours to most of a day. He understood that the
craving for oblivion would never entirely leave him, that his best
defense lay in good habits and eternal vigilance. When he felt
confident that he could handle it, he checked himself out five days
ahead of schedule.

Montoya drove to Austin with him and helped him clean the
apartment of booze and drugs. His presence alone was enough
to keep Cole from holding back a couple of beers or a few pills.
He got rid of his works and the spoon he'd cooked the junk in
and the candle he'd used to heat it, for fear the smell would make
him nostalgic. They opened the windows to air the place out and

cleaned the spoiled food out of the fridge and went to HEB to restock, and then Cole made them Portobello mushroom burgers and baked sweet potato fries for dinner.

"You've done so much for me," Cole said hesitantly, "and I paid you back by turning into a junkie. I feel ashamed."

Montoya spoke even more reluctantly than Cole. "I don't mean this in a critical way, but... it is hard. It's hard for me to understand. God knows we gave Alex everything he wanted. Even if your father didn't have the luck that I had, he kept you well fed and sent you to a good school. Compared to where I came from, it seems like you and Alex both had incredible advantages. But now they look more like liabilities, the way both of you have struggled so hard."

"It does seem crazy. And the happiest I've been, I think, was when I was on the commune, working ridiculous hours and not having much of anything that was really mine."

"I don't think that's crazy," Montoya said. "You can't get something like that again?"

"It didn't... it just wasn't built to last, that's all. But I think I am going to go back to construction work for a while. Being in bars, hanging out with musicians, it would be a constant temptation."

"I think you're going to be okay now."

"You've always believed in me. And look where it's got you."

"Well, tonight it got me a good meal." He smiled. "Even if it didn't have any meat in it."

The next morning Cole put him on a plane to Dallas, and within two days had landed a job on a remodeling crew, steady indoor work through the coming winter.

On weekends he cruised the pawn shops, and near the Army base at Fort Hood he came up with a 20-year-old Martin D-35 in decent shape with a sweet sound and a good price. He found a luthier who rebuilt the bridge and leveled the frets and put on new machines, and Cole bought it a nice hardshell case to ride around in. He named it Palestrina after the line in *Under Milk Wood* where Organ Morgan goes on and on about Bach, "It's Bach every time for me... and then Palestrina." He'd had a running joke with Alex where Palestrina was synonymous with second best, make-do, and consolation prizes. If the guitar's feelings were hurt by the comparisons to the lost Pelirroja, it didn't let on.

By New Year's Eve he'd put on some weight, a fair amount of it muscle. He'd experimented with a Van Dyke beard and a Fu Manchu mustache and in the end had shaved it all off and put his hair in a ponytail. He'd turned 31 the previous Tuesday, and celebrated with vanilla ice cream and chocolate cupcakes from the HEB bakery. That night he intended to bring somebody home with him from the Armadillo and not be terribly fussy.

It turned out that Valentina was doing a solo slot at 11 PM. Cole saw her backstage and thought what the hell. He wandered over and said, "The new records sound great. I mean that sincerely."

She looked him up and down. "Thanks, Cole. You look good. You doing all right?"

"Better now than I have been. How do you like the big time?"

"I love it. I absolutely, totally love it. Hey, you want to sit in with me at the end?"

"If you can find me a guitar."

"I've got a spare."

At 11:55 she finished "Take Me with You" and said, "I'd like to bring up an old friend to help me kick off the new year. He started my band with me, and he's a great singer and guitar player. Jeff Cole!" The audience clapped and yelled and it didn't sound like they were just being polite. Cole was grateful, and yet he wanted so much more. Valentina hugged him and handed him a guitar and together they counted down to midnight. The reception for the New Year was less enthusiastic than the one Cole had gotten, but then the Armadillo was dying as they clapped.

Cole and Valentina led the crowd in "Auld Lang Syne," and then Valentina called for "Cielito lindo" and everybody sang along on the choruses. The crowd brought them back for an encore and Valentina announced Cole's song "Time and Tide." He was amazed she remembered it.

When it was over and they walked backstage together, Cole said, "Thanks. That meant a lot."

"For auld lang syne, Cole. It was good playing with you again. Take care." Then she was borne away by admiring fans.

Asleep at the Wheel came on and when Cole went looking for a dance partner, he found Charlene. He hadn't had any contact with her since his OD. If she was still a bit heavy, her bustier made the most of it. She'd colored her hair a dark brown with red undertones and she was wearing her cowboy hat and boots and skin-tight jeans. "How you doing, Charlene?"

She shrugged. "I'm here. You want to dance?"

They two-stepped to "Miles and Miles of Texas," a Bob Wills chestnut, and Cole remembered that they'd danced to Asleep at the Wheel the night they'd met. She was wearing the same perfume, and though he knew it was a dangerous and unhealthy idea, Cole couldn't get away from images in his head of the two of them naked together.

The song ended and Charlene said, "Buy a girl a drink?"

They walked to the bar together and Cole bought her a Lone Star. "You look different," she said. "I guess I never seen you without the beard before."

"I've been clean now for four months," Cole said.

"It won't last."

He felt like she'd backhanded him. "Well. I hope you're wrong."

"You can change your hair and drop all your old friends, but you're still the same person you was. You got the same demons you always had, and they ain't going to let go that easy."

"Thanks for the dance, Charlene. Happy New Year."

She raised her paper cup in salute. "Good luck, Cole. Good luck to us all."

Commander Cody hit the stage at 2:30. A few songs in, Cole caught a dance with a petite blonde with a big, happy smile. She clearly knew how to two-step, though she was somewhat the worse for alcohol and unsteady when she came off the fast spins. After the dance she threw her arms around his neck and gave him a smacking kiss on the mouth. "You're a great dancer," she said.

"Thanks," Cole said. He gave her a squeeze and let her go. Six months ago he wouldn't have hesitated to take her home. Now he saw that the counselors at Baylor were right. If he lay down with drunks and junkies he would get up using again. He'd hoped

1980

it wasn't going to be that hard. Where was he supposed to meet women, church socials?

As the sun came up on 1981, he was sitting outdoors with Jim Franklin in the Armadillo Beer Garden. Somebody from the kitchen had brought them nachos, saying, "We got to use this stuff up somehow."

Cole's sweat had dried in the damp morning chill and Franklin looked exhausted, as if the ten-year struggle to keep the place open had caught up with him all at once. Through the gaps in the wooden fence, they watched the last of the crowd stagger out to their cars.

"What now?" Cole said.

1984

From the day he was born—Bastille Day, 1982—Ethan had been dark mystery to Ava's golden splendor, shy where she was fearless, inward-facing where Ava always looked to others. Ethan's happiness was undeniable, and also private; his smile was keyed to some inner secret thought.

He was the result of an extended thaw during which Paul had spent more time at home, had helped Madelyn in the brutal cramming for her oral exams, and had renewed his campaign for "a child of our own." Unfortunately his attentiveness barely outlasted the pregnancy; Ethan's neediness drove him back into a colder country even as it melted Madelyn's heart. Ava, eight years older, was captivated by him too, and fiercely protective. She took charge of his stroller from the first and was ever alert for dogs, threatening weather, and strange persons.

Ethan gave Madelyn an excuse to stop torturing herself over not having begun her dissertation, and because of Ethan she had time to read for pleasure again. As long as she was willing to be constantly called away, reading was the only activity that let her feel her boundaries as an individual human being. Ava still loved libraries and loved to show Ethan around; she was especially fond of the Gelman, and she was on Christmas break from the third grade that January day when Madelyn had agreed that they could all go there together.

The afternoon was dry, cold, and blustery, and Madelyn had heard the wind pop the banner above the table near the library, but she hadn't looked at it until Ava said, "Isn't that what Daddy does?"

The banner read INTERNATIONAL MONETARY FRAUD— LEASH THE IMF! Madelyn was more amazed than anything else; she had gotten used to having to explain what the IMF was, and had never imagined that they might be anyone's anathema. She stopped at the table to peek at their handouts and got drawn into conversation with a young woman whose multicolored dreadlocks poked out at odd angles from the hood of her parka.

Twenty minutes later, armed with scrawled notes on the back of a flyer, she dropped the kids off at the encyclopedias and hit the *Reader's Guide to Periodical Literature*.

Over dinner, ignoring the ice cube of fear in her stomach, she said, "They were protesting against the IMF on campus today."

"Seriously? Do they not have anything better to complain about?"

"I'm not sure they do," Madelyn said. "One of the things they were upset about was the 'Chicago Boys' and Pinochet and the IMF in Chile."

Paul was quiet for a long time. "Not our finest hour, I admit."

"I'm not trying to pick a fight here. I'm just saying, this is giving me some real anxiety about what you do every day. And to say Pinochet was 'not your finest hour' is a bit of an understatement."

"He was not a nice guy. But he was a pro-US guy, backed by a popular uprising against a Communist government—"

"Paul. Pinochet was put in power by a CIA-sponsored coup. Allende, whom he replaced, was a socialist, not a Communist, and was enormously popular. If Pinochet had been popular he wouldn't have had to fill all those stadiums with political prisoners and terrorize the people who were left on the streets. The 'Chicago Boys' were former students of your man Friedman, and they systematically looted Chile's economy, so the IMF could step in and dictate terms favorable to the US."

Paul put his silverware down and looked at his lemongrass chicken.

"This is not you," Madelyn said softly. "You're the guy who went up against Reagan at Berkeley. You're the guy who believes in the underdog, who spoke up for Trotsky on the day we met. You tell me all the time you're still that same guy. So help me understand how you can be that guy and support Pinochet too."

"The... the IMF... it's not the same. It's not the same organization that it used to be."

He looked up, and Madelyn nodded sympathetically, afraid that if she said anything at all it might block the words he'd been holding back for so long. In her peripheral vision she saw Ava start to squirm and play with her food, so she slipped an arm around her to calm her.

"At first…" Paul said, "it did what it was supposed to do. It helped poor countries through a crop failure or a trade imbalance. Then Nixon…"

"'Then that bastard Nixon,'" she urged.

"Well. This one was probably not Nixon's fault. Which is why this is all so incredibly complicated. Nixon singlehandedly took the US off the gold standard in 1971. Which he had to do because the postwar boom was over and our balance of payments had gone into the toilet. So it ended up that a lot of things we… the IMF… used to do, like keep exchange rates stable and consult on monetary policy, that all went out the window. All that was left was lending money and setting conditions for the payback. And the conditions… sometimes the conditions were…"

"Invasive?"

"That might be a little strong."

"Forcing Britain to cut social programs and get rid of all their import controls? Forcing austerity programs on Mexico and dictating where they can go to buy food and machinery? There was a long list."

"Okay. Okay. I have problems with that. But look at Africa, all those countries that fought their way to independence in the sixties and ended up broke. We rescued pretty much every one of them. Kenya, Uganda, Chad, Swaziland, you name it, literally dozens of countries."

She forced herself to keep her voice gentle. "And where did most of that money end up? In the pockets of crazy murdering dictators like Idi Amin? Buying guns and cattle prods for the death squads in Argentina?"

"What am I supposed to do?" Paul said. He was clearly in distress. "Give up? Go to work for some NGO that's smuggling a few bags of rice across the border into El Salvador? Give up this house, the nanny for the kids, our trips to Europe, so we can live like college students again in some ratty apartment? And still not change anything?"

Madelyn was barely paying her own way through school with

scholarships and grants and teaching assistantships. Without the money that Paul brought in, she would have to give up her dream too and go back to work. How much of this was her own fault, her own willingness to look the other way for so long?

Ethan, emotional barometer, began to whimper. Madelyn took him on her lap and hugged him. "I don't know what to do," she said.

Paul pushed himself away from the table, his dinner only half eaten. "Yeah," he said. "Me either."

She listened to his heavy footsteps climb the stairs. "Mommy's sorry," she whispered to Ethan. "Mommy is very, very sorry."

THOUGH MADELYN had skipped her morning coffee out of respect for her nerves, the sacrifice was in vain; she was literally shaking in her waterproof boots by the time she'd crossed the February slush to the new English Department offices in Rome Hall. She was, according to the neatly typed chart on Dr. Willcott's door, his first meeting of the day. A legend at the bottom read, "If you believe this document to be in error, you have incorrectly noted your appointment. Please adjust your schedule accordingly."

She set her watch to the wall clock and waited until precisely nine before knocking. Willcott's high, asthmatic voice said, "Come in, Ms. Brooks."

Willcott was believed to be in his early 70s, though some argued that his origins were more likely prelapsarian. He was a man of enormous girth whose fringes of white hair surrounded a pale, veined pate, and joined at the ears to a white prophet's beard. His office was furnished with a Persian carpet, a floor lamp, and custom oak bookcases from a William Morris design, one of which was filled to capacity with a single copy of each of his publications. He also had an industrial coffeemaker filled with French Market chicory coffee that came oily and purple from the tap.

Madelyn spent two careful minutes asking after the Hawthorne seminar that was the only class he still taught, the health of the two large Bassett hounds that were his only companions, and his plans for what he would be planting in the spring in his raised garden beds. The length of time that Willcott spent on pleasantries was a measure of his respect for his favorite students, whose number was about to decrease to the tune of one.

When the allotted time was up, Willcott said, "This is about your dissertation, you said?"

"Yes, sir. As you know, I've had some trouble making my deadline."

With the faintest of sarcasm he said, "It'll barely be three years overdue in May."

"Yes, sir. I think I finally understand why it's been so hard for me to finish."

"Indeed? In previous discussions you seemed reasonably sure your pregnancy was to blame, followed by the demands of caring for your son. Who would now be two, if memory serves. How is Ethan, by the way?"

"He's very well, sir, thank you. The thing is, I think one of the reasons I got pregnant was to avoid writing the dissertation."

His silence let her know that she was the last person in the room to have arrived at that conclusion.

"And the reason for that," she said, "is…" She had begun to perspire, and the heavy sweater she'd worn under her coat was suddenly suffocating her; she tried not to show her panic as she struggled to get out of it.

"Your usual self-possession," Willcott said, "eludes you this morning. What precisely is this newly discovered flaw in the dissertation?"

She couldn't think of another way to say it. "I don't like it," she said. "I'm not excited by it. I don't want to write about it anymore."

The topic was *The Convergence of Centrifugal Themes in Moby-Dick*, and Willcott had essentially bullied her into agreeing to it. Among other issues, including the fact that it was not her idea, was its reliance on an unpopular interpretation of the word "stricken" in the final chapter to mean that Moby-Dick was fatally wounded, one that Willcott had held for his entire career and which was believed to have kept him from a leadership role in the Melville Society.

"I see," Willcott said. "And might I inquire as to whether you have come up with another topic sufficiently stimulating that you might bring yourself to write about it?"

"I just want to be clear," Madelyn said, a drop of sweat stinging one eye, "that it's not a problem with the topic itself, it's that it's not suited to me personally." Oh Lord, she thought, I sound like I'm breaking up with him. It's not you, it's me. "I thought I could write it because of the intellectual challenge, but I need... I need emotional involvement too."

"To wit...?"

She took a deep breath. "*They Must Here Remain Stationary Until Utterly Extinct: Anti-Colonialism and the Other in Melville.*"

"Colonialism?" Willcott packed a lifetime of disdain into the single word. "The Other? Please tell me you haven't joined the brain-dead followers of Lacan and Derrida. Tell me you're not contemplating a fashionable dissertation full of meaningless 'theory' and 'texts' and obscurantist jargon and hectoring wordplay."

"No, sir, not at all. But the issues that Melville deals with in 'Benito Cereno' and *Omoo* and *Typee* are more relevant than ever now. White men are still enslaving developing countries, only now they're doing it with loans—"

"Please spare me the lecture, Ms. Brooks. I am well aware of the evils of the white race. Can I remind you that we no longer live in the nineteen-sixties, thank God? Nor is it a requirement of this department that your dissertation be 'relevant,' nor that it have some specific percentage of political content. In fact, I am strongly opposed to politicizing literature, and if you insist on this new topic, I'm not sure that I would be willing to direct such an effort."

"I expected that, sir, and—" Her voice was fading and she forced herself to speak up. "—and so I broached the subject, hypothetically, with Dr. Rosenberg. He said that if... if it came to that, he would direct it."

She'd anticipated anger or cold dismissal. What she had not expected was the look of hurt in Willcott's eyes. "I see," he said.

"Only if that's okay with you, sir," she said in a guilty rush, wondering what she'd say if he refused to let her go.

"No," he said. "I'm sure it's for the best." She had a vision of

Willcott's loneliness, his New Criticism credentials grown old, his students dwindling away, his place at the cultural table seized by wild-haired anarchists at war with meaning itself. "I believe our business is done. You can send me any required paperwork and I'll sign it."

"Sir, I—"

"Good day, Ms. Brooks."

Sleet was now falling, and in her anxiety she'd forgotten her umbrella. She made her way up to Pennsylvania Avenue and tried to find a cab, the ice clotting in her hair.

She'd gotten what she asked for, she thought. But there was always a price.

COLE JOGGED ALONG the embankment above the Mississippi, the Café du Monde and Jackson Square to his right, an oil barge chugging downstream on his left, the vast gray-brown river smelling of mud and diesel in the hot April afternoon. He was a mile into his run and completely soaked in sweat. Sultry, they called it here in New Orleans, what in Austin they would call so humid you might as well try and breathe underwater.

It was Saturday, meaning the Old Absinthe House would be mobbed. A slow night was its own kind of challenge, trying to convince the crowd to shut up and listen. A packed night, feeding on its own energy and consuming everything in sight, drained him emotionally and physically both. The tourists were all over the Quarter like powdered sugar on a beignet, crisscrossed in camera straps, men wearing Bermuda shorts and KISS ME I'M CAJUN T-shirts with the creases still in them, women in floppy straw hats and giant sunglasses, college girls in halter tops and cutoffs. Cole slowed and sprinted and weaved his way through them, trying to bear in mind that some tiny percentage of their dollars eventually wound up in his pocket.

He'd moved to New Orleans the week after he passed the audition for the Old Absinthe House band, a year and three months ago. He hadn't been in Louisiana since his parents left Lafayette when he was three, and he might have kept it that way had the phone not rung one Saturday night as he was headed out to Antone's in hopes of a slow dance or two. The voice on the other end said, "Oye, vato, it's me, Gordo," and Cole became unmoored in time and space.

"Gordo?"

"Sí, hombre, maybe you remember me from Woodstock? Not the movie, though, I didn't get to be in that because my lead guitar player was too fucking ugly."

"Gordo! ¿Qué carajo? Where are you?"

They spent half an hour catching up. Gordo had stayed in San Francisco for a couple of years after the Quirq implosion, watching the whole scene follow the band into collapse, before going home to New Orleans. There he'd worked his way up through the clubs, playing whatever came to hand—disco, zydeco, blues, jazz—and getting a reputation for reliability. "Not the easiest thing for me, but I was all like Scarlett O'Hara, did not ever want to be hungry again." For the last six months he'd been at the Old Absinthe House, one of the top clubs in the Quarter.

Gordo had a lot of questions. Was Cole still playing? Was he in a band? How were his chops? "I'm getting the feeling," Cole said, "that this was not a completely casual phone call."

"Our lead singer and our lead guitarist decided to start their own band and left us flat. I told the manager I could bring in a guy who did double duty, save him some bread. Can you fly out tomorrow, on us? Bring your guitar."

The gig was strictly electric Chicago-style blues, so Cole auditioned on a Les Paul he'd turned up on one of his pawn shop runs. He'd put on new Grover machines to keep it in tune, and had otherwise not fooled with its sweet tone or tiger-striped finish.

The band was a six-piece, counting Cole. Hammond B-3, tenor sax, and drums, all black guys, Gordo on Fender Jazz Bass, and one of three or four different white guys from Tulane or Loyola on trumpet—Gordo said they never knew from one night to the next which one would show up. The players all had ferocious chops. Duncan, the sax man, was light-skinned with a dusting of freckles on his cheeks, tall and big-chested, with short processed hair. He'd learned circular breathing in the Fourth Army Band, taking air in through his nose and blowing it out through the horn at the same time, so once per set he would walk through the audience, holding a single note for three or four minutes and collecting astonished applause. The drummer, Henri, pronounced Cajun style, had purplish black skin and a short natural. He could play a melodic solo with his left hand and right foot while the right hand maintained a perfect shuffle on the ride cymbal and the hi-hat knocked down the two and four. Zeke, goateed, with his head shaved clean, played organ like Booker T., Jimmy Smith, and J. S. Bach put together.

They fucked with Cole at the audition, throwing in key changes or clean breaks without warning, all of which he handled with good humor, and when they were done, Zeke looked at the manager and said, "Hire this honky motherfucker. He's pretty, and we can always teach him to play and sing."

"Well," the manager said, "I guess you're in."

Cole had boarded the plane believing that, if they made him an offer, he would have to think on it. He'd risen to foreman at the remodeling company, making good money for less work, and had been looking around for a house with enough land to grow some vegetables, hoping to ease the rootless feeling he couldn't seem to shake.

Playing "Wang Dang Doodle" and "Smokestack Lightning" and "Get Out of My Life, Woman" again changed his mind. He'd just needed a few years to break the bad associations in his head. Fronting a great band felt like nothing else in the world, part conversation, part choreographed dance, part team sport, part armed combat. It was where he belonged.

He ran across the foot of Canal Street, where the low nineteenth-century sprawl of the French Quarter transformed itself, as if by some evil sorcery, into the skyscrapers, banks, and chain hotels of the Central Business District. Up Poydras to Loyola and then back into the Quarter, around the St. Louis Cemetery where Marie Laveau was interred, her tomb marked with Xs and littered with dimes left by those seeking favors. Then up Rampart Street, the western boundary of the Quarter, where the trees and the charm had long since dried up, then down to the river once more and up

Toulouse Street and through the wrought iron gate into one of the hidden courtyards that had fascinated Cole on his first days in the city, red and purple geraniums in hanging baskets, bougainvillea climbing the pink stucco walls, white lilies growing in the fountain in the middle of the rough concrete floor. He ran up the stairs to the second-floor balcony and unlocked the deadbolt on the eight-foot-high antique wooden doors of his apartment.

Tina sat on the couch with Jezebel, one of her stripper friends. Tina had her arms around her and Jezzie was crying. Tina, who had never stripped, had somehow ended up den mother to a gaggle of abused women, who sometimes slept two at a time on their foldout sofa. Her orphans, she called them. Cole didn't mind having beautiful women hanging around the place, especially these, who were careless about their personal modesty. They were New Orleans in a nutshell—sexy, permissive, risky, going nowhere. Tina, who'd had her own substance problems, was a stickler about not permitting booze or drugs in the apartment, and on the rare occasions when one of the girls fucked up, she didn't hesitate to flush the problem down the commode. As for Cole, Tina had told him that as long as he kept his hands to himself, he was free to look all he wanted. The truth was he preferred Tina's factory accoutrements—tall, rangy body, honey-blonde hair, wide hips and champagne-glass breasts—to the aftermarket parts on her friends.

He'd met Tina at the 544 Club where she tended bar. Their R&B band was widely considered the hottest in the Quarter, and when Cole and Zeke had a free night they liked to drop in. The first time Cole ordered a club soda from her, she sized him up and said, "How long you been sober, sugar?"

He had to stop and think. "Three years and change. You?"

"Five years, three months, two days."

"Not that you're counting."

"Who, me?"

He looked again, saw that she was older than he'd first taken her for, mid-thirties at least, and saw that a light went on in her crinkly eyes when the ends of her mouth went up. Though he was not ordinarily one for Southern accents, he wanted to hear hers again.

"Hell of a place to be sober in," Cole said.

"I don't know." She put her forearms on the bar and leaned forward so she didn't have to shout. "Being surrounded by all these negative examples does the trick for me."

A few nights later she came to check him out at the Absinthe House and hung around till closing. When she came home with him that night he assumed she was easy. In fact she had come to stay, and she slipped into his life without either of them missing a beat.

They didn't have a lot in common, though she was a college dropout and had a troubled relationship with her parents, same as Cole. She was the oldest of five kids and still thought she might want some of her own one day, though she knew time was running out. She had wanted to be a brain surgeon when she was little and had somehow lost her way on that one too. Her family had been dirt poor outside Knoxville, Tennessee, where her father was a long-haul trucker and her mother was a part-time waitress. The first order of business when Daddy got back from a trip was to administer the spankings that her mother had been saving up, and it didn't take Sigmund Freud to work out how much they'd looked forward to his coming home.

She liked CNN over Cole's MTV, funk and blues over Cole's current fascination with Duran Duran and Thomas Dolby, Coca-Cola over Cole's fruit juice and soda water. She was into actions more than words and they had never said "I love you" to each other. She was more concerned with walking the walk of daily kindness than putting a name on what they had. It was that day-to-day comfort, the mutual respect and the lack of fights, that had set the hook in Cole.

"Troubles with Jake again?" Cole asked Jezzie. She was 19, with the kind of delicate beauty that wouldn't last long in the Quarter, especially with the company she kept. Dark brown skin, broad African nose, innocent eyes, massive silicone breasts on a petite frame.

Jezzie nodded and sobbed, and Tina said, "He was passed out with a hooker in their bed. Again."

"Same hooker?" Cole asked.

"They all look the same to me," Jezzie said.

The idea of AIDS made Cole very nervous, and he'd been using condoms until Tina came along, and they both got tested, and agreed to keep it one-on-one. He was amazed by the way that people like Jezzie had unprotected sex and shared needles, and it made him think about what Charlene had said about junkies and death wishes.

Tina said, "How was your run, sugar?"

"Soooltry," he said, and her eyes crinkled up.

He took a shower and they cooked a couple of pans of cinnamon rolls from the freezer and squeezed some fresh orange juice. While they ate he felt Tina's foot rub up and down his leg, and after washing the dishes they left Jezzie to watch TV and retired to the bedroom. As a lover, Tina was more languorous than madly passionate. Cole was fine with that, and the sex was plentiful and satisfying all around.

Dinner was lentils, brown rice, salad with fresh avocado. At 7:30 Cole took his Les Paul out of the locked, reinforced metal cabinet, kissed Tina goodbye, got a hug from Jezzie, and walked to the club.

He was just in time to see a cat fight in the street outside. Two trannies, bare to the waist to show off their breasts, had thrown their wigs onto the sidewalk like football players discarding their helmets and gone after each other with fists and fingernails, screaming insults. Drunken tourists stopped in the middle of Bourbon Street to cheer them on, and two uniformed cops watched from the sidelines, talking back and forth as if trying to pick a winner. The owner of the strip club where they worked stood in the doorway, arms folded, and Cole imagined he was weighing the benefits of the free publicity against the possible damage to his assets.

Cole still struggled with the paradox of the city's genuine warmth and its harsh cynicism. In some ways the Quarter was a parody of the anarchist paradise the counterculture used to talk about, openly libidinous, a proud mixture of races and genders and sexual preferences where altered consciousness was the norm, except perverted into a carnal Disneyland where everything had a price and little was what it seemed, all of it only a few hundred yards from the grinding poverty of the Ninth Ward.

Cole was part of the fraud, a white suburban kid masquerading as a blues man, costumed in Hawaiian shirt and Ray-Bans, shoe-horning the authentic music of despair into perfectly calibrated 45-minute sets. Yet Cole owned a piece of the paradox, putting his heart into every note he played, as did every other man in the group, night after night.

Like a lot of clubs in the Quarter, the Old Absinthe House was open 24 hours a day, so everything that happened, from mopping the floors to restocking the bar to rehearsing the band, happened in front of an audience. Zeke was already there, working up a couple of new arrangements with Duncan and tinkering with the set list. By the time Cole tuned up, Gordo had arrived and they played through the new songs. Henri never needed to rehearse and the trumpet player would be working off a chart anyway.

At nine sharp they changed gears from rehearsal mode to performance and the soulful clockwork took over, the precisely delimited spaces for improvisation, Zeke's piercing whistle when somebody threw down a good solo, the crosstalk and shouts of encouragement. The manager had ruled out cumbia footwork as "culturally inappropriate," but Cole and Gordo still exchanged the occasional «¡échale!» and «¡sabrosón!».

Halfway through the second set, Cole saw Alex in the audience.

He raised his guitar neck in greeting, and Alex waved. At the break, Cole squeezed into a chair next to him. There wasn't room to stand up for a hug. Cole gripped Alex's elbow with one hand and they grinned at each other. A couple of months had gone by since they'd last talked on the phone, and something was clearly up because Alex's hair was long again, curling past his collar in back.

Over the noise of the crowd, Cole pieced the story together. Alex had split from Callie—details to follow—and was work-ing as a programmer for the company that provided his father's computers.

"It's like playing music," Alex said. "It's all rhythm and logic and progressions. It turns out I'm good at it."

Cole explained that the couch was taken, but they had an air mattress if he was game. He set Alex up with a couple of free beers and went back to work.

During the next break, before the final set, he asked Alex if he wanted to come up and jam. "Those guys would eat my lunch," Alex said. "I think all of that really is over for me. I sold all my gear except the acoustic that Jesús made. Most of my records, too. The divorce cleaned me out. It's okay, though, I needed to lighten up, you know?"

Perversely, Alex's apparent satisfaction with his own life left Cole melancholy. Had he been nursing some idea that he and Alex would be in a band again? He also hated that Alex's endless push-pull with his father was in the push stage again, for both their sakes.

At 1:30 AM they walked to Cole's apartment. The streets were still mobbed, the tourists staggering drunk, the hookers physically aggressive, an undertone of vomit beginning to color the predominant odors of booze and cigarettes and cheap perfume.

"How can you live in a place like this?" Alex asked.

"I find it very calming," Cole said, trying not to shout and damage his voice after a long night of singing. "All the chaos is on the outside. Tell me about Callie."

Other than the expense, the divorce was straightforward. Custody was the problem. Because of the bust, any tales of drug abuse that Callie told would carry weight. And if a private detective started poking around and noticed his car rentals, all hell could ensue. A substantial amount of money was required for Alex to get the occasional weekend with Gwyn, most of which came, to Alex's great discomfort, from his father.

They'd arrived at Cole's apartment. He unlocked the door to the sight of Jezzie on the unfolded bed watching TV, her flimsy cotton bathrobe wide open. "Oh," she said, making a slow and half-hearted effort to cover herself. "Sorry. I got overheated in the shower."

"Alex, meet Jezzie," Cole said.

By the time Tina got home, Cole had put together some red beans and rice, and the four of them sat around the table for supper. If the number of times that Jezzie's robe slipped was any indication, she was quite taken with Alex, and there was no way that Alex, being straight, male, and human, was going to resist, so when Cole had an opportunity, he took Alex aside and told him there were condoms in the drawer of the table by the couch and strongly suggested he use them. "No issues that we know about, but she is at a lot of risk, entiendes?"

"Jesus, she's beautiful."

"She's also got a sometime biker boyfriend and she's not exactly emotionally stable. But yeah."

Cole woke out of a deep sleep to pounding on the front door. It was 4:49 AM. "Jezzie!" a drunken voice bellowed. "Jezzie, I know you're in there!"

"Jake," Cole said. Jake was six-two, 300 pounds, and had shown himself on previous occasions to be largely impervious to pain.

"I'll handle it," Tina said. She put on a robe and went into the living room. Cole slipped on his boxers and followed.

"Jake," Tina said in a firm, quiet voice to the door. "If you don't quiet down, the neighbors will call the cops. If you get arrested again, they'll send you to Angola. You don't want that."

"Then let me in!"

Jezzie sat up in bed, naked. "Jake?" she whispered.

Cole perched on the edge of the thin mattress. "Shhh. Give him a minute, he'll go away."

Alex, on the other side of the foldout, was sitting up now too, his eyes wide in the darkness.

"I should go to him," Jezzie said.

"He's drunk," Cole said. "Give him a while to sober up."

"Jezzie!" Jake yelled.

"He loves me," Jezzie said, trying to climb out of bed, managing to bump her breasts into Cole's arm and thigh repeatedly. "I should be with him."

Cole gently held her down by the shoulders. "Wait till tonight. Let him cool down a little."

Jake began to cry. "Jezzie…"

"Aww," Jezzie said.

"Go home, Jake," Tina said, and a minute later Cole heard stumbling footsteps on the stairs.

Now Jezzie was crying. "Hey," Alex said, reaching to comfort her, "it's okay."

Tina and Cole exchanged a look and retreated to the bedroom. "They're like little kids," Cole said. "Jake and Jezzie and all your other lost souls. Little kids with adult hormones."

"When anything goes," Tina said, "where's your incentive to grow up?"

Cole sighed. Between fear of Jake and the skin contact with Jezzie, he was full of hormones of his own.

"What's wrong, sugar? Can't get back to sleep?" Her hand moved down his chest to his belly. "Aha. I believe I found the problem."

POLITICS WAS SOMETHING Steve Cole had always considered a spectator sport. He voted and he kept up with the news, but when they called up and wanted money for campaigns, even when it was Nixon going up against Kennedy in '60 or up against Humphrey in '68, he always left that to the people with loose cash lying around.

Reagan was different. Reagan made him feel something he hadn't felt since the 1950s, made him feel like the normal people were back in charge, that America was going to be okay again.

From the end of the sixties all through the seventies, he could see now, he'd been afraid and it had made him angry. It had seemed like a bunch of spoiled kids were going to pull down the whole temple and take everybody else with them, just like Samson in the Bible, wreck everything that Western Civilization had built up over the centuries.

He remembered seeing the news about that Woodstock festival, all those kids half-naked and covered in mud, and thinking, is this what the future holds? We didn't have to be bombed back to the Stone Age by the Russians, our own kids did it without firing a shot. Then Betty blurted out, "Jeff was there," obviously regretting it the minute the words were out.

"Figures," Steve said, and that was that, except that it opened all the old wounds again, Betty silently blaming him for running the kid off, Steve silently pissed off that Betty had her clandestine contact with him that he was not allowed a part of.

Then Reagan had come along and proved that the temple was not, in fact, in ruins. He won the war in Granada, and for the first time in history, a country that had gone over to Communism came back to freedom. He'd shown that the so-called Energy Crisis was just hysteria. He'd taken the handcuffs off the oil business and was on the verge of getting the economy back on its feet. It was funny how the kid had dressed up like a cowboy when he was little, and those hippies had worn cowboy outfits too, and yet it turned out to be Reagan who was the real cowboy hero, cleaning up the town like he used to do on TV.

Steve had retired when he turned 65 in June. There had been speeches and a plaque and gag gifts like a green eyeshade and nice gifts like a fifth of Canadian Club, and when it was all over he'd ended up at home all day sitting in front of the TV, without the heart to even go out to the wood shop. Betty had the idea for him to get involved with the Reagan re-election campaign and now here it was, 7:30 on a warm September Wednesday evening, and instead of thinking about going to bed, he was sitting down at the desk in the office Betty had finally let him make out of the kid's old bedroom. He got the list out of the drawer and dialed the first number that hadn't been checked off.

"Ben?" he said, when a man's voice answered. "This is Steve Cole down the street. Can you spare me a couple of minutes?"

The best part of it was when he made real contact, and it happened at least once every night, talking about people's hopes and fears.

If he had one wish, it was that things with Betty could be the way they were before his heart attack. They were of an age where even if the kid hadn't run away, even if he'd finished college and gotten a decent job, he would have his own family by now and they wouldn't see him that much anyway. Instead it was like the kid had died, and they were both carrying around that load of guilt and blame. Deep down, at the very foundation of the marriage, it had never gone away.

"Well, Ben," he said, "I'd like to talk to you about how it's morning again in America."

JOE STAYED UP to watch all the returns, long after Peggy had gone to bed, long after Reagan had made his victory speech from Los Angeles, long after it was obvious that Joe had not only lost his seat in the state House, but lost it by a considerable margin. The polls had been going against him after a particularly nasty campaign by his opponent, who implied he'd tried to desert in Vietnam, claimed he had an illegitimate black child with a welfare mother in Jackson, and worst of all for Mississippi voters, called him a communist.

He had lunch the next day with Judge Winter at Johnnie's Drive In, where they sat in the Elvis booth. Though Joe tried to stick to small talk at first, the election wouldn't let him alone.

"They were gunning for you, no question," Winter said. "They spent a ridiculous amount of money for a state election."

"Can I come back from this?"

"Well, Lincoln lost his first election, as I'm sure you remember. Losing a second election is harder. It tends to read as more of a vote of no confidence. It would take a hell of a lot of money to overcome, and money is not exactly piled up for the taking these days. But we can try, and I'd be behind you a hundred percent."

"It was hard, the smear campaign, the lies. Especially on Peggy. I didn't tell you—she's pregnant again."

"Congratulations. And no, that part would not get any better."

"What I'm hearing from you is that you think I should quit."

"No, it's me hearing you say you're ready to quit, and I don't blame you."

"Is this how democracy works? Is this truly the best way we can find to govern ourselves?"

"The problem is that the kind of man who can stand up to these tactics and give as good as he gets is probably the kind of man you wouldn't want in public office anyway. You're a damn good lawyer, you got a happy marriage, what in hell do you need this aggravation for?"

Joe flushed with embarrassment and could hardly get the words out. "I want... I want to make a better world."

"That's like saying you became an auto mechanic because you want to drive a limousine. You want a better world, take up preaching. Or stick to lawyering."

They finished their dough burgers and drank off the last of their iced tea. Suddenly Winter leaned forward. "If it's any consolation, they were afraid of you. That's why they put everything they had up against you. They thought you might be headed for a national career and they decided it would be cheaper to step on you now than when you were running for Senate. Or Governor."

Joe's throat felt like that last bite of hamburger hadn't gone down all the way. He nodded and swallowed hard. "I'll try to remember that," he said.

As far as Madelyn could tell, Paul had failed to consider the potential consequences of her finishing her dissertation. Not without reason, she had to admit, given how she had lost her way on her first attempt. Still, as autumn turned to winter and the typewritten pages began to accumulate, and as Dr. Rosenberg enthused about the first completed chapters, she understood that she would be on the job market in less than a year, interview at MLA next Christmas, defend in the spring of '86, and start her first teaching job that August. Now that it was happening, it was happening too fast.

She hated to bring up a potentially explosive subject at the dinner table, but it was the only time they saw each other when they were both awake. She waited until the dishes were stacked in the sink and the coffee was poured and Ava had taken Ethan in to watch their nightly Disney video.

"What's this about?" Paul asked. "I've got a lot of work tonight."

He had a lot of work every night. "You do understand that the odds of my getting a teaching job anywhere that is even vaguely in commuting distance are effectively zero?"

"You can't just teach a class here and there at GW? That wouldn't satisfy you?"

"That's not the way it works. You're either faculty or you're not. Surely you know that. And nobody hires their own graduates."

"What are you saying?"

"I'm saying that in two years I might be on the other side of the country."

"And that's more important to you than our marriage?"

Yes, she thought. What she said was, "We need to think about a way to make it work."

"What about the kids?"

The conversation had become an iceberg, nine-tenths submerged, and Madelyn did not point out that Paul only saw the kids for an hour a day anyway. "I would want them with me, of course."

"No way. Not acceptable. I love our kids."

That much, Madelyn had to admit, was true. And if he had any preference for Ethan, fruit of his own loins, he didn't let Ava or Madelyn know.

"Well," Madelyn said, "I guess time will tell."

1990

D AVE WAS PICKING UP a few things at Zabar's when he saw her by the cheese cooler. He wasn't sure it was her at first— this woman was a little on the zaftig side and her hair was short, dark brown, and lightly threaded with gray—but when she turned her head enough for him to get a three-quarter view there was no doubt about it, and he dropped his shopping basket and headed for the door.

He'd been back in New York for five years. Given the kind of city it was, and the circles they ran in, he was only surprised it hadn't happened sooner.

He'd been making a good living in San Francisco, working with Van Morrison, Huey Lewis, Greg Kihn, Boz Scaggs, plenty of others too. Even Jake was back in the limelight with a retro-sounding kid named Chris Isaak. Still he couldn't escape the fact that the city had passed its prime in the mid-seventies. The only thing keeping him there was inertia. He'd decided to spend a couple of weeks in Manhattan to see how it felt, and the minute he landed at La Guardia he started to kick himself for waiting so long to come home.

Outside Zabar's it was January, verkakte weather, sleet and rain and no taxis. He unfurled his big golf umbrella and started up Broadway toward 81st, thinking about his feet and nothing else, how cold and wet they were going to be by the time he got to his apartment on West End.

"Dave!" He recognized Sallie's voice behind him, squelching his last hope of getting away unseen. He stopped, took a breath, and turned around.

She hesitated five feet from him, the freezing rain matting her hair and splashing her big, red-framed glasses. Apparently she had not thought far enough ahead to have a conversational opening ready.

"For God's sake," Dave said. "It's a big umbrella, at least get out of the rain."

She stood next to him, close enough to touch, yet not touching.

A number of sarcastic remarks came to mind, but the truth was that after all these years it felt like luck to stand this close to her again. He was in no hurry for it to end. She didn't have to know that he was such a schmuck that he was still in love with her. He completely lost track of time standing there, waiting for her to say what she had to say, until it became so clearly absurd that they both started laughing at the same time.

"Come on," Sallie said, taking his arm with both hands, "let me buy you a coffee. It's the least I can do."

"The very least," Dave said, and they both laughed again, as if that was all there was to it, as if it could be that easy.

The waitress at Zabar's Café brought her some napkins to dry her hair. When she was done she leaned back in her chair and stared at him. "You don't know how many times I've tried to imagine this."

He couldn't stop himself. "So you could tell me how I kept you from being yourself all those years?"

He'd never seen anyone turn so red. "Oh, Dave, I am so, so sorry. That interview... I have to take the blame, and I do. But I was also set up. The PR flacks at the label coached me and coached me on what I was supposed to say, and they kept telling me how huge the record was going to be. I went through with the interview, and the next day I told my manager to call *Billboard* and have them kill it, that it was all bullshit, and he promised me he would. Only he didn't, because he thought he knew better, just like Bones talked me into arrangements I didn't want because he knew better, and the record came out and it was even more huge than anyone imagined, and so I believed maybe they were right, and they did all know better. But in my heart I knew the whole thing was fake, this big statement of liberation where men were still calling the shots. I felt like I was this stunt double impersonating Sallie Rachel Krupheimer for the next two years and five hundred and twenty-seven shows, and meanwhile the follow-up stiffed because we'd put all the good songs on the first record, and the well had gone dry. And I'd burned all my bridges." She stopped and pulled a face. "And there was no water to put out the fires on the bridges because of that well being dry and all."

"But it wasn't fake," Dave said. "Those were your words and your songs, and the timing was perfect. People saw past the perm and the bullshit and responded to the music, which was exactly what they needed to hear right then. And I say this as somebody who could not get away from that goddamn record no matter how hard I tried. Coming out of cars I passed on the street, in grocery stores, on boom boxes. Imagine how I felt, seeing that record in the collection of every woman who ever invited me back to her place."

"Oh my God, that's funny. I mean it's sad, but it's funny-sad." She put a hand on his forearm and seemed to forget to take it away. "If it's any consolation, I've had a pretty crummy fifteen years myself. You're still making records, still on everybody's A list. I'm a nostalgia act, when I work at all. The *Krupheimer* record is still making royalties, thank God, and three or four times a year I do these corporate gigs where everybody is in khakis and polo shirts with logos on them and the contract specifies which songs I have to play, and I'm 42 now and I won't get to make another record, even if I had the songs, because my boobs have started to go south."

"Except that it's moot," Dave said, "what with the bridges and the well and the fire department."

"That goddamn fire department. Where are they when you need them?"

He was looking into her eyes and she was looking back, through his glasses and hers, and it was like feedback. He could hear the hum. Already it had gone on too long, and they both knew it. He looked at his coffee and she noticed her hand and took it away and put it in her lap. Then they both spoke up at the same time, him saying, "Where are you—" and her saying, "How long have you—"

They both stopped. She was smiling that I've-got-a-secret smile that made him so crazy with desire that he wanted to wreck the joint. "You first," she said.

"Where are you living now?"

"Inwood. *Krupheimer* pays the rent, with enough left over for food. Half an hour from Columbus Circle on the A train on a good night."

"If you don't have to work, what do you do all day?"

"I play piano. I read. Today I came down to spend the day at the Met and I thought, Zabar's is just on the other side of the Park."

"Just a burnt bridge away." He'd only wanted to keep the ball moving over the net, but he'd put too much power behind it and knocked her façade to bits. Tears ran down both cheeks and her eyes squeezed shut and her nose leaked onto her upper lip. She scrabbled in her purse and blindly threw a few bills on the table and said, "I have to go."

She was up and headed for the door. "Sallie!" he said.

He caught her in the middle of the crowded café and turned her around and pulled her into his arms. She was sobbing. "I really did it, didn't I?" she said, wriggling to pull a tissue out of her bag and wiping at her face. "The only man I've ever really loved, and I pissed you off beyond any hope of redemption."

If that's not what you've been waiting for, he told himself, then you're never going to hear it. Tears and snot and glasses be damned, he kissed her until she dropped the purse and put both arms around him and kissed him back.

The people at the other tables looked like they might applaud. "You idiot," Sallie said. "Why didn't you do that twenty-five years ago?"

"I didn't know you twenty-five years ago."

"Don't you dare quibble with me at a time like this. Where's your apartment?"

There were still no cabs. Magic had limits in New York City. But walking was not so bad, holding her tightly to his side, the umbrella low over both of them.

"I almost jumped you a dozen times," she said, "when we were working on that first album. I don't know what stopped me. You were a big producer and I was just a kid, and you were always a perfect gentleman, and I couldn't bear the idea of you patting me on the head and setting me straight. And my career. My fucking career. I always thought, what if I seduce him and it screws everything up, everything that is so perfect and that I have worked so hard for? And then I went on the road and I thought, I won't ask, but if he shows up to see me, that will be the sign."

"I went to see you in Minneapolis," he said. "I saw how beautiful you were, what a star, and I was so afraid of humiliating myself, I turned around and flew home again."

"Idiot," she said. "Idiots the pair of us."

In bed with her, his most potent fantasy for most of his life, he was suddenly crippled with self-consciousness, even as she seemed in a terrible hurry. After a fruitless half an hour they took a break and opened a bottle of wine and brought it to bed with them. They talked about Skip Shaw and Woodstock and their first meeting at the Bitter End. He watched her extraordinary eyes that still leapt forward, now with extra texture in the skin around them, and she saw him looking and smiled and put her glass on the end table, and he reached across her to do the same, and then it was happening, and as the hormones washed over him he had a thought, a thought that he was sure would seem mundane without the hormones, nevertheless, there it was: as beautiful as her flesh was, the fact that the flesh was inhabited, that this distinct other person that he loved existed within it, that the intimate connection of their bodies could also connect the abstract beings inside—his awareness of that was the most erotic thing of all.

Later, curled inside his arm, she began to fidget. "What's wrong?" Dave said. "Was it that bad?"

"Idiot," she said. She sat up and folded her arms. "For twenty-something years you did nothing, and we could have been doing this."

"I don't know. I think maybe it was worth the wait."

"I was so beautiful then."

"You're so beautiful now."

"Southbound boobs and all?"

"I'd follow them to Patagonia. Gladly."

"All those wasted years."

"We can't change that." He gently drew her back down next to him. "But let's not waste any more."

WHEN SHE WAS LITTLE, Madelyn's father had insisted that Idaho didn't exist. "What proof is there?" he would say. "Have you ever

1990

been to Idaho? Have you ever *met* anyone from Idaho? Can you offer me a single thread of physical evidence?"

"What about the potatoes, Daddy?"

"Potatoes can come from anywhere. Thirty-five states in the US grow potatoes commercially, not even counting this mythical Idaho of yours. They can even come from Ireland. Can your potatoes produce a driver's license with an Idaho address? Can they show me a passport with an Idaho entrance stamp?" He would then duckwalk into the kitchen and take a potato out of the hanging steel baskets above the counter and shake a finger at it. "If you can prove you're from Idaho, speak up!"

And now here she stood on the corner of 4th Street and Main in Moscow, Idaho, across from the Garden Lounge. The bar occupied the lower floor of a two-story red brick building in the exact center of downtown, and everybody at the university hung out there, students and faculty alike. She could look left or right and see in the distance where the town ended and the Palouse began, the gently rolling grasslands where the local farmers grew wheat and soybeans and sileage for their livestock. Straight ahead and four blocks away was the University of Iowa campus, which took up a third of Moscow's land area. It was the second of March, mere days before the beginning of Mud Season, a typically bright, cold afternoon in the process of surrendering to cloudless night. Dirty snow still lay piled on the curb and a restless wind picked at their clothes.

Madelyn was riding high from opening a box of author's copies of her brand-new book, expanded from her dissertation and retitled *Melville and the Other*, published by SMU Press, an actual, honest-to-God book with her name on the cover. She and Ethan, now going on eight, were en route to a celebratory dinner at the Café Spudnik with Lila Davenport, the Victorian Lit prof who had been her mentor when she first came to Idaho, plus a couple of other faculty, to be followed by a party at the Garden Lounge. She was trying to keep Ava's decision to stay home from casting a shadow on the evening.

The divorce had been especially hard on Ava, as she'd had to testify at the trial. The fault was entirely Paul's; left to babysit

Ava and Ethan on short notice one night, he'd decided to visit his mistress anyway, leaving Ava and Ethan in the woman's living room to watch TV while he had noisy sex in the bedroom. Ava, hurt and puzzled, had come to Madelyn the next day for an explanation; Madelyn, clueless until then, had quickly worked out the truth. She'd confronted the woman, a lobbyist for nuclear energy, and gotten a full, tearful, and embarrassed confession. The woman had testified too, and lost her job over it. Madelyn had gotten full custody of both children in time for the move to Moscow.

Ava blamed herself for the divorce, no matter how forcefully Madelyn argued to the contrary. She didn't want to hear Madelyn blame Paul, which Madelyn understood. She hated tiny Moscow, population 18,000, after the fast-lane rush of DC. And, for the final touch of drama, she'd had a particularly turbulent puberty, her hurt feelings festering in a sea of hormones.

Now that she was 15 she'd begun to reveal herself, in ways not obvious early on, to be her biological father's daughter: introverted, slightly melancholy, and wild for the opposite sex. Moscow, whether because of the name, or the cheap land around it, or the progressive politics of the university, had drawn a disproportionate share of the counterculture during the seventies. Some of those refugees had found jobs on campus, others farmed, did small engine repairs, worked construction, or found other ways to hold on. Their sons, now Ava's age, were Madelyn's worst nightmare: beautiful, well-read, experienced with marijuana, completely unselfconscious about their bodies, precocious sexually and otherwise, and barely supervised. Madelyn had used the last of her credibility to cut her losses, providing Ava with condoms and informing her that whatever she did, it was not to involve her brother in any way, shape, or form.

It was hard enough being a 40-year-old assistant professor. She was not, not, *not* going to be a 41-year-old grandmother.

She and Ethan were the last to arrive at the Spudnik, to no one's surprise. Trying to balance the kids, her teaching schedule, and work on the book had left her perpetually out of breath. Lila teased her about her "just-in-time delivery system," like at Toyota, where parts went straight from the delivery dock to the assembly line; for Christmas she'd gotten Madelyn a nameplate that said "Dr. JIT" and Madelyn had put it proudly on her door. It was that kind of a department: easygoing, collegial, supportive, free of the bloodthirsty politics that were legendary at other schools.

Also easygoing was the unofficial attitude toward alternative lifestyles, perfectly symbolized by the openly lesbian Lila, and by Tony Langer, from Sociology. Tony was the victim of a classic academic marriage bind; the closest school where his wife had been able to find a job was Sacramento State, 825 miles away, a 12-hour drive in the best of weather. As a result they were widely known to have an open marriage, and Tony had confirmed it when he asked Madelyn out. He was in his late thirties, dark, athletic, and bearded, and he allegedly had 1200 pages of an unfinishable novel in his desk, his excuse for spending so much time in the English department. Madelyn, unwilling to become entangled in either the marriage or the novel, had declined the sex while consenting to the occasional dinner and movie, which had the effect of reminding her that she was missing her own sexual prime. Everyone assumed they were sleeping together anyway.

The table was filled out by the department's latest hire, a blond young writer, and his artist wife, who were both entirely too charming. A couple of plates of antipasto had already made the rounds. Madelyn snagged some marinated mushrooms before they disappeared and poured a glass of wine. She was toasted, a speech was demanded and refused, and dinner was ordered.

"What's the next book going to be?" Lila asked. She was sixty, large, and had an unselfconscious voice that easily reached the back rows of the Administration Auditorium. She had a trace of a Southern accent from a distant past that she refused to discuss. She was feminist but decidedly not postmodern, and considered *Middlemarch* to be the pinnacle of world literature.

"Well..." Madelyn said, knowing she should keep her mouth shut, but seduced by the gratifications of the day and the intimate company and the first buzz of the wine, "what I really want to do is teach a graduate seminar on the Literature of the Sixties, and then turn that into a book."

Lila responded with her trademark squint. "A bit early for that, isn't it?"

"I don't think so," Madelyn said. "I think the election of Reagan was a kind of cultural iron curtain, cutting off the sixties from the history of the future."

"What about Solidarity in Poland?" Tony asked. "The Velvet Revolution in Czechoslovakia? Tiananmen Square?"

"We saw what happened in Tiananmen Square," the young writer said. "The rest—the fall of the Berlin Wall, the so-called end of the Cold War, all the stuff in Eastern Europe—that's just more of Reagan's triumph of capitalism. It's hardly the hippie dream made manifest."

The discussion quickly descended into the party game of Pick the Syllabus. *Catch-22* and *One Flew Over the Cuckoo's Nest* were elected by universal acclaim; "Howl," *Another Country*, *Portnoy's Complaint*, and *The Bell Jar* brought out the swords and knives, to everyone's immense pleasure, including Ethan's, who had learned early on that these arguments were categorically different from the ones at the dinner table in DC. His head moved back and forth with the flow of conversation as if he were watching a tennis match.

Even so, by ten Ethan was exhausted and Madelyn called it a night. She accepted a ride home from Tony, who then carried the sleeping Ethan into the house.

The minute she set foot inside, Madelyn heard the absence. While Tony tucked Ethan in, she checked Ava's room, and the den, and finally found the note in the kitchen.

"Mom," it said. "Don't worry. I've saved up some money and you didn't raise no fools, as you have often said. I will be very careful and I will be in touch as soon as I land somewhere. Love, Ava."

She didn't permit herself to panic. She called the Chief of Police at home, a perk she'd gained from going to the same church that his family did. As it rang on the other end, Tony stuck his head around the corner and mouthed, "Where's Ava?"

Madelyn held up one finger and said, "Hi, Nancy, this is Madelyn Brooks. I apologize for calling this late. You know I wouldn't do it if it weren't an emergency."

"Are the kids all right?"

"No. Ava's run away."

"I'll get Jim."

Jim required no explanation. She read him the note, told him where she'd last seen Ava and what she'd been wearing, said she had no idea where she'd be heading. He said he would call the State Police immediately and get a local officer over to the house "to see what he could see."

"Thank you," Madelyn whispered.

"I'm going to say this even though I know you're not listening. Kids pull this kind of crap every day. Ava's smart and nearly grown and she'll be fine. Now I'm going to hang up so I can call the ISP."

She put the phone in its cradle and slumped onto the floor with her back to the dishwasher and hugged her knees.

Tony knelt in front of her. "God, Madelyn, are you okay? What can I do?"

"Is Ethan in bed?"

"Fast asleep."

She closed her eyes. "A glass of water would be nice."

He gave it to her and she drank half and said, "What I really want is to get in the truck and go look for her myself."

"No way. You have to be here if the phone rings, and to talk to the cops. I can go take a look if you want. It would mean leaving you here alone…"

"Would you? Would you just get on 95 South and go for fifteen, twenty minutes, in case she's hitching and didn't get picked up?"

"Sure," he said. He stood up awkwardly and said, "I'll be back in a while."

He hadn't been gone five minutes when the city cop pulled up with his lights strobing. His name was Officer Keating and he was young and ambitious and competent, and he gave Madelyn an unjustified but welcome moment of hope. They took an inventory of Ava's room and found her wilderness backpack and sleeping bag were gone, along with several days' worth of jeans and T-shirts and underwear, her waterproof boots, her down jacket, and her Mariners baseball cap. Keating got on his radio and gave the ISP the details to add to their description. Also missing was a photo of Madelyn and Ethan, and the thought that she intended to be gone that long provoked a stinging in her eyes. She made coffee while Keating asked her a long list of questions with little obvious purpose other than to keep her distracted.

At 11:30 Tony returned. He shook his head and said, "I went all the way to the 195 merger. Sorry."

Keating took that as his cue to leave. "Between us and the Sheriff, we've got every road in the county covered. If she's anywhere in the vicinity, we'll find her."

Madelyn knew Ava was no longer anywhere in the vicinity. She thanked him nonetheless. Once he was gone she looked in on Ethan, who had apparently slept through the whole thing.

She and Tony sat at the dining room table and drank coffee. "I know you're thinking you could have prevented this," he said. "It's not true. Kids that age, it doesn't matter how good the home environment is, they're at the mercy of all these feelings they don't understand."

"What I was *thinking*," Madelyn said, "was that it's already below freezing out there and how cold and alone she must feel."

Tony looked down into his cup, properly rebuked, and Madelyn felt even worse because she had, in fact, been blaming herself, and she didn't like him being able to read her so easily and didn't like that she'd been feeling sorry for herself instead of Ava.

"Christ, I'm sorry," she said. "Obviously I am not handling this as well as I would like to be. That's no excuse for scratching your eyes out like that."

"Well," Tony said. "It's not like I have any standing to be lecturing you on kids."

"I don't know. You're great with my kids."

"Viki and I both wanted them. But it didn't seem fair to them, with things being... what they are."

All too rarely, the hand of the kitchen clock ticked forward a single minute. Doing nothing was the hardest part. She had been praying continuously since she'd walked into the empty house, and by the tenets of her shaky faith, that was supposed to count as doing something. It was hard, putting herself in the hands of a deity she could not picture, whose track record for saving children, including his own, was nothing to write home about.

The conversation was desultory and after one AM Tony began to nod off. Madelyn put him on the couch with a pillow and blanket and after that it was easier, not having to worry about anyone but Ava. She walked through the past week in her mind, looking for clues and not finding any. Madelyn had proofread, at Ava's request, a paper for school on Atticus's "parenting style" in *To Kill a Mockingbird*, and had not detected any barbs aimed at her. One night Ava had spent an hour on the phone with one of the local farmers' sons, and when Madelyn had looked in on her, Ava had held the phone at arm's length and crossed her eyes and stuck out her tongue.

If anything happened to her, those memories would not be bearable.

Finally she too began to drift off. When the phone rang at 3:20 AM, she jumped and banged her knee on the table. She ran to the wall phone and said, "Hello?"

"Miz Brooks?"

"Yes?" She sucked in a breath and held it.

"This is Sergeant Travis with the Twin Falls police. We've got your girl here."

"She's all right?"

"She's just fine. Pissed off that her adventure is over a lot sooner than she planned."

"Oh thank God."

"We're short-handed here tonight, so it's going to be late morning before we can get somebody to bring her up there to you—"

"I'm on my way. Just tell me how to find you."

Tony wanted to come along. Madelyn convinced him to stay with Ethan and see that he got breakfast and lunch. She poured herself a thermos of coffee and emptied everything she could out of her bladder, and before she had the Suburban out of the driveway she felt like she had to go again. Twin Falls was nominally a seven-hour drive, but it was four lanes all the way and she made it in five and three-quarters, and that was with stopping three times to pee and fill the tank and splash cold water on her face. The scenery, had it not been dark, would have been spectacular, with half the trip cutting through the Nez Perce-Clearwater and Payette National Forests. The highway curved between pine-covered mountains that were lighter shadows against the night sky, then fell to rivers roaring with snow melt, climbing again to breathtaking drop-offs where her headlights disappeared into nothingness. She promised herself she would enjoy it on the drive back.

The day shift had arrived at the police station by the time she got there, and Sgt. Travis was long gone. The duty sergeant told her how a cop had spotted Ava at the Flying J Travel Plaza in Jerome, where the Interstate met the outskirts of Twin Falls. She was wandering from truck to truck and talking to the drivers, an obvious runaway, what with the backpack and the nervous glances over her shoulder. She was currently asleep in her own private cell. "Just show me a picture ID, and she's yours to keep."

"Thank you," she said. "I can't possibly thank you enough."

"I got three little girls of my own. I know every square inch of where you're coming from."

Maybe it was a trick of the light, but Madelyn thought, as they brought Ava out, that she saw a flicker of love and gratitude in her daughter's eyes. Maybe she was kidding herself. Ava's face was creased from the pillow and she looked so young and helpless that it was all Madelyn could do not to wrap her up in her arms.

Ava didn't say anything until they crossed the Snake River on the way to the Interstate. "So what happens now?"

"What do you mean?"

"Am I grounded forever? Are you going to send me to a convent school? Pack me off for psychiatric evaluation?"

"Oh, sweetheart. No, none of the above."

"What are you going to do, then?"

"*We*," she said, "are going to talk."

Getting to the crux of it was slow work. In the end, it turned out to be none other than Cole. Why was she not surprised?

"I want to meet him," Ava said.

"And that's where you were headed?"

A nod.

"Where is he?"

"Guanajuato."

"How did you find him?"

"Gwyn."

"Gwyn?"

"Gwyn *Montoya*. You know, Alex's daughter?"

Madelyn refused to rise to the sarcasm. Eyes on the prize, she told herself. Don't fight the wrong battles. "How long have you and Gwyn been talking?"

"A few months."

"Have you been in touch with Cole? Did he know you were coming?"

"No."

Well, that was something. She wouldn't have to kill him, then. "And it's that important to you? That you would put me through the fear of you being out on the road alone?"

"If he's as much of a dick as you think he is, then I won't want to be around him, so why are you so afraid of me meeting him?"

"When did I say he was a dick?"

"You didn't have to."

She'd refilled the thermos with burnt, sour cop coffee and she took a minute to drink some and try to think through her options. Her exhaustion was too complete and the possibilities too numerous, so she went with her instincts. "What if I said yes? That we'll fly down there and you can meet him and I'll give you time alone with him and you can judge for yourself?"

"For real?"

"Maybe. First of all, I have to be convinced he's not using heroin. Did you know about that?"

"Gwyn said, yeah."

"I have to finish this semester. And I have to talk it over with Cole."

"When's the last time you talked to him?"

"You were still in the womb."

"Wow."

Madelyn saw that it was the proper thing to do, that Ava's defenses were coming down. Nevertheless. What in God's name had she just agreed to?

"Mom, you're weaving. Pull over and let me drive."

Ava, like most of her friends, had been driving since she was 12, first in the open fields outside town, then on back roads, finally in traffic, always with Madelyn there ready to grab the wheel. Now it was Madelyn herself who was the danger. She got off onto the shoulder, then slid across the bench seat while Ava walked around the front of the truck. She had Cole's features, softened by the lack of a Y chromosome, and Cole's rangy body; she was not an obvious beauty, but a true and lasting one once she revealed herself. She was fully formed, Madelyn reminded herself. Surely Cole could not do that much harm.

Ava got in and put the truck in gear. "How about some music?"

The cassettes in the truck were all Ava's. Madelyn pulled a plastic case from under the seat and read down the familiar labels: REM, Fine Young Cannibals, Elvis Costello, Jo Jo Zep and the Falcons. She pulled out Doug and the Slugs, an upbeat, witty Canadian band that Ava had discovered somewhere, and fed it into the player as Ava accelerated onto the highway.

"If I'm going to meet him," Ava said, "I want the history. All of it."

Madelyn took a couple of deep breaths. She made sure her door was locked and settled herself against it. "Do you remember learning about the War of the Roses?"

"That's not the history I was—"

"Patience," Madelyn said. "York was the white rose and Lancaster was the red…"

THE ANSWERING MACHINE was flashing when Alex came in. He'd been at a late after-work dinner with a couple of the younger programmers and he was buzzed from their energy. The message was that his uncle Jesús was dead of a massive heart attack. The family was flying down for the funeral. Did Alex want to come?

He'd been sleepwalking. He'd let the years pass, agreeably enough, and he'd failed to count the toll. In Alex's mind, Jesús was the same as when he and Cole and Alex had first played together in his grandparents' living room. Now he was going to forcibly trade that image for the sight of him in his coffin.

In Mexico they loved their iconography of the dead, not just on El Día de los Muertos, but all year round, with skeleton figurines everywhere dressed as mariachis or brides and grooms or folk-loric dancers. "As you are now, so once was I," was the repeated message. For Alex the fixation on death itself missed the point. What frightened him was the deterioration of the body, the slow-ing of the brain, the ever-shrinking list of things worth fighting for, the need for more and more physical comfort. Alex resisted seeing those changes in himself, wanted to believe that he too was the same as he'd been that night, 17 years old, dick constantly hard, sure of his own invulnerability. And Jesús was proof that he was lying to himself.

After the divorce from Callie, he and Brenda had split up, too. She'd found somebody else while he was not paying attention. Then one night, five years ago, he'd woken up in the uneasy, low-numbered hours, terrified by the thought of the loaded gun in his storage unit, which suddenly seemed like an early warning sign of insanity. The next day he'd sold it at a pawn shop and told Álvaro he would not be doing any more import work. He'd declared the cash as poker winnings over the course of a couple of years, and got rid of the storage shed and the safe.

He'd turned old and afraid by increments so small that he hadn't noticed them at the time.

He called his father. They'd kept an uneasy peace for a while now. Phone calls every Sunday, dinner at his father's house once a month or so. No more high-stakes poker. When Gwyn was up from Marfa, she always spent time with her grandparents. Everyone understood what was safe to talk about and what wasn't.

"Yes, Papa, I want to come."

"Good. Good, I'm glad. I had the agent hold a ticket for you. Why don't you come over and spend the night here? We have to leave at six in the morning."

His next call was to Cole in Guanajuato.

"Yeah," Cole said, "I just heard this morning. I saw him a couple of weeks ago and he was in bad shape, but... shit, you know?"

"I hear you."

"Does this mean you're coming down?"

"We'll hit town late morning tomorrow. I'll call you."

When he got to his parents' house, Alex's mother greeted him at the door by saying, "We've got a surprise." She sounded like she was trying to talk herself into being pleased. She pointed toward the dining room, where Susan sat with his father. Susan got up to hug him and he said, "Hey, sis. Is what's his name here?"

"You know perfectly well that his name is Peter. And no, we're getting divorced."

"This is a new record," Alex said. "This is the first time you managed to divorce one before I even met him."

"It's only my third," Susan said, stung. Alex hadn't seen her in two years. She'd gained weight in Savannah, she was wearing too much makeup, and her hair was sprayed into the kind of helmet that had gone out of style in 1965. Her expensive taupe pants suit was too tight at the armpits and waist, and her perfume mixed unpleasantly with the smoke from the Kool that burned in the ashtray by her chair. Given Alex's state of mind, it was hard not to see her as death in process.

Peter was some kind of stockbroker, well enough off that Susan hadn't had to work for the three years they'd been married. She'd met him at some Savannah retreat that she'd organized during her brief career as an event planner. This had followed her losing her job with the law firm that had discovered that she had not quite finished law school, nor passed the bar, after abandoning her psychology degree, and it was the point at which Alex's sympathy for her had bottomed out.

"Susan's going to stay here until she gets back on her feet," his father said. If his father's sympathy was not yet worn out, it was clearly running low.

"Well, I hope you find something," Alex said.

"What, do you think I won't?" She was defiant, ready to skirmish.

"No, I'm sure you will. Something you really like, I should have said." To his father he said, "Jimmy's not coming?"

Jimmy was a staff photographer for the Austin *Statesman* now, and did freelance work on the side. He'd married a courts reporter and he had two kids in elementary school and a nice house in West Lake Hills. He stayed close to his own family and cordially distant from the other Montoyas.

"No," his father said. "He's got assignments all weekend. Graduation parties, weddings, it's a busy time. And he was never close to Jesús the way you were."

"He's got his own life," Susan said. "I wish I could say the same."

Alex fought off a moment of claustrophobia. Just being under this roof, no matter how much he loved his family, ate away at his identity. Maybe Jimmy knew what he was doing.

"We've got an early start tomorrow," Alex said. "I'll see you all in the morning."

ALEX FELT THE WEIGHT of time again when Octavio wasn't there to meet them at the León airport. For a few years after his grandparents died, back in '73, the family had still managed the traditional Christmas trip. But Jesús hadn't wanted the house, and as Octavio got increasingly infirm and unable to take care of it, the idea of keeping it for the sake of ten days a year began to seem extravagant. They'd sold it in '78 and given Octavio a pension. Somehow that had been the end of the Christmas trips as well, and Octavio had died soon after. Alex's father had still flown down on occasion to see Jesús. Alex hadn't been back since the time he and Callie had run into Álvaro.

They took a cab from the airport to the Hotel Embajadora in Guanajuato, where the family had booked a suite. They were at the extreme eastern edge of the city, a brisk ten-minute walk from the Jardín de la Unión, surrounded by hills that cupped them like giant hands.

Alex called Cole from his room and invited him to join them for lunch at the hotel. He washed his face and changed into a guayabera shirt and tried to reset his internal clock to Mexican Optional Time.

Cole arrived as they were all sitting down at a couple of patio tables. Everybody stood up again to give Cole an abrazo, Susan last of all. Alex saw it happen, right before his eyes. Cole gathered her up and kissed her on the mouth, not a steamy, passionate kiss or anything, but on the lips, and it lasted longer than it should have by half a second, time enough for something in Cole to ignite and something in Susan to yield. You could see it in the way they looked at each other as they slowly pulled apart.

Uh oh, Alex thought.

THE HEART WENT OUT of New Orleans when Tina left.

In hindsight, Cole supposed it was inevitable. She'd carried too many broken people for too long, and when she burned out, her relationship with Cole was collateral damage.

The last straw was a woman named Jacqui, older, street hardened, who'd brought a gram of coke when she came looking for refuge. When Tina told her to leave, she turned violent and they had to call the cops. Once she was gone, Tina said, "I can't do this anymore."

"I don't blame you. I'll just tell the girls when they show up that they have to go somewhere else."

"No," she said, dry-eyed, her words sounding rehearsed. "Not just the orphans. The Five-Four-Four. The drunks. The tourists. The heat. New Orleans."

"Me?"

Her mouth twitched. The smile didn't make it to her eyes. "You're great. Some lucky woman is going to snap you up."

Cole knew he had contributed to her burden, when his Darkness descended out of nowhere and demanded more meaning from his existence than it could provide, when he needed all his resolve not to take a shot of vodka or something stronger. After four years, it was a bit late to say, "I love you." Tina had clearly made up her mind. Still, with nothing to lose, he gave it a try.

"Maybe I love you too," she said, "but I need to make a break."

"How long have you been thinking about this?"

"A while."

"You didn't want to talk to me?"

"I couldn't, sugar. I just couldn't."

1990

Within two weeks she was on a plane to Madison, Wisconsin, where an aunt had agreed to put her up. She was considering nursing school. She gave Cole the address but not the phone number.

Only after she was gone did he realize how much he'd taken the ease of their daily existence for granted. Their differences, which had seemed profound at the time, now looked trivial. He missed her honeyed voice and the healing touch of her hands. After a few weeks, he'd brought somebody home from the club, a perfectly nice divorcee in her early thirties, and he'd been so sick with post-coital remorse that he'd almost called 911.

He gave notice at the club and on his apartment and put all his possessions into his little yellow camper-top Toyota pickup, and on his last day in New Orleans he still had not made up his mind where to go. Retreating to Austin felt so much like failure that he was afraid of ending up drunk or on the needle again. He couldn't afford New York or LA, and San Francisco had been over for 15 years.

Guanajuato, though. Physically beautiful, with nobody there to ask him where his career had gone. He could teach English on the sly, play guitar for tips, live cheap, plan his next move. On the way out of town, he stopped at a barber shop and got his hair cut as short as it had been in the early commune days, then hit the Mexican Consulate for a visa.

At the border he explained that he was a music student, there to learn Mexican songs. In Guanajuato, he sold the truck for seed money and rented a decent apartment high up one of the winding callejones above La Alhóndiga, the old fortified granary. He was close to El Mercado, the giant indoor market full of fresh vegetables, and ten minutes from El Jardín de la Unión. The plumbing was new and so were the heavy-duty locks on the doors.

As much as he hated moving, he hadn't lost the knack of making himself at home in a new city, of finding the pieces that would fit into a routine. Fresh-squeezed orange juice and hot bread from El Mercado in the morning. A copy of *La Jornada*, the liberal paper out of the Distrito Federal, which he read while eating his breakfast on a bench by the fountain in El Jardín Reforma across from the market. Back at his apartment, he would write a letter to somebody in the little address book he kept in his wallet, maybe Tupelo Joe or Gordo, Tina, his mother, Sugarfoot, or Susan care of the Montoyas. Some laps around the local fútbol field, taking it easy because he was not yet fully acclimated to the 6,500-foot elevation. A shower and a cheap comida corrida at one of the cafés on Avenida Benito Juárez. Siesta in the heat of the afternoon, then playing guitar in the street at night.

Alex's father started arranging him a work permit and said he could set him up with a guy who did construction when his savings ran out.

In his first week, he went by Jesús's guitar shop, where he discovered a slender guy in his thirties with big round glasses. He was shaping a neck out of a piece of maple, and he said, "Jesús is retired. I'm his apprentice." He used the archaic term discípulo, which struck Cole as appropriate. Cole explained who he was and the man introduced himself as Félix Gutiérrez, one of El Maestro's pupils for the last ten years. "Come upstairs," Félix said. "He'll want to see you."

Félix closed up the shop and they climbed the steep street to get to the upper story, where Félix knocked and motioned Cole inside. The house was dim and smelled of old cooking oil. Jesús, stretched out in a recliner, dozed in front of a blaring fútbol match on TV. Félix found the remote and turned the TV down, which woke Jesús. Disoriented, he looked from Félix to Cole and said, «Qué pasó?»

«A former student of yours, come to pay his respects,» Félix said.

Before Cole could remind him who he was, he saw recognition bloom in Jesús's eyes. The old man struggled to get up even as Cole urged him to stay put. «¡El Mariachi Montoya!» Jesús said. He was massive in the chest and belly, unsteady on his feet, hair turned white and mostly gone, liver spots dotting his face. He gave Cole a hug that popped the air out of his lungs, and then sat back on the recliner. «And how is La Pelirroja?»

Cole opted not to explain drug busts and stolen guitars. «Still the most beautiful guitar I've ever played.»

Jesús nodded his satisfaction. «You and Félix have to play together. Promise me this. Make an old man happy.»

«Of course,» Félix said.

Jesús asked after Alex and Alex's father and Susan, and then abruptly said, «Come again soon. We'll have dinner and stay up all night and play guitars the way we used to.»

As they walked downhill to the store, Cole said, «He doesn't have long, does he?»

«Hard to say. His mind is still good, obviously. And he's strong. But he's very tired. And since Leticia died last year, there's nobody to give him the kind of care he needs.»

«There's nothing anybody can do?»

«It's just life. He's had a long one. He's ready to go.»

Cole wandered through the shop, looking at the guitars, each beautiful in its own way. He said, «What kind of music do you like?»

«Jazz, mostly. You know Al Di Meola? Paco de Lucía?»

«Sure, they're great.»

Félix picked up a guitar and told Cole to try any of them he liked. Cole saw that he was the real thing, tuning by ear, long spidery fingers arcing over the neck. Cole grabbed the nearest guitar, tuned to Félix, and on impulse started to play "Perfidia." Félix smiled in recognition and peeled off a few hot licks over the introduction, then played chords once the main melody got going. Cole took the first solo, knowing Félix was going to kick his ass when his turn came. Cole kept it simple and legato, more David Gilmour than Eddie Van Halen, working the timing and the finger tremolo. After a couple of choruses he turned it over to Félix, who cut the melody line into pieces and reassembled it in strange and haunting phrases, sounding more like Django Reinhardt than anybody else. When he did unleash a burst of speed it was indeed blinding, though each note in the flurry was cleanly struck. Cole tried to find some inversions and suspensions to keep the chords interesting for him, and it must have worked, because the longer they played, the deeper Félix dug in. Finally Cole blew off the chord structure entirely and they sailed away into outer space, just like in the days of The Quirq, except with more technical proficiency.

They played for an hour and a half, until Cole noticed a teenager with a guitar staring at them open-mouthed and Félix recalled his four o'clock lesson. «If you're not doing anything tonight,» Félix asked Cole shyly, «maybe we could get something to eat. I close here at eight.»

«Órale. I would like that a lot.»

And so Félix fitted himself into Cole's routine, reminding him that he hadn't had a close male friend since Lenny, all those years ago. At first they played in the street outside the fancy restaurants around the corner from the Plaza San Roque, then, over time, they began to be invited in to play for money. Some nights they sat at a cheap café afterward and talked about music and women and politics.

Félix never drank more than one beer a night, saying, «Beer is the enemy of skill.» Like Cole, he had married young and it hadn't worked out. «She thought I would outgrow the guitar.» He was active in the Partido de la Revolución Democrática, the new left-wing party that had just split off from the PRI, the Institutional Revolution that had ruled Mexico since 1929 through universally acknowledged corruption.

«Corruption used to be the glue that held this country together,» Félix said. «But you can't fight los narcos with corruption. You can only fight them with ideals. And if we don't fight them now, los narcos will end up ruling us all. They are the ultimate capitalists, and right now everything in Mexico is for sale—politicians, human life, immunity from the law.»

«Not that different from the US,» Cole said, thinking of the immunity that Montoya had bought him.

«In this,» Felix said, «for once, we are ahead of you.»

When Alex called to say the family was coming for Jesús's funeral, Cole immediately wondered if Susan would be with them. Less than a premonition, more than idle curiosity. The last time he'd seen her was Alex's wedding in the summer of 1974. Sixteen years ago.

Seeing her at the restaurant on Thursday afternoon, everything was apparent to him in an instant. Her sadness, her loneliness, her vulnerability. He could have been looking in a mirror. It gave him the courage to kiss her on the lips, and like in the fairy tale, he felt the kiss awaken her. He saw that she'd aged, that her body had softened. To him she was as beautiful as ever, still the unattainable princess, only now maybe not so unattainable.

They were seated too far apart for privacy, so they sent each other messages through the general conversation. Susan brought up her divorce in the first five minutes, and Cole mentioned that he wasn't seeing anybody. Susan talked about being at loose ends professionally and Cole talked about how he and Félix were now playing four or five nights a week, making enough for Cole to live on.

When the last of the food was gone and the bill paid, Montoya announced that he was going to have a siesta to prepare himself for Jesús's wake, happening that evening at the house above the shop. Food and alcohol would be abundant and it was likely to go on into the early hours of the morning. He and Alex's mother excused themselves, leaving Cole alone at the table with Susan and Alex.

Alex was hyper and wanted to talk about computers. Though Cole tried to pay attention, the technical details slipped away. Cole eventually got the topic shifted to Susan and her latest disastrous marriage.

"I thought enough money could make up for everything," she said. Cole didn't remember when they'd switched to English. "I was wrong. When he wasn't working late or cruising for hookers, he was buying coke to enable the first two."

"I'll pass on the hookers," Alex said, "but when the work is interesting it can be pretty seductive. And I don't mind doing a line of blow now and again." He looked at Cole. "Don't you ever miss it? Not any of it? A cold beer on a hot summer day? A joint before sex?"

Cole didn't bring up his occasional cravings. "You can have good memories about something and still know that it was in the past, and that it wouldn't be the same anymore, and that it's ultimately no good for you. I mean, you wouldn't want to still be dating Denise, would you?"

"If she was here now, I would be on my way to the hotel room with her."

"Even knowing there's no future in it? That you guys are not cut out for each other?"

"How much future do you need? You can pack a lot into an afternoon." Alex sighed. "I was never good at resisting temptation."

Cole felt the power of Susan's gaze on him. "I want more than that," he said. "I want forever."

Susan said, "I don't know if I still have that much romance in my soul. I feel like it's been squeezed out of me."

"You never know," Cole said, and out of the corner of his eye he saw Alex give him a warning look.

The idea of him and Susan as a real possibility was brand new, and yet it already had weight and momentum. He wanted nothing more in the world than to be alone with her and see what would happen between them. To Cole's surprise, Alex was obviously unhappy about it. But even Alex could not fight the primal energy that flowed across the table, and after another ten minutes he got up. "I guess I'll see you tonight, then."

"I'll be there," Cole said.

He watched Alex walk away and felt his breathing go shallow. He said, "Is there someplace…"

She laughed and stubbed out her cigarette. "What did you have in mind?"

"I just want to talk to you alone."

She stood. As he walked up to her, she slipped one arm around his waist. "I've been wondering for the last two hours," she said, "if that felt as good as I thought, or if I was imagining it."

"What's the verdict?"

She tightened her grip. She led the way to her room, took the key out of her purse, and handed it to him. The symbolism of the gesture only stoked Cole's desire. He opened the door and ushered her in. She tossed her purse on the bed and turned to face him. He closed the door and kissed her, all out, with 25 years of hopeless longing. Some small part of his brain marveled at what he was doing, even as the rest of it was lost in sensory overload, perfume and the softness of her lips and the feel of her hands in his hair.

When they finally pulled back, she put her forehead into his shoulder. "Something tells me," she said, "this might not be the best idea in the world."

"Don't listen," he said. He picked her up and laid her sideways across the bed and kissed her neck and throat. He unbuttoned her blouse and saw that her unrestrained breasts were deeply tanned, matching her arms and face. "Nude sunbathing," she said, "on the back deck in Savannah."

Shortly thereafter, when he raised her skirt, she stopped his hand. "Give me a minute," she said. "I can't seem to think straight, for some strange reason."

"Don't think," Cole said. "Feel."

"What about condoms? Do you have any?"

"I've been using them since I broke up with Tina, and she and I were both tested."

"I'm not on the pill, and I'm still fertile. Theoretically."

Cole sighed dramatically and rolled onto his back. "There's a farmacia down the street."

"What time is it?"

Cole looked at his watch. "Almost four."

"I'll need at least an hour to get ready for the wake."

"What are you saying?"

"Go home, get dressed for tonight. I'll see you there. And when it's over, I'll come to your apartment with you. You have condoms there, right?"

"Do you swear?"

"Cross my heart," she said, "and hope to die."

COLE ASSUMED THINGS would get off to a late start, as usual in Latin America. He arrived at six to find throngs of people already in the streets around the house. When he finally made it inside, he was startled to discover Jesús on display, arms folded across his chest, face waxy with death, his coffin supported by a low wooden table, the lid standing to one side. Two women in black knelt on cushions by the coffin, saying la novena por los difuntos, the nine days' worth of prayers that had started the day Jesús died.

The house glowed with yellow light from dozens of candles. Flowers on every surface, a giant guitar-shaped wreath over one of the food tables. A few of Jesús's least expensive student guitars sat on stands next to stools in an otherwise vacant corner of the living room, and Félix was already playing one of them. A heavyset guy Cole's age played rhythm next to him. His wall eye looked familiar, but Cole couldn't say from where. Cole and Félix nodded to each other and then Cole went back to looking for Susan.

Outside the front door, a group of old men in guayaberas had commandeered a table in the midst of everything and begun to play dominoes. Cole saw the Montoyas then, walking uphill from the shop, Alex and Susan and Alex's parents, and when Susan saw him she ran ahead and threw her arms around him and kissed him in front of God and everybody. It's really happening, Cole thought. He was scared and happy and in love, and he ignored the alarm on Alex's face and the confusion on the face of Alex's parents, and fell into step with them, Susan taking his hand.

«You look very beautiful,» he said to Susan in Spanish. She wore a long black skirt and a simple black knit top and a silver and turquoise necklace. She was thoroughly made up and clouds of perfume hovered around her.

«You're a liar,» she said, «but I'll forgive you this once. I look old and puffy and tired.»

«You look like the woman of my dreams.»

"Flatterer," she said in English. "Rascal." Cole knew it was a quote but didn't remember from where.

Progress through the crowd was slow. Everyone knew the Montoyas and wanted to give them an abrazo and invoke God for a few words of consolation. Once inside, Susan headed straight for the drinks table and poured a glass of wine. Before she drank, though, she turned to Cole and said in English, "You don't mind, do you? I mean, you'll still kiss me if I taste of wine?"

"I can't imagine a situation in which I would not be willing to kiss you."

She took a long drink and said, "Prove it."

He kissed her and yes, the taste of wine in her mouth was weird. Not falling-off-the-wagon weird, more like playing-with-fire weird.

Not that it mattered. This was fire that he could not walk away from.

They rejoined Alex, who had just seen the guitar players. His first reaction was shock, Cole noted, which he quickly hid behind a smile. «Órale,» Alex said, «you remember Álvaro? Who gave you your first porro?»

And who, Cole remembered, Alex had been smuggling marijuana for.

Álvaro looked up and saw Alex and beamed at him, putting the guitar down to embrace him. Alex reminded him of his history with Cole, and Cole introduced Félix around, and then somehow Cole had a guitar in his hands and they were playing "La Corriente," the Javier Solís hit. Alex sang lead and Cole and Álvaro sang harmony, telling the current to take them back, never to return. If the room didn't exactly go quiet, at least the noise level dropped substantially. A few people sang along and a few others let out the traditional yipping gritos and falsetto howls of approval.

Susan watched him like she'd never seen him before. Eyes glistening, mouth in a startled smile, tongue flicking out to touch her lips.

For him.

They played for an hour. Susan watched a while, then wandered off. Finally Cole couldn't stand it any longer and went to look for her, handing off his guitar to one of Felix's students. He saw her in the kitchen, where she smiled at him and moved into the crowd, leading him on, until he caught up with her outside Jesús's bedroom, where she was opening the door.

«Do you think we should...» Cole said.

Susan held a finger to her lips and said, «We're family. Nobody will mind... just for a second.» She pulled him into the bedroom and kissed him ravenously. «Seeing you play tonight... it made me crazy.»

«We could leave right now,» Cole said. Susan was pressed against him and nothing else mattered.

«It would be disrespectful. Our time will come.» She kissed him again, sucking his lower lip into her mouth and raking it with her teeth. «Go play some more. But don't forget me.»

First he filled a plate with black beans and rice and tortillas and stuffed a big bite in his mouth. He was all appetite. He found a bottle of mineral water and drank half of it in one pull, then finished his food while watching the mobs of people move through the house. Some of them, surely, had no idea who Jesús was and were merely freeloading. The vast majority had put their sadness on open display, women weeping into lace handkerchiefs, men clinging to each other. Cole knew that it was a vital escape valve for a macho ethic that disdained weakness, that married for life and practiced open infidelity, that revered mothers and mistreated wives. Cole loved the culture for its sentimentality and acknowledgement of pain.

By the time he picked up a guitar again, people had started to call out requests and step up to sing lead. The band did what they could to make them sound as good as possible, whether they were on or off key, slightly drunk or staggering. Alex came and went, as did Susan, who blew him kisses when no one was looking. Though he was mightily distracted by her, he also had to acknowledge the chemistry between himself and Álvaro and Félix. Álvaro had the discipline of years as a professional mariachi, an encyclopedic knowledge of the songs, instinctive vocal harmony, and a simple, powerful guitar technique. Félix was wildly inventive, finding hidden melodies and turning the chords inside out. Cole's gift was his ability to knit the two together.

During a break, Cole sat with Alex and Susan and tried to rehydrate himself. The candles and the cooking and the crush of people had created a feverish heat. Suddenly a turbulence moved through the crowd and out of it emerged a clean-cut man in his twenties, in an expensive black suit and open-collared white shirt. He had a single thin gold chain around his neck and another on his right wrist. He had a stylish short haircut and intelligent eyes. He and Álvaro embraced warmly.

«Alejo,» Álvaro said, «let me introduce you to Miguel Ortiz. Miguel is a friend from work, very young, very ambitious, with a big future, we think."

So he was a narcotraficante, Cole thought, which explained the space that opened around him. Alex understood it too, and his nervousness showed in his eyes as Ortiz took his hand.

«I was very sorry to hear of your uncle's death,» Ortiz said.

«Thank you,» Alex said. «Did you know Jesús?»

«No. But I have heard much about you from mi primo Álvaro. He says you're a good man, very trustworthy. And a very good card player.»

Alex shrugged modestly.

Álvaro said, «This is Alejo's sister, Susana.»

«Lovely,» Ortiz said, bowing over her hand as Susan inclined her head.

«And this is our friend Cole, a wonderful guitar player.»

Now it was Cole's turn to shake Ortiz's hand, and it reminded him of the time he'd locked eyes with a tiger at the Audubon Zoo in New Orleans. The tiger had looked at Cole with mild, disinterested calculation, as if wondering if it was worth the trouble to kill and eat him.

«I'd hoped to hear some music,» Ortiz said, in a way that suggested he was not used to disappointment.

«We just finished our break,» Álvaro said, which was not remotely true. «Is there something special you'd like to hear?»

«Do you know 'Mexico, lindo y querido'?»

It was a sentimental patriotic ballad, not one of Cole's favorites. «Claro que sí,» Cole said. «We would love to play that for you.»

Somebody found Ortiz a chair while they tuned up. Alex sang lead on "Mexico," and after that they played "Guadalajara" and, inevitably, "Cielito lindo." Everybody in the room sang along at the top of their lungs, making so much noise that the pans hanging on the kitchen walls vibrated along.

Ortiz said something in Álvaro's ear. Álvaro held up his hand, as if refusing money. He probably was. Ortiz smiled and waved as he walked away, again leaving a wide wake.

Later, Cole walked out to say goodnight to Alex's parents. Susan leaned against the front of the house, holding a wine glass, looking like she needed the support. As Cole watched the Montoyas turn the corner, Álvaro put a hand on his shoulder. «Care for a little mota?»

«Not for me,» Cole said. «You go ahead.»

«Not drinking either?»

«Not for a while now. I liked it too much.»

«Smart man,» Álvaro said.

Though the crowd had thinned, the party was far from over. They had Death on the run, but not yet vanquished.

«You made a very good impression on El Cicatriz,» Álvaro said.

«You're talking about Ortiz?»

«Claro. It's all the fashion these days to have nicknames, usually some kind of scary shit. The Scorpion. The Mad Dog.»

«What do they call you?»

«El Mariachi Loco.»

«Not so scary.»

Álvaro laughed. «I'm not a scary guy.»

Which was not entirely true. Álvaro wasn't in the same gym-hardened shape as Ortiz, but his wall eye and dissipated air made him look like somebody to not get on the wrong side of.

«How come El Cicatriz? I didn't see any scars.»

«He says they're all on the inside. When he was fifteen, the federales killed his older brother in the street. Mistaken identity. His mother died from grief.»

«Can you do that? Die from grief?» Cole didn't mean to be cynical. The question just popped out.

«You can if you stop eating, which is what she did. Anyway, he joined the federales himself as soon as he was old enough, and within a year everyone who had anything to do with the death of his brother was dead too.»

Cole thought about Ortiz's eyes.

«Listen,» Álvaro said, «I've never seen a gringo with the kind of feeling for this music that you have.»

«Thanks. Coming from you, that's quite a compliment.»

«The guys I work for, they all love this shit. You and Félix, if you put a group together, I personally guarantee you could make some real money.»

The idea terrified him and ever-so-slightly tempted him. «The group would just play music, and nothing else?»

«Nada más. Private parties, lots of benefits. The drugs I guess you wouldn't care about, but maybe the women?»

Álvaro followed Cole's glance to Susan, who looked at Cole and licked the rim of the wineglass. Álvaro laughed. «Or maybe you're covered in that department too. You think about it, you let me know if you're interested.» He gave Cole a card that listed him as a Vice-President of Sales. «It was a real pleasure to see you again. You've grown into a really first-class musician.»

Cole was touched. «Thank you. I really loved playing with you. You have to go?»

«I've got a long drive tonight. And I think the amateurs have taken over.»

Cole focused his ears and heard a drunken howling from the stage. «Ah. Así es.»

Álvaro hugged him and said, «I think you have an appointment of your own to keep.» He nodded to Susan, lifted his hand, and said, «Que Dios te bendiga,» as he walked away.

Cole took the empty glass from Susan's hand and put it on a nearby table. When he turned back she wrapped her arms around him and kissed him, her tongue sliding into his mouth like a warm serpent. "Take me home and put me to bed," she said in English.

"Shouldn't we say goodnight to Alex?"

"No."

They started downhill to Avenida Juárez, arms around each other's waists. "Does it bother you that I'm a little drunk?" Susan said.

In fact it bothered him more than he wanted to admit. "How drunk are you? Do you just want to go to sleep?"

"No," she said, and stopped in the street to kiss him again. "Do you?"

"I've been waiting twenty-five years. I don't want to wait any longer. What if you change your mind?"

"Don't say that," she said with unexpected heat. "What you fear in others is what you fear in yourself."

"I loved you from the first time I saw you," Cole said, in an attempt to get things back on track. The words set his libido on fire again. "I'll love you till the day I die."

She stopped again, put her hands on his face. "Really?" Her eyes shone as she ricocheted from one emotion to the next.

"Really," he said.

"I want you so much. Make love to me, here in the street, right now."

She seemed serious. "I want you in my bed," he improvised. "I want to go to sleep in your arms after."

"Okay," she said. "Hurry."

They were out of breath by the time they got to his apartment. They each took a turn in the bathroom and shared Cole's toothbrush. The domesticity dampened their momentum. "I should take some aspirin," Susan said. "Can I have some bottled water?"

He brought the water to her in the bathroom and she swallowed three aspirin and drained the glass. She set it on the edge of the sink and looked in the mirror and yawned.

"Susan," Cole said. "This is..."

She turned around, reaching behind her with both hands to hold on to the sink. "It's what?"

"It's not..."

"Not what?"

She stared at him and he saw that she felt the magic slipping away too, the footmen turning into mice, the cakes and pastries to fairy dust, and behind her anger and disappointment he saw her longing and her need. He lifted her by her damp armpits and set her on tiptoe in front of him and kissed her, his fingers digging into her shoulder blades, and her arms went around his neck and he felt her fingernails on his back and in his scalp. The bathroom was too cramped for him to pick her up, so he backed her toward the bedroom, both of them bumping into doorframes and finally falling onto the bed.

They struggled out of their clothes, then Cole was fumbling with a condom and then, incredibly, he was inside her. Making love to Susan Montoya.

When it was over he lay on top of her and she stroked his back. "Was it all right?" she said. "Am I the oldest woman you've ever had?"

"It was wonderful," he said.

"And? Am I the oldest?"

"In terms of years older than me, no."

"But absolute age?"

"I suppose so. Do you really think that matters to me?"

"How many?"

"How many what?"

"Others. How many other women have there been?"

"Not as many as you might think. If you want an exact count I will have to work it up for you. Not right now."

That seemed to satisfy her. Cole held the condom in place and rolled away from her, knotted it and wrapped it in a tissue and threw it away. He put his head on her shoulder and cradled one breast with his hand and started to drift off.

"Can I smoke?" she said. She was as wide awake as he was exhausted.

"I guess." He made himself get up to open the window next to her side of the bed. The temperature was in the mid-60s and the light breeze made him shiver.

"Is there an ashtray?" She had found the cigarettes in her purse and the flare of the match showed her smeared mascara and matted hair, the lines around her mouth. They were the signs of intimacy and vulnerability and it touched Cole's heart and made him want her again.

He found a plastic ashtray in the kitchen cupboard and brought it back to bed. He curled himself around her warmth, one hand stroking her stomach, the little finger trailing into her pubic hair.

"Is the smoking going to be a problem?" she said.

"I don't like it," he said. "I guess I can live with it."

"I'm going to quit, but it has to be on my own terms, in my own time."

"Okay," Cole said. He let his hand move lower. After a minute he said, "I don't want you to go back to the States."

"Be careful what you wish for."

"What do you mean?"

"My mother's got leukemia. She's been after me to move in with her while I'm getting myself together, take care of her."

"I'm sorry about your mother. But if you were to move in with her... that would be fantastic."

"You say that now."

"Yes," he said. "I do." He moved his fingers lower still.

"Cole. Am I really supposed to keep calling you by your last name?"

"You can just call me 'mi amor.' 'Mi vida.' 'Mi querido.'"

She began to move under his hand. She took a big drag off her cigarette and stubbed it out.

"Ay," she said. "Colito."

THE PHONE WOKE Cole at ten in the morning. Susan was nestled against his back, one arm draped over his chest. He squirmed free and grabbed the receiver. «¿Hola?»

"Is my sister there?"

«Buen día, Alejo. She's right here.»

Susan grabbed Cole's pillow, put it over her face, and rolled away. "I'll call him later," she said.

«She'll call you later,» Cole said.

"We're going to have brunch in an hour if you guys want to make it." He sounded like he hoped they wouldn't.

«Doesn't look very likely. I'll see what I can do.»

After a long pause, Alex said, "Listen, Cole, you think you know Susan, but you don't, not really."

Cole gave up and switched to English too. "Aren't you supposed to be warning her about *me* and telling me what you'll do if I hurt your sister?"

"It's not you hurting *her* that I'm worried about."

"I'm a big boy," Cole said.

"Just watch yourself, okay? Please."

Though offended on Susan's behalf, Cole was also touched. "All right."

"Check in with me later."

«Órale,» Cole said, and hung up.

"What did he want?"

"We're invited for breakfast in an hour."

"No way."

"And he said to watch out that you don't hurt me."

"Prick," Susan said. "Are you sure you want to be part of this family?"

She took a long time brushing her hair and fixing her face with what makeup she had in her purse, then put on her pants from the night before with one of Cole's T-shirts. He took her to El Mercado, where she got coffee and a pastry with thick sugar frosting. After that she made him go into an upscale men's clothing store and try on a suit.

«I can't afford this,» he said.

«I looked in your closet. You don't have anything to wear to the funeral tomorrow.»

«Nobody is going to care.»

«I care, if you're going with me. Besides, I'm paying for it.»

«How can you afford it?»

«Peter's rich, remember?»

The suit was elegant black summer-weight wool with a fine chalk stripe. The tailor had to take in the trousers. «Ready tonight,» the salesman promised. «Eight o'clock.» Susan also bought him a white shirt and a silk tie and a pair of tasseled loafers.

"I've never been a kept man before," Cole said. They had drifted into English again as they walked toward the Jardín de la Unión, Cole carrying the new clothes in a slick paper bag.

"I don't give a damn about money. Never have. It's a problem, it makes people around me nervous. If I have it, I spend it, if I don't, I don't care."

"Now you sound like a hippie."

"Not me. I never felt like any of that had anything to do with me. All you hippies and flower children, it was like you were the generation after me. I was oldies-but-goodies and A-line dresses and V8 cars."

"And football players?"

"That goes with the big cars, the status-seeking. I thought if I went with the most popular boys then everybody would like me. Instead they were jealous."

"If you remember, I never bought into your whole sorority-girl act. That was never you."

She suddenly hugged him with desperate intensity. "To think

you were right there in front of me all those years. You tried to tell me and I wouldn't listen."

"Is this where I get to say 'I told you so?'"

"Don't you dare!"

Their harsh and angular English consonants embarrassed Cole. As they moved on, the stores they passed were all open to the street, selling silver jewelry, T-shirts, souvenirs. Susan stopped to look through a rack of earrings.

"I wanted to be useful as well as decorative," she said. "Daddy fought me at every turn. The boys were supposed to go into the family business and get rich, and I was supposed to get married. The only reason he let me go to college was to meet a husband."

"Really?"

"You don't believe me?"

"I believe you, it just doesn't sound like the man I know."

"Oh, I know you have this idealized image of him. Believe me, it was different for me. Some of it was just the culture he grew up in, but you can't explain that to a little kid. The day Alex was born, he lost interest in me. Not completely, he was very protective. But I didn't want to be protected. I wanted to *be* somebody. Did you know I worked on Roe versus Wade?"

"No."

"I knew Sarah Weddington when she was at UT and we kept in touch. You know 'Jane Roe' was a pseudonym, right? Her real name was Norma McCorvey and she was from Dallas. Wade was Henry Wade, the Dallas DA. I was spending a lot of time in Dallas to get away from Jesse, and Sarah let me do some of the scut work on the appeal—interviews, drafting some of the briefs. It was pretty exciting, as you can imagine, women arguing before the Supreme Court on a feminist issue. I thought maybe I saw a future for myself doing that kind of work."

"What happened?"

"Between Daddy and Jesse, they put their feet down. Typical, right? I had to give up my future as a feminist firebrand because my daddy disapproved. I wasn't strong enough to fight both of them. And so I ended up the shattered wreck that you see before you now."

"At least you've got somebody to blame. I managed to squander my talent without any help."

"I heard you last night, remember? Seemed like a lot of talent to me."

"Thanks. But I'm also over forty and whatever songwriting ability I might have had dried up years ago."

"So you're going to spend the rest of your life hiding out in Mexico?"

Cole pretended to think it over. "Sure. Why not?"

"It's going to be a long wait, if you don't even hurry it along with booze or dope."

Nothing like talking about his career, Cole thought, to depress him beyond words. "Maybe I'll get lucky and get hit by a bus."

"I need to shower and change and see my mother. You want to come?"

"Yes," Cole said.

He stretched out on the bed in her hotel room and didn't realize he'd fallen asleep until he jerked awake and saw her standing naked in front of the bathroom mirror, her hair wrapped in a towel, the air thick with perfume and cigarette smoke as she put on her makeup. He'd never been with a woman who did the whole trip, foundation and blush to eye shadow and mascara. Hair dryer, curling iron, hairspray. Going through that much work every day just to go out into the world seemed crippling.

"You know," he said, "you don't have to do all that for my sake."

"It's not for you," Susan said. "It's my armor."

When she was finally dressed, they walked to her mother's apartment hand-in-hand. Kids ran past, laughing, and younger lovers watched them with covert smiles. If science could synthesize the chemicals we're emitting, Cole thought, it would be Woodstock every day.

Susan's mother felt it too. She was propped up in a hospital bed in her living room, too wobbly to make it up and down the stairs any longer. Her skull showing through the skin of her face, a turban over her chemo-depilated scalp. Her raptor's gaze flicked between Cole and Susan as Susan went to her and kissed her forehead.

«Mama, do you remember—»

«El Guapo,» she said in a phlegmy voice.

«Hello, Iliana,» Cole said. «It's a pleasure to see you again.»

«I doubt that. I look like La Catrina.» La Catrina was the iconic female skeleton from the Day of the Dead.

«Only even more beautiful,» Cole said, and she laughed.

«I see Susana finally changed her mind about you. When did that happen?»

«Last night,» Cole said, and Susan blushed.

«Is it that obvious?» Susan said.

«I'm jealous. He's grown up very nicely.»

«Well, you may be seeing more of him. I've decided to take you up on your offer and live with you for a while. We can see how it works out.»

«Oh, m'ija,» Iliana said, and reached for Susan with both arms. Susan held her gently, then used a tissue to dab at Iliana's overflowing eyes.

She hadn't told Cole about her decision, hadn't brought it up after the first time. He looked down to make sure his feet were still in contact with the floor. Only the faintest of clouds shadowed his joy, the nagging reminder that getting what he'd asked for had not worked out that well so far.

«So El Guapo will be living here too?» She sounded like she had some concerns of her own.

Before Cole could say that he had his own apartment, Susan said, «Yes. El Guapo too.»

ALEX HAD NOT EXPECTED Cole and Susan to show up for brunch, yet he was disappointed just the same. He felt like Cole had traded him in for Susan and taken off.

The wake had played perfectly into the feelings of seclusion he'd been having, of loneliness, of time tearing things apart. At the same time, it had reawakened his sense of being a Montoya, of what that meant. And now Cole and Susan had to go and put the entire, delicate equilibrium of the family at risk.

After brunch, Alex's mother left to go shopping and Alex stayed behind with his father, his heart swelling with love in a way that it hadn't in years. «What are you thinking, Papa?» he asked. «You seem down.»

His father sighed and then, reluctantly, said, «Jesús was only two years older than me.»

«He also took really bad care of himself.»

«It's not like I go to the gym and work out. Sooner or later it's going to be me in that coffin, and what happens to my business then?»

The only problem with his father's second-in-command was that he wasn't named Alex Montoya. «Fred will take over and he'll be happy that he doesn't have to fight you anymore whenever he wants to modernize something.»

His father managed a sad smile. «You know me. Social liberal, financial conservative.»

The excuse had annoyed Alex down through the years. «Maybe it's time to let that go. The Internet is going to change everything. These online services like CompuServe and Prodigy—have you seen them? You can play games, you can buy things with your credit card, you can send instant messages to your friends, show your photographs, send files, all over your phone line in your own home. It's like... it's power in the hands of the people, like we used to talk about in the sixties. People will be able to vote directly on issues and we'll cut out the politicians. Everyone can be an author and a publisher or make records and be their own record company. Now that we're on an information economy, anybody with a computer will be able to work at home, and everybody will have a computer because they're so cheap. The government may even give them away.»

His father shook his head. «Can you drink a beer over the Internet?»

"You'll be able to order a case of beer in the morning and have it delivered that afternoon. And that night you can have a video conference call and drink it with friends anywhere in the world. There's more money to be made from this than you can imagine. All you have to do is put a bucket under the tap.»

«I wouldn't have the first idea how to do that.»

As an attempt to cheer his father up, the conversation was failing badly. In desperation, Alex started to throw out some of the half-baked ideas that he hadn't yet shared with anybody, stuff he'd been brooding about for months. «I can help you. We can start a new company, you and me. I've got a dozen ideas, mostly to do with music. The first thing we need is a way to compress digital music files the way GIFS compress pictures. Then I have this idea for an internet music service where you don't have to own physical albums or CDS anymore, you just pay a subscription fee and you can listen to any song you want, any time you want. You should be able to have a recording studio on the Internet where the individual band members can be anywhere in the world, and they can still make records together. I've got other ideas, but you can see how one project feeds off the next, and all that has to happen is for any one of them to take off.»

At last Alex saw that his father's mind had engaged. He leaned forward and put his elbows on the table. «We could share the legal and accounting departments with the import business, spread the expenses around, pick up some tax credits. How many people would you need to start with?»

The longer Alex talked, the more he started to believe it himself. His father took notes on napkins and after an hour of fevered discussion he smiled and ordered two bottles of Bohemia. «Do you have a name for this company?»

«I was thinking maybe... Mariachi.»

THE FUNERAL SERVICE was in La Catedral de San Diego, where Susan's first wedding had been. Cole couldn't stop noticing the contrasts. Susan then, in white and barely functional, and Susan now, in black and hanging on his arm. Jesús then, playing for the ceremony with Cole and Alex, and Jesús now, in a box, and Cole and Alex lost in the crush. The artificial happiness then and the genuine sorrow now.

«There's Papa,» Susan said, and ran ahead to talk to him.

Cole stood apart from the Montoyas and wondered how long his relationship with Susan would continue to make things awkward. As if in answer, Alex wandered over. «Nice suit,» he said. «Looks new.»

Susan was out of earshot. «I understand Susan's ex is footing the bill.»

«Not likely. Mac McKinney has a motion before the judge in Savannah to try and pry some money out of him. He cut her off when she left.»

«Then what's she living on?»

Alex glanced at his father. «What do you think?»

«Mierda,» Cole said.

«Don't say I didn't warn you,» Alex said, and turned away.

Cole trailed the procession, Susan falling back to walk with him. Inside, Félix sat where Cole had sat for Susan's wedding, playing a Bach fugue. They filed into a pew at the front where Leticia's sister had taken the aisle seat. Alex first, then his father, his mother, Susan, and Cole. Cole felt like Pluto, orbiting in the outer darkness.

The Mass went on endlessly, less enchanting than his first Christmas Eve there, but still affecting. Between the might of the organ and the delicacy of Félix's guitar, the quiet sobs of the women and the forceful solemnity of the priest, everything drove home the finality of Jesús's death in a way, Cole saw, that was meant to let them all be done with it and move on.

Two hours later they emerged blinking into daylight. They walked in formation through the pedestrian-only streets to the cul-de-sac where limos waited to take them to the graveyard.

The Municipal Cemetery in Guanajuato was so full that, as late as the 1950s, the city was still evicting the corpses of families that had only paid for a "temporary" interment and was reusing the space. The unearthed bodies, which had mummified due to the chemistry and aridity of the soil, ended up in a museum for the tourists. Jesús, on the other hand, was headed for a permanent grave in the new cemetery near the Plaza de Toros.

The sun had started to bear down and Cole's new white shirt wilted in the heat. More incense, more praying. Finally the casket went in the ground. Alex and his father were among those who threw a shovelful of dirt into the hole, and Cole was not. It shouldn't have mattered to him, and yet it did.

Afterward Álvaro and his narco friend Miguel Ortiz came up to give Cole an abrazo, and Álvaro said, «Have you thought about my offer?»

Cole needed a second to remember. Playing guitar for los narcos. «Still thinking,» Cole said with a smile.

«Nice suit,» Álvaro said, rubbing the lapel between thumb and forefinger. «Everybody deserves some nice things now and then, no?»

«I guess,» Cole said, «that would depend on the price.»

Álvaro's laugh was harsh and out of place. He and Ortiz moved on. Alex greeted them with a neutral expression and his father failed to hide his disapproval.

The Montoyas had arranged a buffet at the hotel. At some point during the evening Cole and Susan ended up standing with Montoya and Alex. «Your friend Álvaro,» Montoya said to Alex, «he's a narco now?»

«Why do you say that?» Alex shouldn't try to bluff, Cole thought, if he couldn't do a better job.

«Please,» his father said. «The gold, the arrogant attitude, the ostrich cowboy boots...»

«He's still a good guy,» Alex said. «We just can't talk business, that's all.»

«Business?» Montoya said. «What kind of business uses automatic weapons? They have better guns than the police.»

«Papa, they *are* the police,» Alex said. «Raúl Salinas has his hands in every drug deal in Mexico.» Raúl was the brother of Mexican president Carlos Salinas, and Cole was shocked by Alex's cynicism.

«What's going to become of this country?» Montoya said.

«It's only going to get worse,» Alex said. «It's capitalism to the limit. Why not just kill your business rivals? It's cheaper than trying to undercut their profits. Why pay taxes when you can own your own government officials?»

Montoya, showing more frustration and disappointment than Cole was used to seeing from him, turned to Cole. «Where do you know them from?»

«I met Álvaro the first time I came to Guanajuato with you.»

«I worry about you, both of you,» Montoya said. «These are very dangerous men.»

«Cole knows better than to get involved,» Alex said.

Cole had Desi Arnaz in his head, and Desi was singing, "Perhaps, perhaps, perhaps."

AVA HAD TO GIVE her mom credit. Once she said she would do something, she was good for it. The first week in August, they flew from SeaTac to DFW, where they stayed overnight with Grandpa and Grandma and dropped Ethan off for the duration.

"What about Cole's parents?" Ava asked. "Aren't they here in Dallas too?"

"One thing at a time," Madelyn said. It turned out Madelyn had never met Cole's father, that's how bad it was between Cole and him.

Ethan, who didn't usually make a fuss, was weepy pretty much from the time the plane hit the ground in Dallas. Her mom kept saying the wrong things, telling him how hot it was down there and how the food would make him sick. Finally Ava sat him down and explained why this was important to her and that she needed to know he was okay while she did it. He said it was okay, and that was that. She hated it that at 8 years old he had such a highly developed sense of self-sacrifice.

The next day she and Madelyn flew into León, because Guanajuato didn't have its own airport, and stuff started to get interesting. Ava had never been out of the US before, except once when they went to Vancouver for summer vacation, and that didn't really count because they spoke English and everything. Anyway, even before they got out of the airport, Ava realized that she'd had premonitions or clues all along. Like insisting on taking Spanish for her language classes instead of French, like her mom wanted her to. The way she'd always loved tacos and burritos and the way she perked up when Santana came on the radio. Madelyn said Cole was like that, that he should have been born in Latin America.

Ava tried out her Spanish on the guy at Customs, la aduana, who ended up being super-nice, so after that she was «gracias» and «con permiso» all the way to the big glass doors at the entrance, and it felt in a weird way like she was coming home.

Then she saw Cole. There was no mistaking him. He was leaning against a wall by the entrance, with a Mexican guy and a woman who looked Mexican and who Ava understood to be Alex's sister Susan. Cole was in faded jeans and a clean white T-shirt, hair in a short ponytail, looking older, duh, than the few photos her mom had of him. He looked so nervous that she hoped a car didn't backfire in the street or anything.

Cole pushed off the wall and held out his hand. "Hey, Ava. Long time no see."

«Fifteen years,» Ava said in Spanish. «More or less.» They shook, and Cole held on.

«I believe you're right. How was the flight?»

«Boring. Best kind, no?» Cole was grinning at her and Ava was grinning back.

"Okay, you two," Madelyn said. "Mom's Spanish isn't up to this. Let's keep it in English."

Cole introduced everybody. The Mexican guy was a guitar player named Félix who was Cole's "primo" and whose main reason for being there seemed to be that he had a car. Susan was checking Madelyn out pretty aggressively. "How do you do it?" Susan said. "I swear you look the same as the last time I saw you, which must be what, 1969?" She had on too much makeup and way too much perfume. Madelyn had warned her that Cole and Susan were an item now, and as far as Ava could tell he had traded down in comparison to her mom, who was, no matter how you sliced it, really beautiful, whereas Susan looked about ten years older than Cole and maybe was on drugs or boozing it or something.

"You're much too kind," Madelyn said. "You're looking good yourself." This was apparently one of those Texas customs she had tried to explain, where outrageous lies were suddenly okay.

Susan put her arm around Cole's waist and said, "Nothing like being in love to keep you young." That so totally embarrassed everyone except Susan that Ava began to count the seconds of silence.

Before she got to ten, Félix reached for one of their suitcases. "The car is very nearby," he said in pretty good English.

The car turned out to be a thrashed Dodge from the late seventies. They'd barely gotten the luggage in the trunk when Susan lit up a cigarette and Madelyn asked her, very nicely, to put it out because she was allergic. Susan made a face and moved downwind, where she proceeded to toke up on nicotine for a couple of minutes while the rest of them waited.

Cole and Madelyn were awkward as hell around each other, her asking about the weather and how long was the drive to Guanajuato, stuff she'd already looked up back in Moscow, and he asked about the flight, which he'd already asked Ava about. Félix looked at his shoes and tossed his car keys from one hand to the other.

Finally Susan got in the front with Félix and Ava ended up in the back between Cole and Madelyn. Cole smelled of deodorant and soap and clean clothes, not at all unpleasant, but it was weird to be aware of your father's smell. He had a lean, muscular body and a kind of cocky way of holding himself. Ava wondered how much she looked like him, because he was attractive in a way that might work for her. Cole got Madelyn talking about the new book she wanted to write, which meant conversation was covered for at least the next half hour.

Once they were through the tunnel and into Guanajuato, they drove to a restaurant called Mexico Lindo y Sabroso, which was pretty fancy, with lots of shiny tile and palms in big orange pots. There was a lot of stuff on the menu she'd never heard of, which Cole explained to her. Madelyn and Susan split a bottle of expensive white wine, with Susan doing most of the work and Cole and Félix drinking bottled water. After dinner a second bottle of wine arrived. Susan didn't act drunk, exactly, but she got more and more assertive, and she kept talking about what a great singer and guitar player Cole was and how happy they were when nobody was asking.

At the end there was a three-way fight for the check between Cole and Susan and Madelyn, and Susan seemed seriously pissed off when Cole won. They stopped off at the hotel long enough to get Madelyn checked in, and then she wanted to see Cole's apartment, which meant going down into the tunnels under the center of town, which was the coolest thing yet.

The apartment was pretty nice, up on a hillside, wood floors and lots of windows. Cole had rented a bed for Ava and set it up in the living room and made it with clean sheets and everything. Madelyn made a face and said, "It smells smoky in here."

Cole opened a couple of windows and said, "Susan won't smoke in the apartment as long as Ava's staying here."

Madelyn was a little tipsy, which tended to make her giggly, which made it difficult for her to continue to be a hard-ass. She put both hands on Ava's shoulders and said, "Don't forget."

"I won't forget," Ava said, rolling her eyes. Madelyn had made her promise that if she wanted out of the deal she would use a code phrase, "tastes like licorice," on the phone, and her mom would "swoop down like the Erinyes on Orestes," Erinyes being her fancy name for the Furies, because she was never one for doing things the easy way.

Another thing Ava liked was the way men hugged each other in Mexico. Cole hugged Félix and thanked him some more, and then Félix left with Madelyn.

"Uh, can I use the bathroom?" Ava asked.

"Down the hall," Cole said. "You know not to drink the water, or even rinse your mouth with it, right? If you want to brush your teeth, use the drinking water out of the dispenser in the kitchen."

"Okay."

When she came out of the bathroom she heard Susan's voice in an angry whisper. "... nothing but good things to say about you all night and you had nothing to say in return."

Cole said, "I feel like you keep springing tests on me that I keep failing."

"Well, I don't. And it's a good thing, because you *are* failing them."

Ava went into the kitchen and made some noise getting a glass of water. The living room went quiet, and when she came out of the kitchen, Susan had taken out a cigarette and lit up.

"Look," Cole said, "I promised Madelyn..."

"*I* didn't. And you didn't ask me."

"Please put it out," Cole said.

"One cigarette is not going to make any difference at this point."

Cole walked up to her and snatched the lit cigarette out of her hand and threw it out the window. It happened so fast that Ava and Susan were both stunned. Susan reached into her purse and came out with a pack of Kools. Her hands trembled and she didn't look too steady on her feet. She started to shake out another cigarette, and like a flash, Cole grabbed the whole pack and threw that out the window too.

"Ow," Susan said, clutching her hand as if he'd seriously hurt her, which was pretty unlikely.

Cole just stood there and stared at her. He was taking deep breaths, and they sounded a little shaky too.

"Fine," she said. "Either you can go get my cigarettes, or I will. If I go, I won't be coming back."

Cole folded his arms. "See ya."

She turned around too fast and wobbled for a second, then went out and slammed the door.

"Holy cow," Ava said. "What got up her butt?"

"Long story," Cole said. "She's spent her whole life thinking nobody wanted her for who she really was. So she's always trying to act like she doesn't care. Habits like that, the way you think of yourself, that can be hard to shake. Also tonight she's jealous." He tilted his head toward the kitchen. "I've got some cokes and beer in the fridge, and plenty of mineral water. You want something?"

"A beer would be cool," Ava said, putting the water on the coffee table and perching on the edge of her bed. "What's she jealous about?"

From the kitchen Cole said, "She thinks I'm still in love with your mother."

Ava felt a tightness in her throat. "Are you?"

Cole handed Ava something called a Bohemia and then he swigged from a clear bottle with a mountain on it. "I've been in love with Susan Montoya since I was fifteen. You should have seen her back then. She was always like this unattainable goddess to me." Cole sat in an overstuffed armchair, scrunched low in the seat, his feet up on an ottoman. It was exactly the way Ava sat when her mother wasn't around to make her stop.

"You didn't answer my question."

Cole laughed. "Susan's got nothing to worry about. That's all I'm trying to say."

Ava took a sip of the beer. It wasn't like she'd never had one before or anything, but it felt grown up to be so casual about it. "So..." she said. "What are the rules?"

"No smoking!" Cole said in a mock-stern voice and they both laughed.

"No, I mean, what am I allowed to ask questions about?"

"You can ask anything you want. If I feel too uncomfortable, I may not answer. I won't lie to you and I won't set any limits on what we talk about. Okay?"

"Okay. What I really want to know is, why did you run out on my mom?"

"The gloves are off already," Cole said with a smile. "Which time, in sixty-nine, or after you were conceived? The first one, I'll take a big share of the blame. The second one, she threw me out."

"Start with the first."

Cole was quiet for a long time. "I guess the best way to explain it is that it's possible to be in love with somebody that you don't have that much in common with. Maybe you love them because you want to be more like them. Smarter, more sophisticated. Maybe the things that you do have in common, like a certain kind of intensity, maybe that can be as hard to live with on a daily basis as it is attractive in certain situations."

"What did she see in you?"

"Man, you are ruthless. Beyond my incredible good looks and irresistible charm, you mean?"

"Yeah, besides all that stuff."

"I think I was not the kind of guy she expected to end up with. She could have had her pick of brainy English majors with trust funds, but for a guy like me to want her, I think it made her feel like a different person than she'd been raised to be. It was exciting and a little dangerous. It also didn't fit her in the long run."

Ava kept after him for a while, not sure herself what she was looking for. He was sort of kidding about the irresistible charm and also sort of not. Cole wanted other people to like him and he gave that easy affection back. Pretty quickly he turned things around and started asking her questions, what did she want to do with herself, what were her favorite classes, did she like music, movies, sports?

By this point the beer was gone and Ava had that feeling she got sometimes, that there was something missing from her life, and the absence was like a wound that hurt so much it made her eyes burn. She'd always believed it was her father that was missing, and yet here she was, in the same room with him at last, liking him, even, but the wound was still there.

"Hey," Cole said gently. "What's up?"

"I don't know what I want to be. It feels like everything's already been done. They've walked on the moon, they've put safety pins in their ears, they've invented the atom bomb and granola. Money's not the answer, drugs are not the answer, sex is not the answer."

"Love is the answer," Cole said.

"Then what's the question?"

"It's all part of the same question. What's it all about? Why get up in the morning? Where did I leave my keys?"

"I love my mom. That doesn't make the feeling go away."

"It helps, though. Loving other people is really important, and the other part of it is loving what you do. It doesn't matter what it is if you love doing it. When I saw Bob Dylan playing guitar, I knew what I wanted to do."

"You're lucky."

"There are days I might argue with you, but today is not one of them. Today I got to meet you and I feel like the luckiest guy in the world."

IF THE FIRST HOUR was any indication, Madelyn was not going to make it through five days of leaving Ava with Cole. She was twisted up inside like a wrung-out washcloth, imagining all the things that could go wrong. What if Cole thought it would be funny to get her drunk on mescal or stoned on peyote? What if Cole left her alone so he could go have sex with Susan and Ava got kidnapped and sold into sexual slavery in Mogadishu? It could happen.

After Félix dropped her at the hotel, she went to the bar for one more glass of wine, knowing she would not get to sleep without it. The first glass went down far too quickly; over the second she took out a Moleskine notebook and made a list on the soothing blue grid of the page.

1. *Ava is loyal.* So if Cole started trashing Madelyn, or suggesting things that she knew Madelyn would disapprove of, she wouldn't put up with it.

2. *Ava is responsible.* She had expressed a healthy nervousness about being in a strange country and she wasn't going to do anything stupid.

3. *Cole has changed.* This one made her pause with her pen hovering over the paper. Admittedly, most of Cole's adult life had passed since she had seen him; still, there was something calm and steady about him that she hadn't seen before. Part of it had to be the sobriety. Part of it also seemed to be Susan Montoya.

4. *It's the oldest trick in the book.* She stared at the page. Where had that come from? She was completely losing the thread. Oh, yes. Susan Montoya. All these years of Cole wanting Madelyn and her wishing he would just go away, and now here he was, not interested in her anymore, and now she was asking herself what had happened. Had she lost her looks? Had she gone so long without sex that she was now putting out dried-up spinster vibes?

5. *Don't go there.* She was exhausted and worried sick and yes, finally, drunk. She tore the page out of the notebook and crumpled it up and threw it in her purse. Bedtime.

Ava called at nine the next morning. Madelyn had been up since seven, moderately hung over, starving, pretending to reread *Sometimes a Great Notion*, waiting for the phone to ring and unwilling to leave the room until it did.

Ava was fine. Cole had let her have one beer. Susan had gone to her mother's house when Cole wouldn't let her smoke. They'd talked. "You know. About stuff." In Ava's defensiveness she saw the one catastrophe she had failed to prepare herself for: father and daughter had bonded.

Dear God, now what?

She spent the next four days seeing the sights of Guanajuato: the Mummy Museum, the Diego Rivera house, the Alhondiga, the People's Museum, the silversmith's shops, the cathedrals, the University. Enough Spanish returned to her for her to function. Ava phoned in every morning with a report. She and Cole had been to the Mummy Museum too; they'd gone to a folkloric festival at the plaza by the Don Quixote statue; Cole had taught her the words to some Mexican songs and she'd sat in with Cole and Félix at an upscale restaurant and made 17 US dollars in tips. They'd walked to the reservoir and did Madelyn know that people swam in the city's drinking water? They'd climbed to the Pipila statue and wandered the twisting streets for hours.

Madelyn joined them for dinner on the last night. Susan had reingratiated herself, and she and Ava had evidently made peace. Seeing Ava and Cole together was revelatory. Already they had private jokes that excluded both Madelyn and Susan, and Ava looked at Cole with something very like love, or at least infatuation, and Madelyn fought not to be jealous, or angry at Cole for not having been someone she could stay married to, or critical of herself for having raised Ava without the father she so clearly wanted. Well, there had been Paul, though Ava had never responded to him the way she did to Cole, and Madelyn and Cole were simply not possible. Because, she told herself. Because of lots of reasons. Because, for one thing, though he had matured in some ways, he had not grown up to the point of having a steady job or a stable life, the things that would have allowed him to be a contributing parent and to meet Ava long ago.

It was a difficult evening, and she needed, for Ava's sake, to act as if it weren't. She limited herself to two glasses of wine. She smiled at Susan when she came back from her cigarette breaks. She let the conversation find its own way.

They had an early flight in the morning. Félix and Cole picked them up at six AM and Susan sent her apologies. At the airport, Cole and Félix both hugged Ava, so Madelyn thought what the hell and hugged both of them. Cole didn't hold on any longer than strictly appropriate, and he was the first to let go.

At DFW she got another surprise; instead of her parents, Alex and Gwyn were waiting with Ethan in tow. "Gwyn was in town for the week," Alex explained. "It seemed like an opportunity."

Ethan ran to Ava first and hugged Madelyn as an afterthought. "Lord," Madelyn said to Gwyn, "I haven't seen you since you got up on two feet." Gwyn was five-eight and slim. She wore no makeup and her dark hair was cut in a shag that was as casual as her flannel shirt and jeans. She had a hawkish nose, a wide mouth, and deep, dark eyes.

"Me either," Ava said, and stepped up to awkwardly shake her hand, still holding on to Ethan with her left. Madelyn watched them check each other out, pen pals mapping reality to expectations.

Madelyn also needed to update her mental image of Alex. He'd gained some weight and lost some hair, but looked good in spite of it. Cole had not been the only one with demons; between his father and Callie and his non-specific rebelliousness, Alex too had been haunted, and he looked like he was at last finding some stillness.

They drove to Madelyn's parents' house and took two cars from there to La Madeleine near SMU. Her father kept insisting that the restaurant was named after her, though the joke failed to catch hold. At 68, his sense of humor was more insular and obscure every year and his vision bad enough that he could no longer drive at night. Madelyn could not look at him without being afraid of losing him.

At her parents' house afterward, Ethan crashed first, and her parents shortly thereafter. Gwyn and Ava decided to watch Cocteau's *Orpheus* on videotape, which Gwyn had already seen three times. Alex and Madelyn withdrew to the couch in her father's study.

Alex wanted to hear about Cole and Ava, "the straight dope, the stuff you couldn't say at dinner."

Madelyn told him what she knew, then asked about Gwyn.

"She's brilliant. She's going to a private school in San Antonio, Incarnate Word, and making straight As."

"Isn't that a Catholic school?"

Alex looked embarrassed. "Yeah, that part is weird. What could I do? She wasn't going to get challenged in the Marfa Independent School District and Callie wouldn't let me bring her to Dallas."

"Girls only? Cole always complained about having to go to a boys-only school."

Alex dropped his voice to a whisper. "Yeah, well, I'm not entirely sure Gwyn is exactly, uh, interested in boys. Or girls either, for that matter."

"Are you worried, or relieved?"

"Both, probably. I don't really care, I just want her to be happy and have a good life. And whether Cole wants to admit it or not, we got a hell of an education."

"Academically, sure. But a lot of the St. Mark's boys I've known —present company excepted for the sake of argument—could have used a bit more social development."

"You mean like learning how to talk to girls before putting the moves on them?"

Alex's eyes held something more than a smile. A dare, perhaps. His arm was on the back of the couch and he was sitting so close that their thighs almost touched. Madelyn's breathing sped up.

"Speaking of which," Alex said, "there's something I've been wondering about for years."

Madelyn thought perhaps she should look away. Instead she said, "What's that?" Now she was whispering too.

Alex leaned in and kissed her. It was gentle at first, then Madelyn's lips opened and it got more intense. She lost track of things for a minute or two and then abruptly she remembered where she was, that their kids were in the next room and her parents down the hall, that Alex was Cole's best friend and that she lived two thousand miles away. She turned her head away and put a hand against Alex's chest.

"I'm not complaining," she said, "but I think I need some time to get used to this idea."

"I don't know," Alex said. "I think I could get used to it pretty quickly."

Madelyn massaged her temples, trying to get her intellect to kick back in. "It's been an exhausting week. I should get to bed. I've got a long flight tomorrow."

Alex put a hand on her thigh. "Why don't you change your reservation? Stay a few more days. Let's see where this goes."

"Oh, I know where this goes. What I *don't* know is whether I can go there right now." She picked up his hand and put it on the couch. "Let me think about this. We're not kids anymore. There's time."

"Okay," Alex said. He wasn't cranky or impatient and she thought, Alex has changed too.

Alex gathered up Gwyn, and Madelyn hugged him at the front door. Ava said, "I'm going to stay up and finish watching this."

"Okay," Madelyn said. "I love you."

"I love you too, Mom." She said it without looking up.

Madelyn put on sweat pants and a T-shirt and brushed her teeth, checked on Ethan and got into bed. In the last moment before she closed her eyes, she touched two fingers to her lips.

IT WAS EARLY OCTOBER and the crabgrass was the last green thing in the lawn. Somehow the damned stuff could hold dew right into the afternoon, and Steve Cole knew it was going to be a bitch to mow.

Betty saw him changing into his yard clothes and said, "What are you doing?"

"Last cut of the year. Going to get it over with."

"I don't suppose there's any way to stop you. The Boone boy down the street would do it for twenty dollars."

"He doesn't overlap his rows far enough, leaves those seed stems standing. I'd be looking at them all winter."

As usual, the mower was balky about starting. Betty had said that if he was going to insist on cutting the grass himself, he should at least get one of those riding mowers, and maybe next spring he would.

The air was chilly but the sky was clear and he felt like an ant under a magnifying glass, the way the sun was boring into him. He cut the little strip on the far side of the driveway and then started on the main lawn. It was going pretty well until about halfway through he hit a patch of crabgrass that was particularly thick and wet and the damned mower died on him. He jerked the starter rope and the engine sputtered. He set the choke and tried again, and then the third time, in his frustration, he really gave it a yank, and at first he thought the mower had jumped back and hit him in the chest, but no, the damned thing was still stalled and now he was on his back in the damp lawn, struggling to breathe, and he thought, you have really done it this time.

He saw the cold blue sky through the branches of the mimosa tree. It was rushing away, like he was falling down a well, and his last thought was that there was something he had forgotten, something he had been meaning to do, and for the life of him he couldn't remember what it was.

WHEN HIS MOTHER called with the news, Cole immediately went numb. Then, once he was off the phone, he spent the next few hours alternating between relief and guilt. And a sense of possibilities now lost forever.

Alex picked him and Susan up at the airport in his new Lexus. They didn't talk much. Cole saw that Alex was only setting aside his displeasure because of the circumstances. Then Susan surprised him by telling Alex that she wanted to stay at the Montoya house, that Cole needed time alone with his mother. Cole thought that he and Susan might have talked about it first, but he kept the thought to himself, like most of his thoughts these days.

Alex and Susan came in only long enough to say hello and offer hasty condolences. Cole hadn't been in his parents' house since 1966, 24 years ago, more than half his life. The smell of the place, of ripe fruit and scented soap and furniture wax, instantly brought back feelings of oppression and anger and loneliness. As bad as things had been with Susan lately, he wanted her there, if only to surround him with her familiar fragrance of smoke and Obsession.

The last time Cole had seen his mother had been the weekend of the drug bust, 13 years ago, and though he'd talked to her regularly on the phone, he was not prepared for how fragile she'd become. She'd gained weight, yet the bones of her wrists and forehead pressed hard against her translucent skin. Her hair, dyed an odd yellow-brown color, was thinning, and arthritis shortened her steps.

Cole followed her into the living room. Here was the chair his father had been sitting in when he told Cole his guitar was forfeit for his Russian History exam. The couch where he and Janet had made love once when his parents were out at a dinner party. The patch of carpet where he'd lain to watch *The Man from U.N.C.L.E.* on Monday nights. He wondered if he had any memories that weren't painful.

"How are you holding up?" he asked his mother.

"Mostly okay. Only I get so angry, sometimes. I try to tell myself that if it hadn't been this one stupid thing it would have been another. He was so stubborn."

She looked at Cole. "I wish—"

"I know, Mom."

"I wish you two could have worked things out before he died."

"I know, Mom." He struggled to not put all the blame on his father. "There just wasn't any common ground."

Later he took his suitcase to his old room, which his father had turned into an office. He still saw it the way it had been. The window he'd lowered his guitar out of on the night he ran away, the closet where he'd sung along with his green reel-to-reel. They'd replaced his old bed, the one where he'd tried to fall asleep by fantasizing about sex night after night, with a daybed that his mother had made up for him.

He was supposed to be here to comfort his mother and deal with his father's death, yet all he could think about was his adolescence and the promise that had failed to materialize. He had been so sure, lying in bed and playing "I Can't Let Go" or "Do You Believe in Magic," over and over, so convinced of his own importance, of his destiny. Where had that gone?

HE WORE HIS new suit to the funeral the next day, the third time he'd worn it, and his third funeral of the year. Jesús in the spring, Susan's mother in September, now his father two weeks later. Whether the suit itself was bad luck or it had accumulated too many bad associations, Cole had come to hate the sight of it.

As he stood outside the Restland chapel, waiting for the service to begin, a stretch limo pulled up and disgorged the entire Montoya family, father and mother, Susan, Alex, and Jimmy, and then, to Cole's amazement, Madelyn and Ethan and Ava.

"This has got to be so weird for you," Madelyn said as she hugged him.

"I can't believe you came."

"Ava wanted to meet her other grandmother. And I wanted to see my father, and... other stuff. We'll talk."

Ava hugged him too. "Sorry," she said. She was in a long black dress and low heels, the first time Cole had seen her in anything other than jeans. She looked like she was playing dress-up.

"I'm so glad you're here," Cole said.

Madelyn introduced him to Ethan, who was beautiful, with long, dark hair framing Madelyn's eyes, and who regarded him with frank curiosity. Cole then introduced Ava to his mother, who teared up for the first time since Cole had been back. She touched Ava's face and said, "Oh, Ava, how lovely you are. Thank you."

Ava, embarrassed and speechless, looked at her shoes.

Cole's mother seemed prepared to stand there and stare at Ava for the next hour. Madelyn stepped in smoothly and said, "We're going to be here for a week. We'll spend some time together, I promise."

The ceremony would have been annoying if Cole had let himself get emotionally invested. A chaplain who'd never met his father and kept referring to him as "Stephen." Two hymns, which would have been two too many for his father. A canned sermon about an afterlife that his father had little faith in.

Through the ordeal, Cole tried to focus on his mother and to not keep wondering what Madelyn had meant by "other stuff."

The burial, at least, was quick, and this time Cole did get to wield a shovel. He had thrown three angry shovels full of dirt into the grave when he realized he was making a spectacle of himself and stepped aside. The chaplain tried to lighten the moment by saying, "That's okay, less work for the hired help." Cole was alarmed by the way his feelings had snuck up on him.

The wake was at his mother's house. The brass from the oil company made a good showing and Cole put up with their homilies for his mother's sake.

Around four, Susan came to him and said, "I think my family's getting ready to leave."

"Let's talk," Cole said.

They went out the glass doors to the back yard, which was mostly patio that gave way to a small stand of oak and sycamore trees. Cole led the way to a marble bench near the back fence and shook out his handkerchief for Susan to sit on.

"I'm moving back to Texas," Cole said.

"Just like that?"

"Pretty much."

"To be with your mother?" She sounded incredulous.

"Mostly, yeah. To get a real job, buy a house, settle down, grow up."

"Where did that come from?" Suddenly she nodded. "Oh, I get it. Ava."

"It changed me, being with her."

"You're going to live in Dallas?"

"Austin. But I'll be coming up most weekends for a while. Mom's going to need a lot of help. She's going to sell the house, move into one of those retirement places."

She lit a cigarette, her hands shaking. "And me? What happens to me?"

"I hope something wonderful happens to you."

"I thought something wonderful had."

"We fight all the time."

"We do not."

The sliding glass door opened and Alex stuck his head out. "We're leaving. Are you coming?"

"Yes," she said. "Give me a minute." When the door closed, she said, "So you're dumping me, is that it? No warning, no discussion, no second chances, not even a reason why?"

"Do you remember when you used my credit card a month ago

to buy a new dress without telling me? And I told you I couldn't live with somebody who was not honest and open with me? Do you remember what you said?"

"No, but I suppose you do."

"You said, 'I will always lie to you.' I've been trying ever since to figure out how I can live with that. And I realized that I can't."

She took a deep drag on her cigarette and said, "Your father's death has upset you way more than you realize. You're taking all the anger you never expressed to your father out on me. You should know better than to try to make a decision like this when you're under so much emotional stress." She stood up, took a last hit off the cigarette, and ground it into the dirt.

"You told me I was the love of your life," she said. "You told me you would always love me. So that makes you a liar too. I'll be at my father's house when you come to your senses."

Cole watched her walk away. Then he sat for a long time and stared up into the bare branches of the oak.

1993

"YOU'RE PROBABLY WONDERING why I gathered you all here today," Madelyn said, trying for a lightness she didn't feel. Her nervousness annoyed her; she hated the bad news she had to deliver; she resented having to ask Cole for anything. She'd picked Harthomp and Moran, a North Dallas health food store with a café, as the scene of their confrontation, hoping it might appeal to Cole's granola side.

Cole looked fit and tanned. His hair was fairly short, his jeans new. He glanced around, as if to make sure that it really was just the two of them. "I take it I'm a murder suspect in a bad play? That would explain a lot."

A waiter brought their sandwiches and Cole asked him, "Didn't this place use to be further down Greenville?"

"Yep. Whole Foods bought us out and we moved up here."

"I thought I remembered it. Everything's changing."

"Life in the retail food biz."

"Eat or get eaten, right?"

The waiter laughed. "You got it. Let me know if you need anything else."

The charm thing, Madelyn thought. Still working.

Cole bit into his sandwich and closed his eyes. He chewed and swallowed and said, "Real tomatoes. Nothing like it."

"You're growing your own, I hear."

"Tomatoes, corn, peppers, squash, onions. I've got half an acre under cultivation." He waved his hand. "It's been small talk for fifteen minutes. You were about to reveal the reason for this mysterious rendezvous."

She hadn't seen Cole since before she and Alex had gotten married. The last time had been in February, when he took Ava to see *Groundhog Day*. It had been awkward beyond words; Alex hadn't even come out of his study to say hello. She'd sent him an invitation to their wedding in April, and he had politely declined. As of August, Ava was in Austin, living in the Castle, starting her freshman year at UT. Cole still came to Dallas to visit his mother, though with Ava gone, he had no excuse to visit Alex and Madelyn. Thus she had called him at his mother's on this Saturday in early November, and invited him to lunch.

"Ava said you've gone to dinner a couple of times."

"Yeah," Cole said. "It's pretty weird picking her up at the Castle, I have to tell you. At least she's in Alex's old room. It would be too much if she was sleeping in the same bed that…" He let it trail off and now they were both unwilling to look at each other. "That's not what this is about, is it?" he asked. "Me seeing Ava is not news."

"No, I'm just…"

"Afraid to tell me?"

"Yes." She still hadn't touched her food. "Susan's dying."

"Oh, Christ." Cole set his sandwich down and stared at the table.

"Sorry," Madelyn said. "I could have eased up on it better."

"What happened?"

"Cervical cancer. By the time they diagnosed it, it had spread to her bladder and, uh, rectum."

"When did they diagnose it?"

"Two weeks ago. They felt like it was too late for surgery. They tried chemo to slow it down and it was too hard on her."

"How long has she got?"

"Weeks at most. Maybe days."

"Do you think she'll see me?"

"Well, that's what this is about. Alex doesn't know I'm here. I want you guys to fix whatever it was that went wrong between you."

"Don't look at *me*."

"I *am* looking at you, Jeff Cole. What started it?"

"Susan," Cole said. "Alex didn't want us to get involved."

"And he was right, wasn't he? Both of you got hurt."

How had she forgotten how intense Cole's stare could be? "You don't refuse to do something," he said, "because you're afraid of getting hurt. That's the first thing. The second is, I fell in love with Susan Montoya when I was 15. I imprinted on her, like I was a duckling. There was no way I was not going to get involved. Then Alex was pissed off at my leaving her, when it was clear that the situation was impossible."

"He wasn't pissed off. Just conflicted. Susan wanted him to be loyal to her, though he knew it was all her fault."

"He said that?"

"Don't you dare let on that I told you."

Madelyn watched his brain churn. "Then," he said, "there's you."

"I thought we'd put that behind us. When I came down there with Ava…"

"I was in love with Susan and so I didn't care about the past. Now I'm alone again and the past is this Bengal tiger trap I keep falling into. Logically, it shouldn't be an issue, you and Alex. I should be happy for both of you. But it feels weird. It feels like… a betrayal." He held up his hand and Madelyn caught herself staring at his scarred middle finger. "I know it's wrong to feel that way. I'm working on it."

"I have to ask this. Are you drinking again? Are you using? If you are, I need to know."

"No, I'm clean. It's still hard sometimes, but I'm not going to screw that up now. It's just…"

"Just what?"

"I don't give a damn about contracting. I haven't written a complete song in twenty years. I play once or twice a month, to smaller crowds than I played to in high school. I can look objectively at my life and say, okay, I blew it. Part of it was bad luck, part of it was just me. I wasn't cut out to be a star, obviously. But how do I live with that, day after day?"

Before Madelyn could say anything, Cole went on, "No, I'm not thinking of harming myself. I wouldn't do that to Ava, if nothing else."

The waiter materialized, looking concerned. "Is the food okay?"

"The food is great," Cole said. "We're practicing for a slow eating contest."

"Let us know," Madelyn said, "when you need the table."

Cole took a drink of his Snapple and said, "What about you? You're commuting from Houston on the weekends?"

Madelyn nodded. Parts of her story felt safe to talk about, others less so. Cole didn't need to hear that it had been Alex's intellectual curiosity that had won her over, or how Alex had called her in Idaho to talk about what he'd been reading, Alvin Toffler and Stewart Brand and Ivan Illich and Jane Jacobs. The night of Steve Cole's funeral they'd made love for the first time, and then argued about artificial intelligence and NAFTA and Vaclav Havel until four AM.

She told Cole how the closest open job to Dallas had been at the University of Houston at Clear Lake, a long four-hour drive away and a considerable drop in prestige. The campus was in the Houston suburb of Pasadena, where the sodden brown air smelled of oil refineries. She drove to Dallas most weekends. Now that Ava was at UT, it was just her and Ethan.

She kept to herself that she and Alex did not have the grand passion she'd had with Cole. In retrospect, those highs had been worse than the lows. Instead it surprised her to find how smoothly things went when there was no assumption of hostile intent if the dishes piled up in the sink or somebody caught an inconvenient cold or they couldn't juggle their schedules to be together.

"The other part of it," Madelyn said, "is trying to spend as much time as I can with my father. Like I was with Julia."

"With Julia?"

"Oh, Lord. Nobody told you."

Julia had come home for Christmas the year before, looking pale and thin. She said she had trouble swallowing because of a persistent sore throat. She hadn't been to a doctor, had no insurance. When the AIDS test came back positive, she fell apart.

Madelyn had to fly to New York to pack her meager belongings and terminate her lease. Julia stayed on in Dallas in her old bedroom, penniless and hopeless. Alex, out of sheer kindness, had paid for the obscenely expensive AZT that her parents couldn't afford.

"How did this happen?" she'd asked Madelyn. "How can it be that making love can now kill you?" She'd been having a bad day, her recurrent yeast infections having given way to pelvic inflammatory disease, with alternating high fever and chills.

"I don't know," Madelyn said. She'd been visiting every time she was in Dallas, at least a couple of times a month, at least an hour at a time, month after month.

"It's like the world turned upside down. Art is now a dirty word, soldiers are heroes just by putting on a uniform, government is evil, greed is good, ignorance is bliss. How did this happen to us?"

"I don't know, sweetie," Madelyn had said. "I don't know."

Among the many ironies was the fact that for the last three years Julia had been more discriminating in her sexual partners and unfailing in her use of condoms—too late, as it turned out.

A yeast infection killed her, Candida albicans; she was in hospice at that point, too weak to fight one more opportunistic disease. Madelyn had been holding one hand, her mother the other, her father standing at the foot of the bed.

If she and Julia had been close, Madelyn thought, her grief would have been less compromised, easier to work through. If Julia had been courageous and witty like in *Steel Magnolias* and *Terms of Endearment*, closure might have been nearer to hand. Instead Julia had faced the ordeal with terror and bitterness and a need to apportion blame that had left Madelyn as relieved as she was sorry when it finally ended.

Julia died in September and Susan was diagnosed in October, a mere 19 days later; Madelyn had not had time to learn to get through a Sunday without the nagging sense that she was late for something. Meanwhile, her father's increasing forgetfulness and disorientation were almost certainly the first signs of Alzheimer's.

She tried to stick to the high points, but she couldn't keep her exhaustion from showing.

Cole took her hands in both of his. "I'm so sorry. What can I do?"

"Fix this thing with Alex. He's going to need you."

"I would love to be friends with Alex again. I would like to see Susan before she dies. If you can make either of those things happen, I would be more grateful than I can say."

COLE GOT THE CALL from Madelyn that night. "That was quick," he said.

They had Susan in the Texas Oncology facility at Medical City, only a few blocks west on Forest Lane from Harthomp and Moran. "Can you be there at nine tomorrow morning?"

"Yes," he said.

He got there early. He sat in the truck for a couple of minutes listening to KEGL, remembering when it would have been out of the question to get up this early on a Sunday morning. The slick, deliberately offensive DJ finally drove him out into the cold drizzle.

The moment the hospital doors closed behind him, he smelled it. Bedpans and rubbing alcohol and the hot-ironing-board odor of carbolic acid. It took him back to hospitals in Oakland and Tyler, to Demerol and the slow, sleepy warmth spreading through his chest and neck and fingertips, and suddenly he wanted a shot so badly that his legs gave out. He sat in a blue plastic chair and folded his arms and closed his eyes.

He'd been clean for 13 years now and he hardly ever thought about smack, except for now and then when the loneliness wore him down, or he heard a few bars of "Achilles Last Stand" on the radio, or he saw Valentina's photo staring out at him from a magazine rack, or he got a Pavlovian high from a tetanus shot, or he came home from work with an ache in his back and his hands too sore to touch a guitar. Always something that blindsided him the way this hospital smell had.

Sometimes he let the fantasy play out in his head, all the way to the place where he was strung out again. Mostly he didn't have to. He knew by now that the craving would eventually pass. In five minutes he was under control again, if still shaky.

Alex and his father were waiting outside Susan's room. Cole flinched internally at the sight of them but toughed it out, extending his hand to Alex first. Alex wrapped him in an embrace, and they held each other a long time in silence.

Eventually they stepped away. "What did Madelyn say to you?" Cole asked.

"Let's just say I pity any of her students who 'squander the potential they were entrusted with.'"

Cole was startled by how far Alex's shaggy black hair had

receded, how deeply the lines had sunken into his forehead in the last three years. His father looked even worse for wear, his head nearly shaved, white hairs outnumbering the black, with a couple of days of grizzled beard to match. His shoulders hunched forward and liver spots dotted his hands. Cole hugged him too, and said, "I've missed you."

"I've missed you too, son."

"Can I go in?" he asked Alex.

"She's waiting for you."

The bed was cranked into right angles, her head barely higher than her knees. She wore a green knit turban and had attempted eyeliner. Slack skin hung from the bones of her arms. He reminded himself that what looked like irritation on her face was probably no more than insecurity. CNN blared from the wall TV. She muted it and left her hand lying on the sheet where Cole could reach it, so he picked it up.

She studied him for a few long seconds and then looked away. "What I wouldn't do," she said, "for a cigarette." She slurred the words. Her fierce internal energy kept her blundering on, wide awake and hurting, despite the heavy dose of morphine dripping into the crook of her elbow. Cole would have surrendered to it gladly.

Susan, seeing that her initial conversational gambit had failed, squeezed his hand. "Cole. How the hell are you?"

He pulled up a chair, still holding her hand, and told her about his house, directly under the flight path from Mueller Airport, and how he'd gotten it and the vacant lot next door for next to nothing, and how he'd learned to sleep with earplugs. About his vegetables, and the music room he'd added on in back. About his contracting job, and playing out at Antone's or Liberty Lunch. The longer he talked, the more relaxed she became, as if their six months as lovers in Guanajuato had never happened, as if they were sitting around the Montoyas' dining room table with the crucifix looking down on them, catching up the way they'd done a dozen times before, minus the flirtation, minus any input from her, as if the wounds they had opened in each other had, if not healed, at least slipped both of their minds.

In half an hour she was snoring softly. Cole put her hand on the bed and retreated to the hall.

Alex was gone. His father said, "Can I buy you a cup of coffee?"

They made small talk, Montoya still more tentative than Cole would have liked. Finally Cole said, "What did she say about me?"

Montoya tried to evade the question and Cole dug in. "Go ahead, she can't hurt me anymore."

"She said… well, for one thing, she said you forced her to sell her mother's house. That you kept all the money and then put her on the street." Montoya looked like it hurt him physically to get the words out.

Cole smiled. "We were both living in that house when I broke up with her. That's easy to prove. I assumed she sold it, but I wouldn't have taken any money from it, even if we'd still been together."

Montoya interlaced his fingers and put his elbows on the table, like he was praying. "She said you were still drinking, maybe doing drugs, and you were hiding it from her. That was the one that hurt the most."

"I can take a blood alcohol or a drug test right now if you want. I'm guessing that's not necessary."

Montoya still couldn't meet his eyes. "She said you were verbally abusive. That you said terrible things to her about being useless and a parasite."

"Not me. Those were the voices inside her own head talking."

"I didn't want to believe any of it, but I didn't want to call my own daughter a liar."

"I expect she was counting on that."

Montoya finally looked at him. "She's been this way all her life. So unhappy, always angry, always disappointed."

"Well, she had to choose between you and her mother at a very young age."

"That may be how she remembers it. What really happened is that her mother didn't want her. She said she couldn't take care of Susan and get her law practice going at the same time."

"Jesus Christ."

"We tried to keep it from her, but deep down…"

"She had to know," Cole said.

Montoya shifted his bulk in the plastic chair. "She doesn't have long now. I think it'll be a relief to her when she goes."

Cole could only nod.

"What kind of terrible thing," Montoya said, "is that to say about your own child?"

1999

Dave got to Tavern on the Green a few minutes early, though not so early that he could walk around and take in the spring that had once again erupted through the concrete and asphalt of New York City. What was the word for being amazed by the same thing over and over again, year after year? He knew that being early might make him look overeager, and he might have cared about that in his twenties or thirties. He was well beyond it now.

A cab pulled up and Alex Montoya got out, whose photo Dave had found in a *Time* magazine in the library. They shook hands and sized each other up. Dave was taller than Montoya and had 15 years on him. Montoya was in a pricey suit, and Dave had on a pair of khakis and a brown corduroy jacket over an open-collared checked shirt. They both looked like they could have done with a jog around the park instead of another rich meal.

"Incredible day, isn't it?" Montoya said.

"It makes the heart sing," Dave said.

Montoya took his time getting around to business. Dave asked how long he'd been in the city this trip, and it turned out Montoya had been in film school at NYU in the early seventies, along with Scorsese and that crowd, so he had some nostalgia for when it was still a real city and not just a Disneyland for the rich. They ordered and got their salads and then Montoya said, "You've at least heard of Mariachi, I assume."

"You had the ma7 file compression. Clearly superior to mp3 and it's a goddamn shame you guys lost out. There ain't no justice."

"Well, thanks. We've got a lot of other balls in the air, fortunately, and the stock is hot, so we're riding high at the moment. Which is why I wanted to talk to you. How would you like to run your own record company?"

Dave froze with a bite of Caesar salad halfway to his mouth and slowly lowered the fork. He'd assumed Montoya was looking for an endorsement or some other PR fluff. "Did I just hear what I thought I heard?"

"A boutique operation, maybe half a dozen releases a year. You can farm some out to other producers. I would secure distribution through one of the majors."

Lately Dave had cut back to one, maybe two production gigs a year, mostly favors for old friends. He'd been trying to convince himself he was ready to retire. He'd taken Sallie to Paris, to Japan, and, yes, to Patagonia. They had plenty of the world still to see, though the passivity of being a tourist didn't sit right with him, all that time and effort and nothing to show for it beyond some camcorder footage, identical to the footage shot by thousands of other tourists. Still, what else was there? He would be 64 in September, he'd made whatever mark he was going to make. Or so he'd thought.

Montoya was still talking, and Dave had missed some of the details. "You would have a complete free hand with the artists," Montoya finished up, "with one exception."

"Mr. Montoya—"

"Alex."

"Alex, then. You are talking about a very expensive vanity project." If the bubble was going to pop when he poked at it, he thought, let it be now and not later.

"Well, I wouldn't be heartbroken if you turned a profit. I'd give you a couple of years before that became an issue."

"So who's the exception?"

"A guy named Jeff Cole. You produced—"

"Yeah, yeah, I know. Good luck getting Cole to work with me. That Quirq record was chazerai by the time I was done with it, and all because I wet myself over having sixteen tracks and I didn't listen to him. Whatever happened to him, anyway? He had a gutsy voice and a nice way with the guitar."

Alex shrugged. "I don't have to tell you that it doesn't matter how good you are if you don't have luck, and Cole has always been short in that department."

"What kind of budget?"

"You'd be able to offer competitive advances, like in the thirty thousand range. I mean, obviously, you wouldn't be going after Springsteen or Madonna."

"How about Sallie Rachel?"

"If she'll work for thirty K, that'd be great. I loved the *Krupheimer* record."

Dave flinched. "I didn't do that one. That was Bones Howe."

"Sorry," Alex said. "Sore point, huh?"

"Used to be," Dave lied.

The waiter brought their lunches, risotto for Alex, pastrami and lox for Dave. To make conversation, Dave asked Alex what he listened to, and Alex responded with a few names like Jeff Buckley and Radiohead. Dave suspected that Alex was skipping over some of the same old Stones and Grateful Dead albums that everybody his age listened to, which was okay, because it was all about painting a picture, setting expectations, giving himself some credibility in the present day.

"How about you?" Alex asked.

"Lately?" Dave said. "Lately I've been listening to bop records from the fifties. Diz, Monk, Bird, all that." He laughed. "Not what you wanted to hear, right? Don't worry. I'll find you some new bands."

"Listen," Alex said. "There's one more thing. I don't want Cole—or anybody for that matter—to know that I'm the one putting up the money for this."

"He doesn't want charity?"

"I think he would see it that way, yeah. My idea, if anybody asks, is for you to say that you're being backed by some music industry entrepreneurs who want to remain anonymous. That's more or less true. Are you okay with that?"

"I suppose. I take it you're not going to call it Mariachi Records."

Alex laughed. "No, I think that might be tipping my hand. Got any ideas?"

"How about Official Records?"

"I don't know, maybe. Is there a story behind that?"

"Fischel is my real name, Fischel Cohen. I was kind of robbed of it when I started in the music business back in fifty-seven. So it's what you might call an inside joke."

"Works for me. But now I don't know what to call you."

"Call me Dave. It's the only name I answer to."

"Well, Dave, assuming we can agree on a salary for you, and assuming you can have a few days to sleep on it, what do you think?"

He thought the business with Cole was hinky and that Alex was underrating Cole's potential ill will. He thought Sallie would give him holy hell for taking on this much work when she was trying to get him to quit altogether. He thought if it did happen, it could make him happier than anything had since he first kissed Sallie in Zabar's café.

"I don't need a few days," Dave said, and stuck out his hand. "You've got yourself a record company."

MADELYN SPENT the endless drives between Houston and Dallas working out her next project in her head. It started as a prequel to her book on the sixties, but the more she thought about it, and the more she talked about it—to Alex, to her colleagues, to Ava and Ethan—the bigger it got. Her working title was *A Crisis of Idealism: Defiance in American Literature 1850–1951*.

She started by taking issue with the Renaissance idea of America as the New Eden, with its innocent Adams and Eves. Instead she saw the defining American trait as an idealism that stood up to dehumanizing authority. The political case was obvious, from "Don't Tread on Me" to the Boston Tea Party; the literary one was more intimate, starting with Hester Prynne and Bartleby, moving through Frank Norris's embattled farmers to the Wobblies of Dos Passos to Steinbeck's Tom Joad, and ending with Private Prewitt in *From Here to Eternity*.

Her intent was to place the revolution of the sixties in a continuum, and a noble one at that. The depressing and inescapable conclusion was that the rebellion, like the ones of her beloved protagonists, had failed, and now was in danger of being written off as one of history's comic interludes. She thought of Peter Cooke in *Beyond the Fringe*, reading a book about the heat death of the universe and being pleased that the author ended on a hopeful note. "He says, 'I hope this will not happen.'"

Madelyn too.

The book was her great consolation. As in the Road Runner cartoons, where painting a landscape on the side of a cliff opened a roadway into a three-dimensional world, she could fire up her ancient beige Toshiba notebook computer and cross into a universe of her own making, where nothing was more important than art, and learned discourse was the coin of the realm. For hours at a stretch she could forget her ratty apartment—the consequence of her insistence on living on her own salary—and department squabbles and problem students and weekends apart from Alex.

On a Thursday in early March of 1997, with 14-year-old Ethan at school, no classes on her schedule, no papers to grade, and cold drizzle falling outside, she had sat down to finish the rough first draft. She would still have miles to go—a year or two of rewrites, followed by peer reviews and more rewrites—but halfway through the concluding chapter she knew for the first time, without question, that she'd made her case and the book would stand.

The phone had interrupted her on the next-to-last page. The voice on the other end belonged to the chair of the English Department at SMU, telling her she'd gotten the job that would take her to Dallas at long last, with the promise of promotion to full professor upon publication of the book.

Her immediate reaction upon hanging up was an exhaustion as profound as anesthesia. She collapsed onto her bed and ran the numbers in her spinning head; the total came to over a thousand hours spent on the road in her own tale of two cities. She tried to remember how long she'd been pushing herself forward on will alone. Since moving to San Francisco with Cole, probably. Nineteen sixty-eight. Nearly thirty years.

This, then, was the payoff. Full professor, the top of her profession; a first-class faculty that included Marshall Terry, one of her favorite novelists; sharing a house every day, year-round, with her husband.

And, finally, the chance to spend more time with her father.

When she wasn't researching her book, she'd been reading Augustine and Aquinas, Locke and Kierkegaard. Her faith had been sorely tested by the remote and abstract evil of the Holocaust, by babies with AIDS, by global warming, but nothing had brought home the cruelty of the universe like watching her father lose the vocabulary that he had accrued and honed and savored over a lifetime.

He was the first one she'd called with the news about SMU, and it was the pride in his voice that let her appreciate the magnitude of what she'd accomplished.

The rest was anticlimax: finishing her last semester at Clear Lake; moving herself and Ethan into Alex's gated mansion on Inwood Road; splurging on new clothes, a new car, her own copy of the OED, all the luxuries she'd denied herself for so many years.

None of which compensated her for the day, less than a year later, when she arrived at her father's house for one of her twice-weekly visits and found him on the front lawn, her mother holding him by one arm as he leaned into the balls of his feet and stared into the distance, ranting in incoherent rage.

By the time he died, in January 1999, nothing remained of the man who had taught her to love William Blake and Laurence Sterne. The light in his eyes and his secret smile had been replaced by the lost and scowling face of a stranger.

The night after the funeral, her mother told her that she intended to move to Three Fountains, the same retirement home where Cole's mother now lived. The house had become a prison where she was confined with the memories of her dead husband and dead daughter. She left it to Madelyn to dispose of her father's things. The clothes went to Goodwill; Fondren Library at SMU agreed to take the books, after Madelyn had plucked out the orange-jacketed *Odyssey* and a few dozen others; the phonograph records and stereo ended up with Cole, whom she charged to find them homes, via eBay, where they would be appreciated.

In March she walked through the empty house for what she knew would be the last time, taking a silent inventory of its secrets. Here, barely visible beneath a coat of almond-hued enamel, were the pencil marks where their father had recorded the girls' heights age 2 to age 14; here was a tiny dent from where she'd stumbled at age 10 and driven one of the high heels she'd surreptitiously borrowed from her mother into the soft wood of her bedroom floor; here was the lingering scent of the cedar sachet her mother had kept in all the closets.

The Realtor was waiting outside to take possession of the keys. Madelyn had always believed in moving forward, but dear God, this one was hard. When she finally locked the door and started down the sidewalk, she had the absolute conviction that if she turned around she would see her father at the living room window, one venetian blind lifted, the way he used to do when she was in high school and headed out for the evening. She couldn't bear for it not to be true, so she just kept walking, one foot in front of the other.

BY THE THIRD DAY in the cabin, things were getting a mite tense. Joe was not all that sure what he was doing there in the first place, and Cole was not helping.

It had started with Cole getting a call three weeks before from Dave Fisher, who had produced the Quirq record, saying he was looking for talent for a new label he was starting. That he'd followed Cole's career, such as it was—that was Cole editorializing there—and that he'd always felt bad about the album they'd made and wanted to know if Cole might want to put together a demo for him. He'd done a pretty hard sell, only to have Cole tell him he hadn't written a song in years and he didn't think it was happening, thanks very much.

Shortly after that, Cole had called Joe down in Tupelo and kind of casually mentioned the demo thing, and it had laid there so heavy in the middle of the proverbial conversational table that Joe had felt compelled to poke at it a little. Why hadn't Cole written anything? Well, the words didn't come together for him anymore. Another long silence. Then Cole asked if Joe was still writing his lyrics or poems or whatever he called them. When Joe got him to flat-out admit that he wanted to try collaborating on some songs, Cole still played hard to get, said maybe they could try, to see where it went, and to keep that ripcord handy if either one of them wanted to bail.

Cole had the bright idea to get the cabin at Lake Travis, north of Austin, supposedly to get them away from distractions. Once they got up there, that was where the planning ran out. Joe had brought a couple of dozen poems, and Cole had read through them and liked them well enough, even said they should be published, though Joe didn't think he was ready yet to take the chance of being pissed on by some Yankee editor in an Italian suit. But when they sat down with Cole's guitar and tried to make them into songs, it wasn't happening. Silences that dragged on for minutes at a time, Cole's noodling on the guitar that either went nowhere or went into somebody else's song, Joe making a couple of attempts to sing and vetoing the results before Cole had a chance to.

Cole had brought a boom box and some homemade cassettes that Joe had looked through on the first day. Half of them were something called the *Anthology of American Folk Music*, which Joe found screechy and weird. "It took twenty years to grow on me," Cole said, "but now I love it."

"We don't have twenty years. What's the rest of this? Doc Watson? Big Bill Broonzy? Leadbelly? Jean Ritchie?"

"They were Madelyn's dad's records. She let me have any of them I wanted if I sold the rest."

"Clearly you are aiming at Casey Kasem's American Top Forty by filling your head with this stuff."

"Who should I be listening to? Britney Spears? Ricky Martin? The Backstreet Boys?"

Joe started to sing "Livin' la Vida Loca." Cole was not amused.

By the third night, driving back from dinner at a place called The Oasis, Cole said, "Maybe we should pack it in. This was not that good of an idea in the first place."

"I feel like I let you down," Joe said.

"It's not your fault. It's just me not wanting to let go, when the truth is I haven't got it anymore. I'm washed up without ever having arrived."

"I know the feeling," Joe said. He'd had a couple of margaritas on the deck overlooking the lake and they'd loosened up his tongue. "That's how I felt when I got my diagnosis."

"Diagnosis? What the hell?"

"Two years ago," Joe said. "Prostate cancer. They caught it early, but it was pretty aggressive and I had to have it out."

"Jesus, man, how come you didn't tell anybody?"

"It's not something you want to talk about." In fact he was already sorry he'd brought it up. "For almost a year after, I was in those adult diapers and I couldn't get it up half the time. I wasn't so sure I wanted to go on like that. But little by little it got better and after a year I was pretty much back to normal."

"Pretty much? I mean, forgive me for prying, but I always wondered what it was like, after."

"I can still get hard, still have an orgasm. But nothing comes out, you know? Because all that stuff came from the prostate. So you don't get that swelled-up feeling, like you're going to explode." He shrugged. "It's still pretty nice."

He couldn't seem to shut up. "The thing is, I hadn't been with that many women. I'd always been faithful to Peggy, and I felt ripped off, getting the cancer before I was fifty, not knowing if I was going to be okay after, feeling like it was my last chance. So a month before the operation, I started playing around with this woman I knew, a court reporter, a lot younger than me, not beautiful, not an intellectual, a real flirt, sexy in this obvious kind of way. And Peggy found out, and went to live at her mama's, and I felt horrible and broke up with that other woman, so in that last couple of weeks before the surgery I was all alone, thinking a lot of pretty terrible thoughts, hoping I wouldn't wake up from the anesthetic, that kind of thing.

"The day before the operation, I found those songs that you and me did for my wedding. I took the tape to a guy and had him transfer them to CD, and I sent them overnight mail to Peggy and told her how sorry I was, because I was pretty sure that if I didn't die on the table I'd find another way shortly thereafter, and I didn't want to leave things the way they were.

"Well, long and short, when I came out of the anesthetic, Peggy was there. So that's why I agreed to this dumb idea of trying to write songs together, because we did pull it off at least once before, and I owe you for that."

Nobody said anything for the rest of the drive to the cabin, night coming down fast, so it was full dark by the time Cole pulled into the driveway. Instead of getting out of the truck, though, Cole shut off the engine and just sat there, looking straight ahead through the windshield. "When me and Alex were in San Francisco for the so-called Summer of Love," he said, "I was talking with this girl. She was telling me about the Human Be-In, which had happened back in January, where it really had been peace and love, and not Methadrine and overcrowding and hunger and cold. She said, 'We thought it was the beginning, but it was already the end.'"

He looked up. The words, rhythmic and powerful, hung in the air. Joe grinned and Cole grinned back and then they both started to nod and laugh.

"Let's go write a song," Joe said.

ALEX FLEW INTO LaGuardia and took a cab to Dave's apartment, three blocks from the Dakota and Central Park. He called ahead on his new cell phone, an awkward contraption the size of a king-size Snickers bar.

It was Sallie who opened the door of the apartment. Alex had talked to her on the phone but only seen her in photos and the *Woodstock* movie. She was around Alex's age, no longer svelte but still nicely curved, wearing jeans and a sweater and bunny slippers, her eyes crinkling when she smiled, and exuding more charisma than anyone Alex had ever seen. She took his hand in both of hers.

Dave came out of the kitchen in a white apron and said, "Alex, this is—"

"I think he figured it out," Sallie said.

Dave looked at Alex's face and said, "Beautiful, isn't she?"

Alex struggled not to stare. "We have to get you on the road," he said. "Just standing here makes me want to buy every record you ever made."

Sallie laughed and said, "I do love my flattery. Don't stop, either of you."

Sallie poured the wine while Dave brought in stuffed mushrooms from the kitchen. Once they were all settled in the living room, Dave said, "Look, if you don't mind, I'd like to fast forward to the feature attraction. I want you to hear this one song."

The basic instrumentation was acoustic guitar, standup bass, piano and drums. The sound was spacious and raw—the snare buzzed in resonance with the low bass notes and Cole's fingers squeaked on the strings. A lead guitar came and went and at one point a trumpet and sax played two measures low in the mix.

The song itself was medium tempo, the changes moving from major to minor to sevenths, from hope to sadness to resignation, the melody sweet, with an ache to it that came from the timbre of Cole's voice.

The various elements combined to deliver a set of lyrics that quietly took Alex apart, like a lover's fingers that knew instinctively where to find the pain. In a succession of vivid moments— huddled in a doorway on Haight Street at three AM, caked with mud and stumbling with exhaustion on the road that led from Yasgur's farm, listening to the evacuation of Saigon in a car that had run out of gas—the song picked apart all the dreams that had failed and yet, somehow, impossibly, it refused to let them go.

Alex couldn't say anything when it was over, for fear that his voice would break. Eventually Dave said, "It's not going to be a hit single. Kids these days are sick of hearing about the sixties. And what this is, really, is folk music, like I used to listen to in the Village. But... holy shit."

Sallie said, "We've listened to it about thirty times. It gets better and better. I just love the sound that Dave got. It's like you're sitting right there in the room with them."

"Cole knew exactly what he wanted," Dave said. "This time I was smart enough not to argue. I think we can make some noise with this. Terry Gross'll love it, we can get the NPR crowd. It should get some great reviews."

"Is there more?" Alex finally managed to say.

"There's a whole album," Dave said. "Three covers, a remake of 'Laura Lee,' then eight originals, all written with this T.J. Maynard guy. None of it maybe quite as good as 'Already the End,' but close."

"When can I hear it?"

Dave smiled. "How about now?"

2000

COLE WALKED OUT onto the stage of the Wiltern Theater for a look. Four in the afternoon, 2000 empty red velvet seats. The vaulted ceiling barely visible, the ornate light fixtures turned off, the faux columns and filigree and polished wood dance floor in front of the proscenium all in shadow. It had been an Art Deco movie theater in the 1930s, meticulously restored in the eighties, and now, clean, silent, and expectant, it made Cole feel like he was trespassing.

Sallie came up behind him. "You should see it when the lights are on," she said. "It's glorious." She was whispering, and he could hear her perfectly.

"I'm going to have to step up my game," Cole said.

He and Sallie were the opening acts on the first leg of a Tracy Chapman tour that would finish up in Anchorage on April 25, a week away. Chapman would then fly on to Europe without them, and Cole would go home to Austin and Sallie would go home to Dave Fisher.

The initial offer from Chapman's organization had been for Cole to do a solo acoustic opener. Cole had understood that he was getting in the door on Sallie's coattails, still he wanted to use the dream band from his album. Luke on standup bass. A drummer named Rick, with a snap in his wrist that reminded him of Gary Travis of The Chevelles. A jazz pianist who was into Eddie Palmieri and who hit the keys so hard that Cole called her by Palmieri's old nickname, Rompetecla, the Breaker of Keyboards.

At the same time that Cole was making his record, Sallie had been cutting her own comeback in New York, *Second Bloom*, with her old sidemen Bernard Purdie, Chuck Rainey, and Cornell Dupree coming out of retirement as a favor to Dave, and Booker T. Jones filling in for the deceased Richard Tee. She couldn't take them on the road, so Cole had talked her into using his band and letting him share.

Cole had never forgotten the way she dazzled him at Woodstock, had thought of it every time he heard her on the radio or saw one of her LPs in a thrift store. When she walked into the Austin rehearsal studio that February, now more lioness than gazelle, when he saw the easy way she got his band to fall in love with her, when he heard how the years had added poise and wisdom to her voice, he understood that she'd only become more desirable over time. By that point he was in love with her himself.

The first time he'd said it to himself he hadn't been serious. After three weeks in the close quarters of the tour bus, after thirteen shows where they'd duetted on "Quién será," her singing the English lyrics and Cole the Spanish, as they transitioned from his part of the show to hers and he sang and played guitar behind her, it was no longer a joke. She laughed easily and listened with her full attention and gave credit to everybody but herself. Her mere presence was electrifying. Walking across the stage, she looked like the caress of her clothes against her skin was giving her pure sensual pleasure. She was two years older than Cole and looked five younger. She'd dropped ten pounds since the start of the tour and lately she'd been running with Cole every day. She was unselfconsciously physical, free with her hugs, touching him on the arm when she talked to him, on the face sometimes before she walked away, until Cole began to believe the attraction was mutual.

He'd overheard her on the phone with Dave and it certainly sounded like she was in love with him. Cole's desire made its own excuses. Who knew what kind of arrangement they had while she was on the road. If she wanted him to respect her relationship, she had to make that clear. And so on. Especially when he was trying to get back to sleep in his narrow bunk after the bus's squealing brakes had woken him up on some desolate stretch of Interstate.

So that Tuesday afternoon as they stood together in the Wiltern Theater and Sallie slipped her arm around his waist, he turned to her and very slowly leaned in to kiss her. She saw him coming. Her eyes had started to close. Then, at the last millisecond, she turned her face away.

"Oh, Cole," she said, "no."

Cole, restored to his senses, his face hot with shame, took a step back. "I'm so sorry."

She grabbed for his hands and squeezed. "No, no, this is my fault. I really like you a lot, and admire you, and I'm definitely attracted to you. I've been acting like I could have those thoughts and there wouldn't be any consequences. But the truth is that Dave is the only one for me."

"He's a lucky guy."

"I think I'm the lucky one. But... oh God. This is going to be awkward now, isn't it?"

"No," Cole lied. "I'll be fine. I just need to take a cold shower and recalibrate."

He started to back away.

"Wait," she said. "Can we go for a run first? It'll do us both some good."

IN FACT it *was* awkward. Cole's stomach was fluttery when he moved up to the microphone to introduce her that night. "Ladies and gentlemen, please give a warm welcome to an amazing singer, a woman who's written some of the most enduring songs of her generation, the incredible Sallie Rachel..." As always, he swallowed the "Krupheimer" as the audience, at least the female portion of it, burst into applause and cheers. Sallie came out and hugged him as she always did, sweaty as he always was, and kissed him on the cheek. "Jeff Cole, everybody," she said, her arm extended toward him as the applause for her continued, as if it were meant for him.

Cole was thinking he should step back to the harmony mike on stage left, but Sallie had made room for him at the lead mike that they had always shared before and as she motioned him forward she gave him a wink that no one else could see. He ignored the pang it evoked and stepped up, hit an E minor, and sang, «¿Quién será la que me quiera a mí?» the longing in the words and the melody hitting him hard.

After the first verse he stood aside and Sallie kicked off the

English version, "Sway," a big hit for Dean Martin in 1954, with less poignant lyrics. "When marimba rhythms start to play…"

By the end of the song they were side by side, Sallie's hand on his shoulder, trading lines instead of verses, and she was so at ease with herself, so joyful in the music, that she brought Cole fully into the moment himself, until there was nothing in the universe except the song and the woman beside him. He was able to sustain the good feeling through the rest of her set, but in the dressing room after, staring out through the metal bars over the window, he felt bleak. He washed his face and armpits and put on fresh deodorant and a clean shirt, then sat with the band, head back and eyes closed, and waited for Tracy to finish her set.

The next night would be Berkeley, and Tracy's tour manager had passed along an interview request from a DJ named Jack Hardesty at San Francisco's KFOG FM. Cole had failed to recognize the name until the tour manager said, "He told me to mention Johnny Hornet and to tell you he loves the new record."

Cole was pleased that Jack remembered him, though the words "Johnny Hornet" summoned all the pain of that time, all the possibilities that hadn't worked out. Listening to "Laura Lee" with Janet over the phone. Learning that McLendon had pulled the single the same night that Cole ran away from home.

The memories were still bouncing around in his head as he dragged himself to the meet-and-greet in the basement "green room," a long narrow space with green patterned wallpaper and black leather couches. He stayed in a close orbit around Sallie, if only because she drew a crowd of age-appropriate women, often beautiful and well-heeled. Cole had been celibate thus far on the tour, and was now prepared to reconsider that position.

He was deep in conversation with a woman named Teresa, fifties, slim, black-haired, with alert eyes and an intriguing mouth, when he looked up and saw Alex walking toward him, accompanied by a decidedly age-inappropriate knockout in a miniskirt and ribbed tank top, looking like an acid flashback to the Haight of 1967.

"Can you excuse me just one second?" he said to Teresa. "Don't go away."

He was unexpectedly happy to see Alex, and grabbed him in a bear hug. When he finally let go, Alex said, "You remember Gwyn."

The last time he'd seen her had been fleetingly, at his father's funeral, and she'd changed from an awkward teenager to a self-possessed woman. "I thought I did," Cole said. "It looks like I was mistaken."

She extended a long, narrow hand and Cole squeezed it gently. Then her cool got away from her and, eyes wide, she said, "Can I meet Sallie Rachel? I'm such a fan."

He came up behind Sallie as she was signing her umpteenth copy of *Krupheimer* that night and tapped her shoulder. "Sallie," he said, "I want you to meet my best friend..."

He was unable to finish because of the look that passed between Sallie and Alex, a knowing smile just short of a wink, lasting a fraction of a second and revealing everything.

"Alex Montoya," Alex said. "And this is my daughter Gwyn."

"Hi. I'm Sallie."

Cole took a step back, unable for the moment to process any of what he'd heard. He understood that Sallie was charming Gwyn as she charmed everyone. When he managed to tune in again, Sallie was saying, "You flew out here just to see Cole?"

"I know that's hard to believe," Alex said, ha ha, good old Alex, what a kidder. "You guys didn't have a stop in Texas and I had some business out here anyway."

Record company business? Cole wondered. He didn't say it because the realization was still too new and he hadn't figured out yet how he was going to deal with it.

"Can you guys get away for a while?" Alex said. "Maybe get something to eat?"

"Bad timing," Cole said. "We're in Berkeley tomorrow night and we're hitting the road in a few minutes."

Sallie was now looking at him curiously. It was barely midnight, and the bus wouldn't leave for at least three hours.

Alex looked hurt. "Wow, that's a tight schedule. It's been a long time and I was hoping..."

"Next time," Cole said, unsure how much longer he could keep up a good front. "Maybe in Austin or something." He smiled with the bottom half of his face and said, "Got to run. See you."

He walked away from their puzzled looks and found Teresa pouring a glass of cheap Chardonnay from the hospitality table. "Can we take a walk?"

"Sure," she said. "Are you okay?"

"Nope," Cole said.

They escaped into the corridor and Cole randomly picked a staircase that took them down into the cavernous space under the stage. Air ducts and work lights hanging from the raw wood of the ceiling. Music stands, scaffolding, lengths of PVC pipe, plywood floor. Cole leaned against the wall and Teresa gently touched his arm. "Want some of this?" she asked, offering the wine glass, and Cole shook his head. "What happened up there?"

"It's a long story," Cole said. "I just figured out that somebody I trusted with my life has been lying to me."

"I don't have to be anywhere. If you want to talk about it."

How was it that total strangers were capable of such kindness, and the people you loved and depended on were capable of such immense betrayal? Was it all just a matter of expectations?

"Could you hold me for a minute?" he said.

She set her wineglass down and slipped into his arms, where she fit perfectly. He allowed himself a brief fantasy. He would go AWOL from the tour, let Teresa take him home, spend a couple of weeks making love with this very sweet, very desirable woman before slinking away to Austin. Sallie would notice he was gone, but the audience wouldn't care, particularly. And it would read the last rites over the final, pathetic gasp of his career.

"I've never been a groupie before," Teresa said. "I'm a little nervous."

"Don't be," Cole said. "The sad truth is that I have a bus to catch."

COLE WAS THE FIRST on board, and he managed to doze for a few minutes before Sallie rapped on the side of his bunk and said, "Talk to me, Cole."

Cole followed her to the front of the bus, where the empty, predawn highway was already rolling up under their wheels. He stretched out on the couch and Sallie sat cross-legged facing him. "What happened to you tonight? One minute you were fine and then you just walked away. Alex was so disappointed. Is this about you and me?"

"I figured it out," Cole said.

"Figured what?" The quaver in her voice told him he was right.

"I figured out that Alex was the 'anonymous industry entrepreneurs' who were supposedly funding Official Records. You two obviously knew each other and were pretending you hadn't met. It's the only explanation."

He didn't bother to look at her and she didn't try to tell him he was mistaken.

"I should have known," he said, "that nobody who was really in the music business would shell out for a Jeff Cole record."

"I told them this was wrong," Sallie said. "I told them they needed to tell you what was going on."

"You told them that, but you didn't tell me."

"No," Sallie said. "I didn't tell you."

Cole finally looked at her. She was crying, the tears running untouched down either side of her nose.

"I don't know why it matters who paid for it," she said. "It's a brilliant record. Dave says he's as proud of it as any record he ever made. And he says he didn't do anything, that you did it all."

"It does matter," Cole said. "It makes me a charity case."

"Alex said you'd say that. But that's just as true of me. Dave made it a condition of the deal that I was one of the artists he signed."

"Oh, please. Who were all those people lined up to talk to tonight?"

"Tracy Chapman, mostly. And the ones who were there for me were there because of an album that's thirty years old."

Cole stood up.

"Cole? You're not going to do anything stupid, are you?"

"Like ditch the tour? Like throw myself under the bus? Don't worry. I won't spoil things."

Back in his bunk, he thought about how he had changed over the years. In the seventies, when he'd first suspected that his life was not going to work out, the thought had required booze or dope or smack to be put down. What he'd learned was how to go numb without external aid, to drain the panic from the dire voices in his head, to put one foot in front of the other no matter how desperate he felt, no matter how futile it seemed. It was all a matter of practice.

2001

ON MARCH 5, the Ninth Circuit Court out of San Francisco ruled that Napster was liable for copyright infringement and the brief era of commercial file sharing software was over. After the ma7 debacle, followed by the reluctance of the major labels to license their catalogs to his subscription service, Alex had moved Mariachi into the file sharing space. His father had always told him that you had to be agile, that nobody ended up with the business model they started with. In the wake of the Napster verdict, the company stock, which had been riding high on the Internet boom, dropped from 143 to 5 in the course of one agonizing week, and agility was no longer an option. Mariachi filed for bankruptcy and Alex, who had been rich on paper the week before, was wiped out.

Official Records had scored a modest hit with Sallie Rachel's *Second Bloom*. It wasn't enough to support the rest of the list, which had been well-received critically but needed career-building over time to earn out. Without Mariachi, nobody was left to write the checks to buy that time. The company folded and the CDs went out of print, except for *Second Bloom*, which Sony picked up when they signed Sallie to a three-record deal. Dave had tried to interest them in Cole, and the head of A&R had said, "It's great stuff, but I don't hear dollar signs."

Alex had put off telling Cole. After the fuckup in LA, Cole had not returned any of his calls, and the letter he'd sent was returned unopened. Sallie had been really pissed off about ending up in the middle, and he understood that. He also knew that without the subterfuge, none of it would have happened—not Cole's record or Sallie's, no tour, no Sony deal for her. That was why he was in business and she was an artist. Without people like Alex, she was the proverbial falling tree in the deserted forest.

When Cole again ignored his phone messages, Alex called the local indie weekly, the Austin *Chronicle*, and they told him that Cole was booked at La Zona Rosa Café on Saturday. The Villa Capri was long gone, turned into a football practice field, so he reserved a room at the Motel 6 north of town, a better fit for his current budget.

That next morning he reluctantly told Madelyn he was going. She was always after him to miraculously make things all right with Cole, and sometimes Alex resented Cole's ever-present shadow over their marriage.

Back in Palo Alto, at Madelyn's graduation, Alex had felt the first stirrings of attraction to her, and immediately put them aside because of Cole. Likewise, when she used to drop Ava off for babysitting, and Alex, in his loneliness, couldn't help but notice the way her beauty shone through her exhaustion and stained sweat clothes, he was always aware of Cole brooding in Austin. Not until Ava's trip to Mexico, when Cole was deep into his obsession with Susan, did the two of them have room to let a few sparks fly. That the sparks ignited a comfortable, living-room-fireplace blaze rather than a roaring inferno was okay with Alex. He did wonder sometimes what it would have been like to have her beside him on the front lines of the Kent State protests, or supporting him in his fight for independence from his father, how different both of their lives might have been.

She was, predictably, happy about the Austin trip. Then she said the most bizarre thing.

"You're in love with him, you know." She was gathering her books and notes for her summer session class on Myth and Allegory and Alex was finishing his morning coffee over the sink.

"What?"

"It's perfectly all right. I suppose in my own way I'm still a bit in love with him myself."

"You're saying I'm gay? When you have every reason to know otherwise?"

"It's not about sex. You can be in love with someone without wanting to have sex with them. I think you were in love with him at first sight, from the way you talk about it. I think it's part of the reason you married me."

Alex was so dumbfounded that he couldn't summon the anger that the moment deserved. "I think you're completely out of your mind."

"I know you do. And yet every once in a while I do manage to get through to you." She kissed him lightly on the lips and walked away.

His mind kept circling back to that conversation as he drove. It was like not being able to remember if he'd closed the kitchen window before he left the house.

He checked into the motel before seven PM and ate a late dinner at Dirty's, ordering the turkey burger and denying himself the onion rings as a concession to his cholesterol. By the time he got to the Zona Rosa, which was a restaurant on one side and a cavernous performance space on the other, Cole was starting his first set. He had the same young black drummer and fashion disaster of a string bass player that he'd had in LA, minus the keyboards. He went back and forth between a beat-up Martin acoustic and the same beat-up Strat that he'd played in The Chevelles. Alex didn't see any signs of backsliding into booze or drugs. Cole drank nothing but bottled water, and he was fully present at the microphone, almost scarily so, joking and casual between numbers and then nakedly emotional when he sang. The crowd loved him, and why not? He had passed from feverish youth to craggy maturity without losing his looks or, the bastard, putting on weight. The Lennon-esque roughness of his teenage voice had smoothed out and gained gravitas. He had all the pieces of stardom and yet had somehow failed to pull them together.

He wrapped up the set with "Already the End," and Alex had to fight back tears. He nearly walked out then, thinking, better to drive back to Dallas than to deliver more bad news. Instead he asked a waitress how to get backstage. She used her professional skills to assess the thread count in his shirt and the label inside his sport coat and pointed him the way, getting herself a five-dollar tip for her trouble.

In the dressing room, Cole was talking to a rough-looking blonde in big, tight jeans and a leather jacket, his eyes searching for an escape. The bass player and drummer played cribbage in the corner. Alex got close enough for Cole to notice him, and Cole excused himself and walked over. He folded his arms and said, "I guess taking hints is not your strong point these days."

Fuck this, Alex thought, and fuck Madelyn and my being in love with this asshole. Drop the bomb and go. "I had to do this in person. Mariachi went under, and it took Official Records with it. I'm sorry."

"You think I didn't already know that? Sallie told me a month ago. Did you drive all the way down here just for that?"

"Mostly. But as long as I'm here, I guess maybe I am curious as to what exactly you're so pissed off about."

"You lied to me, man. You sold me a record deal under false pretenses. You made me believe there was somebody who actually gave a shit about my career."

"There is," Alex said.

They stared at each other for a good five seconds without anybody blinking, then Cole went back to the blonde.

Alex followed him. "Why is it that I don't count?" He nodded to the blonde to acknowledge that he was interrupting her. "Why is everybody else's opinion worth more than mine? What does it matter where the money came from when the result was a brilliant fucking record?"

"The end justifies the means?" Cole said. "I expected better from you. That's what put us in Vietnam. That's Reagan pushing dope to fund the Contras."

Alex flashed back to the Battle of the Bands in Richardson, to Cole taunting Gary until Gary physically attacked him. Alex felt like taking a swing at Cole himself. "So, let me get this straight, you're sorry you got to make the record, is that what you're saying?"

"I love that record," the blonde said.

"Me too," Alex said.

"I'm not sorry I made it," Cole said. "That's not the fucking point, and you know it." And then Alex saw Cole's armor of resentment fall away and his shoulders drop. "I'm just... disappointed, that's all. One more disappointment in a lifetime of disappointments." He looked at Alex. "And what about you? What happens to you, now?"

Alex fought to keep his own emotions from showing. "Back to work for my father. I convinced him he needs his own IT department and I'm going to run it for him."

"CIO, in other words."

"Yeah. I didn't know you spoke corporate."

"Know the enemy. When you were in college, did you ever think you would end up like this?"

"Wearing a suit? Working for my father? It was my worst nightmare. But I didn't know shit back then."

"I think we knew a lot. I think we look smarter with every year that goes by. But I would never have predicted I'd end up like this. You want a beer?"

"Sure."

Cole pointed to a green plastic trash can. "It's Heineken. I asked for Bohemia, but…" Cole fished a bottle of water out of a second barrel and asked the blonde, "Do you want anything?"

"Heinie's good," she said, and Alex held one out to her. "Could you open it for me? I don't have a lot of strength in my hands."

"Sure," Alex said. A little kindness all around. Why not?

"How's Madelyn?" Cole asked. "I sent her a note last year when her mother died. That must have been tough, so soon after her dad."

"Yeah. She's been kind of lost in her work the last few years. At least she got something out of it. Columbia University published her *Defiance* book and it got reviewed in the mainstream media. She's got tenure now and she delivered the keynote address at MLA last year."

"She's the one of us all that got what she wanted."

Alex didn't say the first thing that came to mind, how hard she'd worked with absolute single-mindedness and dedication to get where she was, raising two kids in the process, despite two worthless husbands, then nursing her sister and father and mother in one city while teaching a full load in another. "She earned it," he said.

He filled Cole in on the rest of the family, his father seeming invulnerable and getting richer by the day, Gwyn graduating from UNC medical school in two weeks, Ethan starting his sophomore year at SMU in the fall, probably headed for an English major, Ava still working at Half Price Books, unable to figure out her next step.

"Ava I knew about," Cole said. "I try to see her when I'm up there with my mom. Poor kid seems to have inherited my fuckup gene."

Alex was tired of listening to Cole beat himself up. "She's not a fuckup. And neither are you."

"No," Cole said, "I still don't know how I ended up here. Some are born to failure, some achieve failure, and some have failure thrust upon them."

"Greatness," the blonde said. "It's greatness, as you well know. 'Thy fates open their hands. Let thy blood and spirit embrace them.'" Cole stared at her in shock and Alex didn't hide his surprise much better. "Maybe you should embrace your own greatness for a change," she said. She chugged the rest of the beer, set the empty gently into a recycle bin, and walked out.

The bass player in the unfortunate pork pie hat said, "Time, Cole."

"Be right there," Cole said.

"Are we all right?" Alex said.

"I'm not all right," Cole said. "And it sounds like you could be doing better yourself. But I guess I'll return your phone calls, if that's what you mean."

"You should write some more songs, you know. With Tupelo or without him."

Alex watched Cole stop himself before asking why. "I'll think about it," Cole said.

DAVE AND SALLIE watched the World Trade Center burn on CNN. Dave's first instinct was to flee, and Sallie, as usual, had the cooler head. She reminded him that traffic was impassible and every seat on every form of transportation out of the city was booked for days.

It was, Dave thought, an inauspicious way to start a new century. First Bush the Younger stole the presidency in broad daylight, and now the vultures of US policy in the Mideast had come home to roost. Life was suddenly precarious and music irrelevant. The future was too monstrous to contemplate and the past was irrevocably out of reach.

Sallie shut herself in the bedroom for a while. When she came out, she said, "Dave, you've got to turn it off."

He started to argue with her, and then he thought, what is it I'm so afraid of missing?

She put some matzo and cheese on the coffee table and they picked at it for a while. From the street came nothing but sirens, relentless, sawing at Dave's nerves. He was about to put the TV on again, just to block the awful noise, when Sallie abruptly got up and put Ahmad Jamal's *At the Pershing, Volume 2* on the turntable. The room filled up with piano, bass, and drums.

The sound hit him at first as a shock, as hideously inappropriate. Then, slowly, he understood it for the act of pure kindness that it was. Dave reached out to her, and as she moved toward him he saw that they would get through it somehow. Through the coming days and the coming years, somehow.

2010

Alex had lost the distinction between work and not-work years ago. He rarely went into the office. Instead he spent 12 to 14 hours a day at the computer in his study, most of it running the various businesses, some of it in personal email, and at least an hour a day on Facebook.

He wished he'd thought of it. Not just because he could have used a billion dollars, but because he would have done such a vastly better job with the interface.

Still, what a maker of miracles it was, and this morning's miracle was Denise Glover Polonskaya of Brooklyn, who worked as a Russian translator in Manhattan.

"I've only been on FB for three days," she wrote. "I can't believe you found me already."

Her messages were clotted with smiley faces and exclamation points. She'd moved to New York on impulse in 1978 with a girlfriend from teacher's college, failed to make the cut as a UN translator, lived on the verge of starvation for a year or so after her friend moved back to Texas in despair, then met a socially awkward arbitrage banker at a Peter Tosh concert in Central Park, married him, and through him found a job in an international law office translating contracts.

"I never had the vaguest idea what he did all day," she wrote, "not even when the indictments came down in '89. Or where the money went, other than for our ritzy apartment on W. 68th. Turns out he was spending quite a lot of it for high-dollar prostitutes to spank him with a tennis racket.

"By that point he had practically an entire law firm working to get him out of the securities fraud charges, so they threw in a divorce as part of the package. You know what court is like, it's a contest to see who has the most money, and I was never in the running. I was lucky to get out with enough to buy a condo in Park Slope before it got yuppified."

She mostly worked at home. On one of her weekly visits to

the office she met a nice Russian contract lawyer and ended up marrying him. "Viktor has the misfortune to be honest," she wrote, "so he's not rich. But between us we do okay."

Facebook was not Alex's only distraction. The past was everywhere on the Internet. He'd lost an entire night to watching black-and-white TV footage of The Lovin' Spoonful. He'd found page after page with photos of SoHo in the early seventies. A site devoted to the Studio Club had a picture of the Chevelles logo on Cole's old hearse.

All those things had driven him to get his student film, "Nimbus," and the edited interview with Miguel from the Young Lords transferred to DVD. He'd uploaded both of them to YouTube, using a custom email address. He hadn't told anybody about it, not even Madelyn. His fantasy was that somebody would stumble on them one day and get in touch. Watching them now was like finding an old check he'd forgotten to cash, or a love letter he'd neglected to answer. It made him feel dislocated.

So did looking in the mirror. He'd begun to resemble Ben Franklin more every year, bald on top with a fringe of dark, curly hair from ear-level down. He'd resisted the occasional impulse to cut it short because he no longer gave a damn for anyone's approval. Like one of the characters in Madelyn's book, he grooved on the defiance that his image projected. He'd even gotten a pair of rectangular framed glasses that evoked both Franklin and Jim-slash-Roger McGuinn.

Though his father was officially retired, he hovered over Alex and the business like a carrion bird, watching for the first sign of distress to swoop down and start tearing things up. He questioned Alex's investment choices, second-guessed his hirings and firings and promotions, and vetoed his every attempt to move the company into the twenty-first century. Beer was the foundation of the business, he said, over and over, and if you mess with the foundation, the house comes down.

Over the last five years, as Alex had continued to gain weight, his father had lost it. They'd all been alarmed once he dropped below 200 pounds, and they had to fight for every test they got him to submit to. He'd developed sleep apnea, which had driven

Alex's mother into her own bedroom and robbed his father of REM sleep. He had chronic digestive problems that no amount of fiber, probiotics, prunes, yogurt, or Metamucil could relieve. He'd started to develop cataracts, and when tremors appeared in his hands, the doctors put him on Parkinson's medication.

This morning Alex was driving him home from yet another doctor's appointment. He'd been messaging with Denise from the waiting room on his BlackBerry. Alex's mother was in the back seat. She was 85 and in reasonably good physical health, though she'd been too frail and too easily confused to drive for some years now.

"It's too much," his father said. "It's nothing but one disaster after another."

"It's not a disaster," Alex said. "You're 89 years old. You need to stop worrying all the time. You should be taking it easy. You could move to Guanajuato, watch the avocados grow."

"You just want me out of the way so you can run my business into the ground." Reluctantly, he added, "I'm kidding."

"No, you're not. That's okay. I love you anyway."

"I love you too. I love life so much. It's hard to believe, looking at the wreck I am, but it's true. I don't want to let go."

Alex wished he could say the same. He and Madelyn got along fine, comfortable, considerate of each other. Madelyn's work left her fulfilled and happy, despite her complaints about budget cuts and committee work. Gwyn had her own practice now in Wilmington, North Carolina, and a house on the beach. Ethan was teaching high school in Dallas and getting married in the fall to a woman he'd met while folk dancing. Ava was in the deceptively named city of Riverside, in the middle of the California desert, doing maintenance work for a solar energy farm that Alex owned a piece of.

Alex himself was sleepwalking. He pulled himself from day to day, hand over hand, not daring to think too much about it. He needed a Restoril, a joint, and a beer or two to sleep at night, and in the morning it took willpower and the smell of coffee brewed on a timer to get him out of bed. He kept his alarm clock on the dresser across the bedroom so that he had to get up to shut it off, because otherwise he might go back to sleep and never get up again.

Something had to give.

SALLIE HAD ALWAYS known she would outlive Dave. She was 12 years younger, women outlived men anyway, and she took better care of herself, as she'd told him a million times. Still, she'd relegated his death to some distant future, and when it came on January 15, 2008, at 4:10 in the morning, she was not ready. She'd woken up and Dave's side of the bed had been empty and cold. She'd waited for him to come back from the bathroom, and when he hadn't, she'd finally gotten up, afraid to look, afraid not to, and found him in the kitchen, stretched out on the floor. A massive stroke, the EMT guy said, he probably hadn't felt a thing. Of course he would say that.

They'd only had 18 years, 18 years that had passed like a long, sleepy weekend.

Everybody came for the funeral, everybody that was left. Ahmet was gone, Tom Dowd was gone, Bill Graham, Al Grossman, Tim Hardin, so many others. But Jake and Sebastian were there, and Booker T. and Bernard and Chuck and Cornell, God bless them, and Sal and Rocky from the Meteors, and Skip Shaw, Ellie Greenwich, Don Covay, Wavy Gravy, Boz Scaggs. Paparazzi everywhere, and a double handful of artists that Dave had nothing to do with who were there for the photo op. And Alex Montoya and Cole were there, and when Cole hugged her she felt so safe, so surrounded and loved that she wanted to melt into a puddle of grief.

Still, all those years of showmanship counted for something, and she held it together, at least until she drank too much at the reception and went to lie down for a second and woke to find everyone gone and the caterers cleaning up. She didn't discover Cole's note on the music rack of the baby grand until the next day. "Anytime, for any reason," it read. "You know where to find me." She squashed her immediate urge to call him because she didn't trust anything she was feeling. The empty silence of the apartment made her anxious, sleep deprivation amplified the anxiety, and underneath it all lurked an unbearable pain waiting to slice through her numbness. She left the note sitting by her computer, putting off calling from one day to the next until it became part of the cluttered landscape of her desk, invisible in plain sight.

That summer, to get herself out of the apartment, she proposed a songwriting class to the 92nd Street Y. It filled up in a matter of hours. To prep for it, she got the piano tuned, and once she started to fool around, she was suddenly jotting down half-formed ideas for new songs. The class came and went without bringing the fragments to life. She taught it again in the fall and ended up with more bits and pieces and nothing that could carry its own weight.

Finally, on a night in early December, after one glass of wine too many, she sat down at the piano with a portable cassette recorder and talked and played through the most promising bits, using up one side of a 60-minute tape. She rewound it, made sure it was audible, put it in a padded envelope, and sealed it up. She sent an email to Cole asking for his mailing address and went to bed.

In the morning Cole had replied with his address and a line of question marks. She knew if she listened to the tape she would chicken out. She addressed the envelope and stood in a long Christmas line to mail it. It was all she could do, having posted it, not to turn around and ask for it back.

That was on a Friday. On Tuesday she got another email from Cole, subject line CALL ME and his phone number in the body.

She was freshly back from running and she thought it over in the shower. She knew she was playing with fire. If they started working on songs together, they were unlikely to stop with music. It had been almost a year since Dave died, and the ache of missing him had never gone away, the emptiness of the apartment without his presence haunted her every night. As the hot water surged over her and the steam rose, she closed her eyes and ran her hands over her body, imagining they were someone else's hands. Cole's hands, say. That brought on a different kind of ache. You can't hide out forever, she told herself. Besides, Cole might have something of his own going on, or might not want you anymore. It might end up just being about the music after all.

She allowed herself one glass of wine for courage and made the call.

She didn't remember a lot of detail afterward. Cole's voice was so warm. He seemed so nice. He loved the songs, heard possibilities in them. What did she want from him? Critique or collaboration? Long distance or face-to-face? New York or Austin?

She thought she might feel less conscious of Dave looking over her shoulder in Austin, though she didn't put it in those terms. He suggested the week between Christmas and New Year's, when he'd be off work. She'd forgotten his day job. How did she feel about cats? He had a guest room, and they'd relocated the airport so he was no longer in the flight path. There were motels nearby if she preferred. She said she was fine with cats and they should play it by ear.

She arrived on December 26, a Friday. A blizzard in the Midwest had caused a three-hour domino-effect delay and she didn't touch down until 6:25. It was dark and cold and drizzling. They were both hungry so he took her straight to a Mexican place called El Mercado where she had a margarita the size of a fishbowl and a combination plate buried in tomato and lettuce, as red and green as Christmas. She was relaxed and ready for anything, and Cole was on edge.

The margarita loosened her tongue. "Is there still a problem because of, you know, Alex and the record company and all that?"

He shook his head.

"C'mon, Cole, talk to me. We used to be friends, remember?"

"We *are* friends. And I don't want to sound like an idiot."

"And I don't want to sound like a seventies bumper sticker, but friends are the people you can sound like an idiot with."

"I'm jealous of you," Cole said. "I wish I'd had your life and your career. I say that without the slightest desire to take it away from you. You earned it. You're an amazing songwriter and a great singer and possibly the most charismatic person I've ever met. I'm still jealous."

At that worst possible moment, she looked up to see a woman hovering over their table. "I'm so sorry to bother you," the woman said, "but aren't you Sallie Rachel?"

She was tempted to say no, mistaken identity, it happens all the time, only she couldn't bring herself to lie to a fan, not when she could possibly make the woman's night. She signed a napkin and shook the woman's hand, and when she was gone Cole was smiling.

"You see?" he said. "That's what I'm talking about."

"You want to be constantly interrupted at dinner? Believe me, it's not as much fun as it looks."

"It's one more reminder of the difference between you and me."

"Are we so different? 'If you prick us, do we not bleed?'"

"One of us will have a lot more people running up with Band-Aids."

"When I listen to 'Already the End' I don't feel different from you." Cole looked down at his plate. "When we were on tour together, playing together, we felt like two arms of the same Hindu god. That's what it felt like to me, anyway. At this moment the biggest difference I feel between us is that I'm happy to be warm and a little drunk and in the company of an attractive, intelligent, talented man who I really, really like a lot, whereas you are sad. And I wish I could change that."

He looked up at her then with a longing that, God help her, reminded her of the way she'd looked at Dave for all those years of missed signals. She shoved the thought away and reached her hands across the table. "Now cheer the fuck up, okay?" she said. "And do they have any flan at this joint?"

When they walked out to his truck they had their arms around each other. Once they got to his house, he brought in her luggage and introduced her to Punkin, his plump orange cat. He helped her out of her winter coat, and she waited until he kissed her, and then she kissed him back. "We have to go slow," he said. "I need to be less in awe of you."

"That should be easy to fix. But slow is good for me too."

He was a sweet and thoughtful lover, making sure of her orgasm before his own, and oh, oh, the big O, how she had missed the gift of it, so different from treating herself, and if Dave was not entirely absent from her thoughts, she never lost sight of who she was with, and the pleasures far outweighed the awkwardness.

The next morning Cole fixed potato and egg breakfast tacos

and said, "Now, was this all an elaborate pretext to seduce me, or would you like to try and work this morning?"

She felt as lazy as Punkin, who dozed in a patch of hot sunlight on the kitchen floor. "Oh, I suppose we could do a little work."

She thought Cole would break out the guitars. Instead he sat her down on the couch and said, "When Dave and I were working on my record, we ended up in his hotel room one night, really late, and he started talking about 'tikkun olam.' Do you know what that is?"

Sallie shook her head. "Is it Hebrew? I never did the bat mitzvah thing." The mention of Dave made her anxious.

"Yeah, it means 'healing the world.' He said that for him it meant that by setting a good example, by honoring all, what is it, six hundred and thirteen commandments, by basically being a good man, you could be 'a light to the nations.' A model of how to behave. And that way you could contribute to healing the world. I felt like he had got inside my head and understood perfectly what I wanted to do."

She went to the bedroom and brought the Puffs box back to the couch with her. She dried her eyes and blew her nose and said, "That sounds like him."

"All those pieces of songs you sent me, the ones with words, anyway, they're all about Dave."

"Oh God, I'm so embarrassed."

"Don't be. You should go with it."

When the guitars finally did come out, he continued to gently peel away her layers of artifice until she completely melted down. He held her, and then she was kissing him, and then they ended up back in bed for most of the afternoon. Afterward he cooked spinach and parmesan ravioli with fresh homemade pasta, topped with tomato sauce he'd canned from his garden, night falling hard outside and her falling too.

After dinner, she asked to hear some of the Mexican songs that he loved so much, and he got out a lot of scratchy old LPs and played her Trio Los Panchos and José Feliciano and Mariachi Vargas, and then CDs by Lila Downs and Cucu Diamantes. Her high-school Spanish was rudimentary, and he translated enough for her to follow along. He taught her how to cha-cha-cha.

The next day she turned it around and got Cole to talk about his marriage, and his daughter, and his father, and his relationship with Alex and Susan and the rest of the Montoyas. This time when the guitars came out, they both knew they were on to something. Neither of them felt like leaving the house, so Cole cooked dinner again, a dish of his own invention that involved layers of beans and cheese between corn tortillas with hot sauce and avocado on top. He didn't cry that afternoon, though he did that night when Sallie went through his record collection and DJ'd for him, playing songs that had special meaning for her and talking about them, and she caught him in the gut with The Hollies'"On a Carousel," taking him back to his senior year in high school and his first band and leaving home. Then she proceeded to do herself in with "Then You Can Tell Me Goodbye," the Casinos' doo-wop cover of the great John D. Loudermilk country song, where the singer says to kiss him each morning for a million years and only then, if it didn't work out, to say goodbye.

On Monday they bore down and finished two songs, not Sallie Rachel songs, as it turned out, but something new, a hybrid that carried both their musical DNA. They went for a run in the clear, cold afternoon and then Sallie cooked omelets for dinner, stuffed with more of Cole's garden veggies out of Mason jars. They hurried through washing the dishes because Cole was eager to get to the stereo. He started off with the Dave Mason and Cass Elliot LP, which Sallie could not believe she'd never heard. After a couple of cuts, he took it off and played Larry Campbell and Teresa Williams singing "When I Go Away" from one of Levon Helm's Midnight Rambles at his Woodstock studio. Was there anything that could turn you inside out like music? Love, maybe. Weren't they somehow the same feeling?

That sent her to YouTube, and sure enough, somebody had posted Emmylou Harris and Daniel Lanois covering Hendrix's "May This Be Love," which Cole had never heard. He came back with Laurie Moss and Skip Shaw doing "Don't Make Promises" from her first CD. "Her father was in The Chevelles, my high-school band."

"It's a small world. I met Skip when Dave recorded his first album. Can you believe he's still alive?"

"Some days I find it hard to believe that I'm still alive."

She straddled him where he was sprawled on the couch and kissed him. "Oh yeah," she said. "You're definitely still alive." She sat at the opposite end and lifted his feet up onto her lap. "I'm getting a strong subliminal message from tonight's playlist." She closed her eyes and bunched up her fingertips on her forehead like a psychic at work. "The word 'duet' keeps coming into my head."

"I didn't want to be the first to say it."

"Well, it's out there now. Jeff Cole and Sallie Rachel, together again for the first time."

"Except your name first, because you're the star. You tell me. You're the one with something to lose, I'm the one with everything to gain."

"I wish we had somebody to play the songs for. If only Dave were here…"

She couldn't believe she'd said that.

"Oh, shit. Oh, Cole, that was so stupid. I'm so sorry."

"Sallie. Sallie, look at me." She turned her head toward him, wincing. "I don't want you to stop loving Dave. You don't have to take away from him to give to me. The more you give, the more there is."

"Is that from a song?"

"I expect it will be, before the week is up. What about Columbia, is there somebody there you could send a demo to?"

"Columbia released me after *Hearth*."

"Oh, hell, Sallie, I didn't know. That was a great record."

"It 'didn't find its audience.'" She let herself talk without thinking it through. "What if… we did it ourselves? Recorded the album, then found some indie label to release it on? We could get Luke and Rick and Rompetecla to play on it. You could produce it, Dave said you virtually produced *Already the End*. We could do a club tour to promote it, work the radio stations… Cole, are you laughing at me?"

"Never. But I'm too old to spend months on the road anymore. I've got my gardens now, and my cat, and I like sleeping in my own bed, now that the airplanes are gone."

"I like sleeping in your bed, too. Nothing too strenuous, then. A night or two here and there."

"Let's get some more songs," he said, "and we'll see."

The next day Cole brought out some fragments of his own, and they were working on them when the phone rang. Sallie kept playing while Cole went in the kitchen to answer it, and came back a minute later with the handset pressed against his chest. "It's Steve from the Continental Club. Their opening act for tomorrow night cancelled. He wants me to do a solo acoustic set. Want to do it with me?" She lit up at the thought of it, and Cole said into the phone, "Have I got a deal for you..."

The Continental Club, it turned out, had been made over in the eighties as a retro joint—rockabilly, vintage country, roots music. To blatantly pander to their audience, they worked up covers of Elvis's "Return to Sender" and the Five Satins'"In the Still of the Night." They put two of their new songs on the list, three numbers from *Krupheimer*, Cole's "Time and Tide" and "Already the End," and tried to put them in a logical order.

The crowd went crazy when Sallie's name was announced and they pelted her with requests after every song. If it bothered Cole, he didn't show it. They loved the cover tunes, screamed during the *Krupheimer* selections, and despite Cole's badmouthing himself, they accorded him local hero status when he sang his own material. Sallie warned them that it was their first gig, and told them about the new songs, and the reaction, given that they'd never heard them before, was terrific. They closed with "Return to Sender" and got called back for an encore, so they did "Quién será/Sway" like on the Tracy Chapman tour.

Steve, the owner, with his wild white hair and pointed beard, was waiting for them when they came offstage, grinning and shaking their hands. "Any time you guys want to headline, say the word."

They saw in the new year at the club and Sallie had champagne and signed some autographs and then they drove home on deserted streets at 12:30. Sallie had her head on Cole's shoulder and was holding his upper arm. "I can't remember when I've had so much fun onstage."

"Me either."

They let that sit for a while and then Sallie said the thing she was afraid to say. "I'm not entirely sure I want to go back to New York." It was Thursday now, January first, 2009, and she had a plane ticket for late Friday morning.

"Don't," Cole said. He reached his left hand around to stroke her hair. "I want you here."

"I'm besotted with you," she said.

"I don't think anyone's ever been besotted with me before. What a lovely word."

"I need to sober up and think about everything that's happened in the last week."

"Sallie—"

She put two fingers on his lips. "Don't. We're taking this slow, remember?"

"Too late."

It was too late for her too.

At the airport on Friday morning it was a struggle to keep from breaking down. When she finally pulled free of his arms and fumbled her way through the security check, she looked back and saw him watching her, like James Dean pushing sixty, shoulders hunched, skinny and alone, and every cell in her body wanted to turn around and go to him.

On the plane she listened to their new songs on her iPod and began to ask the hard questions she could no longer avoid.

Cole called her that night. "How was the flight?"

"Miserable. And I hate this empty apartment."

"It's empty here, too. What are you going to do about it?"

"I'm thinking. I'm thinking very hard."

On Saturday she toured her favorite places in the city. The West Village, where she'd met Dave and then chased him down Bleecker Street on a cold, blustery day like this one, was unrecognizable, full of tourists and chain stores. The boathouse in Central Park, where she used to come with her guitar on weekends in high school to escape her parents, was closed and the lake frozen over. Zabar's was no more than a cramped little grocery.

On Sunday night she called Cole and said, "Let's talk hypotheticals. What's your dream scenario? Don't fool with me, Cole. I need absolute honesty, here."

"Honestly?" In his pause her heart stopped beating. Then he said, "The limit. I want to wake up with you every morning. I want you next to me every time I'm on stage. I want my address on your driver's license."

"Then we have a problem."

He was quiet for a long time. "Tell me," he said.

"I grew up in the city. I don't drive."

"If I'm not going to fool with you, you have to not fool with me."

"Okay. Okay, if I do this..."

"Say it."

"If I... leave New York and come live with you..."

"Yes. Please."

"If I do, I want you to quit your job." She rushed to fill the silence. "Dave left me enough money to be comfortable. I get sizable royalty checks, mostly from *Krupheimer*, but from other stuff too. I own this apartment, which is worth over half a million."

"I've always carried my own weight," Cole said, finality in his voice, the closing of the subject.

"It's time you stopped," she said. "If I'm going to pull up my roots to be with you, I don't want to sit around the house all day while you're out somewhere risking cutting off a couple of more fingers. You should be writing songs, and performing, and making love to me, not doing something a million other people can do."

"If that was the case, my records would have sold."

"That's crap. Whatever time you owed for the crime of having bad luck, you have paid it, with interest. Your bad luck is over. Get used to it."

"Sallie, I—"

"This is how art works. Sometimes you get a huge following. Sometimes you die in obscurity. And sometimes your work touches the right people and changes things. Maybe it heals the world a little, like you were saying. It's not about how many people are listening, it's about *who* is listening. And what they can do. In this case, what I can do is liberate you from your lousy day job so we can write more songs together than if you were pounding nails all day. Or am I reading the situation wrong? Do you like dragging yourself out before dawn to do menial labor?"

A long pause. "No. I hate it."

"Good. Do we have a deal?"

"Can I think about it?"

"Do you really have to?"

Another long pause. "No. No, I guess I don't. How soon can you get back here?"

"I need a few days. I need to sell a baby grand piano. I need to talk to my accountant. There's a lot of stuff in this apartment that needs to go. Why don't you fly up here? Quit your job, get a cat sitter, get on a plane tomorrow afternoon?"

"Just like that?"

"Why not?"

"Are you going to boss me around like this for the rest of my life?"

"Absolutely not. Only now and then, when you need it."

Having Cole in what she still thought of as Dave's bed was a little weird, and the balance of power was different on her turf, but the ease and comfort of it was the same, and the sheer physicality, the constant hum of sexual awareness between them, the casual caresses and kisses, made her feel half her age—old enough to know what she wanted and young enough to expect to get it.

Cole had brought his acoustic and Sallie got them a Monday night gig at the Iridium, where they ran out of encores and ended up winging it through a half hour of oldies and Sallie's hits, the audience loving the improvisation even more than the songs they'd rehearsed.

In March she arrived in Austin for good, a couple of days ahead of the van with her boxes. Her apartment was rented out through a management company, she'd sold most of her furniture, and Cole had built new shelves in the bedrooms and the den for her books and records and CDs, and a shed in the back yard for their overflow. Both of them were feeling the riskiness, the suddenness. As she climbed into Cole's pickup at the airport, knowing she no longer had anywhere to retreat to, it hit her hard.

"You okay?" Cole asked, hand on the ignition, not yet turning the key.

"Has it occurred to you that we might be crazy?"

Cole smiled. "Getting cold feet?"

"Not cold, exactly. Maybe just a touch of a chill."

He handed her a small package wrapped in the Sunday comics. "I was afraid of that."

She tore the paper off to find a pair of heated socks with attached D-cell batteries. She couldn't stop laughing. She was still dressed for New York, puffy coat and boots, and in Austin the night was cool and tasted of spring. She squirmed out of her coat and pulled her boots off and put on the electric socks. She kissed him and said, "Take me home."

In May, she dipped into her savings and paid for the studio time to record their album, all new songs except for "Then You Can Tell Me Goodbye," which had become Their Song, as if they were in high school. Luke and Rick and Rompetecla played on it, and when the money was right, she and Cole brought the band— or parts of it—along when they played out, mostly in the Austin area, sometimes for the corporate gigs that continued to pop up every few months.

Sallie's manager got them a deal on Matador and *Duet* came out to very little notice in December, swamped by big Christmas releases from Rihanna and R. Kelly and Chris Brown. But the reviews were good, and they kept coming, and it made Best of 2009 lists from *Rolling Stone* and Pitchfork and All Music Guide and a dozen others, and the same sales figures that would have offended Columbia made Matador quite happy. She got her money back and then some, enough to do another one when they were ready.

They had bad days, rarely both of them on the same day, and all in all Sallie was happier than she would have thought possible in a world that didn't have Dave in it. Though they'd talked about marriage, they'd both been there before and didn't feel like inviting comparisons. Cole said, "I want to choose you every day, of my own free will, all over again," and that sounded good enough for her. She was still, more often than not, besotted with him, and he, incredibly, was still in awe of her.

Then, two days before the anniversary of her move to Austin, the phone rang in the middle of the afternoon. They were just home from playing the Midnight Ramble in Woodstock and hanging out with John Sebastian and Levon. They'd fallen asleep on the couch, Cole with his head in her lap. He jerked like he'd taken 110 volts and stumbled off to answer. Before she could fall back asleep, he was sitting next to her.

"It's Alex," he said. "His father's dying."

UNTIL SMU, any concerns Madelyn might have had about the dangers of getting one's heart's desire had been purely hypothetical.

The high points of the job, she admitted, were everything she'd imagined, of which the highest were the receptions for visiting writers at Marshall Terry's house, where large quantities of wine and beer were required to keep the massed intellectual heat from burning the place down.

The low points were the rub. With the unelected presidency of George W. Bush, a new era of know-nothings had descended upon the US, where otherwise normal-seeming humans in public office proudly refused to believe in evolution, climate change, or science in general. Government funding for universities plummeted even as the economy took a nosedive in 2008. The outcry for universities to be run like businesses had, predictably, resulted in the same abuses as in the corporate world: bloated salaries at the top and austerity for those doing the yeoman work, as salaried professors were transformed into adjuncts, paid per class, and rendered unable to earn a living wage. Meanwhile, the majority of undergraduates, increasingly headed for MBAS or law school, regarded the humanities as a waste of the time they could have spent binge-drinking or texting on their iPhones.

Madelyn hated to hear her inner voices fall into such easy, cynical generalizations on such a depressing, drizzly March day. In hopes of relief, she stopped off at the English Department Common Room before heading home. There she found Adjunct Professor Diane Travers staring speculatively at the burned sludge at the bottom of the Mr. Coffee. Diane had a deadbeat ex-husband, two daughters in high school, and a second job waiting tables on weekends; she and Madelyn had a friendship that was more cordial than intimate.

"I take it you are not my three o'clock," Diane said. As an adjunct she had no office and thus met with her students under a tree outside Dallas Hall, weather permitting, which it currently did not. She abandoned whatever idea she might have had about the coffee and sat on the couch. "I don't get it. I make appointments with these kids to try and help them get the grades their daddies are demanding, and half the time they don't show up."

"This kid just now in my poetry class," Madelyn said, "kept getting up and looking out the window every five minutes. I finally asked him if he would kindly stay seated, and he said no, he was parked illegally right below the window, and he was watching to make sure he didn't get towed."

"Let me guess," Diane said. "Brand new Mustang, right?"

"You called it." smu's mascot was the Mustang, so Diane's prescience was not that remarkable.

"Damn car costs more than I make teaching here in a year."

"This is the same kid," Madelyn said, "whose father called me at home after his first paper to explain how important it was that his son get an A instead of the B I'd given him, though he deserved a C. I told him he would have to take that up with his son, and he complained to the Dean. It's the sheer, unadulterated privilege of it."

Diane gave her the "who do you think you're talking to?" look that was so effective at withering her students. Because one part of her ancestry originated in Africa, she had spent her academic career being offered courses like "Crisis in Black and White" and "The Enduring Influence of the Harlem Renaissance" when her real interests were Chaucer, Donne, Dante, and Shakespeare. She had never said anything to suggest that she resented Madelyn's full professorship, or her rich husband, or her ownership of the Shakespeare seminar, still, the tension was there, if only in Madelyn's mind.

"Sorry," Madelyn said. "That was thoughtless."

"It's not like I don't sympathize. Half these kids, they're just serving time."

"Maybe I'm burned out," Madelyn said. "Maybe it's time to retire." She listened to her words hang in the air. "Dear God, that sounds dire. That's not what I want to do at all."

Diane looked at her watch. "Have you got plans for tonight?"

Alex and Madelyn tended to thaw frozen dinners when the impulse took them; eating together was the exception rather than the rule. "Not if I make a phone call."

"Make the call," Diane said. "I want to show you something."

They took Diane's car, a worn, well-cared-for, 15-year-old Buick. Diane refused to tell her where they were going, only that it started at seven and they ought to eat something first. Diane suggested Taco Cabana, which was fine with Madelyn. As they ate they traded their "superhero origin stories," as Diane put it. She was a third-generation academic, her father having taught history at Hunter College and his mother in turn having been a math teacher at North Carolina College for Negroes, as NC Central in Durham was then known.

"Remember," Diane said, "when we took for granted that we would all do better than our parents? I was born in sixty-four, early enough that I still internalized a piece of that dream. We lived in Harlem, but we would go to Lincoln Center, and Shakespeare in the Park, and Off-Broadway. I thought I was bound for Harvard, or at least Columbia, only I didn't get the scholarships, and tuition at Hunter was free because of my dad.

"I was just getting my own career going at U. of Oregon when I met Gomer Pyle." Madelyn had never heard her refer to her ex by any other name. He was a white, Southern ex-Marine who'd had a paradigm shift after the first Gulf War, grown his hair, and worked for various radical causes while crashing on other people's floors. "Oh, he was good. He convinced me that I could have it all, family and career, because he had my back. Two kids and a Reno divorce later, I am as you see me now."

They washed up and got on Central Expressway headed south. They were going against traffic and the rain had eased up. After they passed the downtown skyscrapers and got off Central, they might as well have been in another city as far as Madelyn was concerned; other than going to the Cotton Bowl and the

State Fairgrounds, she couldn't remember ever driving on surface streets south of downtown, let alone getting out and walking around.

Diane parked in front of a long, low, precast concrete building whose sign read EL PUEBLO COMMUNITY COLLEGE.

"You teach here?" Madelyn asked.

"ESL. English as a Second Language."

"I'm impressed."

"I get paid," Diane said. "A little. That's not why I do it."

The drizzle had turned to mist and they left their umbrellas furled. In the lobby, three men and two women stood waiting for Diane. The youngest was still in her teens, and the oldest was a Buddha-shaped man in his sixties. Most of them hugged Diane, and when she introduced Madelyn as a friend, they waved to her and smiled. A dark man with a pony tail and a couple of missing teeth took her hand in both of his and said, "How are you doing today?"

"I'm well," Madelyn said. "How are you?"

"Good," he said. "I'm good."

The chairs in the classroom were made of orange plastic and had built-in linoleum-covered desks. One of the fluorescent fixtures in the tiled ceiling was dark, and the worn green linoleum floor was clean. On Madelyn's left as she faced the room were four African women in brightly colored head scarves and floor-length dresses, one of them with a four-year-old child. Two African men in sport shirts sat nearby. The Latinos, who were slightly outnumbered, all sat on the right, the men talking to each other in a mixture of Spanish and English. The women had their own conversation, too quiet for Madelyn to hear. She took a seat in the middle of the room, where the two cultures met, and watched a few more students trickle in.

At 7:15 Diane stood up and smiled and said, "Good evening!" and the entire glass responded, "Good evening, Ms. Travers!" She went to the blackboard and wrote the word FAMILY. "Tonight," she said, "we're going to learn about each other's families."

★

CLASS RAN UNTIL 9:45 and it was after ten by the time the last of the students, the man with the pony tail, finally said goodbye to them in the parking lot. They got in the car and fastened their seat belts, and Diane let out an enormous sigh.

"You must be exhausted," Madelyn said.

"Exhausted, frustrated, jazzed, grateful." She started the car and waved to one of the African men as they drove past him.

"The jazzed I can understand," Madelyn said. "To be in a class-room where everybody actually wanted to learn what you were teaching them..."

"The frustration is trying to bridge that chasm between the cultures. You saw it in class tonight, the way the Latinos were all speaking up and I had to fight to let the Africans get a word in, because they don't have that kind of boisterous culture. I wish they would all sit together, and sometimes by the end of the semester it loosens up, but... The Sudanese guy in the white T-shirt and khakis? He's not even taking the class, he's just there to stand guard over his wife. The old Salvadorian guy, he's not registered either, but Inez can't leave him at home or he'll wander off. I will never know what any of them has gone through to get as far as that class. Coyotes, border crossings, refugee camps. Last year I had a guy from Somalia whose hands had been cut off above the wrists. Both hands. He took notes by holding his pen between the two stubs. I never got the courage to ask him what happened. Not because I was afraid of offending him, but because I didn't think I'd be able to stand having that knowledge in my head. Which is where the grateful comes in. This class makes me grateful for my boring, middle-class life."

"And it makes me wonder what I've done in my long and privileged existence that compares to this."

"Don't go all melodramatic on me. If they hadn't ended up in my class, there are plenty of other ESL teachers."

"But you've got a gift. And they loved you, that was obvious."

"First of all, understand that there are twenty people registered for the class and tonight twelve of them showed up, which is close to a record. The class meets twice a week, and there isn't anybody who makes it to every class. They'll have to work, or they'll be exhausted from working, or they'll have a sick kid, or it'll be Ramadan or some other reason that's more powerful than their desire to be in class with me. Secondly, I read *A Crisis of Idealism*, and if you're not proud of having written that book, you're batshit crazy. Thirdly, if you want to try it yourself, it's a hundred and twenty hours to get certified. You can do the whole thing in a month, or you can spread it out. It's not for everybody."

"But it is for you."

Diane swung into the left lane and accelerated into an open stretch of road. "Yeah," she said. "Yeah, it is."

It was 10:50 by the time Madelyn punched in the entry code and drove down the twisting gravel road to the house. Her brain was hyperactive from the class, from Diane complimenting her book, from the sense of invisible worlds and complex lives all around her, of possibilities she hadn't begun to think of yet. She felt 20 years old again.

She needed a second to realize that Alex's car was gone and the house was dark except for the outside lights on the timer. As she opened the front door she saw the blinking red light on the answering machine in the hall.

She juggled her keys and her armload of books and pressed PLAY. "I'm at the hospital," Alex's voice said. His words were flat with suppressed emotion. "It's Papa. It's bad."

AVA KNEW in her heart that she, and everyone her age and younger, was not going to die of old age. Maybe it would be a direct result of climate change, in the form of flood, hurricane, or wildfire. Maybe it would be indirect, like homicide or starvation or global war. Her mother used to talk about how awful it was to grow up in fear of nuclear Armageddon. That seemed quick and painless and far less inevitable than the future Ava had in front of her.

That knowledge had paralyzed her for years, kept her working dead end jobs and living over garages, refusing to get attached to friends or lovers, getting drunk or high when she could afford it.

It was Cole, of all people, who turned her around. She'd been spending a few days in Austin in the summer of 2008, and she and Cole were throwing a baseball around. Years before, when Cole had first produced what Madelyn disdainfully referred to as a "sports object," he explained, uncomfortably, that he was trying to make up for something he'd missed out on as a kid. Though Ava had little interest in watching sports on TV, it turned out to be fun enough when she was doing it herself. That particular June afternoon, Cole was pretending that he wasn't really bugging her about "doing something with her life," and Ava, 33 years old, already past her prime by the standards Cole had grown up with, was letting him get away with it, because it was pretty cool to run and sweat and feel the ball bury itself in the pocket of her glove with a loud smack. To be good at something that wasn't expected of her.

"I just feel like, why bother?" Ava said. "There's seven billion people in the world. They all want cars and cable TV. We couldn't turn things around now even if we got all seven billion with the program. It's over."

For a while the ball went back and forth while Cole thought about it. Eventually he said, "You ever hear of the Serenity Prayer?"

"I don't know, maybe."

"It's an AA thing. It says you have to figure out what you can change, and work on that. The stuff you can't change, you have to let go."

"You were in AA?"

"Same as. I was in the hospital to get off heroin, a long time ago."

"I heard. Mom was way nervous about my spending time with you because of that."

"Yeah. But I got off it. As your mother has probably told you, I can be a stubborn son of a bitch."

"I might have heard something along those lines."

The ball went back and forth a few more times. "You can't do anything about those other seven billion," Cole finally said. "What you *can* do is sit down with yourself and say, 'If things were different, if it wasn't already too late, is there something I could do to make things better? And would I maybe rather go ahead and do that thing anyway, even though it's too late, rather than lie around and wait for the world to end?'"

The "lying around" part stung. "So what are *you* doing?"

"I don't believe in political change. You can see that with Obama, he talked a lot about change, and once he got in office he couldn't do shit, because you have to change the culture first. If the culture thinks socialism is the greatest evil in human history, you're not going to sell it free health care."

"So that's it? You're changing the culture?"

"I'm trying."

Talking politics always made her frustrated and angry, made her want to lash out. She threw the ball back hard and low and said, "How's that working out for you?"

"Ha," Cole said, scooping it up. "Not so great."

That was the end of it for the moment. Ava came restlessly back to it over dinner. "So the only thing you can do is lie to yourself? Tell yourself there's hope when there isn't?"

"The Buddhists say you should act without hope or despair," Cole said. "That's a hard line to walk, and I can't manage it for long. I find I need to cheat and allow myself a small maintenance dose of hope. Not enough to hurt. Not so much that I'm always getting let down."

"Where do you get it? Because I don't see it."

"It's not rational. You don't argue yourself into it. It's a feeling. It shows up on its own. Listening to a beautiful piece of music, watching the sun go down, throwing a ball with your kid, bam, there it is, whether you want it or not. You can refuse to let yourself feel it, and that's as dishonest as giving in to it completely. You just want that... that little hit every once in a while, enough to keep going."

Some time later, Ava was at one of the family dinners at the Montoya house when Alex went off on one of his rants about the evils of capitalism and how Big Oil and Big Coal and the power companies were conspiring to keep alternative energy from happening. Usually Ava checked out from those one-sided non-conversations because, please, who did Alex think he was if not a capitalist? Only this time she felt a flutter in her chest and decided to run with it. She started asking questions, and it turned out Alex actually did know something about it. A couple of weeks after that, Alex had suddenly bought into some solar energy company and there was a low-level position open and was Ava interested? That was the way Alex worked. If you let it slip that you liked a certain brand of beans, Alex bought the company and said, here, have some beans. At the time Ava was stocking shelves and bagging groceries at Whole Foods, a perfect job if you were like 17 and into guys with wooden plugs in their earlobes, and she thought, why not?

It turned out that feeding a power grid like LA's from a solar array in the desert was not as easy as it sounded. There were issues with transmission and land access and environmental permits, and it took a full 1500 acres of photovoltaic panels to generate the electricity for 100,000 homes.

Ava started as a Basic Installer and pretty quickly worked up to Assistant Solar Technician. Crew members spent four days each week in the desert working 12-hour shifts and sleeping in the bunkhouse, then had three days off in Riverside, a town with a plentiful supply of beer and college-educated men. Work hard, play hard was the unofficial company motto. On the nights she spent out at the array, she invited herself into conversations between the scientists, keeping her mouth shut and taking mental notes.

She liked the work. The array itself was like a deserted dining hall for giants, where the shoulder-high tables were made up of side-by-side, front-door-sized modules that were attached to a frame. When they finally switched the site on, that frame would tilt the panels so they were constantly facing the sun. The men she worked with—and the workforce was almost exclusively male—were pretty much easygoing and smart and idealistic. Once she made it clear that sex was something she did in Riverside and not on the job, they were able to set that aside. They liked her and took the time to answer her questions in detail, even the ones that were totally off the wall.

Ava's cell went off late in the afternoon of March 10, 2010, when she and the lead tech had their hands full, and she forgot about it until she was getting dressed for dinner. The call was from Alex and the message was that Adalberto was in the hospital with stage 4 renal failure.

The company travel agent got her on a noon flight the next day, changing at LAX, and she took a cab straight from DFW Airport to Medical City. It was nine at night and Adalberto's room and the surrounding hallway swarmed with extended family, Cole and Sallie, Madelyn and Alex, Ava's stepsister Gwyn, Ethan and his fiancée, Alex's mother and brother Jimmy, a couple of Adalberto's friends from work. The mood was apocalyptic. Ava wandered from one to the next until she'd hugged everyone in the hall, ending up with her mother.

"Oh, baby," she said, "I'm so glad you came."

All she could do was nod. Alex approached through the crowd and took her aside. "He doesn't have a lot of time left," he said. "He's on dialysis, but his other organs could give out any time."

"Is he conscious?" Ava asked.

"In and out. Let's take a look."

After years of getting skinnier and skinnier, Adalberto looked puffy and his skin was dark as wet leather and gave off a faint, sharp smell. He opened bloodshot eyes as Ava moved in next to the bed. "Ava?"

"Yes, grandpa, it's me."

"You're so brown. You finally look like one of the family."

"I'll forgive you for that because you're in the hospital, but once you're out..."

"I'm not getting out, honey, we're not kidding each other about that. It's okay. To see my whole family together like this, it's a... benediction..." He lost the thread, then recovered. "I'm so happy you made it here. It's so good to see you." His expression was painfully sincere and it made Ava's eyes sting.

"I wouldn't have missed it. You always throw the best parties."

"I'll be leaving early from this one."

Alex stepped in. "You rest now, Papa. Don't worry, Ava's going to be around."

"I wish *I* was." He managed something like a laugh. "It's been such a good life. Nobody could have asked for a better one."

His eyelids fluttered and closed. His breathing was slow and even.

Alex said, "Even that little bit of talking wears him out. He'll be asleep for a while now."

Ava squeezed Adalberto's hand, watching out for the IV, and retreated to the hall. She sat on the floor next to the couch where Cole and Sallie were huddled up. Ava had only seen them a couple of times since he'd hooked up with her, but she could definitely see the attraction.

"Did you get to talk to him?" Cole said.

Ava nodded and swallowed hard. "What would it be like to be the kind of person that so many people cared about?" As soon as she said it, she realized it was a pretty stupid question to ask a couple of celebrity musicians.

Cole let it pass. "This is nothing," he said. "If everybody who owed him showed up in one place, it would look like Woodstock. Just speaking for myself, he saved my life on three separate occasions."

Who would come to my funeral? Ava wondered. The people in this hallway, maybe a couple of people from the array.

"You must be worn out from your flight," Sallie said. "We were talking about going to the house and getting some sleep."

"I don't know…" Ava said.

"There's nothing you can do here," Cole said. "Visiting hours are over, they want to clear the halls if they can."

Ava gave in and they took the elevator downstairs. They put her suitcase in the back of Cole's camper and all squeezed in the front. Ava fell asleep on the drive to the Montoya house and they'd just unlocked the front door when Cole's cell rang and Alex told them that Adalberto was crashing.

When they got back to the hospital, a white-haired doctor was listening to Adalberto's chest with a stethoscope. He stood in the doorway and said, "He's still breathing, barely. The other organs are shutting down now—they can't handle the waste that the kidneys are supposed to be filtering out. If you want to say goodbye, now's the time. He's not conscious, but it's possible he can hear you on some level."

Alex and Alex's mother and Cole went in the room. Linda looked like rusted metal, about to crumble. She stood on one side of the bed, holding one of Adalberto's hands, and Cole and Alex stood on the other. Linda's lips were moving, but Ava couldn't hear what she said.

Madelyn came to Ava, and Ava gathered her up, and she put her head on Ava's shoulder. In the room, Alex reached out without looking and took Cole's hand. Cole shifted over until their arms were touching along their entire length. Ava felt like a finger was pushing on her throat right at the collarbone.

Everybody was holding their breath. Ten minutes crawled by and then Alex stroked his father's forehead and said, "He's gone."

Madelyn stifled a sob and her sudden tears melted through Ava's shirt. In the room, Linda wailed and Alex went to her and helped her into a chair. Cole came out and Sallie wrapped him in her arms. Pretty much everybody was crying.

In her long, wasted years after college, Ava had smoked a lot of dope with a guy named Rich, whose favorite saying was, "After today, everything's going to be different." They'd laughed and laughed because the only thing that ever changed was whether they could afford to buy another baggie of weed.

She didn't know she'd said it out loud until her mom said, "What did you say? What's going to be different?"

Ava shook her head. "Everything," she said.

IT TOOK THREE DAYS for Ava to get a chance to talk to Alex alone. Friday was the wake, where Alex and Cole played guitars and sang Mexican songs, with Sallie joining them on a few. Saturday was the funeral, and like Cole had predicted, half of Dallas was there, with the local TV stations filming the crowds outside the chapel.

On Sunday afternoon, she found Alex by the swimming pool, which was covered in dead leaves from the previous fall. "Can I talk to you?" she asked.

Alex was reading a book called *The Shock Doctrine* that had a fake bullet hole in the cover. Ava was pretty nervous anyway, and the violence of the image made her feel worse.

Alex stuck in a bookmark and said, "Sure, what's up?" Ava knew that Alex had used to fold over the corners of pages to mark his place and Madelyn had made him stop.

"This is just... this is some stuff I've been thinking about, okay? It may be totally worthless."

"Sit down, relax. Whatever it is, I want to hear it."

Ava pulled up a lounge chair and perched on the edge of it. It was low to the ground, which made her knees uncomfortably high. "Okay, so, I call it Project Ark." Once it was out, it sounded so stupid that she wanted to go stick her head in the pool and drown herself. She felt herself blush with embarrassment.

Alex nodded, acting patient and interested.

"I don't know," Ava said. "Maybe I'm not ready to talk about it yet..."

"Please," Alex said. "Give it a shot."

"Okay, so, it's about the future. I mean, everybody knows this part, right, about running out of oil and rising seas and all, and everybody is like, someday we're going to have to do something about this. These guys I work with, I mean, they're all optimists to some degree or they wouldn't be in the solar business, but the message I'm getting is, one, if we were going to save the planet we would have had to start twenty or thirty years ago, so that fight is over, and two, if we're going to save anything at all, we have to move fast and do it now.

"So I've been thinking about how you could have a sustainable community that could survive what's coming, and what it would look like. The first thing is, it would have to be a place that you could cut off from the rest of the world. Like an island, say, only that won't work with the oceans rising. Maybe a city that was like completely surrounded by mountains or something. Two, it would have to be in another country, where the laws are kind of flexible and money talks even more than it does here. Someplace like... Mexico, say."

"You're talking about Guanajuato," Alex said, obviously interested now, all lit up behind his eyes.

"Yeah. Guanajuato would be perfect. So the next thing is, the old model of having a power company who delivers electricity to your door, that's out. Everybody has to be a provider as well as a consumer. With large solar arrays you have to deal with storage and transportation on too large a scale and you need too much real estate, so you need to put collectors on every roof. Plus wind turbines to supplement, in case you get a long stretch of heavy clouds or whatever. Technically what this would be is a community grid. That means you have to have consensus, and it has to be voluntary because this whole thing is fragile and a few saboteurs could take it down."

"Who pays for all this? The average homeowner in Guanajuato can't afford solar panels."

"That's one of the two biggest holes in the idea. Some incredibly rich person has to decide they're willing to fund it."

"And the rich person would do this because…"

"Because the rich person wants some remnants of civilization to survive the end of the world as we know it. Maybe the rich person grew up in the sixties and a part of him still believes that capitalism is not the answer, and is still hanging on to his own idealism."

"And the second big hole?"

"The drug cartels. They're already the real government in large areas of Mexico and it's only going to get worse. As everything starts to break down, they're going to be the ones with the firepower to take over. This idea won't work if Guanajuato gets turned into a war zone."

Ava hugged her knees and looked at the tile under her feet. "So that's my idea."

Alex was quiet for a while, thinking. He wasn't laughing and he wasn't dismissing the whole thing with a bunch of lame excuses, which made Ava feel pretty good.

Finally Alex said, "So how much money are you talking about?"

"Okay, so, you've let slip here and there how much your businesses are worth. And of course it's impossible to talk in anything but the most approximate terms…"

"Yeah, yeah. What's it going to cost me?"

Ava took a deep breath. "Everything. It's going to cost you everything."

2016

I F 1967 HAD BEEN the Summer of Love, surely the turning of
2015 to 2016 was the Winter of Hate. With the election still a
year away, the Republican Party had goaded itself into a verbal orgy
of racism, xenophobia, and misogyny, while the NRA demanded
more and more human sacrifices and white cops continued to put
bullets in the backs of black men.

Spring was making a late start when Cole flew to Dallas on
Alex's dime, spent the night, and flew home again. He and Sallie
went through the motions of eating dinner and Cole got a couple
of glasses of wine into her and then they sat on the couch.

"It must be bad," Sallie said. "You're rubbing your crippled
finger."

Cole looked down. "I didn't know I did that."

"Only when you're scared."

He told her what Alex wanted of them, and what Alex's hush-
hush activity in Guanajuato had been about for all these years.
Sallie started to cry. Every time she got herself together and started
to speak, she broke down in sobs again. Cole held her and waited
her out.

Finally she said, "Are things really that bad?"

"The polar ice caps are melting, and the more they melt, the
faster they melt. Gun nuts are running the country and we average one mass shooting a day. Donald Trump has virtually locked
down the Republican nomination. He could never win, of course,
but the fact that he's come this far is proof that the US has lost its
mind and its moral compass. We're like the lobster that started off
in cool water and now the water's about to boil, and if we don't
get out..."

"We're cooked."

"Basically, yeah."

She burrowed her head into his chest and they sat that way for
a long time. He stroked her long, beautiful hair, which she had
finally let go gray. Sallie loved him, he knew, and their physical

chemistry was undeniable. Yet there was something in Sallie that did not need him. She had been so successful so young, and been loved so much by so many, that she was the most emotionally secure person he'd ever known. She would always land on her feet, with or without Cole.

"I love this house," she said.

"We would have our pick of houses in Guanajuato. And it's beautiful there."

"When Reagan got elected I threatened to move to Paris. Same thing with Bush II. But now that I'm looking it in the face, I don't want to go. I love this country."

"I don't love what it's turned into."

"And what is it he wants you to do, exactly?"

"I would be Minister of Agriculture or something. Because of what I learned at the commune. I would be in charge of figuring out how we're going to grow enough crops to feed everybody. I would have professional agronomists to help, but I would be the one who made the policy."

"So we'll all be vegetarians."

"Sorry, babe. There might be an occasional chicken. We can't afford otherwise, it's too inefficient. You never eat meat anymore anyway."

"I know it's there waiting for me, down the street at the HEB. Oh, Cole, I may be too old to change."

"Then we'll stay here and go down with the ship, together."

"When I was a kid, the Revolution seemed like the most exciting thing. Woodstock, that incredible sense of possibility. Now if I had to miss a meal or go without air conditioning, I don't think I could stand it."

"We're old," Cole said. "We've done more than our share of sleeping on floors and missing meals. We're entitled to a little comfort."

She kissed his neck and then his mouth. She finger-walked one hand down his chest and into his lap. "Maybe not so old after all," she whispered.

Cole scooped her up and carried her into the bedroom. The lovemaking was urgent, the calm afterward profound. Cole dozed for a while and woke up to Sallie's deep, even breathing.

He untangled himself without waking her, slipped on his jeans, and padded into the music room at the rear of the house. He opened the louvers on the back door to smell the sweet honeysuckle on the night air. His D-35 was sitting out on a guitar stand, next to Sallie's 12-string, and he tuned it up and played a few quiet chords.

In some ways he was happier than he'd ever been. After eight years together, with both of them well into their sixties now, they still made love once or twice a week, and when the moon was full and the night was warm he often found himself helpless with desire for her. With the spring, he'd been working long hours in the garden. They were both healthy, the house was paid for, and Sallie's investments brought in plenty to live on.

Yet in the world outside Austin, Sallie was perceived purely as a nostalgia act, and Cole was not perceived at all. They'd released a live album in 2013 that sold 20,000 copies, enough to pay for itself and not much more. The motivation to write new songs and put together another original album was elusive.

They played 20 or so dates a year, mostly in the summer. During the winter they spent a lot of time on their separate computers. Sallie was satisfied with her life, finding old friends on Facebook, interacting with her fans, tweeting about her life with Cole. She also practiced piano an hour or two a day, worked on her Spanish, read, watched DVDs, did Pilates, and she and Cole took long walks together these days instead of running.

Cole had initially been sucked in by the Internet as well. He found Janet, his old high-school flame, early on. She was married—not to Woody—with three grown kids and a thriving Realty business. She was proud of him, she said, for all he'd accomplished. Sugarfoot, under his birth name of Terry Brewster, was still at the University of Illinois, now Dean of the Ag school, and married to an actor he'd met at a local theater group. He connected Cole to Laramie, now known as Lakshimi, who was co-owner of a Yoga center in Evanston. She'd had breast cancer and a double mastectomy, chemo, and radiation, and had just had a successful 15-year checkup. She'd been married twice, had two kids, done sporadic clerical work. The cancer had made her stop and think again about what it was that she'd been looking for at Woodstock and Eden Farm. Those questions had brought her to Yoga and spiritualism and her current partner. She was "still seeking, more calmly now." Nobody knew what had happened to Sirocco.

Lenny did mechanical drawings and technical writing for an air-conditioning company in Houston and had no hard feelings about anything. Gordo was in El Paso, working in a bank. Glen from Mountain Lakes ran a high-end appliance repair service in Portland, Oregon. His sister Sharon was teaching fifth grade in Michigan. Pauley had been killed in a car wreck in his late twenties.

Cole had found somebody on Facebook who might have been Tina, who never responded to his friend request. He'd found no trace yet of Corrina Shotwell.

He kept up a regular correspondence with Tupleo and Ava, and intermittent exchanges with his other friends, but the constant parade of Facebook updates was like empty calories, and he felt sick if he watched it too long.

Wounded Bird Records had done a CD release of the Quirq album, and some nights it was enough to look at the small shelf of his recorded work, to play a cut or two from one of the albums and try to imagine that he was hearing it for the first time. Or to sit and play guitars with Sallie and sing together and teach each other their favorite songs. Other nights he felt like he'd failed at the one thing he'd been put on earth to do. Worse, that his entire generation had failed, had not been able to outlast the apostles of greed, from Goldwater to Reagan to Trump.

The hardest thing was to think that he'd reached the end of his road, that however wonderful it was to be in this house with Sallie, nothing but more of the same lay ahead of him until he died.

He looked up and Sallie was there, wearing one of Cole's flannel shirts and glowing in the moonlight. "I'm not ready to give up yet," she said. "Let's go to Guanajuato."

WHO IT WAS on the phone was Cole, it turned out. Joe still answered it whenever it rang, though most of the time it was some machine talking to him about his credit card or Medicare or something else to try and get in his pockets. Sometimes it amused him to turn on the radio and put the phone down in front of it without hanging up, so the one machine could talk to the other.

Cole wanted something too, only what he wanted was for Joe and Peggy to move to Mexico. Cole was pretty sure it was the end of the world, and soon.

It seemed like the end of the world to Joe sometimes too, what with everybody and their Aunt Sue walking and driving and eating without looking up from the gizmo glued to their left hand. TV was unwatchable because of the ugliest election campaign ever, ISIS beheading anything that moved, hurricanes on the east coast and drought in the west.

He remembered when his daddy had been the age that Joe was now, and the way he would go on about Bill Clinton playing the saxophone on MTV like it was the death of western civilization, and Joe supposed that it was the way of things, that if a man lived long enough, he'd be yelling at the kids to get off his lawn.

Since 2000 he'd been putting more and more time into a group he'd founded that worked to overturn faulty convictions. His clients were like in the Steve Earle song, mostly black, and brown, and poor, and it was the most satisfying work he'd ever done. He didn't know that it would keep going without him.

Then there was Peggy. She was frail these days, had been down with pneumonia twice in the last two years, and who knew how long either of them had left? Having cancer had done that to him, made him evaluate everything in terms of what if he got a diagnosis tomorrow.

And if there was the tiniest part of him that still held the faintest of grudges against Alex over Denise, well, he expected he could live with that, too.

"We're doing pretty good here," is what he said to Cole. "Janis is an RN here in Tupelo now, and Peggy babysits for her a couple of times a week. Jerry is doing green Realty over to Oxford, so we got both kids and all their kids within an hour of us. I don't think relocation is an option."

Cole was quiet for a while, then he said, "I don't want to lose touch with you, Joe."

"Well, that's why the good Lord made Skype and Facebook and email. If you don't want to lose touch, then don't do it."

They talked some more about this and that, and after they hung up, Joe took a beer out to the screen porch and sat in the glider. The first stars were lighting up. He'd watch one for a while, then another one would fade into view.

Would he have been any happier if he'd been Governor? He didn't think about it often, it was just that Cole had got him started. If there was any one thing that was the downfall of the human race, it was that it was so hard to say, "Enough. I'm satisfied."

"Joe?" Peggy was at the door. "You all right?"

"I'm good," Joe said, and drank off the last of the beer. "I'll be right in."

SALLIE FOLLOWED COLE down the steps, across the tarmac, and into the cavernous León airport.

"How you doing, babe?" Cole asked.

"Holding up," she said. This was her third trip to Guanajuato since spring, and this one was for keeps. The Austin house was only rented, not sold, so theoretically they had an escape hatch, and Cole promised that if she needed to bail, he would bail with her. Still, she didn't want to be the one to cry hold, enough.

Alex and Madelyn and Ava waited for them by the entrance. Hugs were had all around. Sallie still didn't know what to make of Madelyn. Cole assured her that his feelings in that department were no more than mild affection these days, but he *would* say that, wouldn't he? Madelyn was smart and beautiful and her crooked smile burned into the memory. Then there was the fact that she was now married to Cole's best friend, who was in turn clearly attracted to Sallie, though he'd never done more than give her the occasional admiring look.

Alex said, "I've got a truck out there loading up all your stuff off the plane. They'll take it straight to your house. There are professional movers already there to help get the basics unpacked."

"Thank you," Sallie said.

Ava took their carry-on bags and they got in a minivan with the

Project Ark dove-and-olive-branch logo on the side. Sallie ended up next to Madelyn, and once they were on the highway, Madelyn said, "Can we have dinner tonight? Just the two of us?"

Sallie was emotionally exhausted and hadn't slept well for days, watching the house gradually empty of the things she loved. Her feelings must have showed because Madelyn said, "Nothing heavy, I promise. We've never had a chance to really talk."

Madelyn arrived at 6:30 that evening, per Sallie's grudging agreement. The movers had finished setting up the bed and Cole was putting on the sheets. All Sallie wanted was to crawl between them.

She showed Madelyn around. An architect had remodeled the place ten years before to serve as a combination office and home, and when she hadn't found enough clients, she'd moved to San Miguel to live off the expats. The floors were that new bamboo stuff, the exterior walls mostly windows, the interior walls largely non-existent. Freestanding shelves divided the living room from the dining area, which flowed into the kitchen. The guest room and recording studio were upstairs.

"It's fabulous," Madelyn said.

"It won't look quite so *House and Garden* once all our junk is out of the boxes."

She felt self-conscious about kissing Cole goodbye in front of Madelyn, though neither Cole nor Madelyn seemed to care. He was relaxed and friendly with her and nothing more.

Madelyn was on foot and hoped that was okay. "We try to set a good example, not driving any more than we have to."

Setting an example was part of Project Ark's mission statement, and Sallie couldn't hear the words without thinking of tikkun olam and wondering what Dave would have thought of all this. "Walking's good," she said. They were descending a winding street, headed for the Jardín de la Unión in the center of town. "As long as we slow down a little. I haven't acclimated yet." Her first day in Guanajuato, Cole had a meeting with local farmers and Sallie had gone for a brisk walk. She'd made it half a mile before collapsing, her lungs on fire from the thin mountain air.

"Oops," Madelyn said. "Sorry." They slowed their pace, and

Madelyn said, "Can we get rid of the elephant in the room? Or in the street, as the case may be? Cole and I never had very much in common. We were a couple of kids in love with the idea of being in love. I've seen the two of you together, and it was never like that for us."

"It's a tad weird, that's all."

"Tell me about it. Alex and I raised three kids, none of them with the same two parents, none of them with both our DNA. Are you religious?"

Sallie shook her head. "Raised reform Jewish, couldn't even sustain that."

"I'm Christian, something I tend to keep to myself around this crowd. Still, I have to say this. I feel like there's some kind of destiny operating here that brought all of us into each other's lives. Maybe that's an artifact of having been born when we were born, that sense of fatedness. Or maybe the mess we've made of everything really is just the transition to a new age. A new sun, as they say down here."

Sallie laughed. "People used to talk like that all the time. I kind of liked it. What happened?"

"Not enough money in it, I guess. How did you get to be a songwriter?"

Sallie told her, and that led to Dave and the rise and fall of her career, and the rise again with *Krupheimer*, and the long fall again after. By that time they'd arrived at the Van Gogh Restaurant and gotten seated at an outdoor table facing the square.

"I loved that *Krupheimer* record," Madelyn said. "I hope you don't mind my saying so. It was the right record at the right time for so many women. It showed us we could be powerful and vulnerable and that both were okay. It was the first music that a lot of us felt was ours."

"I'm always flattered when I hear that," Sallie said. "And yet the album was produced by a man, the other musicians were men..."

"Sure they were. But in the end they were serving you, serving your songs. I can't help but compare that to what we're doing here. Sometimes I worry that the whole Ark Project is white paternalism, that we're just colonizing Guanajuato. Even though

Alex has legitimate roots here. It comes down to who's being served, right? At least I hope it does."

They ordered dinner, Sallie managing to do it in Spanish. Madelyn's Spanish, she noted, was fluent and virtually without accent, though her English carried a hint of Texas twang. When Sallie complimented her on it, she said, "Years of work. The things that used to come easily have gotten so hard now that I'm old."

The conversation, however, was effortless, and Sallie was impressed to learn that Madelyn had been on hand for the SoHo art underground in the early seventies. They talked painting and literature, and after Madelyn snagged the check and paid it, she said, "There was one other thing. Would you consider teaching a songwriting class?"

"At the University? I don't know if I'm qualified. I did one at the Ninety-Second Street Y…"

"Actually," Madelyn said, looking embarrassed, "it would be at the free school. The school was part of my price for coming here. We set it up so the board is all locals, and most of the teachers are local too. This friend of Cole's, Félix Gutiérez, is teaching guitar, there's classes for basketmaking and silversmithing, there's agronomy classes, all at no charge."

"Well, sure, I'd love to. But Cole is a songwriter, too."

"If Cole wants to be part of it, that'd be fine, but he's going to be plenty busy. It was you the board specifically asked for."

Madelyn walked her home. Sallie invited her in, and Madelyn said, "No, I shouldn't have kept you out as late as I did. Take care, and I'll see you soon."

"You're okay walking home by yourself?"

"This is a very safe city," Madelyn said. "It's one of its many charms." Her smile fell away. "I hope we can keep it that way."

THREE BLACK SUVS belonging to Miguel "El Cicatriz" Ortiz came to a hard stop outside La Alhóndiga, the old grain warehouse where Alex had his offices. Their tires cried out in a chorus that sounded nearly human. Two gunmen each got out of the first and last vehicles and stood at attention in front of the flight of steps that led from the cobblestone street to the main door. They wore black from caps to boots, with Kevlar vests, M-16s, and holstered Glocks. The Christmas wreath hanging from the railing provided a touch of incongruity.

You didn't see los narcos on the streets of Guanajuato, and a crowd immediately formed at a respectful distance. Another gunman got out of the middle car, followed by Álvaro in jeans and a bright green hooded sweatshirt bearing the logo of the Mexico fútbol team. The two of them climbed the steps and the gunman pounded on the door with the heel of his fist.

Alex had been watching it unfold from the time the trucks entered the tunnel that opened into the southwest corner of the city. The room was crowded. Rosa, his deputy mayor, was in the seat next to him and Cole and Sallie stood behind him.

«Should I let them in?» Rosa asked, «or do you want to do it yourself?»

«Go ahead,» Alex said. «Bring Álvaro to my office and give the sicario a cup of coffee.»

They both stood up and Alex saw the look of dread on Cole's face. "It's okay," he said in English. "All the guns and trucks and bullshit are just for intimidation."

"It's working," Cole said.

"Alex?" Sallie said. "I want to make this really clear. If anything happens to Cole—I mean anything—you better pray you don't come back here alive. You guys may be pacifists. I'm not."

"Nothing's going to happen to either one of us." She was bristling and he knew to keep his physical distance. "I promise."

Cole hugged her and said, "I'll call you after I get there if I can."

"I love you," Sallie said, with an edge of defiance.

"I love you, too," Cole said.

They passed through the reception area, where Madelyn was curled on the couch with a book.

"How can you read at a time like this?" Sallie said.

Madelyn's smile was more crooked than usual. "Easy," she said. "I don't plan to remember any of it." She reached up for Alex's hand. "What's the appropriate wish, here? Break a leg?"

"I think 'good luck' would be okay."

"Good luck," she said. "Come back to me." She glanced at Cole. "Both of you."

Álvaro was admiring the office stereo when Cole and Alex walked in. Cole embraced him first, than Alex. Álvaro ran one hand over the stubble on Alex's head. «With the short hair and the mustache, you look so much like your father.»

«That was the idea. To remind everyone. I did it for the election and I guess it worked.»

Álvaro nodded. «You boys ready?»

Alex unlocked his desk drawer and took out an attaché case. «Andamos.»

They had to pass through the reception area again. The sicario sat on the edge of an easy chair, gloves off, drinking coffee and laughing with Rosa. He jumped up when he saw the look on Álvaro's face, slopping some coffee on the floor. Rosa told him she would take care of it.

Alex had stressed to Madelyn and Sallie how important it was to not make a fuss in front of Álvaro, and they both did their jobs. Madelyn waved and said, "See ya," and Sallie kissed Cole without lingering too long over it, and if her eyes were a little intense, maybe Álvaro didn't notice.

The sicario opened the rear door of the middle SUV. Cole got in first, then Alex and Álvaro. Alex put the attaché case on the floor and fastened his seat belt. The drive to Guadalajara, where Ortiz had his ranch, would take three hours. He tried to get comfortable.

«Music?» Álvaro said. He didn't wait for an answer. He snapped his fingers at the soldier in the front seat, and Trio Los Panchos began to sing "Celoso" over the audio system. The SUV eased into motion, tight behind the lead truck, and they were off.

WITHIN TWO MONTHS of his father's death, Alex had made his first moves, buying more and more solar and wind turbine companies and taking some risks to pile up short term gains. He bought a private jet to take him to Guanajuato, spending more time there than in Dallas, renewing his father's relationships, spreading money around, planting seeds both figuratively and literally as he bought up abandoned lots on the upper slopes of the city and bulldozed them into terraces and got alfalfa growing there. He convinced a few of the University professors to put solar panels on their roofs and sent Ava, now on the company payroll, to install them at cost.

The only people who knew the entire plan were Ava and Madelyn, and Madelyn had been a tough sell. "Why would I want to teach in Guanajuato," she'd asked, "when I've got a shot at a fellowship here?" This was a week after Ava had pitched Project Ark to him, and only a few hours since he'd realized that he was going to go through with it. It was a Saturday night and they were eating take-out Chinese at the kitchen table.

"Because instead of teaching the sons and daughters of white privilege, you'd be teaching kids with a real hunger to learn?"

"Nice try, but you know as well as I do that the majority of those kids are the sons and daughters of corrupt officials and narco profiteers and capitalist exploiters of the poor, to borrow a phrase of yours. They're privileged in ways these SMU kids could only fantasize about. Plus I've got my ESL classes at El Centro."

"Okay, how about because it's only a question of time until there's a mass shooting at SMU? Until SMU goes broke because the middle class has no money and the ultra-rich believe that education is treason? Until the drought gets so bad that only the rich have water? Until there are tornados every week? Until there are armed vigilantes roaming the streets and stopping anybody who doesn't look like them?"

Madelyn opened her mouth to say something and then closed it again.

"It's not unreasonable to think we could live another twenty-five, thirty years," Alex said. "Long before then, this country is going to be divided into red zones and green zones. It's happening already, with gated communities and these exclusive subdivisions that have their own restaurants and shopping and private schools and security patrols. Hell, we're living in our own green zone here. I don't want our kids and our grandkids to grow up in that world."

She pushed her food around the plate without eating any. "You're determined to do this, aren't you?"

"If you can talk me out of it, please do. I don't think you can. This is life and death, mine and everybody I love. Maybe even the death of western civilization. Ava called it the Ark for good reason. This could be our last chance to preserve books and music and cultural diversity and art and science and all the other things that we cared about when we were growing up."

"And that's your hole card. Ava. If I don't go along with this, I won't see her anymore."

"You'll see her. As long as it's possible to travel to Mexico."

He read the pain and despair in her face. He wanted to be a comfort to her and didn't know how. If he tried to touch her, she would submit and nothing more. "I need to think," she said.

Alex tried to project love and sympathy. "There's time," he said.

How much time was anybody's guess. The need to move slowly and carefully tied him in knots. Yet by 2014 he'd been elected mayor of Guanajuato and had stepped up the solar conversion, charging homeowners what they could afford, adding what little tax money he could divert to it, and making up the rest out of his own pocket. Gwyn and Ethan and Ethan's wife and daughter were ready to move down when he gave the word, and their commitment had sealed Madelyn's as well. Still he couldn't go all the way, not to the wind turbines, not to sending invitations to everyone he cared about, not to the withering away of capitalism itself, not until he solved the problem of los narcos.

On his darker days he'd had a fantasy. He could buy a hundred Kalashnikovs on the black market, train a militia in secret, plant explosives in the tunnels. If one of the cartels tried to take over the city he could trap them and massacre them, and on some angry days he let himself picture the bloodbath vividly.

The fantasy always gave way to practicality. To unleash that kind of violence would be, as they said in Spanish, to open a box of thunder. Taking the guns back from the militia afterward would not be easy, not once they'd tasted that power and been hailed as heroes. And he would have a pile of corpses on his hands, his own personal Vietnam. He had to find another way.

carpets, rattan furniture with white leather cushions, Remington-esque paintings of cowboys in massive nineteenth-century frames.

Ortiz met them in the den. He wore a crisply pressed, long-sleeved white shirt, black suit pants, and shiny shoes. If the cares of his business had aged him, Cole didn't see it. He seemed genuinely pleased to see them, shaking both their hands. «Come in, come in, my house is yours. I'm sure you'll want to refresh yourselves from the trip. Valeria will show you the way.»

Valeria was a petite, radiantly beautiful woman in black leather pants and a loose white blouse, her shiny black hair in a ponytail. She was one of four women arrayed in front of a big screen TV where an action movie was frozen in mid-car-chase. The only other occupants of the vast room were two black-uniformed soldiers, standing at ease by the far wall, eyes glazed.

The bathroom was something out of a four-star hotel. Marble floors, gold fixtures, huge fluffy towels with "El Cicatriz" discretely embroidered on them in white on white. After he eased his aching bladder and washed his face, he called Sallie, told her so far so good, and promised to call later if he could. "But don't freak out if I don't, okay?"

"Yeah, right," she said.

They settled in with drinks and Ortiz said, «I thought we might relax this afternoon, maybe play some music, then have dinner, start the game around nine o'clock. Does that suit you?»

Like we have a choice? Cole thought.

«Fine,» Alex said. «You should know that Cole is a vegetarian. I hope you can accommodate him.»

«Not a problem,» Ortiz said. «Juana is a vegetarian also.» He pointed to the woman who'd brought their drinks, another beauty in a low-cut black dress, and she smiled shyly.

Ortiz tried to draw them into conversation, asking Alex about his trips to Monterrey as a kid, asking Cole about his time in Villahermosa. Artificial and awkward as it was, all three of them put their shoulders to it and got it slowly rolling forward.

Cole asked where Ortiz had gotten his love of music, which turned out to be tied to his older brother, the one who'd been killed. He'd gotten Ortiz a transistor radio for Three Kings Day when Ortiz was 9. The earplug gave him a way to make his own space in their little house, and those memories came back every time he heard the old traditional songs.

As if on cue, a heavyset guy in a black T-shirt brought in an acoustic guitar and a stand and put it next to Álvaro's chair. Álvaro picked it up and checked the tuning and started to play it idly. The man came back and put a second guitar within Cole's reach, then returned again to set one near Alex.

«If you're in the mood to sing and play a little,» Ortiz said, «that would please me greatly.»

Command performance, Cole thought. He was annoyed that the guitars had been brought out before the invitation was made.

Alex must have felt the same way because he said, «I don't play anymore.» His tone was final. Cole glanced at him for a cue and Alex gave him the slightest of shrugs, telling him to make his own call.

The correct thing to do was to play. To be more polite than his host or his friend, to rack up a score on behalf of the larger mission, whether he felt like it or not. As sacrifices went, it was not substantial. Alex had needed to make a point, to insist that he be treated as an equal. Cole had nothing to prove.

He picked up the guitar, took out the pick that was threaded into the strings, and said, «'Mexico lindo y querido' is a favorite of yours, if I remember correctly.»

Ortiz gave him the first authentic smile of the day. «What a memory you have. I'm flattered.»

Cole inclined his head and began to beat out the chords in three-quarter time. Álvaro let out a long, falsetto grito, and they went into the verses. Cole was not feeling it. He played as simply as he could, hoping to warm to it. He threw in a pro-forma lead at the end and then they wrapped it up. Ortiz and Alex and Valeria applauded, Ortiz with genuine enthusiasm. Cole wondered what it was like for Ortiz to have to pay for everything he wanted. Did he genuinely not mind fake smiles? Henri, the drummer at the Old Absinthe House, liked to go with prostitutes. "It's a power trip, man," he'd told Cole. "It's all about *you*." Maybe Ortiz felt the same way.

«¿Malagueña?» Álvaro suggested.

«¿Cómo no?» Cole said. He did a long instrumental intro, then took the falsetto vocal parts, thinking that Ortiz would surely not want to kill anybody who could play and sing like he could.

They went on like that for an hour and a half, taking a couple of minutes between songs to drink and talk, alternating requests from Ortiz with whatever he or Álvaro wanted to play. Álvaro was the first to give out. «I'm not used to this, my fingers are going to bleed.»

Ortiz thanked them profusely and everybody applauded, including, with some prompting from Ortiz, all of the women. Then Ortiz said, «Are either of you interested in horses?»

Alex, clearly struggling to be polite, said, «I don't know much about them.»

«I just acquired a beautiful pair of Morgans from a woman in Texas. I would love to show them to you.» He stood up.

Alex got up too and Cole, who'd been waiting for his chance, said, «Álvaro and I will join you in a moment.»

Ortiz gave Cole a look of mild curiosity, then nodded to Álvaro. «Bueno. We'll be at the corral.»

He and Alex went out the front door. Valeria started the movie again and Cole said, «Can we walk?»

The sun was nearly gone and a chill wind came down at them from the mountains. Cole shoved his hands in his pockets and said, «Are the dogs out yet?»

Álvaro laughed. «We're safe for a while.»

«What I'm about to tell you has to be a secret. From El Cicatriz, from Alex, from everybody. Can you promise me that?»

Álvaro mulled it over long enough to show Cole that he took him seriously. «Yes. I promise.»

«I have an illness. Some days worse than others. There's a good chance that the day may come when I can't go on.» He wasn't lying, exactly. If the disease was failure and depression, that didn't make it any less painful or debilitating. «Can you give me something, in case it gets really bad? I want to go out peacefully, not puking or convulsing. I want to know that if I have to, I can go to sleep and not wake up.»

Álvaro said, «Is it cancer?»

«It's like cancer, but it's not cancer. It's not AIDS or anything contagious.»

They walked for a while. «Fifty years I've known you,» Álvaro said. «On and off, still, most of my life. We're friends. And you ask me to help you kill yourself?»

«It's the disease that's killing me. I'm asking you to make the death less painful.»

«I hate it that you're sick. As for the rest, I need to think about it.»

Cole was touched. How many deaths had Álvaro caused, directly or indirectly? Yet there were lives he still valued, and Cole's was one of them. «Thank you,» Cole said. «I guess now we need to go look at the fucking horses.»

«For what he paid for them,» Álvaro said, «they better be fucking day and night.»

AS HE SAT DOWN at the table, Alex still wasn't sure how to make his case, or where the evening was headed. Things started badly when Ortiz won the first deal and called Texas Hold 'Em. You never saw more than seven cards out of 52, making it impossible to know what your opponent had. It came down to luck, psychology, and bravado, and Alex preferred old-fashioned skill. Besides which, they were playing standard "friendly" poker with limits on bets and raises, which took away the crazed bluffing that made the game so popular with 20-year-olds.

Along with Cole and Álvaro, the fifth player was an older, well-off rancher named Nicolás who was friends with Ortiz. He wore an unconvincing toupee, polyester slacks, and a Harvard sweatshirt. Alex quickly pegged him as a fish, there to fatten the pots for everybody else.

A few trends emerged early on. Ortiz continued to call Hold 'Em, sensing Alex's annoyance. Álvaro did the same, and there was more than one hand where Alex was sure that Álvaro had folded a winner to let Ortiz take it. Cole, apparently overly fastidious about Alex having staked him, was playing too conservatively and slowly losing ground. Ortiz didn't like to fold, normally an exploitable weakness, except that the cards were running hot for him. Nicolás was indeed over his head and losing steadily.

An hour into the game, Alex said, «Did you mean it when you said we could talk seriously while we played?»

Ortiz glanced at Nicolás before he said, «As long as we exercise a certain amount of discretion.»

You could hardly have illusions about where Ortiz's money came from. Alex assumed that Nicolás just wanted deniability.

«You know that I have ambitious plans for my city,» Alex said. It was his deal and he added, «Seven card stud.»

«I've heard some rumors.»

Alex dealt everyone two cards down and one card up. «My goal is to eventually make us self-contained and self-sustaining.»

«An admirable goal. I know I value my own independence. I'm not sure what this has to do with me.»

Cole was high with a jack. «Check,» Cole said. Everybody checked around the table to Ortiz. Ortiz, who could never leave well enough alone, threw in a $50 white chip.

«The political situation in Mexico is deteriorating,» Alex said. «As it is everywhere, and bound to get worse with Trump as president. You could, if you wanted to, be in a position to protect Guanajuato from being invaded by... your business rivals.»

Everybody saw the bet and Alex dealt another up card. Cole's jack was still tall.

«Speaking only in terms of possibilities,» Ortiz said, «if I were able to do such a thing, why would I want to?»

«Guanajuato is easy to defend. You wouldn't want a rival to control it.»

Cole checked again, and it went around to Oritz, who threw in a red chip, worth a hundred dollars. Based on nothing, Alex was sure, just wanting some money out there on the off chance that he might win. Cole folded and the others stayed. Nicolás ignored the conversation, staring into the middle distance with glazed eyes.

«Then maybe I should control it myself,» Ortiz said.

«There's no profit for you there, and you are too good a businessman not to know that. Otherwise you'd have moved in already.»

Ortiz laughed at the flattery, as he was meant to. «Maybe you're right. Okay, how about we let the cards decide? We play until either you or I run out of the money we bought in with. If I go broke first, I will do everything I can to protect your city. If you lose, then you're on your own, and maybe I will move into Guanajuato anyway. It's a beautiful place. Either way, as soon as you or I lose, the game is over, any other players cash out with what they have. What do you say?»

Alex dealt another round to give himself time to think. The only thought in his head was, "I can take him."

Ortiz now had a pair of tens showing, making him the high hand. «Two-fifty,» he said, the maximum bet, and tossed in a blue chip.

Nicolás folded. Alex had the king of hearts and ten of hearts in the hole and two hearts up. Nobody else was showing any. «I call,» Alex said, «and I accept your wager.» Alex ignored the nervous look that Cole shot him. Wade, the crusty old oilman at his father's poker game, used to say, "Got a hunch, bet a bunch."

Álvaro folded. Alex paired his king on the final up card, which gave him an excuse to stick around. The last down card filled in his flush and he started raising then, which went the three-raise limit. Ortiz had two pair, tens over, not a hand to raise on, even though Alex's flush had been well hidden. Alex raked in the chips and Ortiz said, «I hope this isn't an omen.»

It was. Ortiz's luck had turned, and he didn't have the skills to compensate. As his piles of chips steadily eroded, his mood grew increasingly sour. He joked bitterly about his lousy cards and blamed whoever was dealing. Cole and Álvaro were conspicuously nervous and stopped talking, even when they dealt. Nicolás, oblivious, lost the last of his ten thousand within the hour, excused himself politely, and left the room.

«Bueno,» Ortiz said, «now that the amateurs are out, we can get serious.»

It took another forty-five minutes for Ortiz to lose everything but two white and two red chips. «I can't fucking believe it's come down to this,» he said. «Table stakes, no?»

«That's right,» Alex said.

Cole was dealer. «Seven card stud,» he said, «no splits, nothing wild.»

Everyone anted and Cole dealt the first round. Ortiz was high with an ace and bet one of his whites. Alex saw him, and Álvaro, clearly afraid of accidentally winning the last hand, folded. Cole called and dealt again. Ortiz paired his ace and bet another 50 dollars. Alex, looking at four completely random cards, reached out to fold them.

He stopped.

For the last half hour he'd been ignoring a persistent feeling of disquiet, and now he was absolutely certain that what he was doing was wrong. The game had degenerated into pure macho bullshit, played by Ortiz's rules. The fact that Alex was winning didn't make it any better. He sat back in his chair.

«Bet or fold,» Ortiz said. «I've got a lot of money to win back.»

Alex threw in a white chip and felt his pulse speed up.

In his peripheral vision, he saw Cole trying to get his attention. Alex ignored him.

«Fold,» Cole said.

«Deal,» Ortiz said.

Cole dealt the third up card, no visible help to either hand. Ortiz threw in his next to last red chip and Alex called.

Cole dealt Ortiz a third ace and gave Alex a pair of twos. Ortiz was flushed, excited, thinking he was back in the game. He was petty, vindictive, intelligent, and spoiled. For all his calculation, he was also passionate and self-aware. If Alex was wrong about him, it could cost him everything, including his life, and maybe Cole's life too.

Ortiz threw in his last chip. «I'm all in.»

Alex's vocal cords were stuck together. He had to clear his throat to speak. «What would you say... to suspending the limits? Just for this one hand.»

Ortiz stared at him, then said, as if explaining to a child, «I don't have anything left. We're playing table stakes. I have you beat in sight. Even if you *could* beat me, you'd have nothing to gain.»

«Then you have no objection?» Alex didn't wait for an answer. He pushed all of his chips, somewhere over thirty thousand dollars, into the middle of the table. «I call.» He looked at Cole, whose mouth was open. «Deal.»

Cole, not looking away from Alex's eyes, dealt the final down card. Ortiz immediately turned it over, along with his other hole cards. «Aces full of sixes.»

Alex tossed his cards, face up, to Ortiz. «Pair of twos.»

Cole continued to look as if he'd been punched in the gut. Álvaro was terrified. Ortiz said, «Are you insane?»

«Maybe,» Alex said. «Here's what I think. I don't want you to protect my city because you lost a bet. I don't want you to do it against your will. I don't want you wondering if there's a way out of keeping your word. I want you to protect my city because it's the right thing to do.

«I know that you love music. You don't just love it, you feel it in your heart. If Guanajuato doesn't survive, if places like Guanajuato don't survive, then a hundred years from now, maybe fifty years, maybe in our lifetimes, all the songs that you love could be lost forever.

«I have freed you from your obligation. It's up to you, now. You decide what's right. Then you decide what you want to do.»

He held Ortiz's eyes for a couple of seconds, then he pushed his chair back from the table. «In the meantime, the game is over. Somebody needs to cash Cole out, and I would like to go home.»

Alex tried to gauge Ortiz's reaction. Humiliation? Respect? Homicidal rage? For the first time all night, Ortiz was keeping it on the inside.

«Álvaro,» Ortiz said at last. «Cash him out.» He got up and left the room.

Álvaro followed him out and came back with Alex's attaché case. He dumped the money out on the table, counted Cole's chips, and put six thousand dollars or so back in. The rest he left on the table. Petty cash, Alex thought wildly. Probably leaves that kind of money around all the time.

Nobody spoke. Alex was so full of adrenalin that he had to put his hands in his pockets to keep them still.

After he closed the attaché case, Álvaro beckoned to them and walked them outside. A single suv waited by the door. Alex was soaked in sweat and the night air felt bitterly cold. The driver opened the door to the back seat. Alex got in first and Álvaro handed him the attaché case. Then, curiously, Álvaro hugged Cole tightly, not the usual Latino abrazo but something more, something full of regret. When he did let go, he slipped a small package into Cole's jacket pocket.

Álvaro reached in and Alex shook his hand. Cole got in and Álvaro slammed the door of the truck and the driver pulled away.

Alex closed his eyes and took a slow, shaky breath. "Are we still alive?"

"That was some kind of performance," Cole said. "Expensive, too. You just threw away in the vicinity of thirty-four grand."

"Funny," Alex said. "For a while now I've been thinking that money doesn't matter to me anymore. I guess it's true."

"Well, El Cicatriz got the message. Speaking of messages…"

Cole got out his phone and called Sallie. "We're fine," he said. "We're headed home. We should get in about four o'clock. Try and get some sleep." He listened for a few seconds and said, "I'll tell you all about it when I get there." He looked at Alex. "You want her to call Madelyn?"

"Please," Alex said.

Cole told her he loved her and hung up. It was only, Alex noted with surprise, one AM. They rode in silence for half an hour. No more classic tunes on the car stereo, no convoy, no Álvaro to escort them. Better this way, he thought. However it turns out.

Eventually he looked over and saw that Cole was still awake. "What did Álvaro give you?" Alex asked.

"I can't tell you that."

"It was heroin, wasn't it?"

"I'm not going to start using again. You don't have to worry."

Alex was having a night for insights. "It's not what you had in mind, is it? Thousands of miles from the music business, no touring, no band, no record deal."

"Living with someone more famous than I'll ever be, who's loved by millions." He shrugged. "It comes and it goes. Good days and bad days." He turned away and Alex could see his reflection in the tinted window.

Alex took a minute to line the words up. "It's because of you, you know."

"What is?"

"This whole thing. Guanajuato. The Ark Project. It's because of your song, about how it was already the end. I kept hearing it in my head and I didn't want it to be true. I didn't want everything I'd ever believed in, and gotten teargassed for, and gone hungry for on the Lower East Side, to come to nothing."

Cole turned away from the window and looked at his hands.

"You did this," Alex said.

Cole was quiet a long time, then he said, "Alex..."

"Yeah?"

He shook his head. "Nothing. I love you."

In fifty years, they'd never said those words to each other. Alex nodded. "I love you too."

He leaned back and closed his eyes and the SUV drove on through the darkness of the new day.

LATER

Alex woke up at 6:15 every morning, even when he forgot to set the alarm. He had a top-of-the-line Serta mattress that he'd flown in from the States, with a memory foam pad on top. Still, after six or seven hours, his joints hurt in any position he tried.

Today, more than most days, he had a reason to get up.

He and Madelyn had twin beds because of Alex's tossing and turning, but their beds were next to each other for the comfort of each other's presence. Madelyn was still asleep. Today was the start of the fall semester at the university, so she would need all the sleep she could get. He got up and dressed without waking her. He ate a bowl of oatmeal and drank a cup of coffee and went outside.

The day was clear and cool. It was the first of September and with luck, the rains would come and go in the early afternoon. Two of the city's wind turbines were visible from the vegetable patch outside his front door, the blades turning quickly enough to be invisible.

At the bottom of the callejon stood a rack of yellow bicycles. Alex got one out, adjusted the seat, and rode to the mouth of the alley that started the uphill climb to the Pípila statue. He'd brought Cole there on his first trip to Guanajuato, lo these many decades ago.

He struggled to clear his head of distractions. At noon he would meet with a delegation from Estes Park, Colorado, the latest city interested in following Guanajuato's example. Meanwhile, the night before last, a three-way gun battle had broken out on the streets of nearby San Miguel between the federales, the ultraviolent Zeta cartel, and soldiers belonging to El Cicatriz. The federales had been eliminated, the Zetas had retreated, and Alex had received an email from Ortiz that said, «This will not affect you.»

Alex's hamstrings ached as he climbed the steep, winding paths, and he had to stop twice to get his breath. Neither his physical condition nor his preoccupied mental state was reason enough to turn back. He'd learned, over the years, the importance of ritual. September 1 marked the day that Cole and Sallie had arrived in Guanajuato to stay, the moment when Alex had felt that all the pieces were in place.

He made it to the top and sat on a bench for a few minutes to recover. Then he walked over to the statue and out to the edge of the plaza, leaning on the waist-high, cast-concrete guardrail to look out over the city.

Coming here once a year gave you a way to measure the yearly change, and every year you could see it more clearly. Where once the view was dominated by blocks of pastel color from the densely packed houses on the slopes of the hills, now it glistened with solar panels and shone green with rooftop gardens. The highest parts of the hills were terraced like some ancient Asian landscape painting. Every year you saw fewer cars, less traffic in and out of the city. The air was sweeter and the streets were cleaner.

You needed these moments, he thought, when you could see what you'd accomplished, when you could allow yourself to feel some pride, alone with yourself and the work you'd done. When you could be grateful that Gwyn and Ava and Ethan and the baby were all here, and safe, at least for today. To bask, if only for a moment, in the warmth of the sun.

Then it was time to go. Because, as the statue said, there were still more Alhóndigas to burn.

MADELYN HAD 27 students in her Literature of the Sixties class, five more than she'd had the previous spring. Walls were gradually breaking down between the university proper and the free school; the arts and literature classes had benefited the most. Some of the students, Madelyn was sure, were there out of curiosity about herself and Alex and Sallie and Cole, and the quaint ideas they'd brought with them, ideas like, "from each according to his abilities, to each according to his needs," ideas that had largely faded from the rest of the planet, but were suddenly relevant again in Guanajuato.

There was specific curiosity today about the middle-aged gringa who was auditing the class, tall and blonde and somewhat weathered, trying and failing to be inconspicuous on the back row. Ava had delegated most of her solar panel work and had more time on her hands these days. When she'd asked to take the class, Madelyn had been honored.

Students continued to trickle in. Madelyn sipped her coffee, the first fruits of Cole's attempt to grow the beans locally. Some issues needed to be ironed out; flavor, for one. The amazing thing was that it existed at all. The same could be said for Ava's vision of Guanajuato, as it became more real every day.

The bell rang and the last couple of students darted in. She took attendance, omitting Ava's name, and introduced herself. Then she said, «When I talk about the sixties, what do you think of?» She taught the class in Spanish now; she'd added *One Hundred Years of Solitude* and Cortázar's *Hopscotch*, and the students read the US novels in translation.

A girl in the front row raised her hand. She wore gold jewelry and designer yoga wear that had been hugely popular in the States not that long ago. Her makeup was impeccable and her accent patrician. «My father says that the hippies were a lot of spoiled children. He says that all they did was take drugs and burn flags and have unprotected sex. He says the world went crazy for ten years, but then people came to their senses, and it's a waste of time for me to take this class.» Everyone laughed, including Madelyn.

When the idea of teaching had first taken her, she'd been drawn in by her love of books. She'd embraced the cliché of the ivory tower without shame; she wanted to live in an insulated world of big ideas and dazzling intellects. Somewhere along the line she'd lost her taste for abstraction; she'd come to crave the experience of ideas gripping the human mind and transforming it. El Centro had spoken to that, as had Guanajuato's free school. And this, too, was a part of it: the future soldier she subverted with Louise Glück; the barely literate kid who suddenly glimpsed the pain in a Raymond Carver story.

She took out her notebook. «I'm going to write that down, and on the last day of class we'll talk about it.»

She didn't know how many years of this she had left in her. But this year, ah, this year. This year was going to be good.

SALLIE KISSED him awake. Cole opened his eyes to see the sweet-smelling waterfall of her hair cascade around his face.

"I'm off," she said. "I'll see you tonight."

"Okay," he said sleepily. "You're very beautiful this morning."

"Hold that thought," she said, and kissed him again, running her fingertips down his cheek. He rolled over to watch her walk away, admiring the grace of it. She volunteered most days in the free store at the Mercado, giving away donated food. They had stolen the idea from the Diggers in Haight-Asbury. Sallie was as big a star in Mexico as anywhere and people brought in contributions just to see her smile.

It was already after eleven and he was too hungry to think coherently. He got up and took a long piss and then went into the kitchen, barefoot in his pajama pants. He squeezed a few oranges and ate some cashew butter and dark brown bread.

He washed the dishes and sponged off the countertop, and then he slowly climbed the stairs to the recording studio. The equipment sat out ready to use, though it had been a while. They kept the empty instrument cases in a closet by the mixing board. Cole took out one of the microphone boxes and sat on the couch. He removed the plastic lining and found the small zip-lock baggie of white powder that Álvaro had given him.

He was again, and had been for a while, in the grip of what he called his Darkness. A while back, at Sallie's urging, he'd tried anti-depressants. They made him feel like he was standing outside himself, and they impeded his ability to climax, which was already fading with age. He'd tapered off them after three months and been relieved to be back in his own prickly skin. When she talked to him about it, which was not often, she couldn't resist trying to reason with him. He had meaningful work, a beautiful house, good physical health. He was loved, and not just by her, not just by Alex and Ava, but also by the people he worked beside every day.

She wasn't wrong. The thing that she couldn't understand was that she had asked one thing of life, the same thing Cole had asked, to spend it making music. She had gotten her wish and Cole had not.

He couldn't help seeing a parallel with his entire generation. Instead of the things they'd asked for, they'd gotten endless war in the Middle East, resurgent racial violence, the death of the middle class, environmental disaster. Even Ava's Project Ark depended on the good will of a murderous criminal.

And yet.

The windows were open to a warm breeze that fluttered the curtains and carried in the smell of sun-baked pavement and loamy gardens. The sound of squabbling birds rose up from the street. He had culling to do on the terraces, and that night he and Sallie would likely make love. Maybe afterward they would take their guitars down to the Jardín de la Unión.

He shut the baggie away in the closet. Then he put on clean work clothes and went out to see what the day might hold.

Author's note

First and foremost, my undying gratitude to Richie Unterberger, the king of rock historians, without whose friendship and generosity this enterprise might well have foundered. Richie sent me music and videos, took me on a walking tour of Haight-Ashbury, answered endless questions in email, and shared transcripts of interviews he did for his definitive documents of sixties folk rock, *Turn! Turn! Turn!* and *Eight Miles High*. His recommendations of books, dvds, and cds were invaluable, and his taste, expertise, and love of this music is boundless.

Richie also introduced me to Lyric Seidensticker, then in her early twenties, and already a leading authority on The Lovin' Spoonful. She was also tireless in sharing the fruits of her research.

Among the people I interviewed, extra special thanks to Susan Hardin, Tim Hardin's widow, who shared her memories, her kind heart, and her Rolodex. Erik Jacobsen, one of the great record producers of all time, gave me wonderful stories, keen insights, and the gift of his friendship. John Sebastian is one of the warmest people I have ever interviewed, one of the most generous, and quite possibly the funniest. David Dennard, a St. Mark's classmate, was the bass player of the Novas in the 1960s, the best band in Dallas. I came back to him again and again for details of the clubs, the bands, and the times.

The Big D 60s group on Yahoo was a great resource, and led me to Margaret Moser, rock journalist and woman on the Austin scene, who was unsparing with her time and insider perspective.

Dave Fisher is an entirely fictional character, though I let him take credit for some of the recording feats of the real Roy Halee, engineer on "Summer in the City" and other Spoonful songs, to whom I apologize. Morgan Conrad, head of A&R at Columbia, is also an entirely fictional character.

For a wonderful discussion of folk music, authenticity, and politics, I recommend *When We Were Good* by Robert Cantwell. Dave Van Ronk's *The Mayor of MacDougal Street*, assembled and edited by Elijah Wald, is a great history of the folk scene in Greenwich Village and a joy to read.

Kate Spencer's *Art and Politics in Have Gun—Will Travel* is loaded with insight and information about mid-20th century TV westerns.

My friend George R.R. Martin provided me with invaluable detail about Bayonne, New Jersey, in the 1960s, far more than I was able to use. The Meteors are fictional; Mrs. Jay's was real, and located next door to The Stone Pony.

Background for the oil rig scenes comes from the wonderful and affecting memoir *Roughnecks, Drillers, and Tool Pushers: Thirty-Three Years in the Oil Fields* by Gerald Lynch. Thanks also to Robert Squyres, who got me onto a working oil rig decades ago as research for a novel that was never published. You never know when something is going to end up being useful after all.

Johnny Hornet is entirely fictional. KLIF, Gordon McLendon, and Mike Scott are not.

Luis Manuel García Rangel made heroic efforts to improve my Spanish, provided a walking tour of Guanajuato, and answered questions about history and geography. Mil gracias, primo.

Wilton Barnhardt gave me an amazingly useful Rand McNally 1967 Texaco Touring Atlas, crucial encouragement, and a ferocious intellect to bounce ideas off of.

Jim Savage, another St. Mark's classmate and lifelong friend, turned me on to Bob Dylan back in 1965 and took me to the concert in Dallas that fall. Fifty years later, he provided details about UT registration and housing and discussed the folk music of the sixties with me.

For general information on San Francisco, the Fillmore, and Bill Graham, nothing can beat *Bill Graham Presents* by Bill Graham and Robert Greenfield, a benchmark for oral histories. The best nonfiction book I read on the Summer of Love is Charles Perry's *The Haight Ashbury: A History*, though I also highly recommend the novel *Summer of Love* by Lisa Mason, thoroughly researched and full of heart.

Paisley Octopus, if it wasn't obvious, is fictional. The Sons of Champlin are not, and neither is the Italian artist Michelangelo

Pistoletto. And, for the record, Dave Fisher and I do not agree about Blue Cheer, whose early albums I still love.

Barry Harrington, on the ground in the Bay Area, sent me books, CDs, and magazine articles. He called around to track down obscure details of local history. He sent me long, funny emails offering insights about the local music and geography and people. His contribution cannot be overstated, and I am ever grateful for his friendship.

Two books were especially helpful for technical details about the various recording studios in the novel: *If These Halls Could Talk* by Heather Johnson, and the fascinating *Studio Stories* by David Simons.

Frank Werber is a historical character and my main source for his story is *Greenback Dollar: The Incredible Rise of the Kingston Trio*, by William J. Bush.

My chronology of Woodstock is based on the Woodstock Wiki (woodstock.wikia.com), the most reliable source of information on Woodstock that I was able to find. I substituted Sallie Rachel for Melanie Safka on Friday night and The Quirq for Quill on Saturday morning. No disrespect was intended, as I am a big fan of both.

Of the many books on the festival, my favorite is *The Road to Woodstock* by Michael Lang (with Holly George Warren), which is not only beautifully written, but manages to capture Lang's remarkable spirit, which was so essential to the enduring importance of the festival. Also particularly helpful was *Woodstock Revisited*, a collection of eyewitness accounts, edited by Susan Reynolds.

Special thanks go to Michael Tassi, who helped me get my hands on Project Woodstock Complete, 25 hours of music and stage announcements, the most complete audio record of the festival available at the time.

Bob Wayne really outdid himself for this one, chauffeuring me to the town of Woodstock, to one of Levon Helm's last Midnight Rambles, and to the site of the festival and the Woodstock Museum in Bethel. He also drove me to Liberty, where the staff of the Day's Inn (formerly the Holiday Inn) went out of their way to open up the lounge where the Woodstock musicians hung out (long since converted to a storage area), to show me a sample room, and to answer questions.

Bob also provided me with stacks of UK music magazines covering the sixties, including *Shindig!*, *Mojo '60s*, and the amazing *History of Rock* series from *Uncut*, all of which were extraordinarily helpful.

I invented Hugh Romney/Wavy Gravy's dialog for this novel, but it's inspired by his own books, interviews on the web, and the Wavy Gravy Movie, *Saint Misbehavin'*. I consider him one of the greatest heroes of the 1960s.

For details of the student movement at UT, I relied on *History of Student Activism at the University of Texas at Austin (1960-1988)*, a student thesis by Beverly Burr, from Spring 1988. From Burr's thesis, I learned that my friend Jon Lebkowski had been an eyewitness to both the Waller Creek and Chuckwagon demonstrations, and he in turn provided me with lots of great information and sent me to David P. Hamilton's blog post from 2011, "1969 in Austin: The famous Chuck Wagon police riot."

The quotes from Raoul Vaneigem's *The Revolution of Everyday Life* are based on the Donald Nicholson-Smith translation, though I used my high-school French to compare the original and tinker with them here and there. Quotes from Guy Debord's *Society of the Spectacle* are from the 1977 Black and Red translation.

Gary McDonald endured endless questions about cameras and editing equipment for the NYU scenes and never complained, just dug deeper and gave me more and more great stuff. Another St. Mark's classmate, Jerry Carlson, pointed me to great info on Loisaida, including *Palante*, a fascinating oral history of the Young Lords.

For information about the SoHo art scene of the 70s, I am indebted to *Art on the Block* by Ann Fensterstock, as well as to Jessamyn Fiore's *112 Greene Street: The Early Years*. The SoHo Memory Project (sohomemory.com) was the best of many extremely helpful websites about the era. Paula Cooper, Donald Judd, and the other artists I name-checked in the SoHo section are all real, with the exception of Callie Janus, whose paintings are my own invention.

Of the many friends whose lives I plundered for this story, my biggest debt is to Margaret Downs-Gamble, who fully participated in the process. Her help, especially in the matters of pregnancy and childbirth, was crucial. Love and thanks also to Michael Minzer, Tricia Jumonville, and the late R. P. Alberts.

Eden Farm and Sheriff P. J. Mackie are entirely my own creations, though the town of Wytheville is real. My good friend Bill Bischoff gave me a short course in farming, answered rafts of questions, and read the first draft of the commune section to help me get it right. Fred Brockman, ex-communard, also read the section in first draft and made many helpful suggestions, many of which I appropriated verbatim. Terry Bisson, another commune veteran, pointed me to some valuable resources, including his own *Any Day Now* and his friend Peter Coyote's deeply moving *Sleeping Where I Fall*. Also essential was *Voices from the Farm: Adventures in Community Living*, edited by Rupert Fike.

Steve Pease, in addition to endless moral support, read the Led Zeppelin section in preliminary draft, fixed the odd bit of tin-eared British dialect, and wrote my favorite line in it. He then dragged Andy Tompkins in to verify some details of the gear, for all of which many thanks to both.

Jim Matzorkis is real, and his beating at the hands of John Bonham, Peter Grant, Richard "Ricardo" Cole, and John Bindon is described in chilling detail in *Bill Graham Presents*. I used Mick Wall's *Led Zeppelin: When Giants Walked the Earth* for additional details about the band. The Led Zeppelin website, ledzeppelin.com, contains a wealth of photos, videos, and eyewitness accounts of the concert. In reality, Judas Priest opened both the Saturday and Sunday shows.

David Menconi was kind enough to loan me a copy of his master's thesis on the Armadillo World Headquarters, which was not only great reading, but was crammed with terrific insight about progressive country, Austin, and the 1970s. He also provided me with a pre-publication copy of *Comin' Right at Ya*, the Ray Benson autobiography that he co-authored, also a thorough delight to read.

For details of the academic jungle, many thanks to John Kessel and Lance Olsen. In addition, John provided Madelyn with the revised title of her dissertation, and Lance furnished me with vivid descriptions of Moscow, Idaho. Margaret Downs-Gamble was endlessly patient in helping me concoct Madelyn's academic pitfalls, promotions, and publications. El Pueblo Community College is fictional, but my friend Debra Taylor provided crucial details about teaching ESL in a similar environment.

For information about climate change and alternative energy, I want to acknowledge the work of Bill McKibben, especially *The End of Nature* and *Eaarth*. Jill Engel-Cox generously coached me on solar power and the competing technologies available in 2010.

For background on Mexico's drug war, I referred to Ioan Grillo's *El Narco: Inside Mexico's Criminal Insurgency*, as well as many issues of the Mexican news weekly *Proceso*.

James Gardner, who contributed his vast musical knowledge, his amazing record collection, and his unqualified enthusiasm for this book, did not live to see the end of the first draft. I miss him more than I can say.

My dear friend Eric Rabkin supplied unfailing encouragement, expertise on countless subjects, and the concept of tikkun olam, which snapped into the book like the final piece of a puzzle.

Thanks to the following, who responded to emails or phone calls or both with bits of crucial information: Paula Kamenish, author of *Mamas of Dada*; Darice Murray-McKay of the San Francisco Public Library; Lea Rude of the San Francisco History Center; Bryan McKinney, Assistant Manager of the Texas/Dallas History and Archive; former St. Mark's class president Bart Wade; Michael Fulton, owner and manager of the Historic Route 66 Motel; Emily Casey and Wade Lawrence of The Museum at Bethel Woods. Special thanks to David Stevens for legal details on the drug bust. Thanks also to Cash Edwards and Jorma Kaukonen for Woodstock gear info; Mike Autrey, as always, for his faith and friendship; Joe Lansdale for Sirocco's martial arts; Alden Taylor for inspirational conversations; Barry Ragin for a timely critique of the lyrics to "Already the End"; Jeff Archer Black for support and eagle-eyed proofreading; Arthur Hoffman for too many reasons to name; Dennis "T.T." Taylor for love and encouragement; and many, many more whom my failing memory has neglected to include here.

Richie Unterberger, Lisa Tuttle, David Stevens, Carol Stevens, Barry Ragin, Eric Rabkin, David Rabkin, Steve Pease, Gary McDonald, Iain Matthews, John Kessel, Marian Henley, John Hamby, Margaret Downs-Gamble, and Richard Butner read the manuscript in various drafts, gently pointed out mistakes, offered excellent suggestions, and gave me much-needed encouragement.

Thanks to Danny Baror for agenting the manuscript and for believing in the book. My US publisher, Bill Schafer, went all out for this one, time and time again. Additional thanks to the rest of the Subterranean crew, especially Yanni Kuznia and Geralyn Lance. In the UK, Head of Zeus awed me with their enthusiasm, with special thanks going out to Nic Cheetham and Madeleine O'Shea.

I have saved the best for last. My partner, Orla Swift, has been sounding board, cheerleader, traveling companion, photographer, nursemaid, and unfailing source of faith in this project since I first conceived of it, and to her go my boundless gratitude and love.